MW01110252

THE FOREVER RANGER

by

Robert L. LeBrun

DORRANCE
PUBLISHING CO
EST. 1920
PITTSBURGH, PENNSYLVANIA 15238

The contents of this work, including, but not limited to, the accuracy of events, people and places depicted; opinions expressed; permission to use previously published materials included; and any advice given or actions advocated are solely the responsibility of the author, who assumes all liability for said work and indemnifies the publisher against any claims stemming from publication of the work.

All Rights Reserved
Copyright © 2019 by Robert L. LeBrun

No part of this book may be reproduced or transmitted, downloaded, distributed, reverse engineered, or stored in or introduced into any information storage and retrieval system, in any form or by any means, including photocopying and recording, whether electronic or mechanical, now known or hereafter invented without permission in writing from the publisher.

Dorrance Publishing Co
585 Alpha Drive
Pittsburgh, PA 15238
Visit our website at *www.dorrancebookstore.com*

ISBN: 978-1-6453-0306-0
eISBN: 978-1-6453-0833-1

For Christ gave his life for me, so I will dedicate all to Him.

Where there is faith, there is an abundance of hope. Our walk through life is forever being plagued by evil, and if you choose faith over all else then your resolve will surely endure. The good in our souls will constantly be challenged, and therefore we must stand strong against those who would so easily destroy us.

Sᴛ. Fʀᴀɴᴄɪs, ᴡʜᴏ ᴡᴀs ʙᴏʀɴ ʙᴇᴛᴡᴇᴇɴ the years 1181 and 1182, was an Italian Catholic and was given the birth name of Giovanni di Pietro di Bernardone. His father nicknamed him Francesco, which means "the Frenchman." His father, Pietro di Bernardone, was a silk merchant and became a successful businessman, which brought much wealth to the family. Like most typical young wealthy men, Francesco lived a high-spirited life and even joined the military in the year 1204 and fought as an Assisi soldier.

When he returned to Assisi, he lost his taste for the worldly life and renounced his family's wealth. He took a pilgrimage to Rome and joined the poor in begging at St. Peter's Basilica, which had a profound affect and moved him to live a life of poverty. When he returned home, he began preaching on the streets. He gained a following and in the year 1210, founded the Franciscans, which were an order of priests and friars authorized by Pope Innocent III.

After many years of service to the Lord, Francesco received his final call, and on October 3, 1226, he passed away peacefully in his bed while listening to a reading of Psalms 140. Two years later on July 16, 1228, Francesco was proclaimed a saint by Pope Gregory IX. Although he is known as the patron saint of animals and the environment, one can also say he was a champion for the poor and oppressed.

The Franciscan priests continued to thrive, and like most Roman Catholic orders, they branched out to foreign lands. They developed and funded missionaries for evangelical purposes, and in the year 1534, they established six provinces in Mexico.

With the fall of the Aztec empire in the year 1522, the collapse of the Mayan Empire by the year 1541, and the conquering of the Inca Empire in the year 1572, Spain set its sights on the territory north of Mexico, looking for more wealth. The British and French, who were also looking for wealth, competed with Spain to colonize the same territory. With greed came opportunity. Evangelical missions trips by the Franciscans were attempted to El Paso in the years 1630 and 1656 but failed. In the year 1659, a third missions trip into El Paso was successful for the Christian faith and the teaching of God's word. With foreign powers bickering and fighting with various Indian tribes and each other, the Franciscan priests continued to do their own colonizing.

In order to help finance their missions, the priests used some of the local Indians who had already been converted to the Christian faith to help locate silver. One Indian boy in particular surprisingly knew the mountain region well and would accompany the priests on their expeditions. During the year 1680, several rich mines were found and the priests started to mine the silver ore. Because El Paso was a territory of Spain, Spanish law required one-fifth of all silver be shipped back to the King of Spain. After several years of no communication or shipments of silver, Spain dispatched soldiers along with missionaries from another Roman Catholic order called Jesuits to try and locate the Franciscans and their silver mines.

Travel by ship was long, dangerous, and cumbersome. By the time the Jesuits and soldiers arrived at New Spain, which was the official name of all the conquered territory previously belonging to Mexico, the Franciscan priests had already received word they were coming. Fearing they would lose control of the silver, the priests concealed the mines, telling nobody but the senior members of their order the whereabouts of the locations.

Over the years, stories surfaced then faded then resurfaced, but prospectors and treasure hunters alike couldn't locate the mines. Somehow over the next several generations, the Franciscan priests failed to pass the secret information on to their successors and it seemed the mines were lost forever.

Under Spanish rule, the Franciscans continued their work to try and convert Indians to the Christian faith mainly by force. While Spain continued to add to its territory, France, the Netherlands and even Russia claimed other territory north and east of New Spain. By 1732, England had established thirteen colonies along the east coast of the New World. By now, the Franciscans had crisscrossed the new territory and were established in most major townships. Over the next century, the new territory was plagued with wars. The thirteen colonies battled Great Britain for their independence and created the United States. New Spain won their independence from the mother-land in 1821 and reestablished themselves as Mexico. Texas, which was a territory of Mexico, fought a seven-month war and won their independence in 1836. Texas then joined the United States in 1845. In the wake of the United States' annexation of Texas, the Mexican American war was fought from 1846 to 1848, during which time, Mexico lost and the United States gained California and New Mexico.

With all the wars along with various uprisings of Indians, the Franciscans faded into the background of dilapidated churches and monasteries. Since their arrival in North America in 1630, many other congregations had formed as various religious orders littered the United States. Even the Franciscan name faded into oblivion. Most people just referred to them as priests, monks, padre, or simply men of the cloth.

In 1848, while Mexico and the United States were settling their differences, gold was discovered in the soon-to-be-acquired California. Although California wasn't an official state of the United States yet, over three hundred thousand people flocked across the country to stake their claim. Nicknamed the Forty-Niners, the gold seekers fought off Indians, droughts, disease, and even bandits for a possible payday of wealth.

By now, silver had taken a back seat to gold. There was still silver mines operating, but gold fever ran rapid like wildfire. While traveling through Texas on their way to California, an old English Bible-wielding couple and their family, the Masons, was crossing over some rugged terrain attempting to find a smoother trail when they came across a little boy. He was half-dehydrated, leaning up against some rocks. He was trying to catch some shade, but being mid-day, there was no shade to be found and the afternoon sun was beating hard. The boy only had a piece of buffalo skin covering his front and backside.

Thinking the boy might be an Indian child and knowing rations were low, the father took it upon himself to leave the boy in God's hands and keep moving. The mother, on the other hand, had a different plan in mind. She scolded her husband with shameful words and made him stop the wagon. When she climbed down, she scooped a cup of water from the water barrel and quickly ran over to where the boy was laying. As the boy responded with a glimpse of life, the kind woman noticed he was also wearing some Apache beads around his wrist and a leather string with a patch around his neck. She knelt down to get a closer look and noticed the leather patch had a strange symbol on it. It resembled a cross with a small circle within a larger circle in the center. She also saw the boy was not an Indian, but only had burned skin because of the hot sun.

After giving the boy a few minutes to drink and gain some strength, the kind lady scolded her husband once again and made him help the boy into the back of the wagon. Onward they went until the next day, when they happened across an old monastery. The family could tell it was once a grand place of worship, but the years gone by were unkind and the weather had beaten it down to a skeleton of its old self. The two old priests who lived there quickly helped the boy to one of the rooms and tended to his health.

When the priests asked about the boy's origins, the family had no answers. They explained they had found the boy half-dead out on the Texas plains. After a day of rest, the Mason family paid the priests for some supplies then shared a prayer. They expressed their gratitude and left at dusk in order to travel during the cool of the night.

Over the next week, the two priests tended to the boy's needs until he regained his strength and was well enough to talk. As Father Santos prepared breakfast, Father Andres sat at the old rickety table staring at the young boy. "So boy, do you remember what happened to you? Do you remember your family or where you come from?"

The boy thought for a few seconds then answered. "I'm not sure where I come from, sir, or who my family was. An Apache tribe found me wondering out on the plains."

Just then, Father Santos placed food and drinks on the table, then sat down. "Do you think the Apache killed your parents?"

The boy didn't show any sorrow or anger. He just stared momentarily with a blank face. "I don't remember anything, sir, before the Apache found me. They said I was a ghost. They called me a wondering spirit from the past."

The two priests looked at each other as the hair stood up on the back of their necks. They slowly consumed their breakfast as they attempted to choose their words carefully. Father Andres took a drink of his water, then quietly placed the cup down on the table. "Apaches don't like the white man, so why didn't they just kill you?"

With his deep dark eyes, the boy once again stared with a blank face. "They were afraid of me. They thought it might bring them bad fortune if they harmed me, so they had one of their warriors and his son take me back to where they had found me. They rode horses while I was forced to walk. As we neared the plains, the daylight started to fade. When we finally stopped, the son climbed down off his horse and walked with me while his father stayed behind. The son told me as a part of his test of manhood, he was to take me out into the darkness and leave me tied up so I would parish, but the son took pity on me. He said he had had a vision the night before and that he thought I had purpose in this world. He said I was on a mission from the spirit world. So he cut me lose and gave me a beaded bracelet. He told me we would see each other in another life."

The priests listened intently as the boy told his story. After breakfast, the boy returned to his room as the priests tended to their chores. They knew there was something different about the boy and it worried them, but nevertheless, God delivered him into their care and he was their responsibility for now. They found some old donated clothing and shoes he could wear and gave him his own Bible.

The next day at breakfast, the priests had more questions. Father Santos quietly ate his food while Father Andres stared at the boy with curiosity. "So boy, do you have a name?"

With sadness, the boy shook his head no as he looked down with sorrow. "No sir. The Apache just called me Hok'ee. They told me it means 'abandoned.'"

At the boy's expense, Father Andres laughed. "No boy. God will never abandon you. Even in our darkest hours, God watches over us. So boy, we're not the Apache, so we need to figure out a new name for you. It was the Mason family who found you, so it only seems proper you would take their surname. Now, we need a strong Bible name for you."

As Father Santos cleaned the breakfast dishes, Father Andres pondered the dilemma. "Let's see now. Do you know who John of Patmos is?"

The two priests were shocked when the boy told them the answer. "Yes sir, John of Patmos was exiled and abandoned on the isle of Patmos. That is where he wrote the book of Revelations."

Father Andres nearly fell out of his chair as Father Santos, who was in awe, almost dropped the dishes. Father Santos stopped what he was doing and walked over to the boy. With a stern face, he looked down at him. "Wait outside, boy, while Father Andres and I talk."

Like a scolded soul, the boy slowly walked out. With worry in his heart, Father Santos sat down in the chair. "Something isn't right about that boy, Andres. I know the Apache don't believe in our God, but they have their ways. They know things. Unholy things. If they were afraid of that boy enough not to kill him, then maybe they know something we don't. I've never known the Apache to be afraid of anything. That boy doesn't remember anything, and yet he's diverse with the Bible?"

Father Andres thought for a moment as a little hint of a smile occupied his face. "Old friend, he's just a boy. God has brought him to us for reasons we can't comprehend at this moment. We have to believe God has a higher purpose for him. You'll see. We shall give him is own identity. We will drop the letter H and shall grant him the name Jon Mason. We will continue to pray and you shall see old friend. You shall see."

And so it came to be, the mysterious unknown boy was now Jon Mason. Because the priests were up in age, Jon took over most of the daily chores. He was a hard worker and never had to be told twice to do something. One day while working in the garden, Father Andres knelt down to help pull some weeds. When Jon first arrived at the old monastery, Father Andres noticed the strange necklace he was wearing, but didn't want to overwhelm the boy with questions he couldn't answer. "Jon, I've been meaning to ask you about that necklace you wear."

Feeling a bit fatigued from the sun, Jon stopped for the moment to wipe the sweat from his brow. "What about it? Just like everything else, I don't know where it came from. I guess I just keep holding onto it just in case I remember one day."

Thinking the padre would accept his answer; Jon could see that Father Andres had more on his mind then just curiosity. While thinking about Jon's words, Father Andres reached across and gently moved his fingers across the symbol embedded in the soft leather. "I know what this symbol means. I've seen this symbol before. It is an ancient symbol used by the Pueblo Indians. It is a symbol used to describe silver."

Surprised at the direction of the conversation, Jon stood up and once again wiped the sweat from his brow. "What's an old priest like you know about silver?"

Wanting to conduct a more thorough investigation, Father Andres stood up and motioned Jon towards the old monastery. As they entered the old church, Father Andres led Jon into what use to be the head priest's private quarters. "Please Jon, help me move this book case."

Since his arrival, Jon had gained much strength, so he very easily pushed the old book case aside to reveal a set of steps leading down into darkness. As Father Andres lit a candle, he led Jon down the cobweb-filled steps. "When Father Santos and I found this old monastery, we had great visions of bringing it back to life. But time got away from us and our age became our enemy. We very seldom spend time in the old church now because of the crumbling walls. We found this room by accident one day when we still had our youth. There's not much down here. Just dust and a couple of old books and manuscripts. Our guess is this room was used to hide church valuables from bandits and foreign militaries."

As Father Andres lit a few more candles, the room brightened and Jon could see some old tables with some manuscripts and some old books scattered on the floor. He also noticed an old ornate cross, which probably sat atop the church at one time. While Jon looked around, Father Andres picked up one of the old dusty books and placed on a table. "Look here, Jon. Look at the symbol on this book."

Jon could see the book was starting to fall apart and the leather cover was cracking, but he could see the symbol on the book, which matched the symbol on his necklace. When he opened the book to look inside, some of the pages had already started to disintegrate. He made an attempt to read some words, but the language was unfamiliar to him. "What language is this book written in, Father Andres?"

Father Andres took a few moments and viewed some of the pages, then gave his best educated answer. "The symbol comes from the Pueblo Indians. The ancestors of the Pueblo were called Nahuati. The Nahuati were linguistically diverse, and one of the many languages they spoke was that of the Aztec. I think this is the Aztec language. Very old. Now, let's get out of this dark hole so we can study the book and talk more."

Feeling the need to exit such a closed-in space, Father Andres closed the book then ascended up the steps. Being the helpful person he was, Jon pushed the book case back into position then followed Father Andres out into the courtyard where they found some shade and sat down. When Father Andres opened the book, he started skimming through the pages. As Jon's eyes tried to keep up, he noticed a word on several of the pages that was more prominent then the rest. "Stop. I know that word."

Father Andres held the page while Jon removed his necklace. He flipped the strange necklace to the inside to reveal a word etched into the leather. It was the same as the word in the book. Arizuma. With his investigation yielding some exciting results, Father Andres placed the necklace next to the word and studied it. "I'm not as diverse as the Nahuati were, but I know this word to be the word for silver."

After a few more page turns, the old priest decided to call it a day. "Come, my boy, it's almost dinnertime. We can talk more in the morning. Besides, Father Santos is making us tamales."

The next day, Jon was up earlier than usual and finished all his morning chores in record time. He was anxious to talk to Father Andres and Father Santos about the mysterious book and its contents, but after breakfast, the two priests jokingly played coy at Jon's expense. They knew Jon was determined to talk about the book, but purposely avoided him and laughed as Jon chased them around every corner.

After a while, Jon got frustrated and gave up his quest. With his emotions high, he walked out into the courtyard and sat on an old stone wall that was half falling down. He started to whittle a fallen branch when the two priests snuck up from behind and flashed the old book in Jon's face.

Like a little kid, Father Andres was almost giddy. "Is this what you want, Jon?"

Almost immediately, Jon jumped off the wall with excitement and grabbed the book from Father Andres. In a feeble attempt, he tried to scold the two priests. "Why do you constantly joke at my expense?"

Feeling just as giddy as Father Andres, Father Santos laughed. "Because there's nothing out here but dust and coyotes, so we two old goats have to do something to keep our sanity."

After a few more laughs, the two priests took Jon on a more in-depth tour of the old monastery. Even though there were barely any recognizable features left, they pointed out some of the old architecture of the building, such as the oval-shaped bell tower, which resembled Franciscan-built churches. Then they walked to some of the more secluded areas and pointed out some of the old engraved scenes on the wall. Some were murals of friars accepting guidance from some of the local tribesmen and others were engravings of conquistadors. Still, there was one more thing they had to show Jon. Over the centuries, the harsh weather had chiseled away and destroyed most of the statues, but there was one left in the courtyard that had been knocked over and buried by weeds. After a few grueling minutes of uncovering the artifact, Jon helped the priests stand it upright. The podium for the statue had long been destroyed, so they picked it up and placed it on an old tree stump. With feelings of familiarity, Jon stared for a few moments as though he recognized the likeness. "This is St. Francis."

Father Santos was astonished, but Father Andres had grown used to Jon's surprising answers. As Father Andres brushed some dirt from the statue, Father Santos decided to go down the road of curiosity. "How do you know this statue to be St. Francis, boy?"

Unable to grasp his insight, Jon didn't answer right away. He stood staring at the statue as though he was trying to understand his knowledge. "I'm sorry, Father Santos. I know you have grown leery of me, but I also lay awake at night wondering where my knowledge comes from. I know this statue to be St. Francis, but I don't know why."

With no desire to press the situation, the two priests and Jon found a shady spot along the old stone wall and sat down. Wanting to educate Jon more about his surroundings, Father Santos began to tell the story of the old monastery. "St. Francis was from Italy and started a religious order called the Franciscans. They conducted mission trips to Mexico, then, with the help of Spanish soldiers, pushed their way up into what is now known as California, Arizona, New Mexico, and Texas. They built churches and monasteries throughout the area to help permanently establish their existence. Because of its location, this particular monastery was also used by the Spanish soldiers as a fortress. It was one of their strongholds and used in fighting off Indians and invading armies. It saw many battles and, as you can see, has been diminished to nothing more than a few scattered buildings and walls of rubble."

With sadness in his heart and disgust for the story, Father Santos stood up to take a breath of air while Father Andres continued. "The Franciscans were known for their silver mines. With the help of some of the local Indians, they discovered silver in the year 1680. It's said that a young Indian boy guided them through the mountains and helped find the famous mines. But after a

period of time, the King of Spain became furious with them because they refused to send any of their silver back to Spain. He sent many soldiers to hunt
them down, so the Franciscans hid their mines. They kept them hidden for
many years, but unfortunately, they kept them too well hidden. Even the information became lost, or so the stories go. I think this book might reveal the
secrets of the Franciscans."

Wanting to concentrate more on the present and not so much on his past,
Jon took the book from Father Andres and opened it up. His eyes skimmed
through the pages as his mind ran rapid with thoughts. "So, what is it you want
me to do?"

Just then, Father Santos sat back down to provide some guidance. "Father
Andres and I have no need for wealth. We are old and will soon be given back
to the Earth and turned to dust. You, my boy, are young and have your life
ahead of you. God has given you breath. Not once, not twice, but three times
your life has been spared. Use the gifts God has provided for you and live
your life."

After Father Santos gave his blessing, he left Father Andres to give further
guidance to Jon as to what he should do. Wanting the best for Jon, Father Andres took the book back from him and held it in his hands. "Listen to me, Jon.
Father Santos is right. We're not getting any younger. With each passing day,
we both grow nearer to the end of our journey. You my boy have yet to start
yours. Take this book. It is said there is an old Indian man who lives up in the
mountains. As the legend goes, he speaks many languages and knows many
things. Some say he is nothing more than a medicine man. Others say he is a
spirit left behind to roam the Earth. Yet others say he doesn't exist at all. And
some even say he is the devil himself. You should have no difficulties. The Indians fear him, so they stay away. Bandits also stay away because some have
ventured to the mountain, never to be heard from again. You shall present this
book to the Old One and then be guided by what he tells you. Come, my boy.
We shall prepare for your journey."

During the following week, Jon studied old maps of trails leading up to
and through the mountain region he would be visiting. He also gathered food

and supplies to take along for the trip. As Jon prepared himself, Father Santos traveled by foot to the town of Presidio, which was forty miles south of the old monastery.

While at breakfast one morning, Jon asked Father Andres to tell him more about the old Indian and the mountain he lived on. Father Andres laughed, but at the same time, welcomed the young boy's curiosity. "I get the feeling you're not afraid of the story I told you." Father Andres once again smiled and leaned up close to Jon. "Well, let's see how you feel after I tell you more. The Old One lives at the top of El Capitan. That is what the white man calls it. The Indians call it Totokonoolah, which translated means The Chief. Most other people call it Hell because nobody ever returns. It is said that no matter which direction you enter El Capitan, the Old One will find you. Now Jon, listen to me and listen carefully. You will pass by outposts and towns—some small, some big—and you will see things. Do not enter the towns and do not stop at any of the outposts. Most are bad and you are inexperienced. You are not yet ready to handle the evil within this world. Promise me, boy, and swear to me you will keep your promise."

After breakfast and swearing several times, Jon went out to finish his chores. After a few minutes of tending to the gardens, he noticed off in the distance a man on a horse-pulled wagon, and he was headed toward the monastery. Not knowing who the man was, Jon called out to Father Andres, who was still cleaning the breakfast dishes. When Father Andres came out to see what Jon was yelling about, he saw the wagon getting closer. He also noticed a second horse tied to the rear. As the stranger approached, Father Andres stood by Jon's side. When the stranger climbed down from the wagon, Father Andres could see he was well dressed.

Out of respect, the stranger took off his hat and introduced himself. "Good morning, Padre. My name is Doctor Micah and I've come from the town of Presidio."

Out of kindness and curtesy, Father Andres welcomed the good doctor and extended the hospitality of food and drink. Unfortunately, Doctor Micah wasn't out riding for pleasure. "I appreciate the hospitality, Padre, but I've come to see you with some possible bad news. I have a coffin in the back of my wagon with a body. I'm hoping maybe you might know who he is."

Fearing the worse, Doctor Micah walked to the rear of the wagon, followed by Father Andres and Jon. When the doctor lifted the cover, Father Andres immediately saw that it was Father Santos. By the sad look on his face, Doctor Micah could tell Father Andres knew the man.

"I'm sorry, Padre. He stumbled into town a few days ago. I think he knew there was something wrong, but instead of coming to see me, he went to the livery stable to purchase a horse. Unfortunately, there was something very wrong with his health. His heart gave out and he collapsed. Nobody knew where he came from, but we could tell from his clothing that he was a man of the cloth. And this is the only church I know of other than our own within a hundred miles from town. I thought this old place had long been deserted. In any case, I was on my way to a small Indian village about twenty miles further south to deliver some medicine. Thought I would take a chance and bring the padre along. I wasn't sure if anyone would even be here."

Father Andres stood staring at the body of his long-standing friend, then said a small prayer. He then turned his attention to Jon, who had never seen a dead body before, let alone one of somebody he knew. Surprisingly, Jon kept his emotions in check.

Despite the earlier wishes of the doctor, Father Andres insisted he come in for some well-deserved food and drink. Afterward, they took on the task of burying Father Santos in the shade where the statue of St. Francis was. When the prayers were said and done, Jon retreated back to the monastery while Doctor Micah said his good-byes. "Well Padre, I wish I had visited under better circumstances, but in any case, it was a pleasure meeting you. I'm sorry for your loss. Incidentally, your friend had already paid for the horse, so I guess he belongs to you now."

Father Andres watched as Doctor Micah climbed up on to his wagon, but before the doctor left, he had some more disturbing news. "Padre, I'm not sure how much news you receive out here, if any, but there's talk of a war between the States. Just thought I'd let you know."

As Doctor Micah made his exit, Father Andres thanked him for his kindness. When Father Andres returned to the monastery, Jon was nowhere to be found. Thinking about the day's events, he sat at the kitchen table and pondered the news of war, and worried about Jon and his up and coming travels.

As the hours passed, Jon was nowhere to be seen. When dinnertime approached, Father Andres went looking for him. After what seemed like he had looked everywhere, he found Jon in the older part of the monastery, staring at the engraved scenes he had learned about the week before. He was particularly interested in the engraved scenes of the Spanish conquistadors standing alongside of the Franciscan priests. "What do you think about this scene, Father Andres?"

Father Andres laughed for a moment, then pointed at the engravings. "I think the Franciscans mocked the conquistadors because they never found the secret locations of their silver mines. Because the Franciscans were authorized by the Pope and their founder immortalized as a saint, the King of Spain dare not harm them in any way because it would have been a sin against God. The Spanish had no choice but to leave the Franciscans to their own fate."

After dinner, Father Andres and Jon reconvened in the courtyard to talk about Jon's travel plans. The sun was starting to set and the nighttime breezes were winding their way through the monastery. They could hear coyotes off in the distance talking to each other through various high-pitched howls as Father Andres sat quietly for a few moments remembering his old friend Father Santos.

Afterward, he reiterated what Jon needed to do. "My son. You came to us as a boy and now you must start your quest to become a man. Tomorrow, you will take the horse Father Santos bought and travel to the El Capitan. Once there, you will give the book to the Old One and be guided by what he says."

Thinking ahead about his trip, Jon gathered his thoughts as he contemplated the advice of Father Andres. "Not that I'm afraid, but if you say nobody has ever returned from El Capitan, then why do you insist I go?"

Seeing Jon grow and his mind expand since his arrival, Father Andres smiled with pride. "Many men have traveled to the El Capitan and even some women. All had evil in their hearts. All had different reasons for going, but in the end, the Old One saw through their hidden agendas and their souls were condemned. You, my boy, have God watching over you. Your heart is pure and your soul is good. The Old One will know your purpose in life. He will teach you and give you further guidance."

The next morning, Jon was up early doing his usual chores when Father Andres approached. "Jon, your time is done here. I've packed your supplies and readied your horse."

Jon was leery about leaving Father Andres alone, mainly because of his age, and he wasn't sure how long his trip to the mountains would take or what would happen once he got there. "Father Andres, I know you think I must go on this quest of manhood, but I'm not sure I should be leaving you now."

Father Andres stood staring at Jon, then momentarily looked towards the sky as to look for guidance from the heavens. "My boy, God has given me many blessings during my lifetime, but none as important as the day you were left in my care. Our Lord has granted me the privilege of being his voice in guiding you to the next stage of your life. Now listen to me. I have given a lifetime of service to our Lord in Heaven and I am not afraid of what awaits me, nor should you be afraid of what awaits you. Now, enough of your mothering an old man. You have a long day of riding ahead of you and its time you have at it."

With love in his heart and faith in the Lord above, Father Andres kissed Jon on the forehead and gave him a long hug. He then recited a small prayer for a safe journey. As Jon climbed up on the horse, Father Andres told him he looked forward to his return.

After saying good-bye, Jon had his maps and rode all morning and into the afternoon, only stopping at an occasional waterhole. By late afternoon, he was hungry and needed a break. As he sat and studied his maps, he couldn't help but have the feeling somebody was watching him. He looked around several times but didn't see anyone. After some rest, he decided to ride until dark.

When the sun went down, he made a small campfire and listened to the chorus of prairie dogs and coyotes sing their songs as he fell asleep.

The next morning was like clockwork. Jon was early to rise and back in the saddle. During his morning travels, he came across one of the outposts Father Andres warned him about. It consisted of two small buildings, a barn, and an outhouse. Remembering his promise to Father Andres and not wanting to be seen, he got just close enough to watch the activity of the locals. Every few minutes, a half-dressed woman would come running outside laughing, followed by a half-dressed man holding a bottle of liquor. The chase wouldn't last long before the man would scoop the woman up and carry her back inside. Jon watched as several what seemed to be couples playing the same game. Eventually he grew bored and moved on.

As Jon rode into the afternoon, he got the same old feeling somebody was watching him. Just then, he caught a glimpse of somebody riding up on a hill that was parallel to him. He could see it was an Indian, but he was unsure from which tribe. Over the next couple of days, Jon noticed several Indians keeping pace, but always from a distance. Eventually the townships and outposts came and went, and the distance to El Capitan grew shorter. As Jon got increasingly closer to the mystical mountain, the Indians finally left him to his own demise.

Late one afternoon, El Capitan came into view. It was still a distance away, but Jon could finally see his destination. The sun was going down, so he decided to stop for the night. Just when he climbed down from his horse, a group of men came riding up. They came out of nowhere and before Jon could react, they had surrounded him. Jon showed no fear as he stood and stared at the men while they stared back. He knew right away they were some of the bandits Father Andres spoke about.

At first, they tried speaking in the Spanish language, but when Jon didn't speak back, the leader of the group climbed down from his horse and spoke in English. He was very dirty and smelly and was missing some teeth. In a stern voice, he scolded Jon. "What are you doing way out here? You are just a boy. Where do you come from, boy?"

Jon stood strong with his chin up, then answered the man. "I come from a monastery about ninety miles southeast from here."

The rough-looking man stared at Jon for a few seconds, then turned to his men and bellowed out a laugh. "I know this monastery you speak of. Two old fools use to live there."

Suddenly, the man's voice became louder as he threw his arms up in the air. "They spoke of God and love and peace." The man placed his hand on his gun and shook it up and down. "This is the only God I know. Now you listen, boy. What do you have besides this old horse? Any gold?"

Before Jon could answer, the man grabbed him by his shoulders and violently shook him. He then backhanded Jon across his face. "Why are you out here, boy? Tell me."

Feeling contempt for the bully, Jon held his cheek as he waited for the sting to go away. All he could do was the one thing he was taught: When faced with violence, recite scripture. Knowing he may provoke the much larger man, Jon took a step forward and looked him in the eyes. "Matthew 5:39," he said. "'But I say to you, do not resist the one who is evil. But if anyone slaps you on your right cheek, turn to him the other also.'" Then Jon turned his cheek towards the man and waited.

Hearing the words from the Bible, the man scarfed and was amused at first, then became outraged. "So, the two old priests taught you something. Too bad they didn't teach you how to fight, boy." The brute of a man grabbed Jon by the shirt and once again, violently shook him while slapping him several times across the face.

Afterward, Jon fell to the ground. Like a towering beast, the man stood over top of him as his temper subsided. "I'll ask you once again, boy, and don't give me your holier than thou attitude. What are you doing out here?"

Not caring about revealing his destination, Jon slowly stood up and brushed the dirt off his pants. He then pointed towards El Capitan. "I'm going there."

With his eyes, the man followed Jon's arm down to his finger then saw the mountains off in the distance. "El Capitan?" The man laughed again, but this time, his men joined in on his laughter. "But you are just a boy. Many men have traveled to El Capitan to try and find its secrets and many men have perished. The Apache and the Comanche are fearless and not even they will travel to the El Capitan. Banditos have sought refuge there and have never returned. What makes you think a boy such as yourself will survive?"

Still with his chin held high, Jon stood staring at the man because he didn't have an answer. After a few seconds, the man realized Jon had tolerated his verbal and physical abuse and had nothing more to give. As he climbed back up onto his horse, the man couldn't help but feel ashamed. He gave Jon one last look with a hint of a smile and some advice. "That mountain is cursed. You will do well to stay away from it." As mean and nasty as he was, the man felt the need to further insult Jon. "Not that I care, my young friend, but we may see each other again. Just so you know, my name is Rodrigo. This necklace I wear, I took it from Padre Andres. The old fool thought he could hide it from me." Rodrigo spit on the ground and just as fast as they rode in, Jon watched as Rodrigo and his men rode off into the darkness.

The next day, Jon rode hard because now he was more determined than ever to reach El Capitan. After his experience with Rodrigo and his men, he felt that Father Andres was right. God must have a plan for him. By nightfall, Jon had reached the base of the mountain. Although he didn't lack the courage, he thought it best to wait until morning to start his ascent. As he tried to sleep, strange sounds came out of the darkness and shapeless shadows appeared without warning. Morning time couldn't come fast enough, but eventually, sunrise chased away the moon and let its presence be known high in the sky. With the thought of finally getting some answers, Jon gathered himself and climbed onto his horse. He could see the trail was just wide enough to ride up through the rocks. Jon didn't know what to expect, but the mental picture he had had in his mind wasn't what he was experiencing. During his travel, he had pictured makeshift totem poles or bones of long-forgotten animals hanging on sticks as a warning to stay away, but there was none. There were no bandits waiting in hiding. There were no monsters. There were no ghosts. More importantly, there was no old Indian man. Just rocks, dirt, and dust.

After guiding his horse through the rocky slopes all morning, the trail began to get steeper, the rocks turned to boulders, and the passage became narrower. It was obvious to Jon he had to continue on foot. Not knowing how much longer he would be or if he would ever return, he chose not to tie the horse to anything just in case the latter happened. Looking ahead at the steep trail, Jon took a small portion of food, his canteen, and the mysterious book, and started his climb. Eventually, the trail started to widen again, which led to a small plateau. As he sat down to take a break, the late afternoon sun was doing its best to melt the landscape. Jon sat for a while and pondered the idea that all the ghost stories were exactly that, just ghost stories. Stories told long ago to anyone who would listen for reasons unknown. As he lay on the ground thinking, he propped his head up on a rock in order to figure out what his best course of action would be.

With a full belly and the sun beating down, Jon fell into a deep sleep. He started to dream about a happier time in his life. A future time with lots of love, happiness, and good fortune. But then a dark cloud hovered over his life. The dark cloud took away his love and happiness and replaced it with hatred. In his heart, Jon knew he had to face the dark cloud and defeat it, but he didn't know how. Just when the dark cloud enclosed around him, he awoke screaming.

Realizing he was asleep longer then he cared to be, nighttime had come and the moon was larger than usual. The stars were out in force and shining bright. When he stood up to shake off the dirt and the bad dream, he noticed a campfire light coming from further up the trail. Without thinking, Jon was drawn to the fire like a moth. As he carefully climbed up the trail, it led to a small cave. He stood at the mouth of the cave and saw the campfire burning bright with an old frail-looking Indian man with long white hair sitting beside it. Jon's heart sank because he didn't know how or what to feel. Should he be afraid? Should he run? Is this the man Father Andres was talking about, and if it was, should he approach and greet the man? All these questions filled Jon's thoughts, but this was the purpose for making the trip. So Jon took a deep breath then slowly approached the elderly man.

The elderly Indian man never turned his head but steadily stared into the fire while slightly rocking back and forth. Using his best manners, Jon confronted the man. "Hello sir. My name is Jon."

Still rocking at a slow pace, the elderly man didn't say anything at first. After a few seconds, he finally mustered enough energy to softly speak one word. "Sit."

Not wanting to cause trouble, Jon immediately sat down and crossed his legs while the old Indian man studied him. The mountain breezes started to howl, but the fire was keeping the small cave warm. Jon stared at the man, waiting for him to speak, but the old Indian man said nothing.

Without any conversation, Jon decided to utilize his other senses such as sight and took notice of the garments the man was wearing. It was a bright white robe with what looked like a silver-plated sash around his waist. He also noticed the designs around the collar and the sleeves matched the type of writing in the mysterious book. The old Indian continued to sway back and forth as he seemed to peer into the fire while at the same time keeping watch over Jon. His eyes were black like coal, and although he was old, his skin had a type of shine to it. He was also wearing some jewelry, which matched his garments.

After a few more minutes of silence, Jon decided to once again test his courage. "Sir, are you all right? I have some food and water that I brought with me. Would you like some?"

Upon hearing Jon's generosity, the old man immediately stopped swaying. He then stood up next to the fire and looked down at Jon while Jon stared up at him. Jon wasn't sure if he should stand or remain seated but then the old man spoke. "You are Cheveyo. Stand so I may look at you."

Feeling a little uneasy, Jon slowly stood up but made sure the fire stayed between them, mostly because he didn't know what to expect. "I'm sorry, sir. My name is Jon Mason. I'm not sure who Cheveyo is."

The fire flashed and crackled, which made Jon blink, but in the blink of an eye the old man was gone. The fire started to burn hotter and grow larger, but just when Jon was about to vacate the cave, the old man reappeared in front of him and blocked the entrance. Jon was startled but instead of showing fear, he stood his ground and took a more bold approach. "For an old man, you sure do get around fast."

The old man wasn't amused and stood staring at Jon with his black eyes. Then suddenly, the cave went dark. The fire had quickly gone out and Jon couldn't see anything. Now his heart started to flutter as he tried to focus on where the old man was. As he stood waiting, nothing happened. Suddenly he could hear the old man's voice speaking, but he couldn't tell where it was coming from. It seemed to come from all directions. "Why are you here, Cheveyo?"

Still waiting for his eyes to adjust to the darkness, Jon blurted out his answer. "I guess I'm here to mainly find out who I am. You keep calling me Cheveyo. Who is Cheveyo?"

As quickly as it went out, the fire burst back up, lighting up the cave, but this time, the light brightened every dark corner, revealing Aztec gold and silver along with jewelry stacked high. Jon noticed the old Indian man sitting back in his original position, but was confused as to why all the parlor tricks.

After a few seconds of letting Jon view the riches, the old man spoke. "I think you're here for wealth. I think you're here to take what is not yours."

Disappointed at the old man's accusations, Jon walked over to the fire and stood next to him. This time, he took it upon himself to sit without waiting for permission. "No sir. I have no need for wealth. I'm not sure where I come from, but I have this strange necklace with the Aztec symbol and word for silver. The two priests that took care of me found this old book with the same symbol. They say this mountain houses an old Indian man that speaks many languages and may be able to tell me more about the book and myself. Are you the Old One they speak of?"

As the wind howled through the mountain passes, the fire grew dim within the cave. With one hand waving over top the fire, the old man used his other hand to throw silver-like dust into the flames. Suddenly Jon's eyes became heavy. Slowly, he faded backwards onto the floor of the cave and entered into a dreamlike state. His eyes were open, but he couldn't move. He could see the old man dancing around the fire wearing a more colorful garment with a feathered head gear and chanting some type of song in a long-forgotten language that Jon couldn't understand.

Out of nowhere, Jon could see battles taking place. Conquistadors and Aztec warriors clashing with swords and armor. As one scene ended, another would start. This time it was the Franciscan priests paying Spanish soldiers with silver to kill the Jesuits and the kind Indians who helped find the Franciscan silver mines. Appearing out of the fire, the same dark cloud that was in Jon's earlier dream engulfed the Franciscans and they perished.

After a few more minutes, the old man reappeared wearing his bright white garment with his silver sash. Being somewhat more hospitable, he sat down beside Jon and introduced himself. "I am the one you seek. I am called the Old One by many. To the spirit world, I am Askuwheteau, which means 'I Keep Watch.' You are Cheveyo, which means 'Spirit Warrior.' You come from nowhere and you come from everywhere, and I've been expecting you."

The Old One paused as he took a brief moment to enjoy what appeared to be a sigh of relief. He then began to tell the story of a violent past. "The Spanish were greedy. They came in search of wealth and treasure. They used deception to gain the confidence of the local people so they could plunder their riches and the land. They were like a great war machine creating destruction wherever they went. They brought with them holy men called Franciscan monks in order to convert people to their faith. Anyone who refused was killed or enslaved. The holy men used Spanish soldiers for protection during their missions. Eventually wars and never-ending battles took its toll on Spain and the holy men realized the Spanish could no longer support their missions. So the monks took it upon themselves to enlist the help of some of the converted Indians to help find silver mines. The monks knew much of the jewelry and sacred objects the Spanish took from the Indians were made out of silver. With the help of a local youth, it didn't take long for the monks to find the mines.

Like most conquerors, they made false promises and told the Indians they would use their newfound wealth to rid the land of the evil Spanish empire, which killed and plundered so many Indian villages and cultures. After the

Franciscans had secured their wealth, they paid the Spanish soldiers to kill the naive Indians and the Jesuit priests that posed a threat. Afterward, the monks poisoned the Spanish soldiers, leaving no witnesses. Because they were unable to keep their promises, the dark cloud consumed them. There were twelve senior monks that kept the locations of the mines secret. When one died, another would take his place and be granted the secret wisdom. They fought and bickered among themselves, then disappeared into the cloud of darkness, never to be heard from again. But hear me, Cheveyo, and hear me well. Not everything is what it seems. The mountain in which the silver was discovered was sacred, but revenge was used by a tortured soul to betray the priests."

After the Old One's story, Jon's eyes started to flicker as he slowly regained his strength and ability to move. When he was finally able to shake off the dream-like state, he noticed the Old One had taken the mysterious book. Not wanting to risk another episode, Jon decided to exercise patience. He waited for the Old One to reveal what-ever wisdom he was willing to give.

The old Indian man sat for a few seconds while skimming the pages of the book and reading through its deceptive history. "This book belonged to the Franciscan monks. This is how they kept their records and secrets. When the Spanish learned about the Aztec sacrificial ceremonies, they were horrified. The senseless killing of women and children to appease their false gods was viewed by the Spanish as barbaric and paganism. The Spanish soldiers gathered anything they could find related to Aztec writings and destroyed it, but a Franciscan monk took pity and saved some of the tablets. He later learned how to translate the language. This book was written using the Aztec language and was supposed to be handed down between generations."

Out of respect, Jon listened to the Old One tell of a history he wasn't interested in, but he still had more questions concerning the present. "Father Andres told me many men have come to this mountain. What happened to them?"

Thinking back on all the thieves, bandits, and outlaws that came to the mountain with deception in their hearts, the old Indian man closed the book and placed it at Jon's feet. "Many men have come to this place and all have perished. They had evil intentions in their hearts and tried to take what was not theirs to take. You, Cheveyo, are the spirit warrior and have come here in good conscience. This tells me your soul is pure. You do not try to take what is not yours; instead, you offer me food and water. This tells me your heart is good. You wear the mark of the Aztecs. This tells me you are on a quest. You have seen the dark cloud in your dream and in your vision. This dark cloud will one day try to consume you. You must defeat the dark cloud that follows you everywhere. Then and only then will you be able to ride the White Spirit and fulfill your destiny."

Jon was listening but didn't exactly understand the colorful metaphors the old wise man was using. He was hoping for more direct answers, such as his heritage or why Father Andres thought he could find the answers that connected his necklace to the mysterious book. "What about my necklace or the book? What's the connection to me?"

Unwilling to shorten the journey Jon must take, the Old One picked the book back up and held it in his hands. "You must first see the evil of this world. Then you must do battle with your inner demons and become the man in which the spirit world needs you to be, Cheveyo. Then and only then will you return to this place and find your answers. The secrets of the mountain will be revealed to you, and you shall set right what has been wronged."

Jon pondered the words of the Old One but couldn't think of any reason he would ever return to the El Capitan. He stood up and walked to the cave entrance and recapped everything that had happen to him since his arrival. When he turned back around, the Old One was gone. There was no fire nor were there any signs that a fire was ever there. Just a cold dark cave with a dirt floor. He also realized the Old One took the book that may have held answers to his questions.

Feeling as though he may have been jilted, Jon took a few seconds to breath in the mountain air. Night had given way to morning and Jon was no closer to finding answers, and now the one thing that may have helped him was gone. With some frustration, he made his way back down the mountain to surprisingly find his horse waiting for him. Taking the time to think about all the strange events and knowing nobody had ever made it off the El Capi-tan, he was happy just to be leaving and had no intentions of ever returning.

The trip back to the monastery was long, knowing he wasted much time for nothing. There were no signs of Indians or bandits, but during his travels, he could hear an occasional explosion. Sometimes off in the distance, he would take note of uniformed soldiers he didn't recognize. Some wore gray uniforms and others had on blue. Jon would never approach, but instead, stayed as far away as possible.

After a few days of travel, he made it back to the monastery. To his hor-ror, it had been destroyed. Some areas were burned while others had been blown to bits. He could tell a battle had taken place, but his thoughts ran rapid. What kind of men would come to a monastery to fight, and where was Father Andres?

Jon wasted no time in climbing off his horse and sifting through rubble where the monastery use to stand. He found several types of weapons lying about including swords, rifles, and pistols, but no bodies and no sign of Fa-ther Andres. With anxiety getting the better of him, Jon ran from one end of the compound to the other, digging through the destruction and search-ing for Father Andres. After taking a few seconds to rest, he remembered the secret place where Father Andres showed him the book. Trying to get his bearings straight, he ran to where he thought it might be and started digging through the burnt timbers and crumbled rock. After a few tense minutes, he finally uncovered the old bookcase that covered the secret lo-cation. It had been knocked over, but was still covering the monastery's se-cret room.

By now he was overcome with emotions. Feeling anxious, Jon tossed the bookcase aside and descended the old stone staircase. The stairwell was filled with buzzing flies and the stench was almost unbearable. When he got to the bottom, he located some candles. One by one, he lit the candles as he stumbled his way through the dark. There, in a dark corner of the room, Jon found Fa-ther Andres's decaying body. Although the body was nearly unrecognizable, Jon could tell somebody shot Father Andres in the gut.

As Jon stood staring at his old friend, all his anxieties shrank down to just one emotion: sadness. With tears falling like rain, Jon was somehow able to fight through his emotional breakdown and carry the priest out into the courtyard. He laid Father Andres's body down on the ground and sat down beside him as his thoughts ran rapid. With his tears starting to subside, a new round of questions entered Jon's thoughts. Who did this and why? Was it bandits? Or maybe Indians? Or maybe it was the strange-looking soldiers he had seen on his return trip? So many questions with no answers.

After a few more minutes of mourning, Jon made the decision to bury Father Andres beside Father Santos, but like everything else, the grave site had been destroyed. Just then, a man on a horse came riding towards the destroyed monastery. Looking older and distinguished, the gentleman had a white beard and was dressed like some of the soldiers Jon had seen earlier. Wearing a gray uniform with a long sword at his side, the man rode tall and proud. Showing no fear, Jon watched as the man climbed down off his horse and approached. The stern-looking man took a moment and gazed at Father Andres's decaying body, then turned his attention to Jon.

"What's your name boy?"

Taking a step towards the man who seemed to tower over him, Jon politely gave his answer. "My name is Jon, sir."

Appreciating Jon's conviction, the man's eyes shifted from Jon to Father Andres, then back to Jon. With pride, he boldly introduced himself. "Good to meet you, Jon. My name is Colonel Andrew Beck of the 4th Battalion infantry. Were you here when this happened?"

Jon took a few seconds and stared at Father Andres's body and felt guilty for leaving him, but felt no desire to create an excuse. "No sir. I was at the top of El Capitan. I don't know what happened here. This is Father Andres. He was my friend."

With some skepticism and a hint of sarcasm, Colonel Beck looked down at Jon and smiled. "El Capitan is feared by many. Even the most fearsome soldiers dare not trespass on Satan's property."

The afternoon sun was beating hard, so the colonel took off his jacket and found an old shovel in order to dig a hole for Father Andres's grave. As Jon and the colonel stood over the grave site, the colonel recited a small prayer. "O Lord, we commit this body back to the ground and pray you except his soul into your house, amen."

Jon wanted something to mark the grave with, so he looked around for something heavy. To his surprise, the statue of St. Francis was still intact so the colonel helped Jon maneuver the relic to the head of the grave.

The colonel couldn't help but feel compassion for Jon, so he felt obligated to offer him the opportunity to come with him. "I'm sorry about your friend, Jon. May I ask how old you are?"

Momentarily thinking about it, Jon never gave his age a thought because he didn't know how old he was. "I'm not sure, sir. Some people found me and dropped me off here with Father Andres and Father Santos, and now they're both dead."

Thinking Jon would make a fine young soldier, the colonel looked Jon up and down and smiled. "Well now, you look to be about sixteen or seventeen years of age. You must be eighteen in order to join the Confederate Army, but I guess rank has its privileges. I might be able to doctor up some paperwork for you, and if need be I would vouch for you."

Jon thought about what the colonel was saying, but didn't comprehend what the purpose of the Confederate Army was for. "I'm sorry, sir. Why would I join your army and not the other?"

The innocence of Jon brought comfort to the colonel, but he was concerned with Jon's question. "What do you mean son when you say other?"

Looking down at the ground as though he had said something wrong, Jon explained about the other men in uniform. "I saw some other men, but they were dressed in blue clothing. I stayed away and never spoke to any of them."

Suddenly, the colonel's demeanor became anxious as he gathered his belongings. "How long ago did you see these men and in what direction where they traveling?"

Jon thought momentarily, then remembered what he had seen. "I saw the men dressed like you about a day's ride from here. They were headed in a northwest direction. A lot of them looking injured. A couple hours later, I saw the men dressed in blue. It looked like they were headed in the same direction."

With a bit of urgency, the colonel slipped into his coat and climbed up on his horse. "Are you coming with me, Jon, or are you staying here?"

Jon didn't have to think too long about the question because he had no intentions of joining anyone's army. Glancing over at Father Andres's grave, the sorrow he felt earlier began filtering back through his thoughts. "No sir. Thank you for your kindness, but I think I should remain here."

The colonel appreciated Jon's candor but still had some advice before leaving. "Well son, I have to catch up to my men. Remember, life is full of choices. The day might come when you'll have to choose a side. Hopefully you will make the right decision." The colonel turned his horse towards the northwest and with the crack of a riding whip, his horse kicked up dust and galloped away.

Jon sat for a while at the grave site until the sun set, and then he set up a small camp. After a restless night, the morning finally arrived and decisions had to be made. Most of the monastery was now collapsed, and what wasn't collapsed was burned to the ground. Jon knew he couldn't stay, but where could he go? The monastery was the only place familiar to him. The Indians feared him and he didn't have it within himself to become a bandit. The only other option he could think of at the moment was the town of Presidio. He had heard the two priests talk about the town a few times in the past, and he remembered the kind doctor who brought Father Santos's body home.

With his mind moving in survival mode, Jon scoured through the section of the monastery where the kitchen use to be. He managed to find some beef jerky, and then he filled two canteens with fresh water from the well. He then gathered as many weapons as he could carry in hopes of turning them into money. He found several knives, handguns, and rifles. He had no knowledge or use for them, but he figured he could sell them once he got to Presidio. Jon loaded up his horse, then stood over Father Andres's grave and said his good-byes. With tears beginning to fall, he climbed up on his horse and slowly rode away.

During his travels, Jon saw more and more soldiers but managed to always keep his distance. Over the next couple of days, he used his maps to guide himself to Presidio. He had never been in any town, so he didn't know what to do or who to talk to. He remembered when Father Andres told him to stay away from townships because they were evil, but that advice didn't apply anymore. All the shops were closing for the night and he had no money for a hotel, so Jon found an old barn and fell asleep.

Jon awoke early the next morning so he could find the only person familiar to him: Doctor Micah. The town was full of soldiers wearing gray uniforms, and there was a lack of friendly faces walking the streets. He finally wandered into one of the several saloons to ask the whereabouts for the doctor's office. Jon stood watching for a few seconds as the saloon girls danced wildly, throwing themselves at the customers and the belligerent drunkards stumbling around like buffoons. When he finally approached the bartender, he was half-drunk on his own alcohol and annoyed at the fact Jon was a nonpaying customer. The bartender, being half man and half jackass, wasn't very kind, but he surprisingly pointed Jon in the right direction just to get him out of the bar. Not liking what he had experienced, Jon wasted no time vacating the premises. He quickly made his way to the doctor's office where he found Doctor Micah.

It took a few seconds, but Doctor Micah recognized Jon from the monastery. "I remember you. You're that boy who was with the padre at the monastery. What are you doing here? Is the padre all right?"

With an influx of emotions, Jon nearly broke down, but he was able to keep his composure. "Well sir, not really. What I mean is Father Andres is dead."

The doctor could see Jon was upset, so he offered him a chair and some water. "Are you hungry? I can get you some food."

Jon accepted the doctor's kindness and sat down at the table and drank the water. "No sir. I had some beef jerky earlier this morning. I hope you don't mind me coming here."

With his compassion starting to show, Doctor Micah smiled as he took a seat at the table. "No son, I don't mind at all. If you don't mind me asking, what happened?"

Jon decided to keep his time at El Capitan to himself and instead took a breath and another drink of water. "Well sir, I was gone for a few days from the monastery and when I returned, I found Father Andres dead. Some kind of battle had taken place and Father Andres was shot. A kind soldier came along and helped bury Father Andres. He said that I might have to choose a side one day."

Doctor Micah listened to Jon's story with sadness as he attempted to express his sorrow. "I'm sorry about the padre. He was a decent man. I have a room in the back I use for sick patients but I don't seem to have any right now, so why don't you make yourself at home and get some rest? I must make some rounds around town, but I'll check on you throughout the day. I have some fresh water in the other room and a little bit of food. Help yourself and we'll talk some more tomorrow."

With his internal clock right on time, it was rise and shine the next morning for Jon as he was ready to work. He retrieved the weaponry he had brought with him and took them back to the doctor's office with the idea the doctor could help him make a sale. But Doctor Micah was less than enthused to have weapons of destruction in his office. "What are you doing? I told you to make yourself at home, which doesn't include bringing guns and knives in my office."

Jon could see the doctor was upset but offered good reason. "I apologize, sir. I found them at the monastery and thought I could sell them. You see, sir, I have no money and I only have a little bit of jerky left."

Doctor Micah could be a hard man, but he also knew how to extend mercy when mercy was needed. "All right, son. We might be able to sell them to the town's gunsmith for a few dollars. Afterward we can take a walk over to the hotel and I'll introduce you to our shameless town gossip, Harold Hinklemeyer. He's the manager there and his staff serves a mighty fine steak for breakfast. By the way, my name is Doctor Micah, but most people just call me Doc."

Jon was glad to see that Doc wasn't upset with him and he was also glad to be having something other than jerky for breakfast. "My name is Jon, and thank you for your help."

After wheeling and dealing with the gunsmith, Jon settled on $2.50 for all the guns and knives he was selling. Doc wasn't pleased with the deal, but unfortunately the weapons were mostly Confederate and considered worthless. As promised, Doctor Micah took Jon to the hotel and introduced him to Mr. Harold Hinklemeyer. The ever-so-flamboyant manager was happy to meet Jon, mainly because he loved to talk, especially if it was a juicy rumor. Not wanting to over stay their welcome, especially if it meant being subjected to Hinklemeyer's endless stories, Doc rushed Jon off to the dining area. After being seated, they ordered two of the biggest steaks they could order along with eggs and potatoes.

Realizing Jon was unfamiliar with events outside of the monastery, he wanted to try to update him as to what was going on between the states. "Listen to me, Jon. These are very uncertain times we're dealing with. A war between the states has started and it seems like everyone is choosing a side."

Jon sat and listened while he gobbled down his food, while old Doc Micah watched in amazement the speed in which Jon devoured his meal. "What's your hurry, son? I promise, nobody's gonna steal your food."

Hearing the humor in Doc's voice, Jon finished up what he was chewing, then took a drink of water. "Sorry, sir. I'm just use to having vegetables and jerky. I've never tasted food like this before."

Doctor Micah smiled as he watched Jon enjoy his meal, and when the two finished, Doc paid the bill then enjoyed an after-breakfast drink and cigar. With his first time being in a fancy hotel, Jon sat quietly as he looked around in amazement at the exquisite decor. At the same time, some Confederate soldiers were also finishing their breakfast and leaving. As Jon watched them walk out, questions started to plague his thoughts. "Why is there a war and why did they have to kill Father Andres and destroy the monastery?"

Puffing on his cigar, Doctor Micah couldn't help but hear the innocence in Jon's voice. "Listen, Jon. Trouble between the states has been brewing for a long time. I could sit here and educate you about economical grievances, unfair taxation, and individual state rights, but ultimately it comes down to money, power, and the right for all men to be free."

As time went on, Jon stayed with Doc Micah, as the kind doctor was gracious enough to pay for Jon's meals. In return for Doc's hospitality, Jon ran errands and kept the office clean. He was also a good helper when Doc needed to take goodwill trips out to the small Indian villages. As the months went by, Jon learned all he could about the politics involving what was now a civil war. Eventually the Confederate troops were needed elsewhere and vacated the town of Presidio, leaving it unprotected. Being so close to the Mexican border, bandits often raided small townships for supplies and whatever else they deemed to be of value.

Like most of the townspeople, Jon understood some of the arguments made by the southern states and even agreed with most, but he just couldn't fathom the thought of slavery. In his thinking, he constantly reasoned with himself, "How could a man take away another man's freedom and equality and not feel ashamed?" As Jon's mind matured, so did his passion to be on the right side of humanity. Unfortunately, the State of Texas entered the war as a southern state, so that meant fighting for Texas was out of the question. It would have gone against Jon's deepest values, but at the same time, he didn't want to leave his friend Doc Micah or his life he had come to know in Presidio.

Whenever Confederate soldiers would march through town, Jon carried no hatred for them but instead sympathized with them and even felt sorry for them. Most of the time, they looked beaten and battered. A lot of them were young boys barely eighteen that didn't even know what they were fighting for. Most had signed up to fight without knowing the cause, and most wouldn't see their nineteenth birthday.

One day while sweeping out Doc Micah's office, Jon saw several men come riding into town. They looked dirty and mean, and they rode through the streets with malicious recklessness. He thought to himself, "*Bandits.*" As they dismounted their horses, people scurried away or just simply turned around and fled in the opposite direction. Jon watched as one man entered the saloon and the other two men walked across the street to the general store. As usual, whenever men such as these entered town, there were no soldiers around and the town of Presidio hadn't had a sheriff in years. The last sheriff was strung upside down by his feet and beaten like a piñata until he was dead.

A few minutes passed before the saloon-bound bandit came walking back out with several bottles of liquor. Jon watched as he made faces at the children hiding and peaking around corners, then walked across the street to join his partners. As he approached the general store, the store owner came out head-first through the glass window and bounced several times into the street. All three men began to laugh and kick the store owner without mercy. Jon watched in horror and was nearly in tears because there was nothing that could be done.

Suddenly a haunting quiet came over the townspeople. After a few more seconds of laughter and a couple more kicks, the three men took notice that there was no more noise. No wagons were moving. No screaming children. Not even a whisper from the horses. As the storekeeper lay unconscious and bleeding, the three men stood up straight and watched as the townspeople suddenly disappeared inside anything with walls. They slammed the doors and windows shut, leaving the three men to their doom. With curiosity, the three men glanced at each other, then turned to see two men on horseback in the middle of the street. It seemed like they had appeared out of nowhere, but in essence they had quietly slipped into town unannounced and without vanity.

The two strangers sat atop their horses staring at the three bandits while the three bandits stared back with uncertainty. With elegance and grace, the two strangers slowly climbed down from their horses and stepped towards the bandits, leaving a distance of ten paces between them. Almost simultaneously, they pulled back their jackets to show their guns and their intentions, but most importantly to show the badges they were wearing. These weren't the average sheriff badges and the two men weren't the average lawmen. These two men were Texas Rangers. Unofficially created by Stephen F. Austin in 1823, the Texas Rangers were considered one of the most feared fighting forces in the territory.

Now, with uncertainty, came fear. The three bandits had heard the rumors, the myths, and the stories, but now they were faced with the real deal.

Knowing there were three of them and only two Rangers, their confidence was quickly starting to climb. One of the bandits burst out laughing while another just stood staring with an angry silence. Still holding several bottles of liquor, the third bandit dropped all but one bottle. He pulled the cork and took a swig, then handed it off to his friends. By the time the third bandit had finished drinking the liquid courage, it was time to die. Swiping his sleeve across his lips, he threw the bottle against the wall of the general store, smashing it to pieces, then attempted to draw his gun. The other two bandits followed suit, but with no chance of success. As the bandits attempted to draw their guns, the two Texas Rangers had already drawn and shot four holes into the chest of each man. Their speed and accuracy were unequal to anyone the town of Presidio had ever seen.

As Jon ran to get Doc Micah, the two Rangers retrieved the remaining two bottles of liquor and returned them to the bartender. Again, without words or vanity, they mounted their horses and galloped out of town.

In his excitement, Jon grabbed a hold of old Doc Micah's hand and nearly dragged him down the street. "Come on, Doc. You gotta see this. They were so fast!"

Doc had never seen Jon so excited about anything and tried to keep up with his young helper. "Hold on, son. You act like your britches are on fire. What's your hurry?"

As they rounded the corner, Doc could see the three men lying in the street, but there wasn't much to do except call the undertaker.

For the rest of the day, Jon did nothing but ask questions. "Who were those men? Where did they come from and where did they go?" The townspeople were reluctant to talk, so that meant Jon had to exercise his patience and hope that Doc would volunteer some information.

When dinnertime came around, Doc had finished his medical rounds and now he had to deal with Jon. While sitting at the dinner table, Doc forbid Jon to speak about the incident because it was inappropriate, but he could tell Jon was about to burst at the seams. Jon downed his food in record time, but that only compelled Doc to eat slower.

When Doc finally finished his food, he pushed his plate aside and stared at Jon. "Now listen hear, son. Those men you saw today were lawmen. Not just any lawmen. They were Texas Rangers. They're a very proud and distinguished organization. There's not very many of them and since the war began, it seems there's even less. You don't see them often but when you do, stay out of their way."

Jon had many questions and knew his window of opportunity was small. "So, why don't those men fight in the war?"

Gathering his thoughts, Doc leaned back in his chair and lit a cigar. After taking a couple of puffs to get it started, he blew out a cloud of smoke, then took a deep breath. It seemed Jon's eagerness had begun to wear him down. "Well Jon, some joined the war efforts, but the Civil War isn't the only problem the State of Texas has right now. The Texas Rangers were never considered a military force. Instead, they've been commissioned to patrol and protect our borders between us and Mexico. They've also helped subdue some of the Indian uprisings. Unfortunately, what you saw earlier happens all the time, especially in towns like ours, which are situated along the Mexican border."

Thinking about his position on the war, Jon's face lit up as though a great revelation had consumed him. He often thought about becoming a soldier, but he had no interest in fighting for the Confederacy, and at the same time, hated the idea of leaving Texas to fight for another state. It had been close to a year since the war began and there was no end in sight. He thought, "*What a great opportunity to serve the great state of Texas without actually fighting for their cause.*"

Over the next few weeks, Jon begged Doc to buy him a gun so he could practice, but old Doc Micah was dead set against violence and anyone or anything that promoted it. One day some Confederate soldiers came riding into town. As they slowly trotted down the middle of the street, an elderly man, Mr. Albert, spit in their direction then cursed them. In retaliation, one of the soldiers climbed down from his horse and started beating on the defenseless man. Soon, another soldier joined in and soon after, another. Once again Jon watched as the townspeople looked on but was powerless to do anything. When Doc Micah came out of his office, he saw what was going on and rushed over to try and help, but the soldiers just pushed him away. After the soldiers had finished, Mr. Albert laid unconscious and bleeding in the street. After the soldiers left, Doc and Jon picked Mr. Albert up and carried him to Doc Micah's office to be treated.

Like most of the townspeople of Presidio, Mr. Albert felt Texas had entered the wrong side of the war. He had three sons and tried to compare Texas fighting for its freedom in 1836 and the freedoms being fought for now, but they wouldn't listen. His three sons joined the Confederacy and were killed in action within the first few months.

Hours went by and Jon sat waiting outside for any news, even if it was bad. Finally, Doc emerged from the back room, feeling physically and emotionally drained. When he walked outside, Jon could see the look on Doc's face as Doc gave the bad news. "Mr. Albert didn't make it. When you're as old as he was, the body just can't take that kind of punishment."

Jon didn't really know the man, but he had seen him around town and often exchanged pleasantries. With a sense of anger, Jon stood up and started kicking dirt around. "I bet those Texas Rangers would have stopped those soldiers. I bet they would have stomped them into the ground."

With his emotions running high, Jon's anger didn't subside. Instead, he ran down the street and eventually came face to face with the town's one and only church. When the war began, it seemed less and less people attended services each week, which meant church funds ran low. The pastor could no longer keep up with the maintenance, and considering there were no more congregations, it really didn't matter. Having motives of greed and power, he informed the townspeople that God's will was for him to move on and so he did.

Jon hadn't thought about church, religion, or prayer since the death of Father Andres, so he decided to venture into the little one-room church. As he walked in and sat in one of the pews, the storm that was raging inside of him seemed to slowly fade away. He sat for a few minutes staring at the old dusty statue of Jesus Christ, which seemed to stare back at him from behind the pulpit. He didn't know what to think or how to feel, so he bowed his head in prayer. "My Father in Heaven, please forgive me. It's been too long since I sought counsel with you. Father Andres and Father Santos are with you now, and I'm still not sure who I am or what I'm supposed to be doing. Doctor Micah has been very kind to me and I can't thank you enough for his friendship. Father, I know we're not supposed to test thy Lord, but please send me a sign. Walk with me and talk with me in my times of need. For I have fallen and I need your strength to control my anger. I watch as thieves take what they want and drunkards curse your name. The prostitutes flaunt in defiance of you, and good people are beaten and killed all in the name of fun. And all I can do is weep in fear. Please forgive me, Lord, for my lack of courage."

When Jon finished his prayer, he couldn't stop the waterfall of tears. Suddenly he felt a hand on his shoulder and when he looked up, it was Doc Micah. "I thought I might find you here."

Taking a moment to ease into the pew, Doc sat down beside Jon and glanced up at the statue of Jesus. "Listen here, son. When Jesus came into this world, there was chaos everywhere. Christians were being persecuted and killed. The sick and the lame were plentiful, and there were always wars or threat of wars. Jesus wasn't discouraged, nor did he lack courage. Instead, he traveled the land and healed the sick. He had compassion for the people, and for those whose faith was strong, he blessed their lives. He used the word of God to battle the ignorance of man. I guess what I'm trying to say, Jon, is it's all right to be afraid. Being afraid doesn't mean you lack courage. Everyone is scared of something, but courage comes from overcoming your fears and standing up for what's right."

By now, Jon's tears had stopped falling and a hint of a smile had crept onto his face. "Father Andres told me God would never abandon me, but abandoned is how I feel right now. Is that wrong?"

Taking a few seconds to think about his Bible knowledge, Doc Micah offered Jon a smile. "Don't you think Joseph felt abandoned when his brothers left him to die in a pit? And just look at Job. He lost his family, his wealth, and his health. You don't think maybe he felt just a little abandoned by God? Listen to me, Jon. There are all kinds of disparity throughout history. That doesn't mean God has abandoned you, me, or anyone else, for that matter."

In processing the information Doc was trying to instill into him, Jon took a moment and glanced back up at the statue of Jesus. "My God, my God, why have you forsaken me? Even in his last moments, I wonder if Jesus really felt abandoned. It seems God hasn't abandoned mankind, but in times of uncertainty, mankind always seems to abandon God. Why is that?"

It was a good question and as Doc looked around at the empty church, he briefly thought about the pastor with disgust for leaving town. "When people are doing well with prosperity, they attend church on a regular basis and praise God, but when difficult times fall upon them, they seem to fade back into the shadows and curse the world like a bunch of hypocrites. What do I know? I'm a doctor of medicine, Jon, not a psychiatrist. I can't go around helping everyone make life decisions, but I've grown to think of you as a son, and I think I've been on this earth long enough to be able to give you some fatherly advice. So, you seem to have a passion for the Texas Rangers."

Jon knew better then to interrupt, but he just couldn't help himself. "I admire them. They help people and people respect them, and I want to be able to help people in times of need just like them."

Doc could see where the conversation was going, but he didn't mind because it was a conversation he needed to have. "Well son, you're getting older now and you can't spend your life sweeping out my office and doing meaningless chores around town. I still disagree with the violence, so I'm not going to do you any favors like buying you a pistol. What I will do is buy you a rifle to hunt with along with some traveling supplies. About two hundred fifty miles northwest from here located on the Texas border is the town of El Paso. There, you will find Fort Bliss along with the Texas Rangers."

The joy in Jon's heart was overwhelming and had taken the place of his sorrow and anger. He was finally able to see a little light where there had been nothing but darkness. Jon knew it would be a long trip and he wanted to get started right away, so he leaped up out of the pew and ran to the door. As he approached the door, he stopped and turned around to see Doc still sitting. "Come on, Doc. You coming?"

Feeling his bones popping and cracking, Doc slowly got up and walked to the door. "You're really pushing my buttons, boy. Can't you give an old man a break?"

Laughing out loud, Jon could hardly contain his excitement. "I love you too, Doc. If I ever had a pa, I'd want him to be you."

Doc and Jon spent the next few days gathering supplies, then as promised, Doc bought a rifle for the trip and he even bought Jon a new horse: a two-year-old jet-black Mustang named Sapphire with a saddle. Once again Jon was set for a long journey. He gathered his supplies, packed his clothing, and loaded his rifle.

As he brushed Sapphire and got him ready for the trip, Doc came walking into the stable. "Well Jon, It's about that time. I fabricated some paperwork for you just in case you need proof of age. When you get to Fort Bliss, you give them this paperwork and tell them you're nineteen years old. If they ask about your heritage, tell them your father is the doctor in the town of Presidio."

Feeling as though his life was changing for the better, Jon took the papers from Doc and smiled. "Thanks, Doc. I like that. Not that you're the doctor, but that I have somebody I can call my father. Thanks for everything, Pa."

The afternoon was approaching, so Jon gave Doc a hug good-bye then mounted his horse. He rode hard until nightfall then pitched camp and made dinner. As he enjoyed the warmth of the campfire, he decided to view the paperwork Doc had given him. When he pulled it out and unfolded it, a hand-written letter fell out.

> *Jon,*
>
> *All my life, my one and only love has been medicine. I never gave two thoughts to having a wife or children. It humbles me to be looked upon as a father figure and I'm proud to say I love you like a son. There's a lot of good in this world, but unfortunately there's just as*

much bad. Sometimes it's hard to tell the difference. I'll miss you, son.
God speed in your adventures. Doc.

After reading the letter several times, Jon neatly folded it and placed into his pocket.

The next morning, he was up bright and early and ready for a long ride. After some distance of travel, he came across the old monastery. Looking around, he saw that nothing had changed. It was still crumbled and burnt, and the overgrowth had gotten worse, especially around the statue of St. Francis. In honor of his friend, Jon took a little time out of his travel and groomed around the statue. He then stood beside the grave of Father Andres and paid his respects. Afterward, he climbed atop Sapphire and took one last look around before riding off.

Jon made sure to stay clear of Indian Territory, especially Indian burial grounds. But every now and then he would see an Indian or two ghosting him, but they never approached. There were also times he could hear gunfire and cannon fire off in the distance, but he knew better than to be too curious. As Jon tried to keep pace with a northwesterly direction, he tried equally as much to stay as far away from the Mexican border as possible because he never forgot the beat down he received from Rodrigo. He wanted no parts of Rodrigo or his men—or any other bandits for that matter.

Days later, Jon entered the territory of El Paso and eventually found Fort Bliss. There was much hustle and bustle as troops entered and exited the fort. Almost right away, he noticed the fort was like a small town within a town. There were Indian guides, small shops, and makeshift housing for displaced civilians, along with the garrison itself. After a few failed attempts to speak to the soldiers, Jon was finally able to get the attention of a kind women who directed him to the building that housed the Rangers. This was it. Jon wanted to make a good first impression, but what should he say? How should he approach the Rangers and most importantly, who exactly did he need to speak with?

With a plan playing out in his mind, Jon's nerves set the stage for total disaster. When he knocked on the door, there was no answer. Jon knocked again and suddenly a loud voice screamed out, "Come!"

Jon wasn't the nervous type and was rarely afraid of anything or anyone, but the voice he heard screaming didn't sound very pleasant. Jon slowly opened the door and peaked in just to see a bearded not-so-robust man sitting at his desk rummaging through some papers. Without even giving Jon the respect of acknowledgment, the man kept playing with his papers as he spoke.

"What do you want, boy? I'm very busy. There's a war going on. If you're enlisting, the line is at the front gate." In an attempt to be his normal self, Jon swallowed the lump in his throat and walked in to greet the man. "Hello, sir. My name is Jon and I'm here to join the Texas Rangers."

Finally glancing up from his paperwork, the bearded man looked at Jon and laughed. "You don't even look old enough to hold a gun. What makes you think you can be a soldier?"

Still humored by Jon's words, the man got up and walked to a table near the window and sat down. When he opened a drawer, he pulled out a bottle of whiskey. "Here, son, drink this."

Pausing a moment to think, Jon walked over to the man and looked at the bottle. "I'm not interested in drinking or being a soldier, sir. I'm interested in joining the Texas Rangers."

After trying to figure Jon out, the bearded man stood up and grabbed the bottle. He took a long swallow then slammed the bottle down on the table. "My name is John Ford. Most people just call me Rip, but you can call me Sir or Colonel. You see those men out there? They're soldiers. Most will probably die by the end of the week. Some will live but die of some God-forsaken disease later on in life. Yet others just might see the end of this war. In which category will you fall in, boy? Or aren't you willing to take a chance?"

With the colonel pushing Jon's emotions, Jon could feel his anger building. "I'm here to join the Texas Rangers and I'm not leaving here until I do."

Watching Jon get angry gave the colonel a sense of respect for Jon as he picked his bottle up again and took a small swig. "Boy, this is the headquarters for Terry's Rangers, not to be mistaken for the Texas Rangers. I served proudly with the Texas Rangers, but they were decommissioned several years ago. We put up a good argument on our behalf, but in the end, the great state of Texas saw no need to keep us around. Now, my suggestion to you, boy, is to go back to your mama and be a good farm hand."

Jon listened, but he wasn't buying what the good colonel was selling. "I saw the Texas Rangers in the town of Presidio. There were two of them and they killed three bandits at the same time."

Hearing Jon tell his tale, a proud smile came across the colonel's face as reminiscent times wandered through his thoughts. "I said they were decommissioned. I didn't say they weren't still around. There's still a remnant of what we use to be still roaming these parts fighting the good fight. There's not many, but I guess there's just enough to protect the decent folk from troubling times. Just before this war started, we argued for our survival, but like I said, the state of Texas didn't see the need. Then, when the war began, most of us joined the Confederate cause, but some decided to just keep law and order throughout this proud land. Listen, boy, leave this place and go home. If you're lucky enough to see the Texas Rangers in action again, you tell them Ol' Rip Ford says kill 'em all."

Taking one last look at the colonel as he tried to drink away his memories, Jon realized his one and only opportunity had slipped away. Afterward, he left the colonel to his bottle and walked out. Disappointed but not beaten, Jon was determined to find the Texas Rangers. As he left Fort Bliss, he watched the soldiers march in formation to wherever the next battle was. He couldn't help but realize that the colonel was probably right. Most would die before the end of the week.

As Jon started his trek back to Presidio, he decided to ride the border hoping to run into the legendary Rangers. Instead, three days later, he accidentally wondered into a Union camp. Before he could turn around and sneak back out, the Union soldiers surrounded him. Jon was mystified because these men weren't ordinary soldiers. They wore the Union uniform, but had dark brown skin. When Jon climbed down from his horse, he stood staring at the men. Then out of the crowd, came a short, stocky man.

"What's wrong, boy? You ain't ever saw no Negro soldier?"

Before Jon could answer, another man came from behind the trees on his horse. He was much older and more distinguished-looking then the short, mouthy man. He had grayish hair with a white beard and also had dark brown skin. He spoke well and corrected the younger soldier. "Have never seen a Negro. I think my young friend is asking if you've ever seen a black man wearing a uniform before."

Jon thought for a moment because he wasn't sure what was going to happen. "No sir. I've never seen a black man, ever."

With grace and posture, the old soldier climbed down from his horse and approached Jon. "What's your name, son, and what are your values?"

With a smile on his face and no hesitation, Jon held out his hand and introduced himself. "My name is Jon Mason and I get my values from the Holy Bible."

The old soldier shook Jon's hand and invited him to sit and have some food. "Well now, Mr. Jon Mason, my name is Jacob Jabari and even though we hold no rank, some of these find soldiers have adopted me as their leader. It's very nice to meet your acquaintance. You don't look like a Johnny Reb and you have no resemblance to a Yankee, so what are you and why did you try and sneak into our camp?"

Feeling a bit more comfortable, Jon sat down by the campfire and helped himself to some left-over possum. "Well sir, it's like this. I went to Fort Bliss to join the Texas Rangers, but I was told they were decommissioned. But I saw some real live Texas Rangers kill some bandits a while back. They were fearless and protected the townspeople and that's what I want to do."

With a bit of exuberance, Jacob gave Jon a smile. "Well Jon, we've certainly heard of the Texas Rangers, but I don't think we've ever come across any. Mind you, Texas is a Confederate state and we're not too keen on having unwanted holes in our uniforms."

Enjoying the conversation with Jacob, Jon knew he was half-joking. "The Texas Rangers I saw weren't soldiers, and I don't think they would try to hurt anyone who didn't deserve it."

Once again Jon's attitude had innocence about it and was inoffensive, but Jacob kept staring, trying to get a sense of dishonesty in Jon's voice, but there was none. "All right, Jon. Let me introduce you to the rest of the men. You've already met Ezekiel, but he doesn't take kindly to people calling him that, so we just call him Zeke."

Jacob started to point around the camp at the men leaning up against trees, sitting on the ground, and cleaning their weapons. "That's Jesse over there, and those two are Uriah and his younger brother, Chatter. He doesn't talk much. Mr. Music man with the harmonica is Harvey. He keeps us in good cheer with the tunes he plays. The man cleaning his gun is Shelby. He's meaner than a hungry rattlesnake, so do your best to stay out of his way. There's Bo. He's been shot twenty-three times, but he just won't lay down and die. And last but not least, there's Milky Way. We call him that because he's always gazing up at the stars. He's a mute and uses his hands to communicate. He's a hell of a shot with a rifle. Guess you can say we're the lucky nine."

Wondering about the small amount of men, Jon looked around at the gloom on everyone's face. "So, what happen to everyone? Shouldn't there be a lot more soldiers?"

Jacob didn't say anything at first. He just stared into the fire as though he was replaying memories in his mind. "We had orders to secure a passage along the Rio Grande where those Johnny Rebs were crossing over into Mexico, but our reinforcements never came. There was a Battalion of a thousand Confederate soldiers headed our way and we had nowhere to run. There were twenty-five of us and some left over from a broken Company out of Fort Craig. A hundred or so men. Not many and certainly not enough to stop an entire battalion of Rebs. The highest-ranking officer we had was a major. Major Roy Wesley. I tried to talk some sense into him, but he was a real piece of work. Very young and very cocky. Came from good stock and had a chip on his shoulder. He had aspirations of moving up in the ranking system, so he decided to make a stand. Knowing it would have been hostile territory, I tried to talk him into retreating into Mexico. It would have been better than the alternative, and I think he knew that to. Sometimes, pride can blind a man. Anyway, as expected, we got chopped to pieces. Ten minutes into the battle, Major Wesley took a cannonball to the face. We lost a lot of good men that day. I lost a lot of good friends." Enduring the pain of losing his friends didn't sit well with Jacob, so as he relived the battle for a few more minutes, he drifted backward and faded off to sleep.

The next morning, Jon was awakened by the sounds of the men moving about. He saw Zeke wiping down his horse and decided to strike up a conversation. As he approached Zeke from behind, Zeke quickly turned and drew his gun. With the speed of Zeke's motion, Jon's heart dropped as his eyes got big. "Wow! That was fast. Almost as fast as the Texas Rangers I saw."

After seeing it was Jon, Zeke's demeanor relaxed as he placed his gun back into his holster. "Sneak'n up on somebody is a real good way to get yourself killed, boy."

Feeling as though he did nothing wrong, Jon still apologized as he fed the horse some grass. In an attempt to try and lighten the mood, Zeke smiled as he inquired about the Texas Rangers. "So, I was almost as fast?" With some confidence, Zeke stopped brushing his horse and drew his gun even faster than before, firing six bullets into a tree. Jon didn't think much of it until he took a closer look and noticed five of those shots made a circle and the last shot hit the center like a bulls-eye.

"You're really good. You think you can teach me how to shoot like that?"

With a bit of pride hanging off his shoulder, Zeke continued brushing his horse as Jacob came running over. "I know you don't care, Zeke, but I would like to make it back to Union territory in one piece. No telling how many Rebs heard those shots."

Jacob was right. Zeke didn't care. He was full of confidence and arrogance. "Come on, Pop. Ain't nobody for miles. Besides, this boy try'n tell me those Ranga boys is faster than me. Ain't nobody faster than me."

Feeling his anger becoming heated, Jacob glanced down at the ground and smiled. "Boy, your English is getting worse." He then slapped Zeke across his face with lightning speed. His hand moved so fast that Zeke never saw it coming. "Now you listen here, boy. Don't ever bite the hand that takes care of you." With some disgust, Jacob left Zeke wide-eyed as he walked away.

Thinking Zeke might be embarrassed, Jon stayed quiet and continued feeding the horse. Zeke, on the other hand, wasn't embarrassed at all. He smiled then burst into a laugh. "Pops is really someth'n. He taught me every-thing I knowed and made me a better man. I might have been exaggerat'n just a little. Pop is much faster than me with a gun, but sometimes I guess he has to knock my attitude down a notch."

Jon was glad the awkwardness was gone, but he didn't quite understand why Zeke was okay with being slapped. "So, you and Jacob go back a ways?"

Getting ready to tell his story, Zeke finished his brushing and started to clean up. "Yeah, you can say that. Me and my folks belonged to a rich white family in Mississippi. I's was too youngs to understand what was going on back then. Guess'n I was one of the lucky ones, though. I wasn't separated from my parents. Think'n back on it, days were long, and work was hard, but as long as weez did what weez were told, everythin seemed okay. One night, my parents woke me up and said we were leav'n. We were supposed to be meet'n up with some peoples who was tak'n us up north but someth'n went wrong. My ma and pa trusted the wrong peoples and instead of meet'n up with some of thems abolitionist, we were met by the landowner and his henchmen. I still remember that ol' white man like it was yesterday. He put his arm around me like I was his son and made me watch as they hung my ma and pa from a tree. He say he had no choice. That there was, how you say, consequences for be'n disobedi-ent. Consequences my ass. That be a word from them white folk."

Jon was saddened by Zeke's story. Not being able to remember his own parents, he could almost relate to it. "So how did you meet Jacob?"

Feeling the need to finish his story, Zeke motioned Jon over to a tree with some shade and sat down. "When that white man took me back to his plantation, he throwed me in a cage like I was some kinds of animal. The cage sat in the middle of a field, so this way everyone could see me and anyone else think'n 'bout runn'n away would think twice. Couple days with no food and water and with the sun beat'n on me during the day, the rain slap'n me around at night, they finally put me back with everyone else. When the war started a few years lat'a, the farm was overrun by the Union. Pops just happen to be one of the soldiers. I's remember him slapp'n that old white mans around like he was nutt'in, but that wasn't good enough for me. That was the day I swore I's would someday kill that old white man for what he did to my ma and pa. Pops could see the hatred in my eyes, so he tooks me in. He told me I's was much too youngs to waste my life on hatred. Over time, he taught me how to be a man and how to respect people, but best of all he taught me how to use this here gun."

Jon's ears were glued to every word Zeke was saying because his story was so colorful and full of action and that's what he wanted. He was fascinated with the story, especially the part about Jacob teaching Zeke how to shoot.

Just then Jacob came walking over. "If you two are done dilly-dallying around, we need to figure out a plan to make our way up into Kansas."

Eventually everyone got themselves ready to ride, but Jon was undecided what to do. Go back to Presidio as a failure, or take a chance and ride with his new friends all the way to Kansas? Jon didn't have much time to decide, but he took a liking to Jacob, so he chose to stay with him. Besides, Jon saw an opportunity to learn some shooting skills.

Breaking camp, they crossed over the Rio Grande into Mexico, then made their way up through New Mexico. As they traveled, Jacob showed Jon the basics of shooting a gun and even showed him some techniques on how to be a fast draw. Because New Mexico wasn't established as Union or Confederacy, Jacob decided it would be best to travel through Indian Territory.

After hearing Jacob's plan, Jon had his concerns. "Not that I'm trying to question your decision making, but why take the chance with upsetting the Indians?"

Growing accustomed to Jon's innocent questions, Jacob laughed as he shook his head. "Well Jon, it's like this. Indians don't like the white man, but they sometimes tolerate the Confederacy because they kill the blue coats. And although we wear the Union uniform, my hope is they won't bother us because they know we're fighting for our freedom. Something they're all too familiar with. Sometimes I think Indians look at us as being some kind of magical people because of the color of our skin."

Thinking of his own past, Jon chuckled as he rode alongside Jacob. Glancing over at Jon, Jacob chuckled back. "What's so funny?"

Still smiling, Jon began to tell Jacob his story about being found by an Indian tribe and how they were afraid of him because they thought he was some kind of magical being. He told Jacob they gave him the name of Hok'ee and left him out on the plains to die. He also explained about the Mason family saving him from a certain death. Hearing Jon tell his story, Jacob laughed for a moment and smiled. He really liked Jon and was hoping once they made it to Kansas, he would join the Union.

Before Jacob could express how he felt, several cannonballs came whistling by and exploded behind them. Jacob's horse was immediately spooked and reared backward, throwing him to the ground. Everyone else scattered while Jon stood fast. He noticed right away the Confederate troops firing the cannons were too far off to be an immediate threat, so he quickly guided Jacob's horse back to him. As Jacob picked himself up off the ground, a barrage of bullets consumed the area around them. An infantry unit was closing in on them fast from the left flank.

Suddenly Zeke and the rest of the men came galloping in formation from behind, firing back at the enemy. With deadly accuracy, they were able to chop down a large number of Confederate soldiers. With cover fire laid down, Jacob climbed back up on his horse and called for everyone to retreat into the nearby woods. After the exchange of gunfire and the number of casualties inflicted by just eight men, the Confederate soldiers decided not to pursue.

As Jacob guided the men deep into the wooded area, they came across a freshwater stream and stopped to rest. First thing was first: Take a head count and make sure everyone was accounted for.

Jacob looked around but didn't see Chatter. "Did anyone have eyes on Chatter?"

Uriah, who was drinking face down in the river, suddenly jumped up with worry. "My brother was right behind me."

Bo, who had fallen off his horse and was now lying on the ground bleeding from his gut, saw what happen. With weakness in his voice, he explained. "I'm sorry, Uriah. Your brother was in front of me when he took a bullet to his shoulder. When he fell off his horse, I tried to pick him up, but just when I was about to grab him, one of those Johnny Rebs shot him in his back."

Seeing Bo was hurt, Jacob sat down beside him and looked at his wound. He then glanced over at Zeke and shook his head with sadness. Bo started spitting up blood and tried to talk, but it was too late. Although Bo had survived many past injuries, it just wasn't meant for him to continue on. His eyes rolled back into his head as they slowly closed.

Uriah was so enraged, he wanted to go back but Jesse and Shelby stood in his way. They knew he was grieving, but they weren't about to risk anyone else for the purpose of revenge. Feeling frustrated, Jacob stood up and walked over to the stream and filled his canteen with fresh water. As the water entered the canteen, he watched as, one by one, the bubbles burst and disappeared.

With some apprehension, Jon walked over and sat down beside him. "I'm sorry, Jacob. I know you're tired of losing friends."

Jacob appreciated Jon's words, but the war was starting to take its toll. "Well, losing men during war time is expected, but this unit has been together since the start. There were twenty-five of us and seventy-five white soldiers. Most of the company was made up of just young boys barely eighteen and ignorant to the reasons why the war started in the first place, but we had a bond, especially after our first battle. We somehow got through our differences and even learned to like and respect one another. We're all that's left of that company. I promised these men I would get them back to Fort Riley, Kansas. I've been sitting here thinking that we're just like these bubbles you see. One by one, we keep bursting in our own blood and dying off."

Jon could tell Jacob wasn't in the mood to talk, so he left well enough alone. Leaving Jacob to his mood, Jon filled his canteen and made sure Sapphire was tended to. After a few minutes of rest and silence, Zeke, Milky Way, and Harvey dug a shallow grave and laid Bo to rest. They covered him with river rock and said their good-byes.

Afterward, Jacob gathered everyone together. "Anyone here tired?" Jacob looked around and could see the worn out looks on everyone's face, but nobody said anything. "Well, I am. I'm tired of this damn war. I'm tired of watching my friends die, and I'm tired of running."

With a full head of steam, Jacob began to lay out a bold plan that would turn conventional warfare upside down. "Now pay attention, because what I'm about to say might make you think I've lost a few of my marbles. We're about fifteen miles from Comanche territory and those Johnny Rebs are in our way. We don't have the time to go around, and considering we're not sure what other surprises they have waiting for us, I don't think it would be in our best interest. We don't have the manpower to confront them, and I'm damn sure not going back toward Mexico. Now, I'm thinking those Rebs probably think we have more men, which works in our favor."

As Jacob paused to take a breath, Zeke smiled because he knew where Jacob was going with his thinking. "I hopes you talk'n bout a little sneak and destroy, 'cause if'n you are, hell yeah, counts me in."

Listening to Jacob and his angry voice and hearing Zeke speak in an unfamiliar code, Jon had no idea what either man was talking about.

With confidence in his voice, Jacob continued to explain his plan. "Shelby, those Rebs probably have scouts out looking for us, so do what you do best and go get me a Reb uniform and don't kill anyone just for the fun of it." But Shelby was all too happy to go and dispose of a Johnny Reb and take his uniform. With his usual angry face, he wasted no time in climbing up on his horse and galloping away at top speed.

As Jacob looked around, his mind continued to process the part that everyone would play. "Milky Way, you're a crack shot with your rifle, so I need you to find some high ground and take care of any uninvited guests."

As the cogs in Jacob's brain turned, he glanced over at Jon and smiled. "Jon, you're the only white guy we have, so you, my friend, are going to walk right into their camp and blow their munitions."

Feeling a bit confused, Jon was still trying to wrap his mind around what Jacob was proposing. "I don't know about this, Jacob. Won't they know I'm not a soldier?"

Accepting Jon's innocence, Jacob just shook his head. "Jon, I know you're new to the game, but you're going have to keep up. Don't worry, though, I'm going make a soldier out of you yet. Shelby's going bring back a little gift so that you'll feel right at home. Harvey, Jesse, and Uriah, you're going to be my horsemen. When all the fun starts, I'm going to need you three to grab the Rebs horses and make it look like we have a cavalry. Zeke, you're with me. We're going to find the bastard that's in command of those butchers and give him a little taste of his own medicine."

Jacob could tell Jon was worried about his participation in the plan, so he pulled him aside and tried to reaffirm that everything would work out just fine. "Jon, why didn't you run away when those Rebs fired at us?"

Jon was thrown off by the unexpected question and just stared at Jacob for a moment. But in thinking about it, he realized the answer. "You're my friend and you needed help. I saw there was no immediate threat, so I took advantage of the opportunity and grabbed your horse before he could run off."

That was the answer Jacob was looking for. "Listen, Jon. We didn't ask for this war and we damn sure didn't ask to be anyone's personal property. Now, if you follow my direction, I'll get you through this tough time and you'll be helping us get back to Fort Riley. Isn't that what the Texas Rangers are all about? Teamwork and helping people that need help?"

Jon thought about what Jacob was saying and although he could tell Jacob was a master of manipulating words and was leading him on, he also knew that he was right. "All right, Jacob. I'm in."

An hour later, Shelby arrived back at camp with a Confederate uniform. Not that Jacob had any doubts in Shelby's abilities, but he was glad to see he had made it back safe. After the brief "good to see you" reunion, Jacob held the uniform up to Jon to measure it out. "I don't know where these Johnny Rebs are growing these boys, but this guy was huge. Shelby, you couldn't find somebody smaller than Goliath?"

Shelby wasn't much for sarcasm and very seldom laughed or even cracked a smile. "Sorry Jacob, but I couldn't help myself. The horse he was riding was begging for help. So, I felt obligated."

Jacob shook his head with concern then turned his frustration to Harvey. "Harvey, put down that harmonica and get cracking on this uniform. We need to make sure this thing fits Jon."

When night fall came, Jacob could see off in the distance some of the campfires that were lit in the Rebs' camp. While Jacob looked on, Harvey was finally able to cut, tuck, and sew the Confederate uniform close enough to Jon's size to look authentic. Even Jon felt a little more at ease. The plan was set, and it was time for Jon to play his role. Once Jacob explained about the munition tents, he gave Jon a thirty-minute window to inconspicuously waltz into the Rebel camp and locate them. Once there, he would just light a fuse and quietly walk away.

As the minutes went by, everyone else took their places. It wasn't very hard for Jon to just walk into the Rebel camp unnoticed. With the bang-up job Harvey did on the uniform, Jon looked more like a Confederate soldier than the actual soldiers. All he had to do was avoid eye contact and conversations. As he walked the interior of the camp, he saw there were many tents, but they all looked the same. Jon's time was running thin and so were his nerves. Most of the soldiers were either sleeping or standing guard on the outer parts of the camp, so he moved around with very little notice.

As the thirty-minute mark came and went, Jacob began to worry. Zeke could see the anxiety on Jacob's face and tossed in his own opinion. "Come on, Pops. Let's cut our losses and get the hell up out of here. Maybe make our ways back down through Louisiana way. I heared rumor that Major General Butler and his forces are gonna take New Orl'ins. We can hook up with them."

With some frustration and a lot of disappointment, Jacob glanced over at Zeke. "Cut our losses? Don't you mean cut that white boy loose and leave him for dead? And what about Bo and Chatter? Remember them?" As Jacob waited for an answer, Zeke was feeling no remorse, so Jacob continued his verbal assault. "You're really something, Zeke. You really disappoint me. I understand your anger toward white folks, but that boy has done nothing but admire you and you would so easily turn your back on him? And I think I recall a few times when old Bo pulled you out of some sticky situations. Don't you at least think we owe him a little peace?"

Suddenly the night sky lit up with fire as explosions were rapidly going off. Turning his attention toward the commotion, Jacob looked toward the Confederate camp in amazement. "Damn, he did it."

As the Confederate soldiers scrambled around in confusion, Jacob and Zeke confronted them straight on, shooting every gray coat that moved. Uriah, Harvey, and Jesse were right on time. After the initial explosions, they were able to secure the Rebs' horses then stampede them through the camp, making it look like an entire cavalry was attacking while all along, shooting everyone in their path.

Jon, who was still wearing the Confederate uniform, decided it would be much safer leaving the uniform behind before vacating the camp. As he was rushing to take it off, several Confederate cavalry men saw him and concluded that he was acting in a cowardly fashion as a deserter. When the soldiers tried to confront Jon with their swords and guns, Shelby came running out of the darkness and killed two of them with the quick brutality of his Bowie knife. But the third one was able to slash Shelby's arm, knocking him to the ground. The soldier then laughed as he withdrew his pistol and shot Shelby in the leg so he could no longer stand or fight.

"Well, well now, lookie what we have here. I been wait'n me a long time to kills me a Negra."

Just when the soldier was about to strike the final blow, a bullet split his skull from behind, blowing out half of his face. As the blood splattered in every direction, the soldier slowly dropped to his knees then collapsed forward. Realizing the accuracy of Milky Way and his rifle, Jon quickly helped Shelby to his feet and carried him out through the mayhem to safety.

As the munitions continued to explode, the Confederate soldiers scattered in disarray. Harvey, Uriah, and Jesse were successful with their cavalry disguise and made sure the Rebs' horses were dispersed. Milky Way continued his assault, picking off soldiers one by one, creating a safe path of escape for his friends. After their initial charge, Jacob and Zeke continued fighting their way toward the interior of the camp. It wasn't too difficult with all the confusion and pinpoint shooting of Milky Way. When Jacob spotted a colonel barking out orders that nobody was paying attention to, he knew that he had found his man.

By this time, most of the camp was on fire and many of the men were either wounded, dead, or running around after their horses. The colonel who was already angered by the attack saw Jacob and Zeke and fired several shots in their direction before retreating into his tent. With his adrenalin pumping and his appetite for revenge, Zeke quickly dismounted his horse and ran in behind the colonel without any hesitation. The colonel withdrew his sword, but Zeke was quick on his feet. He grabbed the colonel around the neck and choked him until he dropped the sword, then tossed the colonel over a small table. As the colonel attempted to regain his composure, Zeke drew his gun in a quick-draw fashion. But before he could pull the trigger, Jacob entered the tent and stopped him. "Zeke! Don't be stupid. Holster your gun."

Respecting the order given by Jacob, Zeke paused and then smiled. "Maybe we'll meet on the battlefield another time, Colonel. Maybe." With his eyes on a prize, Zeke placed his gun back into his holster then picked up the colonel's sword. "But for now, this beauty belongs to me."

With a distasteful look on his face, the colonel peered into Zeke's eyes. "You filthy animal. You don't even know what you hold in your hands. That sword you think of as a trinket has been handed down through generations of my family. That sword was presented to my family over three hundred years ago and you dare soil it with your dirty hands."

Tired of the colonel and his insults, Jacob approached and stood eye to eye with him. "What is your name, sir?"

With an arrogant look on his face, the colonel inhaled slowly then exhaled a breath of frustration, but refused to answer the question. Jacob smiled then glanced over at Zeke, who was still admiring his trophy. "Listen, Colonel, I'm not really a violent man, but if you don't answer my question, I'm going let my young friend here treat you like the dirty pig you are and carve you up."

The colonel's eyes shifted over to Zeke, who was now smiling back and gripping the sword with intense anger. "I am a gentleman and an officer of the

Confederate States of America, and I don't answer to Union scum or to trash like you."

Jacob could hear the mass confusion starting to die down and he knew his window of opportunity was starting to close. "Zeke, make sure we don't get any uninvited guests."

Zeke took a peak outside and saw that most of the remaining soldiers were either fighting the fires or attempting to gather their horses. "We good for now, Pops, so let's just carve his white ass up and stuff'm with an apple."

Feeling even angrier, the colonel didn't appreciate the distasteful comments at his expense, especially coming from two black men. "That sword is going to be your demise, sir, I promise you. My name is Colonel Augusta Pittman of the twenty-third Infantry Company G out of Fort Stafford Texas. I guess I shouldn't expect much from a couple of savages such as yourselves. It won't be long before my men converge on this tent and then your little game will be over and mine will just begin. Before I execute the both of you, I will personally flog you both without mercy."

Just then, Zeke noticed one of the Confederate captains walking toward the tent. "We's got company, Pops."

With his quick thinking, Jacob promptly picked up the small table and chair and placed them upright on the ground. He then gagged Colonel Pittman and tied him to the chair.

As the captain entered the tent, he began to assess the attack. "Colonel Pittman, sir, we lost a lot of men and horses but—"

Before the captain could finish his sentence, Zeke slashed his throat with the sword. Grabbing his throat, the captain fell to his knees, gasping for air and spitting out blood. He was dead within a few seconds. Zeke then took another look outside to make sure nobody else was approaching. "Okay Pops, we good."

Feeling pressed for time, Jacob turned his attention back to Colonel Pittman. "All right, Colonel. You want to talk about being savage? Make no mistake and have no regrets. This is a war and in God's eyes, we're all savages. Several hours ago, you attacked my men. We were ten men in an open field and all you had to do was surround us and take us prisoners. But you chose to attack us in a cowardly fashion."

Wanting some answers, Jacob pulled the gag out of the colonel's mouth so he could answer for his actions. But Colonel Pittman was outraged. "Your ignorance is beyond comprehension. You killed Captain Watkins in cold blood. He had a wife and three young children. Do you even realize your inhumane provocations?"

As Colonel Pittman's anger escalated, Zeke became more anxious. "Come on, Pops, we gotta go."

Jacob knew his time was running short, but he was enjoying the mental chess game with the colonel. "Ten men, Colonel. You tried to blow us up with your cannons, then you tried to shoot us down with your infantry. A barrage of firepower for ten men. Two of my men died, Colonel. One of them was shot in the back. They were my friends. Did you know their names, Colonel? Did you know how many children they had or if they had wives?"

Once again, Colonel Pittman refused to answer, but he did have some last words for Jacob. "Kill me. Kill me now, Negro, or so help me God, I will hunt you down to the ends of God's great earth and when I find you, you will pay for what you've done here."

Realizing the conversation was over, Jacob glanced over at Zeke and smiled. "You ready to do this?"

As Harvey and Uriah tended to Shelby's wounds, Jon and Jesse anxiously waited for Jacob, Zeke, and Milky Way to arrive at the rendezvous point. After waiting what seemed like forever, Zeke and Milky Way came riding up, followed by Jacob. Feeling relieved, Jon was happy to see everyone was safe.

Once again, Jacob's priority was to make sure everyone was okay, so as he looked around, he saw Shelby had been shot. With a hint of a grin, Jacob climbed down from his horse. "Well, well, Shelby, looks like somebody meaner than you tried to do you in. Can you ride?"

Enduring his pain, Shelby stood up and grunted out some words. "I can always ride."

Glancing over at Shelby, Harvey shook his head and laughed. "He was lucky, Jacob. The bullet went straight through. Those Johnny Rebs can't shoot for noth'n."

Jacob was glad his plan had worked, but he wasn't happy with losing Bo and Chatter. "All right. Everybody listen up. About fifteen miles northeast from here is Comanche territory. They have more numbers than the Apache and they're a lot more ruthless. If we ride out now, we should be there in no time. The darkness should serve as good cover. Once we get there, not even the Confederate army with dare risk a confrontation with the Comanche."

Although everyone was thinking the same thing, only Harvey decided to ask the question. "If the Comanche find us, what'ya think they'll do to us?"

Jacob had been friends with Harvey for a long time and they were just about equal in age, but even Jacob had limitations when it came to friendships. "We could take our chances and go back and risk execution from the Rebs, but if we're so lucky as to make it back down into Mexico, then we risk being found by the Mexican army or maybe shooting it out with a pack of bandits. Take your pick, Harvey. If you have a better plan, then this would be the time to speak up."

Knowing Jacob was just venting his frustrations, Harvey didn't have any response. With no interest in perusing the subject, Harvey's eyes slowly dropped to the ground in hopes that Jacob was done with his banter. After a few more seconds of staring Harvey down, Jacob mounted up and swung his horse around in a northeasterly direction. "Now, let's get the hell out of here before those Rebs come looking for revenge."

After a while of riding, Jacob was feeling comfortable enough to finally slow their pace and somewhat relax. As they rode in a two-by-two formation, Jacob rode alongside Jon. At the risk of being scolded, Jon confronted Jacob. "Seeing how Harvey is one of your friends, don't you think you were a little too hard on him back there?"

Jacob thought for a moment, then glanced over at Jon. "They were all my friends. I told you, there were twenty-five of us to start. Now look at us. Seven of us left. You're damn right I was hard, but Harvey knows I didn't mean anything by it. Harvey's humiliation is the least of my worries. In more ways than one, we're fighting for our lives in a war we may or may not win."

Even though things were looking pretty grim, Jon tried to be of good cheer. "Well, all things considered, I think you're doing a good job."

Jacob knew Jon was trying his best to be positive, but no matter how hard he tried, Jacob just couldn't see the pot of gold at the end of the rainbow. "Listen Jon, I appreciate what you're trying to do, but I promised these men I would get them back to Kansas and I'm just not so sure I'm doing such a good job. Honestly, I was hoping Harvey had a better plan. Contrary to what I told you about Indians not minding the black folks, the Comanche are a breed apart from the rest. They don't like anybody in their territory. No matter the color of your skin. The Apache will brutalize you and kill you, but the Comanche will do ungodly things to you and make you suffer. Anybody not Comanche is considered an enemy. If we're discovered, maybe we can make some kind of deal. If not, then hopefully they'll be compassionate and kill us quick."

After a few minutes of enjoying a nighttime breeze, they arrived at what looked like an abandoned camp, so Jacob gave a silent hand signal to stop and dismount. There were several fire pits along with red-colored rocks and stakes lying about with various books and trash cluttering the area. With an uneasy feeling, Jacob ordered everyone to form into a defensive position while he slowly and rigorously investigated the surrounding area. When he came back, the news wasn't good.

Zeke was the first to speak up. "So, what's the verdict, Pops?"

Jacob didn't say anything at first, then he grabbed the reigns of his horse and started to backtrack. "Everyone form up and follow me. Don't make any sudden movements and try not to make any unnecessary sounds."

As everyone followed, Jacob led them a few hundred yards in the direction from which they came from. When they finally stopped, Jacob had Zeke take care of tying up the horses and securing their gear. While Jesse and Milky Way built a fire, Uriah made Shelby comfortable then patrolled the outer perimeter of their camp.

Jacob was a solid man and after years of friendship, this was the first time Harvey had seen him spooked. "Jacob, talk to me. What's going on?"

Feeling a bit anxious, Jacob's eyes were wide like he had seen something heinous. "We're here."

By now, Zeke had finished with the horses and Uriah had returned. The campfire was in full swing and everyone took a seat. Like a bunch of friends telling ghost stories, everyone waited on Jacob to elaborate. When he had finally gathered his thoughts, Jacob broke the silence. "Well, what we saw up ahead wasn't a campsite. At least not in the sense of what we think of as a camp."

Before Jacob could explain, Harvey interrupted. "What did you mean before when you said that we were here? Where's here?"

Warming his hands over the fire, Jacob paused then continued his explanation. "What we saw is the Comanche equivalent to posting a keep-out sign. When I was checking around, I saw some bones along with a couple of skulls. And those fire pits weren't for roasting pig."

While Jacob explained their position, Jon sat and listened while his nerves started to breakdown. "So, what do you think they were used for?"

While gathering his thoughts, Jacob stared into the fire as he slowly shook his head. "Remember our conversation about the Comanche? I told you they were capable of doing some ungodly things. Well, you just saw some of them. Those skulls I mention are attached to bodies, which are buried underground. As part of the torture process, the Comanche will bury their victims up to their chins then cut off their eyelids. This way, the sun will burn their eyes out before they eventually starve to death. Those fire pits are also used for torture. They tie their victims to a thick branch and turn them over an open fire, so they roast to death."

With his men hanging on every word, Jacob stopped for a moment and tried to swallow the lump that was forming in the back of his throat. The fire was burning hot, so he took a minute to wipe the sweat from his brow and think about what he had said. After hearing Jacob's words and seeing him nervous, Jon's nerves wasn't feeling any better. "What about the red paint on all those rocks? What does that mean?"

Harvey saw that Jacob had had enough, so he continued to school the youngster. "That wasn't red paint, Jon. My guess is they beat some of their victims to death. I've also heard they sometimes like to stake their victims to the ground over top an army of red ants."

As the fire burned, an eerie silence fell over the camp. Everybody's nerves were on high alert and sleep wasn't an option as Jacob's thoughts ran rapid with doubt. Unfortunately, it was one of those times when a plan sounded better than what it was. After a while, the silence started to become too heavy to bear.

When the fire started to crackle and pop, Jacob took the opportunity to speak. "Zeke, you take first watch and I'll relieve you in a few hours. Everyone else, try and get some rest. We move out at first light."

Everybody heard what Jacob said, but there was no rest for the weary. Although nobody said anything, they were all thinking the same thing: Sleep with one eye open and have a rifle by your side with a revolver lying across your chest.

As soon as the sun pierced the morning sky, Jacob made sure everyone was mounted and ready to go. The plan was simple: close knit two-by-two formations with no one person breaking rank for no reason. Jacob also made sure Jon would be riding alongside him just in case of any trouble. "All right, Jon, you're with me. Everybody stay close and keep your eyes open. If anything happens, make sure we stay together and use your horses for cover if necessary. Zeke, I know your high emotions can get the best of you, but I need you to stay focused."

With his usual arrogant attitude, Zeke smiled then let out a small laugh. "Come on, Pops. Ain't no Comanche gonna take me down."

Harvey, who was still feeling the effects of his nerves from the previous night's conversation, had just about had all he could take from his egotistical partner. "Zeke! It's your arrogance that just might get us all killed. Now shut the hell up."

Before the argument could go any further, Jacob put a stop to it. "Now, everybody listen. Fighting and arguing with one another isn't going to get us anywhere. They already know we're here. They knew we were here last night.

They also know there's only eight of us. If they wanted to kill us, they would have done it by now. I need everybody to keep a cool head so maybe, just maybe, we'll get through this without incident."

With careful movement and a slow pace, they made their way back to Comanche territory. When they arrived back at the torture site, they slowly continued through without stopping. While riding through, everyone, including Jon, glanced around and couldn't help but wonder who the victims were. "So, why do you think they do such terrible things?"

Jacob thought for a few seconds then came up with the best answer he could think of. "Intimidation maybe. Warnings definitely. Or maybe they just simply enjoy it. But whatever their reasons, I sure don't want to piss them off."

As they began to get deeper into Comanche territory, the sun started to beat down on them. So, Jacob decided to give the horses a break by dismounting and walking for a while. With Comanche being a plains tribe, there was no real cover to take comfort in for shade. Just a few rock formations or a couple of boulders every now and then. As they battled the heat, the horses started to become restless. Finally Jacob gave the order to stop. Jesse and Milky Way were the two at the rear of the formation.

After Jacob gave his order for rest, Jesse, turned to see a large number of Comanche closing in from behind. "We have incoming, Jacob."

Before Jacob could react, Zeke grabbed his rifle. As he lifted his rifle and took aim, Jacob quickly grabbed it and pulled it from his hands. "I told you, Zeke, I need you to stay focused. We're trespassing on their territory and we don't have a chance in hell to survive a gun battle out here in the open."

Just then, Jacob turned to see more Comanche coming from every direction. With his anxiety on the rise, Zeke wasn't thrilled with Jacob's decision not to draw first blood. Forming an arrogant smirk, he decided to speak his mind. "I love you, Pops, but you ain't been right yet. Ever since you made the decision to get us back to Kansas, we been do'n noth'n but dy'n."

If it wasn't for the fact that they were now surrounded by the Comanche, Jacob would have slapped the silly smirk off Zeke's face. In a low baritone

and his arrogant son. His trigger finger was just itching to put a bullet in between Two Feathers' eyes, but something inside of him was telling him to exercise patience. Two Feathers gave Jacob one last smirk, then joined his father and two other warriors as they circled Jacob's men, screaming and yelling as a sign of dominance.

As Seven Bulls screamed out his warrior mentality, everyone else joined in as though they were already victorious in battle. While the Comanche readied themselves for fun and torture, Jacob watched as Seven Bulls and his son circled his men and carried on like savages. Once again, a brief thought entered his mind to just shoot it out and take down as many Comanche as possible.

Looking around, Jacob saw that Zeke was running low on patience and he could tell the other men were now getting restless. With his restless thoughts, Jacob slowly moved his hand toward his side arm, and just as he was about to draw, Seven Bulls came to an abrupt stop. Suddenly it was quiet. Nobody screaming. Nobody acting out. No movement. Just the sound of a light breeze blowing across the plains. Seven Bulls had spotted Jon in the middle of Jacob's men and became suspicious. Now, it was Seven Bulls with a look of worry.

Two Feathers waited for his father to speak, but Seven Bulls just sat and stared with concern. With curiosity, Two Feathers finally approached his father. After a few moments of whispering to each other, Two Feathers approached Jacob, who had already rejoined his men. Out of respect for his father, Two Feathers didn't say anything and waited for Seven Bulls to speak again. After an eerie silence, Seven Bulls approached Jacob and spoke. After listening to Seven Bulls, Jacob turned to Two Feathers for the translation.

"My father not afraid of no man. He is a great warrior and a wise leader. He seek council with the one who different."

Jacob, who still had his hand on his side arm, slowly pulled it away and glanced over at Jon. "Jon, they want to speak to you."

Jon's heart was still pounding from the earlier intimidation and now he was shocked that the Comanche even noticed him. Feeling even more apprehensive than before, Jon slowly guided his horse over to Seven Bulls.

Once again Seven Bulls just stared at Jon as though he was looking at a ghost. Finally he spoke. Afterward there was silence. Two Feathers waited for Jon to respond, but Jon just sat and stared back at Seven Bulls.

After a few more awkward moments, Jacob decided to speak. "What does Seven Bulls want with Jon?"

At the risk of disrespecting his father and possibly upsetting the spirit world, Two Feathers ignored Jacob and spoke directly to Jon. "My father say you are the one called Hok'ee. You wear the mark. You are the lost spirit that roams the land like a ghost. You enter the visions of our warriors and kill them while they sleep. You carry death within you. My father say you will destroy us and our land if we try to harm you. Why do you ride with such cowards?"

Thinking Two Feathers might be referring to his necklace, Jon thought back to his childhood. Two Feathers brought back some bad memories for Jon, but instead of taking offense, he realized Seven Bulls gave him a great opportunity to get Jacob and his men out of harm's way. "Your father is very wise and speaks the truth. I am the one called Hok'ee, and these men are not cowards. They are great warriors which whom I have chosen to help me on my quest. They are powerful spirits who help guide me. If you dare to interfere, I shall bring great destruction and death to your people."

Staring at Jon as though he was a fake, Two Feathers then turned to his father and spoke to him in length. When he was finished, Seven Bulls looked at Jon and, with his head held high, spoke words of pride. He then bowed his head out of respect, then turned and rode away.

With suspicion, Two Feathers peered at Jon then spoke. "My father say you may go in peace. It is agreed we honor the spirit world and we wish to remain at peace. You shall not enter these lands again. If you do, then it is the spirit world who breaks the promise and we shall strike without mercy. The Comanche do not tolerate disrespect and as you say, are not afraid to die for what we believe. Over the next ridge, you will find water for horses. Now go and do not return."

With a bad feeling of unnecessarily giving free passage through their territory, Two Feathers turned his horse around and gave the other Comanche the sign to disperse.

After the Comanche were out of sight, Jacob breathed a huge sigh of relief. Not that Jacob is the kind of man that looked for a pat on the back, but he remembered the words Zeke said to him earlier. As Zeke mounted his horse, Jacob rode up beside him. "Listen Zeke, I know you've lost friends and I know you're frustrated but attacking me or anyone else in this group doesn't help matters. War is war. If you couldn't handle the thought of losing friends, then maybe you shouldn't have joined this fight. And maybe I should have just left your ass behind to work the white man's fields. Either way, I can give a damn about how you think I'm doing as a leader."

Once again Zeke knew he was out of bounds, so he didn't say anything. What could he say? He knew Jacob was right. As the shame wrapped around his outside, the anger slowly simmered on the inside. He waited until he knew Jacob was finished with his scolding and trotted off toward the waterhole. After hearing Jacob speak to Zeke in a not-so-friendly tone, everyone else dared not say a word. So they mounted up and followed Zeke to the waterhole.

As Jon prepared to follow, Jacob asked him to stay behind. "Well now, Jon, you seem to have made yourself quite useful. I just wanted to thank you for saving our hides. Not that I would ever admit to it, but sometimes I think Zeke is right. I'm not doing such a good job of keeping us alive."

With a great feeling of knowing he escaped certain death, Jon thought for a moment then smiled. "I never thought I would welcome the thought of being labeled as a wondering spirit."

Also feeling the weight of the world falling off his shoulders, Jacob smiled then burst into a laugh. "Well, whatever you are or wherever you came from, I'm sure glad you wound up with us. Now, let's get the hell out of here before those Comanche change their minds about you."

After a few more days of riding, relief was insight. Jacob and his men finally arrived at Fort Riley, Kansas. After taking care of the horses, most of the men headed for food and drink. Jacob had to report in with the fort commander, so Jon tagged along. Dusty, dirty, hungry, and just plain worn out, Jacob dragged himself into Colonel Isidore Shaw's office. The colonel's men called him by rank, but his friends just called him Izzy. As Jacob stood in front of the colonel, Jon took to a nearby seat and waited. When the colonel stood up from his desk, Jacob saluted him. Being a subtle man, the colonel moved with grace in order to stand face to face with Jacob.

"You and your men have been quite busy. Word of your exploits has spread across the states like wildfire." As the colonel paused, he looked Jacob up and down. Suddenly a big smile stretched across his face. "Damn good job, Jacob. Damn good job."

Accepting the kind words in honor of the men he lost, Jacob shook his friends' hand and felt good about being home. "Thanks, Izzy. It's good to see you too."

Most people might think it's odd for a black soldier to call a colonel by his nickname, but Jacob and Colonel Shaw became best friends many years before the war. Born in Kansas, which was a northern state, Jacob still struggled as a young adult. One day, four brothers who were pig farmers tried to accuse him of stealing some pigs. It was a false accusation, but it was hot, the day was dragging, and they were bored. They chased Jacob for several miles, hoping to catch him and hang him just for fun. By the time they caught up to him, Jacob had stumbled onto some farmland owned by the Shaw family. Very prominent, the Shaw family owned several thousand acres.

With his clothes torn and hanging off and the hot sun beating down, Jacob was tired and knew he wouldn't be able to fight off all four brothers, so he gave into the notion of running and just waited for whatever fate would follow. Knowing they had caught their prize, the brothers surrounded him and pushed him from one brother to the other. They laughed and taunted Jacob, calling him names and of course telling him how he was going to die.

Izzy, who was out riding and checking the fence posts, heard the loud yelling and guided his horse to where the noise was coming from. When he arrived, he saw Jacob on the ground and the brothers taking turns at kicking him. When he approached, he yelled for the brothers to stop. He then climbed down from his horse and identified himself. He tried to explain that his family owned the land and they were trespassing, but they just looked at one another and laughed. Izzy, who was quite good at target shooting, didn't take kindly to being laughed at, especially on his own property.

As Izzy stared, his temper began to rise. He was young and at this stage in life had only shot at inanimate objects. Considering the circumstances, he wasn't opposed to killing the pig farmers. He noticed that only two of them had pistols. A third brother had a rifle but was using it as a club to beat on Jacob. Izzy was hoping that it was inoperable. The fourth brother, who was the biggest, had a large hunting knife stuffed down the front of his pants. Izzy took a couple steps toward the brothers, who were now preparing themselves for a different kind of fight.

Without warning, Izzy withdrew two dueling pistols from his waist and fired. He hit two of the brothers in the gut, which killed both, but not before one of their stray bullets struck Izzy's horse. Without hesitation, Izzy quickly moved back to his horse, which was now dead, and pulled out a third pistol from a side pouch and took aim at the brother with the rifle. After Izzy fired his gun, the bullet struck the brother in the leg, causing him to fall over. Unfortunately, the rifle that was in question worked well and Izzy took a bullet to his shoulder. As he stumbled backward, he realized the biggest brother was still left to deal with.

As Izzy lay on the ground bleeding, the last brother looked around at the demise of his siblings and became infuriated. He pulled his large hunting knife from his pants and began to walk toward Izzy as Izzy attempted to reload. Before he could do any harm, Jacob picked himself up and tackled the much larger man. He tried his best to fight, but the large man shook Jacob around like a rag doll. After toying with Jacob for a few more seconds, it was time to end the game and move onto Izzy. With a heavy fist, the big man struck Jacob several more times, knocking him to the ground. Just for pleasure, he kicked Jacob one last time then readied his knife to finish him off. Suddenly, a bullet from Izzy's gun entered his back and made its exit through his heart. Glancing up at the sky, the large man stumbled in circles, then finally he stole his last breath as he fell to the ground.

Jacob, who was still feeling the pain of being beaten and nearly killed, slowly got up and made his way over to Izzy. He helped Izzy to his feet, but there was still one brother with a bullet in his leg and he was still alive. Just like Izzy, up until this point in life Jacob had never killed a man. The wounded man, who was now lying on the ground holding his leg, happened to be the youngest brother out of the four. Jacob was quite content with walking away, but Izzy had other plans. He had reloaded his gun and wanted to put it to good use. He handed his gun to Jacob with the expectation that he would kill the last brother. But Jacob looked at the gun then at the wounded boy and felt nothing but pity.

When the young boy saw that Jacob didn't have it in him to shoot, he began to insult Jacob and called him several foul names. The feeling of pity that Jacob had felt slowly faded away, and the idea of how many other people would have to succumb to this boy's torture quickly filled his thoughts. Without hesitation, Jacob pointed the gun at the boy's head and fired. Izzy, who was still struggling with his wound, saw that Jacob was frozen with fear and peeled the gun from Jacob's shaking hand. After taking care of Izzy's wound, Jacob carried him several miles back to his house so he could receive proper care. To show their gratitude, Izzy's parents took Jacob in and treated him like a son.

After Colonel Shaw and Jacob did their catching up, Jacob introduced the colonel to Jon. "Izzy, I'd like for you to meet my friend, Jon. He's the reason we're standing here. If it wasn't for Jon, we'd all be roasting over a Comanche fire right about now."

Even though Jon wasn't in the military, he still stood up out of respect for his elders, then held out his hand and gave the colonel a good, firm handshake. After shaking Jon's hand and feeling his grip, the colonel smiled and looked Jon up and down. "Well now, son, why aren't you wearing one of our uniforms?"

Not knowing the colonel, Jon wasn't sure how to react to the question so Jacob took it upon himself to let Jon wiggle off the hook. "Well now, my friend Jon wants to join the Texas Rangers."

After hearing that, the colonel glanced over at Jacob, who was winking his eye, then turned his attentions back to Jon. "Well now, son, the Eighth

Texas Calvary, better known as Terry's Texas Rangers, why, they're a real lively bunch with a reputation bigger than Texas itself. I take it you don't believe in all men being equal and free?"

Before Jon could speak up, Jacob once again came to his defense. "No Izzy. Jon wants to join the original Texas Rangers. He wants to be able to protect people and help them in their times of need."

Realizing the bond between Jacob and Jon, the colonel offered Jacob a cigar then sat down at his desk and lit one up for himself. "If it wasn't for this war, I would have great admiration for those boys. Very proud group. Good fighting men. Stood for honor in every sense of the word, but I heard once the war broke out, most of them took up arms with the Confederacy. Word has it they don't even exist anymore."

Now the colonel was talking about something Jon had firsthand knowledge of, so Jon didn't hesitate to respond. "No sir. I can assure you, they do exist. I saw two of them kill three bandits like it was nothing."

Once again the colonel glanced over at Jacob, who was now enjoying his cigar. "Well, I think Jacob would agree that killing a man isn't exactly nothing. To look into a man's eyes knowing you're going to send him to be judged by his maker can be a heavy burden, to say the least. Maybe one day Jacob will explain to you what I'm talking about, but in the meantime, I wish you the best of luck on your quest. Now, if you'll excuse us, Jacob and I have some military matters to discuss."

Jon took the hint that the colonel wasn't too pleased with his current decisions, so he excused himself and joined the others. After Jon made his exit, the colonel expressed his displeasure. "So, what about this boy, Jon? Sounds like he needs a little convincing that our cause is for the greater good."

After taking a couple more puffs on his cigar, Jacob thought for a moment then smiled. "I could say he's young and stupid, but he's not. He's ambitious and you can't fault him for that. But he has a sense of mystery about him. I can't quite put my finger on it. He's a good kid, Izzy. Saved our hides more than once."

After hearing Jacob's praise, the colonel decided not to pursue the issue, so instead he pushed the conversation into a more important direction. "Listen, Jacob, far be it from me to judge your actions, but this war isn't going to last forever, which brings me to my counterpart: Colonel Augusta Pittman of the twenty-third infantry out of Fort Stafford, Texas."

Thinking about what he did, the name brought a smile to Jacob's face. "What about him?"

Colonel Shaw gave a half-smile, then shook his head in disgust. "Jacob, you took the liberty of embarrassing him on behalf of the Union army, and from what I'm hearing, it was a quite large embarrassment. I heard Jefferson Davis himself caught wind of it and was thinking about removing Colonel Pittman from command. If it wasn't for the fact they're running short on supervision, I'm sure he would have done it by now."

After a brief silence, the colonel continued with his concerns. "You should have killed him, Jacob."

Before Colonel Shaw could continue, Jacob reacted with displeasure. "Like I killed that boy years ago? Come on, Izzy. You kill a man during battle or you kill a man in self-defense. You don't kill a man in cold blood, damn it!"

The colonel could hear the anger in Jacob's voice, but continued to voice his concerns. "We're in a war, Jacob, and he's the enemy. That should have been enough reason for you. Colonel Pittman is not somebody you want to cross then leave breathing."

Still feeling the fatigue from his battle to get home, Jacob finished his cigar then stomped it out. As he walked over to the window and glanced out at the troops coming and going, Jacob tried to reason out his decision not to kill an enemy colonel "Like you said, Izzy, there's a war going on. Colonel Pittman has bigger issues than me or his vanity to think about. Besides, we're not those two young boys that met years ago. Your parents took me in. They treated me like a son and made me a part of their family. Father taught us hard work and how to be men. Mother taught us compassion and mercy."

Colonel Shaw could see his words were falling on deaf ears, so he decided to tone the conversation down and try to express the worry he was feeling. "He's a rattlesnake, Jacob, with a very dangerous bite. He'll come after you just to save face. If he doesn't get you during this war, then he'll create his own personal war afterward. Either way, you're going to wind up face to face again. Mark my words."

Reviewing the conversation in his mind, Jacob knew Izzy was right. Colonel Pittman was either going to get revenge or die trying. "All right, Izzy, you made your point. Now, get that bottle out that I know you have hidden in your desk drawer and don't be stingy with it."

Realizing Jacob knew him all too well, Colonel Shaw smiled and pulled a bottle of whiskey from his desk. He poured two hefty drinks and handed one to Jacob. "Here's to the men you've lost. They were good men, Jacob, and I pray our endeavors will honor them in the end."

After a few more drinks and some laughs, Jacob left to find what was left of his men and it didn't take long. They were in the mess hall trying to school Jon on women and drinking. Jacob was tired and didn't have a lot of good news, so he got right to the business at hand. "Listen up. We have a day's rest coming, then we're moving out. Colonel Shaw is attaching us to a regiment of a thousand men. We're supposed to meet up with two other regiments down in Arkansas. From there, we're going to filter down through Mississippi and Louisiana. Jon, I need you to come with me. We need to talk."

Jacob didn't sound too pleased, but that didn't worry Jon. He wasn't a soldier, so what the colonel needed them to do didn't affect his decision to go back to Texas.

As Jacob walked and talked, Jon followed and listened. "Listen, Jon, every man has to follow his own destiny, and I think your destiny involves something I just can't comprehend. In any case, I want you to ride with us down into Arkansas, and then you can split off and make your way into Texas. With that said, I wanted to thank you properly for saving my life, not just once but two times."

Having a certain gift in mind, Jacob led Jon into the stables where he had his gear stored. When he pulled out one of his saddlebags and opened it up, Jon's eyes widened when Jacob pulled out a gun belt and gun. The belt was black and was laced with silver inlay, and Jon was instantly mesmerized.

Seeing that Jon couldn't take his eyes off the belt, Jacob smiled and handed it to him. "Try this on for size and see how it looks."

Jon took a moment before he could breathe, then he wrapped the belt around him and buckled it nice and snug. He then tied the leg strap to his leg. "Is this right? How does it look?"

Jacob smiled with pride then handed Jon a Remington 1858 with ivory grips. "It looks damn good on you, son. Damn good. I wanted to someday give it to Zeke, but I think you've more than earned it." Jon admired the gun and studied it like it was something special, then he slowly placed it in the holster.

Jon's clothes didn't exactly match the fancy gun belt, so Jacob suggested they walk over to the general store to buy Jon some decent clothing. As they walked, Jacob told the story behind the gun belt. "Right before the war started, I took a trip down to Mexico. Little town just across the border called Puerto Palomas. I knew it wasn't the brightest idea, but I was hoping to find me one of those beautiful señoritas that I kept hearing people talk about. Well, I found one. She was stunning, but she was also attached. I didn't know it at the time until her man walked into the bar and crashed our little party. He was a pretty big guy, but lucky for me, he wasn't interested in fist fighting. However, he was wearing that gun belt and invited me outside. There I was, a black man in a strange land with no friends in sight. I remember thinking how fast he must be since he had that fancy belt on."

Before Jacob could finish his story, Jon's excitement got the best of him. "But you have the gun belt, so that means you beat him, right?"

Jacob laughed as they entered the general store. "Yes Jon, I have the belt, but it wasn't without consequences. When I walked outside, he was there waiting for me. He had a big grin on his face because there were three other men standing beside him. Even though the fight was between him and me, I knew that if by chance I won, his three friends would try and finish me off. Well, I was right. After a few seconds of staring me down, he drew his gun and I drew mine. Come to find out, that fancy holster didn't help him. He wasn't fast at all. Just stupid. He underestimated me and that cost him his life."

As Jacob sifted through some clothing, Jon wondered about the consequences. "You said there were consequences. What did you mean?"

Jacob held up a few shirts, but didn't like the look. He then found a pair of brown pants that was just right. "Well, I told you he had three friends. They weren't too bright either. They also underestimated me and thought I was going to lose. By the time they realized what had happened, it was too late. After I shot the big man, I kept firing. I emptied the rest of my bullets into those sorry bastards. Now, here's where the story gets a little sticky. The man with the fancy holster that was now dead on the ground had a brother who happened to be the local sheriff. He came running out of the resident whore house with his pants hanging off his ass and saw his dead brother on the ground."

Jon was so wrapped up in the story, he had stopped looking through the clothes and was all ears. "So, did you explain that it wasn't your fault?"

With a surprised look, Jacob smiled. "Explain? Were you listening to me when I said black man in a strange country? What was there to explain? I had just killed his brother and what I had to say didn't matter. As he was trying to pull up his pants, he took a couple of shots at me. Now, listen carefully because this can be a future lesson for you. Always carry more than one gun. I was out of bullets and out of ideas. Several of his shots missed, but one caught me in my collar bone."

Jon was like a statue, and the intensity of the story had him grinding his teeth. "Come on, Jacob, what happened?"

Jacob, who was still looking through shirts, laughed. "Well, if you stop interrupting, I'll tell you. Come to find out, the four men I killed, along with the sheriff, had been terrorizing this little town for years. They made it their own personal playground. Raping, pillaging, extorting—you name it and they were doing it. Well, after I killed those four men, I guess the locals decided they had had enough so that little cutie I was with grabbed a rifle out from behind the bar and shot the sheriff. After passing out, I woke up the next day and to my surprise, that little señorita was hovering over me."

Shaking his head and smiling, Jon continued the quest to find a shirt. "Wow, Jacob! Have you ever met anybody faster than you?"

Jacob paused for a moment and thought about the question. "Well, I'm still here, so I guess not. But don't think of me as being arrogant. There's always somebody faster. You just have to be smarter than that guy."

Just then, Jon picked out a shirt and held it up. It was beige with a collar and tie string. "What'ya think, Jacob?"

Jacob took the shirt and held it up as he admired it. "I think this is perfect. Soft, warm color that fits your personality. Now, let's find you a hat and some nice boots."

After just a few minutes, they had picked out a pair of shiny brown boots and a light-colored beige hat to complete Jon's outfit. Not wanting to waste another minute, Jon stepped into the back room to try on his new clothes. When he came back out, Jacob handed him his new gun belt, which Jon couldn't strap on fast enough. "Do I look okay?"

With a gleam in his eye and pride in his heart, Jacob looked Jon up and down. "I think you look just like a Texas Ranger."

The next day Jacob and his men packed up and readied themselves for a long trip and a long campaign. The men often teased Jon about his new clothes, but Jon was okay with that. He looked good and he knew the other men were just jealous. Jon spent most of the trip riding along side of Jacob and talking. During their down time, he would seek advice from the other men about drawing his gun in a timely fashion. Whenever possible, he would practice the advice he received.

As they approached the Arkansas line, it was time for Jon to say his good-byes. He personally went around to every man and shook their hand and thanked them for their advice, experience, and friendship. Uriah, Milky Way, Shelby, then Harvey and Jesse.

When he came to Zeke, Zeke shook Jon's hand with a smile. "Well now, looks like you growed up real fast. Keep practic'n, boy, and maybe you be as fast as me one day."

Being accustomed to Zeke and his ways, Jon paused for a moment then laughed. "Thanks for all your help, Zeke. Take care of yourself."

Then came time to say good-bye to Jacob. Instead of just a handshake, Jacob decided to ride with Jon a few miles to the Texas border. During their time, Jon still had some questions lingering in his thoughts, but before he could ask, Jacob pulled out a small Bible. "Jon, I probably should have given you this the night I found it, but I just didn't have the heart. The night we stumbled upon the Comanche torture site, I came across a small box of papers. Among the papers was this Bible."

With some curiosity, Jon took the Bible and opened it up. Inside the cover was some worn-out words that could no longer be read and an old photo of a family. On the back of the photo simply read "The Masons." Jon didn't say anything, but with a grieving heart, he placed the photo back into the Bible and stuffed the Bible into his saddlebag.

After Jacob finally swallowed the lump in his throat, he dared to ask, "When I found it, I could tell it had been there for a very long time. Is it them?"

Jon couldn't get the words out, but by the look on his face, Jacob already knew the answer.

With an overwhelming feeling of sadness in his heart, Jon tried vigorously to suppress the horrible feeling by changing the subject. "So, tell me, Jacob, why didn't you give this gun belt to Zeke?"

Although Jacob hadn't planned on a serious talk, it was a valid question that deserved an answer. "Well now, that's a good question. You already know I think of Zeke as a son, and giving him such a gift would have been the natural thing to do. Did Zeke tell you about his parents?"

Thinking back to Zeke and the story he told, Jon didn't answer right away, but it was a story that profoundly affected him. "Zeke told me that horrible story. I feel sorry for him. I can't imagine watching your own parents die."

Knowing Zeke probably withheld some of the facts, Jacob, who was feeling somewhat sad, gathered his thoughts and told Jon the story that Zeke didn't tell. "Well, Zeke and I were camped out one night down on the Missouri/Kentucky line. I had been trying to teach him proper language skills and how to respect people and himself. I taught him how to handle a gun and shoot, and he was doing quite well. I woke up one morning and he was gone. I thought he was over all that anger, but I was wrong. I didn't realize I taught him a little too well."

Thinking back on the incident, Jacob paused for a few minutes and laughed. "That sly fox came up with the idea of making his way all the way down the Mississippi River. At that time, those Johnny Rebs had pushed the Union out and was gaining back the territory they had lost. Apparently that old white man that killed Zeke's parents was working on rebuilding. Zeke waited one night till he was alone then snuck into his house."

Once again Jacob paused and smiled. "What I would have given to see the look on that old man's face when he awoke and saw Zeke standing over top of him. Well, Zeke whipped him pretty bad. He dragged that old man out of his home and into the nearby woods. He put two bullets in the man's kneecaps, but I'm not sure if that was for Zeke's pleasure or so the man couldn't run away. Being a black man in Confederate territory, you would have thought Zeke would just kill the man so he could get the hell out of there. But Zeke had other plans. After the old man suffered for a while, Zeke tied his hands then tied him to his horse and dragged him to the tree where his parents were hung."

Jon listened as it became more difficult for Jacob to tell the story. With the break in Jacob's voice, Jon took the opportunity to speak. "Zeke told me about his plan to kill the man, but what you're saying sounds more like torture."

Jacob shook his head in disgust as he thought about what he was going to say. "You're right. It was torture. Zeke hung the old man upside down by his feet. He lit the man's hair on fire and watched as the man screamed for mercy, but Zeke had no mercy to give. That night he had nothing but hatred in his heart and revenge on his mind. After the man's hair had burned away, Zeke lit the man's clothing on fire and watched him burn. The man screamed more as he twitched and suffered, but there was nobody coming to his rescue. Zeke told me the smell of the flesh burning was unbearable, but his anger kept him there watching. Once again, after the fire had died out, the old man was still alive and moaning. Zeke told me the old man could barely speak, but he was still begging for mercy. But mercy wasn't apart of Zeke's vocabulary. He cut the old man down then strung him up by his neck. The old man didn't even have enough strength left to struggle. He gasped for air until he finally died.

And just for the fun of it, Zeke emptied his revolver into him. Five bullets to the chest and one to the head. He left the old man hanging and made his way back up the Mississippi River. After finding out what he had done, I could no longer look at Zeke the same way."

After hearing the story, Jon regretted asking the question. It was obvious Jacob was bothered, so Jon didn't say anything more. They rode quietly for a while until the Texas border was insight. As they halted their horses, they sat for a few minutes without saying a word. They just enjoyed the quiet and the gentle breeze blowing across the grass. Finally, Jon spoke out. "I'm sorry, Jacob. You could have just told me to mind my own business back there. I would have understood."

Feeling as though no harm was done. Jacob glared at Jon as though he was trying to dissect him. "No Jon, I'm sorry. It's never good to have regrets, but I thought I could mold Zeke into something that he's not. The night he killed that old man, something inside of him changed. Some kind of monster crept in and Zeke was gone. The things he did, not even the Comanche could conceive such evil."

After another few minutes of eerie silence, Jacob smiled. "You deserve the belt, Jon. You earned that belt. I feel proud to be able to give it to you. I have no doubt you will use it for good."

Jon climbed down off his horse in order to give Jacob a proper handshake, but Jacob didn't feel that a handshake was the proper thing to do. When he dismounted his horse, he shook Jon's hand then gave him a hug. "Remember, there's fast, there's faster, and then there's dead. Take care of yourself, son. I would say God bless, but I get the feeling you already have a direct line to our creator."

After parting ways, Jon rode several days until he reached the town of Presidio. It hadn't changed much and it was still lawless without a sheriff. The townspeople were still bothered by the war and angry about being occupied by Confederate troops. Jon's new look surprised people and most didn't even recognize him. He looked good like a man should.

After a long and welcoming reunion with Doc Micah, Jon decided to walk the town so he could get reacquainted with the people. As he greeted people, he noticed the school yard was alive with the sound of children laughing and enjoying the day. Then he realized before he had left, there was no school. It had been closed for several years. As a friendly gesture, he decided to introduce himself to the new teacher.

When Jon entered the schoolhouse, he was stunned to see a beautiful young woman writing on the chalkboard. As he stood speechless in the doorway, he removed his hat and watched her move with a subtle grace. Eventually she turned and was startled by Jon. "May I help you?"

Jon was captivated by her beauty, but managed to gather his thoughts. "I'm sorry, ma'am, my name is Jon Mason. I was looking to introduce myself to the schoolteacher."

Armed with only her smile, the young woman came from behind the desk and stood staring at Jon. He was young, handsome, and well-groomed, but he was wearing a gun. "My name is Miss Beckham and I do not allow gunfighters in my schoolhouse."

Still taken by the young beauty, Jon smiled because he appreciated her candidness. "I'm sorry, ma'am, but I don't consider myself a gunfighter. I'm sorry to have disturbed you. Good day." Jon placed his hat back on his head, then turned around to leave.

Just then Miss Beckham came running from behind. "Mr. Mason, please wait. I'm sorry. I didn't mean to offend you. Please, let me start over. I am the schoolteacher, Miss Beckham."

Hearing the small footsteps coming from behind, Jon abruptly stopped and turned, causing Miss Beckham to briefly come face to face. As the awkward moment ran its course, Miss Beckham took a step back. "Please, Mr. Mason, accept my apologies. This town seems to attract some of the most vial and nastiest of men. And the soldiers that come through here seem to be no better. Sometimes the children look upon them with envy, so I try to keep certain elements away."

Once again Jon was momentarily speechless, but he managed to conjure up some words. "I'm not offended, Miss Beckham, just surprised. Not that I spend my time thinking about school, but I would have thought a schoolteacher to be much older."

Miss Beckham smiled and took Jon's words as a compliment as she began to blush. "Well now, Mr. Mason, you really know how to flatter a woman."

Still captivated, Jon once again removed his hat. "Please, my friends call me Jon. I'm very pleased to meet you."

As Jon waited for a response, an overwhelming feeling came over him. It was something he had never experienced. "I'm sorry, Miss Beckham, I know you don't know me, but you can ask around about me. Would you consider having dinner with me tonight?"

Now it was the schoolteacher who was speechless. After a few seconds of gazing into Jon's eyes, she could tell his intentions were innocent. "I have to admit, Jon, you seem to be mysterious in a good way, but before I give you an answer, I think I will take you up on your suggestion about asking around."

Before Miss Beckham turned to walk away, she reached out and shook Jon's hand. "My friends call me Emily."

After school let out and all the children had gone home for the day, Emily asked several prominent people, including Doc Micah, about Jon. They had nothing but praise and kind words for the handsome young man.

Eventually Jon and Emily had many dinners together. Emily was like a breath of fresh air and Jon would get lost just staring into her eyes. After several months of courtship and consulting with Doc, Jon decided to propose marriage. Jon's love for Emily was second to none.

As the war between the states raged on, friends and townspeople pitched in to liven up the old one-room church that was abandoned long ago. They had to hire the preacher from the next township, but when all was said and done, it was music to Jon's ears when the preacher announced Mr. Jon and Emily Mason. And of course, Doc couldn't help but cry.

After the wedding, Jon got a job working for the local stagecoach line. He practiced his gun skills every day and became very diverse in weaponry. He never forgot the story Jacob told about his trip to Mexico and the advice he gave. Always carry more than one gun. He also never gave up on his quest to find the Texas Rangers. Emily didn't like the idea of Jon becoming a lawman, especially after hearing some of the gruesome stories told about what bandits do to them, but she never held Jon back from pursuing his dream.

While riding shotgun one day along the Mexican border, the stagecoach was chased several miles by some Mexican outlaws. They were more than Jon and the driver could handle and the horses started to tire. There were several prominent people on board, but Jon made the decision to stop and make a stand. Along with his six-shooter, Jon had a modified stagecoach shotgun strapped to his back and another six-shooter nestled within a shoulder holster. As the stagecoach came to a stop, the outlaws tried to surround it but they weren't prepared for what Jon had in mind. With precision and malicious intent, Jon shot several of the men who tried to flank the stagecoach. The driver had a rifle, but before he could use it, he took several bullets to his leg and arm. With his passengers crouched down inside the stagecoach, Jon desperately tried to hold off the bandits.

As with calm before the storm, an eerie silence briefly filled the air. As Jon reloaded, the bandits prepared for their final pass. Just then a sudden gust of wind kicked up some old tumble weed and dust. Without warning, three Texas Rangers came galloping from behind Jon and filled the air with gunfire. Without hesitation or fear, Jon came from behind the stagecoach and fired everything he had, killing several more bandits. The bandits that were left were no match for the Rangers. With lightning speed and deadly accuracy, the Rangers disposed of the outlaws without mercy.

After the dust cleared, Jon made sure the passengers were all right and had them tend to the driver's wounds. This time, Jon could approach the Texas Rangers on equal terms. Before he could react, one of the Rangers approached him. He was an older gentleman with a kind face. He sat tall on his horse as he gazed down at Jon. "That's some mighty fine shoot'n, young'n. My name is Gunther, but most just call me Gunny."

Accepting the compliment with pride, Jon reached up to shake the man's hand. "My name is Jon. I wanted to thank you, sir, for your help. If you hadn't come along, I think our outcome would have been a bit different."

Listening to Jon, Gunny cringed then smiled. "Listen, boy, calling me 'sir' is like putting wings on a buffalo. It just ain't proper. Listen, son, it's rare to see a greenhorn like yourself with such good skills. We could really use your talent if you're interested."

Thinking about the offer Gunny just made, Jon was ecstatic. After what seemed like forever, he had finally gotten a chance to speak to the impossible-to-find Texas Rangers. Not only did they pay him compliments, they were asking him to join their cause.

Gunny could see the excitement in Jon's eyes, but he could also see the hesitation. "Its long hours of riding and we're rarely home, and can't say it pays more then what your making now. As a matter of fact, pay ain't much. Just what the townsfolk give as a thank-you."

Jon was listening but his immediate thought was of Emily because he knew it wasn't the kind of life that would support their new marriage. "Well Gunny, once again, I would like to extend my appreciation for your help, but I'm afraid I'm going to have to decline the offer."

With no ill will, Gunny smiled and shook Jon's hand. "There's word of this war ending soon and we been hearing some jabber about the reformation of the Texas Rangers. If that happens, you be sure to look us up."

Once again, Jon appreciated the kind words, but after searching for so long, he decided to give up the one thing he desired most for his new bride. "Thanks Gunny. By the way, I met a man some time ago, Rip Ford. I'll be kind and tell you he sends his best regards."

Gunny thought for a moment as his memories took him back to another time. "Ol' Rip still kick'n? That ol' mountain goat. His motto was to kill 'em all without mercy. Leave no outlaw standing. Well Jon, we best be gett'n on. You take care now." As fast as the gust of wind brought them in, the Texas Rangers were gone.

After getting the passengers safely back to town, Jon made sure the driver made it over to Doc Micah. He couldn't wait to get back home to Emily and tell her about the Texas Rangers that came to the rescue. As he burst through the door, Emily nearly jumped out of her shoes. "Jon Mason! Have you lost your mind? You nearly scared me to no end. Now stop fool'n me and sit down. Dinner's almost ready."

With some vigor, Jon glided across the floor and placed his arms around Emily. "You are so beautiful when you're angry." Before Emily could respond, Jon gave her a kiss on her cheek, them another longer passionate kiss on her lips. When he was finished, he sat at the table and watched as Emily stood in awe.

"Well now, I guess a girl can't stay mad forever. What's gotten into you, Jon?"

While Emily set the table, Jon told his experience from earlier that day. She was happy that he was safe, but knew he had been searching for the Texas Rangers for a long time. "Jon, I know it's been a long-time dream of yours to maybe someday become a Texas Ranger, but I'm glad you didn't take that man up on his offer. At least, not at this time."

Emily took a moment to rest as she sat down at the table across from Jon. "Jon, I was hoping for a better time to tell you. I've been having some difficulties lately, so I went to see Doc Micah a few days ago."

Suddenly Jon didn't feel quite as excited as he did when he came home. "Well, when you say difficulties, what exactly does that mean?"

Thinking about the words she wanted to say, Emily reached across the table and gently grasped Jon's hand. "Well Jon, you're going to be a father."

With eyes wide, Jon was stunned but only for a moment. Happy, worried, and overall excited, he jumped up and gave Emily a big hug. Jon could see the worry on Emily's face, but he was too caught up in the moment to let doubt claim their happiness. "Don't worry, we'll be just fine. My job isn't the best job to have, but it pays and it's steady. And I know Pa will always help out if we need it."

The months that followed, Jon did everything he could to make sure Emily was comfortable. When he wasn't at work, he was working around the house and making sure Emily didn't overexert herself. Finally the big day arrived. Doc made sure he was at the house so there were no mishaps. After a grueling two hours of waiting, pacing, and rocking back and forth in the rocker, Jon's nerves could barely stand the pressure. Just when he was about to step out for some air, he heard a faint cry. After pausing momentarily, a much louder cry followed. Baby was here and Jon's patience was just about gone. He burst into the bedroom just in time to see Doc Micah hand the newborn child to Emily.

With a glow of pride, Doc stood up to shake Jon's hand. "Congratulations, Son. I'm proud of you."

After a grueling two hours of waiting, Jon shook Doc's hand, then gave him a hug. "Thanks, Pa."

As Jon sat on the edge of the bed, he gave Emily a kiss on the cheek, then marveled at the miracle of his firstborn child. "What shall we name him?"

Emily smiled with joy as she glanced down at the baby. "Well first off, it's a girl, silly. And I like the name Abigayle. We can call her Abby for short."

With joy in her heart, Emily handed the child to Jon to hold for the first time. Attempting to be as gentle as possible, Jon stood up and cuddled the child as he bounced up and down for a few minutes. As he walked around the room, he smiled and made funny faces and noises and pondered the name. He then handed the child to Doc, who already had a tear falling down his face. "Pa, I would like to introduce you to Abigayle Mason."

Overwhelmed with happiness, Doc gently took Abby into his arms. "I like the name. It fits just fine."

As the time went by, there was more and more talk of the war ending. The year was 1864 and once again, Emily was pregnant. To everyone's surprise, she had twins: Adam and Abram Mason. Jon worked long hard hours just to be able to provide, and of course Doc helped with whatever he could.

While home working in the field, Jon stopped for a few minutes and found a spot under an old cedar tree to rest his eyes. As his mind started to wonder, he thought about how much his life had changed. He reminisced about his younger days when he was lost and searching for who he was. He remembered his time on the El Capitan and laughed. He briefly thought about his encounter with Rodrigo and his men. He also wondered about Jacob, Zeke, and all the friends he had made during his trip back from the cursed mountain. He wondered if he would ever see them again or even if they were still alive. War was brutal and the stories Jon would here about the battles were horrible. The sun was starting to set and it was time for dinner. As he stood up, Jon could see his cabin off in the distance and he smiled when he noticed Emily hanging laundry, and Abby there by her side. He felt good as all the other thoughts became unimportant.

On April 6, 1865, General Lee of the Confederate States of America surrendered in Northern Virginia after realizing the battle he was fighting was hopeless. One by one during the next couple of months, all the other Confederate generals surrendered, including General Stand Watie, who was the last to surrender on June 23, 1865. After four years of a divided America, the Civil War was finally over, and it had changed the political and social landscape of the United States.

With the end of the war came new problems for Texas. Indian attacks were on the rise. Outlaws became abundant, Southern sympathizers and ex-Confederate soldiers were constantly trying to create ways to regroup in order to fight another day, and Mexican bandits took advantage of the lawlessness that was plaguing Texas. Of course, with opportunity came another kind of problem: bounty hunters. Men who would kill another man simply for the price that was placed on their head. As spring turned into summer and fall into winter, the lawlessness in Texas got worse as time went by.

One day while in town, Jon made a short visit to see Doc, then decided to pick up some supplies for the up and coming winter. While in the general store, he heard some ruckus outside, but thought it might be some of the local drunks from the nearby saloon. When he came out to load up his wagon, there were several men waiting. Feeling as though they were planning something, Jon didn't say anything. Instead, he quietly loaded his wagon, then walked back into the store to get the rest of his supplies. While gathering his merchandise, he asked the store clerk to take a short break and to wait in the back room.

When Jon loaded the last of his supplies, one of the men began to taunt him. "That's a real nice wagon you gotcha self. Gett'n ready for the winter, I see."

The man smiled and waited for a response but Jon kept quiet and just stared. As he looked on, the smirk on Jon's face just irritated the man. "Hey boy, I'm talk'n to ya. My momma needs them there supplies and we not leav'n here empty-handed."

Jon knew the man was just trying to bait him, so he decided to accommodate the three men. He stepped out into the street and invited the three men to join him. "Your dirty momma can buy her own supplies, and as for you leaving, you can either ride out of here or leave in caskets. It's your choice."

The three men didn't take kindly to Jon's comments but were delighted that he was willing to face off against all three of them. They figured it would be easier just to take what they wanted and, for an added bonus, kill Jon in the process. So they climbed down from their horses in order to start their fun. Unfortunately for the three men, it was anything but fun. Jon waited a few seconds so he could look them in their eyes, and as soon as the man with the mouth twitched, Jon drew his gun and fired three shots. Three bullets left his gun and three bodies fell to the ground. Jon's draw was so fast, the three men didn't even have time to regret their decision.

After the fight was over, some of the townspeople gathered around, including Doc. Doc checked the three men for life, but there was no need. Three shots dead center to each of their chest. When Doc stood up, he looked at Jon with disappointment, then walked away. The townspeople were so in awe, some of them asked Jon to be sheriff, but seeing the disappointment from Doc, Jon had no answer at the time and needed to speak with the man he had come to know as his Pa.

When Jon got to Doc's office, Doc was sitting at the table just staring out his window. Jon took a moment, then sat down and waited for Doc to say something, but Doc didn't say anything. Finally Jon spoke out. "It wasn't my fault, Pa. They thought they could just come into town and take whatever they wanted. What was I supposed to do? Just let them take the supplies I bought for Emily and the children?"

Doc stared off into space for a few more seconds then gathered his thoughts. "Back when you took your trip to find the Texas Rangers, I bought you a rifle to hunt with, but I refused to buy you a pistol. I did that because I just can't stand violence, especially when it leads to someone's death. Not having children of my own, I guess I thought I could somehow protect you and keep you from becoming something that you would regret. I never wanted this for you."

Jon could see the sadness on Doc's face, but could offer no comforting words. "Pa, I'm sorry. I don't have it in me anymore to just stand by and let these outlaws do whatever they want."

Doc looked at Jon, but this time it was with pride. "Son, there are things worse than killing a man. Being a coward is one of those things. I'm proud of you for standing up for yourself, but what about Emily and the children? What happens when one day somebody comes along who's faster? Then what?"

Jon thought about what Doc was saying and he understood his point. It seemed to be a catch twenty-two situation. Damned if you do and doomed if you don't.

Jon knew it was an argument he couldn't win and Doc knew he had struck a chord with Jon just by mentioning Emily and the children. So the two men accepted the stalemate as Jon gave Doc a hug and tried to reassure him. "Thanks for setting me straight, Pa. I can't promise you I'll always make the right decision, but I can say without doubt that I'll always place Emily and the children's needs first."

With a deep sigh, Jon left Doc's office feeling better than what he felt going in. He made it home safe with his supplies and with no time to spare because winter's first storm started to show its ugly face. As the large flakes started to fall, the wind howled with a ghostly sound as the clouds blocked out the sun. After securing the animals, Jon made sure the house was secure and ready to withstand the storm.

The next day, Jon took care of his daily chores, then gave Emily a kiss. Emily knew what the kiss meant, but she liked to give Jon a little hassle. She knew Jon wasn't one to stay in one place for very long. "Where are you going?"

Jon smiled and leaned over to give another kiss, but this time Emily backed away. Just then, Abby came running out from her bedroom. "Daddy, Daddy, Daddy! Don't leave, Daddy."

As Abby raised her arms, Jon picked her up and gave her a big Daddy hug. "You can't get rid of me that easy. I will never leave you. But I do have to go and check on Grand-Pa Micah. He's not getting any younger, and these old winter storms can take their toll."

It was time for Jon to go, so Emily gave a gentle kiss. "You tell Doc it's been too long since he's been out for dinner." With a smile and a hug, Jon made his exit.

The snow wasn't deep so the ride to town wasn't a bad one. When he finally arrived, Thomas, the blacksmith, came out of the stable to talk. "Hi Jon. Bad news about Doc."

Before Thomas could explain, Jon quickly dismounted his horse. "Thomas, what's going on with Doc?"

Thomas was large and in charge and a straight-forward kind of guy that didn't mince words, and he wasn't dramatic to any degree. "Well, some riders came in during the storm. One had a bullet wound to the gut and the others were pretty banged up. They went looking for Doc and found him. He tried everything to save the man, but I guess the Lord had other plans. They didn't take too kindly to their friend dying. They beat Doc pretty bad and stole everything that wasn't nailed down. He's resting over at Molly's place."

Molly owned the local brothel and was very well known to be a house of sin filled with some of the most erotic girls around. In order to calm Jon's nerves, Thomas smiled as he turned to walk back into the stable. "A couple of the women are taking care of his needs."

Jon didn't waste any time as he thanked Thomas for the information and made his way over to Molly's. When he arrived, he could hear old Doc barking out orders to the ladies. After hearing Doc's voice, the anxiety he was feeling was suddenly gone. When he entered the house of ill repute, Jon was met by none other than Molly herself. Molly not only owned the brothel but had some of the finest whores in Texas. Molly was quite a looker herself and always had eyes for Jon.

"Hey handsome, I'd offer you a drink and take you upstairs, but you need to get that old goat out of here. He's scaring away a lot of my customers with all his medical talk on sexually transmitted diseases."

Beginning to realize the situation wasn't too bad, Jon didn't even have to ask. He just followed the sound of Doc's loud voice upstairs to the back room. When he burst through the door, he couldn't help but laugh. One of the girls was trying to give him medication while another was attempting to fluff his pillow, and yet another was trying to maneuver Doc's legs to a more comfortable position.

Jon folded his arms across his chest as he leaned up against the door jam and enjoyed the show. "Well Pa, never thought I would see the day. You in bed with three lovely ladies."

Being exhausted from Doc's resistance, all three women knew Jon and were glad to see him. As they one by one funneled their way out the door, they gave their hugs and kisses and left him to deal with Doc.

Doc was none too pleased with Jon's comment but in any case, was also glad to see him. "You should be at home with your wife and children. These storms can be hard on a family. But since you're standing there gloating, come here and help me up. I bet this old sagging bed has seen more action than a Civil War cannon."

After Jon helped Doc sit up, he sat down on the chair beside the bed. "Thomas told me what happened, Pa. You're lucky they didn't kill you. I should have been there for you."

With a roll of his eyes and a look of despair, Doc blasted Jon for his words. "You were right where you needed to be. I thought we had this talk already. Your number one priority, Son, is your family and not this God-forsaken town. And certainly not me. I can take care of myself. You can't be everywhere and take care of everybody at the same time."

Jon knew Doc had taken his fair share of beatings over the years and he knew he wouldn't be able to take much more. "Why don't you move in with Emily and me? You can still make your rounds around town each week, and this way I know Emily and the children are safe when I'm away."

Doc was slow to get up and he was also slow to speak. His mind ran rapid as he thought about Jon's offer. "Jon, I appreciate your offer, and nothing would please me more than to play a bigger part in the lives of your three children, but my work is here and my life is here and that's the last I want to speak of it. Now, get me out of this house of sin before our Lord strikes me down."

Trying to keep his laughter on the inside, Jon shook his head and smiled. "You're as stubborn as an old mule stuck in mud. But okay. If I leave you here, these women are libel to strip you down to your skivvies and tie you to the bedpost. Who knows, you may even like it. But let's get you back to your office before I change my mind."

When Jon and Doc got back to the office, they assessed the damage. The place was in bad shape. All the furniture was broken and the windows were shattered. More importantly, all the medications and supplies that Doc had stored away were gone, including his surgical equipment. It would take weeks to have everything replaced, so Jon proposed a deal. "Listen, Pa. You need supplies and you also need rest, so why don't you keep Emily and the children company for a few days while I take a trip over to San Antonio? You can get the care you need while visiting with the children, and I'll pick up the supplies you need and bring them back."

Doc didn't want to admit it, but it was a good plan and it would give him the break he needed; not to mention the townspeople couldn't wait weeks for medical supplies. "All right, Jon. You have a valid point. Let me just gather a few things, then we'll ride out."

After Jon got Doc settled at home, he didn't waste any time gathering some supplies and heading back out. It was only a few days ride to San Antonio, but Jon didn't mind. He was comfortable with Doc staying at the house and he didn't mind the time alone. Since having three children, he had forgotten how good it felt just to be out riding. After riding all day, the sun began to set so Jon decided to stop for the night and rest Sapphire.

It was a bitter cold night and the wind howled with force. Every now and then, Jon was awakened by some ghostly sounds. He tried to contribute them to the wind blowing through the trees, but after a while he couldn't help but think how similar they were to the sounds he had heard years before at the El Capitan. He tried to ignore them most of the night, then finally morning came.

It was still early and the sun hadn't risen yet, but that didn't matter. Jon was anxious to leave the area.

Eventually the sun came up and it warmed the morning air. Jon rode for a while, then came across a horrible sight: a large field littered with dead men. Luckily it was winter so there were no flies and hardly any stench. Jon dismounted his horse and walked through the field of bodies, looking for anyone that may still be alive. They weren't soldiers; at least, they weren't wearing uniforms. The war was over, but Jon had heard stories of skirmishes between Union soldiers and Southern sympathizers. But this was too massive. Too much carnage. As he methodically searched, he couldn't help but think about the force that could have done this. Soldiers would have collected any weaponry and buried the dead, but the weapons of the dead were still in their holsters as if they had never gotten a chance to pull them out. Indians would have scavenged the bodies and took valuables, but Jon noticed most of the men were wearing some kind of necklace or other types of jewelry. And a gang of thieves or robbers would be much too small for such a large massacre.

The ground was much too hard and there were just too many bodies for one man to deal with. Jon knew he was limited on time and he still had to get the medical supplies and get back to Presidio, so he decided to relay the information to the San Antonio sheriff. Just when he was about to leave, he heard some movement coming from behind. Like a flash of lightning, Jon turned and withdrew his gun. He saw no threat to fire at, so after scanning the area he holstered his gun.

Suddenly one of the bodies lying on the ground let out a small moan. Cautiously, Jon took small steps and approached the body. The man doing the moaning had several bullet wounds and was barely alive. As Jon knelt down, he surprisingly recognized the man. It was Rodrigo. He was a little older and a little rougher looking than Jon cared to remember.

"What happened here? Who did this?"

Rodrigo couldn't speak so, Jon fetched his canteen. After letting Rodrigo sip some water, Jon repeated his questions. "Who did this to you?"

Still moaning in pain, Rodrigo seemed to be delirious. He wasn't making any sense with his words. "You? Run...run."

There was nothing Jon could do about Rodrigo's wounds. Although Rodrigo seemed to recognize Jon, it was just a matter of minutes before he was going to die. But Jon felt the need to find out what kind of force could have taken out so many men. "Rodrigo, listen to me. Who did this to you? Who killed all these men?"

Rodrigo tried to speak, but he continued to speak in confusing terms. With his voice starting to fade, Rodrigo spoke with his last breath. "Too late to stop…dark cloud coming…You must run…You must run."

Trying to understand Rodrigo's words, Jon could see the life starting to exit his eyes and then he was gone.

As Jon stood up, he noticed Rodrigo was wearing a necklace. He remembered when he gloated about the necklace he had taken from Father Andres, so he bent down and plucked it off the dead bandit's neck. It was a gold chain attached to a small round coin. On the coin was the faded likeness of St. Francis. He took a moment to remember the padre, then placed the necklace safely in his pocket.

It seemed to be too much of a coincidence with the night before with the howling wind, the ghostly sounds, and now Rodrigo talking about a dark cloud coming. What did it mean, and who could have killed Rodrigo and all his men? So many unanswered questions, but Jon had to stay focused. He had to make it to San Antonio and back to Presidio.

The rest of the ride to San Antonio was filled with questions and thoughts of Jon's past. He thought he was over the fact he couldn't remember his parents or where he came from, and over the years his heart had finally healed after losing Father Santos and Father Andres. El Capitan, the mysterious mountain that Father Andres sent him to, was a distant memory until now. Jon thought about how he had finally moved on and created a nice life with Emily and his three children. He wanted nothing to do with mysterious dreams about a dark cloud or an unattainable treasure on top of a haunted mountain.

When Jon arrived at San Antonio, he notified the sheriff about the bodies, but the sheriff wasn't surprised. He told Jon about some other mysterious deaths that had recently happened. Most were old homesteaders. The sheriff explained that they contributed the deaths to Indians at first, but as time went on it became apparent that Indians weren't involved.

After speaking with the sheriff, Jon found the nearest saloon for a drink and some hot food before taking his trip back. As he sat at the bar eating, a black man walked in. He had on presentable clothes, nice boots, and a black hat. He also had a gun hung low as though he used it often. Out of respect, the man removed his hat and sat down at the bar next to Jon. When he asked for a drink, the bartender just stared. "You walked into the wrong establishment, mista. We don't serve you people here."

Before the man could react, Jon became quite offended. "What do you mean by 'you people'? He's with me. Give him what he wants."

The grateful man smiled and introduced himself as Gideon.

Just then, two other men walked in. Full of dust and dirt, they looked around with arrogance, then sat down at one of the tables.

"Where's the dirty whores?" one of them yelled.

The other one abruptly laughed and had an equally loud voice. "Barkeep, bring us a bottle."

As Jon watched with disgust, he turned his attention back to the ignorant bartender. With a voice of authority, he spoke up. "I thought I told you to get my friend a drink."

Without warning, the two loud men walked up behind Jon. One of them had the audacity to take Jon's beer and drink it. "You listen here, boy. Ain't no black man gonna get served before us."

Now it was Jon who was slow to react. Before Jon could say a word, Gideon swung his fist around and knocked the foul-mouthed man backward onto his backside. He then stood up and struck the other man just as hard.

As the two men lay on the floor wondering what just hit them, Gideon walked over and stood over top of them. "Now you listen, boy. I didn't come in here looking for trouble, but if its trouble you want, I have all you can handle."

With amusement, Jon watched as the lips on both men started to swell. With anger and frustration, they stood up and squared off against Gideon.

One of the men wiped the blood, which started to run down his chin. "You just signed your death warrant, Negro. We'll be waiting for you outside."

With haste, the two men stormed out, but Gideon didn't seem to be affected by the threat, so he walked back to the bar and sat down next to Jon. With a warm welcome, Jon smiled and introduced himself. After shaking hands, Gideon turned to the bartender. "How about that whiskey, barkeep?"

The bartender was less than enthusiastic as he displayed his angry face while reaching down under the bar and pulling out a double-barrel shotgun. "Now you listen good, mista. You and your sympathizing friend get the hell out'a here before I send you both to ya maka."

Feeling a bit disappointed, Gideon glanced over at Jon, who was just finishing with his meal. "Sorry Jon, I may have inadvertently worn out our welcome."

Feeling no remorse, Jon placed his fork down, then wiped his face. He then let out a small laugh, then stood up. "Oh well, as nasty as this food was, I don't have any plans on coming back."

With the aftertaste of his meal attacking his taste buds, Jon scoffed then placed a silver dollar down on the bar. "Thanks for the hospitality."

As Jon and Gideon walked out, the two men were there waiting with the sheriff. Having no tolerance for black folks, the sheriff looked Gideon up and down, then turned to Jon. "I don't have any quarrels with you. You can go ahead and get on out of my town." He then turned his attention back to Gideon. "You, Negro, are my problem. I know you think you're a free man, but you can't just go around punching upstanding citizens in their face. That, to me, is a challenge, and these men have the right to accept that challenge."

Jon had just met Gideon, and though he wore his gun like a gunfighter, he remembered the story Jacob had told about looks being deceiving. "Look, Sheriff, I know you have a job to do, but I don't think this is right. This man didn't start the fight. Your so-called upstanding citizens initiated this whole situation."

Thinking he had the advantage of his badge, the sheriff paused for a moment then smiled. "Boy, you can either get the hell out of my town or spend the night in jail."

Taking a deep breath, Gideon shook his head then laughed. "Don't worry, Jon. The good sheriff is right. I laid out the challenge and now these two men have a choice. They can just walk away or die."

Jon knew it wasn't his fight, but he somehow felt responsible. "All right, Gideon, I hope you know what you're doing." With some reservation, Jon stepped aside in hopes that Gideon was as fast as he looked.

As Gideon stepped out into the street, he unsnapped his holster and gave a warning. "When I'm done here, Sheriff, you're next."

Listening to Gideon and his threat, the sheriff laughed and shook his head, then spit on the ground. "I'm not even gonna waste my time burying you, boy. I'm just gonna lay you out so the wild dogs can nibble on you come nightfall."

As Gideon stood looking at the two men, the two men looked back with their halfway smiles and rotten teeth. Just as the first man flinched, Gideon drew his gun and fired twice, killing both men instantly with shots to both their heads. As the two men fell to the ground, the sheriff reached for his gun, but before he could pull it out, Jon drew his gun and shot the sheriff in his gun hand.

"Now, now, Sheriff, I wouldn't want you to do something that goes against that badge."

In pain, the sheriff held his hand and tried to stop the bleeding. Seeing the sheriff in a more acceptable position, Jon took the opportunity to throw the sheriff's words back into his face, so he walked over and plucked the badge off his chest. "You no longer have the authority to do a damn thing. How about we give this badge to a real man?"

Feeling confident about Gideon's skill level, Jon turned to Gideon and handed him the badge. "I'm headed back to Presidio. If you're looking for work, I think you would make one hell of a sheriff."

Gideon smiled as he took the badge and placed it in his pocket. "Why not? The hospitality in this town stinks, and the people aren't much better."

After buying some medical supplies and much needed medications, the two men rode out of town. Jon decided to avoid going back the way he came due to the fact he didn't want to have to answer any questions Gideon may have had about the bodies. When the sun set, Jon and Gideon set up camp. As the campfire burned bright, the coyotes sang their nighttime songs while the two men talked about the Civil War and told each other their stories. Gideon was a scout and was hired by the military just after the war broke out to track the Apache and the Comanche. When he realized the war wasn't going to end anytime soon, he enlisted and played an even more important role tracking the Confederate Army. When the war ended, he decided to continue working for the Union. He used his skill set to hunt war criminals and deserters. He told Jon he had been tracking the two men in the bar. They didn't have a price on their heads like most outlaws; instead, they were wanted because of the crimes they had committed against humanity. They were Gideon's last assignment.

A day later the two new friends rode into Presidio. Jon figured Doc would be at his office, so he wasted no time in getting him his much-needed supplies. He introduced Gideon and told him how he thought Gideon would make a great sheriff. Doc was a part of a makeshift town council and was very influential when it came to making decisions concerning town business.

Doc didn't say anything at first. As he glanced through the various medications and supplies, he thought about the idea Jon had presented. He smiled as he walked over to his window and looked out upon the town. With a spiteful grin, he turned to face Gideon. "Well, it's the 1870s and times are changing. Sir, this town has been without a sheriff for way too long. You'll find that overall Presidio is a good town, although we're not without our troubles and personal conflicts. Most of our people are good folk and work hard. Others can be hurtful in their thinking. Not only would I welcome you into the position, but I would be mighty proud to be friends with the first black sheriff in the state of Texas. I can't make any promises, but I will present your case at the next town meeting, which is tomorrow."

Although Gideon was welcomed to stay with Jon and his family, he decided to instead take up room and board, which was attached to the Lucy Goosy saloon. So Jon said his good-byes and headed home to see Emily and the children while Gideon settled into his room and got comfortable. After resting, he made his way down to the bar for a late-night drink and some food.

Well-mannered and respectful, he introduced himself to the barmaid, Ms. Lita, who in return introduced herself. The saloon was empty and the brisk air carried the nighttime sounds in from the outside.

After a few minutes of good conversation, the quiet night was cracked by three belligerent bounty hunters who entered the saloon with mouths wide open. Two of the men sat down at a table while the third man slammed his hand down on the bar. "Hey bitch, gimme three beers and a bottle, and don't be all night."

Ms. Lita was a mature woman and didn't take kindly to having been called a degrading name. "Listen, mister, I've had a long day and I'm tired. I'm only gonna guess your momma taught you better manners and if not, then shame on her."

The man cringed as he brushed off some trail dust then he reached over the bar and grabbed Ms. Lita by the arm. "You listen here, bitch. I had a good momma and she was killed by some dirty Indians, so I don't take kindly to you talk'n 'bout her."

Before the man could continue his assault, Gideon grabbed the man by his coat collar and shoved him back away from the bar. "I think the lady would like you to be a little more respectful while in her establishment."

The man was so caught up with himself that he failed to notice Gideon when he entered the saloon. "What the hell is this?" With an arrogant attitude, the foul-mouthed man began to berate Gideon. "Boy, that war was years ago, but that don't mean anything is changed. Them damn Yanks might've won that there war, but this is Texas and I'm gonna gut you like a dead pig."

Just then the other two men stood up and unsnapped their guns. With a devious grin, Gideon glanced over and gave Ms. Lita a wink. He then turned his attentions back to the three men and smiled. "I have nothing against the great state of Texas, but I do have something against ignorance. Why don't we step outside so we can avoid Ms. Lita having to clean up any mess we make?"

The three men were very happy to see that Gideon wasn't backing down, so they agreed and walked outside. After the three men stepped out, Ms. Lita came from behind the bar with a double-barrel shotgun. Seeing the massive barrels of steel, Gideon appreciated the nice gesture but didn't want Ms. Lita to get hurt. "I welcome your kindness, Ms. Lita, but a lady such as yourself shouldn't get involved in these disputes."

With a devious smile of her own, Ms. Lita let out a quiver of a laugh. "I appreciate your kindness, Gideon, but I've been cleaning up around here for years and I don't need any man to protect my honor. These three trail dogs have it coming."

Gideon liked her spunk and he wasn't about to argue with a woman holding a double-barrel shotgun, so he gave a soft smile and nodded his head toward the door. "Shall we?"

As Gideon and Ms. Lita walked out, the three bounty hunters were waiting in the street. As Gideon stepped into the street, Ms. Lita stood behind him with her shotgun pointing out. When some of the townspeople saw Ms. Lita with her shotgun, they knew there was trouble brewing and sought shelter. When the three men saw Ms. Lita, they burst into a loud, obnoxious laugh. When they were finished, the man with all the mouth stepped forward. "I ain't ever shot me no stupid bitch before, but I ain't oppose to the idea. If it's something long and hard you wanna play with, I can bend you over later after I take care of this here Negro."

As the man waited for a response, there was none. He then looked toward Gideon. "What are you staring at, Negro? Do you even know who I am?"

Gideon didn't answer right away, but he could feel his anger starting to rise, so he just stared at the man for a moment then gave a bone-chilling response. "I know who you are. Your name is Floyd Robertson and the two men with you are your brothers. You hunt bounties. Some people call you the Killing Man because of the amount of men you've sent to the grave. Some say you're the fastest around, but I say you're just fast with your mouth."

Floyd was stunned that a black man would know anything about him, so he took a step back and stood beside his two brothers. "Well now, Negro, you seem to know an awful lot about me. After I'm done, I might have to go and buy me a new gun. I seem to be running out of room for my notches. Why don't we just get on with it so I can get me some of that lady friend of yours?"

Although Gideon wanted nothing better than to kill the three men standing in front of him, he still had more to say. "You and your brothers are wanted in three states. You not only kill your bounties in cold blood, but you've tortured and killed family members for information on their whereabouts. One of your bounties had a sixteen-year-old daughter that you and your brothers raped and killed."

Gideon paused because he could see his words starting to take effect on Floyd. After a few moments, he continued. "I've changed my mind, Mr. Robertson. I was going to kill all three of you, but I think I'm going to let Ms. Lita take care of your brothers. For you, I'm going to put two bullets in your gut and one in your balls. Then as you lay on the ground wondering how this Negro got the best of you, I'm going to put a bullet in your head."

There was no more history to be said. No more insults and no more words. Testosterone levels were at their highest while the anger ran rapid, and Ms. Lita had heard enough. She didn't even wait for anyone to draw. She just simply pointed and pulled the trigger, and neither brother stood a chance. As both brothers fell to the ground, Floyd Robertson drew his gun for the last time. Gideon's draw was so fast, the three bullets he promised hit their targets as Floyd's one shot harmlessly hit the ground.

As Floyd lay on the ground suffering, Gideon slowly walked over to him. "What do think about this Negro now?" As Floyd glanced up, Gideon showed no mercy. A promise of a fourth bullet to the head was the last thing Floyd felt.

After the showdown was over, some of the townspeople came out to see the results. Some people congratulated Gideon while others seemed to flock toward Ms. Lita. Yet others seem to not care one way or the other and just simply went home. It was late and there were no customers to serve, so Ms. Lita decided to close the bar. The undertaker was left to attend his duties while Gideon helped Ms. Lita with her chores.

As the town once again grew quiet, Ms. Lita poured two shots of whiskey and slid one across the bar to Gideon. "You seem to be a pretty knowledge-able man."

Gideon drank down his shot of whiskey and gently placed the glass down on the table. "Well ma'am, you seem to be pretty handy with that shotgun."

Having a warm feeling about Gideon, Ms. Lita smiled then let out a small laugh. "Well, I wasn't lying when I said I was tired. Been doing this for years and I've seen my fair share of bloodshed. What about you? How did you know all that information?"

It was an innocent question and Gideon didn't mind talking, especially to a woman who just helped him take down three idiots. "My pa taught me to know who you're up against, so I try to keep up with the Wanted posters and names that come my way."

Still smiling, Ms. Lita drank down her whiskey like it was water. "Sounds like your father was a wise man."

Gideon thought for a moment as though his memories were passing through time. "He was harsh and that was okay. He taught me how to be tough. He also taught me to have compassion when necessary and to give mercy when warranted." Once again, Gideon paused as Ms. Lita refilled his glass. After taking another sip, Gideon continued his story. "He died trying to protect my mother and me."

Ms. Lita could see Gideon was bothered, but she could also sense that he was ready to unload a heavy burden. "Gideon, you don't know me and I would understand if you didn't want to talk about it."

Still in deep thought, Gideon didn't mind telling his story. "Pa wasn't a hateful man. He was God-fearing and treated everyone with respect. We belonged to a really nice family, the Fosters. I was even friends with their son, Lonnie. We were the same age and we played together every day. Mr. Foster was an older man that couldn't get around much, so he would let my pa take us out hunting and fishing all the time. He taught Lonnie and me how to live off the land and how to track. Sometimes he could be hard, but he instilled values into us. One day Lonnie took sick. He had a fever that just wouldn't break. He died a week later."

Ms. Lita sat and listened while Gideon seemed to feel relief with every word.

Finishing his second glass of whiskey, Gideon let out a half-smile as though he had made peace with his past. "Come to find out, the Fosters were feuding with some other landowners. During Lonnie's funeral, they came calling. There was no reasoning. No talking or even a warning. They were wearing masks as they came storming in on their horses in a full gallop. A few of the farm hands tried to stop them, but they got trampled to death. I remember Mr. Foster trying to block them from his son's casket, but they were brutal in their actions and there was no stopping them. They shot Mr. Foster point blank then knocked the casket over. When Lonnie's body fell out, my pa ran over and tried to stop them from doing any more damage. I remember seeing my pa pick up a revolver that one of the farm hands dropped. He wasn't going to use it. He just wanted the men to stop and go away."

Ms. Lita could see Gideon was getting emotional, so she poured him a third drink. "Don't do this to yourself, Gideon. What's done is done. Leave it in the past."

As Gideon glanced down at his drink, he took a deep breath as though he was getting a second wind, then laughed as he continued his story. "One of the men rode up behind my pa and hit him with a horse whip. My pa stood tall and was as thick as a tree trunk. That man got one hell of a surprise when my pa turned around and just stared at him. Even though the man was wearing a mask, I could still see the terror in his eyes. He tried to crack the whip again, but my pa shot him. It all happened so fast. My pa got off three more shots before they got to him. They tried to beat him, but he fought back. He got his licks in and then some. He kept them busy just long enough for my ma and me to run and hide. We watched as they finally got my pa on the ground. They beat him some more and then they horse whipped him until he was dead."

It was a sad story from the past, but Gideon didn't seem to mind getting it out of his system. Before Ms. Lita could show any sympathy, Gideon quickly moved onto another subject. "Jon thinks that I would make this town a good sheriff. Doctor Micah is supposed to be recommending me to the town council tomorrow. May I ask what your thoughts are?"

Shaking off the story Gideon just told, Ms. Lita lined up four more shot glasses and filled them with whiskey. "Well, I happen to be a part of that so-called council, so with endorsements from Doc and me and the fact that you're willing to stand up for this town, I don't think anyone would be opposed."

The next day Jon was up early and starting his chores. After breakfast and some time with his family, he finished his chores and headed into town. He stopped to see Doc, who wasn't happy when he told Jon about the night before. Explaining to Jon how Gideon had already become a target, Doc wasn't pleased about the violence. "I figured this would happen. Gideon's not even sheriff yet and he has men already looking to use him as a trophy."

Jon sat and listened, but once again disagreed. "Come on, Pa. How is that Gideon's fault? He was just trying to help Ms. Lita. Why is it you oppose people helping other people in need?"

As soon as those words came out of Jon's mouth, he knew he had made a mistake. With disappointment in his heart and anger on his mind, Doc became irate. "Who the hell do you think you are? You don't have enough time on God's green earth to sit in judgment of me!" Screaming at the top of his lungs with even more anger, Doc stepped toward Jon and shook his finger in his face. "I've lived through more wars, battles, and Indian uprisings than you'll ever see and I'm tired! I've seen death take too many people and I'm not about to wait around to watch death take you. You want to live your life as a hired gun, then you'll do it without my blessings."

Jon stood frozen as he absorbed whatever punishing words Doc could throw at him. When Doc was finished, Jon gave him a few moments to calm down. Afterward, he realized Doc was just hashing over the same old argument. It wasn't about Gideon; it was about Jon agreeing with what Gideon did and being happy with three dead bodies in the end. "I'm sorry, Pa. I know how strongly you feel about me carrying this gun, but this town needs a sheriff. If you're not going to recommend Gideon, then I guess I'll step up and take the position." Jon didn't feel there was anything more to say, so he turned and quietly walked out.

During the town meeting, there was enough encouragement to swear Gideon in as the new sheriff. As a celebration, Ms. Lita invited Jon, Doc, and Gideon back to the bar for drinks. Doc declined the offer, but Gideon and Jon were looking forward to having a good time. By the end of the night, it was time to check out the sheriff's office. Unfortunately it had been boarded up for many years. As Jon and Gideon sifted through all the trash and junk, Jon told Gideon the story about the last sheriff, but Gideon wasn't surprised. Most small towns along the border experience many forms of violence toward the law.

As time went on, the townspeople grew to respect and even like Gideon. After all, he was a good sheriff. Kindhearted, respectful to all, and more importantly, he kept the peace. Winter was coming to an end as the trees were showing signs of spring and almost on a daily basis, more and more Wanted posters were being posted. Mostly men trying to make a name for themselves as bank robbers, train robbers, or stagecoach bandits. Since Jon still worked for a stagecoach line, Emily became increasingly worried. Every now and then, she would try to talk Jon into finding better work, but the only other thing that paid decent money was hunting bounties. Jon would often think about it, but would always revert back to conversations with Doc and the integrity issues.

Living on the outer boundaries of Presidio, Jon kept a constant vigil on the surrounding areas and activities. Whenever his job took him away from home for more than a day, he made sure Doc or Gideon and sometimes distant neighbors would check on Emily and the children. As the town of Presidio grew, so did its needs. Doc, being up in age, even hired an assistant: Ms. May Belle Hobbs. She was an older lady with college degrees in the medical field and her name sounded prudish, but she was in reality a very sweet woman. Most people just called her Belle, and Doc Belle was okay with that. Being overjoyed with having someone to converse with, the two doctors were often seen walking and laughing together, and everyone thought maybe Doc Micah had a sweetness for his new assistant.

Spring was in full bloom and Presidio hustled with farmers selling goods and buying supplies. Livestock was being bought and sold daily, and ladies were ordering new dresses for the up-and-coming spring and summer dances. With his children a little older, this was the perfect opportunity for Jon to take Emily and the children into town. Jon could pick up some much-needed supplies for the planting season, and Emily could take the children and visit with Grandpa Micah and Belle. Afterward, she could join the ladies in picking out a new dress for herself. After leaving the wife and children with Doc, Jon made a beeline to see Gideon. Gideon and Jon had become good friends and Jon was always excited to visit and get caught up on the latest news—especially if it had anything to do with law enforcement.

With a smile on his face, Jon popped his head in and saw Gideon running his fingers through various stacks of paperwork. "Sitting at that desk isn't doing this town any good."

When Gideon looked up, he saw Jon standing bright and cheery in the doorway. "Hey Jon, grab a seat. You got me into this mess, so the least you can do is help with all this paperwork. I have Wanted posters, legal papers, and I even have the governor's secretary sending me letters."

Delighted to help, Jon pulled up a chair and sat down. He immediately grabbed the Wanted posters and started sifting through them. As he glanced through the posters, he started to point out the various patterns of each wanted man. He also picked out some of the ones that were already in jail or dead.

Amazed at Jon's insight, Gideon sat back in his chair and smiled. "You really have a knack for this, don't you? Why don't you take this job and I'll go and be the happy homesteader?"

After a few more laughs, both men decided to take a break so Gideon could check on the town and visit with Emily and the children. After walking the town, Jon and Gideon caught up with Doc and Emily, who were just walking out of the bank. After tipping his hat, Gideon gave Emily a hug. "Where are the children? Jon told me they were getting big."

Thinking about her children, Emily blushed with pride. "Abby is going to be as tall as me soon, and the boys are getting bigger and stronger every day. They're spending some time with Belle so I can shop in peace for a new dress. Doc was kind enough to be my handsome escort."

Before the conversation could continue, a gust of wind kicked up some dust as gunfire broke the cool spring air. Suddenly a band of horsemen with guns blazing came galloping from around the corner heading toward the bank. Without giving it any thought, Jon grabbed Emily and quickly pushed her into a nearby store front. With his lightning fast gun hand, Gideon drew his gun and started firing. After several bullets nearly missed him, Gideon decided to take cover behind a horse trough. After making sure Emily was safe, Jon exited the store and fired several shots. As the men spun their horses in confusion, more dust kicked up, which caused a temporary cease fire. When the dust settled, all but one of the horsemen had retreated out of town. Realizing he was all alone, the last man attempted to gain control of his horse, but it was too late. Gideon had reloaded and, utilizing all six bullets, had emptied his gun into the man's chest. As the man fell from his horse, death stole him away before he could hit the ground.

After the gunfire had stopped, the townspeople slowly emerged from their hiding places to assess the damage as Emily came running out to give Jon a well-deserved hug and kiss. Even though the gunman was dead, Gideon still had to check the body for any hint of identification. As he checked the man's pockets, he found a wanted poster. He was a part of a gang that was wanted for bank robberies in Kansas and Arkansas. Wanting to share the information, Gideon walked over and handed Jon the poster.

With a smirk on his face, Jon glanced down at the imprinted face. "These guys aren't very good at robbing banks."

Frustrated, Gideon just shook his head. "I've heard of these guys. They pick a town that they think is easy, then they create a distraction by shooting up the place. Usually the sheriff and deputy are busy chasing them down while a member of the gang slips into the bank and robs it. We just happened to be in front of the bank, which presented a big problem for them."

Before Jon could relax, he noticed a crowd of people starting to form in the street. When Gideon walked over to investigate, Jon followed. As the crowd parted, Jon saw Doc lying on the ground. He had two bullet wounds to his gut. Jon quickly fell to the ground to check for life and realized Doc was still breathing. With some urgency, Jon and Gideon quickly picked him up and carried him to Doc's office where Belle was waiting. It was obvious that it was going to be a long day, so Jon had Emily take the children home. Minutes turned into hours as Jon patiently waited. Every now and then, Belle would come out to get fresh water just to rush back into the room where Doc was. Every hour, Gideon would walk the town but then return to sit with Jon. Even Ms. Lita wanted to help, so she brought food and drink, but nobody had an appetite.

Finally Belle came out of the room, wiping her hands on a bloody towel. With a look of exhaustion, she glanced over at Jon and Gideon and slowly shook her head no. Exhausted from her efforts, Belle sat down beside Jon and placed her head on his shoulder. "He's asking for you."

While Gideon sat with Belle, Jon rushed in to see Doc. When he entered the room, he looked around at the several water bowls filled with red water and all the bloody towels. No doubt Doc had lost way too much blood and was still bleeding.

As Doc lay with his eyes closed, Jon sat down and gently took hold of his hand. "Hey Pa. It's me, Jon."

When Doc slowly opened his eyes, he saw Jon and smiled. "I'm sorry, Son. I'm a stubborn old man that was blinded by thoughts of peaceful existence."

As the pain came and went, Doc would squeeze Jon's hand in order to somehow feel relief. "I was looking forward to seeing the children grow and to be there for you."

Breathing heavy off and on, Doc let out a cough as his body grew weak. Jon tried to hold back his emotions but it became more difficult with each squeeze of his hand. "It's okay, Pa. Try and save your strength."

But Doc had no intentions of staying quiet. Even until his last breath, he was going to speak his mind. "I'm proud of you, Son. I always have been. You have the heart of a lion and you have a rare set of skills rarely seen. When I was a boy, my father taught me to never be afraid and never back down. To always stand up for what's right."

As the minutes ticked by, Doc grew weaker as he tried to look upon Jon with pride. But in the end, his words started to slur as his mind became delusional. Jon listened as Doc's words sent chills down his spine. "Jon, run…Run, Jon. Take Emily and the children and go." Doc squeezed Jon's hand tight but this time, it wasn't because of pain. "There's a dark cloud coming. It's evil. Leave this place, Son, and don't look back. Run."

As his last breath made its exit, Doc's eyes slowly closed as he drifted off into his final moments. There was no more squeezing of Jon's hand. No more words of wisdom and no more life. Grandpa Micah was gone.

Distraught, confused, angry, and sad, Jon sat quietly for a few minutes as his emotions were overwhelmed with questions. The dream he had had years before about a dark cloud consuming his family. The old man on the mountain warned him of a dark cloud that would have to be defeated. Rodrigo's last words about a dark cloud, and now Doc speaking about a dark cloud with his dying breath. After a few more minutes of pondering all the questions, Jon reached into his pocket and pulled out the letter Doc had written him for his trip to Fort Bliss. As the tears started to fall, he unfolded the letter and read it. Afterward, he neatly folded it and placed it back in his pocket. "I never thanked you for the kind words you wrote. I love you, Pa."

The days that followed Presidio were sad days. The entire town, including the people who kept to themselves, loved Doc. Through the years, he had helped many people and when he couldn't save somebody, he would always be there to comfort family members. The day of the funeral, the town of Presidio shut down. Everyone was in attendance, even the drunkards and prostitutes. Presidio was still without a religious figure, so some of the elders from the town council stood up to say some kind words. As the last of the speakers closed out with a prayer, they lowered Doc's casket into the ground. With Emily by his side, Jon watched as some of the store clerks covered the casket with dirt.

Suddenly thoughts of revenge momentarily filled Jon's mind. *Walk away from trouble. Don't have a revengeful soul. Be a peaceful man.* These were things that Doc would always preach, but now Doc was dead at the hands of greedy bank robbers that were probably too lazy to do an honest day's work. Greedy men always willing to hurt people for profit. Bad men willing to hurt people just for the hell of it. Bullies always taking advantage of the weak. People thieving, robbing, and creating havoc wherever they go. Jon was tired of it. Tired of always turning the other cheek. Just when he could feel his anger reach its peak, he turned to see Jacob standing beside him. Before Jon could react, Jacob spoke some words of wisdom to his young protégé. "Please tell me you're not thinking of doing something crazy."

As he looked around, Jon took a breath as he released all the hatred he was feeling. "Jacob! Where did you come from?"

Watching as the men shoveled the last of the dirt into the hole, Jacob used his humor to try and defuse the situation. "I came from my mother's womb. Where did you come from?"

Taking some time to enjoy the moment, Jon shook Jacob's hand then gave him a hug. "You know what I mean. It's been too many years to count. What are you doing here? Where is Zeke and all the guys?"

As the townspeople started to filter out of the graveyard, some stopped to give their condolences to Jon while others just gave a respectful nod. Jon knew he was going to be a while, so he sent Emily and the children home. Finally, everyone was gone except Gideon. Before Jon could get his introductions out, Gideon shook Jacob's hand. "How the hell are you, old man?"

Once again, hugs were in order. Afterward, Jacob told Jon how Gideon was the military's finest scout and how they had served together during a few campaigns.

When the three men got back to Gideon's office, Gideon pulled out a bottle and poured the drinks. He then raised his glass for a toast. "Here's to Doc, may he rest in peace."

As Jon finished off his shot, he once again made some inquiries to Jacob. "So, how did you know about the funeral, and where is everybody?"

Feeling the smooth whiskey slide down his throat, Jacob smiled as he placed his empty glass on the table. "Well, I'm glad to see you too, Jon. I'm sorry about your friend. I know the both of you were close. Word travels fast when tragedy strikes down a man like Doctor Micah. As for the rest of the crew, what's left of everyone is up north on a cattle drive. I broke away so I could come and see you."

Jon didn't like the words that Jacob chose and Gideon knew all too well what that meant. To break up the awkward silence, Gideon poured several more drinks and Jacob wasted little time drinking his down. "Damn Rebels. The war was supposed to be over when Lee surrendered in Virginia. But there was a few other stubborn generals that just weren't ready to give up the fight. We were on our way home when we took on some small arms fire. That day we buried Uriah and Jesse. We were lucky that any of us made it out alive. They chopped us down like we were nothing. After the war was finally over, we still had to be careful because of all the Southern sympathizers, ex-Confederate soldiers, and just plain ol' Southern folk with the hatred to pick us off. So we decided it would be safer for us to sign up for whatever cattle drives we could find."

Thinking about his present position, Jacob paused for a moment and smiled. "Those cattle barons don't take kindly to losing men. Losing a man means losing money to them. So we've been quite content since the war ended and it pays well."

With frustration, Gideon finished his drink, then slammed his glass down on the table. "It seems that winning a war doesn't change people's minds overnight. It was bad for all of us. I saw a lot of good men die. I didn't know your friends, Jacob, but I'm sorry. I'm sorry that damn war had to take place. If you'll excuse me, gentlemen, I have to make my rounds."

After Gideon walked out, Jon's frustration picked up where Gideon's left off. "Doc didn't pass away. He was shot down by a bunch of sorry pigs."

Worried about Jon's mental status, Jacob saw in Jon what he had seen in Zeke years before: hatred and revenge. "Now, Jon, I could see that look on your face when they were lowering Doc into the ground. I'm asking you...no, I'm telling you, don't go down that path. Once you do, there's no way back. Doc lived a good long life. Just let him go."

When Jon heard those words coming from Jacob, he could feel his insides cringe. "He didn't deserve to die like a dog in the street. I can't believe you would even say such a thing. How about Chatter? Remember him? Zeke told me what the both of you did. He told me you carved up some colonel like a wild pig. Look me in the eyes and tell me that wasn't revenge. Tell me you didn't feel hatred when you did what you did."

Feeling a bit of shame, Jacob turned away because he knew Jon was right. Too many times he had felt anger and hatred. "Jon, I'm not perfect and I've made plenty of mistakes in my life. Mistakes that will probably come back to haunt me. I just don't want you to one day wake up and regret the mistakes that could have been avoided."

As much anger as he had, Jon came to the realization that Jacob was right. "Why, Jacob? Why? Why do bad things happen to good people? Why does God allow good people to suffer and bad people to take whatever they want?"

Living the type of life he had and seeing many of his friends die, Jacob understood the hurt Jon was feeling. "I don't know why God allows evil to exist in this world. I know I've done things in my life that I'm going to have to account for. Over the years, I've learned to stay focused on living right. Sometimes it becomes difficult to stay on the path of righteousness, especially during a war. Jon, I can't sit here and say I've never felt hatred for somebody, nor can I say I've never taken revenge out on somebody for what they've done, but I can attest to the fact that I have plenty of regrets. It's not a good feeling to know you could have taken a different path other than a path of destruction."

Needing a break from the conversation, Jon sat quietly while his mind ran rapid with emotions. A trip back to the El Capitan was the last thing he wanted, but there was no denying the fact that everything seemed to be pointing him in that direction.

Just when the silence was about to become uncomfortable, Gideon came back from doing his rounds. "Judging from the silence and the looks on your faces, it seems I may have missed something."

Feeling good about Jacob's counsel and guidance, Jon stood up and smiled. "No. Just a wise old man giving a young fool some good advice. Listen, I have to go away for a few days. I'm not sure when I'm coming back. Gideon, could you please check in on the wife and children from time to time? Jacob, thanks for being here for me. Thank you for everything." With thoughts of his trip fresh on his mind, Jon shook Gideon's hand and gave Jacob a hug. Feeling the weight of the world on his shoulders, he walked out.

Twisting and turning his empty shot glass and tapping it on the table, Jacob sat silently with his convictions. After watching a troubled Jon ride off, Gideon grabbed a seat and sat down. "I know Jon's upset about Doc, but there's something else. Is there something I need to know?"

With a worried look on his face, Jacob helped himself to what was left in the bottle. "How well do you know, Jon?"

With a firm outlook, Gideon didn't have to think long. "We met up in San Antonio. Long story short, he told me Presidio needed a sheriff and since I was about to be out of a job, I took the offer. Seemed like a good idea at the time."

As the seriousness of the conversation took a humorous turn, Jacob let out a small laugh. "So, how is it being the only black sheriff in Texas?"

With some pride mixed with some apprehension, Gideon smiled. "Well, it's not a bad job if you can dodge all the bullets."

Waiting for Jacob to elaborate, Gideon watched as he drank down the last of the bottle. "Don't worry, old man. I have another." After pulling another bottle from his desk, Gideon poured two more drinks. "So, getting back to Jon. What are you so worried about? He's a grown man and he's more than capable of taking care of himself."

Thinking back to when he met Jon, Jacob remembered the almost impossible scenarios Jon somehow was able to resolve. "I met Jon during the war. He was young and dumb, coming from Fort Bliss, and he inadvertently stumbled into our camp." Reminiscing about the time, Jacob paused as he let out a small laugh. "Damn fool. I'm sure I don't have to tell you that some of the men were almost a little too quick to plug him full of holes. Luckily curiosity got the best of us. Anyway, just in talking with him for a few minutes, I knew there was something about him. Something I couldn't quite understand and still don't."

Gideon listened as Jacob seemed to suggest that Jon was different than most. "So, what are you saying? He's lucky? He's has a guardian angel watching over him? What?"

Jacob didn't know what to say because his thoughts were scattered with ideas. "I don't know. When he was younger, an English family found him wondering out on the plains. He said he was living with the Apache for a while, but they were terrified of him. They called him Hok'ee, which means 'abandoned.' They thought he was some kind of lost spirit. The Comanche think he wonders the night and kills their warriors in their sleep. Me personally, I think that boy is on a journey that's going to come to a violent conclusion."

Listening to Jacob try and describe Jon, Gideon sat back in his chair and smiled. "Come on, Jacob, you don't seem like the type for telling ghost stories. Jon is a man just like any other man. He just lost a father figure to violence. You just have to give him a chance to grieve in his own way. If that means taking a trip out into the wilderness, then so be it."

Feeling the dryness in his mouth, Jacob took one last drink, then stood up. "Something is coming, Gideon. I can feel it in my bones. I wish I knew more, but I don't. So with that said, thank you for the drinks, but I have to get back to the cattle drive."

While Gideon sat and pondered Jacob's words, Jon was home preparing some supplies for his trip. With Doc's funeral still fresh in their thoughts, Emily knew not to question where Jon was going. Instead, she stayed quiet and helped him pack some food for his trip. When she was finished, she gave him a hug. "Do what you have to do and come home safe."

With a delicate touch, Jon kissed Emily on the cheek, then gave the children hugs and walked out.

It was a long ride, but it wasn't anything he hadn't done before. As Jon put miles behind him, he kept an eye out for any shadows. A day and a half into his trip while sitting at his campfire, he could feel a presence close by. Between the owls hooting, the crawlers chirping, and the coyotes howling, Jon knew there was something or somebody just beyond his eyesight. As he slowly stood up, he dropped his gun belt to the ground and yelled out, "I know you're out there. Why don't you show yourself?"

After a few moments of waiting, Jon yelled again. "Who are you? Why do you follow me? What do you want?"

With the wind blowing and whistling its own tune, Jon waited for answers but there were none.

When the morning sun rose high, Jon rode hard, only stopping for short breaks. By sundown he made it to the base of the El Capitan. It was going to get real dark real fast, but this time he wasn't interested in waiting until morning. Just like before, he rode until the path became too steep and then he climbed the rest of the way by foot. After making it to the plateau where he had had his dream, Jon stood and waited for a sign. After a few minutes, the sign he was waiting for appeared as the brightness of a fire lit up the path to the cave. Once again Jon entered the mysterious cave hoping to see the Old One and get some answers. Thinking about the questions he would ask, Jon stood just within the mouth of the cave and watched as the fire burned bright.

Suddenly, he could see movement within the fire. Just as the fire became too bright to watch, the Old One appeared to step out of the fire. Wearing turquoise and silver clothing with a beautiful headrest made up of rainbow-colored feathers, the Old One approached Jon. "I see you have returned, Cheveyo. It is not your time. Why have you come here?"

The fire was still burning bright, and it seemed the eyes of the Old One burned just as bright as the fire. Jon held up his hand to try and block some of the blinding light, but it was too much. The force of the fire pushed him back as he fell backward into a deep slumber. Once again he saw visions around the fire. A white thoroughbred as bright as the stars was running wild. As free as the wind, the mare raced across the plains. As she disappeared, another vision began. It looked like a massacre of men in a small canyon. As Jon tried to focus, he noticed that each man lying dead on the ground was wearing a Texas Ranger badge. Then he saw himself lying on the ground with a badge clenched in his hand. He was startled as his body began to tremble. Suddenly, the familiar dark cloud came upon him and consumed him and his family. In a sweat, Jon awakened and screamed.

After regaining his ability to move, Jon looked around and saw the fire was gone along with the Old One. As he stood up and brushed off some of the dirt, he glanced toward the mouth of the cave. It was daylight and the birds were singing their morning songs. Frustrated and still shaken by what he saw in his vision, Jon walked out. As the morning sun warmed his face and the mountain breeze gently blew by, he turned and looked back into the cave. "Why do you haunt me, old man? What is it that you want from me?"

Jon was hoping to get some answers from the Old One, but unfortunately that didn't happen. What was the dark cloud in his visions, and why was everyone warning him about it? Jon thought back to his first encounter with the Old One and remembered his visions of priests and conquistadors, but why? What did these visions mean and why was he having them? All legitimate questions, but it seemed Jon had wasted his time coming back to the El Capitan.

Once Jon made it back down the mountain, he immediately started his long trip home. With his frustration at its peak, he suddenly lost interests in finding answers. Once again he realized he was content with his life and had no reason to believe anything bad would happen. Emily, Abby, Adam, and Abram—they were his life and he was eager to get back to them. In an attempt to forget his worries, Jon tried to clear his mind of all the thoughts within his dreams and visions. Recently, he had overheard a couple of merchants talking about a herd of wild Mustangs that were seen in the area he would be traveling, so he was excited about maybe catching a peek, especially since he had never seen a wild herd of Mustangs before.

After a couple of days riding, there were no horses in sight. Just when Jon figured he wouldn't even get a glimpse, there they were, about twenty miles outside of Presidio. As he looked down from a ridge, he could see the herd was about twenty-five strong. Beautiful in every way, they were powerful but moved with grace. Jon watched for a few minutes while the herd moved in conformity across the fields, and then it happened. On the opposite ridge from where Jon was sitting, he could see something shining bright. At first he thought it might be the sun bouncing off something metal, but then it moved. It was a horse, but not just any horse. It was a white thoroughbred and she was the leader of the herd. Her coat shined so bright it looked like polished silver. As she reared back and cried out, the herd of Mustangs responded with force. They started off with a slow trot, which turned into a full gallop. The white thoroughbred moved almost without effort. So powerful and fast, Jon had never seen anything like her.

As Jon's heart pumped with excitement, he watched the thoroughbred as she led the herd back and forth across the fields. It reminded him of his vision. So exhilarating just to witness. He thought about trying to get a closer look, but he didn't think Sapphire was up for the task, so he decided to just sit and watch. Jon looked on for a few more minutes, then the mare led her herd off into the opposite direction of where he was going. The sun was going to be setting soon, so he continued on and eventually made it back to town.

With his mouth dry and the excitement of the Mustangs still fresh, he decided to stop to talk with Gideon and maybe have a drink. As luck would have it, when Jon walked into the saloon, Gideon was already at the bar talking with Ms. Lita. Knowing that Jon was grieving when he left, Gideon was glad to see his friend back safe. "Well, welcome back. Have a seat and Ms. Lita will set us up."

Ms. Lita was also glad to see Jon, so with a smile on her face, she poured three beers and three shots of whiskey. Business was slow and except for a few of the passed-out drunkards, Gideon and Jon were the only customers in the bar.

Before anyone could take a sip, Jon raised his glass for a toast. "Here's to family and friends."

As the three downed their whiskey then sipped their beer, Jon began to tell his story. "You would not believe what I saw on my way back to town. Before I left, I heard some people talking about a herd of wild Mustangs, so I went looking for them and found them. They were beautiful, but that's not all. They're being led by an incredible white thoroughbred. She's the fastest horse I've ever seen."

As he drank down his beer, Gideon let out a small laugh. "She's the fastest horse anyone has ever seen. She showed up a few weeks ago. A couple of old boys was out on a cattle drive and saw her. They tried to corner her, but she was just too damn smart for them. Quite a few cowhands have tried to catch her since then, but like I said, she's way too fast and much smarter than most folks I know. A horse like that is worth a small fortune for the person who does catch her."

After some laughs and a few more drinks, Gideon had some bad news to tell. "I know this isn't any of your concern, Jon, but the old Wellington place burned to the ground last night. Luckily it's been abandoned for years, so except for the structures themselves, there wasn't any harm done."

Jon remembered the farm because he had offered to buy it after he got married, but the Wellington family was very adamant about keeping it for future generations. "So now what? Maybe I should make another offer."

With a suspicious look, Gideon drank down the last of his beer, then gave Jon more disappointing news. "Too late. Already been bought. The Wellingtons live in San Francisco now, so I sent them a telegram about the fire. Come to find out, somebody was already in contact with them and bought the land sight unseen."

Realizing he missed an opportunity, Jon didn't say anything, but Ms. Lita was very surprised and had her concerns. "I've known the Wellingtons for years. They're a proud family and never had any intentions of selling that property. They were saving it for their grandchildren."

Just before Jon was set to leave, Gideon had more news. "Listen, Jon, little Julia Taylor was in my office yesterday morning. She told me her grandparents were supposed to visit the night before but never showed up. They live about fifteen miles up north, so I took a ride out to their place."

Jon was familiar with the elderly couple because he would often check in on them during his travels, so as Gideon informed him of their disappearance, Jon listened with the hope they didn't fall prey to outlaws or Indians. "So, what are you thinking? Comanche?"

With ideas and various scenarios in mind, Gideon thought for a moment as he took a drink of his beer. "No. Not this far south. Besides, Comanche doesn't have any need for old folks. Same thing for Apache. They would have just killed them and took the available livestock, but the livestock they had was dead and breakfast was still on the table half-eaten. I took a look around but there was nothing. Like they had just vanished."

Listening to the story, Jon thought about the sheriff in San Antonio and remembered the stories he told. "When I got to San Antonio, that sheriff told me some of the landowners had mysteriously died. He said he thought it may have been Indians, but he was doubtful. I wonder if their land was also bought right away."

Appreciating Jon's early theory, Gideon didn't want to come to any conclusions until he could investigate further, so he had his own idea. "I know you want to get home to your family, but I'd like to take a ride back out there tomorrow. I was hoping you would ride along with me."

Of course, Jon got a big smile on his face because he was always eager to do any type of law enforcement work, especially alongside of Gideon. "Hell yeah, count me in. But for now, I have to get home to Emily."

Later, when Jon got home, Emily and the children were already asleep, so he grabbed a bottle he had hidden in the cabinet and walked out to the porch. He was no longer thinking about the El Capitan or the so-called mysterious cloud of death or any of his visions. He wasn't concerned with what problems Texas was having or what Gideon had told him. And with the Texas Rangers being a distant memory, Jon was quite content with his life and family.

The following morning after breakfast, Jon was on his horse and headed to town. With his excitement riding high, he met up with Gideon and off they went. Before going to the Taylor homestead, Gideon wanted to show Jon the results of the Wellington fire. The old Wellington place was only about a thirty-minute ride northwest of Presidio. When they arrived, Jon couldn't believe the damage. The main house, several barns, and even the outhouse was burned to the ground.

As Gideon dismounted, he pointed Jon to the main house. "Come take a look at this. I want to show you something."

Still in awe, Jon dismounted and walked toward the main house. There was absolutely nothing left. Just ash and dust. Gideon stood at the foot of where the porch would have been and pointed toward the area of where the barns use to be. "Look at this. Look at the distance between the house and the first barn. I spoke to old Ben at the feed shop this morning. He says he passes by here at least once a week and he told me the house and the barns were perfectly fine last week. Now, there hasn't been any harsh winds lately, so for a fire to spread from structure to structure isn't possible at this distance. At least not without help."

Taking a minute to look around, Jon was awed by the devastation. Even the fence and all the posts were burned. "But why would anybody burn down a farm that's been vacant for years? And a better question, who would buy a piece of property sight unseen?"

Gideon took one last look around and surveyed the damage. "This wasn't Indians. There was nothing here for them to take. Come on, let's take a ride out to the Taylor place."

The Taylors lived another thirty minutes north, so Jon and Gideon wasted no time getting there. When they arrived, Jon looked around but saw no signs of life. There were a few dead pigs in the pen, and the two cows they had were now lying on the ground rotting with flies buzzing around. There were no signs of the Taylors, and just like Gideon said, breakfast was still on the table.

Gideon peeked into the bedroom but saw nobody. "Look at this." Gideon picked up an old jewelry box and handed it to Jon.

When Jon opened it, it played an old-fashioned song with a little ballerina dancing around. Also inside the ornate box were a few pieces of gold jewelry, a pearl necklace, and a decorative ring. "This doesn't make any sense. Indians would have taken this. Hell, anyone with foul play on their minds would have taken this. This just doesn't make sense."

Jon handed the box back to Gideon, who then closed it and gently laid it back down on the dresser. "I wanted you to come out with me today because I want to do a perimeter search of the property. Maybe something happened to the Taylors, which prevented them from coming back home."

With the simple plan of circling the property, Gideon went east while Jon rode west. After searching for an hour, neither one found any signs of the Taylors. When they met back at the Taylors farm, both men had somber looks on their faces. Gideon shook his head no while Jon just looked bewildered. "I know the Taylors had a buckboard, but I didn't see any tracks."

Gideon wasn't surprised because two days earlier when he checked the barn, the wagon was there and their horse was dead. "I don't know, Jon. About a few hundred yards east, I noticed a bunch of horse tracks. Looks like there was a gathering, but there was too many to count. I sent some telegrams yesterday to a few other territories. What'ya say we head back to town to see if anything came back?"

When Gideon and Jon got back to town, there were no new messages at the telegraph office, so they decided to walk the town to see if any other odd occurrences recently happened. Last stop for the day was Doc's office to see Belle. Since Belle took over, she had been conducting medical rounds throughout the territory. Belle was always a delight to talk to, but Gideon could tell there was something bothering her. "Belle, I know you're busy but I'm hoping you can help us out with some recent problems we've been having."

Belle didn't have news about the homesteads but she did have some disturbing news about some of the local tribes. "Sorry, Gideon. I heard about the Wellington place and now stories are starting to circulate about the Taylors. Some of the townspeople are blaming the Indians, and others are just talking foolishness. People are running around telling ghost stories, and the children are terrified of monsters coming down from the mountains at night and eating people. Some of the tribes I've visited have told me some of their warriors have disappeared and sometimes when they send scouts out to find food, they don't return. They say the spirit world has become unbalanced and now the spirits are angry. They think bad spirits are roaming the land and devouring people. I've also heard that Mexican bandits refuse to cross the border. I don't know, Gideon. I don't frighten easily, but I can feel something evil in the air."

Taking in all the information Belle was giving, Gideon listened and was surprised at all the wild rumors and speculations being spread. "Listen, Belle, as stubborn as you are, I know it's a waste of my breath to try and talk you out of conducting your medical rounds every week, so I would feel a lot better if you took somebody along with you when you do go."

Happy to accommodate Gideon's request, Belle didn't even put up one word of argument. She was all too pleased to have company along for her trips.

"Thomas is six foot four, three hundred pounds, and is dead on with a rifle. And besides, I think he has a small crush on me. He'll be glad to ride along with me and if he behaves himself, I may even bring a picnic basket along."

After leaving Doc's, Jon suggested the ultimate stress reliever: drinks with Ms. Lita. Jon's treat. When they entered the saloon, Ms. Lita was tending bar as usual while several customers were spread out around the tables. After Ms. Lita poured the beers, she confronted Gideon about all the rumors that were running rapid around town. "Gideon, I know I don't have to tell you, but folks are starting to get scared. There's a lot of talk about you not being able to do your job. I know everyone's entitled to their own opinion even if it is wrong."

Without taking offense, Gideon smiled as he took a drink of his beer. "I don't hold anything against folks like that. People are disappearing. Mysterious fires are starting by themselves. Local Indian tribes are afraid to go out at night. There's talk of monsters, evil spirits, and God knows what else. What is there to be worried about?"

It wasn't a laughing matter, but Ms. Lita knew Gideon was just trying to break up what seemed like a tense situation. "And that Mr. Hinklemeyer isn't exactly giving out comforting thoughts either. He was in here last night telling all kinds of crazy stories. I swear, that man is a gossip expert."

Just when humor had made its mark on the conversation, a man that was at the bar became upset and decided to voice his opinion. He was a local farmer named Harley Daniels and he had a mean streak going down his backbone. "I don't take kindly to ya jok'n 'bout the woes this here town is hav'n, Sheriff. People are scared and ya don't seem to care one way or 'nother. Or is it you people don't rightly care 'bout white folk?"

Gideon was familiar with Harley and knew he could be a mean drunk, so he didn't let his words bother him. "Mr. Daniels, I know you lost your youngest child this past winter and your wife has been sick, so why don't you just go home and sleep it off?"

Gideon didn't mean any harm, but bringing up Harley's children was a big mistake. "You listen here, boy. You might've won yer freedom in that there war, but us Texans aren't too fast to forget. My two eldest fought for Texas and they died because of you people." In his frustrations, Harley approached Gideon and stood eye to eye. "I don't know what ya did to get that there badge and I really care none 'bout it. I don't appreciate you mak'n light of us folks."

Gideon tried to be patient, so he took a step back to create a little distance. "Mr. Daniels, please. I don't think it's a good idea for you to be locked up tonight while your wife is home sick."

After realizing Harley wasn't backing down, Ms. Lita decided to join the argument. "Listen here, Harley. Take your drunken ass home or I'll tell your wife I saw you coming out the back door of Molly's whore house."

With his anger starting to build, Harley grabbed a half-empty beer from the bar and chugged it down, then took a step back. "Go head, you stupid bitch. Mind yer own. My bin'ness is wit the Negro. Well how 'bout it, Mr. Negro Sheriff? I hear'ed you think yer pertty fancy with that there gun."

The last thing Gideon wanted was a gun fight and he was done with talking, so he turned his back on Harley in hopes that he would get the message and go home. Instead, Harley became enraged and grabbed Gideon by the arm. "I knew ya people were yeller."

With Harley still holding Gideon's arm, Gideon spun around with a left hook and struck Harley on his chin. With his eyes rolling back into his head, Harley fell backward onto the floor and passed out. Still frustrated, Gideon bent over and took Harley's gun and handed it to Ms. Lita. "When he wakes up, give him his gun and buy him a beer on me. Then send his racist white ass home."

Gideon then glanced at Jon, who was trying hard to hold back his laughter. "It's getting close to dinnertime, but before you leave, I need to talk to you. I'll be waiting in my office."

Not trying to make eye contact, the rest of the patrons in the bar lowered their heads as Gideon walked out.

Although Jon thought the situation to be funny, it sounded like Gideon was back in a serious frame of mind. Ms. Lita could tell Gideon was bothered, not by Harley but by the strange happenings, so that made her worry even more. After some uncomfortable silence, Jon finished his beer then left to meet with Gideon.

When he arrived, Gideon was sitting outside enjoying the spring air. "Have a seat, Jon. I wanted to talk to you about something."

With some concern, Jon pulled up a chair and sat down beside his friend. "I know you're under a lot of strain, but don't let that Harley get to you. He was born an ass and just grew bigger. Hopefully he sobers up and apologizes."

Gideon sat and stared as merchants got ready for the sun to set. Because of all the rumors, most were closing early so they could get home to their families. "After seeing what you saw and hearing all the wild speculations, what do you think?"

Thinking about the inquiry, Jon didn't respond right away because the tone in Gideon's voice suggested something other than an innocent question. "Well, I don't know what I think. I'm in the dark about all this just like everyone else."

Gideon could feel the apprehension in Jon's voice, but it was a conversation he felt he needed to have. "Before Jacob left town, he told me something. He said the Indians refer to you as Hok'ee."

As Gideon watched for a response, Jon cringed at the thought his friend was now questioning him as a suspect. When he heard that name, he was shocked that Jacob or Gideon would even bring that subject up. "Are you accusing me of something, Gideon? Because it certainly sounds like it."

As the town started to shut down, Gideon watched as the last merchant left for the night. He then turned back to Jon and laughed. "No, but I had you going for a while."

After a few more seconds of laughing at Jon's expense, Gideon laid out his thought process. "I've come to the conclusion that Indians aren't responsible, and I'm certain evil spirits aren't running around setting fires. I don't believe in ghosts, so I certainly don't suspect them of abducting people, and I suppose monsters coming down from the mountains is just juvenile nonsense. So, what does that leave us?"

As the silence settled in, Jon decided to tell Gideon some other disturbing news. "Gideon, not that I want to add to your problems, and this may or may not be connected, but I came across something the day we met on my way to San Antonio."

Not that Gideon needed anymore problems, but he was anxious to hear what Jon had to say. "Right about now, Jon, good or bad, I could use all the information I can get."

Feeling a bit burdened, Jon sat up in his chair and leaned forward. He needed to tell Gideon about Rodrigo and his men without saying anything about his past. "Well, when I was younger, I was out hunting and gathering food when I suddenly found myself surrounded by a bunch of Mexican bandits. They thought I might have something of value, but they soon realized I had nothing for them to take. They had their fun and beat me up some, but that was about it. Strange as it may seem, right before they rode off, their leader seemed to think that we were going to meet again so he told me his name. Rodrigo."

Gideon listened with interest but he didn't recognize the name. After a short pause, Jon continued with his story. "After that encounter, I never thought I would see Rodrigo again—until I came across him and his men on my way to San Antonio."

With the story becoming more enticing, Gideon was now on the edge of his seat. "Well, you're here telling me this story, so I'm guessing you took care of business."

But Gideon's premature thinking led Jon to tell the rest of his story. "I wish I could say yes, but I can't. Some very bad business happened way before I arrived. Rodrigo had over twenty men with him and they were all dead. It looked like a slaughter. Most of them still had their guns in their holsters. I looked around and just when I was about to leave, I found Rodrigo barely alive. He was shot up pretty bad and there was nothing I could do for him. Now, this is where it gets interesting. With death about to take him away, somehow he recognized me. He told me to run. That there was something coming nobody could stop."

With the idea of comparing Jon's story, Gideon sat back in his chair and thought back to his conversation with Jacob. "My parents taught me to always respect my elders and to listen to their advice. Just like Rodrigo, Jacob said the same thing. He also seems to think that something bad is coming. He added you into the equation and has somehow surmised that you are headed for a violent showdown. That said, along with all the strange happenings, I think Jacob is right."

Jon briefly thought Gideon was trying to bait him into another joke, but Gideon wasn't smiling. He could see the look on Gideon's face was serious. "Well, I'll tell you this, Gideon. Everyone seems to think something bad is going to happen and that I need to run away from it. I've never ran from anything or anyone and I'm not about to start. Whatever comes my way, either bad or good, I'll face it head on."

The next day, Jon spent the entire day with Emily and the children. Picnic by the stream, then a ride into town for some ice cream. Afterward, Emily and the children went to visit Belle while Jon headed straight to Gideon's office. When Jon walked in, he saw Gideon was talking to an old familiar face. It was Gunther, the Texas Ranger that saved his life.

"Gunny, how the hell are you?"

After standing up for the greetings and handshakes, Gunny quickly sat back down and got comfortable. "Well young'n, I was just sitting here telling the sheriff that the Texas Rangers are going to become a reality again. Politics have changed and now they want us back. Times aren't getting any better for the state of Texas and the homesteaders could use a little help, not to mention the local sheriffs. I thought I would stop by and introduce myself, and Gideon here has been kind enough to offer these old bones a drink."

After the three men drank and told a few fun stories, Gunther finally got down to business. "Well Jon, the powers to be is asking me to recruit only the finest of men. Men of character. Honest men with integrity. Men that aren't afraid of taking on the toughest of jobs and with the skills that it takes to handle it. Our new governor is already taking some heat from all the rumors that are spreading across the state, and folks are getting worried. And when folks get worried, that translates into politicians not getting reelected."

After gulping down his glass of whiskey, Gunther glanced over at Gideon. "No offense to you, Sheriff, but a Texas Ranger would have a little more latitude when it comes to investigating events outside of your local jurisdiction."

With his momentum building, Gunther than turned his attentions back to Jon. "In simple terms, Jon, the state of Texas would be your playground. You would have access to resources and, more importantly, you would have the support and power of the state behind you."

After turning down the offer once before, Jon never thought this day would ever come again, and he certainly wasn't prepared to give an answer. "I don't know, Gunny. It would be a dream come true and it certainly sounds ambitious, but I have a wife and family to take care of now. Before, it was just Emily."

Once again, Gunther could see Jon was caught between priorities, so he wasn't going to press the issue. "All right, Jon. As I told you before, it's a standing offer. Take your time and think about it. It pays well and we need all the good men we can find. I'll be staying in town 'til the end of the week."

After Gunther thanked Gideon for his hospitality and left, Gideon waited while Jon sat and pondered Gunther's offer. "Well, what'ya think? After all this time I don't see you not taking the job. I'm sure Emily would support your decision."

Before Jon could answer with his response, Emily came strolling in with the children. With big smiles on their faces, the children were always glad to see Gideon because they thought of him as a distant uncle. Before Gideon could get up to greet his three little fans, he had all three giving him hugs. It was perfect timing as far as Jon was concerned. Now he could take some time and ponder his decision.

After a late dinner in town, Jon and Emily finally got the children home and in bed. Afterward, Jon, with thoughts weighing heavy on his mind, sat outside on the porch with Emily not too far behind. She knew Jon had something on his mind, so she cozied up to him and waited for him to finally talk. As the nighttime breeze blew by, Jon held Emily close as he whispered into her ear, "I love you."

After a few more minutes, Jon decided to break his silence. "What do you think about me keeping the stagecoach job?"

Emily hated the stagecoach job, so it didn't take her too long to think about the question. "Jon, I know you need to work to support us, but I wish you would give that job up. It's getting much too dangerous to be out there with all that's been going on. Maybe you can find something temporary in town until something better comes along, or maybe try one of the wealthier ranches in the area."

Manipulating the conversation with some deception, Jon knew the answer all along. He knew even before Gunther finished his last drink. He just needed Emily to be okay with it. "Emily, I have a confession to make. I had already decided to give up the stagecoach job earlier today. Do you remember me telling you about Gunny?"

Emily thought for a moment, then remembered the story Jon told about the failed robbery and how the Texas Rangers saved his life. Jon didn't have to say another word. Emily knew in her heart where he was going with the conversation and she knew being a Texas Ranger was where Jon belonged. "Jon, all your life, that's all you've ever wanted. It's where you should be and it's what you were meant to do. I love you and I will always love you."

After giving Jon her blessing, Emily leaned over and gave him a soft kiss on his cheek. She then got up and stood in the doorway. "I'll be in bed waiting."

With a state election in full swing, the state of Texas saw a newly elected governor, which led the state legislation to recommission the Texas Rangers. Emily, Abby, Adam, and Abram, along with Gideon, Belle, and Ms. Lita, watched as Jon was presented with his shiny new Texas Ranger badge. Unfortunately, Jacob and the other men were two states away helping to drive cattle to market for a rich cattle baron. But Gideon made sure a telegram was sent explaining Jon's newly appointed position.

The job of the Texas Ranger was simple: Anything that compromised the safety of the state of Texas or its people. Indians, range wars, bandits, outlaws, feuds, and any other kind of dispute involving violence. First up for Jon: the town of Del Rio along the Texas Mexican border. Founded only one year before, the town was having trouble with hordes of bandits crossing over into Texas and pillaging the small town. When Jon arrived, there was mayhem in the streets. Several Mexican bandits were terrorizing the bar while several others roamed the streets breaking windows and stealing goods from the general store. As Jon calmly dismounted, he looked around for any law enforcement. Unfortunately, the sheriff and several deputies were already dead, strung upside down with puddles of blood beneath them.

In the midst of all the trouble, Jon spotted Gunther sitting quietly off to the side whistling to an upbeat tune and whittling away on an old piece of wood. As he rocked back and forth in an old decrepit chair, he finally got tired of the noise and stood up. The grin on his face gave Jon some relief. As the two men met in the middle of the street, Jon expressed his delight. "I'm a little surprised to see you, Gunny, but I won't turn down any help you might be able to provide."

Still grinning from ear to ear, Gunther took a quick glance around, then turned back to Jon. "Well, young buck, how are you going to handle this situation? There are seven of them. That's Gods number and I like that. Are you going to try and talk them into surrendering? Or maybe just tell them to drop their weapons and quietly leave town? Or maybe they'll all line up nice and neat so you can march them into a jail cell."

Jon knew Gunther was being sarcastic, but he did have a valid point. How was he going to handle his first assignment?

As the mayhem continued, Jon's thoughts ran rapid. Then out of the corner of his eye, he saw two of the bandits walking toward him with their guns drawn. During their pillaging, the two men noticed Jon and Gunther and decided they were going to have some fun. Unfortunately for them, fun wasn't on the menu. With lightning speed, Jon withdrew his gun and shot both men, killing them instantly. As the two men fell to the ground, Jon glanced over at Gunther and smiled. "I think I'll take D, none of the above."

Feeling excited about the situation, Gunther was ecstatic to see Jon take action. "Damn, son, I like your thinking. Seems to me you and I are gonna get along just fine. What'ya say we get to it? There's five left. I bet you a shot of whiskey and a beer that I get three of them."

Hearing the bet, Jon laughed and shook his head in disbelief. "I'd hate to take advantage of an old man, but you're on, Gunny."

Gunther walked up one side of the street while Jon took the other. As they reached the general store, two of the bandits came walking out carrying sacks of grain with sugar sticks in their mouths. When they saw the two Rangers staring them down, they panicked. Dropping their sacks of grain and nearly choking on their candy, they tried to draw their guns. As Gunny watched the bumbling idiots, he broke into a laugh. Almost feeling sorry for the two bandits, Jon tried to wait as long as possible but finally had to shoot the two sorry men, putting them out of their misery. He didn't even have to be quick about it. "Well now, Gunny, that's two for me."

Still laughing, Gunny apologized. "I'm sorry, young'n, I just couldn't help myself. What'ya say we head on over to the saloon so you can buy me my drinks?"

With a smile on his face, Jon holstered his gun and pointed out one small fact. "You're way behind, old man. All I need is one more."

With a devious smile on his face, Gunther took his gun from his holster and took three bullets out, leaving him with three shots. "I'm not that old and yes, you will be buying me those drinks."

As they made their way further up the street, they arrived at the saloon and could hear the bandits yelling obscenities and breaking furniture. Before Jon could take another step, Gunther grabbed his arm. "Hold on there, young'n. Before going off halfcocked and storming into a situation, a good Ranger always checks his ammo."

Not thinking anything was wrong, Jon slowly pulled his gun from his holster to check it. With a grin as big as a half moon, Gunther broke out into a laugh. Leaving Jon behind, he ran into the saloon and fired a quick two shots, killing two of the men, then ran back out to where Jon was standing. "You're way too easy, young'n."

Still laughing, Gunther bent down and rested his hands on his knees. "Now that was exhilarating. Wow! That'll get the heart pumping."

In disbelief, Jon just stood staring at Gunther. "You're crazy, old man. Hell, if I knew it was that important to you, I would have just bought you the drinks. But there's still one more. Now what?"

Breathing a little easier, Gunther stood upright as he stretched out his back. "Well, he can't stay in there forever. He has to come out eventually."

As the two men waited for their prey, Gunther decided to break the tension. "So, wife and kids okay?"

Once again, Jon stood in awe. "You're really something, Gunny. We're standing out here in the open and you're wondering about my family."

With every intention of waiting for an answer, Gunny smiled as he patiently waited. "So, what about the family?"

Shaking his head, Jon couldn't help but smile. "Gunny, for all we know, there could be a rifle pointed at us."

Still smiling, Gunny whistled a small tune and continued to stare at Jon. "So, about your family, everything okay?"

Finally Jon broke down and gave Gunny what he wanted. "They're good, Gunny. Thank you for asking."

After Jon broke a smile from listening to Gunther's banter, the last bandit finally made his appearance as he exited the saloon and stepped into the street. He was a big man, tall with a prominent chest. He also had the kind of holster that held two guns, one hanging off each hip. Unfortunately he made the mistake of thinking he could intimidate the Texas Rangers with his size and his frivolous talk. With an angry look, he stared the two Rangers down. "Señor, do you know who I am?"

Neither Jon nor Gunther said anything, and their silence made the Mexican bandit angry. The look on the big man's face was fierce as he continued to eyeball the two lawmen. "I am the fastest gunfighter in Mexico."

Hearing the big man talk his talk once again, Gunther broke into a laugh. "Well now, that's one of your problems right there. You're not in Mexico, friend."

Gunther's laughing didn't sit well with the bandit, and his demeanor showed it. With Gunther laughing at him, he became even angrier. "Señor, I am a fair man so I will give you a chance to apologize then leave." After a few seconds of silence, the big man shrugged his shoulders. "Or I can just kill you both."

Gunther appreciated the confidence the big man was trying to display, but it was getting him nowhere. "Friend, you and your men caused a lot of damage and you killed several of the town's lawmen. Please tell me you didn't really think you were just going to waltz out here and talk us into leaving."

With his feeble mind twisting and turning, the bandit thought for a moment then gave his answer. "I guess not, señor. I guess it's time for you to die."

When the talking stopped, the big man drew both of his guns. But by the time he pulled the triggers, there was already bullets entering each one of his eye sockets. With a tight grip on both his guns, brain matter exited the rear of his head as he fell backward to the ground. His life was gone in an instant.

As Jon and Gunther holstered their guns, they walked side by side toward the dead man. While the two Rangers admired their handiwork, the townspeople slowly emerged from their hiding places.

Jon looked around while Gunther just couldn't help himself. "I think my bullet hit him first, which makes that three for me. Looks like you owe me some drinks."

Once again, Jon stared at Gunther in disbelief. "Gunny, you not only have a warped sense of humor, but you're also blind. My bullet definitely hit first, but never mind the bet. I appreciate you being here, so I'll buy you those drinks."

When the two men entered the saloon, the terrified patrons were in awe. The place was a mess and there was broken glass everywhere. When Jon approached the bar, he greeted the bartender and ordered two whiskeys and two beers. Wasting no time, the bartender filled two glasses with beer and placed a bottle of the saloon's best whiskey on the bar. "Listen fellas, I ain't ever seen noth'n like that. You guys are welcome here anytime. Drinks are on the house."

Between Indians constantly on the up rise, Mexican bandits terrorizing border towns, and American outlaws becoming more prominent, the Texas Rangers had their work cut out. Over a short period of time, the Texas Rangers became legendary. One town, one Ranger. That's all it took. The Texas Rangers commanded respect and were feared everywhere.

During his first year as a Texas Ranger, Jon realized Gunther was right.

The entire state of Texas was his playground, so he took advantage of his freedoms and began to help investigate the problems Presidio was having. All the disappearances, the mysterious fires, and even a few deaths. Whenever he got a chance, Jon helped Gideon with whatever he could. Unfortunately, with his Texas Ranger badge, his duties always took priority. In 1874, the military, along with six Ranger companies, fought the Red River War. Even though it only lasted a few months, the Texas Rangers were tasked with helping the military round up various Indian tribes from the southern plains and forcibly relocating them to reservations within Indian territory. There were some small skirmishes and very few casualties, but by the end of the year, the war was winding down.

With his busy schedule, Jon divided his time between his family, duties, and helping Gideon. Eventually several townships, along with Presidio, started to compare notes. After a year of crisscrossing the territory with telegrams, Gideon realized the problems had spread over a wide range of territory. Disappearances of well-known people, unexplained fires, killing of livestock, and mysterious deaths. Using a map of Texas and pinpointing each incident, Gideon noticed a pattern stretching from Houston, Texas, all the way to El Paso. It was too large to ignore and too widespread for any one town or sheriff to handle. Eventually word made it to the governor's ears so the governor made it official. The investigation into the mysterious crimes was to be handled by the Texas Rangers. Unfortunately, the state of Texas was one of the largest states and was still struggling with their post-war reconstruction stage. Along with issues of Mexican bandits crossing the border, the rise of American outlaws, Southern sympathizers, and Indians, Texas was also struggling with its political identity, conforming to new laws, and widespread lawlessness. Because of these issues, the Texas Rangers were stretched thin, as the governor only dedicated twenty-five Rangers to solve the mysterious crime spree.

Jon was part of the Rangers that were assigned and was ecstatic to be working alongside of Gideon on a full-time basis. First order of business was a trip to Waco, Texas. Waco was further up north and wasn't anywhere near the pinpointed line that Gideon had created, but there was someone special in Waco that Jon wanted to see. Jacob and his crew were there working for a large ranch

moving cattle and taking care of other livestock. It was wintertime, but no
snow had fallen yet. The winds were blowing and it was bitter cold, but for
Jon, the trip was necessary.

For the trip, Gideon left the town of Presidio in the hands of his new
deputy, Jubal. Jubal was Gideon's age and fought in the war as a Confederate officer. He was a second lieutenant during the war, but gained respect
for Gideon after Gideon helped his family out of hard times a year earlier.
Known to always wear his old Confederate hat, Jubal owned a small farm
and was experiencing one down fall after another. His well had dried up
and Gideon was the only person who offered to help dig another. The
crops that were being grown didn't do very well, so Jubal had to sell off
most of his livestock. Knowing Jubal's woes, Gideon would stop by once a
week to make sure he and his family had food. Eventually Jubal fell behind
with the bank, so Gideon offered him a full-time deputy position. Jubal
was well known in town and was liked by all, so Gideon felt good about
leaving Presidio in his hands.

After a few long days of hard riding and some cold nights, Jon and Gideon
finally arrived in Waco, Texas. After making their way to the Wild Boar Ranch,
the owner directed them out to the northern pastures. It was getting late and
the sun was going down, so as they approached, they could see a campfire
burning bright. As Jon and Gideon slowly wondered into the camp, they were
met by Harvey and Shelby. The years had gone by and Jon was older now, but
Harvey and Shelby still recognized him immediately. When Jon and Gideon
dismounted, Jon shook hands and gave hugs. When Harvey escorted them
further into the camp, Jon saw Zeke and Milky Way sitting by the fire.

As Zeke stood up, he faced off against Jon. "Well now, what'a we got here?
A real live bonafide Texas Ranga. Damn, I ain't neva seen no real Texas Ranga
before. I'm wonder'n how you is wit that gun?"

As Jon stepped closer, he looked Zeke up and down as he slowly moved
his hand toward his gun. "Seems to me I've seen your ugly mug on a wanted
poster. Only problem is they only placed a five-dollar bounty on you. That
isn't even worth the trouble of hauling your ass to jail."

With one eye on Jon and the other on his drawing hand, Zeke stood staring at Jon for a moment, then stepped closer. "Ain't no way no how. Who say I'm goi'n to jail?"

Now it was Jon staring down Zeke as he stepped closer. "Zeke, I see your English has improved."

When Jon broke a smile, Zeke burst into a laugh and shook Jon's hand. "Damn, son, you went and growed up on me. I see you still wear'n that gun belt Pops gave you. You look good."

After all the silliness was over, Jon introduced Gideon to everyone. Just then Jacob came riding into camp. Looking a little worn, he climbed down from his horse and gave Jon a hug. "Well now, what brings you two to our little clump of paradise?"

After the initial meet and greet was over, everyone sat down around the fire to get warm. Milky Way and Shelby already had dinner going, so everyone got their fill before settling in for the night. While everyone sat around talking, Jon, Gideon, and Jacob took a walk.

Jacob knew there had to be more of a reason for the visit then just the visitation itself. "So, a sheriff from Presidio and a Texas Ranger visiting me in Waco, Texas. I would like to think it's because you miss me, but I'm guessing that's wishful thinking. So, what gives?"

Jacob already knew about the troubles Presidio was having, so Gideon filled him in on all the recent information, like the pinpoint map that showed a pattern of crime across Texas and all the similar problems other towns were having. He also told Jacob the Texas Rangers had full reign over the investigation.

Blowing on his hands to keep them warm, Jacob glanced over at Jon and smiled with pride. "Congratulations, Jon. I imagine the governor is keeping a close eye on these developments. This could mean big things for you and your family."

Jon appreciated the kind words, but now it was time to find out if the trip to see Jacob would produce any useful information. As Jacob listened, Jon explained their visit. "Jacob, things aren't getting any better in Presidio. Rumors are still out of control and now we know that other territories are having similar issues, which makes folks even more frightened. For now, the majority of the problems seem to be affecting the southern townships."

As Jon continued to talk, Jacob waited patiently as he absorbed the information, but Jon could tell Jacob had something to say. "What about you? Since the war ended, you've worked for just about every large ranch from Waco to El Paso. Have you seen or heard anything unusual?"

Still trying to warm his hands, Jacob didn't say anything at first. He took a few moments to think before speaking. "Well, depends on what you would consider unusual. Right before winter hit, we drove a herd of horses down to Del Rio. On the way down, Shelby was on point and came across some tracks. These weren't just any tracks, though. There were way too many to count. At first glance we thought military, but Shelby made a good observation. The tracks were all over the place. Military tracks would have been more organized because they would have been riding in some kind of formation. Second thought was Apache. We were pretty close to their territory, but we would have seen other signs. The problem that I had was Shelby. He's the best I know when it comes to tracking. Nothing ever gets by him, and even he couldn't come up with an explanation."

Jon thought about what Jacob was saying and glanced over at Gideon. "Remember the story about Rodrigo? I kept trying to figure out what kind of force could take out so many men so fast."

As the night air turned bitter cold, the howling winds continued to test the resolve of the three men. Jacob paused for a moment to pull his coat collar up around his neck while Gideon and Jon did the same. He then continued to tell Jon and Gideon about some other happenings. "After we delivered the horses to the new owners, we headed back up north. It got late one night, so we decided to set up camp along a wooded area. Storm was coming in, so we needed some cover. That's when we found them."

Gideon and Jon waited for Jacob to continue, but the ghostly look on his face should have said it all. So, Gideon took the initiative to ask. "Jacob, what did you find? What was out there?"

Taking his time and slowing his thoughts, Jacob looked at Gideon, then glanced over at Jon. Then he swallowed the lump in his throat before speaking. "We found a makeshift grave site. Most of the graves were shallow, so the coyotes must have sniffed them out. They tore the bodies up pretty good, but we were able to make out what they were supposed to be. It looked like an entire family. From the grandparents down to the grandchildren."

As he sat down on an old tree log and removed his hat, Jacob continued to explain. "The storm hit and the fellas got spooked. We couldn't understand why an entire family was buried in such a disgraceful way. When we started to try and rebury the bodies, lightning lit up the night sky and struck a nearby tree. Then Shelby thought he saw movement off in the distance. He said it looked like an entire army of men just sitting on their horses while the rain poured down. Hell, with my eyesight and the storm looking like hell just opened up and poured out all its dirty water, I couldn't tell if it was men on horseback or a bunch of trees. Then Harvey, of all people, swore he heard something crawling around in the bushes."

Once again Jacob had to pause to collect his thoughts before continuing. With a sarcastic look on his face, he placed his hat back on his head and stood up. "And you already know how crazy Zeke can get. No sooner did Harvey say something, Zeke started hearing noises all around us. The fool pulled his gun and fired six rounds into a bunch of goddamn shadows. Hell, for all I know, he could have fired at a bunch of damn ghosts."

Rubbing the cold off his face, Jacob got up and started pacing. Jon could tell he was shaken, to say the least. "I've never known you to be this rattled, Jacob. Not even when you faced down the Comanche. Take your time. We're not here to judge anyone. We're just looking for answers."

Still bothered by his memories, Jacob rubbed the back of his neck while he continued to pace. His hands started to tremble, but Jon and Gideon couldn't tell if it was from the bitter cold or from the story he was telling. Finally Jacob stopped. No more pacing. No more trembling. His eyes were wide and, as cold as it was, he had sweat dripping down his face. "The lightning just wouldn't stop. The thunder was so loud and so frequent that it sounded like a barrage of Johnny Reb cannon fire coming down on us. Suddenly Shelby came running over. He said what I thought were trees were now getting closer. I'm sorry, Jon. I don't believe in ghosts, lost spirits, goblins, monsters, or much of anything else, but I gotta tell you, that night I was scared. I don't know what it was that struck fear into me, but we got the hell out of there. We rode all night through the storm until daylight hit us in the face. Harvey suggested we go back and bury the dead, but I said no. We all just stood around looking at each other like we had done something wrong. Maybe in God's eyes we did, but I guess we won't find out until our time comes."

The next morning, Zeke and Jon were the early birds, setting up cans and shooting holes in them. After they got bored with that, they started tossing whatever they could find up into the sky and shooting it down. Eventually everyone was awakened by the noise, so Milky Way got up and made breakfast.

While Jon played catch up with the guys, Gideon and Jacob took a plate of food and stepped away from the men. Jacob knew Gideon had more questions, so he waited patiently for Gideon to strike up the conversation. As Jacob picked away at his breakfast, Gideon began his inquiries. "Jacob, I'm surely not here to question your integrity, but last night sounded like a campfire ghost story. What about those bodies you found? You think it was Indians or maybe bandits?"

Reviewing the question in his mind, Jacob thought for a moment while he finished chewing his food. "Well Gideon, whether or not you believe what I said last night is up to you. When you've been on this earth as long as I have, sometimes you see things that frighten you. Sometimes you get overwhelmed with feelings that you can't explain. I don't know what it was during that God-forsaken night. Maybe it was a combination of the storm and our imagination. Maybe we were just tired and was seeing ghosts that weren't there and hearing bumps in the night. I can tell you this: Those bodies were real, and neither Indians nor bandits would have taken the time to do a half-assed burial, or any burial at all."

Enjoying the food, the two men took a few minutes to finish their breakfast before continuing their conversation. Gideon didn't want to offend

Jacob, so he chose his words carefully. "What do think Shelby saw that night? He said they were men on horseback, and you thought it looked like trees in a forest."

Using his sleeve, Jacob wiped his mouth then smiled. "Gideon, I don't know what the hell we saw. If it was trees, somehow, it seemed like they were moving closer. If it was men on horseback, then they were enough to rival any small army. Honestly, I just don't know. The rain was coming down so damn hard, I couldn't make hide nor hair. If I could see five feet in front of my face, I considered myself lucky. It was only when the lighting lit up the sky we could see the outline of something large coming our way. You know black folks in Texas aren't going to stick around and ask questions, and I surely wasn't going to wait around for trouble to catch up to us. Like I said last night, we got the hell out of there and didn't look back."

Trying to lighten the mood, Gideon smiled then let out a small laugh. "Jacob, you sure do tell a good story. As frightened as you made everyone out to be, I sure do wish I was there to see the looks on all of your faces."

Swallowing the last of his food, all Jacob could do was smile. "I might take offense to your comments if I didn't find it so damn funny myself. It does sound silly, but believe it or not, it's the truth."

After the laughter was over, Gideon got right back to business. "What about those tracks you told me about? You have any ideas?"

The sun was shining, but it was a cold morning. Jacob noticed the men packing up and getting their horses ready to ride, so he motioned Gideon over to the campfire. "Well, like I said before, Shelby is the best tracker I've ever known. No offense, mind you. If he couldn't figure it out, then I don't know what to tell you. It certainly wasn't Indians, and you can definitely rule out the military. Whatever it was, it was way too large for a posse. You can probably rule out settlers because there were no wagon tracks. Whoever it was, they seem to be laying waste to everyone in their path."

While the two men warmed their hands over the fire, Jon came walking over. "Well, everyone is packed and ready to go. Gideon, the clouds are looking bad. Looks like snow and a lot of it. Could be a rough trip back."

When Jacob stood up, he stretched out his old bones. "Listen fellas, before you go, I have one more thing to tell you."

As Gideon stood up, he shook off the cold and straightened out his coat. "Please, no more ghost stories. I don't think I can take much more."

With a tin cup filled with coffee quickly going cold, Jacob threw it over the fire, then kicked some dirt over it. "Listen, the man I work for now is very wealthy. He started off herding sheep and goats, then bought cattle. He now deals in cattle and horses. He's one of those characters that seem to have his hands into everything. From what I gather, he moves his money around quite a lot. Anyway, from time to time, he seems to like chatting with me. I prefer to think that he likes me, but reality is I'm the only one around that's close to his age."

Feeling the morning air getting colder, Gideon and Jon listened with interest as Jacob continued to explain. "The other day as we were getting ready to move some of his cattle to greener pastures, he invited me into his house for a drink. I kind of figured he was buttering me up to cut us lose, but that wasn't the case. At least, not at the moment."

Glancing up at the sky, Jacob noticed the snow clouds rolling in fast, so the three men mounted up. Jacob had to move the cattle and Jon and Gideon had to get back to Presidio. Harvey took the men out to the pasture to start moving the cattle while Jacob stayed behind. Gideon knew Jacob wasn't a man who wasted time, so he listened as Jacob finished his story. "So as I'm sitting in his house sipping on the man's finest whiskey, he starts telling me about his next investment. Apparently land grants became legal again last year. I do believe that's when all your troubles started. Gideon, if I were you, I would start inquiring about the railroads. I think you'll find out they're buying up land like little kids buying candy."

Gideon had heard rumors of the railroads wanting to expand through Texas, but the politics of business was something that didn't interest him until now. "So you think the railroads are tied into our mysterious crime spree?"

As the snowflakes started to fall, Jacob gave Gideon and Jon a few last things to think about. "Put it to you this way, the railroads have the money, they have the power, and they have men. Lots of them. Take a look at where tragedy has struck over the past year, then find out who bought the land."

As the snowfall started to get heavier, Gideon knew it was time to go. "So, Jacob, why didn't you tell us this last night?"

As he turned his horse toward the cattle, Jacob looked back at Gideon and smiled. "Hell, it got too damn cold last night to talk. Besides, like you said, I can tell one hell of a good story."

After saying their good-byes, Jon and Gideon headed back to Presidio. The snow came down hard for a while, but after a day of riding, the storm faded off in a different direction. After listening to Jacob and realizing there might be something bigger going on than first suspected, Gideon decided to once again stop by the Taylors' farm to look around.

A couple more days of riding and Gideon and Jon arrived at the farm. Because there was nobody around for the upkeep, the house was in disarray and the farm itself had become weather beaten. Because of their search before, Jon wasn't quite sure why Gideon wanted to come back. The search they did during their last visit was pretty thorough. As the winds blew hard, dirt, dust, and snow became problematic, so both men wrapped their bandannas around their face. As Gideon climbed down from his horse, Jon inquired about the visit. As he yelled to Gideon, Gideon pointed, then walked toward the barn. After securing their horses, they made their way toward the main house.

When they arrived, they pushed the door shut behind them, leaving the nasty weather outside. Still feeling the chill in his bones, Jon took his bandanna off and shook off the cold. "What are we doing here? There was nothing here before, so what makes you think there's something here now?"

With a suspicious look, Gideon took a quick glance around. "Well, I thought about what Jacob told us and all this nonsense is starting to make sense to me."

Jon listened but just wasn't catching on to what Gideon was getting at. "Gideon, I know you can't possibly think the railroad is running around killing people and burning their farms."

Still looking around, Gideon didn't say anything. Tired from riding, he sat down at the table to rest himself. "No Jon, I don't think the railroad would purposely get involved with anything so brutal. But I do have a theory."

With his curiosity at its peak, Jon pulled up a chair and sat down. "All right, let me in on what you're thinking."

With suspicious thoughts running through his mind, Gideon sat up and leaned across the table. "Listen, I don't think the railroad is knowingly involved. If their expanding through Texas, then they're gonna buy land from either the person that owns it or the state. It doesn't matter to them."

Jon listened but still had questions concerning motives. "But if the landowner doesn't want to sell, then don't you think that's reason enough to get rid of people? The railroad could stand to lose a lot of money if they can't line up certain properties."

Jon had a good point, but Gideon laid out a more sinister theory. "You're right, Jon, but not about the railroad. The railroad is going to move forward. Whether it is over a mountain, through a mountain, over a river, or around a stubborn farm owner. There're over fifty railroad companies currently operating in Texas and they're willing to spend a lot of money to acquire land. So what if somebody else is buying up the land and just sitting on it? Land they know is desirable for big, rich, railroad companies. Tomorrow morning, you and I are going to the land deed office and we're gonna find out who bought the old Wellington place sight unseen."

As the wind twisted around the old farmhouse like a whirlwind, it attacked the old worn-out shutters without mercy, ripping some of them from the house. Sitting quietly, Gideon and Jon patiently waited for the wind to die down. While Gideon sat and waited, Jon decided to help himself to the bottle of whiskey old man Taylor had hidden way back in the cabinet. Wondering why Jon was appropriating the bottle of whiskey, Gideon watched as Jon popped the cork and placed the bottle to his lips. After taking a nice, hefty swig, Jon gave a smile. "What? It's not like the Taylors are coming back anytime soon."

When Jon handed the bottle off, Gideon laughed then took a drink. "Jon, why is it Texas Rangers have such a warped sense of humor?"

As the two men shared the bottle, Jon listened to the wind howl as his eyes wondered around the room. "So, you never said what it is exactly you expect to find here."

Thinking about his agenda, Gideon placed the nearly empty bottle on the table and got up. Planning a path around the kitchen, he slowly moved around the room opening cabinets and drawers. He moved systematically until he got to the bedroom door. As he opened the door and glanced in, he turned back to Jon. "They never left."

Listening to what Gideon was saying, Jon stood up and walked over to the window. "They're not here, so they had to go someplace. Gideon, people don't just up and disappear."

Gideon could see the wind was starting to die down, so he sat back down and took one last sip of whiskey to warm his stomach. "Listen to my reasoning and tell me what you think. The Taylors never showed up to visit little Julia. Their only transportation is their buckboard and horse. Their horse is dead and the buckboard is still in the barn. The breakfast dishes were never cleared from the table, and one of the things we missed last time was the fact their bed wasn't made. A respectable wife such as Mrs. Taylor would never leave the house without cleaning it first. So, I've concluded that they never left."

With a heavy sigh, Jon sat back down and leaned across the table. "I don't know what to tell you, Gideon. We checked the grounds and two miles in each direction."

Gideon listened for a moment, then realized the windstorm was coming to an end. So, he got up and opened the front door. As he stepped out onto the porch, Jon was right behind him. "All right, Gideon, where to?"

With his plan still playing out, Gideon stepped to the edge of the porch and looked out to the other side of the yard. "You're right, Jon. We looked everywhere—except there."

As Jon stepped to the edge of the porch, Gideon pointed across the yard at the Taylors' well. A shiver ran up Jon's spine as horrible speculations crossed his thoughts. "Are you serious? Come on, Gideon. You think somebody would actually throw two old people down a well?"

Just thinking about it, Gideon cringed at the thought while hoping he was wrong. "Well, I guess it's time to find out."

With some hesitation, the two men walked toward the well, but neither one was in any hurry. When they got there, they both stood staring at each other. After a couple of seconds, Jon spoke out. "Well, this was your idea and you're the sheriff."

Feeling as though he was just duped, Gideon looked around the yard and spotted a small bundle of hay. "Okay, Mr. Fearless Lawman. Go grab that hay for me and find me some rope."

After Jon fetched the hay, he went to the barn and gathered some old rope. When he brought it back to the well, Gideon tied the rope around the hay, then placed it in the pail. He set it on fire, then lowered the flaming hay down the shaft of the well. Gideon and Jon reluctantly peered down the well as the fire got closer to the bottom. Finally, they hit water. As the two men stared, it was obvious nothing was down the well but water. With some reservations, both Gideon and Jon had mixed emotions. Both were relieved and disappointed they didn't find the Taylors.

With his frustration starting to set in, Gideon took a deep breath and let it out. "Well, we're no better or worse off then what we were before, so I guess it doesn't matter that my idea was wrong."

As the two men retrieved their horses, Jon sat atop Sapphire and thought for a moment. The sun was about to set and it was going to be dark soon, and Gideon was just itching to leave. "Come on, Jon. The wind is starting to pick up again and I don't feel like spending the night here. This place is starting to creep me out."

Jon smiled then let out a small laugh as he decided to return the banter. "Well, well, Mr. Fearless Lawman. Now who's shaking in their boots?"

As the wind got more forceful, it started blowing around debris. The horses started to get spooked, so the camaraderie had to wait. As much as Jon agreed about leaving, he couldn't leave without checking one more place. "Listen, Gideon, a few years ago, old man Taylor was in town bragging about how he got a few of the town drunks to dig him a new well. He was proud that he only had to pay them a few bottles of whiskey. Anyway, I asked him if he needed any rock and dirt to fill in the old well, but he wasn't interested. He said he was going to reuse the old materials for the new well and lay planks of wood over the hole, then mark it with a large rock."

As tempting as it was to just ride away, Gideon knew he had to check out all possibilities. "Well, hopefully old man Taylor had the sense to go back later and fill it in. So, where's this old well you're talking about?"

With a slight hesitation, Jon pointed in the direction of the barn. "It's about twenty yards beyond the barn. I remember wondering why it was so far from the house. Anyway, let's get this over with."

As the dust and dirt swirled around, the howling wind once again started to cry out. Jon led the way around the barn and once he found the general area, it wasn't hard to find the large rock that marked the hole. Feeling hesitant, both men dismounted and stood staring at the old planks of wood. Not feeling good about the well still intact, Jon glanced at Gideon as Gideon stared back. "Well, I guess we were both hoping this wasn't here but it is. You wait here this time and I'll go get the bucket and hay."

Jon stood by the horses to try to keep them calm while Gideon went to look for more supplies. It wasn't long before he returned. "All right, Jon, let's get these planks out of the way so we can get this over with."

There were several planks of wood, but it only took a few minutes to remove them. After the wood was no longer a hindrance, Gideon wrapped the hay with some rope and stuffed it into the pail. He lit it on fire, then slowly dropped it into the old well. The sun had gone down and darkness had settled in, so it was much easier to see the bottom with the fire lit. The rope slowly slid through Gideon's hands, then it finally came to a stop. Once again, the two men stood staring at each other, with each one waiting for the other to look down the well.

A huge grin started to form on Jon's face while attempting to push off the responsibility. "By all means, Sheriff Gideon, be my guest."

It wasn't a laughing matter, but Gideon smiled and shook his head. "Not this time, Ranger Jon. You out rank me. Have at it."

In a playful manner, Jon rolled his eyes. "All right, this isn't getting us nowhere. On the count of three, we'll both look. Ready, one...two...three."

When the counting stopped, both men took a deep breath and a quick glance down the well. Afterward, they turned their backs and let the air out of their lungs. Neither man said anything at first, then Gideon broke the silence. "Well?"

Jon waited, but Gideon didn't elaborate. "Well, what?"

This time it was Gideon rolling his eyes. "Well, did you see anything?"

Jon didn't say anything at first, but he knew he had to give an answer. "Um, well, I didn't see anything because my eyes were closed. What about you?"

Gideon stared at Jon but couldn't hold any discontent. "No. I looked too fast. Everything was a blur."

Feeling a little embarrassed, Gideon smiled, then shook his head with disgust. "Look at us. A couple of grown men acting like two scared children. We should be ashamed of ourselves."

With guilt starting to set in, Jon and Gideon both slowly turned and looked down the hole. The pail of fire was still burning bright, so it wasn't hard to see their worst fears had come true. As both men peered down the hole, they could see the outline of two skeletal remains.

Gideon took a deep breath as Jon turned away to gather his thoughts. "Well, you were right. Somebody is going on their own personal land grab and they're killing people that happen to be in their path."

With the sun gone, the temperature was rapidly dropping as the night air grew colder. Gideon thought for a moment as he glanced around at the surrounding area. "They must have killed the livestock to cover up the odor of the decaying bodies. We have a new undertaker, Orville. I'll have him come out tomorrow to collect the remains. I'll also inform the family."

With the cold weather starting to beat them down, Gideon and Jon mounted their horses with the intentions of quickly leaving the spooky old homestead behind. As the dust and dirt continued to swirl, the wind howled and assaulted the farmhouse and the surrounding trees with force. Suddenly Jon jumped off his horse and ran into the house. With curiosity, Gideon waited for Jon to return.

A couple of minutes later, Jon came running back out and got back on his horse. "Sorry, it was dark in there and it took a minute to find that whiskey bottle."

With the bitter cold piercing through his body, Gideon couldn't do anything but laugh. "Really? There was hardly a swig left in that bottle."

Feeling satisfied with his actions, Jon happily agreed. "Yeah, but it was worth the effort. You were right, though. This place is creepy. Let's get the hell out of here."

It was late when the two men got back to town. Both were tired, but decided to stop by Gideon's office to discuss the night's events. Whenever Gideon was out of town, Jubal slept in the back room of the jail. He happened to be awake, so Gideon told him about the Taylors and his theory. Jubal wasn't much for wearing his emotions on his sleeve, but he had known the Taylor family for many years and was bothered with the news of them being killed and tossed down a well. As his hand slid across the back of his neck then across his face, he attempted to absorb the horrific news. "We gonna find out who did this, right, Gideon?"

Taking a deep breath, Gideon took a moment to collect his thoughts. He glanced down at the floor, then looked back up at Jubal. "You're damn right we are."

The minutes were ticking down and it was nearing midnight, so Jon said his good-byes and headed home to his family. Gideon was about to retire for the night, but Jubal had some news of his own. "Sorry, Gideon. I know you must be exhausted, but there's someth'n you need to know. Day after you rode out of town, some new faces showed up. Five men with fancy clothes wearing long brown leather jackets with guns hung low."

With everything going on, five new faces in town wearing the same clothing definitely peaked Gideon's interests. "They stay in town for long?"

The fire in the stove was starting to die out, so Jubal took a minute to stoke the fire and add a log. "Well, they got a couple rooms over at the hotel. The next day, they were over at the Lucy Goosy. Ms. Lita said she poured drinks for them for about a half hour, then they left. She said they were very respectful but didn't really talk much. Later on, I spotted them tak'n a Sunday stroll around town."

Gideon listened but he didn't like what he was hearing. "Did they go anywhere near the banks?"

Jubal paused as a slight grin crept across his face. "I was think'n the same thing, but that was the only place they hadn't gone. After they were done tour'n the town, they rode out. So I decided to take a ride to see where they were headed."

Anxious to hear more, Gideon stood up to stretch his legs and to warm his hands over the stove. "So, what did you find out?"

With a big sigh, Jubal shook his head then stood up. "Well, whatever they're up to, it's no good. There's about a hundred or so of them camped about two miles out of town over near the old Donovan place. All wearing the same thing."

With his mind starting to turn ideas, Gideon thought for a minute as he paced around the room. "That's a lot of men. Might explain the tracks that Jacob and his men told me about. You think they were railroad men?"

Jubal rubbed his eyes for a moment, then shook off the fatigue. "I hope you ain't too upset at me, but I wandered into their camp and introduced myself. They were real hospitable at first until I started ask'n questions. I spoke to a man who I thought looked more important than the rest. He said they were out hunt'n big game. He smiled at me like it was a joke, but I got the point. As I made my exit, I got a good look around. Wagons filled with ammo and rifles, couple of chuck wagons, spare horses. They're loaded for bear, Gideon, but not the kind that live in caves. I kind'a got the idea they were wait'n for someth'n. A lot of them looked like ex-military. Some of them had that bounty-hunter itch about'm. Others just looked like stone-cold killers. Professionals hired to do a job. Call'm what you like, but they definitely ain't no railroad men."

With a big yawn, Gideon's eyes started to grow heavy and he knew he had a long day ahead of him. "Waiting for something or maybe waiting for somebody. Listen, Jubal, that was a gutsy thing you did riding into their camp like that. I would never question your courage, but next time, maybe wait for some help. I'd hate to lose a good man like you. Now, go home and get some sleep. We have a lot to do tomorrow."

As Jubal opened the door to walk out, Gideon called out, "Hey, Jubal? Thank you. You did a fine job."

The next morning, Jon met Gideon and Jubal at the land deed office. The paperwork for the Wellington place along with several other mysterious territorial purchases had arrived when Gideon was out of town. Jesuit Silver Holdings Corporation was the name on all the paperwork. As the three men reviewed the material, Gideon noticed the pattern he thought he had figured out was starting to become erratic. With a bit of worry, Gideon held up the latest acquisition for Jubal and Jon to see. "Look at this. This is paperwork for that old ghost town way up at the north border between Texas and Comanche territory."

While Jon and Jubal glanced at the paperwork, Gideon sifted through more deeds. "Look, here's more. All those old border towns that popped up before the war along the southern border. They're worthless. They all went under right after the war started. Look at this. The same company owns all of them and it looks like they're buying up land all over Texas. This doesn't make sense. This definitely isn't the railroad."

After the three men were done sifting through the many pages of paperwork, they realized the Jesuit Silver Holdings Corporation had bought all the land in question. Gideon needed to make the rounds around town, so he asked Jon and Jubal to meet him over at the Lucy Goosy for a drink afterward. After Gideon was done checking the town, he arrived at the saloon. Typical day: Ms. Lita working the bar while the saloon girls did their best to get the patrons to spend money. Jubal and Jon already had beers, but Gideon needed something a bit stronger so he bought a bottle.

While Jon and Jubal helped Gideon with his bottle, Ms. Lita poured herself a drink and let Gideon in on some of the town gossip. "While you were gone, Gideon, a couple of old trappers came wandering through town trying to sell some furs. They said they came down from Colorado and bragged about how they did some trapping in Comanche territory. They were in here drinking one night and got pretty wasted. I noticed one of them was wearing what looked like Comanche jewelry. When I asked how he got it, the other one got real scared like. Told his partner not to say anything. By the end of the night, the one that was rattled passed out. So, I asked his friend again where he got the jewelry. He said they were doing some trapping along the Red River and came across what they thought was a large Comanche war party."

Making sure there was nobody close enough to hear, Ms. Lita leaned over the bar and got up close and personal. "Gideon, he said they were all dead. He told me it looked like a massacre."

Jon and Jubal were working on beer number three while Gideon slowly sipped his whiskey. Stories of a Comanche war party being slaughtered would have promptly made their way around the territory if the military was involved. And if it was bandits or homesteaders, the stories would have spread even more rapidly. Gideon grabbed the bottle and glasses, then motioned Jon and Jubal over to a table so they could talk in private. After hearing what Ms. Lita had said, it was time to compare notes and come up with a new theory.

Jubal already knew some of the information, so it didn't take long for Jon and Gideon to get him caught up. Afterward, Gideon laid everything out. "All right, my idea about the railroad is starting to fall apart. So, this is what we have. Certain pieces of property all over the territory are being bought at an alarming rate. We now know the name of the company who's doing the buying. Jon, your story about Rodrigo and his men, Jacob and his ghost stories about a very large force moving toward him, not to mention the tracks they couldn't identify. Also, the bodies they found half-buried. And we have the Taylors down a well. To top it all off, we have mysterious fires and disappearances. Have I forgotten anything?"

By now, half the bottle was gone and nobody had a working theory. Then Jon thought back to when he found Rodrigo. As he leaned across the table, Gideon and Jubal could tell he had something good. "Listen, when I found Rodrigo, most of his men had their guns still in their holsters. I kept asking myself what kind of force could have killed all those men. An entire band of killers that didn't even put up a fight. How about the Comanche war party? We know it wasn't the military. And with the wide spread of crime, it would take a pretty large amount of men to cover the state of Texas."

Gideon and Jubal were both on the same page, but it was Jubal who had the fastest tongue. "Yeah, 'bout a hundred well-dressed men. Men who are now camped outside of your town, Gideon, and have an arsenal that would rival any military."

Pouring himself a drink, Gideon swallowed it down as he thought about Jubal's words. "I think it's time we do a little more digging into the Jesuit Silver Holding Corporation. Jon, I'm gonna need you and Jubal to take a trip up north again to check out the Comanche story. And please, no heroics. While you two are gone, I'm going to send out some telegrams to the surrounding areas to see if the same company has any dealings in their town. Before you leave, Jon, I suggest you send word to the governor's office to give them an update."

Being as early as it was, there was only a couple of patrons in the bar. Besides the conversation Gideon was having, there wasn't much talking going on. While Jon and Jubal discussed their travel plans, Gideon noticed the absence of noise outside. Usually this time of morning, there was a lot of wagon traffic along with store owners haggling back and forth with their customers about prices.

Suddenly the saloon doors swung open and in walked the five men Jubal had told Gideon about the night before. Dressed in their suits and long brown leather jackets, they slowly and strategically spread out to face off against the three lawmen. As Jon stood up, Gideon and Jubal followed as they prepared for the worse. Jon stood where he was while Gideon and Jubal both took a step to the side. All three men had their badges prominently displayed so there was no mistaking their identity to the five strangers. Remembering the lessons Jacob gave, Jon kept an eye on their gun hands, but more importantly he watched their eyes. Jon knew most men blinked before they draw. The few other patrons that were in the bar quickly made a dash for the door.

As the uncomfortable stares became more tense, the saloon doors once again swung open and in walked a well-dressed man wearing a suit made of the finest materials. He stood proud with a stern but distinguished look, but wore no gun. He waited just inside the doorway momentarily, then stepped forward into the saloon. As he moved across the room, he eyeballed Jon and Jubal, then he stopped in front of Gideon. With the idea of trying to intimidate him, he looked Gideon up and down, then stared into his eyes. "Well now, seems to me I've heard of you. First black sheriff in the state of Texas. Now, isn't that just grand."

With a smirk on his face, Gideon was less than impressed. "I seem to be at a disadvantage, but I'll take a crazy guess and say you're the owner of the Jesuit Silver Holdings Corporation."

With his arrogance leading the way, the man smiled as he looked back at his men. With a look of smugness about him, he turned back to face Gideon. "Bravo, Sheriff. An educated black man. Can't say I'm impressed."

Still trying to belittle Gideon, the man introduced himself. "My name is Zachariah Odalis Hayden." As a show of disrespect, Zachariah placed his hands in his pockets. Even though he was the sheriff, Zachariah felt he was above shaking hands with a black man.

Being the man that he was, Gideon didn't take offense because he had no intentions of shaking hands with Zachariah.

After the uncomfortable moment, Zachariah pulled his hands from his pockets along with a silver pocket watch. "Well, Sheriff, I can't say it's been nice to meet you, but it's been interesting. I have some business in your quaint little town that needs my attention, so if you'll excuse me."

As Zachariah turned his back to walk out, Gideon called out. "Mr. Hayden, I hope your men won't be stirring up any trouble while they're in my town. They're not above going to jail and neither are you."

After hearing what he perceived to be a threat, Zachariah stopped short of the door and turned to face Gideon. "No need for provocation, Sheriff. My men are quite well behaved until I give the orders not to be."

Before Zachariah could make his exit, Gideon had a few more words. "I may have some questions for you later, so make sure you're available."

Growing tired of the mental chess game, Zachariah placed his hat on his head and quietly walked out. One by one, his men slowly followed.

As the three men sat back down, Ms. Lita came from behind the bar and sat at their table. "Well Gideon, I can't say I wasn't scared 'cause I'd be ly'n if I did. What the hell was that all about?"

Gideon poured a drink for Ms. Lita, then for Jon and Jubal. He then finished off the bottle with one last swig. "I think we just met the cause of all the problems that's been plaguing the territory. Ms. Lita, keep your ears open while they're in town. Maybe somebody will make a mistake and say something damning. Jubal, plans have changed. Mr. Hayden has already given us a clue about himself. His middle name, Odalis, is Spanish. It means 'wealth.' I need you to take a trip down south and find out all you can about our new friend. Jon, I still need you to go north to find out if those two fur traders were telling the truth. Have a look around, but be careful. Comanche don't take kindly to their people being slaughtered."

It was going to be a long ride, so Jubal decided to leave right away. Gideon had to once again make rounds so he accompanied Jubal out. With an empty bar, there wasn't much for Ms. Lita to do, so she left the bar in the hands of some of the women so she could walk with Gideon. Jon sat for a moment to think about what he needed for his long ride, but first he needed to go home and spend some time with his family.

As he made his exit, two of Hayden's men were waiting for him. Jon watched as they pulled their coats back revealing their guns. He wasn't sure what to think, especially with what Gideon said about making trouble. Gearing up his quirky humor, Jon let out a smile. "You boys lost?" Pointing east to one of the town's exits, Jon continued his banter. "I think your camp is that way."

The two men didn't appreciate Jon's outgoing humor, so one of them tried to anger him. "I hear the Texas Rangers ain't noth'n but a bunch of phonies. Ain't noth'n but a bunch of cowards with badges."

Years before, Jon's response would have been violent, but time with Jacob and Gunther and lessons learned for Doc through the years placed him in a more well-rounded state of mind. "I have a long ride ahead of me, so you gentlemen have a nice day."

As Jon attempted to walk away, the man doing all the talking decided to push one more time. "Yeah, you go 'head boy. Like I said, noth'n but cowards. I should just shoot you like the dog you are and put you out of yer misery."

Jon didn't respond to the worthless words, but he heard the familiar clicking sound of a hammer of a gun being pulled back. The man wasn't trying to be quick about it, but instead he was attempting to scare Jon, which was his fatal mistake. With lightning speed, Jon turned and at the same time drew his gun and fired three shots: two to the chest and one to the head.

As the unlucky man fell to the ground, his partner placed his hands in the air with uncertainty. "Hey mister, we was just fool'n. Weren't no need for that."

Some of the townspeople gathered around as Gideon and Ms. Lita came running. Before Gideon could ask about the circumstances, the scared man tried to place the blame on Jon. "We was just play'n around, Sheriff. This maniac drew down on Charlie and killed him."

Gideon knelt down and viewed the body and saw the man still had his gun in his hand. "So, if you were just playing, then why is there a gun in your dead friend's hand? I warned you boys about making trouble in my town."

Being a Texas Ranger, Jon didn't necessarily have to defend himself against such frivolous accusations, but with somebody attempting to place blame on him, Gideon decided to conduct a makeshift investigation. Taking a moment to look around at the crowd that was forming, Gideon shouted out, "Anybody see what happen?"

Although some of the people saw the incident, they chose not to say anything out of fear of retaliation. As the crowd slowly started to filter away, two small children came running up to Gideon. Gino and Summer. Two cousins that happen to be standing outside eating their candy while their parents bought supplies. A rambunctious Gino pointed at the dead man as though he was mocking him while Summer stepped forward. Shy in her own way, she looked up at Gideon. "That bad man tried to shoot Ranger Jon in the back."

Not that Gideon had any doubts about Jon, but he needed to keep his bias in check. He took the other man's gun and escorted him to jail, then afterward spoke with Jon.

Trying to keep his thoughts in order, Gideon glanced out the window and watched how the townspeople dropped back into their normal routines. "You know what really bothers me? All these grown people that call themselves high and mighty Christians afraid to come forward to speak up for you. Most of them know you and call you a friend. But two innocent children are bold enough to step forward in your defense. Makes a man wonder about humanity and where it's going."

Taking a moment to think, Jon stood beside Gideon and looked out the same window at the same people. "Don't be so harsh. They're just everyday normal people trying to raise their families. They don't need trouble coming to their front door." Jon paused to gather his thoughts, then continued on. "So, why do you think those men had it out for me?"

Sitting down at his desk, Gideon rustled through some drawers and pulled out some paper. He started making a list of townships and territories to contact. "Well, it's the Texas Rangers that are heading up the investigation, so maybe they were trying to send a message. But if you think about it, they could have done that in the bar. I doubt if they were just two idiots trying to blow off steam. It seems Hayden is working on a plan and he's too damn smart not to hire disciplined men. So that leaves just you."

Thinking about the dilemma, Jon thought for a moment, then sat down. "What'ya mean by leaves just me?"

With more questions than answers, Gideon stared at Jon. "I'm not sure. They went after you specifically, but not because you're a Texas Ranger. So I'm wondering if there's something about you in particular they're interested in. In any case, be on your best guard. Don't take anything for granted and watch your back."

Valuing their friendship, Jon appreciated Gideon's advice and took it in stride, so he decided it was time to go home and spend time with Emily and the children.

When he arrived home, Jon got a big "Daddy!" welcome, along with a nice long kiss from Emily. Although Jon enjoyed being on the trail and chasing outlaws, he also enjoyed his home life. He spent every moment he could with his family. After a nice lunch, Jon let the children take turns riding Sapphire, then he and Emily took a long walk. During their stroll, Jon confided in her the events that unfolded and about all the trouble which had been going on. Ever since Jon became a Texas Ranger, Emily would worry, but now since the direct attempt on his life, she was even more concerned.

Holding hands while they walked, Emily turned to Jon and kissed him softly on his cheek. "Jon, I know how you feel about being a Ranger, but I'm really scared. I'm afraid you're going to ride off one of these days and never come home. The children need their father. Abby is such a daddy's girl and the boys look up to you as a hero. They run around with sticks in their hands pointing at each other and making pop sounds with their mouth. All three have these makeshift badges they wear. They love their daddy, and so do I."

Feeling the love in his heart, Jon continued to hold Emily's hand while he thought about what she was saying. "You know how I feel about bullies, and this guy Hayden looks to be one of the biggest. We suspect he's had at least two people killed that we know of, and God only knows how many more. We think he's the one forcing people out of their land. We also suspect his men of killing livestock, setting fires, and are possibly involved with the many disappearances we've been hearing about. He's a real piece of work and he needs to be taken down."

After their long walk, Jon and Emily found their way back to the barn. Winter was nearing its end and the weather was starting to break. With the children in the house, Emily decided to take advantage of her time with Jon. A little while later, they were back in the house enjoying their family time.

The next day, Jon was lingering around the house thinking about his trip. After the previous day, he wasn't looking forward to leaving his family, and recalling what happen the last time he was in Comanche territory, he certainly wasn't looking forward to going back. After a short kiss good-bye and a promise of coming home safe, Jon set out on Sapphire. He not only needed to verify the story of the fur traders, but he also wanted to visit with Jacob and his men. But before his trip could start, he had a score to settle.

Before heading north, Jon rode into town to see Zachariah Hayden. When he arrived it was still early, so he decided to try the hotel dining room. When Jon walked in, Zachariah was sitting at a table dining on breakfast and sipping on a glass of white wine. The next table over consisted of four of his henchmen. As Jon approached, the four men quickly stood up. Not wanting to cause a scene, Zachariah promptly told his men to relax. Jon wasn't against defending himself if need be, but he wasn't there to shoot anybody. He just wanted some answers.

After staring each other down for a few seconds, Zachariah invited Jon to sit. "I heard about the unfortunate incident that occurred yesterday. Let me assure you, I had nothing to do with that."

As Jon sat and listened to Zachariah's foolishness, he could feel his anger starting to rise. As an insult, he reached over to Zachariah's plate and took a piece of toast, then ate it before scolding him. "Hayden, that mess out in the middle of the street is what horses leave behind, and I think your full of it. So I don't appreciate you trying to shovel that nonsense my way."

Appalled at Jon's ignorance, Zachariah watched the Ranger as he swallowed the piece of toast he was chewing. Even though he wasn't use to being treated in such a raw manner, he decided to smile and keep the conversation civil. "Please, excuse my manners. Would you care to eat the rest of my breakfast?"

Once again, Jon wasn't amused. He watched Zachariah take a sip of wine and waited for him to explain his actions.

Zachariah wasn't in any hurry to reveal himself, so after sipping his wine, he maneuvered it around in his mouth to get the full effect of the taste. "Well now, Mr. Texas Ranger, I introduced myself yesterday, but I don't remember receiving the same courtesy."

Jon hoped by now Zachariah would've dropped his guard, but it was clear he enjoyed playing mind games. "My name is Jon Mason, and I'm not too pleased to meet you. As for the unfortunate incident you're referring to, I don't think your men were acting on their own accord."

Once again, Zachariah realized for the second time in two days he wasn't able to wage mental warfare on law enforcement. "Well now, Ranger Mason, I'll say this for you. You have a strong conviction walking in here and confronting me. Because if I'm not mistaken, it sounds like you're accusing me of something. I don't know whether to admire your resolution or be offended."

Boasting a strong will, Jon wasn't concerned about hurting Zachariah's feelings, and he surely wasn't afraid of the consequences. "Listen Hayden, I don't care what you think because I'm here for answers. I didn't appreciate your men calling me out yesterday. So maybe you can enlighten me on why it happened."

Although Zachariah had contempt for Jon, for some reason he admired him. There was something about his resolve that commanded respect. "All right, Mr. Mason, your candor amuses me, but I can appreciate a person who is genuine."

Before continuing, Zachariah took another sip of wine and once again maneuvered it around in his mouth before swallowing it. "Mr. Mason, whether you choose to believe me or not is up to you. It wasn't my intent to have such a violent outcome, but I guess old Charlie got a little rambunctious. I instructed them to make you an offer."

This peaked Jon's curiosity, so he gave Zachariah the benefit of the doubt to explain further. "All right, Hayden, you have my attention. So what were they supposed to offer me?"

Zachariah smiled because he was actually starting to enjoy the conversation and it gave him the opportunity to complete what his men botched with incompetence the day before. "Consider yourself fortunate, Mr. Mason, because I don't normally engage in conversations about my past or my personal business. You see, I have a very rich ancestry. Both monetary and cultural. I've spent quite a few years mining for silver and as a result have become not only wealthy but a very powerful man."

Feeling impatient, Jon wasn't expecting Zachariah's life story and didn't care about his social status. He was hoping for a more direct explanation.

"Hayden, I don't have all day. What does your conquest of the world have to do with me?"

Sarcasm wasn't on Zachariah's agenda, but he was beginning to enjoy Jon's witty humor. "Mr. Mason, please, you give yourself too much credit. You mean nothing to me. If I wanted you dead, I could just snap my fingers and it would be done." Zachariah paused as he leaned over the table to get closer to Jon. "It's that necklace you're wearing. I noticed it right away when I walked into the saloon yesterday. Where did you acquire it?"

Jon shifted his eyes downward as he pulled the strange necklace away from his neck. "I didn't acquire it. I had it when I was younger, but I don't know where it came from. It's just an old necklace. Why would somebody like you be interested in this old thing?"

With a devious grin, Zachariah leaned back into his chair. "As I said, Mr. Mason, my ancestry is, well, shall we say very diverse? If you're not already aware, the symbol on your necklace is from the Aztec language. It means 'silver.' May I be so bold as to inquire about what the reverse side has?"

This wasn't the conversation he was expecting to have with Zachariah, so Jon was caught a little off guard and he found himself thinking back on all the things he tried so hard to forget. The book with Aztec language, El Capitan, and the death of his friend Father Andres. "Listen, Hayden, I don't have any interest in silver or any other riches you may be after, so get to the point."

From the tone of his voice, Zachariah could tell Jon was becoming agitated, but he decided to take a chance and point out one more fact. "Mr. Mason, I apologize if I in some way upset you. I already have an idea what the reverse side has. It's the word 'Arizuma.' Just like the symbol on the front, it means silver."

Jon had a long ride ahead of him and he had had just about enough of Zachariah and his babbling about silver, so he readied himself to leave. "Hayden, do yourself a favor and tell your men to stay away from me. And by the way, white wine doesn't go with breakfast."

As Jon turned to make his exit, Zachariah quickly stood up. "Mr. Mason, please, wait. I'll give you $100.00 for that necklace. It has no monetary value and you obviously have no concern over its historical significance."

As Jon stopped to think, Zachariah continued his assault on his integrity. "The Texas Rangers can't be paying you that well, so I'm sure your family could use the money."

Feeling displeased about the mentioning of his family, Jon kept his anger in check, then turned back to face Zachariah. Thinking this might be Zachariah's way of trying to buy his loyalty, Jon wanted no parts of it. "Necklace isn't for sale and neither am I. Besides, I wouldn't look good wearing one of those brown overcoats."

As Zachariah watched Jon and his mysterious necklace walk away, he immediately turned to his men. "Apparently our friend Mr. Mason is going on a trip. Grab a few more men and follow him. Find out what he's up to. Meanwhile, I'll be paying a visit to the sheriff."

Glancing down at his breakfast that grew cold during his conversation with Jon, Zachariah became irritated. With some discontent, he pulled the napkin from his shirt and wiped his mouth. In fine gentlemanly fashion, he brushed off his fancy clothes and placed two silver dollars on the table, then walked out.

Looking like he was taking a Sunday stroll, Zachariah walked along with a big smile, tipping his hat and saying hello to whomever smiled back. It wasn't long before he arrived at the sheriff's office. When he walked in, he found Gideon sitting at his desk playing catch up with paperwork.

Out of habit and no respect to Gideon, Zachariah removed his hat. "Good morning, Sheriff. I'm here to post bail for Mr. Frank Suthers." With a well-placed strategic smile, Zachariah placed five silver dollar pieces on Gideon's desk.

Glancing down at the money, Gideon let out an apprehensive smile. "Yeah, I figured you and your money would make an appearance this morning."

With no love lost between the two, Gideon decided to poke fun at Zachariah. "It's early, Hayden. I figured you to be someone who likes to sleep in while your men take care of all your dirty work."

With no desire to play games, Zachariah let out a small laugh as he placed his hands in his pockets. "Well, Sheriff, you're right, it is early. So why don't you just keep your wise cracks to yourself and let my man out of jail?"

Gideon didn't appreciate the tone in Zachariah's voice, so he stood up and walked around to the front of his desk. "Listen, Hayden, you and your money don't run this town. I'll let your man out only because I'm bound by the law." With anger still in his eyes, Gideon scooped up the money, then walked back to retrieve Mr. Suthers. When Gideon returned, he had Frank by the arm and shoved him toward Zachariah. "By the way, Hayden, since you like throwing around money, make sure you make your way over to the undertaker's office so you can pay for your man's burial."

Still feeling annoyed, Gideon opened the drawer of his desk and pulled out a small bag and tossed it at Frank. He then grabbed Frank's gun belt from a nearby hook and also tossed it at him. "Here's your personal affects. Now get the hell out of my office."

Attempting to exercise his patience, Zachariah watched as Frank strapped on his gun belt. "Make sure everything is there, Frank. You know how corrupt these small-town sheriffs can be."

After the unpleasant visit came to an end, Zachariah and Frank walked out. As they walked back to the hotel, Zachariah released his frustration on Frank for disobeying an order. "What the hell were you thinking yesterday? I told you and Charlie to make an offer on that necklace. Explain to me what part of that plan included getting yourselves killed or thrown into jail?"

Frank knew Zachariah would be angry, so he quickly gave account of what happen. "I'm sorry, Mr. Hayden. Me and Charlie waited for that Ranger to come out so we could talk, but you know ol' Charlie, always fool'n around. He was just trying to put a little scare into that Ranger."

As Zachariah stepped onto the porch of the hotel, he sat down in one of the outdoor rocking chairs overlooking the street. When Frank tried to sit beside him, Zachariah scolded him. "Did I tell you to sit?"

Hearing Zachariah shout, Frank quickly got the point and stood back up. "Sorry, Mr. Hayden, but that jail cell wasn't very comfortable."

Zachariah sat for a moment and watched the hustle and bustle of the townspeople while contemplating his next words. "I have plans, Frank, and those plans don't include babysitting a bunch of idiots that can't take orders. Now, tell me something. How fast is that Ranger?"

As he stood in front of Zachariah like a little school child, Frank was shaky at best. "Well, Mr. Hayden, sir, he's really fast. I don't think I've ever seen anybody faster."

While he listened, Zachariah slowly rocked back and forth as Frank's words filtered through his mind. "Well, I've seen some of the fastest draws around, but they all had one thing in common."

As Zachariah paused, Frank waited. "If I may ask, sir, what was it they had in common, Mr. Hayden?"

Just then, Zachariah stopped rocking, then stood up. He walked over to the edge of the porch and leaned up against one of the support beams. As he looked out into the street, he pulled his watch from his pocket to check the time. "They were all killed by somebody who was just a little bit faster."

Once again Zachariah paused to gather his thoughts. "Did you know old Charlie had a brother?"

Frank thought for a moment, then spoke with the best answer he could come up with. "Charlie wasn't much of a talker, Mr. Hayden, but he did mention something about kin folk being in the war."

With a serious look, Zachariah turned to face Frank. "His brother was a colonel for the Confederate Army. Colonel Augusta Pittman. He's a brutal killer. He's killed twenty-six men, and that's not including the men he killed during the war. He hated the Union Army and if I may mirror your words, he's the fastest draw I've ever seen and he's still alive. When the war ended, he decided to hunt bounties. Sometimes I think he kills them just for pleasure. He's not going to be very happy when I inform him about his brother. I've already sent word and he'll be here after he catches up to his last bounty. I imagine it won't be long."

Still feeling contempt toward Frank, Zachariah finished his conversation then dismissed him. "By the way, the money I so graciously lent you for bail will be coming out of your next pay. Now, get out of my sight."

Feeling shamed, Frank turned to walk away as several more of Zachariah's men were arriving. Not wanting to conduct business out in the open, Johnson, Martinez, and Adams followed Zachariah to his room.

As the men entered the room, Zachariah closed the door and locked it. He poured some drinks and gave one to each man. "Now, listen to me. I'm assuming you men heard what happen yesterday. I will not tolerate disobedience." While the three men stood in silence, Zachariah continued the scolding. "As I was explaining to Mr. Suthers, I have a plan and I will not let anyone stand in my way."

As Zachariah sipped his whiskey, he slowly paced around the room. With the tone in his voice, it was obvious he was still upset with Frank and the results of his meeting with Jon. "Gentlemen, failure is not an option. I will not be denied my prize. Am I making my point clear?"

As Martinez and Adams gulped down their drinks with confidence, Johnson gently placed his untouched drink on a nearby table. He knew Zachariah Hayden wasn't a man to cross. When Zachariah paused to take another sip, Johnson informed him about Jon. "Mr. Hayden, that Ranger is headed north. Looks like he may be headed toward Comanche territory. We have a couple of trackers following him."

Conjuring up a plan, Zachariah finished his drink, then momentarily stared at Johnson. "Take Frank and a few more men with you. When he gets close to Comanche territory, kill him. Take the necklace and make it look like the Comanche did it."

In preparation, Johnson had Martinez and Adams gather a few more men while he stayed behind to speak with Zachariah. "Mr. Hayden, I'm not trying to pry into your personal business, but there's a good chance we may risk a confrontation with the Comanche."

With firmness in his voice, Zachariah stepped toward Johnson. "I pay well for your loyalty, Johnson, so there shouldn't be any question about risks."

Johnson wasn't weak, but he also didn't want to anger Zachariah by staring into his eyes, so he glanced down at his hat while he rubbed his fingers across the rim. "I understand, Mr. Hayden, but I was just wondering why that necklace is so important."

For a brief moment, Zachariah admired Johnson for being direct. As he poured himself another drink, he picked up Johnson's original drink and handed to him. "Cheers to you, Mr. Johnson. I can appreciate you being forthright."

While both men drank down their whiskey, Zachariah prepared to reward Johnson for his boldness. "Not that I think you're ignorant, but I'm going to take a wild guess that you've never heard of the Aztec god, Tepeyollott."

After Zachariah gave Johnson a moment to answer, Johnson had nothing to say, so Zachariah continued the education. "He was the Aztec god of the mountains. Legend has it that a lowly Aztec man had five sons, and his younger son was very weak. The brothers would physically and verbally abuse him constantly. He couldn't work the fields, nor did he have the strength to help construct the glorious Aztec monuments. His mother loved him very much and tried to protect him from the others, but the father had the plan of sacrificing the young boy to Tlazolteotl, which was the God of lust and sexual misdeeds. When the mother found out, she woke the boy in the middle of the night. She explained that the father and brothers were evil, so she was sending him away in order to save him from the sacrifice. I guess she figured he would have a better chance on his own in the wilderness."

After a short pause, Zachariah could see Johnson had his doubts about the story, but Zachariah enjoyed giving the history lesson so he continued. "I know what you're probably thinking. All the crazy talk about Aztec gods, but for every legend, there's always a little bit of truth. Documents found years ago tell the story of the boy traveling north into what we now call Texas. There he found what was described as a magical mountain. When he entered the mountain, he was transformed into a jaguar. He then traveled back to his village and killed his father and brothers. The terrifying screams woke his mother, and when she saw the jaguar, she looked into its eyes and saw her son. The next day she found piles of silver all over the floor and outside of their little hut."

Once again, Johnson just stood listening and wondering why Zachariah was telling him the story. Although he had no interest in the Aztec culture, he wasn't about to interrupt Zachariah. On the other end of the spectrum,

Zachariah was enjoying hearing himself talk and continued to do so. "Legend also says the magical mountain the boy found was made of silver and the silver flowed like a river down the side into every direction. Now that I've told you the legend, let me give you the truth. During Spain's conquest of the new world, they sent an order of monks called the Franciscans to establish the Christian faith. During their efforts of converting the local natives, the Franciscans found several rich silver mines. At that time under Spanish law, one-fifth of all the silver was supposed to be shipped back to Spain, but those greedy monks decided to keep it all for themselves, which enraged the King of Spain. So King Charles II sent soldiers and another order of monks called Jesuits to hunt down the Franciscans and their silver mines."

Needing some guidance, Zachariah sat down at a small desk and opened his journal. Johnson watched as Zachariah turned page after page until he found what he was looking for. With some relief, Zachariah took a breath and leaned back in his chair. "Every time I think about this story, it fills my heart with exuberance." When Zachariah came to a certain page in his journal, he stopped and momentarily studied it. "Here we are. The Spanish conquistadors and the Jesuits searched for the Franciscan monks but never found them. Legend tells the story of the monks fooling the Indians into killing the conquistadors, then the greedy monks turned on their Indian friends and killed them so to forever hide the location of the mines."

As Zachariah stood up, he closed the book and laid it on his desk. "Now, the intriguing part of the story you've been so patiently waiting for. I took a business trip a few years ago down to Mexico to buy some land. While on my visit, I had heard about one of the locals finding a sizable amount of old silver stashed in a long-forgotten cave. The old man was so excited, he told just about every red-blooded thief the how, what, why, when, and where of his good fortune. As you could surely imagine, the old fool met his demise, but I wasn't interested in the little bit of silver he found. I wanted to see the cave he found it in, so I hired a local guide to take me out there."

Taking a breath, Zachariah paused as he paced the floor. "When we arrived, I was in utter amazement. The cave ran deep and there was hieroglyphics on just

about every wall. Call it what you will—greed, ignorance, or just plain stupidity—but all the time those fools were looking for more silver, they were missing
the real treasure right in front of them. It was written on the walls of the cave.
The story I just told you about the Aztec boy was the story being told on the wall.
In the end, the boy became a god and ruled over all the mountains and the surrounding lands. In the very back of the cave, there was a picture of Tepeyollott
wearing a jaguar skin and around his neck was the same necklace worn by that
Texas Ranger. Now, I know you must think this story sounds silly, but like I said,
there's always a bit of truth to every legend. I don't think there is such a mountain
flowing with rivers of silver, but what I know is the Franciscan monks must have
stumbled upon the same mountain that Aztec boy found. Now, I'm certain there's
no magical powers at work, but I think wherever that mountain is, I'll find a fortune in silver that makes all the silver minds put together look worthless."

Once again Zachariah paced as he gathered his thoughts. "King Solomon's
mines, lost treasure of the Incas, El Dorado, treasure of the Knights Tem-
plar—all legendary treasures of the past that may or may not be real and, I'm
quite certain, will never be found. But the silver mines of the Franciscans are
beyond legendary. They were real and they were documented. Then those
greedy monks hid them away. My ancestors hunted them for years but never
even got close to finding them."

The more he talked, the angrier Zachariah became. His breathing became
heavy as he raised his fist with rage. "But I will succeed where everyone else
has failed. I will not be denied my prize."

As Zachariah reveled in his story, Johnson became more and more nervous. After Zachariah was done, he took a deep breath and sat down at his desk.
"Johnson, I've been researching the Franciscan mines for most of my life. I
became a wealthy man buying up land, then selling the worthless property
after I finished with it. Never have I thought I would ever come across such a
magnificent artifact such as that necklace. That necklace could very well be
the piece of the puzzle that will lead me directly to the legendary mountain
that has eluded my family for centuries. And that buffoon wearing it has absolutely no clue what he has."

After his temper had subsided, Zachariah stood up and walked over to Johnson. "Remember what I said when you first entered this room? I said I don't like failure. Johnson, I hold you personally responsible for retrieving that necklace."

Still nervous and now intimidated, Johnson shook his head and assured success. "Yes sir, Mr. Hayden. I won't let you down."

Zachariah stared into the eyes of Johnson as though he was looking for some kind of reassurance, but all he saw was fear. "I'm counting on you, Johnson, not to fail. By the way, once you have the necklace in your possession, kill that good for nothing Frank Suthers."

When Johnson left out, he met up with Martinez and Adams outside of town. They were with Frank and four other men. With plenty of ammunition and firepower, they set off to catch up with the scouts who were tracking Jon.

An hour away, Jon was traveling north toward Comanche territory. As he casually guided Sapphire across the wide-open land, he was suddenly awestruck by the herd of mustangs he had encountered during winter. Just as surreal as they were majestic, they grazed on the fresh green grass that spring had brought them. With nothing but time on his hands, Jon watched the herd while keeping an eye out for their leader. After a brief scan of the herd, there she was. Like a shining star, she seemed to glow. She was standing on a slight elevation overlooking what belonged to her. She knew Jon was there watching, but she seemed to not mind. As she used her hoof to kick back some dirt, she let out a faint grunt. Then, without warning, she let out a scream as she charged down the hill toward Jon. With incredible speed, she seemed to glide across the land.

Sapphire became nervous as he began to move his head up and down and neigh. As the magnificent white thoroughbred approached, Jon's heart began to flutter as he rubbed the neck of Sapphire to keep him calm. "Steady, boy. It's all right."

The mare stopped just short of reaching distance and Jon watched as she snorted and grunted. Her eyes were dark but beautiful. The brilliance of her coat was beyond bright and her muscles seem to define her stance. After a few moments of staring, the magnificent horse took a few steps forward. Jon wasn't sure what to do, so he calmly reached out his hand as a gesture of friendship. The feeling Jon had was indescribable. Somehow he felt their souls connect. With exuberance running through his bones, Jon momentarily felt as if the thoroughbred was trying to tell him something. But like a moment in time, it had ended. The mare grunted then slowly backed away. She reared back and let out a thunderous scream, then galloped away, taking her herd of wild mustangs with her.

Feeling honored as he took in the moment, Jon watched the herd disappear over the rolling hills. As the dust began to settle, he noticed something else: a lone Indian up on a cliff overlooking the valley. Jon knew he was nowhere near Comanche territory, so who could it be? Maybe an outcast. Maybe an Apache scout. Or could it be the same Indian from Jon's past? In any case, he needed to stay alert during the rest of his travels.

As Jon continued on, Johnson and his men were closing distance and time. While the day passed away, nightfall was rapidly approaching. Johnson and his men decided to camp for the night, knowing they would reach the trackers in the morning. While they slept, the night crawlers hunted their prey as the coyotes howled. Then out of nowhere, some of the men were awakened by gunfire. It was far enough away not to be a threat, but it still invoked a sense of nervousness. As Johnson awoke, he and his men listened. There were no more howling coyotes and all the nighttime sounds had abruptly stopped. Suddenly they could hear what sounded like faint screams. With everyone on edge, Johnson assigned the men to take shifts standing watch until sunrise.

The next day, Johnson and his men were up just before sunrise and were riding hard in order to catch up to the other men. They knew the trackers they had following Jon couldn't be too far away, and they were hoping to catch Jon before he got too close to Comanche territory. Just a few minutes into their ride and less than a few miles from their camp, they found the source of the previous night's gunfire and screams. It was a sight that would make the most hardened of men cringe. The three trackers assigned to follow Jon were hanging upside down from a tree. A few of their limbs were missing and their throats had been cut. With storm clouds rolling in, there was no time for burials.

As the men looked on, Frank was the first to speak. "Holy Mother of God. Who would do something like this and why?"

Seeing movement from above, Johnson glanced up into the sky as the vultures began to circle. "I don't know. Doesn't look like the work of the Comanche, and I don't recall Apache ever dismembering people. Those screams we heard last night and the gunfire must have been them, but what were they shooting at?"

After witnessing several of the men losing their breakfast, Martinez guided his horse closer to the hanging bodies. While staring at them, he crisscrossed his heart then placed some rosary beads to his lips. Afterword, he turned and guided his horse next to Johnson. With a look of fear, he shook his head as he gave Johnson a long cold stare. "Hok'ee."

Frank was already rattled, but seeing Martinez worried made it even worse. With a small tremble in his voice, Frank turned to Johnson. "What the hell is a Hok'ee?"

Before Johnson could answer, Martinez explained. "Hok'ee is a wondering spirit. The Indians believe it roams the night, killing anyone it can find."

After hearing the explanation Martinez offered, Johnson had his doubts. With the rain starting to fall, Johnson warned everybody to stay focused and alert. While the hours went on, Johnson and his men rode further north, hoping to catch Jon before the Comanche caught them. Toward the end of the day, they were in luck. They spotted Jon taking a break just shy of the Red River. Feeling no need to run, Jon saw Johnson and his men coming and waited. It didn't surprise Johnson that Jon didn't try to run or shoot it out. Any commotion would alert the Comanche and then death would be imminent for all of them. As they approached Jon, Johnson and his men slowed to a slight gallop, then stopped to dismount. Normally facing off against eight men would be a little intimidating, but apart from his fast draw, Jon was also intelligent. Along with teaching Jon how to be a man, Jacob also taught him that his brain can be just as powerful and useful as his gun.

Attempting to be strategic, Martinez and three other men flanked Jon to his right while Frank and the other two men took the left flank. Giving his men a minute to get into place, Johnson stood facing Jon for a moment, then approached him. "I thought you Texas Rangers were supposed to be smart. You don't say no to a man like Hayden."

Slow to speak, Jon smiled as he thought for a moment. "Well, maybe Hayden needs to understand not everything has a price."

Having eight men gave Johnson superiority and that made him a bit smug, but his arrogance quickly faded when Jon came right back with his swagger. With a smirk on his face, Johnson glanced around to make sure he still had the confidence of his men. "Now, you listen here, boy. Hayden thinks that necklace of yours is important and he wants it. I'm supposed to take it after I kill you, but I like to think I'm a fair man so I'll make you a deal. I'll take your horse, your gun, and that necklace and point you toward the Comanche, and if you're lucky, you might live for a few more hours before they find you and kill you."

Trying not to laugh, Jon rubbed his brow as he shook his head. "Well now, that's mighty generous of you, but I gotta tell you something. You're an idiot."

Once again Johnson's arrogance took a hit as he was starting to get a bit impatient. "You look here, Ranger. My tolerance will only stretch so far."

Before Johnson could say anything else, Jon decided it was time for a little deceitful strategy. "Listen, none of us is leaving out of here alive. The whole time you've been standing here flapping your lips, a Comanche war party has been taking up positions and surrounding us. So you should probably save your energy for your last stand."

Hearing what Jon said, Johnson froze for a moment as an uneasy feeling suddenly dominated his insides. Once again he glanced around at his men who were now on edge and also looking around at the surrounding territory. Trying to rebuild his confidence, Johnson tried to laugh it off. "I had just about enough of this foolishness. That damn crazy Hayden talking about Aztec treasure, grown men talking about wondering ghosts ripping off people's limbs, and now you with your feeble plan of conjuring up a Comanche war party."

With a nervous sweat running down his face, Johnson quickly pulled his gun and pointed it at Jon. "Now, you listen here, Ranger. You're just wasting time. One way or another, you're gonna give me that necklace."

Then, without warning, one of Johnson's men fell to the ground dead. He had a knife stuck deep into the back of his neck. With dusk starting to dominate the sky, nobody could tell from which direction it came from. With mass hysteria setting in, Johnson watched as his men began to scatter. With his gun still pointing at Jon, he knew it would be better not to kill him just yet. "This ain't over, Ranger." Looking around for his best option, Johnson quickly holstered his gun then ran for cover.

Jon, on the other hand, was a little slower to react. He had lied about the Comanche war party, but there was the question of the knife. Exercising caution, Jon walked Sapphire over to a nearby tree, then took a strategic position behind a boulder near the river. Thinking it may be his best strategy, his back against the water seemed like a good idea. With the sun rapidly sinking over the horizon, the frogs, bugs, and night birds started singing their songs. Suddenly a scream of pain yelled out, but Jon couldn't tell the direction it came from. As he knelt down, he pulled his gun out as a precaution. As he studied the landscape around him, he listened and watched. Another scream. This time, somebody different. Once again, because of the surrounding landscape, it was hard to tell where the screams were coming from.

As the minutes ticked away, another scream. But this time Jon could tell it was coming from a small patch of trees only a few yards away. With his gun in his hand, he carefully made his way over to the tree line. Moving slowly and using each tree for cover, Jon moved deeper into the woods. Not wanting to expose himself too much, he peeked around the tree trunk he was hiding behind toward the direction of the scream. Focusing his eyes on a horrible sight, Jon could see it was one of Johnson's men. He was pinned up against a tree with a hatchet through his skull.

Taking a few seconds to engage in a deep breath, Jon quickly made his way back to the river. He could see Johnson, who took the high ground up on some nearby rocks. It was a good position because he could see everything around him and below him. It was a bad position because now he had to keep an eye on every direction, including behind him.

Johnson maneuvered around every few minutes to keep an eye out, but then he noticed Adams walking out into the open. His arms were wrapped around himself and he looked dazed and confused. Then Johnson saw that his torso had been sliced open from his waist all the way to his throat. After a few steps, Adams fell to his knees, then forward onto his face.

Martinez also saw the demise of Adams, so he took a chance and made a run for his horse. Just when he was about to climb into the saddle, a gunshot rang out and Martinez fell to the ground with a bullet in his leg. Jon watched as a wounded Martinez tried to crawl to safety, but he didn't make it far. Another shot rang out and hit Martinez in his other leg. Martinez cried out for help, but there was no help to give. Another shot hit him in his arm and then another to his other arm. Martinez was now helpless. Jon couldn't tell where the shots were coming from, so with his back against the river, he stayed hidden behind the boulder.

After a few more minutes, Frank finally made his presence known. He came running out of hiding firing several shots into the darkness while he scurried his way up to where Johnson was. "Goddamn it. What the hell is going on? I can't see a damn thing. Where the hell is everybody?"

Looking around, Johnson became disgusted. "Damn it, Frank, shut the hell up and let me think. Martinez is laying out there like side of beef, and all the others are dead except for that Texas Ranger."

With shaky hands, Frank took a moment to reload his gun. "How the hell do we know it's not that Ranger doing all the killing? Remember, those boys were some of the best trackers in the territory. I don't know how that Ranger could have got the drop on them. It looked like a goddamn wild animal tore them apart."

Feeling nothing but contempt for Frank, Johnson closed his eyes and took a deep breath. "Damn it, Frank, you moron. That Ranger was standing in front of us when Lou took a knife to the back of his neck, or does your feeble brain not remember that? Now, shut the hell up before I kill you like Hayden wanted me to"

Hearing what Johnson just said, Frank wasn't about to keep quiet. "What'ya mean, kill me? Hayden was going to have me killed? But why?"

Still feeling annoyed, Johnson looked around, then wiped the sweat from his face. "You and that damn Charlie. What the hell were you thinking? Gonna shoot down a Texas Ranger in broad daylight. A man like Hayden is very wealthy, very powerful, and unfortunately, crazier than a hound dog with rabies. You don't cross a man like him."

With betrayal running through his thoughts, Frank sat up and leaned up against a rock. With anger now adding to his thoughts of treachery, Frank smiled, then shook his head and laughed. "When I get back, that Hayden is a dead man."

Just then, Johnson noticed something. Martinez was gone. Johnson looked around but didn't see him. "Wait a minute, Frank. Where the hell did Martinez go? He was just there a minute ago."

Still steaming at the fact Hayden was going to have him killed, Frank took a moment and glanced down at the spot Martinez was last seen. "I don't know. That bastard probably took off and left us here for dead."

With his hand gripping his gun tight, Johnson took another look around. With sarcasm in his voice, he scolded Frank. "His horse is still here and he had four bullets in him. What'ya think, he just jumped up and flew away?"

Before Frank could respond, out of the darkness came something dripping with blood and it landed in Frank's lap. While Frank jumped around like a scared child, Johnson was finally able to focus his eyes. He could see it was the head of Martinez. Trying desperately to wipe the blood off his hands, Frank scurried backward, kicking the gruesome site to the side. "Christ all mighty, what the hell is going on. That's it, I'm done. Let's get the hell out of here."

Before Johnson could grab a hold of him, Frank got up and ran. Once again he fired several shots into the darkness while trying to get to his horse. Just as he reached his horse, a very large knife appeared out the darkness and struck him in the back. Frank momentarily staggered around, then slowly tried to mount his horse. Once he was in the saddle, another knife appeared to come out of nowhere and struck him in the chest. Johnson watched as the life seemed to quickly drain from Frank's face. It didn't take long for Frank to slump over and fall to the ground.

Still gripping his gun, Johnson knew it was pointless to make a run for it, but what other option was there? Peering down from his rock fortress, he made sure Jon was still near the river. Thinking there may be a glimpse of hope of getting out of the horrific situation he was in, Johnson figured it would be in his best interest to work together with Jon. Looking around on the ground for a small rock, Johnson threw it in Jon's direction to get his attention. "Hey Ranger! Listen. There's a pack mule just beyond the tree line loaded with guns and ammo. If you can get to it, we might be able to shoot our way out of here. What'ya think?"

Listening to Johnson's plan, Jon wasn't naive. He heard the earlier screams. He watched as the horrifying events unfolded in front of him throughout the night. He also knew Johnson was the only one left from Hayden's men. Jon wasn't interested in teaming up with Johnson and knew he had lied about the Comanche war party, but who was doing the killing and why?

After no answer from Jon, Johnson decided to appeal to Jon's inner fear. "Come on, Ranger. Without me, you're not getting out of here alive. What'ya say?"

Smiling and shaking his head, Jon checked his gun to make sure it was fully loaded. With a raised voice, he shouted back at Johnson, "I'm not afraid to face whatever is out there. What about you? Sounds like you're terrified."

Once again Johnson didn't like Jon's attitude, but he was in no position to argue. "Come on, Ranger. Do you really think you're gonna make it out on your own? You saw what happen to Martinez and Frank. The two of us stand a better chance than just one of us alone. What'ya say, Ranger? We gotta deal?"

Once again Jon smiled and shook his head. "All right! But we do it my way. You get the mule and I'll give you some cover fire."

Johnson didn't like the idea, but beggars couldn't' be choosers. "All right, Ranger, but you better not double cross me."

Once Johnson had climbed down from his rocky position, he made a bee-line for the pack mule. With perfect timing, Jon sprung from his position and started shooting at any shadow that moved. When his six-shooter was empty, he pulled the shotgun he had strapped to his back and fired off several rounds while running toward Martinez's horse. Then he quickly grabbed a rifle and started shooting. Afterward, he moved with precision and grabbed the rifle off Frank's horse.

As he knelt down to reload his six-shooter, Jon noticed an eerie calm. The wind had stopped blowing and the night creatures were silent. As he holstered his gun, Jon stood up and looked around. Suddenly Johnson appeared and came walking out of the woods with his pack mule. With a blank look on his face, he walked toward Jon.

With his hand on his gun and a cautious attitude, Jon watched as Johnson approached. "Well, Ranger, looks like you're on your own. Good luck." Just then, Johnson collapsed to his knees and then fell face first to the ground. That's when Jon saw the hatched stuck deep into Johnson's back.

Now, Jon was alone. He briefly thought about moving back to his position near the river, but then he thought why? Whatever was going to happen was going to happen. So, he stood out in the open and waited. It was quiet and nothing was moving. After a few anxious seconds, Jon could feel a small breeze on his face, which was gently blowing off the water, and then it happened. Jon watched as ripples started to form on the river's surface. With caution, he watched the warrior Indian slowly emerge out of the water and reveal himself. With grace, he moved toward the shoreline and approached Jon. With eyes dark like death and his body defined with muscle, he stood with authority in front of Jon. His face was covered with war paint and he had a necklace made of human bones from past victims around his neck. He wore no fancy jewelry, but Jon noticed a familiar-looking beaded bracelet from long ago—one that matched the one around his wrist.

With the tension thick, Jon wasn't sure how to act or what to say, so he did nothing. Remaining still, he waited for the warrior Indian to act, but the warrior Indian did nothing. He just stood face to face with Jon in silence. Using his intimidating looks, he peered into Jon's eyes as though he was at-tempting to gain information, but Jon wasn't easily intimidated. There had been many dangerous situations he had been involved with, but this was different. Now, it was time for answers. The warrior Indian watched as Jon slowly unbuckled his gun belt and let it drop to the ground. Jon also reached back and dropped the shotgun that was hanging off his back.

As he stared at the warrior Indian, he attempted to communicate. "Who are you and why did you kill all of these men?"

With anticipation, Jon waited for an answer but there was none. So, he once again attempted to obtain a reaction. "Why do you constantly follow me?" Jon was hoping the warrior Indian would graciously offer some answers, but he was quickly disappointed. After realizing he wasn't getting anywhere with his questions, Jon stood in silence.

After a few more seconds of staring, the warrior Indian attempted to communicate. Without speaking, he knelt down and drew a figure of a wolf. He then drew two crossed arrows. After standing up, he spoke a few mysterious words to Jon. "You are lost Hok'ee, but soon you will find your way."

Completely caught off guard, Jon was stunned. Before he could react, a sudden gust of wind kicked up some lose dirt. As he squinted and struggled to brush away the dust from his eyes, Jon just caught a glimpse of the warrior Indian disappearing into the darkness on a beautiful painted Pinto.

The next morning, Jon was up early and digging graves. Although the night before had been very bizarre, he still needed to find out if the story told by the two trappers was true. After burying what was left of Hayden's men, including body parts, he gathered his gear and made sure all his weapons were loaded. Before he could mount up, several Comanche came splashing across the river. As they approached, Jon could see it was Two Feathers along with some of his warriors.

Before his horse could come to a stop, Two Feathers jumped off with a very large knife in his hand. Facing off against Jon while wielding his knife, Two Feathers wanted nothing more than to chop Jon into pieces. With a steady calm, Jon did nothing. He didn't try to run, nor did he pull his gun. He didn't move and he didn't blink. He didn't even flinch. He just stood tall and peered into the eyes of Two Feathers.

Seeing that Jon wasn't afraid, Two Feathers decided to speak. "You were warned. Why do you violate our peace and our land?"

With the previous night's events still fresh on his thoughts, Jon glanced around then turned his attention back to Two Feathers. "Look around you. A great battle has taken place here."

Still holding his knife out in front of him, Two Feathers took a moment and glanced around. There was blood splattered on several trees and the ground was also saturated with blood. Two Feathers then saw the eight graves Jon had dug. "I see you have taken more souls. This does not explain your trespass."

Once again Jon had to enter the role of the fabled Hok'ee in order to save his life. "I do not come to war with you. I only seek information."

By this time, Two Feathers, along with his testosterone, had subsided, so he placed his knife back in his side pouch. "My father was very wise and he believed you to be the Hok'ee, so I will honor his memory by not killing you."

While listening to the words of Two Feathers, Jon thought about the massacre he was there to investigate and realized Two Feathers and his father may have been involved. Two Feathers couldn't afford to look weak in front of his men, so he motioned Jon off to the side. He tried to keep a stern face, but it was obvious that Two Feathers was bothered by what he was about to say.

"Seven Bulls has gone to the spirit world. He no longer among us."

Surprised at the death of Seven Bulls, Jon listened while Two Feathers explained how his father died. "Many white men come. They do not talk. Like a ravaging wolf pack, they attack my father's hunting party without mercy. Two warriors escape and return to tell me what happen. After leading many warriors back to battle, it was too late. The white man was gone and Seven Bulls was lying dead on ground. That ground now sacred."

Attempting to think quick, Jon took a moment to grasp the words of Two Feathers. Pretending to know the situation, he took a chance and spoke. "You are correct, Two Feathers. Seven Bulls no longer walks the earth, but he is here. He is the wind in the trees. He is the smell of flowers in the air. He is the darkness of night and the light of day. I was telling you the truth when I said I do not come to war with you. Indeed, your father was a great warrior and he died in battle as an honorable man, and I seek to avenge his death. I seek those responsible and I will punish the cowards for what they did. Seven Bulls was a great warrior and his death deserves to be avenged. As you can see, I've already killed eight of the cowards, and I will kill many more in honor of Seven Bulls."

Feeling a bit suspicious, Two Feathers once again glanced around. He momentarily stared at the graves, then turned his attention back to Jon. "My father was very wise. His words were law never to be challenged. I never questioned his leadership. The day we met and Seven Bulls called you Hok'ee, I did not have the courage to speak against my father, so I held my tongue. I see you as flesh and blood. I see you as someone easily killed. I do not respect you or your white-man ways. I could have taken your life several times and yet I do not. I do not recognize my father's vision. I do not know you as Hok'ee. You are just skin and bone that will someday wither and turn to dust. You are no ghost. I do not recognize your claim to the spirit world."

Jon listened but didn't know what Two Feathers was going to do. His words leaned toward Two Feathers changing his mind and killing him. The idea of Hok'ee wasn't working with Two Feathers, so Jon had to quickly think of something else that would appeal to the angry Comanche leader. "As I said earlier, Two Feathers, I've already slain some of your enemies. The chances of you ever finding the rest of the cowards responsible are zero. You are not free to move about the land as I am, so therefore, you must trust me to avenge your father's death."

Thinking Jon may be right, Two Feathers took a quick look back at his warriors, then turned to face Jon. He didn't say anything, but Jon could tell he was taking mental notes of his words and trying to decide the best course of action. So with the window of opportunity still open, Jon tried one last effort. He slowly reached down inside his boot and pulled out a fairly large hunting knife. Seeing this, Two Feathers took a step back while he watched Jon cut a deep gash into the palm of his hand, allowing his blood to flow strongly to the ground. "You were right, Two Feathers. I'm just flesh, blood, skin, and bones. I'm a man just like you. I will someday die and my body will be returned to the earth. I give this land my blood as a sign of brotherhood and I give my word that I will find and kill the cowards responsible for your father's death."

Surprised at what Jon was saying, Two Feathers watched as the ground turned red from Jon's blood. As he took a step toward Jon, Two Feathers took the knife from him and sliced the palm of his hand. "You would dare to make this pact with me, knowing if you fail there will be grave consequences for you and your family?"

Jon smiled as he held out his hand. Two Feathers once again took a moment to glance back at his warriors. Turning back to Jon, Two Feathers held out his hand in friendship. "We are brothers with a common cause. We shall seek vengeance and you shall protect these lands for which my people claim. If one of us breaks this bond, then he will surely die a thousand deaths."

As a gesture of new friendship, Jon gathered the pack mule along with all the horses and weapons from Johnson's men and gave everything to Two Feathers. Two Feathers graciously accepted, then in a traditional Comanche yell and scream fest galloped back across the river. Jon knew he once again narrowly escaped death, so with a huge sigh of relief he gathered his thoughts and supplies, then headed back to Presidio. With such important information, his visit with Jacob would have to wait.

A couple of days' hard ride and Jon was back in town just in time to meet with Gideon and Jubal at the Lucy Goosy. After a few hellos and drinks, the three men sat down to compare notes.

Anxious to get the meeting started, Gideon was first to talk. "Well, while you two were off having fun, I found out Mr. Hayden has bought land from Louisiana across Texas and all the way to the New Mexico territory. And it seems to be he has a lot of politician friends that are attempting to help him gobble up Indian lands. I've talked with a few of the sheriffs and even a couple of U.S. marshals. Nobody seems to be able to figure out Hayden's endgame. He has men in every town across Texas and he's hiring more each day. I've been in contact with the governor, but unless we have any proof of wrongdoing, there's nothing we can do. Hayden is very well protected in Washington."

With some optimism, Gideon turned to Jon. "Please tell me you have some good news."

Thinking about what Gideon said, Jon shook his head no while he gulped down another drink. With a silly smirk on his face, he gave Gideon what he had. "Gideon, I'm not sure what you consider fun, but whatever it is, my trip wasn't it. Anyway, those two trappers were telling the truth. I think Hayden's men cut down a Comanche hunting party to include their well-respected chief, Seven Bulls. And you can be sure his son, Two Feathers, is looking for retribution."

As the three men took time to let Jon's words sink in, Ms. Lita came over with a new bottle and sat down. "Well now, fellas, care if a lady joins a good-looking bunch like yourselves?" Like a breath of fresh air, Ms. Lita could always turn some frowns upside down.

With a fresh bottle on the table, Gideon poured the drinks. "I know Seven Bulls was well respected. Not only among the various tribes, but he was feared by everyone, including the military. So, we not only have a sadistic killer to deal with; we now have to make sure Two Feathers doesn't go on a war path."

Looking at Jubal, Gideon had the feeling the news wasn't going to get any better. "Okay Jubal, let's hear it. I'm hoping you can live'n up this party."

Slouched down in his seat with his legs stretched out, Jubal slowly pulled himself up and refilled his empty glass. "Well Gideon, you're right about Hayden. He's sadistic in every sense of the word. I guess that can count for something."

Feeling the smooth whiskey trickle down his throat, Jubal couldn't help but be sarcastic given the mood. "On the brighter side of things, it just keeps getting worse."

Giving his full attention, Gideon leaned across the table and listened carefully as Jubal continued. "I crossed the border and hit a few of those border towns, but every time I asked about Hayden, people scurried away. I couldn't get anybody to talk, so I took a train ride down to Mexico City. Figured with all the money he's putting out, there had to be some kind of records on file about him."

Along with Gideon, Jon and Ms. Lita were now paying close attention. Before continuing, Jubal gathered his thoughts, then wet his whistle. "Well, Hayden ain't no small biscuit. He comes from wealth. His family came from Spain. Settled in California back when it was part of the Mexican territory. The family gained their wealth the old-fashioned way—by stealing it." Once again Jubal paused to take a drink and gather his thoughts.

By now everyone was on the edge of their seats as Jubal continued. "Now, here's where it gets interesting. His mother's side of the family came over with the conquistadors. As you know, they conquered and stole everything they could get their hands on. His father's side of the family came over later. Now listen, 'cause your gonna love this. His father's family was a part of a religious order called the Jesuits. They were brought over to hunt down another religious order called the Franciscans."

The story definitely sounded interesting, but Jubal wasn't finished. Now it was time to add the last of the puzzle pieces. "Now, I'm no man of the world so I had to do a little more digg'n, so I took some time to do some catch'n up on my history. Seems to be the Franciscans stumbled upon a couple of silver mines. Those silver mines were a part of a bigger mine that was inside of a mountain. The problem was nobody knew the location except the monks. That's when the King of Spain sent troops and the Jesuits to find the Franciscans and their mines. But by the time they arrived, the Franciscans disappeared along with the locations and the know-how on how to locate the minds. Legend has it that the minds were so rich with silver that it ran like a river down the side of the mountain."

When Jubal was finished, nobody spoke. They were astonished at the story just told to them. Pouring himself a drink, Gideon leaned back in his chair to think about how the story related to Hayden. "Jesuit Silver Holdings Corporation. That's the name of Hayden's company. I'll be damned."

With the cogs still turning in his mind, Gideon was stunned, to say the least. "So you think that maniac is killing people, then buying up their land from the state for pennies on the dollar? All for some fabled treasure that may or may not exist? That's one hell of a stretch, Jubal."

Jubal, who was already back in his slouched position, gave Gideon a smile. "I bet you a steak dinner if you look at all the properties Hayden bought, you'll find a river or stream running through it. And if not, then maybe a small pond or even a lake or mountainside off in the distance."

After listening to Jubal, Ms. Lita gave Gideon a smile. "Well now, Sheriff, seems to me you owe your deputy more than just a steak dinner. Maybe a bottle of my best whiskey to go with it."

Sitting quietly, Jon tried to sort through the information Jubal gave. He shook his head in disgust as he let out his thoughts. "When I was younger, I lived with two old priests. When it was finally time for me to go it on my own, they told me I wasn't ready for the evil in this world. In thinking about Hayden, I think they were right."

Before Jon could reminisce anymore, Jubal jumped in with some more not-so-good news. "Since everyone's on the same page, I can tell you this. All the bad we know about Hayden, he's worse than what we think. After buying a few of the locals some drinks, I finally got a couple of them to loosen up and talk. They say Hayden's worse than the plague. They say he's responsible for killing off entire families. People that had nothing to do with whatever he's involved with at the time. He's traveled long distances just to kill people he thinks may be related to the person he's dealing with. Seems that Hayden fears revengeful kinfolk. And Gideon, I know you're tough and I know you're fast, but I don't put it past that rattlesnake to put a bullet in your back."

After all the talking was done, it was time to get back to everyday life. Ms. Lita went back to tending bar, while Jon said his good-byes and went home to be with his family. As Gideon and Jubal made their rounds around town, they spoke more about Hayden. With both men feeling the stress, they needed to stop Hayden before he killed anyone else.

During their walk around town, Gideon decided to strike up a more personal conversation. "Jubal, you're a good man with a kind heart, and you seem to be more intelligent than most folks I know."

Before Gideon could continue, Jubal laughed because he knew what

Gideon was getting at. "Go 'head boss. I knew this talk was a'com'n. So let's get it out in the open."

Accepting Jubal's nice gesture, Gideon paused then smiled. "Well, all right. I was just curious and had been meaning to ask, why do you continue to wear that old dusty Confederate Army hat?"

Feeling a bit dry, Jubal stopped at a trough to wash the dust off his face. Afterward, he sat down on a nearby chair in front of the dress shop. With a grin on his face and eagerness in his voice, he invited Gideon to sit. "Come on. Have a seat."

Gideon was expecting a short answer, but instead he realized he was in for a story. So he removed his hat, slapped the dust off, and sat down. Waiting for Gideon to get comfortable, Jubal paused for a moment then gave his answer. "Don't much like politics or, for that matter, politicians. We had some tough times when me and my brothers were young. Our ma died, leaving pa, me, and my brothers to take care of what little we had. Pa worked us hard, but he taught us a lot and he kept us alive. When Texas came a'call'n, Pa signed us up. I was the youngest, but I knew a little about what was going on. I didn't agree with it and I let my pa know."

Once again Jubal paused, but this time it was to swallow the lump in his throat. "Pa didn't take kindly to me making a stand, so he hit me a few times, then told my brothers to beat me more until I couldn't get up. I guess that's what they call tough love. I can honestly say, it didn't feel like love when my brothers were kick'n and puch'n. Anyhow, Pa told me if I ever refuse him or Texas again, he would kill me. So we all went off together and fought for Texas during the war."

During another pause, Jubal took a moment to place his hat in his lap. Gideon knew his curiosity probably put Jubal in an uncomfortable position, but Jubal had already started with his story. "Listen, Jubal. The hat doesn't bother me. What's past is past, and you should've told me to just mind my business."

But Jubal wasn't bothered by the story, so he continued to explain. "I like you, Gideon. I don't have anything against any man. Black, white, Mexican,

Indian. Don't mean noth'n to me. When I told my pa that, I guess he didn't like it and decided to beat some sense into me. Anyhow, we stuck together as family and fought hard. During the battle of Sabine Pass, Pa took a bullet to the chest during a charge. I remember seeing him stumble, but the old man got up and kept moving forward. I tried to get to him, but it was too late 'cause the old fool took another bullet to the leg. I yelled for him, but he just wouldn't stop. Guess'n he didn't wanna count himself as a coward. When I saw him go down for the last time, I finally managed to crawl over to him, but he was already dead. He had tak'n two more to the chest. Old bastard probably died before he hit the ground. Yanks were just too much to handle that day, so we found ourselves evacuating the fort and licking our wounds. My oldest brother Bobby-Jo didn't take Pa's death very well. He seemed to think it my fault."

Letting out a sigh, Gideon was hoping the story was over, but Jubal kept going. "'Bout a month later, we were involved with the battle down Galveston. That damn Bobby-Jo, meaner than a wolf at dinner time. Don't know what he was think'n, or maybe he wasn't think'n at all. Dang fool was crouched down behind some rock and popped his head up at the wrong dang time. Bullet grazed his face and his temper was too quick for'em to handle. When he stood up, a six-pound cannonball blew a hole right through his chest."

Thinking about the incident, a big smile came across Jubal's face as he continued. "Although no man should have to endure a death like that, I can say I wasn't sad to see him go. Damn Yanks won that one to. By now, there was only two of us left. My other brother Oliver was a year older than me. Good heart. Strong. From that point on we swore we would never leave each other's side. If we were gonna go down, it was gonna be together.

"Toward the end of the war, we were down at the Rio Grande at a place called Pamito Ranch. There was a truce and everybody was yelling that the war was ending. I remember Ollie and I hugg'n each other, knowing we'd made it through four years of hell together. Well, I guess we were premature in our think'n. For reasons that make no sense, some Yankee coward ordered an attack. Colonel Theodore Barrett. Some say he was never in a battle and he wanted to see action before the war ended. Hell of a reason to attack soldiers that was prepar'n to go home. Anyhow, Ollie and I got separated during the attack. I could see'um, but he was about twenty yards from me and I couldn't get to'em."

Feeling the ache in his heart, Jubal paused, then glanced up at the sky. "Don't know why the big guy allows us to do the things we do, but I'm guess'n he has a purpose. Anyhow, I took a bullet to my leg and it went through without hitting bone, but it was enough to knock me down. I remember laying on the ground and look'n over to see if Ollie was still fight'n."

Once again Jubal paused, as it was getting harder for him to talk while he relived the moment, but Gideon wasn't about to interrupt. After a few moments Jubal took a breath, then finished his story. "I, um, I saw Ollie and he, um, he must'a ran out of ammo. I tried to get up, but my leg just wouldn't let me. And then I saw two Yanks corner him like a criminal. Ollie dropped his rifle, but I guess that wasn't enough for those damn Yanks. Or maybe they just wasn't in the mood to take prisoners. Just for a moment I could see Ollie look my way, but in think'n about it, to this day, I'm still not sure whether or not he was looking at me or even if'n he knew where I was. He had that look. That look a man gets when he knows his life is over. Ollie just stood there while those animals smiled and put two bullets in his head."

With the wind blowing a slight breeze, Jubal and Gideon sat quietly for a few minutes, Gideon taking in the story and Jubal trying to gather himself while remembering the deaths of his family. With his hat still in his hand, Jubal stood up and leaned against a support beam. "Well, Gideon, I didn't mean to throw my life story at you and I hope you don't take offense to my hat, but I guess you can say I wear it out of remembrance of Ollie. Couldn't stand my pa, and like I said, Bobby-Jo was just plain-out mean, but Ollie and I were close. That day Pa told them to beat me, Ollie came to me afterward and apologized. He told me he didn't want to fight for Texas either, but he didn't have the courage like me to stand up to Pa."

With a smile on his face, Gideon stood up and shook Jubal's hand. "Jubal, I don't take offense to your hat, and I'm honored that you thought me such a friend to tell me about your family. Since I've known you, you've never come

here, and I don't think you're so happy to see me. Your men never returned from their trip and that's why you're here now."

Zachariah didn't mind a little cat-and-mouse game occasionally, but Jon was right. He wasn't happy about losing some good men, but worst of all, Jon was still alive and he still had the necklace around his neck. "Now look here, Ranger. Per my orders, my men go out and survey various pieces of land for potential investments every so often. I have men all over the territory, so if you're accusing me of something, I suggest you have some sort of evidence to back up your statements or else I'll be making some inquiries to the governor."

Knowing he wasn't going to be with the Texas Rangers for too much longer, Jon didn't take Zachariah's threats seriously. "Listen, Hayden, if I have accusations, I'll let you know. If you're feeling sentimental about your men, you may want to take a trip up north to the Red River. There, you'll find eight graves to pay your respects to."

Zachariah didn't like hearing what Jon had to say and became visibly upset as he turned to Gideon in order to express his dismay. "Now, Sheriff, you just heard the same thing I did. This man just admitted to killing eight of my men. They were good friends and hard workers. Now, what are you going to do about it?"

Feeling no urgency, Gideon took a drink of his beer, then glanced at Jon for a moment. He then turned his attention back to Zachariah. "I know you're an educated man, Hayden, but I know a little about the law and I didn't hear anyone confess to killing anybody. Ranger Mason simply informed you that eight of your men are buried dangerously close to Comanche territory. Now, you're obviously free to go view the gravesites and bring me back any evidence you may find, but I wouldn't do so without a military escort."

Feeling even more infuriated, Zachariah grew tired of the game. Before he turned to walk away, he had a few last words for Jon. "Ranger, my offer just went up. I'll give you $1,000 for that necklace that means absolutely nothing to you. I'll give you some time to think about it while I retreat to my hotel room for some rest." In a calm fashion, Zachariah placed his hat back on his head then turned and walked out.

After shaking off the chilly conversation, Jon and Gideon got back to drinking and talking business. After a brief silence, Gideon once again had to question his friend. "So Jon, anything you want to tell me?"

Jon didn't say anything at first, but after a nice long drink of his beer, he was ready to talk. "Well, I wasn't lying. Eight of Hayden's men are buried up at Red River. And if you're wondering, I didn't kill them."

With a sarcastic look and a sense of "here we go again," Gideon stared at Jon as though he had more to tell. "Well?"

Staring back at Gideon, Jon let out a small laugh. "Well, what?"

Still with his look of sarcasm and now becoming animated with his hands, Gideon continued. "Well, you gonna tell me what happened out there, or is that a secret like the invisible battle you and Hayden have going on?"

Needing a little more privacy, Jon walked over to an empty table with Gideon following close behind. Hoping for some believable answers, Gideon waited as Jon gathered his thoughts. After finishing off his beer, Jon took a breath and spoke. "The day Hayden's men tried to gun me down, they were after this necklace I wear. I didn't realize that until the next day when I confronted Hayden about the actions of his men. He offered me $100 for it. I guess he's a man that doesn't get turned down much. When I took my trip up north, Hayden sent his men after me. My guess is they were supposed to kill me up near Comanche territory, but it didn't quite work out that way."

With utter amazement, Gideon stared at Jon. "My God, Jon. Hayden doesn't hire just anybody. He has only the best of the best on his payroll. So, you're telling me you waltzed into Comanche territory, managed to kill eight of Hayden's men, and got out before the Comanche caught you? I knew you were good but damn, that's an incredible story to tell around the campfire."

Jon soaked up the compliments and almost didn't say anything, but he couldn't take the credit for something he didn't do. Besides, he had to tell Gideon the truth so they could figure out their next step. Grinning from ear to ear, Jon decided to tell all. "Listen, Gideon, I appreciate the confidence, but it didn't happen that way. When I finally made it up to the Red River, I was tired. Thought I would take a break before crossing over. After a few minutes of rest, I saw Hayden's men coming, but there was nothing I could do. Any gun fight and the Comanche would've come running. They would have killed us all, especially me. Anyway, they wanted the necklace and were willing to make me a deal, but I said no."

Gideon listened as one of the saloon girls placed two more beers on the table and gave both men a wink. Glancing up at the pretty girl, Jon thanked her with a smile, then took a drink before continuing the story. "I don't know what else to tell you Gideon. I'm not afraid to say things got real weird after that. Someone came out of nowhere and started killing Hayden's men. I can tell you for sure it wasn't Comanche and it didn't look like an Apache, but I can say this: he was fast. Faster than anything or anyone I've ever known."

Once again, Gideon stared at Jon with disbelief. "It wasn't Comanche and it wasn't Apache, but you're telling me one unknown Indian killed eight of Hayden's men? Did he get the drop on them and shoot them?"

Jon momentarily paused because he knew Gideon was having problems with the story, but now he had to tell Gideon more. "He didn't have a gun. After he killed the first man with a knife, he moved with lightning speed, killing the rest of them one by one. After the last one fell, I thought I was next. I dropped my gun and just stood waiting for something to happen. And it did."

Like a little boy listening to a ghost story, Gideon hung on every word Jon was saying. With a deep sigh, Jon took a breath and another drink before finishing his story. "Like some kind of damn ghost, that Indian came walking up out of the water. I thought he would just strike me down, but instead he just stood in front of me staring into my eyes. I don't know who he was or why he didn't kill me, but there was a familiarity about him."

With a pause, Jon decided not to mention the pictures the warrior Indian drew in the sand. Instead, he wanted to find out exactly what the pictures meant before voicing an opinion.

Staring at Jon as though he was a master storyteller, Gideon had no words. He had no intentions of doubting his friend, but with Jon's story came new questions. "Jon, there's been a lot of crazy things going on, so one more un-believable story isn't going to make a difference. But I have to ask. Why do you think he didn't kill you? And do you think we may have been wrong about Hayden all this time?"

Jon didn't have an answer about the Indian, but he knew they had the right guy with Hayden. "I think Hayden is a cold-blooded killer, and I don't know why the Indian didn't kill me."

While Gideon and Jon sat and talked, Zachariah was back in his hotel room dreaming and scheming. With his family's background and history, he felt he was above any law and grew tired of being embarrassed. He wanted what he wanted and he was not going to be denied. Knowing if he could get rid of the Texas Rangers, he could very easily make the local sheriff disappear.

With Johnson gone, Zachariah needed a new right-hand man, and he already had just the person in mind. Leadership, brutality, and hatred—the exact combination he needed, and he was already enroute to the town of Presidio. Augusta Pittman. Pittman was due to arrive any day and Zachariah couldn't wait to unleash his plan.

Finishing up his business with Gideon, Jon was off to see Doc Belle. It was good timing since it had been a while since his last visit. Just like Doc Micah, she was preparing to make her weekly rounds to the local Indian villages. As he helped her load the wagon, Jon couldn't help but reminisce about the old days with his pa.

When Jon first came to town, he would accompany Doc Micah on his weekly rounds to the local Indian villages. Old Doc was proud of Jon and would constantly parade him around, introducing him to all the elders. They didn't seem to mind Jon but they kept their distance, except for one of the elders in particular who took a liking to him. Enyeto. He was a not-so-famous but very wise war chief of the Sioux Indians. While Doc conducted his medical exams, Enyeto would sit and tell Jon about the long-forgotten days before the American settlers started claiming lands that didn't belong to them. Enyeto told Jon stories that had been told down through the generations and Jon enjoyed every moment of his visits.

Jon hadn't been out to the villages in a long time, so it was comforting to hear from Belle that his friend would be happy to see him. Halfway to the village, Belle and Jon's trip abruptly came to a stop when Jon spotted the elusive white thoroughbred up on a cliff overlooking the road. She was stunning in every way, but she was without her herd, which piqued Jon's curiosity.

Trying not to voice her excitement, Belle was astonished. She had heard stories about the elusive beauty, almost to a point of being legendary, but before now never had the pleasure of seeing for herself. "Jon, she's amazing. She almost disappears when the sunlight hits her."

Before Jon could respond, the magnificent beast galloped off.

With silence filling the air, Belle was reluctant to speak, but did so with caution. "So, why do you think she decided to make an appearance?"

Jon thought for a moment but had no definite answer. "Well, I've seen her several times now and each time seems to be different. I've seen her up close and from afar, but each time almost feels like she's trying to communicate something to me. Like she knows something that I don't. I know that sounds crazy, but it seems crazy things have been the theme lately."

Still feeling honored, Belle didn't reply and decided to just savor the moment.

When they reached the village, they were met by some happy children running alongside of the wagon. They knew Belle not only came with various medications and vaccines but also with lots of candy. After helping Belle unload the supplies, Jon walked to a very large teepee, which sat in the middle of the village. When he entered, he saw his friend Enyeto sitting upright and meditating by a small fire. As quietly as he could, Jon knelt down opposite of Enyeto and waited.

With his eyes still closed, Enyeto spoke. "It has been long time, Jon Mason. Why you return now?"

Jon couldn't help but smile because it was nice to hear the old chief's voice, even though most of it was broken English. "Hello, Enyeto. I'm sorry it's been too long. I should have made time to come see you sooner, but I carry a badge now and it seems time is never on my side."

When Enyeto opened his eyes, he was pleased to see what Jon had grown up to be. "You look good, Jon Mason. Big. Strong. Badge say people place trust in you. That is good. My friend Micah did fine job with you. I miss Micah. Lady Doc nice but too much nag."

With a small chuckle, Jon appreciated the words of Enyeto. "My pop was a good man and I miss him too. I'm glad to see you still have your sense of humor."

As Enyeto paused to stand up, Jon quickly got to his feet to help the aging chief stand. Afterward, they left the teepee and walked as they talked. With thoughts weighing heavy on his heart, Jon didn't waste any time explaining his visit. "Enyeto, I need some information on a couple of symbols."

Before Jon could continue, Enyeto stunned him with some words. "You have seen great warrior. He make himself known to you."

Realizing Enyeto was talking about the warrior Indian, Jon was astounded. He didn't know what to say at first, then the questions came and Jon was hoping his friend could supply the answers. "Who is he and what does he want with me?"

Enyeto was tired, so he stopped to sit down and invited Jon to do the same. "Most tribes no speak of him. Sioux call him Ohanzee. Means 'Shadow.' When you see him, always too late. Nobody know where he come from. Nobody know what tribe he from. He kill lot of Indian. He kill lot of white man. He kill anybody who hunt him."

Hearing Enyeto's words, Jon was feeling very fortunate to still be alive. "The last time I saw him, he drew a picture of a wolf at my feet. What does that mean?"

With the answers already known to him, Enyeto momentarily peered into Jon's eyes and smiled. "He know your soul. Wolf mean 'companion.' He say you are a great leader and have direction. He say you have strong heart with many values. He say you have power to protect, but you also possess power to destroy. You must choose when time come."

Jon thought about what Enyeto was saying, but it still wasn't making any sense. "He also drew two arrows that crossed."

Once again, Enyeto glanced into Jon's eyes and smiled. "Two arrow cross mean 'friendship.' Your life cross his and his life cross yours. He say both are connected."

Over the next few minutes, Jon explained to Enyeto what he could remember of his past and told the story of the Apache warrior and his son who
led him out onto the plains to parish. He also told how the Apache boy let him
go and gave him a beaded bracelet. Jon told Enyeto that the mysterious Indian
had on the same beaded bracelet as he did.

Jon could tell Enyeto was very tired and getting weaker by the minute, so
he helped him back to the teepee in order for him to rest. While laying peacefully on some bedding, Enyeto took Jon by his hand. "Thank you, Jon Mason.
You good friend and good man. Do not fear. Ohanzee will make known his
purpose. Only then will you know your path together."

Jon saw that Enyeto wasn't looking good, so he ran to get Belle. When
they returned, Jon watched as Belle attended to Enyeto's needs as she pulled
an elixir from her kit and gave some to the weakened chief. As the elixir settled
into his stomach, Enyeto breathed a sigh of relief.

Feeling a little better, he politely asked Belle to step out so he could have
some words with Jon. After Belle left, Jon sat down beside the bed, and once
again Enyeto took Jon by the hand. "Lady Doc come one day. She see I have
problem with stomach. She say I no see next snowfall."

Jon waited for Enyeto to elaborate, but he was weak and needed rest, so
he told Enyeto to get some sleep and said his good-byes.

On the ride back to town, Belle knew Jon would have questions, so she
gave her deepest sympathy and told Jon about Enyeto's diagnosis. "I know you
value your friendships, Jon, but there's nothing I can do for him. I was on a
routine visit to the village about a couple months ago when I saw Enyeto sitting
off away from everybody. One of the elders told me he had been having some
terrible stomach pains lately. Enyeto thought it was some kind of evil spirit
tormenting him, so he was trying to stay away from the other villagers so they
wouldn't suffer the same. Well, I finally convinced him to let me examine him.
Come to find out, some mountain men came through right before last winter
and wanted to trade some of their homemade brew for some furs and blankets.
They had a couple of cases of what I call poison. Before I knew what happen,
two elders died along with two teenage boys and a woman. Whatever those

mountain men made, it wasn't supposed to be drinkable. It slowly deteriorated the stomachs of the Sioux who consumed it."

With a heavy heart, Belle once again expressed her sad thoughts. "Jon, I'm really sorry. I wish I could do more. All I can do is give him temporary relief from the pain and try to make him comfortable."

As Jon listened to the story, his anger began to boil. "The men that traded the poison, were they ever found?"

With her own frustrations starting to arise, Belle continued with more bad news. "Well, after several letters written to the governor, the army, along with a United States marshal, went looking for them and found them. Their account of the story was obviously much different than the Sioux, so there were no arrests made and no trial. Bottom line is our government, along with frontier justice, doesn't value the lives of Indians."

Jon's thoughts raged with the idea of how, time and time again, outlaws and criminals create a path of death and destruction without consequence. After making sure Belle got back to town safe, Jon headed for the Lucy Goosy. After finding out about his friend, he just wanted to relax and drink away the day.

While Jon drank away his thoughts, a very proud-looking man came riding into town. An older man with grayish-blond hair styled in a unique southern way, fancy mustache turned up, and looking meaner than a hungry vulture. As he made his way down the middle of the street, he pointed his horse toward the hotel. Being a stranger, it was natural for the townspeople to take notice. But there was definitely something different about him. Very confident. Giving opposing stairs to anybody who dared to stare back at him for more than a few seconds. He took notice of anybody wearing a gun and also how low they carried it.

Arriving in front of the hotel, the hateful-looking man glanced around before dismounting. After stepping down from his horse, he took one more look around before entering the hotel and making his way to the front desk. It had been a slow day, so the small-in-stature hotel manager, Mr. Rupert Hinkle-meyer, was sitting down behind the desk reading the day's paper. As the annoyed-looking man stood waiting to be noticed, he cleared his throat to signal his dismay to the not-so-observant manager.

As the insecure Hinklemeyer lowered his paper, he immediately stood up and apologized to the displeased-looking man. "I'm so very sorry, sir. Nothing really going on today so I thought I would catch up on the political cartoons. They're so funny."

Seeing that the stern-looking man wasn't amused, Mr. Hinklemeyer promptly tried to rectify the situation. "I'm sorry, sir, how may I be of assistance?"

Feeling nothing but contempt, the angry-looking man took a deep breath in order to hold back his temper. In a somewhat loud and austere voice, he spoke. "You can start by paying attention. If this was a war, you'd be dead. My name is Augusta Pittman, but you may call me colonel. I'm looking for a man named Hayden. He's expecting me."

Mr. Hinklemeyer was very familiar with Zachariah Hayden and knew anyone associated with him was nobody to upset. With his voice starting to quiver, Mr. Hinklemeyer gave the colonel the room number for Zachariah Hayden. Afterward, Mr. Hinklemeyer once again apologized. "I'm sorry, sir. I promise next time I'll be more observant."

Still trying to hold back his temper, Colonel Pittman gave Mr. Hinklemeyer a blood-curling look. "Don't let there be a next time."

After proclaiming his dismay, the colonel made his way upstairs to Zachariah Hayden's room. After several slow knocks, a surprised Hayden opened the door, but there were no introductions needed. Hayden knew exactly who the colonel was. "Please, come in, Colonel. I was under the impression you were hunting your latest opponent."

Glancing around the room, Colonel Pittman cautiously walked through the door. Being enthused about the colonel's arrival, Zachariah made some drinks and invited the colonel to have a seat. Colonel Pittman thanked Zachariah for his kindness, but informed him that alcohol was off limits while conducting business. With understanding, Zachariah didn't take offense, so he set the drinks aside and proceeded with the business at hand. "All right,

Colonel. I'm not sure if you're familiar with me, but I know you and I know your reputation as a military leader. I'm also aware that you're the best gunfighter this side of the border. I know you're as ruthless as they come and I know I can count on you to get the job done if you decide to accept my offer."

Feeling a little more comfortable, Colonel Pittman sat as he twirled his mustache and gathered his thoughts. "Well now, sir, I appreciate your confidence in me. And just so you understand, sir, your name is very prominent and I'm well aware of your family's status. During the war, your family was very sympathetic to our cause and donated much-needed funds and ammunitions to our military forces. So when I received your telegram, I felt indebted to respond. I also feel obligated to apologize to you, sir. I feel losing the war has created a disenchanted government. So, with that said, your telegram was very vague."

With a big smile on his face, Zachariah couldn't have agreed more. "Yes, sir. Although my many business dealings force me to patronize our current government, I can definitely say with conviction I, along with my family, sympathize with you and your fellow brethren."

The colonel appreciated the gracious words of Zachariah, but he wasn't there for fellowship. After the last Confederate general surrendered, which marked a humiliating defeat for the Confederacy and the end of the war, Colonel Pittman became enraged. He left his military life behind just to return to a beautiful home with many acres of land that no longer belonged to him. All of his property and belongings had been requisitioned by the Union after the war then turned over to the federal government to be sold. Shortly afterward, his wife became ill and passed away. Somewhere deep in his soul, he gave up whatever humanity he had left to become a stone-cold killing machine. Known to be the fastest gun alive, he hired himself out to the highest bidder and would kill anyone for a price. So when it came to business, he would prefer employers get straight to the point rather than spend the time attempting to socialize.

After his attempt at conversation, Zachariah realized the colonel was in no mood to waste time, which suited Zachariah just fine. Before he continued the meeting, Zachariah took a moment to comfort his dry throat by swallowing one of the drinks he had made earlier. "Well, Colonel, I can appreciate a man who can be straight forward and likes to get right to the business at hand. So, let me begin by explaining my dilemma and then we can discuss the terms of agreement."

Not knowing how much information Zachariah had or how long he was going to talk, Colonel Pittman stood up in order to fend off some of the minor aches he was beginning to experience. "You'll have to excuse me, sir, I received some unwarranted injuries during the war and in order to relieve such bothersome pain, I sometimes find that standing helps. Please, continue."

Not wanting the colonel to feel uncomfortable, Zachariah used the opportunity to make himself another drink. He then walked to the window that overlooked the town and pulled the certain aside. Zachariah peered out over the town as he continued to explain their mutual problem. "Colonel, the last time I went into detail about what I'm attempting to accomplish, my words were wasted on a man that got himself killed. So, with that said, I'll give you the short version. There's a Texas Ranger by the name of Jon Mason involved in an investigation that quite frankly hinders me from…let's just say my personal business. Ironically, this same Ranger happens to be in possession of something that could very well help me wrap up that same personal business. Now, your brother Charlie was a devoted employee of mine who also happened to get himself killed. And if you haven't yet figured out the common denominator of this equation, it was that same Texas Ranger who gunned him down."

Slightly bending and turning, Colonel Pittman stood in the middle of the room listening and thinking about what Zachariah was saying. "Well, sir, I did receive the news about the early demise of my brother and I can't say that I'm sorry. My brother was stupid, arrogant, and quick tempered. I constantly reminded him that his attitude would someday get him killed. Nevertheless, he was my brother. I take it, sir, you wouldn't want to damage your fine reputation and good standings by being associated with the death of one of Texas's finest, so with the unexpected departure of my brother, you shrewdly saw a golden opportunity to employ my services. And if I may elaborate even further, sir, on the aforementioned issue, you seem to think the demise of this certain Texas Ranger would give me the sweet pleasure of revenge thus resolving your quandary."

Zachariah was charmed by Colonel Pittman's education. "Thank you, Colonel, for those poised and well-placed words. I've somehow grown accustomed to dealing with ignorance over the years, so it's refreshing to finally have a conversation with a well-educated man. And if I may continue, your astute calculations are correct."

Being an educated man had its benefits, and after listening to Zachariah, the colonel realized there was something other than eliminating one man, even if it was a Texas Ranger. After a deep breath, Colonel Pittman walked to the window and stood next to Zachariah. Being a bit taller in stature, the colonel looked down at the smaller man in order to be more direct and to express his dismay for a prolonged conversation. "Mr. Hayden, as you so kindly reminded me, we are both educated men. You certainly didn't ask me here in order to pay me to kill a man I was already going to kill. So let us stop stroking each other's egos and get to the point."

Once again Zachariah couldn't fault the colonel for his candid attitude. "Of course, Colonel. Your observations are impeccable and I can see you're a man who doesn't like to prevaricate. So, I'll tell you what I need and you either accept or decline."

Before Zachariah continued, he offered the colonel a drink of water, which he welcomed, then made himself another drink. "Colonel, I have absolute faith in your ability to be able to kill that Texas Ranger in a gunfight. But, and I say this with the utmost respect to your dignity as a gentleman, being an ex-Confederate colonel and a well-known gunfighter, even if you kill a Texas Ranger in a fair gunfight, the state of Texas will undoubtedly and without waiver hunt you down and hang you without mercy and without the due process of a fair and just trial."

Colonel Pittman, among other things, was a decisive man but was also exceptional at restraining wild impulses. "You honor me, sir, not only with your compliment but with a sense of resolve in the tone of your voice. Please, continue, sir."

Zachariah smiled because he was all too eager to reveal his master plan that would not only solve his issues with the law but possibly lead him to his fabled treasure of the Franciscan monks.

Starting to feel the troublesome sensation of his mysterious but unforgotten injuries, Colonel Pittman decided to promptly sit back down. At the same time, Zachariah was starting to feel the strain of standing so he too sat while he continued to explain his proposal. "Thank you, sir, for your courtesy. Once again, I refer to your keen ability to read between the lines. As you've already concluded, I can't afford to compromise my friendships or my good standings in Washington. The local sheriff and I don't see eye to eye, but he is but a small bug waiting to be squashed. He presents very little problems for men like you and me. As for that Texas Ranger, not only does he have friends but he has the backing of an entire state, which forces me to do the unthinkable. With the information I received from my friends in Washington, there are currently twenty-five Texas Rangers to include Ranger Mason working statewide to solve what they think is a crime spree of murders and disappearances. Now, I have taken the liberty of using my influence and persuading my friends in Washington to help me. Being the concerned citizen as I am, I informed them I felt obliged to do something for the morale of the men, so I coerced them into contacting the governor of Texas in order to invite the Rangers to a formal dinner with yours truly, along with the mayor, of course, and some of the other influential citizens in and around Presidio. As prideful as they are stupid, they will gather first in order to make a grand entrance, so they'll be coming from the west and riding in an easterly direction. Now, there isn't but one road coming from the west that can hold that many horses."

Trying to hold back his enthusiasm, Zachariah took a minute to take a breath and to retrieve a rifle from a trunk at the foot of his bed. Looking on with interest, the colonel could see it wasn't a typical rifle. Colonel Pittman watched as Zachariah took a few seconds to admire it before handing it to him. As the colonel marveled at its appearance, Zachariah explained why it was no ordinary rifle. "What do you think, Colonel? I had this and five others ordered special last month and they just arrived this morning."

Colonel Pittman ran his hand down the barrel, then twisted it around to look at the maker's mark. "It looks like a modified Winchester."

With pride dripping off his shoulders, Zachariah emerged himself into his plan. "This is a Winchester 1873 with a heavy weight Remington 24 twisted barrel. It has a nickel-plated receiver with special fitted sights so there's no missing your target. While I play the gracious host at my dinner party, you, sir, along with five of my best shooters, are going to use these magnificent pieces of hardware to kill not only Ranger Mason but all twenty-five of the Texas Rangers."

He tried not to look surprised, but Zachariah's plan was much more than what the colonel expected. "Well now, sir, you are mighty ambitious indeed. And may I be so bold to say, executing twenty-five Texas Rangers is no small venture. With the preoccupation of your dinner party, you have managed to separate yourself from what may be the crime of the century."

Still attempting to hold back his excitement, Colonel Pittman smiled with delight as he clapped his hands together. "Please, sir, don't do me the injustice of waiting for your second act. I'm anxious to hear the ending to this outstanding masterpiece."

Zachariah gleamed with pride and was overjoyed at the fact Colonel Pittman seemed to enjoy what he was hearing. So he continued. "As you well know, twenty-five dead Rangers lying about would normally cast a huge shadow of suspicion over the territory, but since their reinstatement, they've made ample amounts of enemies all over. The little skirmishes they've had with the Indians and the Red River War last year still haven't been forgotten about. And don't forget the border and the constant suppression of those ever-so-rambunctious Mexican bandits, not to mention our own problems with the unwavering American outlaws and their gangs. Yes, sir, I think for my final act I'll have a wealth of material to offer at any formal inquisition."

Once again Colonel Pittman clapped his hands as he praised Zachariah. "Mr. Hayden, sir, I must say, the superior firepower you have provided along with your devilish hindsight for details combined with your very cold heart makes for a very commendable scenario."

Colonel Pittman smiled as he reached across the table and shook Zachariah's hand. "That, sir, was to congratulate you on a well-thought-out resolution. Now, if we could just traverse the more personal particulars, such as my compensation."

Zachariah paused for a moment, then smiled as he retrieved a small suitcase from his closet and opened it. Along with some clean clothing, there was a small secret compartment with a small pull-string pouch hidden inside. Zachariah pulled the pouch from its compartment and shook it as he returned to the table. Being a man of fine taste and culture, the colonel recognized the sound immediately. It was the sound of gold coins. When Zachariah sat down, he placed the weighted pouch in the middle of the table. "Assuming you know what this is, Colonel, you now know I'm quite serious about my proposition."

Colonel Pittman took it upon himself to pour the contents of the pouch out as he watched the gold coins sparkle and spin. He was almost intoxicated with emotions as the coins eventually flattened flush to the table. "Well now, sir, at first glance, this looks to be about $5,000 in gold."

Once again Zachariah smiled with pride. "Yes, sir. Your count is very accurate. I myself prefer silver, but gold seems to be the standard payment for a job of this magnitude. Take this five thousand as a token of my trust. There's an old abandoned gold mine about ten miles out of town. There, you'll find the five men I mentioned earlier. They're all trained killers and happen to be some of the best marksmen money can buy. They're already familiar with your reputation and are looking forward to working with you. Hell, you may even know a few of them from your past travels."

Understanding the plan, the colonel gathered up the coins and placed them back in the pouch. "Sir, I do appreciate a man that has what it takes to impress me, but as you eluded to earlier, these men you want me to eliminate aren't your everyday ordinary men. Your token of appreciation barely covers me accommodating this meeting."

With a deep breath and pause, Zachariah finished out his offer. "I will pay you $10,000 for Ranger Mason and an additional $5,000 for every other Ranger. Altogether, that's $135,000. Furthermore, I will pay you an additional $5,000 if you bring me back the necklace that Ranger Mason wears around his neck."

Feeling good about the terms of the plan, the colonel shook the pouch one last time before hiding it away in his coat. "Five thousand additional for a fragment of jewelry. It must be an extraordinary piece. Either way, I accept your terms, sir. I will assemble your men and we shall give the Texas Rangers a proper welcome to Presidio. Now, if you'll excuse me, I'm going to take a trip out to the location we shall use for our rendezvous with the Rangers. As you well know, I'm a man of preparation."

Wanting to get started on his game plan, the colonel gave one last handshake to Zachariah and wasted no time in making his exit.

As Colonel Pittman made his way down to the lobby, Gideon was walking into the hotel and stopped to talk with Mr. Hinklemeyer. "Hey Rupert, how are you?"

With a big smile on his face, Mr. Hinklemeyer was relieved to see Gideon and stood up to greet him. "Hello, Sheriff. Sure am glad to see you."

Gideon could see Mr. Hinklemeyer was nervous at best, but took the compliment in stride. "Well, Rupert, I'd like to say I stopped in to say hello, but the town folks are telling me a stranger came into town a while ago headed for your hotel. You wouldn't happen to know anything about that, would you?"

Before Mr. Hinklemeyer could answer, Colonel Pittman came walking down the steps. As Mr. Hinklemeyer rolled his eyes toward the colonel, Gideon turned to see one of his former enemies walking toward him. Gideon stared as Colonel Pittman approached and stopped within five feet of him.

Staring each other down, the colonel didn't hold back words. "So, the rumors I heard are true. This sorry excuse for a Texas town elected a Negro sheriff."

Due to circumstances of war, Gideon was familiar with the colonel and knew the rumors that swirled around his reputation. With memories rapidly filling his mind, anger snuck into his words. "Been some years gone by, but I know who you are. Augusta Pittman. Mass murderer, cruel torturer of Union soldiers, former slave owner, and just an all-around brutal killer with a soul darker than Satan himself."

Feeling disrespected, the colonel slowly moved his hand toward his gun, but decided to confront Gideon with words instead of violence. "You should mind your manners, boy. There are many things I could hit you with besides the bullets from my gun, but I wouldn't think an uneducated ignorant dog such as yourself would understand phrases such as 'defamation of character.'"

With a half-smile barely making itself visible, Gideon took a deep breath. "Pittman, it just so happens that I'm very educated and I know all about defamation of character. It only applies if what I say is false. You may have escaped being convicted of your atrocities, but it doesn't make it any less the truth."

Still feeling some contempt, the colonel paused for a moment, then looked Gideon up and down. "I knew this was a heathen town, but I just couldn't bring myself to imagine just how ignorant I was to the fact. An educated Negro sheriff. How on God's green earth does something like this happen?"

With another deep breath, Gideon looked around and noticed Mr. Hinklemeyer peeking out from behind the hotel desk. Attempting to form the exact words he needed to say, he turned his attention back to the colonel. "Listen, Pittman. The people in this town are decent townsfolk, so if you're here to spread hatred, then maybe you need to move on. If you decide to stay, then I suggest you check your attitude and don't cause me any problems."

With a deep hatred starting to burrow through his soul, the colonel had just about enough of Gideon. With a slight gesture, once again Colonel Pittman maneuvered his hand toward his gun.

Without warning, the hotel door swung open and in walked a cheerful Jubal. As Jubal approached the front desk, he could feel the tension in the air. "Everything all right, Gideon?"

It had been a while, but Colonel Pittman recognized Jubal from fighting alongside him in various battles. Looking at the deputy badge Jubal was wearing, the colonel became even more disgusted. Attempting to keep his composure, the colonel once again scolded the town and it's elected officials. "What the hell kind of heathen town is this? A Negro sheriff with an ex-Confederate lieutenant for a deputy." Offended by the appearance of Jubal, the colonel peered at him with a distasteful look. "You should feel ashamed, boy. You bring dishonor to the hat you wear."

Once again the hotel door opened and in walked a few of the townspeople who were there for dining purposes. Displeased with his surroundings, the colonel glanced around the room. "Yankee cowards, dishonorable traders, and a town filled with infidels." With more anger seeping into his voice, colonel Pittman turned his attention back to Gideon. "Next time, I kindly expect you to refer to me as Colonel or Sir." Afterward, the colonel gathered himself and walked out.

After the colonel was gone, Mr. Hinklemeyer finally came out from his crouched position. "Sheriff, I don't mind saying, I was so scared I nearly soiled myself."

Being the sympathetic man that he was, Gideon had nothing but thoughtful words. With a touch of sarcasm, he smiled at Mr. Hinklemeyer. "Nonsense, Rupert. There wasn't a doubt in my mind you would have sprung into action if I had needed your help."

While Gideon enjoyed a few seconds of humor, Jubal was quick to point out the more cynical side of the moment. With a look of despair, Jubal laid out a grim vision. "Gideon, I know you're not afraid of no man, but you gotta listen to me. What you know about stone-cold killers pales in comparison to Colonel Pittman. I can't even call him a man. More like the devil with a gun. I can't take anything away from him, though. He had a brilliant military mind second to none and I had my fair share of fighting alongside him. Gideon, I'm afraid you may have opened yourself up for a world of hurt."

Gideon knew Jubal was a man of commonsense, so he took his words in stride. After breathing a sigh of relief and saying their good-byes to Mr. Hinklemeyer, Gideon and Jubal stepped outside to talk more. Taking in a deep breath of fresh air, Jubal informed Gideon of just how evil the colonel was.

The two men walked while Jubal spoke in more detail. "Gideon, I wish that war had never came about. That way I would have never met that man. Like I said before, brilliant military mind, but I think a man like that gets too wrapped up in killing. Before you know it, you become obsessed with it to a point you begin to think of unholy ways to do it just to feed that urge. Now, I fought battles with him, but my men and I were never a part of those horrible exploits we use to hear about."

As Gideon and Jubal walked along, they would smile and tip their hats to various people. All along, Gideon was preparing himself for the horrible stories Jubal was about to tell. With an uneasy voice and concern for Gideon, Jubal continued to talk. "You know what happens when a bunch of good'o boys get together. We always gotta outdo each other when it comes to tell'n stories. But whenever one of the men yapped about Pittman, there was no laughing or fool'n 'cause we all knew the stories to be true. Pittman tortured Union soldiers without mercy. So much, it would make even the hardest of Comanche sick."

Before Jubal could elaborate, Gideon told a few stories of his own. "As a Union scout, you already know what my job was. Anyhow, sometimes I would head out a ways to make sure we had a clear path to wherever our destination was. Sometimes I would come across some gruesome sights. Union soldiers hanging from trees with their manhood missing and filled with bullet holes like they were being used for target practice. There were times I found half-eaten bodies of Union soldiers just lying about. I use to think it was Indians, but now I'm beginning to wonder. I heard about some of the rumors, but fighting alongside of him, I'm sure you probably know more"

In listening to Gideon, Jubal knew it wasn't the Indians. Jubal shook his head while he took another deep breath. "The things we did to each other during that war would make the bravest of men cringe. The first time I heard of Pittman and his escapades was back in '62. Very cold winter that year, and we were hunkered down in some woods a few miles from San Augustine. My regiment got beat up pretty bad during a small skirmish at Nacogdoches and a bunch of us got cut off from the rest. So after a couple of days of retreating, we decided to take up a defensive position to try and hold ground. Not trying to offend you, Gideon, but them damn Yankees wouldn't leave us be. Anyhow, we waited and watched, but them Yanks never showed. Since our supplies were low, we decided to try and make our way back in a northwest direction. We finally made it back to Nacogdoches and it was a haunting feeling. Whatever battle took place wasn't the battle we had left. Gideon, when I said we got beat up, that was an understatement. I gotta give it to you Yanks, you guys came prepared that day. We were unprepared, unorganized, and looking like a bunch of schoolboys with our britches hanging down. A lot of our men fell that day, but when we got back, not near a Confederate soldier to be found. But I'll tell you this, dead Yankees spread all over the place. Some hanging from trees half-burnt. Some impaled with their heads cut off. Most were spread out ly'n face down with no feet or hands. Look'n like they were trying to crawl away but just couldn't. Pittman would have his men cut off the limbs so they couldn't get away from being eaten alive by the wildlife. We had heard Pittman was moving south and was supposed to meet up with us, but we weren't sure how close he was. The day we got back to Nacogdoches was the day a few of my men started telling me the stories about Pittman. In looking around at all those dead Yanks and the way they died, I can honestly say you looked pure evil in the eye back at the hotel and lived to tell about it."

Gideon appreciated the concerns of Jubal, but he was the sheriff and his job was to keep the citizens of Presidio safe no matter what reputation he was up against. After making rounds, Jubal headed back to the jail while Gideon went to visit Ms. Lita. When he arrived at the Lucy Goosy, he found Jon working on his fifth beer and half a bottle, so he pulled up a chair and sat down. "Hey Jon, you look like you're on a mission."

With his emotions in disarray, Jon drank down the remaining beer in his glass and asked Gideon about Enyeto. "Belle and I took a trip up to the Sioux village. She told me about the mountain men that poisoned them. Enyeto is the old chief and is a close friend of mine, and now he's dying because of those cowards that hide in the mountains."

Gideon had never been to the Sioux village, but he knew Belle took weekly trips with supplies. "I'm sorry, Jon. I didn't know you were close to the Sioux."

With a heavy heart, Gideon tried to explain his position. "Duty had called you away during that time. Belle told me what happened, but I was limited on what I could do. Those men live at the southern tip of the Limpia Mountain range, which is under the jurisdiction of the U.S. marshal, and the Sioux village is under the direction of the military. I know I don't have to tell you that a black sheriff doesn't mean squat when up against that kind of authority."

Jon wasn't upset because he knew Gideon was limited to his sheriff duties within the town of Presidio. Hoping Jon understood, Gideon ordered two more beers and continued to explain. "Belle and I wrote letters, but it didn't give us any satisfaction. Although the marshal and the military went and spoke to those dirty dogs, it was quite obvious to Belle and me that nothing was going to be done. If it's any consolation, I took my own trip up to their cabin. There's actually two cabins and they're part of an old worn-out mine they took over. I briefly thought about taking care of business, but at the last minute, I glanced down at my badge. I guess I wouldn't be much of a sheriff if I had killed them in cold blood."

As the two beers arrived, Jon took a drink and laughed. "Don't think your face would look very pretty on a wanted poster either."

As the two men laughed and drank away the moment, Colonel Pittman was on his way out to meet with the five men Zachariah had hired. When he arrived, the men introduced themselves. The colonel knew a few of them, but only by reputation. There was Rico, Marcus and Ronnie Beck, Roberto Costas, and Lester Hayes, and they were all excellent marksmen with a rifle. The plan was simple: There was an old cattle road about fifteen miles northwest of town. It was overgrown and was rarely used. This was where the Texas Rangers would form up and ride into town in parade formation. At one point, the road narrowed just enough to form a small canyon with an overlook on each side of the road, but still had enough room for a large number of horses. This was where the colonel and his men would be waiting.

The next day while making his morning rounds, Gideon noticed people were smiling and staring more than usual. As he did every day, he tipped his hat to the ladies and shook hands with the various store owners. While having a conversation with the new owners of the general store, Andrew and Dorothy Bauernshub, Gideon noticed their two children, Summer and Gino, sitting off to the side smiling and pointing. Recently arrived from Germany a few months before, Mrs. Bauernshub was embarrassed by her children's behavior and scolded them. Gideon smiled because he didn't mind, so he used the opportunity to formally introduce himself to the youngsters. "Hello, my name is Sheriff Gideon and I am very pleased to meet you under more pleasant terms. I didn't get a chance to properly thank you for helping Ranger Mason."

Gideon explained to the parents both Gino and Summer were very helpful with the situation when Jon had to defend himself. Both Summer and Gino were very shy, so they didn't say much but reached out and patted Gideon on his arm as to say hello. Afterward, it was time to continue his rounds, so Gideon gave a hearty smile and then said his good-byes. As he tipped his hat and turned to walk out the door, he felt a small tug on his pants leg. As he turned to see Summer, he removed his hat, then knelt down on one knee so he could be equal in height. "Well, hello again, Ms. Summer. What can this humble sheriff do for you today?"

When Summer leaned forward to speak, Gideon could barely hear her soft words. "We heard there was a killer in town and he's gonna kill everybody."

When he heard those words, Gideon's smile quickly turned to a frown, but he immediately navigated the youngster's fears. "No, sweetheart. Where did you hear such nonsense?"

Just then, Gino mustered up some excitement. "Sheriff, we heard you beat'em up and blasted him with your six-shooter. Now you're the fastest gun-fighter ever."

Before Gideon could gather his thoughts, Mr. Bauernshub apologized for his children's outburst. "Sheriff, I'm really sorry, but there's a rumor going around town that you faced down a vicious killer yesterday. Please, the children didn't mean no harm. They were just repeating what they heard."

With a humble attitude, Gideon stood up straight and placed his hat on his head. He then took a deep breath and smiled. "Don't worry, folks, no harm done."

Before he left, Gideon leaned down to Summer and whispered some reassuring words to her. "I will never let anybody harm you or your family, and that's a promise." After excusing himself to take care of a few more errands, Gideon headed back to his office.

As the morning faded and the afternoon arrived, so did the stagecoach, and that meant mail. One letter in particular was addressed to Texas Ranger Jon Mason. It was his invite to dinner in accordance to the liking of the governor of Texas.

When Jubal finally made his appearance, he got an ear full from Gideon. In a slightly raised voice, Gideon stood up and leaned over his desk. "Jubal, with the few serious conversations we've had in the past, I thought I knew you a little better."

Jubal had stopped to get two coffees and was drinking one as he entered through the door. Not knowing what he was being scolded for, he handed Gideon the other coffee, then sounded off with some sarcasm. "Nice to see you too, boss man. Now, I know I can be a little slow in the brain sometimes, but for the sake of time, can you fill me in on what I'm about to be accused of before you continue your brow beating?"

Continuing with his raised voice, Gideon accepted the coffee. "Thank you." After sitting down and taking a few sips, the coffee seemed to calm him down.

Feeling slightly hesitant, Jubal grabbed a nearby chair and pulled it to the other side of Gideon's desk and sat down. As the two men continued to sip their coffees, Gideon was finally able to speak more clearly. "Apparently there's a rumor going around town about me facing down Pittman. I was over at the general store this morning paying respects to the Bauernshubs when their two children started praising my proficiency with a gun."

Still sipping his coffee, Jubal tried to piece together what Gideon was saying. "Gideon, I don't mind stepping up if I knew I did something wrong, but after our conversation yesterday, I grabbed a few supplies and left out of here to go help old man Jasper. He thinks a couple of Hayden's men rustled some of his cattle. Took me a few hours, but come to find out, Jasper is starting to lose his scruples. His daughter told me he forgets to close the gate sometimes and a few of those steers get the notion to wonder'n off. But I don't mind say'n, Jasper's daughter is easy on the eyes, so it's no bother for me going out there."

Not feeling so pressed anymore, Gideon smiled as he continued to sip his coffee. "I don't think there's anything wrong with old man Jasper. Every time I've talked to him, he seems to have his wits about him and he keeps an eye on those cattle like a hawk." After drinking down the last of his coffee, Gideon let out a small laugh. "I think maybe his daughter has something to do with those cattle disappearing every now and then. Maybe she wouldn't mind a certain deputy coming to see her more often."

With an image of a pretty woman gliding through his thoughts, Jubal finished his coffee, then smiled from ear to ear. "Maybe. It does seem she gets very affectionate towards me. She flashes that pretty little smile my way and gives me a peck on my cheek as a thank-you."

Before Gideon could continue his amusement with Jubal, Jon walked in with his own entertaining thoughts. "Well now, I heard congratulations are in order. I heard we have a real live hero for a sheriff."

With a tone of sarcasm in his voice, Jon pulled up a chair and sat down. "Sheriff Gideon, facing down the most notorious killer the west has ever known. Such bravery. Incredible heroism. Honorable courage and ever so fearless. So, what'ya have to say for yourself?"

Absorbing Jon's humor, Gideon sat back in his chair, shaking and scratching his head. "Well, I was just sitting here with Jubal trying to figure out this mess. I ran into one of Hayden's latest acquisitions yesterday and now I seem to be the hero of the year."

Anything to do with Zachariah Hayden, Jon definitely wanted to know about it. "Sounds like Hayden is planning something. So, who's the new gun hand?"

Gideon knew the colonel's reputation but wasn't as familiar as his deputy, so he turned to Jubal to explain. With his anxiety spilling over from the day before, Jubal gave Jon the short version. "Well, I know you weren't in the war, Jon, and be glad you weren't. Looks like Hayden went and hired Colonel Augusta Pittman. He's a relic from the Confederacy turned hired killer. He'll work for anyone who'll pay him top dollar for his services. He's more ruthless than the Apache and more brutal than the Comanche. Even the most infamous and well-known gunfighters won't dare challenge him. Blood-thirsty and ferocious, he's a savage in every sense of the word."

Unbeknownst to Jon, Colonel Pittman was the man who orchestrated the unprovoked attack on Jacob's men during the war, killing Bo and Chatter. Jon wasn't comfortable with what Jubal was saying and his thoughts ran rapid. If this is the type of man Hayden is willing to pay for, then what's the job he was hired to do? As the three men sat and talked, the subject of rumors going around town arose again. If not Gideon and Jubal, then who? While finding it somewhat humorous by now, everyone suddenly came to the same conclusion. Watching their eyes grow wide, Gideon sensed Jon and Jubal was thinking the same thing. "Rupert Hinklemeyer." Along with Gideon, Jon and Jubal were very familiar with Mr. Hinklemeyer. When he wasn't working, he loved to converse with the women and gossip. It was one of his favorite pastimes.

Now that they figured out the source, Gideon had to prepare a plan of action for when Colonel Pittman came calling. While Gideon was busy scheming, Jubal needed to stretch his legs, so while he decided to spot check the banks and see the stagecoach off, Jon voiced his concerns about Pittman. "I've heard a lot of names over the years, but somehow this Pittman character has escaped me. The way Jubal describes him, it doesn't sound like he's the kind of man that takes kindly to unfavorable rumors about himself. Are you worried?"

Feeling no concern for himself, Gideon stood up to stretch out his joints, then walked around the room. While thinking about the situation, he walked over to the window and glanced out at some of the townspeople walking by. "No. Not about me, but you know how some of the locals can get. They fill this jail every Friday and Saturday night. They start drinking and immerse their stomachs with liquid courage, and you know what comes next. They start shooting off at the mouth, then fire a couple of rounds in the air. If just one of them spouts off at a man like Pittman, he's liable to kill every one of them and claim self-defense, and I'd be hard tasked to prove otherwise."

Still concerned for Gideon, Jon let him know just how strong their friendship was. "Listen, Gideon. I've seen you fight with your gun as well as your hands, and I gotta say, you have one of the fastest draws I've ever seen. But if he does call you out, I'll be by your side if you feel you need me."

With gratitude, Gideon appreciated Jon's friendship and his words. As he reached out to shake his hand, he gave a quick smile. "Thanks, old friend, but hopefully it won't come to that. I'm thinking Pittman isn't the kind of man who hangs around in one town for too long, which brings me to the conclusion that he's here to do a job and leave. I don't think that job involves me, and I'm sure his ego and pride wouldn't get in the way of all the money Hayden's probably paying him. And I can't see him picking a fight with you. He'd be lynched before he made it out of Texas for gunning down a Texas Ranger."

Jon wasn't much for wearing his pride on his shoulders, but he couldn't help but throw in a little cynicism. "Now what makes you think he would beat me in a fair fight?"

Brushing off Jon's attempt at humor, Gideon shook his head then gawked. "Men like Pittman doesn't understand the word fair. Listen, we've pretty much come to a dead end with Hayden. Looking at what we know so far, we know he's crazy enough to be looking for some long-forgotten treasure, which we don't even know exists in the first place. We can't connect him to the murders or the disappearances, and he employs a small army for the protection of his interests. And now, he's hired the most ruthless gunfighter known. But why? What is Pittman here to do?"

Now, Jon was up pacing the floor, thinking about Hayden and Pittman and trying to figure out why Hayden needs such a man. Suddenly Gideon zeroed in on Jon's necklace. With some unconventional thoughts, he spoke out. "Seems to be Hayden has tried a few different times to get that necklace you're wearing. You think maybe he thinks it will lead him to his fabled treasure?"

Letting out a deep breath, Jon took a moment and latched onto the necklace while memories filled his thoughts. "No, I don't know. It hurts my head trying to figure out how Hayden thinks. The two old priests that took me in showed me a few things. The symbol on the front is the symbol for silver. The word on the back, Arizuma, also translates to silver. The priests told me it comes from some long-forgotten Aztec language used by the Pueblo Indians. I was told the monastery we lived in was built by the Franciscan monks. It had old paintings on the walls of monks and friars and pictures of conquistadors killing everybody. Probably Hayden's ancestors." With sadness in his heart, Jon momentarily relived all his past memories. "Father Andres and Father Santos are dead. The old monastery was destroyed by the war. The only thing left is a grave and a worn-out statue, which doubles as a grave marker."

While thoughts of doom and gloom took over, Jon glanced back down at his necklace. "No, I think Hayden is just grasping at straws. This necklace is old and probably made by some godforsaken Indian tribe that no longer exists. I don't think it has any meaning."

Gideon could see how the conversation was taking its toll, so he decided to back off for the time being. "All right. I'm sorry, Jon. I know you like to keep your past to yourself." Feeling a bit strained himself, Gideon sat back down at his desk and pulled out a bottle of whiskey. He poured two drinks and handed one to Jon. "I guess I'm just tired of trying to figure out Hayden's next move, and now with Pittman apart of the equation, you better believe there's going to be more killings."

Just then, Jubal came rushing back in with some disturbing news. "Gideon, I was just over at Molly's place. She was pretty upset. She told me a couple of her girls ride out to Jim Duggins' place once a week to do...well, you know, to do business. Anyhow, she said her girls took a ride out this morning and found the place abandoned. She said all the livestock was dead and Mr. Duggin was nowhere to be found. I spoke to the two women and they were pretty shook up. They were upset and crying. They told me they looked around for a few minutes, but they got an eerie feeling like somebody was watching, so they double-timed it back to town."

With a dry mouth, Jubal spotted the bottle on the table and helped himself to a drink. "It doesn't sound good, Gideon."

Jim Duggin was a loner. No wife or family, so Gideon was glad there were no notifications to make. "Damn. I was just out there a few weeks ago.

He rode into town to let me know he was having some problems with trespassers. He said he had seen a couple of riders off in the distance in one of his wheat fields, but when he went out to confront them, he said they disappeared into the woods. Apparently it wasn't the first time. He also told me he thought somebody was creeping around his place at night. During the mornings, he would notice things moved around and sometimes barn doors left open."

After a few more seconds of dismay, Gideon gulped down one last drink, then slammed the glass down out of frustration. "All right, Jubal. Why don't you and Jon take a ride out to Jim's place and take a look around while I pay a visit to our friend Hayden? We'll meet back here later."

After Jon and Jubal rode out, Gideon headed for the hotel with a full head of steam. When he walked in, he saw a few of the town's prominent women crowded around the front desk listening to Mr. Hinklemeyer's whispers. When Gideon removed his hat and approached, one of the ladies, Mrs. Caroline Beckett, spoke up for the rest. Mrs. Beckett was known to be very flirtatious and happen to be married to the owner of one of the three town banks. With her southern accent, she twisted and turned her body blushing with adoration. "Why, good afternoon, Sheriff. Such a fine day. Rupert was just telling us about Mr. Duggin. Such a shame what's going on in our quaint little town. Wouldn't you agree, Sheriff?"

Gideon knew any information he volunteered would wind up being completely misconstrued, so he attempted to sidestep any inquiries. "Well, Mrs. Beckett, we're doing our best to figure out the responsible party for all of our problems."

As Mrs. Beckett delighted in trying to make Gideon blush, she locked eyes with him and moved in closer, making an already uncomfortable situation worse. While she marveled at Gideon's humility, she ran her hand up his chest and across his badge. "As you know, Sheriff, my husband goes away quite often on business trips, leaving me all by my lonesome. If I shall say be in need of your services when things go bump in the night, could I count on a big, strong sheriff such as yourself to come be my protector?"

Trying to be polite, Gideon thought about taking a step back, but instead stood his ground. He had had enough of being toyed with, so he decided to turn the tables. "Well, Mrs. Beckett, I could come over to see that your needs are properly taken care of, but if Mr. Hinklemeyer should accidentally tell Mr. Beckett then you may lose access to all that money your husband has. Then you'll lose that life style you're so use to. And I may be mistaken, but I'm sure you wouldn't want to lose your status in our, as you would say, quaint little town."

Enjoying her mental chess game, Mrs. Becket stretched out her toes and stood on the balls of her feet in order to get within whispering distance of Gideon. "Very well played, Sheriff. I admire a man who knows how to handle a woman with a ferocious appetite. It just makes the chase that much more fun."

After taking her defeat with grace, Mrs. Becket turned to her lady friends. "Come now, ladies. I'm sure our fine sheriff has more important things to do than to play host to Presidio's elite."

As the women made their exit, Gideon turned to Mr. Hinklemeyer, who was staring back in disbelief. Gideon couldn't afford more rumors, so he raised his hand and pointed his finger at Mr. Hinklemeyer. "Not a word, Rupert. You hear me? Not a word. Now, is Mr. Hayden in?"

Still perplexed with what he was just privy to, Mr. Hinklemeyer shook off his wariness. "Um, yes, sir. You have my word. Won't tell a soul. And I do believe Mr. Hayden is in his room resting."

Peering over the front desk, Gideon smiled. "All right, Rupert. I don't wanna have to come back here."

As he mentally prepared for his encounter, Gideon walked toward the stairs and made his way up to Zachariah's room. As he approached the door, he tried the doorknob and found that it wasn't unlocked. Instead of showing respect and knocking, Gideon chose to burst through the door to see a surprised Zachariah jump up from his bed.

"I must say, Sheriff, I knew you were a heathen, but I would have thought you had more manners then to burst into a man's room without knocking. Now, what is so important that you must show your ignorance to me?"

With anger boiling deep down in his soul, Gideon slowly removed his gun belt. As it dropped to the floor, he stepped toward Zachariah and backhanded him across the face. As Zachariah fell back across his bed, Gideon maneuvered around the room and met him rolling off the other side. Before Zachariah could gather his composure, Gideon picked him up by his collar and backhanded him across the face again. "I don't take kindly to people like you in my town, Hayden." Still rattled, Zachariah was stunned as he tried to shake off the attack.

While Gideon fetched his gun belt and buckled it back on, Zachariah stood up and attempted to gather what little composure he had left. With his trembling voice and rubbing the sting off his face, Zachariah approached Gideon. "I don't take kindly to black folks laying their hands on me, you son of a bitch. Ten years ago I would have had you beaten near death then hung from a tree."

Wanting nothing more than to take another swing at Zachariah, Gideon held back his raging urge. Instead, he got up close and personal to Zachariah's face. "This isn't ten years ago and I'm your worst nightmare. A black man with a badge."

Not wanting any confusion, Gideon continued to explain his reasoning for being there. "Now, I've had just about enough of your rich, white, racist attitude. A lot of people have died or disappeared since you and your men arrived in my town. And you seem to have a knack for buying up their land. I also know you hired one of the most brutal killers north of the border. Before anyone else dies, I want to know why. Just what the hell are you trying to accomplish, Hayden?"

As Zachariah stood listening, a smile came upon his face. Still feeling the sting on his cheeks, he turned and walked to a nearby table and made himself a drink to settle his nerves. "I'd offer you a drink, Sheriff, but you seem to be on duty." Zachariah swallowed down his drink, then glanced over at Gideon and laughed. "Sheriff, do the words 'law and order' mean anything to you? Does it not occur to you that we live in a nation of laws? I'm guessing whomever was foolish enough to pin that tin star on your chest failed to advise you of these simple facts."

With his first drink already gone, Zachariah paused to pour himself another. "You burst into my room without just cause. Assault me several times, then accuse me of murder and kidnapping. Then, on top of everything else, you somehow fault me for being a shrewd businessman when making investments in real estate." Once again, Zachariah smiled as he wolfed down his drink. "I don't know what amuses me more: looking at the first black sheriff about to lose his badge or the fact that I'm the last person you're going to think of when death catches up to you."

Gideon didn't welcome the sarcasm of Zachariah, nor did he like the fact that Zachariah refused to provide an answer to his question. "I'm only going to ask you kindly one more time, Hayden. Why kill all those people and why hire Colonel Pittman?"

The sting on Zachariah's face was finally beginning to subside and he was feeling good about having Gideon dangling on a line like a puppet. "You might think that badge means something, Sheriff, but it doesn't give you the right to invade my privacy and demand answers. I will tell you this: I employed Colonel Pittman to supervise my men and to manage some of my more private affairs since your Ranger friend killed Johnson. Now, you have accused me of several awful crimes without a shred of evidence or proof. You've also accused me of being an unscrupulous businessman without feelings, and I may agree with that to a certain extent. As for the latter part of our conversation, my friends in Washington will be contacting the good governor of Texas and shortly thereafter, you will be stripped of your position. Now, I suggest you get the hell out of my room before I decide to have you jailed for assault."

Gideon knew his plan was questionable at best, but he felt he was running out of time and patience. Now, his badge was on the line because of his actions. As he slowly turned to walk out the door, he turned back around for one last confrontation. "Hayden, you're not the only one with friends in Washington. This isn't over." As Gideon turned to walk out, he couldn't help but feel disappointed but there was no turning back now. With even a bigger target on his back then before, he still had to figure out what Hayden was trying to accomplish while trying to keep his town safe.

As Gideon left the hotel, Jon and Jubal were arriving at the farmhouse of Jim Duggin. With an uneasy feeling starting to set in, both men sat atop their horses watching the wind blow around the tumbleweeds. Looking at each other with uncertainty, they climbed down from their horses. Without saying a word, Jubal pointed over toward the stables at the several dead cows and horses. Afterward, Jon glanced over at the pig pen and saw the slaughtered pigs. With dead chickens lying about and an unsettling feeling, the two men ventured inside the house. The stench of uncleanliness filled the air, but it was nothing the two men weren't use to dealing with, with drunks and dirty cowboys fresh off the cattle drives.

Jon and Jubal moved slowly but carefully around the small farmhouse looking for any clues to what happened, but none were found. Thinking back to what happen to the Taylors, Jon decided to check the well out back. As he walked out the back door, Jubal went to check the barn. Before Jon could look down the well, Jubal called out for him. When Jon walked into the barn, he was confronted with a gruesome sight. It was Jim Duggin hanging by the neck from the rafters with arrows shot into his body. With fifteen arrows stuck into his backside and front, he looked like a human pin cushion.

After cutting Mr. Duggin down, they buried him in a nearby field. After Jon said a small prayer, he glanced over at Jubal. "This was meant to look like Indians."

Knowing Indians weren't involved, Jubal shook his head with disgust. "Indians would have taken the livestock and wouldn't have wasted the arrows. This was no Indians. Old Jim wasn't a friend of nobody, but he didn't bother anyone either. He didn't deserve to die like this."

While the two men started their trek back to Presidio, Gideon was trying to calm himself down by making his rounds and greeting the townspeople. As usual, he headed for the post office to see if any new Wanted flyers had arrived. Henry Granville was the postmaster and was up in age. He was set in his ways but sharp as a tack. Growing up in a different era, Henry loved to challenge Gideon whenever he came into his office. With his sense of humor, Gideon didn't mind. He always found Henry to be amusing. He also enjoyed the stories Henry sometimes told about how life used to be before Gideon was born.

Gideon knew Henry had an annoyance about improper dress and manners and would immediately notice if Gideon did something wrong. So for fun, he undid a few of the top buttons of his shirt and untucked one side before entering. And as a bonus, he entered without removing his hat. As expected, when Henry peeked up over top of his glasses and saw Gideon smiling from ear to ear, he became agitated. As he removed his glasses and stood up, he looked Gideon up and down. "Boy, what did I tell you about coming in here without taking off that hat? And button up those buttons and tuck in that shirt. You look like one of those damn European Casanovas."

Still smiling, Gideon took a few seconds to remove his hat and fix his shirt. "Yes'ems Mista Henry, sir. You's Knows us young Negra's, we'ze ignorant and we'ze don't likes to piss off the white folk."

With his hands on his hips, all Henry could do was shake his head and smile. "Damn you, Gideon, I know your folks taught you better. Why do you constantly try to annoy me?"

After making himself presentable, Gideon pulled a cigar from his shirt pocket and handed it to Henry. "The same reason you constantly challenge me. Now, what do you have for me today?"

Running the cigar under his nose, Henry smiled. "Hmm. A cigar a day keeps Doc Belle away. Although, if she sees me smoking this, she'd probably hit me with a frying pan."

Watching Henry light the cigar, Gideon let out a small laugh. "If she knew I gave it to you, then I'll be the one getting hit with the frying pan."

After a few smooth puffs of his cigar, Henry picked up some papers and handed them to Gideon. "New flyers for you. James-Younger gang. It's getting pretty bad. Pinkerton's got involved. Blew up their farmhouse and killed Jesse James's half-brother. The explosion also blew his mother's arm off."

As Gideon viewed the posters, Henry kept talking. "You can bet it's gonna get worse before it's all over. Just hope they don't come here."

With a few more seconds of shuffling through the papers, Gideon finished viewing the posters. "No, I don't think we have anything to worry about, Henry. I can't see Jesse James running south to Mexico. So, what else do you have?"

With Jon in mind, Henry rustled through a stack of papers and pulled out an envelope. After he handed it to Gideon, he took a couple more puffs of his cigar. "That's for your Ranger friend. Looks important."

While Henry continued to enjoy his cigar, Gideon studied the envelope and saw it was from the governor's office. "Well, old man, you have a good eye. It happens to be very important."

Removing the cigar from his mouth, Henry belted out some words. "Old man, my ass. This old man will put a whoop'n on you next time you come in here talking trash."

Once again Gideon smiled from ear to ear as he placed his hat back on, then turned to walk out the door. "Yes, sir, Mr. Henry, sir. Thank'ya kindly, sir."

Feeling that Gideon got the best of him, Henry smiled, then placed his glasses back on his face as he sat down and smoked the rest of his cigar.

While Gideon finished walking the town, Colonel Pittman met with Zachariah to review the plan one last time, but neither man was very happy. The colonel had been in the general store earlier in the day and heard some people talking about the confrontation with Gideon. He had also noticed some of the towns-folk pointing and laughing as he walked over to the hotel. Zachariah, on the other hand, was still upset about the assault he had suffered earlier at the hands of Gideon. As Zachariah invited the colonel to sit, he made himself a drink and offered the colonel some water.

Frustrated at what he had heard, the colonel pulled a fancy pipe from his pocket and filled it with tobacco. As he lit it and took a few puffs, he took a deep breath with some resentment. "Mr. Hayden, I haven't been in this township for very long, but meeting your black sheriff and being privy to some vicious rumors, I'm not liking it. I'm not liking it not one bit. So, if you don't mind, sir, after I dispose of those pesky Rangers, I'll be killing that sheriff of yours for free."

With frustration of his own, Zachariah swallowed his drink with conviction. "No, sir. This is not my town and I couldn't care less about its Negro sheriff. I had a little run in with him earlier and before you kill him, I need you to do me a favor."

With a few more puffs on his pipe, Colonel Pittman sat up with some enthusiasm. "Please, sir, continue."

With the memory still fresh in his mind, Zachariah paused, then walked to a nearby mirror. As he stared at his face, he thought about what Gideon did. He then glanced at his hands as he held them up in front of him. "Kill him however you want, but before you do, cut off both his hands and make sure he knows it was at my request."

Enjoying the plan, the colonel lit a match, then sat back and smiled as he re-lit his tobacco. "I like your style, Mr. Hayden. I like your style."

After going over the final arrangements, Zachariah suggested the colonel stay out of town until the job was done. This would keep any unfortunate mishaps from compromising their negotiations. Afterward, the two men shook hands and parted ways.

While the colonel was making his way out of town, Jon and Jubal were just arriving back into town. After dropping their horses off at the livery stable, they met Gideon back at his office. As the two men walked in, their long faces told Gideon all he needed to know. "I'm guessing you found Mr. Duggin?"

With a long face, Jon took a seat while Jubal started a pot of coffee. "We found him. Full of arrows. Buried him out in the field behind his house. Someone tried to make it look like an Indian attack, but we knew better. Same modus operandi. Everything in place. Nothing missing. Livestock dead. Occupant dead. I don't know, Gideon. It just doesn't make any sense. Some of these properties have mountain ranges off in the distance and some have streams or rivers nearby, but what the hell is Hayden hoping to find that the Spanish, the Jesuits, and several centuries of treasure hunters couldn't? There's no treasure and probably never was."

Gideon didn't have an answer, but he had just as much anger and frustration as Jon, Jubal, and the rest of the citizens of Presidio. After a couple of moments of uneasy silence, Gideon handed Jon his letter. "Here, this came for you today. It's from the governor's office."

Jon wasn't the Texas Ranger in charge of the investigation, so he had no idea what the letter was about. After opening the envelope, he skimmed down the page and realized it was an invitation to a party. "Well now, speak of the devil. The governor is requesting me to attend a dinner party hosted by Zachariah Hayden. And the language seems to be more of a 'must attend with no exceptions.' Isn't that just cozy."

Feeling suspicious, Jon handed the letter back to Gideon so he could read it. Afterward, Gideon laughed. "After you two left earlier, I went over to see Hayden. I can honestly say, I completely lost my mind. I decided to try and beat some answers out of him, but it didn't go very well."

Listening to what Gideon was saying, Jubal finished with the coffee and made a cup for everyone. "Well, you don't look any worse for the wear. I would've given anything to see that fight."

Gideon thanked Jubal for the coffee with a smile, then stood up to stretch his legs. "Wasn't much to see. He's going to try and take my badge, but I'm not too worried about that." Staring out the window, Gideon sipped his coffee. "So, Jon. The letter said the party is tomorrow night. I'm guessing all the other Rangers are on their way here. I'm sure Hayden will have men with him, including Pittman. Maybe somebody will slip up and say something."

Thinking along the same lines, Jon agreed. The party would be a good opportunity to find out information. "All right. I'll head over to the telegraph office before I head home. Hopefully Gunny sent word on a time and place for a meet."

While Jubal manned the office, Gideon walked with Jon to take care of his own problems. When the two men arrived at the telegraph office, Jon was handed a telegram that Gunny had sent earlier that day. He explained that the party was formal and was being held for the purpose of good will. He also noted the Governor of Texas was holding it in high regard. No guns were to be displayed or concealed. Jon wasn't comfortable with the idea but understood. After saying his good-byes, he left Gideon to his business.

After the threats from Zachariah, Gideon didn't want to take any chances. Hayden wasn't the only one with friends in D.C. After Gideon was done sending his telegram, he headed to the Lucy Goosy. While Gideon was winding down his day, Jon arrived home to spend some time with his family. He was looking forward to being just an ordinary person and not having to travel the state chasing outlaws and Indians. Before spending time with Emily, Jon had children duty. Adam and Abram chasing Jon with their toy guns and bows and arrows, and even Abby joined in on the fun. Afterward, it was dinner, chores, and bedtime stories.

The rest of the night was spent with Emily, talking about their future and possibly having another child. The next day, Jon was up earlier than usual. Before leaving, he peeked in on the children while they were still sleeping. He then said his good-byes to Emily. With his arms wrapped around her, he stared into her eyes for the longest time as to give her comfort and strength. "I promise, after this investigation comes to an end, we'll have the rest of our lives to spend together."

Feeling a bit uncertain, something deep down was tugging at her heart, but Emily didn't want to place any more pressure on Jon. "As long as the rest of our lives include you holding me tight and keeping our family safe. I love you, Jon."

After a long, passionate kiss good-bye, Jon rode into town to meet with Gideon and to go over a few last-minute details. The party was being held in the grand ballroom of the hotel and Jon wanted to get a list of working personnel, especially the people who were serving the food and drinks. He also needed to have enough stable personnel available to see to the Rangers' horses.

As Gideon and Jon walked over to the hotel, they were met by Doc Belle. "Hey boys. Nice to see a couple of handsome fellas. Jon, how are Emily and the children?"

After a big smile and a hello hug, Jon was happy to talk about his family. "Funny you should ask, Belle. Emily and I were just talking about how nice it's going to be when I take this badge off for good."

Belle was always glad to see Jon and Gideon, but she had heard about Mr. Duggin and was getting more and more worried about future happenings. "Gideon, please tell me you have some idea of what's been going on with all these deaths and disappearances."

Not wanting to worry Belle more than what she was, Gideon reassured her that he was doing everything in his power to find the people responsible.

"I know you're tough, Belle, but I would feel a lot better if I knew Thomas agreed to ride with you when you went on your weekly trips to the Indian villages."

Feeling warm inside, all Belle could do was smile. "Are you kidding? Thomas jumped at the chance when I asked. He would never miss a Sunday afternoon ride in the country with me. Especially with the way I pack a picnic basket."

After a few more laughs, Belle had to leave to attend to some sick patients while Jon and Gideon spoke to Mr. Hinklemeyer. When asked about the guest list along with the personnel working the party, Mr. Hinklemeyer informed Jon that very few service personnel were requested. As for the guest list, besides the twenty-five Texas Rangers, there was Mr. Hayden, some of the town's council members, to include the bankers Mr. Irwin Beckett and wife, Mr. Arthur Lloyd III and wife, and Mr. Harold Schweitzer. Also included were personal guests of Mr. Hayden, which Jon and Gideon figured to be hired guns. And, of course, the mayor and his wife.

After leaving the hotel, the two men walked down to the stables to speak with Thomas. He informed Jon there were no special provisions made for a large amount of horses, but if needed he could prepare the stables and make sure the Rangers' horses were attended to. After thanking Thomas, Jon helped Gideon make his rounds, then the two headed over to the Lucy Goosy to have a drink and to figure out why Hayden would host such a grand party but not have extra personnel to provide service.

With it still being early in the day, there were no patrons in the bar, so Ms. Lita sat with the two lawmen and had a drink. While the three enjoyed their drinks, Jon became more and more bothered. "Ms. Lita, you've lived here all your life and I know there's been big events in the past. Extravagant parties and town events. Have you ever known these events to be rudimentary?"

Tapping into her memories, Ms. Lita thought for a moment and then smiled. "Not at all. Even that old squatter Leroy that use to live on the outskirts of town in that old beat-up shack. He came stumbling into town one day and swore he found gold. Threw one hell of a shindig at the hotel's expense. That old goat coordinated everything from the food on the menu to the services he promised to pay for." Ms. Lita laughed as she took a small sip of her drink. "I'll tell you, after that party, Hinklemeyer found out the gold Leroy discovered was fool's gold. Hinklemeyer was so hot, you could have fried an egg on his face in the middle of winter."

While the three laughed at the story, Jon couldn't help but think something wasn't right. "I don't know. Part of Hayden's claim to fame is his family background. His education and how proper he is. It just doesn't make any sense that he wouldn't have this party better planned."

Wanting some temporary relief from thinking too hard, Jon wanted to hear the end of Leroy's tale. "So, what ever happen to Leroy?"

With a long face, Ms. Lita shook her head. "He was old and stubborn. Always messing around with that homegrown brew. Doc Micah, rest his soul, tried to get him to stop drinking it, but he wouldn't listen. After that fiasco, Hinklemeyer tried to have him thrown in jail, but everyone knew Leroy was at his end. He eventually destroyed his liver and died. And in the end, the town had to pay for his burial. How ironic." Once again, Ms. Lita smiled. "Here's to old Leroy, who pulled a fast one and got over on all of us."

By now the town was in full swing. The stores were busy selling goods and the townspeople were busy walking from one end of the town to the other. Since the end of the war, Presidio had grown. Along with the town, the competition was growing. Several banks now dominated the town's finances, and several general stores competed for customers, along with two dress shops, three Chinese cleaning shops, and even Molly had her problems trying to get return customers while competing with other newly opened brothels.

The town's regulars started to show up, so Ms. Lita had to open the bar and get ready for her day. Jon had brought his dress attire with him so the idea was to have lunch with Gideon then a bath at the local bath house. Afterward, meet the other Rangers at the arranged meeting place. Gideon had errands to run, so he told Jon he would meet him at the new restaurant for lunch. After the two men parted ways, Gideon headed over to the telegraph office. After he had sent off his telegram the day before, he was now hoping for a positive response.

Post-Civil War was considered the reconstruction era for the United States. More than 1,500 African Americans held public office during this time. Gideon being the first African American sheriff in a southern state such as Texas was big news for the political arena. When Gideon entered the telegraph office, he was met with all smiles and handed the information he was waiting on. Before unfolding the paper, he decided to walk out and read it in private. Before reading, he smiled and tipped his hat at a few of the town's well-known women walking by. Afterward, he took a deep breath and started reading.

> *It has come to my attention that Texas has been plagued by mysterious and unfortunate events, stop. I understand the Texas Rangers are involved and that you're doing everything possible to keep the town of Presidio safe, stop. Do not despair, stop. Times of hardship are often met with corruption which will test your courage, stop. I pledge to you my full support, stop. Signed Ulysses S. Grant, President of the United States of America, stop.*

The day before, Gideon had sent a telegram to Mr. Walter Moses Burton explaining his interaction with Zachariah Hayden. A former slave, Walter Burton was elected to the Texas State Senate in 1873 and was aware of Gideon being the sheriff of Presidio. Understanding the hardships which Gideon faced, Senator Burton sent his own telegram, which caught the attention of the President.

With a smile on his face and filled with relief, Gideon walked back to the Lucy Goosy to have a drink before meeting Jon for lunch. When he walked in, he saw Zachariah Hayden with two of his henchmen standing at the bar. Gideon paused in the doorway as Zachariah turned his head in Gideon's direction. "Well now, Sheriff, don't be shy. Come on in and let me buy you a drink."

Gideon didn't like the tone displayed by Zachariah, but he wasn't about to turn tail and run. As he entered the bar, Zachariah ordered a whiskey for him. With an arrogant smile, he too had also received information from friends in Washington. For spite, Zachariah turned his attentions to his two associates. "Did you fellas know our fine sheriff here is a formidable political opponent?" With some sarcasm, Zachariah slammed his hand down on the bar. "Well, I'm just flabbergasted that this Negro ceases to utterly amaze me."

The new bartender, Tommy, was young and from Kansas and was unaware of Zachariah Hayden, but he could feel the tension in the air. As he poured the whiskey for Gideon, his hand shook while Zachariah continued with his banter. "Now tell me, Sheriff, how does a Negro such as yourself get cozy with such important men in Washington?"

Before Gideon could give an adequate answer, Zachariah rudely cut him off. "Never mind, Sheriff. I'm sure you and your Negro friends are thicker than thieves."

Not wanting to accept anything from Zachariah Hayden, Gideon glanced down at the drink Tommy had placed in front of him but didn't bother to pick it up. "Hayden, up until now, I've been very patient with you and the language you choose to use against me, but I've had enough of your ignorance and insults."

Feeling he had finally gotten under Gideon's skin, Zachariah decided to press on. As his two men were finishing up the bottle they had, Zachariah gave them a nod to step outside. "Well now, Sheriff, why don't you step outside so we can find out if you have the guts to back up that badge?"

Watching the two men walk out, Gideon knew if he stepped outside, he was going to have to take the fight all the way to include killing Zachariah Hayden. Taking a moment to react, Gideon peered into Zachariah's eyes, hoping to see some kind of weakness, but they were giving up no secrets. Running the scenario through his thoughts, killing two men in self-defense was okay, but knowing Zachariah carried no gun, Gideon was going to, nevertheless, put a bullet in his head. He would rather deal with the consequences afterward then to let any more innocent people die. Disappointed in knowing what he had to do, Gideon finally gave in to the hatred he felt for Zachariah. "All right, Hayden. All right. If this is how you want to end it, then we'll do it your way."

Not knowing what to expect, Gideon unfastened his gun and walked toward the door. As he approached the door, he stopped to glance back at Zachariah. With a huge smile on his face, Zachariah raised his drink to Gideon as he waited for him to walk out. "Good-bye, Sheriff."

A man like Zachariah Hayden, Gideon could sense an unfeeling coldness coming from his words. He was also unfamiliar with the two men Zachariah had waiting for him and had the feeling it was purposely planned this way. Fear was never an issue, but the hatred Gideon felt was gone and something else had taken its place. He had never been in a position to where he would be forced to kill a man in cold blood. But now, this was what he had to deal with. In Gideon's mind, he had no other alternative because it was a means to an end. As Gideon turned, he pushed open the saloon doors and walked out. As he looked around, he saw the townspeople walking up and down the street greeting each other, wagons passing by being pulled by horses, and everyday life unfolding as it normally did in Presidio. The only thing he didn't see was the two men from the saloon.

As he stood in front of the saloon, a husband and wife walked by and greeted Gideon, then kept walking. Still surprised, Gideon gave a half-smile, then tipped his hat. "Have a nice day, folks."

Just then he heard the saloon doors open and turned to see Zachariah Hayden staring at him with a smile. Zachariah paused, then pulled out a shiny pocket watch to check the time. "Well now, Sheriff. You have zeal, I'll give you that. You didn't really think I would have you killed in broad daylight, did you?"

As Zachariah placed his watch back into his pocket, he walked past Gideon then turned to face him. "I bet my boys a steak dinner you didn't have the backbone to step out of those doors."

Still stunned at the outcome, Gideon just stood and stared at Zachariah as he basked in his glory. Relishing in his temporary win, Zachariah was about to walk away, but had a few last words for Gideon. "Don't worry, Sheriff. Your time will come. Sooner than you think. Your time will come."

As Zachariah walked away feeling good about himself, Gideon was left feeling even more anger knowing he was backed into a corner just for the purpose of being a puppet in one of Zachariah's warped games. With his tension level starting to decline, Gideon took a walk and checked on a few of the businesses, then walked to the restaurant where he was meeting with Jon.

The sun was high in the sky and the town was booming with business during the arrival of early afternoon. As Gideon walked into Sidewinders restaurant, he was greeted by Miss Isabella, the proud owner of the newest restaurant in town. "Well, howdy, Sheriff. I don't think we've had the pleasure of having you as our guest yet."

Still feeling the effects of his confrontation from earlier, Gideon smiled as he slowly removed his hat. "No, ma'am. I haven't had the satisfaction of having a meal in your fine establishment."

Miss Isabella was a very outgoing woman and loved to make people feel at home. As the smile on her face expanded, she looped her arm around Gideon's arm and guided him to the dining room. "Your friend Ranger Jon is already seated and waiting."

As Gideon was guided to the table, he quietly sat down across from Jon and, without a word, opened his menu. Wanting to make sure Gideon and Jon had the best experience, Miss Isabella offered the first two drinks on the house. "Well, boys, let me get you a couple of beers on me while you decide what fantastic cuisine you're going to pick off the menu."

While Miss Isabella responded to the bar, Jon sat and stared at Gideon. "Rough morning?"

Taking a deep breath and finally feeling at ease, Gideon placed the menu down on the table. With a serious look on his face, Gideon finally spoke. "Don't think too harsh of me when I tell you this, but I think we're dealing with Satan himself."

Not trying to judge Gideon to strongly, Jon let out a small giggle. "Hayden is just a man. A man with many resources, but in any case, just a man."

With Zachariah Hayden still fresh on his mind, Gideon paused then took another breath. "Yeah, I know. But if Satan had a son, Hayden would be it. I had the unfortunate experience of looking into his eyes a little while ago. That man's soul is darker than those black eyeballs you have. I don't think there's any limit to the evil that man spews out."

While the two men sat and talked, Miss Isabella placed two beers on the table. "What'ya boys have for lunch? By the way, we appreciate the presence of law enforcement, so lunch is half-price for you two handsome devils."

With smiles on their faces and a welcoming feeling flowing through their bodies, the two men gladly placed their orders.

After lunch, many compliments went to the chef and to Miss Isabella for the good food and the hospitality. As the two men made their exit, Gideon needed to go meet Jubal at the office while Jon readied himself for a nice, hot bath. Jon was aware that Molly's establishment supplied bathing services, but he didn't want to take the chance of having his intentions being misunderstood, so he made his way over to one of the Chinese bath houses. Once there, a hot bath was quickly drawn as Jon undressed and sat down in a large tub made for two. As his bones started to take in the heat, Jon took a deep breath and began to sink into the hot, relaxing water.

Just when he thought it couldn't get any better, he opened his eyes to see a young, pretty Chinese woman standing in front of him wearing nothing but a long, see-through silk and lace garment. With the woman being very pleasing to his eyes, Jon sat up and grabbed the sides of the tub for support. "Well now, what do we have here? You look very nice, but I'm just here for a hot bath."

Armed with just her smile, the woman didn't say anything at first. She took a few steps toward Jon, then removed her garment, giving Jon a full view of what she had to offer. "You like?" The woman then raised her arm and rubbed her hand across her breast and down one side. "My name Jinjing. You like? I want to be with you. You want me?"

Feeling flattered, Jon smiled while attempting to be pleasant. "No, sweetheart. You're very nice, but I'm just here for a bath."

After accepting Jon's wishes, Jinjing proceeded to step into the tub without any feelings of rejection. She then scooped some of the water and poured it down Jon's back. At the same time, she rubbed soap and some fragrance oils onto his body and began to bath him. Rubbing his shoulders with her hands, she pressed up against him with her breasts, working her hands down to Jon's hips and beyond.

While Jon enjoyed his bathing experience, Gideon was busy meeting with Jubal. With all the past happenings along with the crazy theories and speculations, the two men came to the conclusion that whatever Hayden was planning, it was going to happen sooner than later. And knowing about the dinner function for the Texas Rangers going on later that night, it seemed like a good time for Hayden to execute whatever plan he had.

Trying to think ahead, Jubal thought it a good idea to walk down and talk with Thomas. Knowing there was no plans to welcome the Rangers' horses, Jubal had the idea of having Thomas up on the roof top with a rifle. While Jubal was making arrangements with Thomas, Gideon was visiting Ms. Lita, who didn't take much convincing to close up shop earlier than usual. And of course, she offered up her shotgun services. She was happy to be on standby with extra slugs. Gideon also had conversations with a few more of the business owners, who agreed to standby with rifles.

As Gideon and Jubal readied the town for whatever Hayden was planning, Jon was busy getting dressed in his nice suit so he could go and meet Gunny and the other Rangers. With Jinjing still in the nude, Jon already had his pants on and was buttoning his shirt. As he quickly dressed, Jinjing walked over and handed him a jade coin with a horse on one side and a dog on the other. Wrapping her arms around his neck, she straightened Jon's crooked collar. "You come back to visit?"

Feeling refreshed, Jon stopped for a moment and stared into Jinjing's eyes. He gently placed both hands on her cheeks, then bent over and gave her a short soft kiss on her lips. "Yes, I will come back to visit, but only for a hot bath."

With some worry in her heart, Jinjing smiled. "You bring coin when you trouble."

Feeling clean and rejuvenated, Jon saddled up and headed out of town to meet the other Texas Rangers at the old forgotten cattle road. It wasn't too far of a ride, so it didn't take long for Jon to arrive.

Of course, Gunny was right up front with a big smile on his face. "Well now, young'n, glad you could grace us with your presence." With his nose starting to twitch, Gunny leaned into Jon and took a sniff. "Damn boy, you smell like a French whore house. Not that I've ever been to one, mind you."

Trying not to blush, Jon gave a small laugh, then shook Gunny's hand. "Damn glad to see you too, Gunny. What do you make of this whole good will party thing?"

Always giving his most honest opinion, Gunny momentarily looked away and smiled, then turned back around to face Jon. "Well, if you ask me and I do believe you're asking me, I think it's a pile of horse manure, but what do I know? What the governor wants, the governor gets, and where he points, we go. But I tell you what, I feel more naked than a buffalo's ass without a gun, but the governor never said anything about knives. I have a nice Bowie knife strapped to my leg just in case any of Hayden's men get out of line. If need be, I'll shove this knife where the sun don't shine and spin them around like a piñata."

Typical Gunny. Always with a plan of violence. With laughter in the air and the mood of feeling good, Jon turned his horse back toward town. Starting their trek toward Presidio, the Texas Rangers rode in military-style two-by-two formations, with Gunny and Jon leading the way. Along the way, Gunny and Jon spoke about past experiences and plans both men had for the future.

While the Rangers enjoyed their afternoon ride toward town, Colonel Pittman and his men were setting up for their "Welcome to Presidio" salute as the men took their places along the overlook. Three men were on each side of the canyon armed with their special-made Winchester rifles. As they waited, some passed the time by chewing tobacco and spitting it out at the crawling targets on the ground. Others checked and rechecked their arsenals just to keep their minds occupied. But Colonel Pittman was of a different breed. He didn't chew tobacco and he knew exactly how much ammunition he had. With his time finally at hand, his mind was set on killing Jon in retribution for his brother. For every minute that went by, the colonel's anger and hatred grew stronger and deeper.

Just then, the colonel and his men could see a little dust kicking up off in the distance. With the sun at their backs and shining bright, it made the plan that much better. Anticipating the assault, the men spit out their tobacco while setting their rifles in place. Perched up in their rock fortress, Colonel Pittman and his men waited.

As Pittman's men readied themselves, the Texas Rangers got closer. As with every ride with Gunny, there were always stories being told and this ride was no different. As the Rangers moved along, Jon was listening and laughing at a story Gunny was telling about being in a bar room fight with three prostitutes, a blind dog, and a man with one leg.

As Gunny finished telling his story, he noticed the wind starting to pick up and a strange silence was now filling the air. Along with his intuition, the hair on the back of his neck stood up, signaling the feeling that something was wrong. With the wind kicking up the dust and the dirt, some of the horses became spooked, so he brought the men to a halt. As the Rangers stood fast, the colonel and his men looked on from a distance. Recalling his experience, the colonel instantly reverted to his military days. Who was going to make the first move? And whatever you do, don't flinch. The colonel surveyed the distance and figured the Rangers to be approximately sixty yards away. Too far to open fire because he would then be taking the chance of some of the Rangers being able to retreat and take cover. With time being an issue, Colonel Pittman knew the Rangers couldn't turn back or divert to another route, and with them being unarmed, he decided to exercise patience.

With the sun in his eyes, Gunny was beginning to feel a little anxious. The Texas Ranger inside was telling him to send a scout ahead, but in the best interest of time, the politician inside was telling him to move forward. So, with hesitant thoughts, he signaled the men to slowly proceed with caution. Still in a two-by-two formation, the Rangers began their trek toward a preset battle to the death. They could see the road starting to narrow but had no idea what lay ahead as they continued onward.

As the canyon became narrower, they remained vigilant and attempted to scan the above rocks, but with the sun beating down in their eyes, it was difficult at best. With the Rangers closing the gap, Colonel Pittman watched and counted the distance to which he felt comfortable with. Fifty yards. Forty yards. After letting the Rangers cross over the thirty-yard threshold, the colonel waited a few more seconds then gave the order. "Fire!" Without hesitation or bias, Colonel Pittman and his men open fired on the defenseless Texas Rangers.

Not being able to see their foes, Gunny, Jon, and the rest of the Rangers inadvertently rode head on into a barrage of bullets. Like pigs to a slaughter, one by one, the Rangers fell. Death came instantly for some of the Rangers while others lost control of their confused horses and were thrown to the ground. The colonel thought he made good on his word when Jon took three bullets to his upper body and fell face down to the ground. Gunny was grazed across the left side of his head while another bullet found his left arm. With no way to balance himself, he too was thrown from his horse. As he stood up and looked around at the mass casualties, he noticed Jon lying face down in a pool of his own blood. By now, all the other Rangers had succumbed to their final resting place.

Finally the colonel gave the order to cease fire so the dust could settle and they could view their destruction. As the dust swiveled and swirled in the wind, it began to settle to the ground. Colonel Pittman could see Gunny bleeding from his head and dripping blood from his arm while he stumbled around from dead Ranger to dead Ranger. Then, as a last stand, Gunny pulled the Bowie knife from his side and placed it over his badge. By now the sun had subsided so he could partially see the six men responsible for the slaughter. Seeing their rifles aimed directly at him, he slowly raised his Bowie knife to the heavens and shouted, "Come get it!"

Feeling a little admiration for Gunny and his last stand, Colonel Pittman gave one last order of execution. "Fire!"

Six bullets entered Gunny's chest as the tough and hardened Texas Ranger fell to the ground. With blood gushing from his body, his eyes slowly closed for the last time.

Seeing that some of the horses were still standing, including Jon's horse, Sapphire, Colonel Pittman ordered the men to shoot them down because

Zachariah Hayden wouldn't have it any other way. Afterward, Colonel Pittman climbed down from the overlook to inspect his work and to retrieve the necklace worn by Jon.

Without warning, the wind started to pick up again and the sky grew dim. The sun withdrew behind the clouds, which were beginning to turn dark. With the sound of thunder making the sky grumble, it seemed a heavy storm was about to hit. Off in the distance, Colonel Pittman could see a lone Indian sitting atop a painted Pinto, staring as though he was somehow responsible for the rapidly approaching storm. Knowing he only had five men, he didn't want to risk a confrontation with an Apache war party, so he and his men quickly retreated back to town.

It was later in the day and Zachariah was sitting in the hotel's grand ballroom having a drink when Gideon walked in and sat down. Once again, Zachariah reprimanded Gideon for his lack of manners. "Sheriff, I know you're a heathen, but just out of curiosity, were you raised that way or did you just happen to fall into the ignorant and stupid category?"

Gideon wasn't in the mood for Zachariah's sarcasm, so he got straight to the point of his visit. "What's going on, Hayden? You're minutes away from your big fancy party and none of your guests have arrived. You've made no provisions for the visiting Texas Rangers or their horses, and Mr. Hinklemeyer informed me you've made no arrangements for extra hired help."

Before Gideon could badger Zachariah more, the town's mayor, Mr. Edmund Tucker, and his wife Eleanor walked in. Graciously, Zachariah stood up to greet his guests. "Mr. Mayor, always an honor and a pleasure, sir, to see you and your lovely wife. I wanted to humble myself and thank you for accepting my invitation. It's going to be a wonderful evening."

After shaking hands, the mayor smiled as he glanced around the room. "I see we're the first to arrive, Mr. Hayden." He then turned his attentions to Gideon. The mayor was new and had nothing to do with voting in Gideon as sheriff, and as a southern sympathizer had no real respect for him. But nevertheless, he was always graceful in speaking to Gideon. "Nice to see you, Sheriff. Will you be staying for this evening's festivities?"

Gideon knew the Mayor wasn't a big fan of his, but at the same time always shared a mutual accord. "No, sir, Mr. Mayor. I won't be staying. I have some duties to attend to tonight."

Feeling the need to make his exit, Gideon utilized his charm and excused himself. "Mr. Mayor, Mrs. Eleanor, always nice to see the both of you."

As Gideon was walking out the door, the three bankers—Mr. Beckett, Mr. Lloyd, and Mr. Schweitzer—along with their wives, walked in. With a smile, Gideon gave a short, elegant greeting, then proceeded out the door.

Even more puzzled that guests were actually arriving, Gideon and Jubal stood across the street and watched to see exactly how many guests showed up. Within the hour, everybody who was supposed to be in attendance had arrived. All except Jon and the rest of the Texas Rangers.

Just before Gideon was about to withdraw to his office, he saw Colonel Pittman and his men riding into town. With curiosity tugging at their thoughts, Gideon and Jubal watched as they rode in and tied their horses up in front of the Lucy Goosy. After they entered the saloon, Gideon had Jubal take a walk over to keep an eye on them while he went to check on the men he had posted around town. As he walked through the town, Gideon could see Thomas peering over one of the roof tops and giving him the thumbs up. Gideon quickly checked the other deputized men, then doubled back to meet with Jubal.

As Gideon quickly made his way back through town, Jubal was making his exit from the saloon. Stepping off to the side, Jubal walked back across the street and gave Gideon his analysis. "Well, boss, they're still in there. They're not say'n much at all. Real quiet like. That snake of a colonel is sitting at a table way back in the corner by himself and he's got that look about himself. Like the cat that just ate the canary kind of look, if'n you know what I mean. He saw me walk in but declined to insult me, which tells me he's up to someth'n. I can feel it in my bones. Someth'n ain't right."

With his hands on his hips, Gideon glanced down at the ground and shook his head. "I don't know, Jubal. You're right. Something is terribly wrong, but with Hayden entertaining his very prominent guests and Pittman here in the saloon, I can't imagine what the hell it could be."

After a few more minutes of waiting, the wind started to kick up the dust and the tumbleweeds were making their rounds through town, so Gideon decided to call it a night. "Do me a favor, Jubal. Looks like we're about to get hit with a pretty big storm, so send the men home to their families."

Jubal agreed but before doing so, he had one last observation. "Gideon, not sure if you noticed or not, but take a look at Pittman's horse. Check out the rifle he has hanging off his saddle. If you notice, all of them have the same rifle."

Taking note, Gideon glanced over at the colonel's horse, then at the others. "You're right, Jubal. It doesn't look like your ordinary everyday saddle rifle."

Not that it was a laughing matter, but Jubal let out a small chuckle. "That's a Winchester 1873 with a custom scope and quite a few other specialty items. Nope, I'd say nothing ordinary about it. Saw one at a gun show once. Very expensive. Big game hunters like to use them, but I know some questionable bounty hunters and other lowlifes like to use them for killing their targets from a distance."

Just then, a flash of lightning and a roar of the thunder started spitting down the large raindrops. There was nothing else left for the two men to do but wait for morning after the storm. Holding their hats so they wouldn't fly away, Jubal released the men, then retreated to the office while Gideon made his way back to his room.

The next day, the sun came roaring out of the clouds around noon, chasing away the heavy rain. After checking the town's banks, Jubal manned the office while Gideon went to visit Ms. Lita. Because of the heavy rains, the Lucy Goosy was nearly empty. Just the hard-core morning drinkers were strung about. It was payday for most of the ranchers, so Ms. Lita was behind the bar waiting on her more prominent patrons to arrive, such as cowhands and card players. As usual, when Gideon walked in, the smile on Ms. Lita's face got a little wider.

Before Gideon could get to the bar, Ms. Lita had a drink waiting for him. "So handsome, you're looking uptight and perplexed. Talk to me. What's that sneaky coyote of a man Hayden done now?"

With Jon and the other Texas Rangers not showing up the night before, the frustration and worry started to become cumbersome for Gideon. With the weight of the world on his shoulders, the drink Ms. Lita offered was just a teaser. Trying to control his emotions, Gideon downed the drink quickly and slammed the glass down. "Again."

Sensing some distance and seriousness to Gideon's demeanor, Ms. Lita poured another.

With the same voracious appetite, Gideon quickly disbursed his second drink. "Again."

Becoming concerned, Ms. Lita poured a third with hesitation. "Gideon, you're starting to worry me. If you tell me what's going on, maybe I can do more than watch you get sloshed."

After slamming his glass down a third time, Gideon took a deep breath. "Jon never made it to Hayden's party. And for that matter, neither did the other Rangers."

Not really knowing the importance of the matter, Ms. Lita attempted to offer an explanation. "Gideon, I'm sure there's a reasonable excuse. There was a huge storm last night. Maybe they were held up someplace until the storm passed."

Gideon didn't say anything, but his eyes rapidly moved from side to side while he tried to reason things out in his mind. "Texas Rangers don't make excuses. That word doesn't exist in their vocabulary. Besides, it was a direct order from the governor. Aside from that, you've never met Gunny. Not much for following rules but, nevertheless, one of the toughest men I ever had the pleasure of meeting. Let me tell you, Geronimo and his army couldn't have stopped Gunny from being at that party. He was supposed to be leading them in, but they never arrived."

With thoughts of foul play running through her mind, Ms. Lita was now beginning to worry because Jon was like family. "Gideon, you can't think Hayden had anything to do with them not showing up, do you? He was entertaining at his party last night, and besides, you're talking about twenty-five Texas Rangers. The best of the best. What do you think could've happened?"

Still looking perplexed, Gideon downed a fourth drink, then gently placed the empty glass down on the bar. "I'm not sure. Jubal and I saw Colonel Pittman ride into town last night just before Hayden's party kicked off."

It looked like Gideon was slowing down with his drinks, so Ms. Lita was finally able to take a deep breath and relax a little. As she pushed the whiskey bottle aside, she leaned over the counter and gave Gideon a soft kiss on his cheek. "I've watched Jon grow from a scared little boy into a strong young man. He's got a good head on his shoulders, and he's one of the fastest men I know with a gun. Wherever he is, I'm sure he can handle himself. Besides, a friend like you will always have his back."

Still feeling the effects of Ms. Lita's kiss, Gideon listened to her kind words, but the worry she had in her eyes told a different story. Gideon smiled as he softly took her hand into his. "Listen, I love Jon like a brother and I know there's gotta be a good explanation, and I promise you, I will find out one way or another."

Gently squeezing Gideon's hand, Ms. Lita smiled. "You're a good man, Gideon, and even a better friend. I know you'll find him. In the meanwhile, I saw Pittman and his men walk in last night, but they scurried off to the corner and sat at the table whispering among themselves. I don't like saying this, Gideon, but they looked very happy and pleased about something. They didn't stay long. Just long enough to finish off the bottle they ordered, then I heard one of them say something about Hayden's party as they walked out the door."

With very little to go on, Gideon and Ms. Lita quietly shared a moment while pondering the situation. Just then Jubal came walking in and removed his hat as he made a beeline for the bar. With his usual jolly self, he anxiously greeted his two friends. "Good morning, Ms. Lita. Gideon, I made my rounds around town and I'm ready to go when you are."

Like most people who live day to day, Jubal didn't have any money on him, but he was eyeing up the bottle of whiskey Ms. Lita had out. With a silly smirk beginning to form on her face and without saying a word, Ms. Lita poured Jubal a drink. "Jubal, why is it you always seem to be short?"

As the mood seemed to shift, Gideon began to crack a smile. "Don't worry, Jubal, this round's on me."

It didn't take Jubal long to down his morning drink and afterward, Gideon asked Ms. Lita to keep her eyes and ears open. "We're headed out to Jon's place. I'm praying he's there and if not, I'll talk to Emily to see if he had any last-minute changes to the plan."

Wanting to waste no more time, Gideon paid for the drinks, then he and Jubal took a ride out to Jon's house. As they approached, they could see Emily and Abby hanging laundry. When they turned to see the two men, there was nothing but smiles. As Gideon and Jubal climbed down from their horses, Abram and Adam came running out to greet them. With excitement, the two boys grabbed Gideon by his legs as Abby gave him a big hug.

Being happy to see them, Gideon was all smiles as he welcomed the cheers of the children. "Well now, what do we have here? You three are getting so big." As Gideon knelt down, the two boys were now able to give their hugs.

Afterward, Gideon stood up to talk with Emily. "All right, boys, Deputy Jubal and I have some things to talk to your ma about."

After Emily gave Gideon a hug and greeted Jubal, she asked Abby to finish the laundry and told the boys to go play. She then invited Gideon and Jubal in for coffee.

As Gideon and Jubal entered Jon's cabin, they removed their hats and sat down. The fresh coffee was already made, so Emily poured two cups and placed them down on the table. "Gideon, it's been too long between visits. I'm sure you know Jon is with Gunny."

While Jubal sipped his coffee, Gideon tried to think of what to say. "Speaking of Gunny, before Jon left, did he say anything to you about a change in plans?"

Emily thought for a moment while she wiped her hands on her apron and moved about. "No. He was supposed to meet Gunny and the rest of the Rangers, then head to town to attend a party at the governor's request."

After taking a sip of his coffee, Gideon was hoping Emily could shed some light on Jon's whereabouts. Realizing the visit wasn't just a social call, Emily began to worry. "What is it, Gideon? What's happened to Jon?"

With the hope of finding Jon at his house gone, Gideon had no way of easing into it so he had to come out and say it. "Jon didn't show up last night.

Neither did any of the other Rangers. And nobody has heard from them. I came out here this morning hoping to find Jon or at least find out from you where he might have gone."

Feeling a bit nauseated, Emily started to lose her balance, so she leaned up against the counter as she placed one hand over her stomach. Thinking she looked faint, Gideon jumped up and helped her sit down on one of the chairs. "Emily, are you okay? Can I get you anything?"

By now, Jubal was up and fetching some water from the well and a wet cloth. After a few minutes of tending to Emily, the two men sat back down. After Emily took a drink of water, she explained the problem to Gideon and Jubal. "Gideon, I'm pregnant. I didn't want to leave the children alone, so I had Belle come visit earlier this morning. We're the only two that know."

Feeling happiness for Jon and Emily but still worried, Gideon sat back in his chair. "Jon doesn't know?"

Feeling a little better, Emily took another drink of water while she collected her thoughts. "I had my suspicions, so before Jon left, I spoke about possibly having another child and he was excited about the idea, but I had to make sure. So Belle came to visit this morning and she did an examination. Jon has no idea."

Feeling more concerned than ever, Gideon stood up and walked to a nearby window. Abby had finished hanging the laundry and Gideon watched as she was running around playing and chasing her two brothers. With various scenarios playing out in his mind, Gideon felt nothing but compassion for Emily and the children. After a few minutes of watching, Gideon turned to face Emily. "When Jubal and I get back to town, I'll send out some telegrams to see if I can't get some answers. I should get responses by later this afternoon. When I do, I'll be back and we'll sit and talk. Hopefully this is all just a misunderstanding."

As Gideon and Jubal walked out, Emily walked out behind them and watched the two men mount their horses. Standing on the porch, Emily asked one last question. "Gideon, there were twenty-five Texas Rangers. Twenty-five Rangers can't just disappear, right?"

While atop his horse, Gideon gave a quaint smile. "No, Emily. They couldn't have just disappeared. We'll find them. I promise."

As the two men made their exit, they rode about a mile, then stopped to talk. Feeling even more consumed with burden, Gideon needed to voice his thoughts before riding back to town. "Jubal, the idea was for Jon to meet Gunny at that old cow trail, then ride into town. So, why don't we just take a ride out there to look around?"

Jubal was in complete agreement but had to give Gideon a small warning first. "Not sure if you know this, Gideon, but that land belongs to that nasty old Harley Daniels."

With more frustration starting to set in, Gideon rolled his eyes because he remembered his last encounter with Harley. "Great. Just when I thought things couldn't get any worse."

After thinking for a moment, Gideon decided it was worth the risk of another bad encounter if it would help find Jon. "All right. Maybe old Harley can get past his hatred for me in order to maybe help us out."

Feeling apprehensive and doubtful, the two men rode toward Harley's property. After riding for a while, they finally arrived at the forgotten cow trail. Looking around, Gideon's attitude was hampered with the thought of the ground still wet from the heavy rain it received the night before. Any tracks or signs of horses was now gone, with mud, dirt, puddles of water, and dust remaining. Disappointed with their initial view of the trail, Gideon and Jubal climbed down from their horses and looked around.

Being an ex-scout for the military, Gideon studied the surrounding area carefully. Unfortunately, he couldn't tell if anything was out of the ordinary. "Listen, Jubal. We're not getting anywhere with this. With the risk of being shot for trespassing, what'ya say we take a ride and talk to Harley?"

Taking a moment to climb back up on his horse, Jubal shook his head and grunted out his opinion. "I don't know, Gideon. That damn Harley might shoot first and ask absolutely no questions later. I think we'd be tak'n an awful big chance."

Realizing Jubal was probably right, Gideon agreed, but in his mind it was well worth the risk. "I appreciate your thoughts, Jubal, but if Harley is that much of an ass, then we'll just have to deal with him."

After listening to Gideon's decision, Jubal winked his eye and smiled. "I was hoping you would say something like that. Harley's place is about a mile south from here. Won't take us long at all to get there."

After a short time of riding, it wasn't long before Gideon found himself at Harley's front door. As he slowly climbed down from his horse, the front door burst open and Harley emerged with a rifle. He fired a warning shot into the air, then pointed the rifle at Gideon. "Boy, you is stupid or dumb. Don't rightfully care which it is. You on my property now and you can either get or die."

Looking down the barrel of a rifle wasn't exactly what Gideon had in mind when he arrived, but he knew it was a possibility. Moving at a very slow pace, Gideon showed Harley his hands to convey that he wasn't a threat. "All right, Harley. Let's just stay calm. I'm here on official business only. Not here for any trouble."

With his finger slightly pressed on the trigger of his rifle, Harley's hatred was already in place as his anger started to grow. "Boy, the ways I's sees it, you's has no business be'n on my property. You's got 'bout five seconds and then I'ma plug you full of holes and leave ya for dem dare buzzards to eat."

Just when Gideon was contemplating his next words, Jubal came from around the corner, pointing his gun at Harley with the hammer pulled back. "All right, Harley. Let's just drop the rifle so we can talk some important business."

As Gideon lowered his hands back down to his side, he rolled his eyes and breathed a sigh of relief. "Damn, Jubal. Took a bit long, didn't you?"

Before anyone could react to the circumstance, Harley's wife snuck up behind Jubal with a double-barrel shotgun. "Now, looky what we have here. A back shoot'n deputy. You wasn't gonna back shoot my man, was ya now, Deputy?"

Before Jubal could answer, Gideon pulled his gun with lightning speed and pointed it at Harley's wife. "Good to see you up and about, Mrs. Daniels. Now, why don't you lose that shotgun before things get too far out of hand?"

With a Mexican standoff waiting to play itself out, Harley decided to save his battle for another time. "You's got spunk, Sheriff. I'll give ya that."

Not liking the odds, Harley slowly dropped his rifle and told his wife to do the same. But Harley's wife was having no such thoughts. After spitting a clump of goo on the ground, she held her shotgun and barked out some words. "You listen here now, Harley, I'm not hav'n no Negro man and a trader to the Confederacy come onto my property and tell me what to do."

With his anger being redirected, Harley walked over to his wife and snatched the shotgun from her hands. "Now, you listen, bitch. This here is my land. If'n it wasn't fer the matter of you's still be'n sick in you's minds, I'd slapped the life outta ya. Now, shut your hole an git in that there house before I change this here mind."

With a single tear rolling down her cheek, Mrs. Daniels thought about Harley's disrespectful words while she stood staring at him in disbelief. But Harley showed no sympathy for her as he continued to treat her like a dog. "Go on now, git."

After a distraught Mrs. Daniels slowly walked into the house, Harley turned his attentions back to Gideon. Feeling relieved, Gideon and Jubal had already put their guns away and were awaiting the awkward results of Harley and his wife to end. As the door shut behind Mrs. Daniels, Harley stepped down from his porch and squared himself off against Gideon. "Now you listen, boy. I don't like yer kind. I gots no respects fer ya kind. And I's sure don't have a need fer ya kind be'n on my land, so state yer business an git the hell off my property."

Instead of feeling anger toward Harley, Gideon felt nothing but pity for the man. With keeping his attitude in check, he needed some answers, so he was willing to take the verbal abuse. "My apologies to you and your wife, Harley. I didn't mean to cause you or your family any grief. Jubal and I are here because we wanted to ask if you'd seen or heard anything unusual yesterday."

As a hard look came upon Harley's face, he stood staring at Gideon. "Grief? What the hell do ya know 'bout grief? My two boys are gone an they ain't com'n back cause of that dare damn war." With his emotions becoming more sensitive, Harley had nothing but contempt for Gideon. In his mind,

Gideon represented everything that had gone wrong for him since the Civil
War. "I told ya, boy, me and you got business to tend to sometime lat'a but fer
now, I ain't saw nut'n."

After a disappointing answer, Gideon was surprised when Harley raised
his hand and pointed toward the old cow trail. "But if'n ya really need to know,
some dang fools were shoot'n it up yesterday somewhere near my property.
Whoever it was, it came from up over yonder. Now get the hell off my land
and take that no-good deputy coward with ya."

Gideon knew he would be pressing his luck if he pursued any more questions, so after Harley pointed out the direction of gunfire, he and Jubal decided
to leave while Harley was still somewhat calm.

After thanking Harley for his help, the two men rode off into the direction
he pointed to, which happened to be in the same direction of where they came
from: the old cattle trail. As they arrived back at their original destination,
Gideon climbed down from his horse to take another look around. With
prominent puddles of muddy water still scattered, Gideon recalled an incident
from his scouting past. After climbing back up onto his horse, he sat for a few
seconds with a puzzled look. "I don't get it, Jubal. I must be missing something.
As angry and hateful as Harley is, I don't think he's lying. Something happened,
but we're just not seeing it."

After a few more seconds, Gideon told Jubal thoughts from his past while
Jubal sat on his horse and listened. "Back during the war, I was sent out to
scout for some Comanche that was scene in the area. We were coming down
through Missouri and some folks told us about some Comanche raids. It was
right after some thunderstorms had ripped through the area. I remember
thinking about all the flooding and damage the rains did and I thought there
was no way I was gonna find any signs of Comanche, or anybody else for that
matter. But to my complete surprise, about ten miles east of Comanche territory, I came upon some tracks. They weren't fresh. Maybe a couple of days,
but still, after all that rain, they were there complete with droppings from
their horses, and I even managed to find burnt timbers from the fires they
had made."

Immersing himself into Gideon's story, Jubal sat and listened but didn't have any answers. "I don't know what to say, Gideon. That was a pretty heavy storm last night. Blew some trees down. Blew off a couple of roofs in town. We can ride the trail back to town and look for clues on the way, but I imagine it's gonna be pretty much the same muck all the way."

After a few more seconds of thought, Gideon agreed. "I think you may have something, Jubal. It's not that much of a distance, so we'll ride the exact trail they were supposed to be coming in on."

As the two men rode the trail with caution, neither man said anything. They kept their eyes open for any possible problems the Rangers may have encountered. Still running scenarios through his thoughts, Gideon was trying to keep an open mind, which included a possible encounter with Indians.

After riding a while, Gideon noticed something up ahead and pulled his horse to a stop. Wondering what the problem was, Jubal stopped beside him while he looked around. "What is it Gideon? What'ya see?"

Gideon stood fast as his eyes peered down the trail ahead of them. "Look ahead, Jubal. Tell me what you see."

Jubal's eyes squinted as he was now trying to look a distance down the trail. "Not sure what you're talking about Gideon, but the only thing I see is the trail starting to narrow and a bunch of new saplings. Ol' Harley must have gotten a jump on the planting season."

For a moment in time, Gideon started to smile, but then he realized if what he was thinking was true, then his smile would quickly turn to grief. "Think about it, Jubal. 'Round about the time the Rangers would have been coming down this trail, the sun would have been directly in their eyes. And as you can see, this trail starts to narrow. Now, look at the ridge on each side that slopes downward. What'ya think? Makes for ideal conditions for an ambush."

Looking ahead to where Gideon was pointing, Jubal thought for a moment as his heart sunk. "Gideon, in those conditions six men with special-built Winchesters could take out an entire battalion. So just twenty-five Texas Rangers with no way to defend themselves wouldn't stand a chance. You really think that's what happened?"

As the two men sat atop their horses thinking about what they had just discussed, a small breeze started to form. There were no clouds in the sky and no birds chirping, but feeling the air on his face, Gideon glanced around as though something was trying to confirm what he was thinking. "I don't know, Jubal. I just don't know."

Assuming their theory was right, the two men climbed down from their horses and started to walk toward the narrowed trail. As they walked, their eyes scanned the ground for any kind of tracks or disturbances. They were also looking for signs of a battle, such as shell casings or weapons lying about. But more importantly, they were looking for bodies. Once they got to the ridge, Gideon climbed up to take a look.

When he climbed back down, Jubal could see the distraught look on his face. "What did you find Gideon?"

Unclenching his fist, Gideon opened his hand for Jubal to see. Glancing down, Jubal saw that Gideon was holding a few Winchester shell casings and once again his heart began to sink. With various emotions quickly filling his head, Gideon placed the shells in his pocket, then climbed back up on his horse. "There was about thirty of them up there, and I can probably guess the same for the other side of the trail. But what happen to the bodies? Where are the tracks from their horses, and for that matter, where are the horses? This isn't making any sense at all, Jubal."

At this point, Jubal was just devastated and was all out of ideas. Shaking his head in disbelief, he removed his hat and looked toward the sky. "I can't believe it, Gideon. Jon's gone. I just can't believe it. I knew that snake Hayden was capable of committing atrocities, but twenty-five Texas Rangers? I just can't wrap my thoughts around it. I just can't. What are you going to tell the governor?"

With his heart aching and still trying to piece together what happened, Gideon glanced around the area. "It's not the governor I'm worried about. What the hell am I going to tell Emily and the children?"

After gathering their thoughts, the two men quickly rode back to town. When they arrived, Gideon had Jubal conduct his rounds around town while Gideon sought to confront Zachariah Hayden. By now it was late afternoon, so before heading to the hotel, Gideon checked the Lucy Goosy saloon. As he walked in, he saw Zachariah sitting in the corner enjoying a fine bottle of scotch. Gideon took a deep breath because he didn't need another incident involving violence. So he calmly walked over and sat down across from Zachariah.

With his usual sarcasm, Zachariah had no shortage of words. "Please, Sheriff, help yourself to a chair. May I offer you a drink?"

With his nerves on edge and trying to stay calm, Gideon was in no mood for games. His thought was to just pull his gun and end Hayden's life, thus ending all the problems that had plagued the town of Presidio. But composure and reason started to push out the anger Gideon felt for Zachariah. As he stared out Zachariah, he took a deep breath, then pulled the Winchester shells from his pocket. With a little bit of anger still looming within, Gideon slammed the shells down on the table. "You recognize these, Hayden?"

Zachariah's smile was quickly dispensed as he glanced down at the shells on the table. After taking a drink of his scotch, he gently placed the glass down in front of him. "Forgive me, Sheriff. I don't have a taste for guns; therefore, my knowledge is very limited. But if I had to guess, they look like shells from some kind of rifle."

With anger and bitterness pouring back into his soul, Gideon stood up. As his fingers gently twitched, his thought was to shoot Hayden, but just as his thought process was complete, Ms. Lita came from behind and grabbed Gideon's gun hand. "Well now, handsome, I didn't even see you come in." As she tugged on Gideon's arm, she continued to show grace. "Come now, Gideon, why don't we leave Mr. Hayden to his woes in a bottle so we can go talk over at the bar."

With a little resistance, Gideon stood looking down at Zachariah as though he just didn't care about the law anymore. "Your time is coming, Hayden. I promise you. Your time is coming."

While Ms. Lita was finally able to pull Gideon away, Zachariah poured himself another drink and held his glass up for a toast. "Here's to empty promises, Sheriff."

While Zachariah continued to enjoy his scotch, Ms. Lita pulled Gideon into the back room and began to scold him. "Gideon, what the hell is wrong with you? You shoot a defenseless man, no matter who he is or what he's done, they'll hunt you down and hang you for sure. Now, talk to me. What the hell is going on?"

There was an old table in the corner, so Gideon pulled a chair out for Ms. Lita, then he sat down afterward. Taking a moment to breath, Gideon told Ms. Lita his theory. "They're gone. Jubal and I think Hayden had them killed."

With some confusion, Ms. Lita needed Gideon to elaborate. "Gideon, you're not making any sense. Who did Hayden kill?"

Trying to hold back his emotions, Gideon let his thoughts go. "We think Hayden had the Rangers ambushed on the way into to town yesterday. That would explain the fact there were no provisions made for their horses, which also coincides with why there was so few staff at that party."

Ms. Lita listened but was a bit unsure about how Gideon could come to such a conclusion. As she reached across the table, she intertwined her fingers with Gideon's. "Gideon, you've been working very hard and I know you're tired, but you need some cold hard facts to back up a charge like that. Besides, you're talking about twenty-five Texas Rangers. What makes you think that could even be done?"

With some sorrow in his heart, Gideon gently squeezed the hand of Ms. Lita. "Jubal and I spoke to Harley this morning. He said he heard some shooting going on the day before over by that old cow pass. The same trail the Rangers were going to use. Jubal and I checked it out and I found a bunch of Winchester shells at a point in the trail that was perfect for an ambush. Last night, right before Hayden's party, Pittman and five of Hayden's men came riding into town. Jubal noticed they all had special-made Winchester rifles. He told me bounty hunters like to use them because they can kill a man from a long distance with deadly accuracy. Right now, it's the only thing that makes any sense."

After hearing all the information Gideon gave, Ms. Lita began to worry. "You're talking twenty-five men. What about the bodies?"

Gideon took a breath and thought for a moment because he still didn't have an answer. "I don't know. There were no tracks and no bodies. And beside the rifle shells I found, there wasn't even a sign of a battle. I'm about to walk over to the telegraph office. I need to find out if anyone has seen them or heard from them. I also have to send word to the governor. I'll be praying for good news."

As Gideon got up to leave, Ms. Lita began to cry. Before making his exit, he gently took Ms. Lita by her hand and pulled her toward him. With his compassion pouring out, Gideon held her tight while she exposed her thoughts. "What about Jon? Gideon, you have to find him."

Once again, Gideon held Ms. Lita tight. After a few more seconds of crying, Ms. Lita slowly backed away so she could regain her composure. Taking a few deep breaths, she wiped the tears from her eyes and straightened out her clothes. Before she let Gideon walk out, she looked him in the eyes. "For Emily and the children, you have to find Jon. And if you're right and he's dead, I want you to kill that son of a bitch Hayden."

Gideon didn't have words, but his emotions were all over his face, so he gave Ms. Lita a little nod and then turned and walked out.

Not wasting any time, Gideon made his way to the telegraph office and sent word to the governor's office, the U.S. marshal, and all the surrounding territories.

While Gideon was busy with his task, Zachariah was meeting with the colonel in his hotel room. Not only was Zachariah delighted, it seemed his thoughts were filled with euphoria. As the colonel sat and watched, Zachariah nearly glided across the room in order to retrieve some drinks.

While Zachariah poured the booze, Colonel Pittman lit his pipe and took a few puffs in readiness of enjoying a drink of fine whiskey. "Well, Mr. Hayden. I'm sure you'll agree, with the Texas Rangers gone, you'll be able to conduct your business with a little more ease."

Although Zachariah was enjoying the feeling of victory, the business at hand did not escape his thoughts. As he sat down at the table, he handed Colonel Pittman his celebration drink. "Where's my necklace?"

Before entering into an argumentative conversation, Colonel Pittman paused for a moment, then proceeded to re-light his tobacco. As he huffed and puffed, he finally gave an answer Zachariah did not want to hear. "My apologies to you, sir. We were unable to retrieve the item you requested. But my hope is with the Texas Rangers out of your way, you would pardon the absence of that one item."

Zachariah had already downed his drink, but his inner joy was now gone. "You killed all the Rangers, correct? Why were you unable to obtain the necklace? What? All the sudden, you and your men gained a conscience and were unable to rip an old piece of leather off a dead man?"

The colonel was unimpressed with Zachariah's sarcasm. As a gentleman, he thought it beneath him. "Mr. Hayden, please. I pride myself with efficiency and willingness to get the job done no matter the difficulty. So I appeal to your more patient attributes and allow me to explain the nature of the complication before you pass judgment upon me."

Not wanting to hear excuses, Zachariah forced himself to listen as he took a deep breath. In order to keep himself from looking foolish, he attempted to adapt to the colonel's honorable language. "My apologies to you, sir. I'm sure there's a reasonable excuse for why I'm not in possession of the one item I truly wanted."

Once again the colonel could feel the tension, but was unimpressed with Zachariah's angry disposition. After re-lighting his pipe for a third time, the colonel stood up in order to stretch out his problems stemming from the war. "The men and I did exactly as planned. We had absolutely no issues with killing the Rangers. Sir, I've been called many things to include monster, madman, killer, murderer, and I'm happy to say I'm known as the fastest man alive. But above all else, I consider myself to be a God-fearing man." As the colonel moved around the room, Zachariah could tell he was deep in thought as though he had tapped into a part of his thought system that he rarely visits.

Zachariah continued to watch as the colonel helped himself to another drink. After handing Zachariah another full glass, he continued to speak. "I know nothing about your faith, sir, so I would ask your indulgence on what

I'm about to say. I'm sure you know the good book teaches us about the crucifixion. After the death of Christ, the skies grew dark and the thunder roared and people were suddenly aware of their crime. After those twenty-five Texas Rangers fell, the clouds grew dark and the thunder started to sound off as though we were being scolded by God himself. Just before I was about to retrieve your precious artifact, a heathen Indian appeared on the horizon. I could tell he was a warrior, but there was something about him. He was bigger than most I've seen. He just sat atop his horse and watched as though he was in command of the storm. I can say with honesty, sir, I had no opportunity to lay my hands on your prize. Not wanting to risk a confronting with an Indian raid party, your men and I retreated back to the safety of this God-forsaken town."

After listening to the colonel and his story, Zachariah stood up and paced the floor. Now it was he who was deep in thought. "What about the bodies? We have to think they're still there."

Still enjoying his pipe, the colonel shook his head no. "No, sir. As I expected them to, your sheriff and deputy rode out earlier this morning. With me at a distance, I followed them out to that old cow trail, then over to some old farmer's house. For a moment I thought that old farmer and his wife was going to do us both a favor and kill them. That farmer must have heard the shooting and pointed them back to the trail. So they rode back to the trail to do some more looking."

Trying to comprehend the situation, Zachariah listened with interest. "That sheriff came to me this morning with some rifle shells, but he didn't say anything about the Rangers. What about the bodies?"

Once again the colonel shook his head no as he enjoyed his pipe. "There were none to find. Meaning, they were gone. I followed the sheriff all the way to the location where we killed the Rangers. I saw him collect the shells, then ride back to town. And I'm saying there were no bodies."

Even though he couldn't be connected to the crime, Zachariah was beginning to worry. "Indians don't bury people. Especially the white man. They would have taken anything of value and left them to the wolves and coyotes.

This doesn't make any sense. We would have heard about it if one of the townspeople found them"

Not wanting to speculate on divine intervention, Colonel Pittman decided to get back to the business at hand. "Mr. Hayden, sir, I'm sure you've already made the necessary arrangements for my funds to be deposited into my bank of choosing?"

Still looking perplexed, Zachariah gave the colonel the good news. "Yes. My people in San Francisco has already taken care of it. And by the way, I'll be subtracting the extra $5,000 for not retrieving my necklace."

With all the puzzling talk, Zachariah nearly forgot about payment for the other men. With his mind still stuck on the missing bodies, he fetched a large suitcase from his closet. After placing it on the bed, he opened it in order to show the contents to Colonel Pittman. It was filled with hundred-dollar bills. Setting his pipe aside momentarily, Colonel Pittman stood up to view the money. "Well now, sir. The men will be very pleased to see you have honored our agreement. I'll make sure they receive payment for their work. As we speak, they're on their way out to that Ranger's house to finish off the job. As for me, I don't partake in such barbaric actions. Now, sir, if you'll excuse me, I will distribute these funds when the men return, then I shall catch my train to San Francisco to take care of some business that demands my immediate attention. Afterward, I shall return to this condemned town and finish my business with your sheriff."

While Zachariah pondered the location of twenty-five bodies and the necklace he desired, Colonel Pittman rode a few miles out of town to a pre-designated rendezvous point. While the colonel made himself comfortable, Zachariah's five men were arriving at Jon's house. As they climbed down off their horses, Adam and Abram were standing on the porch.

One of the men, Rico, approached and knelt down in order to talk with Adam. With a big smile on his face, he removed his hat and wiped his brow. "Hey there. little boy. Is your mama home?"

Before he could answer, Abby came waking around the corner with some flowers. When she saw the men, she quickly ran to the side of her brothers.

Noticing how mean and dirty they looked, she spoke with a little attitude in her voice. "What do you want? Why are you here?"

Admiring the little girl's demeanor, Rico stood up and placed his hat back on his head. Still grinning from ear to ear, he gave his answer. "Well now, what have we here? This just keeps getting better. What's your name, little lady?"

Abby didn't answer because her fear was starting to kick in, so Rico continued his sweet talk. "We're here because we were hoping to talk with your ma. Is she inside?"

Just then, another one of the men, Marcus, spoke up. "Forget this nonsense, Rico. Let's get on with it. I'm hungry."

Marcus and his brother Ronnie Beck were dirty, smelly, and downright hateful. They were pure killing machines. When Rico turned to address the outburst of Marcus, Abby grabbed her brothers by their hands and pulled them into the house. But locking the door did no good because Rico quickly kicked the door in and grabbed Abby. As he picked her up, he placed his hand over her mouth before she could scream. Following suit, Marcus and Ronnie grabbed her two brothers and started to shake them violently.

Suddenly the bedroom door burst open and out came Emily with a shotgun. It was loaded with buckshot and she was pointing it at the feet of the men. With anger in her voice, she wasted no time with her demands. "Let my children go and get the hell out of my house."

Surprised at the outcome, an angry woman with a loaded shotgun wasn't something Rico was prepared for. As he slowly let Abby drop to the ground, he quickly informed Marcus and Ronnie to let the boys go. Afterward, he turned his attention back to Emily. "Now listen, lady, these brat kids of yours started it. We were just here to pay you a friendly visit."

Before Rico could continue his lies, Emily once again gave demands. "Now, you listen here, my husband will be riding up any minute now, so you get the hell out of our house and off our property before I send you to hell."

By now, Abby, Adam, and Abram had withdrawn into the bedroom, leaving their mother to take care of business. With their master plan starting to fall apart, Rico had to think fast. After Emily had made the statement about

Jon coming home, he turned to look at the other men and laughed. He gave a short nod to Lester, then turned back around. "There's five of us here, lady. Now put the gun down so we can talk. You can't shoot all of us."

Feeling nothing but malice toward the men, Emily was starting to grow angrier by the minute and she was in no mood to negotiate. "Well now, Mr. Man, that's a real fine observation, but I can get two of you, so which two is going to be making the sacrifice?"

While Rico and Emily were battling it out with words, Lester kept slowly inching his way forward in order to get within reaching distance of Emily. Before she could react, Lester leaped forward and grabbed the shotgun. Twisting and turning, the two struggled to be dominant over the other. Rico and the other three men watched and laughed while they enjoyed the spectacle of the unexpected wresting match.

Suddenly it wasn't funny anymore. While Emily and Lester each pulled on the shotgun, it went off, hitting Roberto on the left side of his face and his left arm. The blast knocked Emily backward to the floor as Lester secured the gun.

After Rico saw it didn't kill Roberto, his anger came shining through. "Lady, I'm tired of this game. It's time for you and your little brat kids to pay the piper."

While Rico and his men were having their way with Jon's family, Gideon and Jubal were sitting at the Lucy Goosy talking with Ms. Lita and having drinks. While Gideon and Jubal had nothing to say, Ms. Lita decided to try and get their minds off Jon, if only for a few minutes. "Well, fellas, I decided to buy the old Willis place. Apparently, him and his family have had enough of Texas and are moving back east."

Gideon thought for a moment, then realized which house Ms. Lita was talking about. "I know that house. Rode past there a few times heading out to the Indian villages with Belle. It has a bunch of walnut trees and spruces out front."

Ms. Lita smiled with pride because she couldn't wait to move in. Living over top of her bar over the years had grown tiresome. "Yes. Isn't it beautiful?

Did you know Mr. Willis planted all those trees? He told me they had meaning, that all trees have meanings."

Overwhelmed with joy, Gideon was happy for Ms. Lita. As he smiled and
shared in her happiness, he took a drink of his beer, then suddenly remembered
something he had seen. As the smile slowly started to droop, he placed his beer
down on the table. "You're right. Every tree has a meaning. Why didn't I see it?"

Watching Gideon's smile slowly turn upside down, Ms. Lita had no idea
what Gideon was talking about, and likewise for Jubal. After a few more seconds of thinking, Gideon became anxious and was ready to go. "Jubal, we have
something to do. Ms. Lita, thank you for the drinks. I'll explain later." As
Gideon hurried out the door, Jubal quickly followed behind in confusion.

By this time, Rico and his men had left Jon's house and were just arriving
at the rendezvous point to meet with Colonel Pittman. As the men arrived
with joyful faces, the colonel readied the suitcase full of happiness. Before he
was ready to open it, he questioned the actions of the Rico. "Did you finish
out the loose ends?"

With a devious grin on his face, Rico was content with his actions and
gave his answer. "Yes, sir, Colonel. Everything was taken care of just like Mr.
Hayden wanted."

After listening to Rico, Colonel Pittman glanced over at Roberto and the
wounds he had. "I see things didn't go exactly as planned. The wife of a Texas
Ranger, I can only imagine, would be a bit feisty. Nevertheless, here is your
payment, as promised."

The colonel was pleased to hear there were no problems, so he laid the
suitcase on the ground and opened it up. "Well, gentlemen, all of your dreams
have come true. You are now very wealthy men."

When the case opened, Rico's eyes got big. As he stood there gawking at
the money, the other men threw their hats in the air and yelled with delight.
After a brief celebration and the dividing of the money, the colonel shook
hands with Rico. "Well now, sir, after your man gets his injuries taken care of,
I surmise your official celebration with be quite a spectacle." The colonel rarely
smiled, but for this occasion he had a small grin on his face. "And if I may

speculate, involved in your soiree will be, shall we say, women with certain talents and liquor with only the finest of ingredients costing much coin?"

Looking back at the men who were now counting their money for a second and third time, Rico turned back to the colonel. "Well, yes, sir. You speculate right. We're headed into town to have that lady doctor sew up Roberto, then we're headed out of state." While Rico and his men headed for town, Colonel Pittman continued on to San Antonio to catch his train to San Francisco.

With Jubal still trying to keep up with Gideon, the two quickly walked to the telegraph office hoping to hear good news, but there was none. Gideon and Jubal stood and watched as, one by one, the messages came in. Unfortunately, they all read the same. None of the surrounding towns heard from or saw the Texas Rangers. And of course, all the agencies had one excuse or another on why they couldn't help. The marshal's office had its hands full with chasing various outlaws across the lands. The governor's office conveyed their worries about the disappearance of its most elite Texas Rangers, but their resources were stretched thin. And the military was occupied with the Sioux Indians and their increasing battles. They also had to deal with the viscous raids Comanche were conducting on settlers crossing their territories and the Apache, who was at war with anyone who they thought was a threat to their existence, namely the United Stated military. The other Texas Rangers were not only attempting to help the military but they also had to maintain their own duties, which included protecting the border from invading Mexican outlaws. So, it all came down to Gideon and Jubal being on their own with no help.

It was no surprise to Gideon that nobody had seen or heard from the Rangers because he was working on his own theory, but he still hadn't informed Jubal about his recent thoughts. With a hefty gallop, Jubal followed Gideon out to the trail where they had recovered the rifle shells. The rain had since dried up and the puddles of muddy water were starting to evaporate. As Gideon sat atop his horse, he glared out into a field adjacent to the trail. The grass was thick and some of the weeds were overgrown, and the woods in the background stood tall.

As he sat quietly, Jubal waited patiently for an explanation. "Gideon, it's not for me to question your methods, but we've been out here twice. What is it you're looking for?"

Gideon paused momentarily, then finally told Jubal his thoughts. Still looking out into the field, he raised his hand and pointed. "Look out there, Jubal. What'ya see?"

Taking a moment to remove his hat and wipe his brow, Jubal glanced out into the field and stared for a minute. "It's a field, Gideon. Grass and the woods off in the distance. What do you see?"

Once again Gideon paused, then climbed down from his horse. As Jubal followed, Gideon raised his hand once again and pointed. "The saplings you mentioned before. If I'm not mistaken, they're oak saplings." Looking on from the trail, the saplings blended in with the distant tree line.

Squinting his eyes, Jubal again glared out into the field. "Yeah, ol' Harley, he may be nastier then a beehive full of bees and honey, but he ain't lazy. Looks like he planted a whole line of them. That's right about the end of Harley's property line. I'm guess'n he got'em self a taste for some acorns."

Looking at the oak saplings, Gideon had a sinking feeling in his heart. "Look at them, Jubal. How many do you see?"

Taking in a deep breath, Jubal took a few seconds and started to count. "Looks to be about twenty-four."

With a quick look at Jubal, Gideon turned his attention back to the trees. "You're right. Twenty-four."

After a few moments of silence, Jubal's mind started to grind. "No, Gideon. Come on. They're just trees. Besides, there were twenty-five Rangers." After a few more seconds of silence, Jubal continued. "Gideon, listen to me. I bet if we go talk to Harley, he'll tell you himself. Come on, Gideon, I'll prove it."

Listening to Jubal and his explanation, Gideon had his own theory he was clinging on to. With a rush of emotions tugging on his insides, Gideon told Jubal his thoughts. "When we were sitting and talking with Ms. Lita, she was telling us about the old Willis house and the trees he had planted. She said they had meaning. That's when it hit me. I learned some of that stuff back in my scouting days. Every tree had its own meaning. When we were out here before, you pointed out the saplings, but I just didn't think anything of it at the time until Ms. Lita said what she said. The mighty oak tree. Symbol of courage and power. Legend says it's the most powerful of all trees. The mighty oak stands strong through all things."

Feeling a bit apologetic, Jubal still wasn't believing it. "Gideon, I know it's been a strain lately with everything going on and now Jon gone missing, but maybe you're just will'n to believe anything just to take some of that pressure off. Believe me, partner, I wouldn't hold it against you."

Having no ill will, Gideon turned to Jubal and let out a small chuckle. "Well, thanks for your support, Jubal. I appreciate the confidence you have in. Now, let's take a walk."

Still feeling apprehensive, Jubal followed Gideon as they walked through the field, getting closer with every step. After a couple of minutes, they stopped within a few feet of the saplings. Gideon studied the line of trees for a few seconds, then turned to follow the saplings to the end. As the two men stood staring down at the base of the last tree, their worst fear became a reality. Stuck securely into the base of the sapling was a large Bowie knife. With his hand shaking, Gideon bent down to pry it out. Afterward, he showed it to Jubal. "This belonged to Gunny. He was showing it off to me the last time I saw him. He said he had it special made at a knife shop on a visit out to California."

With his hand still trembling, Gideon held the knife up so Jubal could see the inscription. It read "Best of the best, Texas Rangers."

Trying to hold back the sickening feeling he had in his stomach, Jubal's legs started to buckle as he dropped to his knees. "Dear Lord, what the hell happened here? What the hell happened, Gideon?" Almost in tears and shaking his head, Jubal continued his verbal outcry. "This can't be. This just can't be. What are we going to tell the folks in town? What the hell are we supposed to tell Emily?"

Taking one last look at the knife, Gideon wedged it back into the base of the tree and then he helped Jubal to his feet. "We're not going to say anything yet. How many trees did you say you counted?"

Jubal thought about the question for a moment and, with a surprised look, blurted out the answer. "There's only twenty-four trees, Gideon."

Looking back down at the knife, then back at Jubal, Gideon nodded his head. "Yeah, only twenty-four, which means there's one missing."

With a surprised look still lingering, Jubal started the guessing game. "A lone survivor? But how? We would have heard something by now. Which Ranger you think it could be? And who do you think buried them? Wouldn't have been Hayden's men. They would have left them for the buzzards. And that damn Harley, as hateful as he is, he would have said something, wouldn't you think?" Jubal had all valid questions and statements, but Gideon had no answers.

After a somber ride back to town, Gideon and Jubal agreed to avoid as many people as possible, at least for the rest of the day. Especially friends.

After not seeing Gideon or Jubal for two days, Ms. Lita went looking. She tried the sheriff's office first and she even went to Molly's place, but with no luck. Heading back to the Lucy Goosy, she decided to stop at the hotel and talk to Mr. Hinklemeyer. As usual, a few of the locals were gathered around listening to Mr. Hinklemeyer and the latest gossip. When Ms. Lita walked in, the look she had on her face told the townspeople all they wanted to know. As she approached the front desk, the local folks decided to make a quick exit.

Mr. Hinklemeyer could also tell Ms. Lita was in no mood, but he attempted to graciously greet her anyway. With a cracking in his voice and a slight stutter, he gave a half-smile. "Well, hello there, Ms. Lita. I see you're looking quite…well, you know."

But Ms. Lita gave no leeway as she honed right in on the little man. As she leaned over the desk and looked down at the half-pint manager, she gave him an evil look. "The only thing I know, Hinklemeyer, is that you better cut the crap. Now, since you know just about everything that goes on in our quaint little town, why don't you start by telling me where the sheriff is."

Mr. Hinklemeyer wanted no parts of Ms. Lita, so with a shaky hand he wasted no time pointing to the dining room. "He's in there having breakfast, ma-ma'am."

Just for her pleasure, Ms. Lita gave one last dirty look to Mr. Hinklemeyer before she turned and headed for the dining room. As she walked in, she could see that Gideon already had a cup of coffee waiting for her. As she approached the table, Gideon pulled the chair out for her. "I figured you were here. I could hear Hinklemeyer's teeth rattling from across the room."

As Ms. Lita gracefully took her seat, she helped herself to two sugar cubes and plopped them into her coffee. After taking a sip, she placed the cup down on the table. Trying to keep her voice as low as possible, she leaned across the table to start her interrogation. "What the hell is going on, Gideon? You and Jubal rush out of my bar like a pair of ravishing wolves and I haven't seen hide nor hair of you since."

Before Ms. Lita could continue her rage, Gideon spoke up. "We found them."

Hearing those three words momentarily sent chills up and down Ms. Lita's spine as she leaned back in her chair. After a brief pause and a look of horror, she asked the question that she didn't particularly want to hear the answer to. "Found them? What's that mean?"

Sipping on his coffee, Gideon didn't answer right away, which worried Ms. Lita even more. Instead, he stood up and took a deep breath while glancing around the room to make sure nobody was around. He saw that most of the morning customers were already gone and the few that remained was busy playing catch up with their faces buried in their newspapers. So he asked Ms. Lita to collect her coffee and follow him over to a corner table by the window.

After they sat down, Ms. Lita leaned across the table and continued her inquisition. "Gideon, what's going on? Who did you find?"

Trying to swallow the lump in his throat, Gideon finally answered. "We found the Rangers. They're dead."

Beginning to hyperventilate, Ms. Lita tried to slow her breathing, but she couldn't. With both hands over her mouth to keep herself from gasping, she was finally able to calm down enough to speak. "My God, Gideon. All of them? But how? Why?" Once again, Ms. Lita became short of breath. "Oh my God. What about Emily and the children?"

While rapid thoughts were dominating the mind of Ms. Lita, Gideon reached across the table and gently took her hand. "We only found twenty-four. There's one missing, but we don't know who it is or where he is or what happened to him. Jubal and I have been sneaking around for the past couple of days scouring the woods around Harley's place, but we can't find any trace of anything."

With all her thoughts spiraling out of control, Ms. Lita had nothing but questions. "Why Harley's place? You don't think that ass had anything to do with it, do you?"

With that said, Gideon lowered his voice and explained everything. Although Ms. Lita already new some of the information, Gideon decided to run through everything again. "The day Jubal and I went looking, we checked the trail where the Rangers were supposed to meet, which runs through Harley's property. Afterward, we spoke with Harley himself to find out if he had seen or heard anything. And let me tell you, he's a difficult man at best, but I don't count him a liar. He told Jubal and me that he heard rifle shots coming from the trail the day before, so me and Jubal hightailed it back to that old cow trail to check it a second time. We followed it all the way down to where it narrows, so we checked the area and found rifle casings. The night of Hayden's party, Jubal and I saw Pittman and his men ride into town laughing it up. Jubal noticed they all had special rifles hanging off their saddles. Rifles that are used for long-distance killing."

After a brief pause, Gideon took a drink of his coffee, which had rapidly turned warm. Afterward, he continued. "That day on the trail, Jubal pointed out something else, but I didn't think anything of it. Newly planted tree saplings. A line of them off in the distance running parallel to the trail and the woods. The day we were in your bar and you told us about the Willis house and the trees is when it hit me. You were absolutely correct. Every tree has its meaning. The line of saplings we saw was oak saplings. When Jubal and I rushed out of the Lucy Goosy the other day, we rode back to the trail. I told Jubal my theory and, unfortunately, I was right. Jubal and I checked the trees and found Gunny's knife stuck in the base of one of them. Under each oak sapling lay one Texas Ranger. Courage and power. The mighty oak stands strong through all things."

After Gideon finished explaining, Ms. Lita was astonished. She had a hard time comprehending Gideon's story, so she attempted to calm herself with sarcasm. "Gideon, you definitely know how to impress a woman. Good looks and a brain. You should be working for the Pinkerton Detective Agency."

Still troubled about what Gideon just told her, one question still remained. Who and where was the last Texas Ranger? Thinking about Emily and the children, Ms. Lita had to ask. "If it was Jon, don't you think he would have contacted you by now?"

Gideon thought for a moment because he knew Ms. Lita was right. If Jon was okay, he would have shown up by now, but that still didn't explain why nobody hadn't shown up at all. "You're right. I've been avoiding it, but I'm going to have to tell Emily."

Now it was Ms. Lita stretching across the table and taking Gideon by his hand. "If you like, I can come along with you for support."

Gideon appreciated the kindness, but knew it was something he had to do on his own. With a sincere smile, Gideon gently squeezed Ms. Lita's hand. "Thank you. You are a kind lady and a wonderful listener, but this is something I just have to do alone."

After leaving the hotel, Gideon had a difficult ride to make. All the way to Jon's house, he kept thinking of ways to confront Emily. After a while, he realized he had arrived at a part of the trail where he usually saw Jon's house from a distance, but on this day he saw nothing. After a brief stop and a pause, Gideon hurried his horse to a quick gallop. As he approached the homestead, he was horrified by what he had found. Jon's house was burned to the ground and all the livestock was dead. As he dismounted his horse, he glanced around and called out for Emily, but there was no answer. He then shouted for each of the children and still received no answers. As he continued to look around, he noticed the barn had only been partially burned. As a precaution, he pulled his gun out and moved toward the barn door. When he opened it, he found a gruesome sight was awaiting him. Adam and Abram were tied by their feet and hanging upside down from the rafters. They had been burned alive and their limbs were cut off. After a few seconds of staring at such a gruesome sight, Gideon turned to see Abby's nude body lying off to the side. She had been raped, then stabbed to death. Collapsing to his knees, Gideon started to cry and pound the ground with his fist. While the tears rolled down his face, he screamed at God and cursed the day Zachariah Hayden was born. As the tears continued to flow like a river, he thought about what Jubal had told him. Hayden not only kills the person but goes after their family.

After taking a few deep breaths, Gideon attempted to collect his composure knowing he still had to find Emily. After a couple of more seconds of breathing, he exited the rear of the barn. There, he saw what was left of Emily. Her nude body had been staked to the ground and left to die. The wolves and coyotes had eaten most of her torso, and now the flies and ants were having their way. There were a few arrows lying around and stuck to the barn walls, but Gideon knew better. This wasn't the work of an Indian raid party; this was Zachariah Hayden. Not being able to take much more, Gideon's bent over as his breakfast came rushing up from his stomach.

Gideon spent the rest of the afternoon digging graves and making sure there was nothing left of the property. He tore down the rest of the barn and dismantled all of the animal's stalls. He even broke apart what little fencing Jon had put up for the vegetable gardens. He placed it all in a pile and then burned it. The only things he saved were the wind chimes Emily had hanging from the porch. They had somehow survived the fire and were lying in the ashes. Jon had once said she enjoyed listening to them at night while the wind blew and that it gave her peace and comfort when he was away. Thinking as a kind gesture, Gideon placed them around her grave marker, then made sure the other graves were properly marked and started his trek back to town.

It was late when he got back and businesses were closed for the night. Luckily, nobody was on the streets and all the rowdies had gone home. Looking around at his empty town, Gideon saw there was a light still lit at the Lucy Goosy, so he decided to pay a visit. The inner doors were locked, but he could see Ms. Lita through the window cleaning the bar. Trying to keep his emotions in check, he lightly knocked on the door.

Hearing the faint knock, Ms. Lita walked to the window and saw it was Gideon, so she quickly opened the door. "Gideon, come in. Where have you been? You should have been back hours ago."

Gideon tried to smile, but he just couldn't will himself to do it. As he slowly walked to the bar, Ms. Lita pulled a bottle and poured some drinks. "Gideon, what's wrong? How is Emily?"

Altogether distraught, once again Gideon broke down and started crying. Completely caught off guard, Ms. Lita came from behind the bar and wrapped herself around him. "Gideon, you're scaring me. What's wrong? Please, tell me."

Feeling as though he had the weight of the world collapsing down on him, Gideon held onto Ms. Lita as though she was the last person on Earth. He held her tight and cried until his emotions were completely drained.

As the two embraced for a few more minutes, Gideon finally gained his composure and was able to talk. After letting Ms. Lita go, his hand found its way to the glass of whiskey on the bar. After swigging down his drink, Gideon told Ms. Lita the details of his day. In a very soft voice, he spoke. "They're gone. They're all gone."

Seeing how upset and emotional Gideon was, Ms. Lita poured another drink. "Gideon, who's gone? You're not making any sense."

After picking up the drink, Gideon glanced down at the floor, then once again finished his drink in one gulp. In a much bolder voice, Gideon repeated himself. "Emily and the children. They're gone. Hayden had them killed."

Ms. Lita was stunned. Her legs became weak as she leaned back onto the bar. "My God. Why? They were no threat to him."

After a pause, Gideon grabbed the bottle and poured two drinks and handed one to Ms. Lita. As Ms. Lita swallowed down her drink, Gideon started the blame game. "I underestimated Hayden. I would have never thought in a million years he would kill an entire platoon of Texas Rangers. And it seems to me Jubal was right. Hayden made good on his reputation of killing the family members. I just didn't see it coming. As many times as he looked me in the eyes and laughed, knowing what he was planning and seeing if I could figure it out. It's just a game to him." Shaking his head, Gideon repeated his words. "Just a game. And we're the losers, with Jon and his family losing their lives."

Attempting to come up with solutions, Ms. Lita began to make suggestions. "I'm not trying to put you down, Gideon, but what about the U.S. marshal? I'm sure you've contacted him. He should be able to help."

Gideon appreciated the recommendation, but had already gotten the bad news earlier in the week. "I take no insult to your words, Ms. Lita. I wish it was that simple. All I have are fairy tales of treasure and wild theories. The marshals' office is too busy chasing criminals on Wanted posters. The military has their own issues at the moment, and the governor is saddened by the news but isn't inclined to help us out. So, for now, we're on our own."

The next day, Gideon went to see Doc Belle. Since Doc knew of Emily's condition, it wasn't going to be easy to tell her the horrible news. When he arrived, Belle was just finishing with one of her regular patients. As the sickly man was preparing to leave, Gideon removed his hat and exchanged pleasantries as the elderly man walked out. Afterward, he closed the door behind him and locked it.

Sitting at her desk, Belle glanced up at Gideon with curiosity. "Gideon, you okay? Why did you lock the door?"

Taking a moment to gather his thoughts, Gideon sat down in the nearest chair. "Belle, I apologize. I need to talk to you without anybody walking in and disturbing us."

Feeling a bit worried, Belle placed her half-finished paperwork aside and gave her full attention to Gideon. As she waited, Gideon stared into her eyes attempting to speak the words he needed to relay. "I know about Emily. She told me a few days ago about being pregnant. She said you came to see her the morning after Jon left."

With a little apprehension running through her thoughts, Belle smiled. "Yes. She was really excited because she and Jon spoke about having another child. She can't wait to tell him when he gets back."

Beginning to feel choked up, Gideon attempted to try and control his feelings. "Belle, that's why I'm here. The Texas Rangers never arrived at Hayden's party. We think Hayden had them ambushed." Before Belle could react, Gideon continued. "We're not sure about Jon. When I went out to see Emily, I found the house had been burned to the ground and her and the children dead. Hayden had some of his dirtiest men execute them."

Having a hard time believing what she was hearing, Belle was horrified. She attempted to stand but didn't have the strength, so she slowly lowered her head down to her desk and started to cry. After a few seconds, Gideon got up and maneuvered around the desk and helped Belle to her feet. He held her tight as her sorrow made its exit and anger took over. As she continued to cry, she pounded on Gideon's chest with both fists. After a few minutes of getting out her frustrations, Belle pulled away from Gideon and sat back down. "Why, Gideon? Why would Hayden do such a thing? And what about Jon? Wasn't he with the other Rangers?"

Once again Gideon paused to gather his thoughts. Belle was a good friend, but Gideon was trying to minimize the information about the investigation. "Well, we think one Texas Ranger escaped, but we don't know who or where he is. Jubal and I are working on it, but we're not finding much to go on. Right now we seem to be in limbo and waiting."

Finally feeling her strength return, Belle stood up and moved around the room as she gathered some of her road supplies. "I'm sorry, Gideon. I need to do a few house calls. I also need to meet Thomas at the stables."

Gideon could tell Belle was still very upset, but she was trying to be strong. "Belle, it's okay. I know you're a woman with strong character, but you're traumatized right now. Maybe you should just postpone your visits."

As Belle rushed around the room gathering instruments and supplies, she suddenly stopped and dropped everything on the floor and started crying. Gideon took a step toward her and once again held her tight. "I'm sorry, Belle. I promise you, Hayden with pay for what he did."

After a few more seconds, Belle gathered herself together, then bent over to pick up the materials on the floor. "I have to go. Julia Taylor is running a fever and Mrs. Bartlett was in the other day. Told me her son, Josh, was thrown by his horse. They think his leg may be broken."

As Gideon helped Belle gather her supplies, he took comfort in the fact Thomas was going along with her. "All right. Please, if you see or hear anything, anything at all, let me or Jubal know."

Just before Gideon was going to turn and walk out, Belle remembered something. "Gideon, wait. There is something. Some of Hayden's men came to me a couple days ago. One of them took some buckshot to his arm and face. He said it happened while he was cleaning his gun. I knew he was full of it, but I didn't care one way or the other. They came in round about the same time you said Emily and the children were murdered. You think there may be a connection?"

Breathing in a deep breath, Gideon thought for a few seconds and pondered Belle's words. "I know Jon had a shotgun at the house for times he was away. He told me Emily didn't like guns, but seeing how Jon insisted she have some sort of protection, she preferred buckshot. I don't know. You have the patient's name?"

Belle was well aware of doctor-client privilege, but at this point she couldn't care less.

While Gideon waited, Belle pulled out the paperwork from days before. As she sifted through, she pulled out what she was looking for. "Here it is. Roberto Costas. He was brought in by a man named Rico. Real suave kinda guy. Roberto had wounds to the left side of his face and his left arm. Didn't take too long to patch him up. They seemed to be in a hurry."

Being the troublesome filth that they were, Gideon recognized the names immediately. "Yeah. I'm familiar with the both of them. They've been in town a few times. Hanging out with two brothers, Ronnie and Marcus, and a friend of theirs, Lester Hays. None of which are choir boys. I saw them leaving town the other day, but I didn't think anything of it. I was actually happy to see them go."

With one last sympathetic hug, Gideon thanked Belle for the information and left.

Days passed as the town's environment became distressed. Working off orders from Zachariah Hayden, more and more of his men were coming into town and starting fights with the local patrons of the bars and restaurants. With being a little overwhelmed, Gideon had to deputize several men in order to keep up with the minor scrimmages being fought. Amid all the issues, thefts and property damage also increased. Lacking any will to stand up and fight, some of the business owners became frustrated and closed their doors for good. Feeling oppressed by Hayden's men, many of the landowners and farmers refused to come to town and spend money. Even Molly's place and the new Asian bath house temporarily shut their doors because they didn't want to have to deal with Hayden's dirty men.

Daylight hours weren't bad. Most of the town was quiet and the businesses that were still open stayed busy. As Gideon and Jubal sat in the office, they stared at the walls and drank some coffee while discussing everything that had happened since Zachariah Hayden came to town. At this point, there was no doubt Hayden was responsible for the killings and the disappearances. Even though they had no proof, they were also sure Hayden was responsible for the assassination of the Texas Rangers.

As Gideon swallowed the rest of his coffee, Doc Belle walked in. Lately, very few things could put a smile on his face, but Doc Belle was definitely one of those people. By now, everyone in Presidio had heard about the disappearance of the Texas Rangers and the murders of their families, and if somebody didn't know or if someone new came to town, Mr. Hinkelmier was sure to tell them. As for the Rangers' graves, Gideon, Jubal, and Ms. Lita made sure to keep the secret to themselves. Knowing Gideon was beating himself over the death of Jon's family, Doc Belle would stop by daily to try and get him away from work for the day.

Trying to maintain an upbeat attitude, Belle explained her visit. "Well, howdy, boys. I'm headed over to the Indian villages to drop off some supplies, and since Thomas has his hands full, I was wondering if I could borrow your companionship for the day, Gideon."

With a welcomed smile on his face, Gideon poured Belle a cup of coffee and invited her to sit for a few minutes. Always happy to sit and talk with Gideon and Jubal, Belle accepted the invite and the coffee.

After letting Belle take a few sips of coffee, Gideon inquired about the local Indians. "Belle, I'm not much of a believer in all the hocus-pocus stuff, but when you go out to the Indian villages, are you hearing anything? Do they talk to you or confide in you?"

Finishing up a sip of coffee, Doc Belle placed the cup on Gideon's desk. "Well, funny you should ask. Being a fine Christian woman, I too am not much of a believer in the whole spirit world thing either, but I gotta say, sometimes they really freak me out with their belief system and some of their predictions."

With random thoughts, Gideon was just bouncing ideas around because he had nothing else to grasp hold of. Still wondering about the last Texas Ranger, he was open to new ideas and theories. "Well, when you say predictions, tell me what you mean. What are they saying?"

Taking a minute to think, Belle picked up her coffee and finished it off, then placed the cup back down on the desk. With the coffee tasting good on her buds, she shook her head and smiled before she answered. "Well, they're always yapping about dark clouds coming upon us and the days being sinister. They have a newly proclaimed chief now. Chief Machakm. Means 'horny toed.' Fits him well. All he does is sit around all day eating and having sex with the unattached women of the tribe."

After a couple of laughs, Belle continued with her story. "Anyway, I was out there last week checking on the chief because he had the scratches down below. When I was finished telling him what it was, he wasn't happy. You see, I found out some of these younger tribal women have been sneaking away at night to have a little fun with some of the locals. Well, what comes around, gets around. Dirty old Chief caught himself a little itch. Serves him right for being a pervert."

Once again Jubal and Gideon found themselves laughing and enjoying Belle's story. Even Belle found herself laughing. "I gotta tell ya ,Gideon, as much as I make fun of that dirty old man, he can really spook me out sometimes. He goes into the big teepee in the middle of the village and smokes the whole damn thing up with some kind of smelly herbs. He then goes into a trance and starts mumbling to the spirits. Afterward, when he snaps out of it, he gets together with his council and talks about the future of the tribe. Well, last week he told me a story of something called Hok'ee."

Before Belle could continue, she saw the blank stare take over Gideon's face. His jaw dropped as he sat up and leaned across the desk. "What did he say about Hok'ee?"

Belle paused for a moment because she realized her story struck a chord with something inside of Gideon. "Well, he told me Hok'ee is a spirit that comes out at night. It somehow enters into the dreams and nightmares of the warriors and kills them before they awake. He said the Hok'ee is coming and that there's no stopping it. He warned for anybody having evil in their heart, that Hok'ee with seek them out and kill them while they sleep. And by that concerned look on your face, it seems you're familiar with this old Indian myth. So, what gives? Should I be worried?"

By now Jubal was up walking around and stretching his legs because the story reminded him of all the ghost stories the soldiers would tell around the campfires. "Come on now, Belle, you're not going to play into that old Indian wise tale, are you? And you, Gideon, I'm surprised at you. You were in the war. You sat around those campfires at night listening to them young fools tell their spooky stories. Hell, we had the same fools in our camps. Nothing new. Just old creepy stories to tell the children at bedtime in order to keep them honest." Jubal laughed as he shook his head in frustration, then placed his hat on his head.

After listening to Belle's story, Gideon was now very interested in meeting with the new chief. "Belle, I think I'd like to talk to Chief Machakm, so yes, thank you for asking. I think I will tag along with you. Jubal can mind things while I'm gone."

Along the way, Belle thought it would be nice to stop and pay their respects to Emily and the children. While standing at the graves, Doc Belle had an idea. While she looked around, she noticed some of the townspeople were starting to cut across the property traveling to and from Presidio. With an inquiring look, she waited for Gideon to finish placing flowers on each grave and say a small prayer. "Gideon, I have an idea and I need your opinion. I have some money put aside for rainy days, so you think maybe I could get a bank loan and possibly buy this property? I'd like to fence it off so the locals don't tread on it."

After placing his hat back on his head, Gideon stood in front of the graves and thought about it. "You're right, Belle. We need to protect this area, but I don't think a loan is the answer. I also have a rainy day fund. It isn't much, but I'm thinking maybe we can ask Ms. Lita and between the three of us, we can buy the lot."

While Gideon and Doc Belle continued their way to the Indian village, the spirits were swirling and churning with images of conquistadors killing off empires of the Aztec, Inca, and the Maya. Bloody scenes raged on as the conquerors killed off the less-advanced civilizations and seized their wealth. Sounds of swords and slashing flesh with screaming and yelling of victims and their families. Just as one display of carnage would come to an end, another would take its place. And with every scene came a dark cloud. While the turmoil raged on, a jaguar stalked its prey and killed every one of its intended victims.

Just when the jaguar was about to strike again, Jon awoke screaming. Having no feeling in his body, he tried to get up but couldn't move. He wasn't tied down, but it seemed like every muscle in his body had shut down. He was drenched in sweat and breathing heavy, and his heart pumped faster than ever before. He was conscious but confused. He lay still on his back staring up at what looked like the ceiling of an enormous cave. As his eyes nervously jolted back and forth, he could see carvings in the walls, which looked to be painted with silver. Accompanied with the carvings was the language he had recognized as a young boy. It was the language of the Nahuati.

A few minutes of looking around, his breathing began to subside. Not knowing what was going on, Jon closed his eyes in order to take a deep breath so as to calm himself. When he opened them, he saw the warrior Indian who had killed Hayden's men and spared his life. The same Indian who had followed him throughout his life. The same Indian he had briefly known and who had refused to take his life when he was a young boy. While the moments ticked away, the Indian stared down as Jon stared up. Jon knew there had been plenty of times the warrior Indian could have taken his life, so he knew there was no danger of the mysterious Indian hurting him now.

After a few seconds of staring, Jon once again, needed some answers. "Why can't I move?"

Refusing to bend to Jon's will, the warrior Indian continued to stare but gave no answer.

With many thoughts running through his mind, Jon remained persistent. "What happened? Where are the other Texas Rangers I was riding with?" All valid questions, but still no answers.

Feeling sympathetic, the warrior Indian knelt down and placed his hand over Jon's eyes. "Rest."

As Jon entered back into a deep sleep, Gideon and Doc Belle were just arriving at the Indian village with their supplies. While some of the men from the village began to unload, Doc Belle and Gideon went to see the chief. They were just in time because the chief had just come out of a trance and was about to address the elders of the village. The chief spoke in their native language so Gideon and Belle couldn't understand.

Afterward, one of the younger men translated for them. "The chief explained that a moment in time will take away centuries of sin and blood. He informed the elders Hok'ee has been aware of the many happenings over time and plans to correct all the wrongs. He cautioned that the Hok'ee is very angry and his wrath will reign down on those who have shed blood on the innocent. And once again, he forewarned when Hok'ee arrives, he will kill all who have evil in their heart."

After the meeting had adjourned, the elders left the room while Gideon stayed behind to ask some questions. While Doc Belle attended to the villagers, Gideon sat down and introduced himself. "Good afternoon, Chief Machakm. My name is Gideon. I'm the sheriff of Presidio."

The Chief had lit a pipe and was starting to puff on it as he took a moment to look Gideon up and down. "You have skin like buffalo and you rule over white man. Lady doctor say you good man. What you say?"

Gideon was a little surprised by the question, but tried to be humble while answering. "Well, I don't rule over anybody. I like to think I protect people and at the same time keep the peace."

Once again the chief looked Gideon up and down while his pipe blew out smoke. "Lady doctor tell me about friends. Very bad sign. Big storm coming soon. Many more will die."

After listening to the chief, Gideon took a moment, then countered with a question. "What do you mean when you say storm? And who is it that's going to die?"

Taking a few puffs of his pipe, the chief rolled his eyes back into his head. "Good stuff. Me get in trade with next village over." After a few more puffs, the chief answered the question. "Battle of good and evil. Many men will die."

Gideon thought for a moment as he tried to absorb what he was hearing. "And when does this battle take place?"

Once again the chief rolled his eyes and breathed a nice, deep breath. "When Hok'ee come, no man safe. He will do battle with evil ones. Buffalo skin cannot hide what is in heart. In time, you will make choice."

With a bit of frustration, Gideon wondered why he was listening to an old man making no sense. "Okay, Chief. What about the Hok'ee? What or who is it?"

The chief could hear the frustration in Gideon's voice, so he placed his pipe down and smiled. "Hok'ee come in many form. Hok'ee walk between worlds. Hok'ee been here many moons and will continue to fight evil. I cannot tell you what I do not know. You know Hok'ee when you see Hok'ee. Only then will you prove yourself as foe or friend. Now, you leave. You take lady doc home."

With more uncertainty than ever, Gideon left the room and met up with Belle, who was just finishing her medical exams. With Gideon's demeanor, she could tell he was upset. As she placed her instruments back into her medical bag, she gave Gideon a smile. "Gideon, don't let that foolish old man get to you. I'm sure whatever he told you was probably due to the fact he smokes that mind-numbing poison all day."

Gideon appreciated the kind words as he shook his head and took a deep breath. "That old man really knew how to push all the right buttons. Some of the stuff he said really got my juices flowing. There's something going on here. Something more than Hayden. I think that old man is right about one thing. I think a battle is coming and it's going to be very bad and very messy."

When Gideon and Belle got back to town, they inquired about the land, then spoke to Ms. Lita. Thinking it was a great idea, Ms. Lita decided to join the two in buying Jon's land. When Jubal caught wind of it, he also wanted to help, so the next day the four signed the papers and became the new owners of the property that housed Jon's family. They bought fencing and over the next week had some of the locals help fence the property off. For Gideon and Jubal, it was a nice break from all the mystery and violence that surrounded Zachariah Hayden.

During that same week, Jon was in and out of consciousness as the black cloud followed him during his dreams. Constant nightmares of Aztecs, Incas and Mayans doing battles with conquistadors. A jaguar stalking villagers and killing its prey. Franciscan priests, Indians, and Spanish soldiers. All with deceiving hearts. As Jon lay asleep, once again darkness consumed his dreams. But this wasn't the dark cloud hovering. This was something different. There was darkness all around and it seemed cold like a grave. Then suddenly, there she was. Out of the darkness came Emily. She slowly moved closer until she was standing in front of him. After a moment of staring into each other's eyes, she placed her soft hand on Jon's cheek. Wanting nothing more than to hold her, Jon could feel the warmth of her love running through his body.

Looking into Jon's eyes, Emily finally spoke. "Hello, Jon."

Jon tried to speak, but he couldn't as Emily gave a small smile. "You're not meant to speak, Jon. Just to listen." After a brief pause, Emily continued. "I love you. I always have. That day in the schoolhouse when I turned and saw you, from that moment I've loved you and would change nothing about our time together."

Unable to speak, Jon's eyes spoke for him as tears of love began to roll down his face. Then, suddenly, another surprise. Abby, Abram and Adam appeared. They stood off to the side of Emily, but like Jon they weren't able to speak. But then Jon noticed a fourth child off in the distance. It was faceless and he couldn't tell the gender.

As he turned his attention back to Emily, she had placed her hand over her stomach and was beginning to fade back into the darkness. "We have to go, Jon. We are no longer a part of your world, but we will always be with you. Keep us close in your heart."

Suddenly Jon awoke in a sweat, screaming. He quickly jumped to his feet and looked around in a panic. He then placed his hands over his eyes and dropped to his knees, crying. "Please God, make it stop. Make it stop. I can't do this anymore."

After a few more moments, Jon wiped the tears from his eyes and stood up. The wounds he had received were no longer an issue. They had healed with full range of motion and he realized his speech was back. He took a moment to glance around to try and get his bearings, but it was dark and he had no idea where he was. That's when it happened. A familiar fire had erupted, which lit up the area he was standing. And there he was. Out of the darkness and fire came the Old One. Still trembling from his vision, Jon watched as the fire receded down to a normal campfire. Having more questions than answers, he recalled his previous encounters so he decided to wait for the Old One to speak first.

Jon observed as the Old One gracefully moved around the fire spreading what looked to be silver dust. He spoke words Jon didn't understand, then sat down and folded his legs. With a hand gesture, he invited Jon to sit across from him. After Jon sat down, the Old One once again started to mumble unfamiliar words. He rocked back and forth and threw more silver dust into the fire, which made it crackle and pop as Jon patiently waited. Some last words and one final throwing of dust, and the rocking came to a stopped. "Cheveyo, I see your wounds have healed well. You still have many questions but I have very little answers to satisfy your desires."

Starting to become a little tired of feeling like a pawn in a game, Jon decided not to speak right away. He thought for a moment because he didn't want to waste the little time he had with questions without answers. "How long have I been here?"

With his usual stern attitude, the Old One paused, then spoke. "There is no time here. Just space which you occupy. You have moved between many realms of space."

Listening to the Old One, this was what Jon was afraid of. He knew his time was limited, but he needed to avoid answers he wouldn't understand. So he realized he needed to ask questions concerning subjects he was familiar with. "There was an ambush. What happen to the men I was with?"

Once again the Old One paused, then answered. "Their souls have moved on from your world. They are at rest."

Unfortunately, Jon understood all too well what that meant. Without thinking, he blurted out his next question with frustration. "Why am I still here? Why did I not go with them?"

The Old One could sense the difficulty Jon was having, but was unwilling to elaborate any further than necessary. "You are Cheveyo. It was not your time."

With annoyance starting to build, Jon stood up and inquired about his wounds as his voice became raised. "I took three bullets to my chest and I don't see any marks and no scars. I should be dead. Whatever you used to heal me could've been used to help my friends. Why did you let them die?"

With no compassion in his voice, the Old One gave his answer. "For good or for evil, they served the purpose of their life. As for you, Cheveyo, you are not done. Your purpose is still ahead of you. Your life still has meaning."

As Jon tried to comprehend the conversation, he took a few seconds to breath. While he turned away for a brief second, the Old One was gone. While the fire grew dim, he could hear whispers from the Old One coming out of the dark. "Sleep, Cheveyo, sleep."

Afterward, Jon's eyes grew heavy and his legs buckled as he fell unconscious. When he awoke, he was laying on the hard ground. With the sun shining down and the birds singing their songs, he stood up and looked around. It didn't take long for him to see he was on the old cow trail at the sight of the ambush. After shaking off the grogginess, he saw the warrior Indian standing alongside a horse, which was tied to the tree Gunny was buried under.

Without hesitation or fear, Jon approached. "Listen, enough with all the talk about Hok'ee and Cheveyo nonsense. I don't care who you are and I'm not afraid of you anymore." After waiting for a reaction, Jon continued on. "Where's my horse?"

With a blank expression, the warrior Indian stood staring at Jon. "Like all things that die, they turn to dust and are given back to the Earth from which they came."

Just then, Jon noticed the Bowie knife at the foot of the tree. As he glanced down the tree line, he began to count. It was then he realized the final resting place of the rest of the Texas Rangers. When he turned back around to confront the Indian, the warrior had vanished. Taking a moment to look around, Jon noticed the horse was saddled and equipped with all the guns he usually carried. So, he suited up and prepared for the ride back to his house. He still wasn't sure how long he'd been away, so he was desperate to see his wife and children.

Jon had the idea of staying out of sight until he could talk with Emily and figure out how long he's been away and what to do afterward. So he stuck to the wood lines and less traveled trails. When he finally arrived home, he was overwhelmed with shock. As he sat atop his horse staring, his heart began to sink. There was no house and there was no barn. What little livestock he had was gone. Looking at the freshly built fence that surrounded the property, once again Jon pondered how long he had been gone.

After finding a gate to pass through, he slowly made his way to where the house use to sit. Still in shock, Jon climbed down from his horse. He could still see the foundation, but could also see it had been burned to the ground. Jon didn't need more questions, but it seemed his life was nothing but an unsolved mystery. While various emotions were rushing through his mind, he turned and saw five graves. They were nestled between two old cedar trees.

He recalled the trees as being Emily's favorite. They had an old wooden swing attached at one time and Emily loved to sit out on warm nights and gaze up at the stars. After taking a deep breath and gathering himself, he walked over to get a closer look.

As Jon got closer, the names on the graves became clearer. When he finally stood in front of them, he dropped to his knees. The sadness he felt was unbearable. Emily, Abigayle, Abram, and Adam. His wife and precious children lie buried beneath him in the ground. After a few moments of grief, he glanced at the fifth grave and noticed it had no name. Suddenly he remembered his vision. The fourth child with no face or gender. That's when he realized Emily must have been pregnant the day he left. Still feeling the pain of losing everything he cared about, Jon slowly stood up and turned to find Gideon standing there.

The two men stood staring at each other for a moment before Gideon spoke with an assertive voice. "Where the hell have you been, Jon?"

Feeling drained, Jon didn't say anything. He was still trying to comprehend the loss of his family. So, with his voice a little more calm, Gideon continued his inquiry. Stepping toward the graves, Gideon removed his hat in order to pay his respects. "I figured you'd make it back here sooner or later."

Feeling completely empty, Jon looked around at the fence line. "You put this up?"

Disturbed by the frivolous question, Gideon shook his head in disgust. With his emotions coming down, he responded in a rational voice. "Belle, Lita, Jubal, and I got together and pitched in. We didn't want people trampling on the land, so we bought the property."

With his remorse starting to turn to anger, Jon glanced down at the graves. "Who did this?"

Reciting a small prayer to himself, Gideon stooped down for a minute, then stood back up and placed his hat back on his head. "That's not a question you should be asking because you already know the answer."

Glancing down at the graves, Jon thought for a moment as he pondered Gideon's response. "Hayden wouldn't dare get his hands this dirty, so who was it?"

Gideon didn't answer right away, but it was obvious Jon wasn't going to let it go. "Jubal and I did some checking around. We think Hayden brought in a special team to take out the Rangers' families. Men that go above and beyond and are ruthless in their quest to punish their victims. I'm sorry, Jon. I underestimated the sadistic mind of that madman, and a lot of innocent people payed the price for it."

Once again Jon didn't say anything. He just turned to the graves and looked down at the ground. As he took a deep breath, Jon turned back to Gideon. "Who were they? I want their names."

With some frustration starting to build, Gideon took a deep breath. "You were never declared dead, Jon. That means you're still a Texas Ranger. You can't go off and kill people when you don't have just cause. You have an obligation to bring them to justice."

Not caring about his status anymore, Jon wasn't listening to Gideon's words, nor did he care. Something was beginning to change within him. Law didn't matter anymore, and with his family gone, there was nothing left for him to fight for. All the good qualities he use to have within him were spewing out and rapidly being replaced with vengeful thoughts.

After realizing Jon would find out one way or another, Gideon took a deep breath and tried to reason with him. "Jon, I'll give you the names, but please, let's do this the right way."

But Jon was no longer interested in what other people thought was right. Without saying any words, he gave Gideon an evil stare as he slowly placed his hand on his gun.

With some disappointment, Gideon glanced down at Jon's gun hand. "Jon, don't do this. I don't want to have to bury you next to you family."

Once again Jon stared as his hand started to grip his gun. "Gideon, I've had enough. I've tried to make a difference. I've tried to play by the rules. I've tried to be the bigger person, but I'm tired. Tired of the lawlessness that this world seems to embrace while good people constantly have to bow down and eat dirt. Please, Gideon, I love you like a brother and I don't want to kill you, but I'm going to need those names."

Feeling torn, Gideon didn't want to force a showdown, so after taking a deep breath, he gave in and rattled off the information. "Marcus and Ronnie Beck. A couple of mountain boys. Their weapon of choice is an ax. Apparently they get off on chopping people up for a living. But don't underestimate them. They're just as deadly with a gun. Then there's Lester Hayes. Loves little children, but in the wrong way. Been in prison half his life but always manages to escape. He's wanted in six states and a few other territories. Roberto Castas. Once killed a man for snoring too loud. Then killed the man's wife after raping her. Just your average pleasant guy. The fifth man is a man named Rico. That's all we know. He seems to have a reputation for smooth talk and being suave with the ladies, but he's as ruthless as they come."

As Gideon spoke, Jon mentally took in all the information. Before Jon could ask any more questions, Gideon tried one last time to talk him out of going down the wrong path. "I loved them too, Jon. You and Emily always treated me like family. Don't let hatred take a hold of you. Please, Jon, let the law do its job."

Jon could hear the words, but they were moving through him like wind through an open door and taking no affect. With a very low but stern voice, he asked one last question. "Where are they?"

Gideon stared for a moment, hoping he could see some kind of humanity in Jon's eyes, but there was none left. Still frustrated, he gave Jon the information. "Marcus and Ronnie went north. I heard they like to hang out in some little town with no name. We think somewhere up in the mountain region. Roberto has family down in Mexico. Town called Nuevo Casa Grandes, and we think Lester may have tagged along for the ride. You can't miss Lester. He has a scar across his forehead, compliments of two very angry Apaches that took a little revenge out on him for attacking their little sister. They run around with a ruthless gang of banditos. As for Roberto, just ask around. He's apparently well known in those parts. We think Rico decided to try his hand at bounty hunting, so he could be anywhere."

By now the two men were exhausted with emotions. Jon had stepped beyond the realm of law enforcement and was on his way to becoming the type of person he had fought against all his life. Gideon was now looking at Jon as though he was about to lose a long lost brother. "Jon, your gun isn't going to bring them back."

Feeling no remorse for his rationalization, Jon thought for a moment and smiled. "You're right, but after I do what I'm going to do, I'm just not going to care anymore."

With disappointment starting to settle in, Gideon tried his best to curb Jon's appetite for destruction. "So, now what, Jon? You either get yourself killed or get your revenge and become a wanted man?"

Once again, Jon pondered Gideon's words. "I'm already a dead man. I just haven't laid down yet. In any case, I will have my revenge and when I'm finished, I'm coming for Hayden."

After hearing that, Gideon was done. He had no more words to offer. "Jon, I can't let you do this."

Knowing what was now in his heart, Jon placed his hand in his pocket and pulled out his Texas Ranger badge, which had meant so much to him at one time. After looking at it for a few moments, he tossed it to Gideon. "Here, I won't be needing this anymore."

Catching the badge, Gideon glanced at it with disappointment. "Jon, please, don't do this. I can't let you do this. I won't let you do this."

Feeling he had nothing left to say, Jon was done talking and his mind was now contaminated with hatred for the world. Turning his back on Gideon, he climbed up on his horse, then took one last look at the graves. He then glanced down at his brother at heart. He didn't physically speak, but his eyes were saying good-bye to a friend.

Not knowing what else to do, Gideon placed his hand on his gun but didn't draw. His voice became elevated as he tried desperately to get Jon to heed his words. "Jon, please, listen to me. I don't want to shoot you. Don't make me shoot you."

With the situation becoming tense, Jon turned his horse north, placing his back to Gideon. "Better a friend do it than a foe."

Gripping the handle of his gun, Gideon watched as Jon started to gallop away. With some desperate last words, Gideon yelled. "Jon! Come back, Jon!"

Gideon's grip became even tighter as he tried to yell louder for Jon's attention. But it was too late. Jon was gone. He was on his way to becoming a wanted man whose life would probably end violently.

As Jon got further and further away, the sky grew dim while the sun sought temporary refuge in the clouds. Climbing up on his horse, Gideon gave one last look at his friend disappearing over the hills. Taking a breath and removing his hat, Gideon glanced down at the graves and had a few last words before heading back to town. "I'm sorry, Emily. Truly sorry." Trying to sort through the encounter, Gideon placed his hat back on his head and turned his horse toward Presidio.

As Gideon was heading back to town, Jon was making his way north toward the mountains. After a day of heavy riding, he came upon an old outpost. He recognized it from when he was younger traveling to El Capitan. Now, being older, he realized what he had been looking at as a young boy. It was a stopover for outlaws, gamblers, and men of questionable character. It had a makeshift bar, a few dirty rooms in the back, and a small barn to house horses overnight. As he approached and climbed down from his horse, he entered the main house with caution. Giving his eyes a moment to adjust to the darkness, he glanced around at the occupants. Same place. Just different faces. The man behind the bar was old. His beard was white and his face looked like he had lived a very hard life. There were two younger men sitting at a table in the back of the room along with two not-so-young-looking women.

After his initial pause, Jon walked over to the bar. With some curiosity, the old man stared a moment, then pulled out a half-empty bottle and poured Jon a drink. "Here'ya go, mista, have a drink. It's not the best whiskey, but it'll do ya. I have a couple of girls over there, Darla and Maggie, if yer fancy is in need. Those two bums ain't do'n nuth'n but waist'n time."

With a smile, Jon gladly accepted the drink. "Well, old timer, I appreciate the offer, but I'm tired and I'm just looking for a place to lay my head for the night."

Just then, one of the men got up from the table and walked over to Jon. "Well now, what'a we have here? A man who don't like women. Well, what'ya like, Mr. Man? Are you one of those guys that like to fuck sheep? Are you a sheep fuck'n man?"

Before the belligerent man could continue, the old bartender intervened. "Come on now, Buck. I don't need ya start'n no trouble in here."

With the hope of curbing a violent encounter, the old man poured Buck a drink in order to defuse the situation. But Buck had other plans as he took the drink and gulped it down, then slammed the glass down on the bar. As he smiled, he turned to his friend, who was still sitting with the two women, and laughed. He then turned his attentions back to Jon, who was slowly sipping his drink. "Don't worry, old man, no trouble here. By the way, isn't it a tradition around here for a newcomer to buy a round of drinks?"

Unfortunately for Buck, Jon was all too familiar with the likes of men like him. So before things could get out of hand, he pulled a coin from his pocket and paid the bartender for his drink. "Thank you, barkeep, for your hospitality, but I think I'll be heading out."

As Jon turned to walk out, Buck had a few things to say. "Now, wait a minute, boy. You gonna break tradition and not buy us a drink and then turn your back on me?"

Stopping just short of the door, Jon turned to face the loud-mouthed man. By now, Buck's friend had gotten up. While walking across the room to join Buck, Buck started talking again. "You believe this ungrateful bastard, Joe? We allow this sheep fuck'n stranger into our fine establishment and he does nothing but insult us."

While Joe took up a position halfway across the room, Buck continued his banter. Shaking his head and laughing, Buck raised his hand and pointed at Jon. "I think you owe us an apology, boy."

Jon looked around the room as he glanced at Joe, who hadn't said a word but was obviously thinking in a strategic manner. Then there were the two women who were still sitting at the table but were now on edge. The old man behind the bar was just that. Old. He was obviously tired and wanted no parts of any trouble. Then there was Buck. Jon knew Buck was the stupid one because he was fast with his lips with no advanced thinking. So, he decided to throw some words out of his own. "I mean no disrespect to the ladies, and as far as the bartender goes, I apologize for any damages that may be caused here shortly."

When Jon turned his attention back to Buck, Buck was still smiling and waiting for some kind of cowardly action, but Jon had no intentions of backing down. "And for the two pigs in the room, I don't apologize to swine."

While Buck's smile started to turn upside down, Jon began to face him down. "Get my meaning, boy?" Just then and without warning, Jon walked toward Buck, clinching his right hand into a fist and struck a blow to the left side of Buck's face. The force sent Buck overtop a table and crashing to the floor.

By now, the two women had gotten up and moved behind the bar for safety. As Joe stood waiting, Buck finally shook off the hard hit and got up. As he rubbed the hurt off his jaw, he smiled and started laughing. "Boy, you pack one hell of a punch, but now I'm looking at a dead man."

Just when Buck and Joe tried to draw, Jon drew first with lightning speed and put two bullets dead center of their chests. The two men stumbled back and destroyed two more tables as they fell backward to the floor.

Gasping for air, Darla was appalled at what she had just witnessed. As she attempted to calm herself, she was finally able to form the words she wanted to speak. "What the hell, mister? You come in here causing trouble, then shoot up the goddamn place. Who the hell do you think you are?"

After holstering his gun, Jon walked over to the two dead men and picked their pockets for valuables. Joe had eighteen dollars and a gold pocket watch; Buck had fifty six dollars and a nice pocket knife. Wanting to reimburse for damages, Jon walked over to the bartender and handed him the money. "Here, old man. This should cover the damages and the leftovers should buy you some better whiskey."

Jon then turned his attention to the women and apologized. "Sorry for any inconvenience, ladies, but here some nice parting gifts for you." Not caring about the insignificant trinkets, he handed them the knife and the watch, then turned and walked out.

While Jon made his exit, Maggie ran out after him. Before Jon could get on his horse, Maggie took him by the hand and pulled him into the nearby barn. She was anxious and breathing heavy as she wrapped her arms around Jon and kissed him passionately. After a few seconds, Jon pushed Maggie away. "What are you doing?"

With a desperate look on her face, Maggie explained her actions. "Take me with you, please. Take me out of this hole. I can't stand being here anymore, please. I'll do anything you want."

Still wanting to impress Jon, Maggie unbuttoned her dirty torn blouse and exposed herself to him. "Take what you want, but take me with you."

Feeling no compassion for the loose woman, Jon turned around for a moment, then turned back around to face Maggie. "I don't know you and I don't want to know you. People like you are part of the problem in this world. Always wanting something. Always needing something, and willing to do whatever it takes to get it, including selling yourself and your soul."

After a few more seconds of staring at Maggie, Jon became sick and continued to berate her. "Go ahead. Go back in there and continue living your filthy life, you dirty whore."

Jon turned to walk away but listening to his degrading words, Maggie wasn't finished as she ran up behind him and stepped into his path. "That's right, tough guy. I do what I need to do in order to survive. You think you're better than me? You're no better. You'll kill a man in a blink of an eye and not even have the heart to think twice about it. Men like you wind up in hell, and I hope you get there soon."

Now Maggie was just as disgusted as Jon and, continuing with her insult, decided to spit in his face. "You dirty pig. Those two men you killed were going to take me places and now they're dead."

Taking a deep breath, Jon wiped the spit from his face and then backhanded Maggie, causing her to fall to the ground. He then stepped over top of her and climbed onto his horse. With her hardened face, Maggie glanced up at Jon as he turned his horse north. Before starting back on his journey, he had a few last words. "I'm sure the next guy that comes along will be glad to take care of a whore like you." With that said, he left Maggie crying on the ground.

While Jon was putting the wind at his back, Gideon was back in town try-ing to figure out a way to deal with Zachariah Hayden. But before doing so, he had to find the words to tell Jubal about Jon. After making their rounds around town, the two men met back at the office. While there, Gideon poured two drinks and handed one to Jubal. It wasn't quite the afternoon, and Jubal's whistle was dry so he gladly accepted the drink. After taking a swig, Jubal placed the glass down on the desk. With a wary disposition, Jubal inquired about the informal meeting. "Gideon, something on your mind you need to get rid of?"

With a heavy heart, Gideon didn't drink his whiskey. Instead, he left it lay on the desk. As he gathered his thoughts, he began to speak. "It was Jon."

Jubal stared at Gideon for a moment, then inquired about the strange statement. "What about Jon?"

Not trying to give too much information at once, Gideon stood up and started pacing around the room. "It was Jon who survived the ambush."

Realizing what Gideon was saying, Jubal's heart sank as he reached for his drink and downed it and then helped himself to Gideon's. "What the hell, Gideon? How do you know?"

By now, Gideon was staring out the window at the townspeople going about their daily business and wondering how things ever got so far out of control. "I'm sorry, Jubal. You're a great friend and a dedicated deputy and I should have told you sooner, but I was trying to keep everything inside in order to somehow contain this volatile situation. But I just can't do it. I've tried to keep everything bottled up like a nice little package, but at times I feel like exploding."

As a kind gesture, Jubal poured two more drinks, then handed one to his friend. He could tell with everything going on, it was beginning to weigh heavy on his mind. After watching Gideon take a drink, he waited for him to continue.

Gearing up to tell Jubal what happened, Gideon paused as he continued to look out the window. "I needed to clear my head, so I took a ride over to the gravesite. I was going to pull the weeds and put some fresh flowers down, but when I arrived I saw Jon."

With the shocking news of Jon finally sinking in, Jubal decided to take a seat while Gideon continued to explain. "My God, Gideon. The graves. What did he say? Where the hell has he been?"

As Jubal continued to question everything, he tried to grasp the idea that Jon was still alive. "Gideon, I know I can be a bit slow in my brain sometimes, but I'm just not understanding any of this."

Gideon knew there would be questions, so he sat back down to try and figure it out. "Jon didn't say too much and I don't think I want to know where he's been. But like you, I'm not understanding too much of what's going on anymore."

With thoughts rapidly moving through their minds, both men paused to gather their emotions. Afterward, Gideon continued his story. "I was so angry but at the same time, I was just happy to see him alive. I gotta tell you, Jubal, I was scared. I didn't really know what to say. It was like my thought process just froze. Before I knew it, he was asking me questions."

With his nerves still on edge, Jubal sat up and leaned over the desk to get more insight. "What kind of questions?"

Thinking back to his encounter, Gideon took a breath and then finished. "Well, even though he asked, it was obvious to me he already knew who was responsible for the deaths of his family. He wanted the information on who did the deed, so I reluctantly told him."

After hearing that, Jubal sat back in his chair and pondered the outcome. "My God Gideon, he's a Texas Ranger. He can't just go gunn'n people down. Gideon, he'll hang if he doesn't get'em self killed first."

Knowing Jubal was right, there was nothing they could do but wait. But there was one more thing Gideon needed to show Jubal, so he reached into his pocket and pulled out Jon's Texas Ranger badge and laid it on the desk."

With a short gasp, Jubal reached over and picked the badge up. As he looked down at it, fear entered his thoughts. "Gideon, when he's finished, he's coming back here for Hayden. And then what?"

With the thought of possibly going up against his best friend, Gideon did-n't have an answer. Just questions. "I think we need to pay Hayden a visit. I think we need to get ahead of the game so we can control the outcome."

Once again it was time to confront the man who had made life a living hell for the people of Presidio. Knowing Zachariah was in his usual spot having lunch, Gideon and Jubal entered the hotel and approached the dining area. Armed with their boldness, both men sat down uninvited.

With his usual sarcasm, Zachariah finished chewing his food and then spoke. "Well now, once again, sheriff, you and Deputy Do Da don't surprise me with your ignorance. So, what can I do for Presidio's law enforcement today?"

With a smirk, Jubal decided to return the insult. "Well, since you're asking, it would be a nice gesture if you packed your belongings and got the hell out of our town."

Pulling a handkerchief from his pocket, Zachariah smiled as he wiped his mouth. "Still the coward I see, Deputy. Always confident with your sheriff sitting beside you. But I have to tell you, your beloved sheriff won't be around forever. I have the distinct feeling he's living on borrowed time."

Not liking what Zachariah was implying, Gideon decided to chime in. "Is that a threat, Hayden? Pittman, your hired killer left town, so is this your way of telling us he's coming back?"

Taking a sip of his wine, Zachariah paused to enjoy the flavor. "My good Sheriff, I'm just merely stating facts. With all the killing and happenings around here, I just don't see you lasting much longer. Besides, you could turn into a nice trophy for one of these young and up-and-coming gun fighters. Why, who wouldn't want the bragging rights of killing the first Negro sheriff of Texas?"

Gideon knew Zachariah was just trying to aggravate the situation, so he decided to say his piece. "We know you're the cause of all the killings because you're looking for some fabled treasure, which doesn't exist. We also know you had the Texas Rangers killed and their families slaughtered. But what you don't know and I doubt if Colonel Pittman informed you, one of the Rangers survived your little ambush. He's going to make a very good witness at your trial."

Gideon smiled as he watched Zachariah's face turn to worry. With a lump starting to form in his stomach, Zachariah was no longer interested in his food.

Realizing the amount of confidence Gideon had while spouting off about the survival of one lone Ranger made Zachariah think that it may be the truth. As he slowly stood up, he once again wiped his mouth with a handkerchief. "If you'll excuse me, gentlemen, I have some business to attend to."

Having a certain plan in mind, Gideon watched as Zachariah quickly made his way out the door. Unfortunately, Jubal was in the dark about what Gideon was doing. "Gideon, I don't understand. Why tell somebody like Hayden about Jon?"

Trying to let a few minutes pass, Gideon sat back in his chair and thought for a moment. "Jon has the idea of working his way back to Presidio because he wants Hayden's head. I'm hoping to be able to convince him that we have enough evidence to convict Hayden for all of the crimes he's committed."

Still not understanding the plan, Jubal scratched his head and thought for a moment. "Gideon, we don't have any hard evidence and I doubt very much if anyone could talk Jon out of killing Hayden."

After waiting a few minutes, Gideon stood up with confidence. "Right now Hayden is on his way to the telegraph office. I imagine he paid a lot of money to have the Texas Rangers killed, so right about now he's probably very upset that there's a possible witness who survived. I have no doubt he's going to send a telegram to Colonel Pittman to let him know his dismay. Then he's going to head to the Lucy Goosy for a stiff drink and try and think about how to fix his newfound problem."

With a smile on his face, Jubal was encouraged by what Gideon was thinking. "I hope you're right, Gideon. If Jon does come back to town, he's gonna want Hayden's head served on a platter."

Following up on Gideon's insight, the two men made their way to the front door of the hotel, then stood off to the side and watched. Just like clockwork, Zachariah Hayden exited the telegraph office and walked toward the Lucy Goosy saloon. Watching Hayden do exactly what Gideon said he would do, Jubal glanced over at Gideon, who was now looking at Jubal with a big smile on his face. "What'ya say, Jubal, we head over to the telegraph office and have a little talk with our friend Mr. Herman."

Anxious to invade Zachariah Hayden's privacy, Jubal followed while Gideon walked with a little swagger in his step. After arriving, they observed the keeper of notes, Mr. Herman, hard at work sending and receiving the day's telegrams. Exercising some patience, both men stood and waited until the opportunity arose to state their business. When Mr. Herman turned to see Gideon and Jubal, he already had an idea of why they were there. Gideon stood quietly with a big smile on his face while Mr. Herman swallowed the lump in his throat.

After a few awkward seconds, Gideon spoke. "Mr. Herman, we've been friends for a while now and I would never ask you to do anything against your code of ethics, but I just happen to know that Zachariah Hayden just left here a few minutes ago."

With a bunch of messages in his hand, Mr. Herman slowly stood up and leaned over the counter. "Now, Sheriff, I'd like to oblige you, but you know the law. Can't give anything out without the person's consent or a court order."

Gideon knew Mr. Herman was right, but before he could say anything else, Jubal decided to throw his thoughts into the conversation. "Herman, you and I go back a long way and you know I have noth'n but respect for rules and them there regulations, but this is really important."

After a few paused seconds, Jubal could see Mr. Herman was still uncomfortable, so he decided to try and appeal to his sense of humor. "Now, Herman, you remember last year when business was slow and I came by to visit and you were sweep'n out your office? You had your door open and that big gust of wind came by and blew a bunch of yer papers all over the floor and I helped ya pick'em up. Well, I see ya have a bunch of notes in your hand and if'n ya accidentally dropped them on the floor, well, you know Gideon and me would definitely feel obliged to help ya retrieve those notes. Get what I'm say'n?"

Feeling the pressure, Mr. Herman stared at Jubal, then glanced over at Gideon, who was still grinning from ear to ear. As he thought about Jubal's words, he maneuvered his hand across the counter and accidentally knocked over a bin full of papers, which also caused him to drop the notes in his hand. "Oh, damn. Clumsy me. Always dropping one thing or another. I'm really sorry, Sheriff, but I just can't help you. But I would appreciate any help you could provide in helping me pick this mess up."

Without hesitation, Gideon and Jubal bent down and quickly gathered up the loose papers and notes. As they did, Gideon saw what was written on the telegram Zachariah sent.

After straightening the papers, Gideon and Jubal handed them to Mr. Herman and thanked him by tipping their hats. Stepping out of the telegraph office, Gideon seemed to be upbeat. "Jubal, that was mighty fine work."

With a bit of pride, Jubal patted Gideon on the back as he smiled. "Sometimes, imagination does the job better than rules and regulations. Did you find what ya were look'n for?"

Looking around at the townspeople going about their daily business, Gideon took a breath and smiled. "Most definitely. I saw the notes Mr. Herman had written. Our man Hayden is in a panic. He sent for Colonel Pittman to come as soon as possible."

Being pleased with the day's events, Gideon wasn't done. Knowing he had finally gotten to Zachariah Hayden, he wanted to continue to pressure him so he would make more mistakes. "I'm thirsty, Jubal. What'ya say I buy us a few drinks?"

Feeling thirsty, Jubal happily agreed, so the two men walked over to the Lucy Goosy. When they walked in, they could see Zachariah sitting in the back of the room sulking in a bottle of whiskey. After saying hello to Ms. Lita, Gideon payed for some drinks, then made his way across the room. Zachariah was so engrossed in his thinking, he didn't notice Gideon until he pulled a chair out and sat down. With a smile on his face, Gideon began to taunt his nemesis. "Well now, Hayden, doing some pretty hard drinking, I see. Something on your mind?"

Zachariah was in no mood for games, especially with Gideon and the information he provided earlier. "Sheriff, I'm getting real tired of your ignorance. You seem to think it's okay to invite yourself when there's no invitation given. Why is that? Was it your upbringing or do all Negros share your rudeness?"

Gideon laughed because he had gotten to the point where Zachariah's racist remarks were more funny than hurtful. "Come now, Hayden, you can do better than that. I always invite myself to sit down because I know deep down, you really like me and you spend every waking moment thinking about me. But right about now, I'm thinking I'm not the only person on your mind. I think you're worried about who survived your little onslaught. I'm thinking maybe you need your friend the colonel to come back and take care of business. I'm also thinking all those men you hired isn't going to be able to protect you while you're serving out a life sentence in prison or hanging from a rope. Whichever the jury decides for you. Sorry, Hayden, no wine or fancy hotel food in prison either. Just the pig slop they throw on your plate and maybe a little sex from behind." Once again, Gideon couldn't help but laugh while pushing Zachariah to his limits.

With a distasteful look in his eyes, Zachariah paused momentarily, then took a drink of whiskey. "Sheriff, your crudeness is appalling to me. Every time I must deal with your kind, it makes me want to vomit. Why God so hated the South that he condemned them to bowel down to barbarians such as you is beyond my realm of thinking. In any case, you're right. Not about me being worried, but about Colonel Pittman returning and taking care of some unfinished business. And I'm not worried about your phantom survivor."

One last drink of whiskey, then Zachariah stood up and threw the empty glass against the wall, shattering it into pieces. Zachariah then cast a look of death down to Gideon. "You can have that whore of a bar maid put that on my tab."

With his anger at its peak, Zachariah grabbed what was left of his bottle and walked out. Afterward, Jubal and Ms. Lita walked over and sat down. Gideon no longer had a smile on his face because, listening to the words of Zachariah, he had realized the endgame Zachariah had in mind.

Feeling a little uneasy, Ms. Lita expressed her concerns for Gideon. "Gideon, what happen? Are you all right?"

Knowing Gideon didn't tolerate a lot of nonsense, Jubal also expressed his thoughts. "Gideon, I can easily go put Hayden in jail for the night. Disturbing the peace, destruction of property. Hell, we can probably make a case for reckless endangerment. You just say the word and I'll lock'em up."

Gideon appreciated all the support, but he wasn't interested in jailing Zachariah for a night. "We put Hayden in jail and fifty of his men will ride in and destroy the town and kill most if not all of its occupants." With a slight smile, he then tried to lighten the mood. "Then we'll all be out of jobs."

Once again Ms. Lita inquired about the incident. "Gideon, it's not like you to just let someone go off on you like that. So, what's going on?"

Jubal had brought over the drinks Gideon bought, so Gideon took a moment and helped himself. Afterward, he paused as though he was staring off into space. "Well, it seems I may have once again misjudged Hayden. He already had the idea of having Colonel Pittman come back to town. I think his plan all along was to kill off the Texas Rangers, finish up his treasure-hunting business, then have Pittman kill me. My guess is that he wired whatever payment he promised Pittman to a bank in California. Pittman then takes a train to California to take care of business and probably told Hayden he would return to kill me. But in telling Hayden about a surviving Ranger, Hayden panicked and asked Pittman to cut his trip short. But I still don't understand why he had all the Rangers killed. There's gotta be more involved than just the fact they were investigating the crimes. So, why them?"

Taking in some quiet time, the three sat and pondered the question and when thinking back to his trip to Mexico City, Jubal may have had an answer. "Gideon, Hayden doesn't do anything unless he's get'n something out of it. The Rangers wasn't hot on his trail and only Jon had any interaction with him and none of it good."

Thinking back, it didn't take long for Gideon to zero in on Jon. "You're right, Jubal. He had no real reason to kill all the Texas Rangers. But to kill them all would cover up killing the one that he really wanted. Commit one crime to cover up another. That old necklace Jon wears. I wonder if Hayden thinks it has meaning? He wanted it really bad, but he needed to find a way to get it without bringing suspicion to himself. So, just like all the homesteader killings, kill all the Texas Rangers and make people think it was an Indian attack. Except there were no bodies to be found. So, I'm guessing Hayden never got his prize."

With even more concern then before, Ms. Lita didn't like what she was hearing. "And after Colonel Pittman finishes his business in California, he's coming back to gun you down. I'm not liking the logic here, Gideon."

Fearing for Gideon's safety, Jubal shook his head and agreed. "I don't like it, Gideon. Take my word, that Pittman is a snake. He'll shoot you in the back, then go have a drink like it was noth'n."

Gideon thought about what Jubal was implying, but knew Pittman wouldn't back shoot him. "No, Pittman likes to try and make people think he's an honorable man. He also likes to make a statement. And besides, Hayden made him a rich man. He's not gonna throw all that wealth away by shooting me in the back. No, I think he'll call me out so that everyone can see how great he is. This way he'll go back to California with his reputation intact and live out his life in luxury."

With a growing concern, Gideon's words wasn't making Ms. Lita feel any better. "Gideon, you can't go up against that monster. I've heard stories. They say he's the fastest man alive."

Being acquainted with those same stories, Gideon took another drink, then glanced over at Ms. Lita. "They seem to say that about everybody. Until someone faster comes along and takes over the title. Listen, don't worry about Colonel Pittman. Hayden seems to be done with his treasure hunt, at least where Presidio is concerned. I'll contact the military to see if maybe we can't intercept Pittman before he gets here, and if we stop Pittman, Hayden will crawl back into whatever crack he came from."

While Gideon spent the rest of the day sending telegrams to the military and his contacts within the government, Jon was already far north of Presidio. Toward the end of the day, the sun was going down, but he could see smoke off in the distance. So, he was hoping for some friendly hospitality. As the sun dropped down behind the Limpia Mountains, he found where the smoke had been coming from: two cabins along with a fairly big barn butted up against what looked like an old worn out mine. Before approaching the homestead, he sat back and watched in order to get an idea of how friendly or unfriendly the occupants were. It was a brisk night and both fireplaces were going strong from both houses, but the barn also had a smoke stack that was lit. Jon recognized the homemade brew smell coming from the barn and was a bit leery about approaching, but it was getting cold and late and he was tired and hungry. Jon was aware that many of the folks who lived in the mountain area often made their own liquor and beer, but it didn't necessarily make them bad people. Most brews were okay to drink, but sometimes the potency mixed with various unnatural ingredients could produce deadly results. Quite often they would trade other nearby communities for medical supplies, blankets, or food and other necessities they needed.

As Jon sat for a few minutes and observed, the barn door suddenly swung open and a heavyset man emerged. Bellowing out his laughter, he was laughing and talking back at somebody still in the barn. As the first man approached one of the houses, the second man made his exit from the barn. He was skinny and wore a gray beard, carrying a wooden crate filled with a fresh batch of homemade whiskey. Laughing as he walked, he followed the heavy man into the house and shut the door.

All the instincts inside Jon was telling him to move on, but the night was getting colder by the minute and he and his horse needed supplies and shelter for the night. So against his best judgment, he decided to approach with caution. Stopping a few yards shy of the house, he sat atop his horse and called to the two men. "Hello in the house!"

As Jon listened to the wind swirl, there was no response. It was quiet and the laughter had stopped as he was waiting for a friendly acknowledgment. Jon could see one of the oil lamps being blown out, which darkened the house, so he once again, yelled out. "Hello in the house! My name is Jon Mason, and I'm just looking for food and shelter for the night! I'm willing to pay you for your hospitality!"

Jon waited and listened, but just like before got no response. Just when the cold wind started to gust and howl with fury, the front door opened and out came the heavyset man with a rifle. Jon didn't try to get down from his horse or make any sudden moves because he understood he was a stranger on another man's property in the middle of the night.

After a few seconds of staring, the heavy man spit a slew of tobacco juice from the side of his mouth and then spoke. "You alone, boy?"

With his night pending on his response, Jon put his best manners forward in order to try and keep the situation friendly. "Yes, sir. Just a traveler looking for some food and shelter for my horse and me. I have money and I'm willing to pay you a fair price."

Just then, the other man came from around the side of the house, also holding a rifle pointing at Jon. He didn't say anything, but he stood strong and stared with confidence.

Still feeling like he should have moved on, Jon tried to appeal to their entrepreneur nature. "Sure is getting cold. I'd be willing to pay for one of those bottles of liquor you made."

Once again the heavyset man at the door spit, then raised his rifle. "Boy, we ain't got no whiskey and we ain't got no food and we ain't got no hospitality. But we'll be tak'n that money you mentioned along with yer supplies, yer horse, and yer guns. Now, you get down from that horse real slow like and drop them there guns on the ground."

After a few seconds of realizing his night just went sideways, Jon complied to the demands and slowly climbed down from his horse. Seeing how he had two rifles pointed at him, he unstrapped his sawed-off shotgun from his back, then threw it to the ground while taking two steps away from his horse. "Listen, fellas, I didn't mean to cause you any grief. I'm just passing through."

After listening to Jon's reasoning, the heavy man stepped down from the porch, but still kept his distance from Jon. "Boy, yer not hear'n me correctly. I said drop all yer guns. That means that fancy side arm you got there."

Jon wasn't in any mood to kill the two men, but it was plain to see they had no reservations about killing him and taking whatever valuables he had. "Listen, why don't you just let me leave here and we can forget all about this little misunderstanding."

Glancing at each other, the two men laughed, then turned their attentions back to Jon. The heavier man was becoming anxious and eager to dispose of Jon, so he continued with his banter. "Boy, we got a couple of them there mountain wolves that like to come and snoop around here at night. Yer gonna make a good meal for them, so why don't you just drop that there last gun?"

Feeling the two men were becoming more and more comfortable with themselves while continuing to joke and laugh, Jon drew down on both men and shot three bullets into each of them. With his lightning speed, Jon gave no warning and showed no mercy as both men stumbled backward, firing their rifles harmlessly into the air. Afterward, Jon approached and stood over the fat man. "Yeah, you're right about those wolves. They're gonna eat good tonight."

Hoping the fat man was correct with his information, Jon took a few moments to drag the two men into the woods. He then collected their rifles and cautiously entered the house. Finding no other occupants, he then checked the other small house. No wives and no children, but what he did find was an old Indian war necklace that had been worn for many years by his friend Enyeto. As he searched through the cabins, he also found a small fortune in furs, blankets, and various types of Indian jewelry. Jon recognized the style of most of the homemade items from his visits with Enyeto. In his thinking, these were the men trading poison to the Indian villages and these were the two men responsible for the death of his friend, Enyeto.

After making sure no other hostiles were around, Jon led his horse into the barn and gave him hay and water. He then helped himself to some food and water and laid down for a long-deserved rest. Before falling asleep, he listened as the wind howled and the coyotes sang their nighttime songs. Jon eventually fell asleep, and during the night he dreamed about a young Aztec boy, a jaguar, and the Old One. With each dream triggering the next, his uncontrolled thoughts turned to the magical mountain with rivers of silver running down the sides.

When morning came, he was up at dawn along with the sun peaking up over the tree line. As usual there was work to be done before he could head out, so he wasted no time getting to it. In thinking ahead, he gathered enough food, water, and ammunition for his travels, then he collected anything of value from both houses. Furs, animal skins, jewelry, and blankets. Over the years, the two mountain men had amassed a small fortune, compliments of the local Indian villages. Barely grasping the amount of items collected, he laid everything out by the wood line and wrote a note:

To whoever finds these riches, may your life be blessed.

Not wanting anymore of the poison getting into circulation, Jon spread the poisonous liquor in and around the three buildings and set fire to them. With the massive fire burning strong, Jon decided to take the two horses belonging to their former owners in case he needed them for riding or trade. On his way out, he checked on the two mountain men and discovered their bodies were gone with only blood stains remaining. As expected, the wolves came during the night and had their feast.

After traveling for a few hours, Jon came across a little makeshift town. It had a saloon, a stable, what looked like a general store, and a small boarding house. Needing a break, he tied his horses to a post in front of the saloon and walked in. When he entered, motion stopped as all eyes turned to him. After a few uncomfortable moments, everyone went back to their business as Jon headed for the bar.

With half her breasts hanging out, the bar maid doubled as a saloon girl and was dressed for the part. "Hey sweetie, they call me Candy because I'm full of sugar. What'ya have?"

Needing something for his dry mouth, Jon didn't hesitate to place his order. "Whiskey."

As Candy poured the drink, Jon made note of the bottle to make sure it wasn't one supplied by the last two unlucky souls he had met. "I'm not familiar with this area. What's the name of your little town?"

After pouring two drinks, Candy smiled. "This town has no name, mister. Never did." Candy slid one drink to Jon as she picked up the other and placed it out in front of her.

"A toast. Here's to having no name."

Like a pro, Candy downed her drink, then watched as Jon gulped his down. "Listen, handsome, I'm the best looking woman in this place, so what'ya say you and I walk across the street to my room and get acquainted with each other?"

Thinking to himself, Jon let out a small grin. "Well darl'n, I'm here on some business, and after I'm finished, I don't think your gonna want any parts of me."

Still smiling, Candy leaned across the bar in order to get a little closer to Jon. "Well, I'll tell you what. You tell me what you need and I'll help you take care of your business, and then afterward you can help me take care of what I want. Deal?"

Not trying to elaborate on his intentions, Jon turned to look around the room and saw four men sitting at a table playing cards. Two of the men were wearing a mix of buffalo hide and beaver fur clothing and had beards hanging down to their chests. Both men were wearing guns across their bellies and had an ax hanging off each of their hips.

Turning back around to face Candy, Jon spoke in a raised voice so the men could hear him. "I'm looking for two brothers, Marcus and Ronnie Beck."

Suddenly the room got quiet again and Candy was no longer smiling. She glanced over at the two brothers as she slowly backed away from Jon. When Jon turned around to face the men, the two brothers were already getting up out of their seats. One of the men stepped forward to the middle of the room and with a strong, raspy voice spoke. "My name is Marcus and this here is my brother Ronnie. State your business and it better be damn good. I don't take kindly to being interrupted when I'm winning at cards."

Feeling good about finding his targets, Jon took one step forward away from the bar, then returned some words of his own. "My name is Jon Mason. Does that name sound familiar to you?"

Not recognizing Jon or his name, Marcus looked him up and down, then answered. "Can't say that it does. I know a lot of men, but you're not one of them."

Marcus then turned to his brother, who was already shaking his head no because he too was unfamiliar with Jon. When Marcus turned back around, he continued to speak. "Mister, if'n you have some sort of problem, you came to the wrong town to solve it. Me and my brother don't take kindly to jokes, and we certainly don't like strangers com'n here and start'n trouble."

By now, Jon's anger was rising, so he gave the Beck brothers one last chance. "I had a pregnant wife, two small boys, and a daughter. Sound familiar now?"

Thinking back, Marcus paused for a moment as his eyes widened. With a smile starting to form on his face, he turned back to look at his brother. "Hey Ronnie, I thought all them there Ranger boys got killed."

Remembering Jon's family and what they did, Ronnie stepped out from behind the table and joined Marcus in the middle of the room. With his brother at his side, Marcus decided to give details. "Boy, how the hell did you survive that godforsaken Colonel Pittman?"

Before Jon could answer, Marcus continued his taunt. "Well, no matter. I gotta tell ya, mister, that there was a nice family and me and my brother, well, we did our part in having some fun."

Jon listened, not because he wanted to hear gruesome details but because he wanted the two brothers to get comfortable with themselves while Marcus continued his talking. "Them two little boys was a hoot. They were noth'n to hold down while we chopped their arms off. Yeah, we hung them boys upside down and lit'em on fire with their bodies twitching as they screamed. Didn't take long though. They only lasted a couple of seconds."

By now chairs were screeching across the floor as patrons were getting up and quickly moving to cover. After hearing Marcus tell the details of his story, some patrons were ashamed while others were appalled and yet others were sick to their stomachs. Hearing enough, Jon was at his limit and was ready to take care of the business at hand. As for Marcus and Ronnie, they had nothing else left to say. The two brothers went for their guns, but it was nowhere near fast enough. Jon drew his gun and fired four bullets hitting the men in both their kneecaps. Dropping their guns, both men fell to the floor as the agonizing pain set in.

Being in no hurry, Jon took a few seconds to reload his gun while slowly taking steps toward the now-disabled brothers. As Ronnie squirmed around in his own blood, Marcus tried to forget about the pain and focus on his attempt to reason with Jon. With both hands up in the air, he begged and pleaded with Jon. "Mister, please. We got paid. It wasn't personal, mister. I swear it. It wasn't personal. It was that crazy Colonel. He paid us."

When Jon finished loading his gun, he fired four more bullets, striking the brothers in both their elbows. Now the two brothers were completely helpless as they lay on their backs in pools of blood with no ability to move their legs or arms. Now it was Jon's turn to taunt. As he stood over top of the two men, he smiled as he peered down at them. "Is this what you were talking about? Easy to hold down while you chopped them up?"

Feeling absolutely no grief or remorse, Jon had no mercy for the two men who maimed and killed his sons. While bending down, he took a moment to look into the eyes of the two brothers who were now showing fear. Afterward, he grabbed the two axes hanging from the belt of Marcus and momentarily stared at them. Without hesitation, he reached back with force and swung one ax forward, striking Marcus in his manhood.

As Marcus screamed in pain, his brother Ronnie finally spoke out. "Mister, I'm begging you, please. You done shot us four times. I'm unarmed. Please, mister, I'm begging you for mercy."

By this time, Jon was beyond any type of reasoning and was showing no emotions whatsoever. Once again he reached back and swung the second ax forward and chopped Ronnie in his manhood. Still not being able to move his arms or legs, Ronnie let out a god-awful scream. Jon then took the two axes from the belt of Ronnie and once again studied them. "Mercy? Did my two sons beg for mercy? Did they plead with you not to chop off their limbs? Did they beg you not to kill them?"

With tears now running down Jon's face, he continued with his revenge. With both men in complete anguish, Jon had one last task. He reared back and, with full force, chopped Marcus down the middle of his chest, causing the ax to crack his chest plate and pierce his heart. After a few seconds of spitting up blood, there was no more pain for Marcus. His eyes rolled back into his head and shut for the last time.

Ronnie, who was still screaming in pain, was now yelling for help. "Somebody, please. Get this son of a bitch. Somebody kill'em."

Crying uncontrollably, Ronnie kept begging. "Please, mister, I swear, you'll never see me again. Please. For God's sake, mister, you ain't gotta do this."

With an unfeeling smile, Jon paused as he glanced down at Ronnie. "God isn't here right now. And after telling everybody what you did, I doubt very much if there's any help to be had."

With one last swing, Jon reared back and swung the ax forward, striking Ronnie in the chest. As with his brother Marcus, Ronnie spit up blood, then faded off into his final sleep.

After he was finished the task at hand, Jon stood up and glanced down at the two brothers as though he was justifying his actions in his mind. Suddenly he heard a very familiar sound. When he turned around, Candy had a shotgun pointing at him. After watching Jon slaughter Marcus and Ronnie, she pulled the shotgun from behind the bar and was now looking to use it on Jon.

With a mixture of emotions in her voice, Candy was trying to hold back her tears. "Mister, I'm sorry for your family, but they was my brothers. They were the only kin I had left and you killed them."

Jon knew if Candy had any intentions of shooting, she would have done so by now, but he could see she was torn. One of the patrons who was an older man had taken refuge behind the bar and was standing next to Candy. He could also see Candy had no desire to shoot, so he slowly took a hold of the shotgun and gently pulled it away from her. Feeling weak in her legs, she could no longer hold back her tears. She broke out into a heavy cry as she fell against the older man for comfort. Once again she mustered up the strength to scold Jon. "You bastard. You didn't have to kill'em. You didn't have to, mister."

Jon knew he had a long ride ahead of him so he made his exit and headed back down south.

While Jon was coming down out of the mountain region, Gideon was receiving word from the military that Colonel Pittman was not a war criminal and wasn't wanted for any type of military crimes. Unfortunately, Gideon also received a telegram from the secretary of Walter Burton, his friend within the Texas Senate. Once again, Mr. Burton outlined several other issues the state of Texas was plagued with and asked Gideon to do his best with what resources he had. But at the end of the letter, there was a side note. Senator Burton informed Gideon that the law isn't always correct and sometimes common sense and human intervention should take precedence.

Gideon understood what the senator was getting at, so it was time to hunker down and prepare the town of Presidio for an impending war. By now rumors had rippled through the territory that an unknown man was responsible for killing several mountain men. Visitors, traveling salesmen, and drifters all had stories to tell as they came and went from the town of Presidio. When Zachariah Hayden heard the rumors, he immediately offered reward money for anyone who could tell him information about the man, such as description or direction of travel.

While the townsfolk were busy with their gossip, Jon was on his way to the Mexican border. He knew he would have to travel through both Comanche and Apache territories, so he kept a few items from the mountain men to use as leverage. The sun was beginning to set, so night wasn't too far behind. It had been a long day of riding, so Jon found a nice stream and some trees and set up camp for the night. While he sat quietly on a rock, he listened to the crackling of the fire he had made. The nighttime breeze was slightly blowing off the water as the nocturnal creatures made their presence known. The wolves off in the distance were calling for each other as the coyotes were singing their songs. There was even an old hoot owl in one of the nearby trees.

As Jon was about to lay down, he heard what sounded like foliage snapping behind him. When he stood up to investigate, he saw it was only a beaver conducting his nighttime rounds. As he turned to sit back down, the mysterious warrior Indian was now sitting by the fire. Jon wasn't startled because, by now, he was use to the untimely interruptions. "Don't you ever knock?"

Even though it was just a joke, Jon waited for a response but got none. So, he took up a position sitting across from the lone warrior. "You have a name?"

With a cold silence, the Indian just stared at Jon and gave no respond. Feeling a bit uncomfortable, Jon attempted to continue the one-sided conversation. "I've told you before, I don't believe in your Hok'ee theory, so I don't know why you and that old man are so interested in me."

Still with no talk, Jon placed another log on the fire and waited. Finally, the warrior Indian spoke. "You, no revenge. You Hok'ee. Must go back."

With no interest in talking about his current problems, Jon just took a moment and stared. Though his anger was beginning to fume, he had no desire to physically lash out. So, he took a moment to take a deep breath. "What do you know? They mutilated my family and killed them."

Before continuing, Jon took another deep breath to try and control his emotions. "You have no idea what it's like to lose your family to a bunch of filthy worthless outlaws."

After taking a third pause to gather his thoughts, Jon tried rationalizing his actions. "The law operates with rules, and sometimes those rules just don't work. I'm not seeking revenge; I'm seeking justice."

Reminiscent of Jon's story, the warrior Indian listened, but had his own tragedy to tell. "My family killed by white man. White man come, attack our camp at night. They kill my father. They kill my mother and sister. Take what they want. Burn down camp. I watch from high up in tree."

When the warrior Indian was done talking, Jon had a new perspective. "Did they ever catch who did it?"

The warrior paused for a moment, then came back with a surprising answer. "The spirit world will take revenge when they ready."

With a bit of frustration, Jon shook his head in disbelief. "But I've seen you kill many men. Men you didn't even know, but you don't seek justice for the death of your own family? I don't understand."

The warrior sat as though he was thinking, but he felt no need to respond. After a few minutes of silence, Jon took notice of the beaded bracelet he had seen during his first encounter. Thinking he may get some answers, he held up his arm and showed the warrior his matching bracelet. "I guess I've always known who you are. Your father had the idea of taking me out onto the plains and leaving me to die, but you let me go. You said we would see each other in another life. What did you mean?"

Still feeling the need to advise the lost Ranger, the warrior Indian stared at Jon. He continued to stare until the fire threw out a few pops and crackles. "Hok'ee have many families from past. Hok'ee will have many more families. Hok'ee is lost and must find way."

With even more confusion, Jon persisted on more questions. "You drew a wolf in the sand along with two crossed arrows. A friend of mine told me the wolf means companion. And the two arrows mean friendship." Jon waited for a reaction, but once again the warrior Indian sat in silence. Then Jon took notice of the animals. The wolves were no longer howling and the coyotes were silent. The old hoot owl was also gone. Then Jon heard the crackling of the foliage again. When he stood up to investigate, there was nothing to see. When he turned to sit back down, the warrior Indian was gone.

The next morning, Jon was up before the sun so he could get an early start. Despite the words from his late-night visitor, he had no plans to turn back. Jon was headed for Comanche territory because it was quicker to go through then to go around, but he was hoping not to encounter Two Feathers or his people. After about an hour of riding, Jon's hopes were dashed when he saw Two Feather and five of his warriors riding hard towards him. Jon had no plans of trying to run and he wasn't sure how Two Feathers was going to react to him being in his territory, so he waited for the quick-galloping Comanche to approach.

As Two Feathers approached, Jon formed a plan and cautiously waited. After coming to an abrupt stop, Two Feathers sat atop his horse and stared at Jon while his five warriors surrounded him. Never knowing what to expect with the Comanche, Jon counted on Two Feathers to keep his word. After a few nervous moments, Two Feathers broke the silence. "You gave word. You hunt man who kill Seven Bulls. Now you again trespass on our land."

With his plan already playing out, Jon didn't respond with words. Instead, he slowly climbed down from his horse and drew a circle in the dirt. Inside the circle, he drew two upside down stick figures of men. He then went to his saddlebag and pulled out a piece of Comanche jewelry and handed it to Two Feathers. Right away, Two Feather recognized the jewelry from being made by the women of his tribe. Two Feathers also recognized the two male stick figures as representing death and realized Jon killed the two men who had been trading poison throughout the territory. The two men and their poison were responsible for the deaths of some Comanche, including several from Two Feathers' tribe. With another gift of respect, Jon handed over the two spare horses belonging to the mountain men.

After seeing Two Feathers was somewhat satisfied, Jon decided to use his temporary fame to his advantage. "The spirit world is with me. I know who killed Seven Bulls and I will make him suffer. As a gift to you in good faith, the two men who poisoned your people no longer walk within this world."

With the expectations of being allowed to continue on without harm, Jon climbed back up on his horse and waited for a response from his blood brother. Satisfied with Jon's actions, Two Feathers nodded his head, signaling his five warriors to ride on. As his warriors turned back, Two Feathers waited for them to move off into the distance before speaking to Jon. After a few moments, Two Feathers extended his appreciation. "You are honorable white man. You do not fear us but respect us. And for that, you may go in peace."

As a gift of appreciation, Two Feathers handed Jon the piece of jewelry as a token of thankfulness. Afterward, he scampered off in the direction of his men. After breathing a sigh of relief, Jon continued on his way and eventually made it out of Comanche territory down into the southern part of Texas. Along the way, he constantly thought about his wife and children and the satisfaction of justice he was looking for. Before continuing on to the Mexican border, Jon decided to stop and visit the Indian villages he used to help Doc Belle with. He knew Doc Belle would be making her rounds and tending to the sick, but was unaware how she would perceive his appearance after his lengthy absence.

It was the middle of the day and Doc Belle was already in all-out work mode. Several of the elders had various illnesses ranging from the common cold to chicken pox to simple food poisoning. During her visit with Chief

Machakm, she found out he was suffering from systems of gonorrhea. As she examined him, Doc Belle had a few choice words. "Chief, all the villagers to include the women know you're a dirty old man and you know you're a dirty old man. And I know you're a dirty old man. You can't keep having sex with these girls that are running wild outside of your village. God knows where they go or who they've been with. You've been lucky so far, but you need to watch yourself. Your luck may run out one day and I won't be able to help you."

With Doc Belle getting on his last nerve, the chief didn't say anything. He was halfway listening to Doc, but it was obvious his mind was someplace else. While Doc finished with her brow-beating and packing her belongings in her satchel, the chief spoke and gave a stern warning. "Man who is not man come see you. Must avoid. He bring much death."

Doc Belle stopped what she was doing because she was shocked at what she was being told. "Chief, what are you talking about? Who is this man?"

After a brief moment, the chief continued with his warning. "You stay away. He no man. He lost spirit."

Belle's experience had always been pleasant with the local Indian villages because she not only gave medical assistance but also adhered to their village rules and respected their spiritual beliefs. Always remaining cautious whenever the chief would make predictions, she was surprised to be included in one of his warnings.

After Belle vacated the teepee, she was a little shaken from the words the chief told her. The chief was a harmless old man, but some of the things he would say would really give her goosebumps. As she was placing her belongings in her carriage, she noticed nobody was outside and the village was now quiet. The children who usually run around and play were silent and nowhere to be seen. The village women who move about and do their chores were now inside. And there were no men coming or going.

As she looked around, nothing was moving except for the dust blowing in the wind. Suddenly, the feeling somebody was watching came over her. When she turned, Jon was standing there. During her initial shock of disbelief, Belle dropped her bag to the ground as she stood speechless and started to tremor. Not knowing what Belle must have been thinking, Jon tipped his hat in a courteous manner and picked Belle's bag up. He then took a few seconds and helped load up the rest of her belongings and supplies.

After being stunned moments before, Belle briefly looked Jon up and down. The way he looked and the way he moved was different, and his demeanor didn't feel right to her. He was bolder and seemed to have much more confidence. His clothes and the way he wore his gun was clean and sharp, like how a gunfighter would look. It was the same Jon but different. Still a little overcome with emotion, Belle just couldn't pinpoint the change.

Realizing Belle was short of words, Jon took the initiative to speak as he gave his usual charming smile. "Hi Belle. How are you?"

Before she answered, Belle recalled the words of Chief Machakm, but could Jon be the man he was speaking of? After a brief pause, Belle finally responded. "Jon? You do know a lot of people are looking for you, don't you? Where have you been?"

Hoping to avoid an informal inquisition, Jon wasn't there for the formalities or to answer questions. He was only there for one purpose, then his plan was to move on.

Seeing that Belle was still feeling uneasy, he tried to put her mind at ease. "Belle, I apologize if I'm making you feel uncomfortable, so I'll keep my visit short."

Reaching into his vest pocket, Jon pulled out the necklace belonging to Enyeto. "I just wanted to give this to you. I know you were close to Enyeto and I wanted you to know the men responsible for his death are dead."

While Belle took the necklace into her hand, she glanced at it in remembrance of her dear friend. While Belle was busy with her fond memories, Jon climbed up on his horse and prepared to leave. Before moving onto his agenda, he had some last words. "Gideon will explain everything. Thank you for what you did for Emily and the children. It was very kind of you."

Still dealing with the thoughts of the necklace, Belle tried to speak, but it was too late. Jon had turned his attention south and galloped off.

After watching Jon disappear into the backdrop of the Texas scenery, Belle glanced around at the village, which currently resembled a ghost town. Still feeling stunned at what she had just experienced, Belle collected her thoughts and climbed into her carriage. While Jon continued with his quest, Belle quickly rode back to town as her anger propelled her speed. With the speed she was pushing her one-horse buggy, it didn't take long for her to reach Presidio. Everyone knew Doc Belle and her mellow demeanor and the fact she was always poised, so when she came galloping into town almost out of control, everyone's head turned. Like a mad woman, she steered her carriage through town and came to an abrupt stop in front of the sheriff's office. Without wasting a moment of time, Doc Belle climbed out of her buggy and swung open the door, just to see Jubal sitting at the desk with his feet up and half asleep.

With her temper about to fly, Belle didn't hold back the thundering sound of her voice. "Jubal! Where the hell is Gideon?"

Like a fox that just got caught in the chicken coop, Jubal jumped up out of his seat. "Belle, what's gotten into you? That's not very ladylike, scar'n the hell out me like that."

Not caring what Jubal thought, Belle was in no mood for ladylike behavior. With an angry look on her face that would scare away the bravest of men, she approached Jubal and got up close and personal. "Now you listen here, you old hound dog, you tell me where Gideon is now before I get a hanker'n to slap you silly."

Knowing better then to mess with an angry woman, Jubal had no problem giving up Gideon's location. Feeling like he had just gotten kicked by a mule, he decided to give his best answer. "Well, last I saw, he was headed to the hotel for an early dinner."

Making sure Jubal wasn't trying to fool her, Belle gave one last evil eye before turning and storming out.

Not stopping to talk with anyone, Belle charged through town until she got to the hotel. Without showing any signs of her rage subsiding, she bypassed Mr. Hinklemeyer without saying a word and proceeded through the lobby and into the dining room, where she saw Gideon relaxing and enjoying his dinner and beer. She quickly glanced around the room, but with so much animosity built up, she could barely contain her emotions. Before making it halfway to Gideon's table, her anger spilled over into a loud bellow. "Gideon!"

Gideon was just about to take a bite of food but stopped in mid-stride and placed his fork down on his plate. Feeling there was a storm coming, he watched as Belle forcefully took a seat across from him. Like a child about to be scolded, he offered up his best smile. "Hi Doc. Everything okay?"

Like a raging bull about to charge, Belle gathered her steam and spoke in an offensive manner. "Gideon, the people of this town have treated you with respect and dignity, and barring a few of the local idiots, Presidio has taken you in and treated you like you were one of its own."

With tears starting to fall from her eyes, Belle started to tremble and shake. "How dare you think you're so high and mighty to keep such a secret? Jon is my friend and my heart bled when he went missing. And you knew all along. Even when we bought his land and made sure his wife and children wouldn't be trampled on and forgotten, you knew. God damn you, Gideon. You knew."

It was obvious Belle was extremely upset and there was no way around telling her about Jon, so Gideon leaned across the table to try and calm a very upset doctor. While the tears continued to flow down Belle's face, Gideon tried to manage the situation the best he could. "Belle, I'm sorry. There was a reason so, please, can you give me a chance to explain?"

Before Belle responded, Gideon took a moment to look around and decided they needed a bit more privacy. "Belle, why don't we go someplace so we can talk?"

By this time, Belle's anger had subsided and was now being replaced with sorrow. Not wanting to hear excuses, she slowly stood up and walked out while Gideon watched in disbelief. Afterward, he got up and ran after her in an attempt to keep a volatile situation from becoming worse. While Belle scurried out of the dining room and past Mr. Hinklemeyer, Gideon tried to keep up and talk, but Belle wasn't having it. As Belle made her exit with Gideon not too far behind, neither one noticed Mr. Hinklemeyer, who had been listening the entire time.

With Gideon trying desperately to keep up, Belle headed straight for the Lucy Goosy. With some force, she swung open the saloon doors and made a beeline for the bar. With caution, Gideon stood at the door momentarily as Belle ordered herself a drink.

Young Tommy was working and he knew Doc Belle wasn't a drinker, so he looked a little bewildered when she asked for a whiskey. "Doc, you okay, ma'am?"

With violence in her eyes and a thunderous roar, Belle wailed at Tommy, "I said give me a goddamn whiskey."

By now Gideon had come from behind to try and talk. "Tommy, why don't you give us a bottle, then we're just going to go in the back room for some privacy."

While Tommy fetched a fresh bottle of whiskey, Belle turned and slapped Gideon in the face. "The hell I will. I'm not going anywhere with you, you son of a bitch."

Watching what was unfolding, Tommy gently placed the bottle on the bar and backed away as he watched Gideon rub the sting off his cheek.

With his patience coming to an end, Gideon had had enough. He snatched the bottle off the bar, then grabbed Doc by her arm. As he manhandled her and dragged her through the bar and into the back room, he gave her a few choice words of his own. "Now, you listen here, you pompous snooty little bitch. Your pappy may have let you get away with doing something like that, but not this man."

As they stepped into the back room, Gideon swung Doc around and pushed her into a chair, then slammed the door behind him.

Just then, Ms. Lita was coming out of an adjacent room and saw what was going on. With some shock, she quickly stepped in between Gideon and Belle. "Gideon, what the hell are you doing? You don't throw a lady around like that. That's Belle. What the hell is wrong with you?"

Taking a breath to try and calm himself, Gideon took a step back and apologized. "I'm sorry. It's just a misunderstanding. I just think we all need to calm down and have a drink."

After taking a few seconds to look Gideon up and down, Lita turned to face Belle. "Belle, are you okay? What's this all about?"

While Belle was catching her breath, Gideon took a few glasses off the cobweb-filled dusty shelves and poured some drinks. He then invited Lita to sit while he explained. Before he could start, Belle spoke out. "I saw Jon. He came to the Indian village while I was there doing exams. While I was there, Chief Machakm told me a man who is not a man was coming to see me, but I couldn't understand what he was talking about and he wouldn't explain. As I was leaving, Jon came out of nowhere. I didn't hear him come up from behind. I turned and he was just there staring at me."

Feeling her body starting to slouch and become weak, Lita was stunned. "What'ya mean, staring. Did he say anything? Where is he now? Why doesn't he come back?"

These were all valid questions, but overwhelmed with emotions, Belle had no answers. With her mouth dry, Belle took a drink of whiskey, then made the face of death. "My God. How do you men drink this poison?"

Still needing to talk, Belle took a second to absorb the alcohol, then continued. "I was scared. The chief said words about some kind of spirit, and then Jon appeared. It was Jon, but it wasn't. I can't explain it. It looked like him, but he seemed more enlightened. So refined and astute. I'm sorry, I just can't explain it."

With more questions than answers, Lita took a drink, then poured Belle and herself another. Afterward, anger crept back into Belle's voice as she pointed her finger at Gideon. "You knew he was alive and didn't say anything, and that, my friend, is the worst kind of betrayal."

Suddenly the door started to slowly creak open and in popped Jubal's head. "Gideon, you in here?"

After listening to Belle, Gideon took a breath out of frustration. "Yeah, Jubal, come on in and join the party."

Once again Belle lashed out in anger as she turned her animosity on Jubal. "Did you know, Jubal? Did you know about Jon?"

Without knowing the context of the conversation, Jubal looked to Gideon for support. "Gideon, what's going on?"

With Belle and Lita not knowing and Jubal trying his best to hold back, Gideon was walking a very fine line with his friends. Now, all eyes were on him as he tried to figure out a way to apologize while explaining about Jon. With his frustration building, he had to finally let it all go. "I'm sorry, everybody. I should have relied on our friendship, but I didn't. Jubal, I owe you the biggest apology for including you in my delusional exploits without warning you of the consequences."

By now, more drinks were poured with everyone being a bit more relaxed while waiting for Gideon to explain. "Belle, you're right. This town has treated me very good and I've tried my best to protect and serve, but sometimes a man just makes mistakes. No matter how much I try, I can't seem to control the events that have recently unfolded."

Not yet willing to relinquish her anger, Belle was still waiting for an explanation, while Lita had a little more compassion. "Gideon, whatever is going on, you can count on us to help. Just tell us what you need."

Appreciating the confidence Lita was displaying, Gideon gained some much-needed momentum in order to explain about Jon.

Before Gideon could say another word, Belle burst out in a bit of resentment. "Before you go handing out Man of the Year awards, Lita, you should probably know something."

Feeling the animosity toward Gideon, Lita turned her attention toward Belle. "Belle, your antagonism is pretty plain to see. You obviously know something we don't, so please, do tell."

With anger starting to settle back in, Belle gave Gideon a fiery look, then stood up. Like a school teacher scolding a child, she once again pointed her finger shaking it at Gideon. "Our fine sheriff has always known Jon was alive and he kept it to his selfish self."

With her heart starting to ache, Lita glanced over at Gideon. "Gideon, is this true? Even after you told us you weren't sure? Did you know?"

As bad as Gideon felt, it was no comparison to the hurtful look Lita had on her face. He tried to look her in the eyes, but it wasn't easy. "Not at first. Jubal and I were telling the truth. We knew there was a survivor, but we couldn't figure out who it was. And in the back of my mind, I had a strange feeling, but that's all I had up until last week when I took a ride out to the gravesite to do some cleaning and weeding. There he was, just standing there like it wasn't any big deal. It wasn't until I found Jon at the gravesite that this whole secret started. Before I got there, Jon already had his mind set on revenge, and it didn't matter what I said or how much I pleaded with him. So, I figured I could buy some time if I told as few people as possible."

As Ms. Lita and Belle listened, Gideon continued to plead his case as his words sounded reminiscent to what Belle said. "Before any of us spoke, there was something about him. I can't really explain it, but he had changed. There was no more Jon. He was no longer that innocent-looking guy who sought justice for the world. It seemed a monster had taken his place. A monster filled with anger, hatred, and revenge. He's going after the men who killed his family, then he's coming back to Presidio to kill Hayden."

Listening to Gideon tell his story, Ms. Lita was stunned. Not only about Jon being alive and well, but the fact that Gideon kept it secret. Now he had not one but two angry women to contend with. With an abundance of emotions stirring around inside, Lita turned toward Jubal. "Did you know?"

As she waited for Jubal to answer, tears started to fall from her eyes. Jubal had known Lita for many years and he now had the misfortune of having to choose between friends. Feeling his stomach starting to turn, he chose his words carefully. "Well, Ms. Lita, not at first, but Gideon did finally tell me."

Still talking to Lita but now looking toward Gideon, Jubal continued. "Not trying to fault anyone, I'm sure Gideon had good reason not to say anything. Right, Gideon?"

When Jubal was done, an overwhelming feeling of thankfulness came over Gideon, so he stood up to speak. "Thank you, Jubal. You are truly a great friend. As for you, Belle, I'm so sorry you had to find out the way you did. I probably would have reacted the same way."

As Gideon spoke with grace, the tension in the room began to dissolve. "In a way, Jubal is right. My reasons for not saying anything weren't selfish. I figured the fewer people who knew would somehow protect Jon. If Hayden found out, he would've had every bounty hunter from this side of the border and the other hunting him down. But as I said before, I should have relied on our friendship, but I didn't, and for that I apologize."

Gideon could see the looks on the face of Lita and Belle starting to give way, so he gave both a gentle kiss on their cheeks in hopes of redemption. He then turned to Jubal and smiled. "You don't get one."

As Jubal let out a small gawk, Gideon stuck out his hand in friendship. After the two men shook hands, Belle stood up and gave Gideon a hug. "Gideon, can you ever forgive my ignorance for all the nasty things I said?"

With a big smile on his face, Gideon responded. "Belle, there's nothing to forgive because you didn't do anything wrong."

With the strain of the conversation gone, Gideon glanced over at Lita who was now peering into his eyes. With a quaint little smile, Lita took a step toward Gideon. "Well now, handsome, aren't you something, carrying all that weight by your lonesome." Ms. Lita then stood on her toes and reached up to place her arms around Gideon. Not being able to hold back their feelings for each other, the two shared a passionate kiss.

While the obvious attraction was taking place, Jubal rolled his eyes as he turned to Belle. "Well Doc, think we should maybe get on out of here. Guess I'll go and keep the dust bunnies from getting out of hand at the jail."

As Belle and Jubal were about to sneak out, Gideon and Ms. Lita took a breather. After feeling good about sharing her kiss, Ms. Lita became uneasy. "Wait a minute, you two, we're not done."

Hearing Lita's voice, Jubal and Belle postponed their duties as they turned back around and closed the door. With thoughts of doom on their minds, all four sat back down at the table to talk more about the near future. With Jon being the subject, Ms. Lita voiced her concerns. "Gideon, you said Jon was coming here. Then what? If he does make it back, he'll probably have a price on his head."

Once again Gideon would be caught between duty and friends. "Unfortunately you're right, Lita. I've been pondering that question ever since I let him ride off. He's most definitely gonna be wanted. And I can guarantee Hayden's gonna try and force our friendship against each other. There's no real answer to the problem and I know there's no assurance Jon will make it back, but I'll roll the dice and place a bet that he does."

With all that said, Lita leaned to the side and placed her head on Gideon's shoulders. "Now, what?"

Glancing over at Belle, Gideon recalled what Chief Machakm told him about a coming battle between good and evil. "All we can do is wait. And when the time comes, get ready for Armageddon, because hell is coming to Presidio."

As the informal meeting adjourned, Belle went back to her office while Gideon and Jubal followed Lita out. Before she returned to the bar area, Lita turned to give Gideon a smile. With his heart pounding with delight, Gideon smiled back. "See you later, Lita?"

Lita, in all her glory, twirled around like a little school girl and giggled. "Sure thing, handsome."

As Lita made her way around the bar, Jubal giggled as he headed for the door. "See'ya later, Lita?"

Before Jubal could get out the door, Ms. Lita gave him a sour look as she berated him. "That's Ms. Lita to you, you old crow."

While Presidio went about its business, Gideon was unaware Mr. Hinklemeyer had been listening earlier when Belle went on her tirade. As Mr. Hinklemeyer spread the word about Jon, Jon was approaching the Mexican border. Before he crossed, he sat and took a break at a nearby stream. Gathering his thoughts, he reminisced about his family and thought about what life would have been like if he had never become a Texas Ranger. He reflected on his life being dull, but Emily and the children would have still been alive. While Jon continued with his tortured thoughts, a familiar friend made herself known off in the distance, her coat shining like silver. At times it was so bright, Jon could barely make out her beautiful silhouette. He watched as she pranced back and forth as though she was trying to speak to him.

After a few more moments, the incredible white thoroughbred disappeared over the horizon. So, Jon got up and got ready to cross into Mexico. His mindset was two men down and three to go, then onto Presidio. It would be another hour before reaching his destination, but Jon kept his anger going strong by thinking about his prey. He conjured scenarios in his mind on how he was going to dispose of the savage men.

About thirty minutes from the town of Nuevo Casas Grandes, Jon encountered three Mexican bandits. They came from behind some tall rocks as they rode up on him fairly quick. As Jon pulled his horse to a stop, he quickly studied the men who were now staring him down. Finally, the one who seemed to be the leader spoke. "American?"

With his soul darker than coal, Jon cast his ice cold eyes upon him and purposely kept his answers short. "Yes."

The grungy-looking man didn't like the way Jon was staring at him, but in his mind there were three of them and only one of Jon. He paused for a moment to try and calm his horse, as his horse seemed to feel uncomfortable with Jon's presence. Afterward, he saw that Jon had a nice horse, two saddlebags, and several guns, including two rifles and some supplies. "I see you travel well, hombre. Me, I am just a poor farmer in need of what you have."

Being in no mood for games, Jon didn't say anything and just kept up his callous stare. With no movement and no answer and what seemed like an unconcerned disrespectful display from Jon, the grungy-looking man became angry. "You offend me, American hombre. I wasn't gonna kill you, but now I think otherwise."

With still no reaction from Jon, the grungy man was at the end of his patience. The two other men had rifles aimed at Jon while their leader insulted Jon and gave him orders. "Get off your horse, hombre."

Feeling no rush, Jon momentarily paused, then slowly climbed down from his horse. In one complete uninterrupted motion, Jon's feet hit the ground as he displayed lightning speed, drawing his gun. He fired three bullets, with two head shots to the two men with rifles and one shot to the leader's gut. The men with rifles were dead before they hit the ground as their leader fell off his horse in agonizing pain.

Showing no emotions, Jon walked over and stood over top the grungy man, who was now on his way to dying. "I didn't kill you right away like your friends. I figured since you were so arrogant about your disposition, I'd let you suffer a bit. Justice for all those people you robbed in the past that couldn't defend themselves."

Jon smiled as he once again pulled his gun and shot the man in both of his feet. Screaming in anguish, the grungy man rolled around on the ground, attempting to alleviate the pain, but there was no relief for him. "Please, señor, help me. I'm just a poor farmer with a family."

Shaking his head, Jon holstered his gun as he glanced down at the dying man. "About five minutes after I leave, the coyotes and wolves are gonna come and feast on your warm body while you're still alive. Then about five minutes after that, the buzzards are gonna come and finish you off."

As the man lay on the ground bleeding from his torturing wounds, Jon gathered the horses of the three bandits and tied them behind his horse. He then saddled up and headed to his destination. A few miles later, Jon made it to the town of Nuevo Casas Grandes. It wasn't much to look at, but the people who lived there called it home. Jon could tell it was one of those towns where the people were constantly being oppressed. As he slowly rode through pulling the horses, people were frightened of the new face they were looking at. As the people walked by, nobody would make eye contact or stop to greet him, and most would just run and hide.

Eventually Jon found what appeared to be the local law enforcement shack. As he dismounted, he separated the three allocated horses and tied them off to the side. He then took his horse across the street and tied it off in front of what looked like a makeshift saloon. When Jon walked in, he looked around and saw it was pretty much like every other hole in the wall saloon. A few raggedy-looking local men, along with the local whores that were working. There was also a few drifters playing poker and drowning in a bottle.

Looking at Jon standing just inside the saloon door, the bartender who was smelly and bulging at his waistline stood by waiting for Jon to approach. After eyeballing everybody in the room, Jon walked to the bar and asked for a whiskey and beer. With only half of what Jon asked for, the large, out-of-shape man turned to grab a half-empty bottle of whiskey and poured Jon a drink. "We have no beer, señor."

With a disappointing look, Jon swallowed down the glass of alcohol. The whiskey was weak and he could tell it had been sitting around for a long while, but he had time to pass so he sat the glass down and pushed it toward the bartender. "Another, please."

With caution, the man paused as he nervously looked at Jon. "I need to see payment, señor."

Being new in town, Jon didn't want to cause a scene just yet without finding who he was looking for, so he gave a polite smile because he understood and took no offense. Reaching into his pocket, he pulled out a coin worth one dollar and dropped it on the bar. Afterward, the bartender picked it up and bit into it. He then smiled and poured Jon another drink.

While the few patrons sat and enjoyed the half-dressed women, Jon paid the bartender for the half-empty bottle, then went and sat down at a nearby table and waited. He watched in disgust how the other men laughed as they ran their hands up and down the backsides of the working women. The women seemed to enjoy it, but Jon knew it was their job to enjoy it. The men were supplying them with drinks and the promise of taking them elsewhere in private and hopefully paying them for other services.

By the time Jon was working on his fourth drink, a man walked in and made his presence known. Looking a bit worn, he was dressed in an old, dusty, and dingy-looking suit, but he wore no gun. He took a moment and stood in the doorway until his eyes adjusted to the room, then walked over to the bar. Jon could see the nervous look on the bartender's face as the mysterious man leaned over the bar and quietly made inquiries. Afterward, the man turned and looked in Jon's direction as though he was the subject of the conversation. Before venturing over, he turned back to the anxious bartender and pointed. The bartender quickly reached down under the bar and pulled out a new unopened bottle of whiskey and handed it to the man.

With a smile on his face, the man turned and stared at Jon for a moment, then walked over and sat down. Still focused on Jon, the dusty man introduced himself. "The name is Victor Wittenhagen and I run this little town. I guess you can say I'm the unofficial mayor."

Before Jon could respond, Victor reached for the bottle of whiskey Jon bought and slid it to the side, then took hold of his own bottle. "Here, try this. It's the good stuff. Sorry, our one and only bartender tends to give that horse piss you bought to the filthy peasants who wander in here on a daily basis."

With little grace, Victor filled Jon's glass, then poured a drink for himself. "Here's to new friends."

Not wanting to be rude, Jon cautiously picked his drink up and waited for Victor to indulge before drinking. "Thank you. That was very kind of you. My name is Jon, by the way. I see you're an American. It's my understanding Mexicans don't like us Yanks, so where do you fit in down here?"

With Jon making a good first impression, Victor smiled and then laughed. Before answering Jon's question, he poured two more drinks, then raised his glass. "Salute."

After Victor and Jon downed their drinks, Victor told his short story. "Well, normally I would say you're right. Unfortunately for me, I picked the wrong army to fight for and my team lost the war. After the war, a bunch of us decided the new lay of the land just wasn't for us, so we upended our families and moved south. The Indians didn't mind us leaving and was almost sorry to see us go, so they left us alone during our travels. In fact, they related well to anybody who killed the blue coats."

After another short burst of laughter, Victor poured more whiskey, then continued. "Well, anyhow, we made our way across the border and that's when I said my good-byes. Their plan was to continue on down to Brazil and settle somewhere near the Atlantic Ocean, and I just couldn't picture myself trying to restart my life all over again. Besides, my family was gone. Yanks blew up my damn farmhouse with them in it. They said it was an accident, but I say bullshit. Of course, nothing happened to them. I mean, it was war. What the hell are you gonna do, right?"

Jon continued to listen, but still wasn't sure how to perceive Victor or his random kindness. Being the unofficial mayor, Jon was sure Victor would have the information he needed, but for now he would just let him continue to talk.

After explaining his brief history, Victor continued to talk about his exploits. "I personally wouldn't say these people fear me, but my presence seems to give off that effect. Probably because I came riding in here with my chin held high and looking important in my Confederate uniform. I think they thought I was some sort of general or something. Boy howdy did they start bowing down to me. It didn't take long for me to sweet talk the local bandits into working for me. Before I got here, they were killing and battling among themselves. They were nothing. They had nothing. Now, they live like kings. Working together and terrorizing the locals and anyone coming into their territory. And, of course, I get a cut of the profits."

After Victor was done, Jon took another drink of whiskey in hopes Victor would finally volunteer the information he was looking for. For some reason, Jon didn't seem to view Victor as a bad guy but somebody with an unfortunate history and the added talent of being a con artist. After a few uncomfortable seconds of silence, Victor thought maybe Jon would start to talk, but Jon wasn't in the mood to reveal any information about himself. Now Victor realized he would have to do a little more investigative work. "So Jon, those three horses you tied up outside my office, may I ask how you acquired them?"

Feeling relieved with Victor's inquiry, this was what Jon was waiting for. He knew somebody would recognize the horses and come snooping around. With a minuscule smile, Jon gave a short answer. "They were donated."

With a silly smirk, Victor briefly turned his head and chuckled because that wasn't the answer he was hoping for. With another uncomfortable pause, Victor could feel a battle of the minds beginning to play out. "Listen, Jon, I can appreciate your toughness and I'm sure you're a big man back home, but this is Mexico and you're in my town, so why don't we just cut the crap? You come in here with three horses saddled up with rifles and you leave them tied up in front of my office with absolutely no valid reason for them being in your possession. You know as well as I do, horse thieving is a capital offense and down here in Mexico, you don't even get a trial. These people don't take kindly to it at all. They just

just plain loco com'n here. Why? Why would you kill Agusto and two of my men, then come here to die? Why?"

With Roberto and Lester in the room, Jon was also at his end. Seeing them both made his blood boil, and now it was time to get on with his agenda. "Like I said, they tried to do me wrong and they paid the ultimate price."

Knowing his answers would infuriate Danario, Jon paused, then turned his attention to Roberto and Lester. "As for why I'm here, I'm going to kill those two men standing behind you."

With his anger on the rise, Jon spoke up with an elevated voice so his intended targets would hear him. "My name is Jon Mason. Sound familiar?"

Glancing back at his men to see their reaction, Danario waited for a response. Not caring about who Jon was, Lester just laughed while Roberto thought for a few seconds. As Roberto took a step closer to look at Jon, he finally recognized the name. Just then, a big smile came across his face as he started laughing along with Lester. "He's that Texas Ranger. We killed his family. That's him, Danario. That's the guy we told you about."

Before Danario could say anything, Jon gave a fair warning so Danario could choose to leave peacefully. "Danario, your brother and friends made the wrong choice and I can't help that now, so I'm offering you a chance to leave. I have no quarrels with you."

With his own anger issues starting to boil over, Danario had no desire to back down. His brother was dead and the man who killed him was standing in front of him. Unfortunately, he had the same arrogant attitude as his brother. There were three of them and only one of Jon. Little did he know, Jon had already worked out his plan and there was very little chance of failure. Danario's fatal mistake was being too confident and too close to Jon, and he also had some physical flaws. He was large in all the wrong places, so Jon knew quickness wasn't his forte, and his gun belts could be used against him. Before anyone could react, Jon grabbed Danario by his gun belts and head-butted him. Lester and Roberto attempted to draw their guns and shoot, but Jon used Danario as a human shield, causing him to be shot several times in the back. At the same time, Jon pulled his gun and shot Lester in the leg and Roberto in the stomach. Both men went down, but Lester was able to crawl out the door, leaving Roberto and Danario to their fate.

With several bullets in his back, Danario was dead but still leaning on Jon. When Jon saw Roberto was no longer a threat and Lester had crawled away, he dropped Danario to the floor. Glancing over at Victor and the bartender who had hid behind the bar, Jon holstered his gun, then walked over to Roberto. Roberto had already lost a lot of blood and had blood hemorrhaging from his mouth. As Jon watched, Roberto slowly closed his eyes and was gone. Now it was time to deal with Lester. Without knowing where Lester was, Jon cautiously walked out of the bar. When he stepped out, he saw Lester had made it to his feet and was trying to hop across the street to his horse, but Jon had plans for Lester. He pulled the shotgun from around his back and zeroed in on Lester's good leg. After pulling the trigger, Lester's leg exploded from the kneecap down. In agonizing pain, Lester fell face first, then rolled over on his back, crying and begging Jon not to kill him. As Jon approached, he stood looking down at Lester, who was trying desperately to alleviate himself of pain.

Still whimpering and crying, Lester yelled out. "What the hell, mister! You blew my goddamn leg off." In shear pain, Lester rolled back and forth, holding the thigh section of his leg, trying to get some kind of comfort, but there was none to have. The pain was nearly unbearable.

Out of nowhere, Lester started laughing and taunting Jon while still holding his leg. "Yeah, that's right, Mr. Texas Ranger. You go ahead and kill me, but I had me some fun. I had me some real fun. Those two little boys of yours, they squealed like little pigs, and that darling little girl was so very fine. So, you go on now."

Shaking and trembling, Lester was still in tremendous pain, but he was no longer looking at Jon. Instead, he was looking toward the sky as though he was waiting for the hand of God to come save him. But God wasn't around. Just Jon's shotgun, which was ready willing and able to handle the situation. Without words, Jon placed his shotgun up to Lester's face and pulled the trigger.

After a brief moment of quietness, Victor came running out of the bar. He took one look at what was left of Lester and nearly puked. "My God. You ruthless bastard. What the hell's wrong with you? You blew his leg off and that wasn't enough?"

Before Jon could respond, three more of Danario's men, with guns blazing, came riding full steam through town. With bullets now flying in his direction, Jon dove to the side and rolled to safety behind a water trough. As the men passed by, they maneuvered their horses around to make another violent pass.

By now, Jon was back on his feet and poised to take care of the problem. With quickness, speed, and accuracy, he withdrew his gun and fired three shots, hitting all three men in their chest. Without elegance or grace, the three men fell backward off their horses to the ground. With his jaw dropped, Victor watched in amazement. Laughing and clapping, he watched Jon retrieve his shotgun and reload his weapons. "Well, goddamn. What's next on the entertainment list? Maybe take on the Mexican army?"

Jon was half-listening, but he wasn't there to entertain and he wasn't interested in hanging around for more encounters.

With one hand on his hip and one rubbing the back of his neck, Victor continued to watch Jon in frustration while realizing his private little town was no more. "Well genius, now what the hell am I supposed to do? I mean, you come riding in here like a damn politician, cool as a cucumber, then you turn into a homicidal maniac and kill all my men."

Never a man to mince words, Jon walked past Victor and collected some of the guns that were now lying in the street. He then took Danario's horse by the reins and guided the horse over to the general store. When the owner finally peaked his head out, Jon negotiated a trade. The horse and guns for one hundred dollars' worth of food, ammunition, and whiskey. Afterward, he loaded up his horse with the supplies and climbed on. Before riding away, he glanced down at Victor, who was now looking perplexed. Victor could feel Jon staring at him but was now a little more composed.

Taking a deep breath, Victor spoke in a calmer voice. "These peasants aren't going to listen to me now. Hell, they have no reason to listen to me. I was it. I was their king and now what? All the king's men are dead and their probably gonna chase me out of town with pitchforks."

Finally showing some compassion, Jon glanced down at a bewildered Victor and spoke gracefully. "Listen, Victor, I'm sorry for your family. Those men who murdered them should have been punished for their deeds."

Even though Victor didn't acknowledge Jon's sympathy, Jon could see the thanks in his eyes. So, he continued with his sound advice. "Take the rest of the horses and weapons and offer them as retribution to the people of this town. Then gather some supplies for yourself."

Feeling as though he was in limbo, Victor listened but wasn't catching on. "And then what, become one of them?"

Finding humor in Victor's current situation, Jon paused as he gave a brief grin. "I heard the weather in Brazil is nice. And I'm sure there's plenty of banditos down there who need commanding."

With a smile starting to form on his face, Victor started to laugh, but this time it was a feel good kind of laughter. Suddenly, Victor was feeling better about his future, but he had one last question. Glancing around at Jon's handiwork, he inquired about his profession. "Are you really a Texas Ranger?"

Looking down at Victor, Jon gave a bleak look. "Seems like a lifetime ago, but no, I'm not that guy anymore."

With no words left for either man, Jon turned his horse north and rode off. With trains and stagecoaches crisscrossing the landscapes of America, it wasn't long before word about Jon's ruthless exploits spread. Family members of the men Jon killed up north asked questions and made inquiries to the U.S. marshal's office. Because Jon was never pronounced dead and was still considered a Texas Ranger, the Mexican government wanted to avoid an international incident, so they made a formal complaint to the governor of Texas instead of the United States government.

Jon had successfully made it back across the border into Texas without incident, but he needed to take a break to rejuvenate his thoughts. While resting beneath a tree by a small stream, he dreamed about his previous life with his wife and children and wondered how his life got so out of control. He was tired of the nightmares about a black cloud and he was tired of the so-called spirits coming in and out of his life. He just wanted to turn back time and change the decisions he had made, which led to the death of his family and the destruction of his life.

Oblivious to what was going on with the local authorities, Jon broke camp after a couple of days' rest. He had one last man to find, then it was onto Presidio to face down Zachariah Hayden. Rico was the only name he had to go by and since he began hunting bounties, Jon knew he could be anywhere. During his days of rest, Jon recalled his early years with helping Doc Micah conduct his rounds to all the Indian villages. Many of the elders knew of the various gangs, wanted men, and bounty hunters because dealing in trade, you also dealt in the exchange of information. So, Jon decided to try some of the local villages to try and locate Rico.

After traveling for an hour, he could see four riders galloping toward him. As they got closer, they seemed to get younger. Seeing they were riding directly at him, Jon decided to stop and wait. As the four riders approached, Jon could see they were just boys. Seventeen or eighteen at best. As Jon sat quietly staring, the four boys seemed nervous as they approached.

After a few awkward seconds, the oldest looking boy spoke up. "Howdy, mister. My name is Ethan and this here is my posse."

Jon took a moment and glanced at the others, who now seemed to be more at ease. He then directed his attention back to Ethan. "Posse? Don't you mean friends?"

Thinking Jon was poking fun at him, Ethan became agitated and pulled his gun, pointing it at Jon. "No, mister. I mean posse. You're that crazy Texas Ranger killing everybody and it seems we found you first. I guess that means God is on our side."

Once again Jon took a moment and glanced at the other boys and saw one of them was now holding up a Wanted poster with Jon's face and name on it. Realizing he was now the hunted and no longer the hunter, Jon became more intuitive. "So, you boys are bounty hunters? Well, you're right about one thing. You found me, but God isn't on your side."

With his gun still pointing at Jon, Ethan was feeling pretty proud of himself. "No matter, mister. Your ass is worth five thousand dollars and we're taking you in."

As Jon stared down the barrel of Ethan's gun, Ethan made the unfortunate mistake of briefly turning his head and joining his friends in laughter as they prematurely celebrated. "We're gonna be rich, boys. We're gonna be rich."

In the time frame it took Ethan to take his eyes off the prize, Jon pulled his gun with accelerated speed and shot Ethan's gun out of his hand. He then turned his sights on the other three boys. Feeling the wrath of hell upon them, the four boys quivered with fear. Ethan had the added unpleasantness of looking down to the ground at his gun, which still had his trigger finger attached to it. Horrified and holding his hand, he started screaming in pain. "Jesus Christ, mister, I'm sorry. Please, don't kill us."

The other boys also chimed in and begged Jon to let them go. One of the boys even scolded Ethan. "I knew we shouldn't have come out here, stupid. What the hell are we gonna tell your folks?"

Jon gave the boys a few more seconds until their anxiety was at its peak, then he holstered his gun. Before leaving, he gave them some advice. "Listen, boys. Consider this a gift. You have a long life ahead of you. Don't waste it with ignorance and stupidity. Go home to your parents. Work and toil the land as God commands. Find a nice girl and fall in love. And don't go looking for trouble, because trouble will surely find you first."

With the four boys arguing among themselves, Jon took the opportunity to quietly ride away. After riding a short distance, he stopped his horse and turned to see the boys still bickering and fighting, and briefly thought about the consequences of being a wanted man. Now he had to be vigilant of everyone he approached and everyone who approached him.

Jon knew of a small Indian village just a few miles west, so he decided to stop and inquire about Rico. With a brisk gallop, it wasn't long before he reached his destination. As he approached the village, he noticed most of the villagers took shelter or hid behind whatever was available. Jon watched as the women grabbed their children by their hands and pulled them to the safety of cover. Jon was familiar with the village, but it had been years since his last visit.

As he dismounted, two elders approached and introduced themselves. "I am Kiche, and this is our chief, Miakoda, which means 'Power of the Moon.' He no speak your language, so you speak through me."

With respect, Jon removed his hat and spoke. "My name is Jon Mason, and I used to come here with my pa when I was younger."

Jon waited for a response, but the two elders just stood and stared. After listening to the wind blow for a few awkward seconds, Kiche spoke. "You are Hok'ee. Why you come here? We wish nobody harm."

With some disappointment, Jon glanced down at the ground, then back up at the two elders. "I'm just an ordinary man trying to obtain some information. I have whiskey and jerky for trade."

Feeling apprehensive, Kiche took a few moments and spoke to Miakoda in order to get further guidance. Miakoda then whispered some words back to Kiche, then walked back into a very large teepee. Kiche then relayed the words to Jon. "You bring food and whiskey and sit with Miakoda."

Placing his hat back on his head, Jon turned and pulled three bottles of whiskey and a large satchel of jerky from his saddlebags. He then walked into the teepee where Miakoda and Kiche were waiting.

Taking a quick glance around, the scene looked all too familiar to Jon as the two elders were sitting around a fire, chanting and praying in their native language. Exercising some patience, Jon placed the food and whiskey down then took his hat off and sat. When the two elders finished, Jon waited for further instructions.

As Jon waited, Miakoda leaned over and whispered something, then Kiche translated. "Whiskey make our people sick. Some die."

Knowing the troubles of the past with the mountain men he had killed, Jon opened up all the bottles and took a small swig from each to show they weren't poison. He then took a piece of jerky from the satchel and took a bite of it.

After watching Jon sample the goods, Kiche handed a bottle of whiskey to Miakoda. After taking a long drink, Miakoda handed the bottle off to Kiche, who then took a small drink. Afterward, he once again inquired about Jon's agenda. "Why do you come here? You are the Hok'ee. You no need to trade. We have no warriors. Who among us do you seek?"

Knowing he needed information, Jon didn't want to take the risk of showing anger or being misunderstood. "I'm here seeking information about a man. His goes by the name of Rico and he's a very bad man, so I need to find him. He wears his gun low and hunts men. I've been told he has good looks and is charming with his words."

Kiche relayed Jon's words to Miakoda, who then threw some dust into the fire and chanted some words, signaling the meeting was now over. Afterward, Kiche stood up and motioned Jon to leave. Though feeling disappointed with the outcome, Jon didn't want trouble, so he quietly got up and placed his hat back on his head and then quietly walked out.

As he readied his horse, Kiche came out and approached. "Miakoda say he know of man you seek. He has deceitful tongue and kill many women and children. Miakoda say he wait for you. Miakoda say war coming. You go now, Hok'ee. You no return here."

Jon realized his welcome was now worn out, so he thanked Kiche for the information and rode on. By now, Jon's Wanted posters were all across the territory and, more importantly, word got back to Zachariah that it was Jon who survived the ambush. Knowing Jon would eventually make his way back to Presidio, more and more gunfighters were arriving in town each day in order to claim their trophy. Gideon and Jubal knew the men they had deputized were mostly family men and were no match against such killers, so he gave them the opportunity to stand down. Realizing their limitations with a gun, all of them took Gideon up on his offer and handed in their badges. Now it was up to Gideon and Jubal to try and keep the town of Presidio from becoming a shooting gallery.

After a light rain had come to an end, Gideon stepped outside of his office to catch some of that fresh air before it was gone. As he stood looking up and down the street, Jubal came back from making his rounds. "Gideon, we got a problem."

Gideon took a deep breath in order to take in the smell of moisture in the air, and with a smile on his face, he let his breath go and breathed another short breath. "Jubal, we have many problems. Which problem do you find more pressing then the next?"

Feeling a little foolish about his statement, Jubal could hear the sarcasm and laughed. "Well, I'll give you that one, boss. The problem I speak of is coming down the street right now."

Gideon glanced down the street and saw three riders slowly making their way down the middle of the street. He could see the residents getting nervous as they slowly rode their horses past them. After a few seconds, Jubal explained the problem. "Gideon, that there is Marlowe and his two brothers Ruben and Galen Bodine. They come down here from Kansas looking for Jon."

As Gideon watched the three men tie their horses in front of the hotel, he took another deep breath, but noticed the air was beginning to return to its normal dusty smell. "Well Jubal, I can see why you think that may be a problem. I think just about everybody has heard of the Bodine brothers. They've killed men all over, including other bounty hunters. Most of them shot in the back. Marlowe likes to face off against their unsuspecting victim, while Ruben and Galen come up from behind. I got a telegram from the mar-shal's office saying they were headed this way."

As Jubal listened, Gideon had some more unfortunate bad news. "Take a look across the street. See the man hiding in the shadows?"

Jubal glanced across the street and saw a man standing by the corner store where the sun was casting its midday shadow, but didn't recognize him. "I see'em, Gideon, but I can't make out who it is."

Gideon gathered his thoughts as he took a moment and sat down in one of the rickety old chairs outside of his office. Afterward, Jubal joined him. "Who is he Gideon?"

Gideon paused for a few seconds before answering because he was well aware of who it was. "Remember back a few months ago when Hinklemeyer was running around town talking about a bounty hunter with a strange accent? He was telling everybody how this stranger had singlehandedly gunned down the Hector Chavez gang and was headed in our direction."

Thinking back, Jubal paused for a moment and laughed. "Yeah, we all said Hinklemeyer was making up stories because he had run out of gossip."

After the initial laugh, Jubal noticed Gideon wasn't smiling. "Come on, Gideon. That was just Hinklemeyer telling some tall tale. I try and keep up with most of the names, but I ain't ever heard of any Hector Chavez gang."

Gideon looked at Jubal, then turned his attention back to the mysterious figure across the street. "Hector Chavez became a wanted man down in Brazil, so he fled the country and came here. He made his way up to Wyoming and convinced some of the local thieves to partner up with him. They started robbing liquor shipments in Wyoming and Utah. They would then return the booze to the intended customers—for a small fee, of course. They had a good thing going until a gunfighter from Ireland showed up one day. Donovan MacCabe heard about bounty hunting in America and decided to try and make a name for himself. He started with Hector Chavez. It was a small bounty, but it was just enough to get his name out there. Nobody really knows how he did it, but in the end Hector and his four men were dead. I do believe that's Donovan MacCabe standing over there."

Jubal was astonished, but Gideon was nowhere near finished. He then pointed down the street at another man leaning up against a post and smoking a cigarette. He wasn't a big man by no means, but he seemed to carry himself well and he had a gun hanging off each side of his body. "What'ya think, Jubal? Think he's any threat?"

Jubal looked at the man momentarily, but didn't seem to think anything of him. "Well, he's short. I'll giv'em that. He doesn't look like much, but he carries two guns."

Now Gideon was laughing as Jubal waited for the punch line. "Good observation. But I don't think being short takes you out of the running for being dangerous. They call him the Sicilian. Nobody knows his real name, but just like MacCabe, he came from his native country and caught the bounty hunting bug. They say he's deadly with either hand."

With both men now wondering about Jon and the future of Presidio, Gideon decided to try and relax, so he offered to by Jubal a drink. While walking to the Lucy Goosy, they ran into Thomas. While the three men greeted each other, Thomas expressed his concerns. "Sheriff, I know I like to keep to myself, but I do talk with Ms. Lita and Doc Bell and they tell me things. And sir, I just want to say I will stand by your side if you need me to."

Gideon definitely appreciated Thomas and his offer, but knew Thomas carried no gun and would be no match for the killers arriving in Presidio. "Thomas, you're a good man and you have helped the town of Presidio many times in the past, but if things go bad, I wouldn't want to see you get hurt. Besides, who would drive Doc Bell to the villages and help carry all of her supplies?"

Just as Thomas was leaving to go back to work, another rider came riding in. As the rider galloped by, Gideon and Jubal both recognized the man. Johnny Rocco. A bounty hunter from Nevada. Very mean and very deadly with a gun. Liked to shoot bounties but not kill them. Instead, he tortured them until they gave up any secrets of hidden valuables they've stolen. As Gideon and Jubal looked on in disgust, Johnny pitched them a devious smile, knowing they knew who he was.

After their brief encounter, Gideon and Jubal walked into the Lucy Goosy and made their way toward the bar. Seeing Lita at the bar put a huge smile on Gideon's face, and as they approached, Ms. Lita already had two beers waiting. With their mouths dry, both men drank down their beers with no hesitation. Although Presidio wasn't without its troubles and some of the shops had closed, Ms. Lita felt the need to improve her business by remodeling and extending the bar area. The business side of her was thinking toward the future when Presidio would eventually become a normal town again. Hoping to see the shops reopen and new entrepreneurs and homesteaders, Ms. Lita invested in an L-shaped bar ,which stretched around the room, and hired another barmaid and bartender.

Taking a moment to look around at the new upgrades, Gideon gave Lita a smile. "Well Lita, it looks really good in here. You seem to be doing well with your expansion. I think after everything is said and done, the Lucy Goosy will most definitely be the crown jewel of Presidio."

Glancing around at her progress, Lita was also very proud and had no problems showing it. "Gideon, thank you. Once all this nonsense is over with Zachariah Hayden, I'm sure Presidio will be booming with business. With the new faces in town, some of the other owners are starting to reopen their stores. And the Lucy Goosy seems to be reaping the rewards. So, what else can I get for you boys?"

Just as Gideon was about to order two whiskeys, the saloon doors opened and in walked a man. He seemed very sure of himself as he stood just inside the door and looked around the room. Seeing Gideon and Jubal, the stranger decided to sit at the opposite end of the bar. Feeling a bit concerned, Lita momentarily glanced down at the end of the bar at the man. He was tall, thin, and looked very angry. The man seemed to send shivers down Lita's spine. "Gideon, do you know him?"

Gideon remained quiet, so Jubal decided to answer for him. "That's Sebastian Cole. People say he's meaner than a pissed-off rattle snake. There's all kinds of rumors about him from here to Mississippi. I heard his first kill was his own father. His pa was wanted for some stupid petty theft and Cole gunned him down. From there, his legendary gunfights gained more and more popularity. They say he's the fastest gun ever."

After peering down the bar at Cole, Gideon was finally ready to talk. "Jubal, I wouldn't believe everything you hear. People say that about most gunfighters. They're always the fastest until somebody comes along and proves them wrong."

While Gideon and Jubal were trying to enjoy their drinks, in walked the local gunsmith, Mr. Fynn McKenzie. He was an older man, wasn't tall or built well, and wasn't much to look at, but he knew guns and ammunition. He couldn't accurately shoot a gun, but his knowledge of weaponry was second to none. He had come from California in order to get away from all the mining that was still going on. It seemed blasting away at every mountain in sight became an everyday normal thing and Fynn grew tired of it.

Fynn wasn't a drinker, so Gideon thought it odd to see him inside the Lucy Goosy. As Fynn walked by, he tipped his hat to everyone and kept walking. Gideon and Jubal watched as he walked to the end of the bar and placed a fairly large case on the seat next to Sabastian Cole. When Fynn opened the case, Gideon could see Cole smile, then reach into his coat pocket and pull out a hand full of cash. Gideon couldn't see the contents of the case, but he saw Cole hand the cash to Fynn. Afterward, Fynn walked out without saying a word. After Fynn made his exit, Cole wasn't too far behind. Feeling curious as to the transaction, Gideon watched Cole finish his drink, then get up to leave. Finding the entire scenario strange, to say the least, Gideon suggested him and Jubal pay a visit to Fynn at his gun shop.

Not wanting to be privy to the ongoing attraction of Gideon and Lita, Jubal walked out as Gideon said his good-byes. A smile and a cute wink of an eye was what Lita had for Gideon. "See you later, cowboy?"

With a big smile on his face, Gideon blushed as he winked back. "Most definitely, pretty lady."

After laying some money down on the bar, Gideon walked out to meet Jubal. Before they could take two steps, another rider had come to town. Jubal didn't recognize him, but Gideon knew who he was. As the rider passed by, Jubal could see he was as white as a ghost and had absolutely no expression on his face. Jubal didn't scare easily, but this particular stranger gave him quite the chill. "Gideon, that man doesn't look right. He looks like he's dead."

With his nerves on edge, Gideon watched as the man slowly rode by. Gideon could feel his adrenaline pumping through his body as he watched the man stop in front of the hotel and climb down from his horse. Standing six foot five and having a broad torso, the man was a force not to be reckoned with. Because of his frightening looks, some of the townsfolk didn't know what to think of him, so they avoided him altogether. As though he was parting the Red Sea, people created distance as he walked into the hotel.

Once again, Jubal chimed in. "God all mighty in Heaven, Gideon, what the hell was that?"

Jubal knew Gideon wasn't afraid of anything but he could see the uneasiness in Gideon's expression. "Jubal, if there was ever a man who gave me goosebumps with shivers up and down my spine, that would be the man. He goes by the name of Solomon. Some people refer to him as King Solomon. Nobody knows his real name or where he comes from. He doesn't just kill his bounty. He chops their heads off because it's easier to travel without a whole body. The Indians are terrified of him, including the Apache and the Comanche. He's the only man I know who can ride through their territories and not be harmed, which makes him one of the most effective bounty hunters out there."

Hearing Gideon talk about Solomon gave Jubal even more anxiety. "So, what's his story? What do people say about him?"

Still feeling the cold chills run through his body, Gideon took a breath and decided to walk and talk. On their way to Fynn's store front, Gideon told Jubal what he knew. "Well, the story goes he was just an ordinary man. A loner with no family. They say he was prospecting somewhere way down in the Falkland Islands when he came across a deep cave system. Now, this is where it gets a little farfetched. People think the cave system he found was a gateway to hell and instead of finding gold, he found Satan. Satan charged the man with trespassing and took his soul as a consequence. But the story doesn't end there. Because the world was created by God and it belongs to God, Satan was wrong for doing what he did. So, to avoid the wrath of God coming down on him, Satan needed a quick fix to the problem. Because Satan had already taken the man's life, there weren't many solutions readily available. You see, God wasn't ready for the man to be judged, so that forced Satan to try and correct his mistake. So, Satan kept the man's soul but let his body go free to roam the earth until it was time for God to pass judgment on the man."

By now, Gideon and Jubal reached Fynn's storefront and were anxious to see what the mysterious transaction was about. Fynn was in the back room busy repairing and cleaning guns that belonged to customers when he heard Gideon and Jubal walk in. After ringing the service bell, Gideon and Jubal patiently waited. A few seconds later, Fynn came from the back room and greeted the two men. "Hello, Sheriff, Deputy. What can I do for you gentlemen today?"

Not wanting to waste any time, Gideon got straight to the point. "Fynn, I know you have a business to run and you have certain obligations to your customers when it comes to confidentially, but I saw you earlier giving Sabastian Cole something he seemed to be very interested in. Can you tell me anything about that?"

With a friendly smile on his face, Fynn paused for a moment because he realized there was no need for secrecy. With his happy-go-lucky charm, Fynn explained the business transaction. "Well Sheriff, as you may well know, many of my customers walk a thin line between law and outlaw, but in my opinion, I don't care. I will sell to anybody who presents me with the right price, and Mr. Cole is no different. He's been a devoted customer of mine for a very long time. Mr. Cole contacted me a couple of months ago in reference to some new merchandise he had heard about. Unfortunately, the merchandise he was referring to wasn't due to hit the market for another six months. But like I said, money talks and, well, you know the rest."

Gideon appreciated the information and the good will Flynn was displaying, but he still wanted to know what was in the case. "So, you sold him a gun that hasn't been offered to the general public yet?"

Fynn wasn't too shy with his business, so he walked into the back room, then reemerged with a similar case from earlier. Gideon and Jubal stood watching as Fynn placed the case up on the counter. "When I ordered Mr. Cole's merchandise, I took the liberty of ordering two for myself."

Wanting to show off his newest acquisition, Fynn opened the case and turned it so Gideon and Jubal could see. "Gentleman, these are two of the finest Remingtons made to date. They're called the Remington outlaw. .45 caliber, nickle-plated with a two-piece walnut grip and a hairline trigger. They have not been offered to the general public yet, but rest assured, they will be in gun shops across America in a few more months."

Overwhelmed with envy, Gideon and Jubal gazed upon the guns as though they were looking at the Holy Grail. After the initial fascination, Gideon picked one of the guns up and held it in his hand. He twirled it around to feel the balance, then pointed it at the wall to view the accuracy. He felt comfortable because the gun felt very nice in his hand. He then reluctantly placed the gun back in the case. "So, Sabastian Cole has some new toys to play with. I'm guessing he's planning on using them soon."

Still smiling with pride, Fynn shut the case and returned them to the back room. When he reemerged, Jubal had a question, but before he could ask, Fynn gave him the answer. "No, Jubal. You or the sheriff couldn't afford these guns on your salary, so don't ask."

At the risk of hurting Jubal's pride, Gideon glanced over and let out a small chuckle. "Now, Jubal, what would you do with a fancy gun like that?"

While Jubal was still contemplating his answer, Gideon thanked Fynn, then turned to walk out. As the two men made their exit, they decided to make some rounds around town.

As the two men checked the banks and some of the businesses, Jubal inquired about the story Gideon was telling earlier. "Gideon, you never finished telling me what happen with Solomon."

Once again, Gideon smiled and let out a laugh. "Really, Jubal? You actually believe that nonsense? What happened to the guy that was mocking the old campfire stories we used to tell during the war?"

Jubal thought for a moment then pondered his answer. "Well, I'm not saying I believe the story, but it would be nice to hear the whole tale so I know what I'm dealing with."

After tipping his hat to some passing ladies, Gideon went on to finish the story of Solomon. "Well, people say he lives off rats and snakes, and because he's supposed to be dead already, he can't be killed. I've heard he was shot a few times, but every time he gets shot, he just gives an eerie smile to the person that shoots him. Then he takes their life. People seem to think he's collecting souls, but nobody knows for sure who he's collecting them for. Some people say he works for God because he's trying to buy his way into Heaven, but then other people say he works for Satan because he only hunts the worst of the worst bounties. Either way, I don't place any truth into such a myth."

After listening to Gideon tell the story, Jubal had his doubts. "Well, I'm just say'n, he really gives me the creeps. I ain't gonna say I believe all the stories I hear, but I'll keep my wits about me."

After sharing a few more laughs at Jubal's expense, the two men finished making their rounds, then walked back to their office. Just when they thought it was safe to relax for a few minutes, Mr. Hinklemeyer came busting through the door. "Sheriff, you gotta do something. With all these bounty hunters showing up, they're scaring off my regular customers. And that Solomon, let me tell you, I don't like the way he looked at me. I think he wants me, Sheriff. You gotta do something. You can't let him take me, Sheriff. You just can't."

Unable to keep his smile from shining through, Gideon glanced at Jubal, who was now looking back at Gideon. "Well, Hinklemeyer, has everyone paid you for their rooms and services?"

Mr. Hinklemeyer was breathing heavy, so he took a few seconds to try and calm himself down. "Well, yes, sir. Everybody paid, but that doesn't give them the right to walk around my hotel like they own it. And what about that dead man, Solomon? He's scaring the hell out of people and he's been looking at me funny. I think he came here for me. You gotta do something. I won't survive in hell."

Gideon could see Hinklemeyer was starting to get to Jubal and he tried desperately to hold back his laughter, but it was hard to say the least. "Hinklemeyer, it sounds like you have legitimate paying customers within your establishment, so until they do something that breaks the laws of the great state of Texas, there's nothing I can do. As for Solomon, he's a bounty hunter, and unless you have a price on your head that I don't know about, I seriously doubt he's here to take you to meet the devil. So, please, try not to spread any gossip about who you think is doing what. Just manage your hotel and let me know if anymore strangers check in."

Jubal offered Mr. Hinklemeyer some coffee to try and calm his nerves, then afterward Hinklemeyer reluctantly went back to his hotel. After Mr. Hinklemeyer left, Gideon burst out into laughter. With a nervous look on his face, Jubal stood quiet. After Gideon was done with his fun, he glanced over at Jubal, who was now looking tense and uptight. Still smiling, he playfully pointed his finger at Jubal. "Not a word, Jubal. Not a word."

While Presidio was trying to cope with all the ruthless killers in town, Jon was making his way east. While riding along, he thought about the meeting with Miakoda and Kiche. Miakoda said Rico was waiting for him, which meant he could only be in one place: Presidio. After a few hours of riding, Jon decided to rest his horse. There was nothing around, but he recognized the territory and remembered the old monastery. With bad memories rushing back into his thoughts, Jon didn't necessarily want to go back there, but it was the only place for miles around to get fresh water, and he was hoping the well was still productive.

A short while later, Jon found himself home. The sun had gone down and it was getting late, so he made a campfire and tried to get some rest. The wind was howling and the night creatures were out, and Jon could hear what sounded like faint calls and cries from long-forgotten spirits while he did his best to ignore them.

Just before he fell asleep, Jon heard the vague sound of Emily calling his name. He could also hear the distant sounds of children playing, but just as he jumped up to investigate, the echoes had faded back into the night. Distressed and confused, Jon shouted out in anger. "What'ya want with me? Why are you doing this? Leave me alone! Just let me do what I need to do so I can die!"

As the night progressed, the spirits and ghosts from the past had finally let Jon sleep. The next morning, he was up with the chilly brisk air. While shaking off the morning bitterness, Jon took a look around at the place he used to call home. The last he'd remembered, there wasn't much left to look at, but now the land was starting to reclaim what once belonged to it. The well was still producing water, so he filled his canteen and gave some to his horse. He then walked around and surveyed all the destruction that time beset on the land. Just a few crumbling walls, which were now overgrown with weeds. Remnants of what used to be buildings were now being confiscated by growth. And of course, the statue of St. Francis, which never seemed to get damaged. It was still being used to mark the grave of one of his mentors, Father Andres.

With all that has gone on in his life, Jon was reluctant to approach the grave of his dearest friend, but he did anyway. As he stood contemplating his words, he finally spoke out. "You were right, Father Andres. I wasn't ready for the evil in this world. I thought I was a good man. I thought I was doing right by God, but instead I let evil sneak into my heart and it destroyed my soul and stole my sanity. Now I'm just waiting for death to come and take me."

Jon stood looking at the weather-beaten statue as though he was waiting on some advice, but there was no response. With disappointment starting to take its toll, Jon turned his anger toward St. Francis. "What about it Francis? You didn't exactly help the padres. So, what about me? You have any words of wisdom?"

Ashamed of his life and saddened by his fate, Jon stood in front of the statue of St. Francis while tears started to roll down his cheeks. Without warning, a light rain started to fall, which began to wash some of the dust and dirt off the old, faded statue. Jon watched as the colorless dull statue began to show a little bit of its past glory. With the moisture from the rain, the faded colors on the statue started to reappear. Jon could see a little more detail come out as the rain continued to fall. Suddenly, he noticed something he had never seen before. Feeling apprehensive, Jon's hands started to tremble. He finally got up enough courage to run his fingers across the neck of St. Francis. Still trembling, he then ran his fingers across the necklace he had been wearing all his life. They were one in the same. The necklace St. Francis was wearing was identical to the one Jon had on.

As his body was now starting to tremble, Jon took a few nervous steps backward. With the rain starting to mix with his tears, he lifted his hand and pointed at the statue. "No. This isn't right. This can't be."

With the rain coming down even harder, Jon began to shake uncontrollably. As he took a few more steps back away from the statue, his mind started to play tricks. Suddenly, the statue opened its eyes and started laughing at Jon. The laughter got so loud, Jon could no longer stand it. With his eyes closed and holding both of his hands over his ears, he started to scream. "No! This isn't real! Stop laughing! Stop laughing, now!"

Then, in the blink of an eye, everything stopped. The rain was gone and the statue of St. Francis was just an old, worn-out statue as it had been for many years gone by. Jon looked around and listened, but there was no sound. No wind blowing, No animals or birds making noise, and nothing moving.

With fear striking him deep down in his soul, Jon became terrified. His mind was now numb. With all the silence, he could hear the faint beet of his heart. As the seconds rolled by, the beet got louder and stronger. His adrenaline started to pump through his body as he started to show the ugliness of his anger. In one swift move, Jon withdrew his gun and fired six bullets into the statue of St. Francis. The old statue, which had stood the test of time, shattered into pieces and fell to the ground.

The statue had withstood skirmishes, battles, and wars. It had defied hordes of bandits conducting raids over the decades and tolerated all that Mother Nature had thrown at it. But in a few short seconds, six bullets from Jon's gun destroyed what had stood for more years than anyone could count.

Just as fast as it was gone, nature was now back in its place. The birds were flying and singing their songs. A light breeze was blowing the clouds across the sky. And the rest of the small critters were scurrying about, conducting their daily business. Not realizing he still had his gun in his hand, Jon took a few moments to calm his nerves and catch his breath. Finally feeling the weight of the gun tugging on his arm, Jon slowly holstered it and walked over to the statue, which was now in pieces.

Remembering the history lessons Father Andres and Santos would give him, Jon knew most statues of the era were solid, so he was surprised to find this particular statue was hollow. Looking down at the ground, he now understood why. Lying on the ground among all the broken pieces was a very old-looking scroll. Realizing the scroll must have been hidden within the statue since its conception, Jon bent down to pick it up. As he unraveled the scroll, he found it was made up of several large pieces of animal skins. The first segment was written on using the Spanish language. Jon also recognized the second piece. It was written in the Aztec language, which was the same language the book Father Andres had found. The third portion was written using the English language. Taking a few minutes to read, Jon came to the conclusion that all three scrolls were the same story, but written in three different languages. The scroll told an original version of a young Aztec boy and a magical mountain. It also told the truth about the Franciscans, who had also found the mountain.

Not really understanding why the scroll was placed inside an old statue, Jon was stunned, to say the least. So many years gone by and there had been a never-ending abundance of treasure hunters and outlaws who spent their lives and gave their lives looking for a treasure that wasn't supposed to exist. Through the years, the statue of St. Francis had been thrown around and knocked around. It had been moved and moved again. It had seen very little good days and multitudes of bad, and yet all who had laid their eyes on it chose to ignore it. Written on the scrolls was a story of a long-lost treasure only dreams and fantasies were made of, and now it was in Jon's hands. Temporarily removing his necklace, Jon studied it for a few minutes. Realizing the two pieces of leather could be pulled apart, he did so very carefully. With eyes wide, Jon found the final piece of the puzzle that would satisfy the greediest of treasure hunters. Inside the necklace was an engraved picture of St. Francis and opposite of that was the word *Totokonoolal*, which was the Indian word for the El Capitan.

Treasure was the last thing on Jon's mind and the scroll wasn't something he was looking for or wanted, so it wasn't going to deter him from getting his revenge. So he rolled the scrolls up and carefully placed in in his saddlebag. With the grave of Father Andres without its grave marker, Jon had to take some time to find a new one. After the destruction of the monastery, what Mother Nature didn't take or destroy, scavengers utilized. But there was still the hidden room nobody knew about. It was buried beneath some old timbers, so Jon made quick work of uncovering the hole in the ground.

Years before while down in the room, he had noticed an old cross made of various colors of beautiful stone, which was probably created by the original builders of the monastery. He could picture it mounted atop one of the towers, which was now gone. It weighed a few hundred pounds, so he tied a rope to his horse and dragged the cross up the old dilapidated steps and over to the grave. It had been many decades since the cross had seen any daylight, but now it was going to be a shiny beacon of light for Father Andres. Jon fetched some water from the well and cleaned the cross in order to bring back its natural colors. He then dug a hole and stood the cross up in order to place it into the ground. After saying a few kind words, Jon mounted his horse and headed for Presidio.

While Jon was riding toward his destiny, Presidio had awakened to more bad news. During the night, more deadly bounty hunters had arrived.

While making his morning rounds, Jubal stopped to talk with the mayor's wife, Mrs. Eleanor, who had just exited the dress shop. While engaged in a pleasant morning conversation, Mrs. Eleanor noticed a stranger walking toward them. "Deputy Jubal, look yonder."

After the inquiry, Jubal turned to see a very young-looking man. "Well, I'll be. You know who that is?" In a moment, Jubal realized who he was talking to. "Begg'n your pardon, ma'am. Of course you wouldn't know who that is. That's Logan Slade out of Oklahoma. He's only twenty years old, but he has five kills already. He doesn't look like much, but they say he's quicker than a barn mouse running for its life. I best go tell Gideon."

Jubal tipped his hat, then quickly said his good-byes as he headed straight for Gideon's office. On his way, he ran into Hank Connors. Hank operated one of the two feed stores in town and had problems in the past with some of the local children playing out behind his store. As usual, Hank heard noises earlier, which sounded like wooden crates being tossed about. Over the years, Hanks tolerance levels had started to disintegrate, so he was hoping Jubal would go investigate for him. "Now Jubal, you know these dang kids don't like me much, and I'm gett'n tired of talk'n to these high and mighty parents that ain't do'n noth'n."

Hank wasn't a mean-spirited person, but he was getting older and becoming more distressed every day. Like scolding a school child, Hank began to shake his finger at Jubal. "Now, you know if'n I go back there, I'm gonna lay some wood down on those kids' backsides. So, you better go handle it."

Jubal was in a rush, but he knew duty came first and his first priority was to the citizens of Presidio. So, he took a deep breath and pulled himself up by his britches. With his shoulders brushed back and standing tall, he walked around to the rear of the store and saw a huge man rummaging through some empty crates. "Hey, you there. What'ya do'n back here?"

Hearing the deputy's voice call out, the man paused for a moment, then slowly turned to face Jubal. That's when Jubal realized his worst nightmare had come true: He was alone in a back ally face to face with King Solomon.

As Jubal's shoulders started to slightly droop, his heart began to sink. While Solomon steadily stared, Jubal tried to swallow the lump that began to form in his throat. "Good morning, Mr. Solomon, King, sir. Um, glad to make your acquaintance, King, I think."

With his faded eyes and pale skin, Solomon had no words as the hulking beast continued to look down at Jubal as though he was peering into his soul. Once again Jubal attempted to swallow the lump in his throat, which seemed to grow bigger by the second. "Mr. King, sir. I'm sorry if'n this sounds disappointing, but there's no rats or snakes back here, Mr. Solomon, King, sir."

Like a statue, Solomon stood strong and gave Jubal absolutely no idea of what his agenda was. By now, Jubal began to worry. "Mr. Solomon, sir. May I ask what yer do'n here? I mean, why me, Mr. King, sir? What did I do?"

Once again Solomon was silent as Jubal's heart was starting to pound and his anxiety started to escalate. "Um, I gotta tell you, Mr. King Solomon, sir. I'm not ready to go yet, sir. I mean, well, I'm sure you can find some feller worse than me."

With Solomon killing Jubal with his silence, Jubal found himself out of words with the tension reaching its peak. For the first time in his life, Jubal was unsure of himself. Solomon watched as Jubal's fingers started to twitch and his drawing hand started to slowly move toward his gun. Suddenly, Solomon moved. With his nerves about to break down, Jubal stopped what he was doing as Solomon flung his jacket back to reveal his gun. Now Jubal was at his crossroads and was pondering which way to go. "Mr. Solomon, sir. You don't really have to do this, sir. I promise you, I can be a better person."

Just then, several horses out in front of the store got spooked from a supply wagon going by too fast. The horses reared back, breaking lose from their ties, which created a chaotic scene. With a natural response, Jubal turned in the direction of the commotion. When he turned his attentions back, King Solomon was gone. With his anxiety down and his heart rate back to normal, Jubal counted his blessings and ran back to Gideon's office.

Crashing through the door, Jubal had to catch his breath while the encounter with Solomon was still fresh in his thoughts. Gideon and Belle, who were sitting and enjoying some morning coffee and conversation, were momentarily startled. After a few moments, Jubal poured himself a cup of coffee and paced the floor. "Gideon, he's after me. That's why he's here. He's here for me. It's my time, Gideon. It's my time."

Having the feeling he already knew what Jubal was talking about, Gideon took a deep breath and smiled. When he stood up to confront Jubal on his fears, he placed his hands on Jubal's shoulders. "You wouldn't happen to be talking about Mr. Solomon now, would you, Jubal?" Gideon could see the fear in Jubal's eyes and patted him on the back as to say, *It's okay.* "First Hinklemeyer, then you." Shaking his head in disbelief, Gideon gave the floor to Belle so she could refute the urban legend. He then maneuvered the frightened deputy over to a chair and sat him down for a little schooling from Doc Belle.

Trying to keep from laughing, Doc Belle stood up to talk. "Listen, Jubal. He's just a man. A very weird man, but nevertheless, just a man. I ran down an old colleague of mine who has a practice in San Francisco. He sent me a telegram that explained our mysterious Mr. Solomon. His real name is Eugene Horowitz. He was born with a rare skin pigmentation. He showed up in San Francisco to have some experimental procedure, but it didn't work out. I guess he figured he would try and capitalize on his condition, so he spread that ridiculous story about himself so he could scare the hell out of people while hunting bounties. You know what they say: Every advantage helps."

Listening to Belle's story, Jubal was starting to feel real foolish. "Dang nabit, Gideon. I'm really sorry for acting a fool."

Still with a smile on his face, Gideon poured Jubal something a bit stronger than coffee. "Jubal, it's all right. Sometimes our imagination gets away from us. If it makes you feel any better, he even had me a little fooled."

With a wink of her eye, Belle gave the boys a smile and said her goodbyes in order to go tend to a few of her sick clients. After Belle left, Jubal helped himself to a sip of his whiskey and thought about his encounter. "But I saw him out back of old man Connor's store sifting through some empty crates. What'ya think he was look'n for?"

Gideon let out a small laugh as he turned to walk out. "Probably looking for snakes and rats." Looking for a quick laugh, Gideon stopped in the doorway and turned to look at Jubal's perplexed expression. "Just kidding, Jubal. Just kidding."

Feeling even more embarrassed, Jubal stood up to follow Gideon out. "You're real funny, Gideon. Real funny man, you are."

As the two men stepped out of the office, they walked toward the hotel while Jubal told Gideon about the young bounty hunter. "Gideon, I ran into the mayor's wife earlier and you'll never guess in a million years who we saw."

Gideon stopped for a moment to greet some passing ladies, then turned to Jubal. "Is that a challenge? 'Cause if so, I will guess a very young Mr. Logan Slade."

With a sarcastic disappointed look on his face, Jubal rolled his eyes. "Okay, funny man. He must have rode into town during the night, so how could you have known that?"

Gideon pushed his hat back a bit, then took a breath. "Hinklemeyer, of course."

After a few laughs, the two men continued their trek to the hotel. Unfortunately, Gideon needed to speak to Zachariah Hayden. Along the way, Gideon mentioned a couple more names. "Apparently another man came riding in during the night. Man named Brice Kincaid."

Looking uncertain, Jubal didn't recognize the name. "I don't think I know the feller. Who is he?" Gideon smiled as he glanced at Jubal. "You should probable read the paper more often, Jubal. Young reporter did a story on him last year. Anyway, his family is huge. Came over from Scotland a century ago and settled up in the Nebraska territory. They own one of the largest farms in the area. Very wealthy. Apparently young Mr. Brice takes his heritage very serious and one day while celebrating one of their holidays, he dressed himself up in a kilt and went into town to do some drinking. Well, his kilt didn't go over very well and some of the locals laughed at him and pushed him around. They tossed him out into the street like a piece of garbage. So, young Mr. Brice went and got himself a gun. He came back just before closing and killed three of the men who were taunting him. A fourth man took a bullet to the leg."

Along the way, the two men stopped at several of the businesses to try and give assurance on Presidio being financially sound for the future. With Zachariah Hayden and his men squeezing the life out of the territory and now talk of all the bounty hunters waiting on the arrival of Jon, Presidio could very easily become a future ghost town. After stopping by and speaking to one of the bankers, Mr. Schweitzer, the two men left out walking toward the hotel and what was sure to be an exchange of hostile words. Along the way, Gideon continued his narrative of Brice Kincaid while Jubal listened with attentiveness. "So, because money talks, it didn't take much for the Kincaid family to push their weight around. Supposedly an undisclosed amount of money was paid out and a deal was struck. Young Mr. Brice was to leave Nebraska, never to come back. In return, there would be no charges filed."

By now they were approaching the hotel, but Jubal had more questions before they entered, so the two men sat outside for a few minutes while Jubal made his inquiries. "Gideon, this man is here for the same reason all the other bounty hunters are here for, so what makes him so unique? I mean, he's just a farm boy that's gonna get himself killed."

Taking a deep breath and looking around, Gideon didn't answer right away. As he watched the townsfolk passing by, he let out a sigh of frustration. "Well, after Brice left the territory, he made his way up into Wyoming. He wound up getting into a bar fight and took on several men much bigger than him. Now, this is where it gets interesting. I'm sure you've heard of Kenna James?"

Hearing the name, Jubal's eyes got wide as his face lit up with admiration. "Sure. I've heard of him. Military hero turned sheriff turned bounty hunter. I heard he always likes to give his bounties the opportunity to go to jail peaceful like."

Gideon smiled as he glanced over at Jubal and continued the tale. "Yeah, I've heard that to. Kenna happens to be a good friend of mine. We served together during the war, and I can honestly say he pulled me out of harm's way more than a few times. Anyway, Kenna just happened to be the sheriff at the time Brice got into his little spat. So, after Brice got whooped, Kenna took him aside and taught him a few things, including how to fight. More importantly, he taught Brice how to handle a gun. Sadly and against Kenna's advice, Brice became a brutal killer. He left the Wyoming territory and started hunting any man with a price on his head. He gets them anyway he can—ambushing them, shooting them in the back and on occasions, fair showdowns where he outdraws them."

With a disappointed tone in his voice, Jubal voiced his concerns. "Why would a man like Kenna James create such a monster?"

Once again, Gideon let out a disheartening sigh. "Well, I don't think Kenna's intentions were to create a monster. He's kind'a like Jon. Kenna sees the injustice within this world and constantly works to destroy it, and I guess he saw Brice as being bullied, so he thought he was doing right by teaching him how to defend himself. He's regretted it ever since."

After the two men finished their talk, they got up and walked into the hotel. As usual, Mr. Hinklemeyer was at the front desk, but surprisingly the women who would normally be hovering around and gossiping weren't there. When Gideon and Jubal approached, Mr. Hinklemeyer was a bit more nervous than normal. "Sheriff Gideon, sir, please, you have to get these killers out of my hotel. They're scaring my other guests."

Feeling sympathy for Mr. Hinklemeyer, Gideon leaned on the counter and let out a small laugh. "Now, Harold, I've already told you, they are paying guests and they've done nothing wrong. I just think you're going through withdrawal because your lady friends won't come in here to gossip with you. Now, is Hayden in his room?"

With his skittish voice, Mr. Hinklemeyer pointed toward the dining area. "No, sir. Mr. Hayden is in the dining room with some guests that arrived a little while ago."

Knowing there was always a chance of confrontation when dealing with Zachariah Hayden, Gideon turned his attention to Jubal who was anxiously staring back. "Well Gideon, this ought to be interesting. Any chance you wanna come back later?"

Gideon smiled as he looked at Mr. Hinklemeyer and then at Jubal, then over to the dining area. "Hell no. I wouldn't pass up this opportunity for anything. Jubal, what'ya say we go and ruin Hayden's day?"

Jubal smiled, then turned to face the dining area. "Anytime I can ruin Hayden's day is a good day for me. Let's go."

With their expectations running high, Gideon and Jubal walked toward the dining room, and when they entered, they saw Rico and a man named Indigo sitting at the table having drinks with Zachariah. Before the two men could stop and think, Zachariah spotted them and invited them over. "Please, Sheriff, come over and say hello."

As Gideon and Jubal reluctantly walked to the table, Zachariah stood up and turned to his two new hired guns. "Well now, boys, I want you to meet Presidio's prestigious black sheriff and the dog that scurries around in his shadow."

When the two men stood up to face Gideon and Jubal, they purposely remained at a distance so they couldn't shake hands. Instead, they just stared with an angry look. While Jubal was busy trying to absorb Zachariah's insult, Gideon was engaged in a staring contest with Rico. "I know who you are, Rico, and I know what you did. You shouldn't have come back because you'll never leave this town alive."

Not taking Gideon's words with any seriousness, Rico just smiled and decided not to respond. Zachariah, on the other hand, had plenty to say. After sitting back down at the table, he took a drink of his wine to wet his lips. "Now, Sheriff, where's your manners? It's not very gentleman like to make threats to my guests, but then again, your kind don't know anything about manners or being gentle."

Taking a deep breath, Gideon wasn't about to exchange insults, so he got right to the point. "Hayden, no doubt by now you know Jon survived your little plan to wipe out the Texas Rangers, and I'm sure you know he's on his way here. So, with that being said, I will do the duty I've been sworn to do, but if you try and take the law into your own hands, I will make sure you never see the outside of a prison cell ever again."

With Rico and Indigo still standing, Zachariah took another sip of wine and smiled. "Sheriff, I don't think you understand the severity of your situation. There is a violent criminal with a price on his head on his way here to try and kill me, so I've hired a few bodyguards to ensure my safety. Now, you may think you still have control of this town, but I assure you, you do not. Over the past few days, a number of bounty hunters have entered the town of Presidio and they will be gunning for your friend. And to add to all the fun, I have added an extra fifty thousand U.S. dollars on top of what the government's offering of just a mere five thousand for such a dangerous animal."

As Gideon stood listening to Zachariah Hayden, he began to wonder if he was right about maintaining control over the town.

Knowing the conversation wasn't going as planned, Gideon was out of words, but Zachariah was still going strong. With an expression of worry starting to appear on Gideon's face, Zachariah continued his verbal attack. "That's right, Sheriff. It's going to be a blood bath, with your friend the ex-Texas Ranger standing right in the middle of it all. With such a big bounty for the taking, I'm sure those bloodthirsty bounty hunters will stop at nothing to collect. And I'm sure they will no doubt kill each other to get their hands on the reward."

While Gideon and Jubal could do nothing but stand there and listen, Zachariah continued to enjoy his moment. "Sheriff, I do believe my friend Rico will be just fine. I think it's your Ranger friend that shouldn't be coming back. I do believe it is he who will not be making it out of the town of Presidio alive."

Feeling a bit beaten down, Gideon let out some of his frustration. "I can tell you this, Hayden. You may think you've won, but the only thing you've done is unleash hell upon you and your men."

Clearly Zachariah was in control of the conversation, so without saying a word, Gideon turned to walk out, with Jubal following behind. As the two men exited the hotel, Gideon stopped to take a breath. Feeling a bit ill, he bent over and placed his hands on his knees while taking several deep gasps of air. Looking on, Jubal became concerned. "Gideon, you all right?"

After breathing in some fresh air, Gideon stood up straight. "Well now, that didn't go exactly as planned."

Just as the two men were preparing to visit the Lucy Goosy, they saw some more bad news. The stagecoach had just pulled into town and when the door opened, out climbed Colonel Augusta Pittman. As promised, he had returned to Presidio to finish a job that was already paid for. Carrying a small suitcase and a rifle, the colonel made his way toward the hotel. In doing so, he stopped to talk to Gideon, who was now anticipating the encounter. Smiling as he approached, the colonel also looked forward to the encounter. "Been a while, Sheriff, and I hear things have changed a little since our last meeting."

Normally Gideon would not respond, but he had to make some things clear. "Listen, Pittman, whatever the reason you have for coming back here, I suggest you make your visit short. No telling when a bullet may find you."

With his anger starting to come out, Gideon didn't give the colonel a chance to respond. Instead, he and Jubal quickly walked away.

While Gideon and Jubal decided to drink away some of their woes, Colonel Pittman checked into the hotel. After acquiring his room, he freshened up a bit, then made his way to the dining area where Zachariah welcomed him with delight. "Colonel, please. Let me introduce you to some of my new associates, Rico and Indigo."

Glancing at the two men, the colonel wasn't impressed, but presented himself in a pleasant manner for the sake of conversation. "Gentlemen, very nice to meet your acquaintance. Now, if you'll excuse us, Mr. Hayden and I have business to discuss."

Feeling good about the colonel being back in town, Zachariah reached into his pocket and pulled out some money, then handed it to Rico. "Please, gentlemen, go have some drinks on me."

Never one to turn down free drinks, Rico and Indigo gladly accepted the kindness and quickly made their exit.

After the two men left, Zachariah wasted no time in getting down to business. He ordered a whiskey for the colonel, then made a toast. "To the future."

Feeling good about himself, Zachariah leaned across the table to begin their meeting. "Colonel Pittman, sir, this couldn't have worked out better if God had planned it himself. I've got every noteworthy bounty hunter waiting to kill that Texas Ranger. And with all those fast guns in town, that good for nothing sheriff will be running around chasing his tail, which brings me to you. As promised, I want you to kill that Negro for me. Once that Ranger arrives in town, he's going to have his hands full trying to protect him, which should make it quite easy for you to catch him off guard."

After hearing the details, the colonel sat and listened to Zachariah and was in full agreement. Taking a drink of his whiskey, Colonel Pittman gave Zachariah a small reminder. "Sir, if you recall, I do not partake in the drinking of spirits that come from the bottle while conducting business, so once we have concluded here today and I walk out that door, my business will start and you shall have that Negro's hands mounted on your wall as promised. And afterward, if that Ranger is still alive, I shall personally place a bullet in his head for free since I failed to collect the ever-so-elusive trinket you seek."

After the two men shook hands on their agreement, the colonel exited the hotel in order to survey the town for his plan of action. As he took a casual stroll around town, Gideon and Jubal were at the Lucy Goosy working on their third drink. At the other end of the bar was Rico and Indigo having fun spending Zachariah's money. And sitting at one of the tables playing cards was Marlowe, his two brothers, and a couple of the local ranch hands. Being loud and obnoxious, they were drinking heavily and becoming belligerent. Ms. Lita had warned them several times about the noise and language, but their behavior persisted to a point where they started to force their unwanted advances onto the women. Not wanting to be a part of the problem, the locals got up and walked out. Before Gideon could intervene, Rico surprisingly scolded the men. Being the suave ladies' man he thought he was, he ordered Marlowe and his brothers to stop harassing the ladies. But now Marlowe was embarrassed, and being a man of odds, he stood up and faced off against Rico, knowing he had his two brothers by his side.

By now, Gideon had seen and heard enough. "Okay, boys. Time to take your little quarrel outside."

Hearing Gideon say that, Jubal was shocked. Normally Gideon wouldn't allow two men to face off in his town, but today was different. While Rico invited Marlowe outside, Jubal leaned into Gideon with curiosity. "Gideon, you really think this is a good idea? I mean, innocent people could get hurt."

Wanting to see how things played out, Gideon didn't say anything. Instead, he followed Rico and Marlowe outside and stood off to the side and waited. Feeling concerned and not knowing his motive, Jubal followed.

Because of Presidio's violent past, the townsfolk were all too familiar when two gunfighters were about to draw down on each other. So, when Rico and Marlowe stepped into the street, the people of Presidio quickly made themselves scarce. Knowing Marlowe had been drinking excessively, Rico waited for him to make the first move. After a few seconds of staring, Ruben and Galen came from around the back ally with guns out. Before they could shoot Rico in the back, Indigo, who had followed the two brothers out the back door of the bar, came from behind and shot both brothers dead. Shocked, to say the least, Jubal watched as Gideon did nothing.

Suddenly Marlowe became irate. "You goddamn Mexican trash."

As Marlowe was grieving and cussing at the same time, Rico pulled his gun and shot him down.

As the third brother fell dead to the ground, Gideon quietly turned to Jubal. "Better have Orville come and take care of the bodies. I'll be in my office if you would like to talk later."

Stunned at the lack of action by Gideon, Jubal headed for the undertaker's office to fetch Orville. While Rico and Indigo were buying celebration drinks, Gideon calmly walked to his office. When he got there, he poured himself a nice tall drink. After a few minutes of thought, Mr. Herman from the telegraph office walked in. Gideon had a few messages he needed to have sent without anyone knowing and had Mr. Herman come by to collect them. After leaving

Gideon to his bottle, Mr. Herman immediately went back to his office to send out Gideon's requests.

As Mr. Herman walked out, Jubal was walking in. After peaking out the door to make sure nobody else was around, Jubal closed the door and locked it. When he sat down, Gideon could see the disappointment in his eyes. "Now, come on, Jubal. You should know me by now."

With a smile on his face, Gideon poured Jubal a drink and slid it across the desk. Witnessing Gideon and his disregard for duty, Jubal glanced down at the drink but didn't pick it up as his eyes slowly turned their attention back to Gideon. "Gideon, I consider you a good friend and even a better sheriff. Never thought I would see the day you would give into these heathens."

With a small sigh, Gideon stood up and walked over to the window. "Every morning as I drink my coffee, I look out this window and thank God for everything he's done for me. Then I watch the people of this town as they get their day started and go about their business. I then pray that I can do the job I've been given by the town council."

As a plan was beginning to form in his head, Gideon paused for a moment in order to think about his next words. "Earlier, I told you about my friend Kenna James. Well, he taught me a lot when I was in the army. We were both scouts stationed up in Missouri early during the war. We had just won a major victory against the Confederate Army and they were starting to retreat. Kenna and I had orders to scout out a safe path toward the southern end of the state. With the Confederate Army still lurking, we had to be careful. We were so busy looking out for Johnny Rebs, we didn't realize we had stumbled into a dispute between the Chickasaw tribe and the Quapaw Indians. You know just as well as I do, there wasn't an Indian alive who didn't want to see us blue coats dead. Didn't matter the color of our skin. Well, the Quapaw had us cornered, but we had the high ground. I gotta tell you, Jubal, I was shaking in my boots that day. I even told Kenna it was nice knowing him and thanked him for show-ing kindness toward me."

By now, Jubal's taste buds was craving the drink Gideon had set in front of him, so during Gideon's pause, he reached over and gulped it down. Feeling the need to wet his whistle, Gideon sat back down and poured two more drinks. Afterward, he continued his story. "Yeah, Jubal, I don't mind telling you I thought that was it. Then I looked over at Kenna, who was smiling and laughing at me. I thought maybe his mind snapped from the stress, but I was wrong. He asked why I was so worried, and in a sarcastic kind of a way, I told him to look out yonder at the fifteen Quapaw warriors about to kill us. He then tells me to look out yonder past the Quapaw warriors. Come to find out, the Quapaw were so busy concentrating on us, they forgot about the Chickasaw. The Chickasaw came up from behind and easily wiped out the Quapaw. Funny thing was, the Chickasaw deemed us useful for their battle and as a gift let us keep our lives."

In following the story, Jubal was still unsure what it had to do with the day's earlier events. "Gideon, you tell a good story, but you got me wondering about your sanity. What do warring Indians have to do with you letting those men kill each other on the streets of Presidio?"

Just like Kenna, Gideon smiled and let out a small laugh. "The point that I'm trying to make is we're outnumbered and outgunned. When your enemies have enemies, why not use them to your advantage? As much as I despise Hayden, he was right. These bounty hunters will have no issue killing each other for that bounty. Listen, Jubal, I'm guessing neither one of us can outdraw half those bounty hunters, so why try just to wind up with a tombstone over our heads? According to Hayden, Jon now has fifty-five thousand on his head. That's a lot of money up for grabs. Those bounty hunters aren't friends and they're not associates; they're just ruthless killers that will kill anyone including each other. For that kind of money, those animals would kill their own kin. So, why not let them? Why not just sit back and enjoy the free show? Hell, before this thing is all over, Orville will be the richest man in town."

Now it was all coming together for Jubal as the worry started to subside and he was beginning to like how Gideon was thinking. Throwing in his own kind of sarcasm, Jubal stood up and took his hat off. "Gideon, I would like to formally apologize for doubting you, sir. That was a great story and I'm liking the plan even better."

The rest of the day was uneventful, with the townspeople coming and going and business being conducted with nobody else getting killed. The plan Gideon came up with seemed to be a good one for now.

While the sun was setting and Presidio was closing its doors, Gideon and Jubal conducted a last walk around town, checking doors and walking the alleyways. Just when they were about to turn in for the night, five riders appeared at the end of town. They sat atop their horses and watched as Gideon and Jubal looked on.

After a few seconds of restlessness, Jubal spoke out. "You know them boys, Gideon?"

Still watching with anticipation, Gideon answered with a bit of anxiety in his voice. "Unfortunately, Jubal, yes I do. Out front is my uncle Vernon, and next to him is his brother Nato, then my cousin, Wardell. Wardell and I don't exactly get along. The other two are friends, or should I say partners in crime. I was never sure of their real names, but the big guy built like a prized bull is from Louisiana. They call him the Rage'n Cage'n. Story goes he got into a fight over a woman and he punched the guy in the face. Problem was the guy never woke up. Ended his life with one punch. The other guy is also a mystery. They call him the Flying Dutchman. There's a few different stories that go along with him. They say he was the captain of the doomed ship when it went down in a storm off the coast of Africa and he was the only survivor. It's said he was cursing God while battling the storm, but when he realized the battle was futile, he summoned Satan himself to save him. He supposedly swam to shore on the back of a great beast and he dare not return to the sea because the ship and its men scour the oceans looking for him."

Overcome with here-we-go-again syndrome, Jubal shook his head as he thought for a moment. "God 'o mighty, Gideon. Maybe I should've joined you Yanks. Y'all surely had better campfire stories than us. But I gotta say, my grandma told me that story of the Fly'n Dutchman when I was just a little turd. Gideon, the Dutchman went down over two hundred years ago, and that would either make him very old or very dead, and if'n it's the latter than him and that there feller Solomon have a lot in common."

Not really smiling, Gideon stared at Vernon while Vernon stared back. "Well Jubal, I think those stories are just that. Stories. Tales that are made up just to scare people."

Momentarily glancing down at the ground, Jubal scoffed. "Well, I ought'a not be say'n this, Gideon, but they got me a wee bit nervous at the moment."

Knowing the seriousness of the situation, Gideon was trying hard not to laugh. "And just to let you know, Vernon has no love for white folks."

Before Gideon could explain more, Vernon and his crew slowly approached. With a staring contest taking place, Vernon was the first to crack. With a smile and a small laugh, he stared down at Gideon from atop his horse. "Well, I'll be. I guess it's true, boys. Looky what we have here. My nephew, the sheriff. Pray tell, I heard you'd be wearing a star on your chest, but I just didn't believe it, so me and the boys came to see for ourselves."

Not accepting Vernon's excuse for being in town, Gideon proceeded with caution. "How are you, Uncle Vern? Been awhile." Turning his attentions to Nato, Gideon nodded. "Uncle Nato, you're looking well."

Not trying to reveal his true intentions, Vernon attempted to use the family connection to gain information. "Well, Nephew, been a lot of fuss gone round. Heard a lot'a names I haven't heard in a while. And you know me, never one to pass up opportunity."

Gideon was tired and he already knew the reason Vernon was in town, so he became a little agitated in his response. "Uncle Vern, I'm not that little boy you remember. So please, don't treat me as such. I suggest you state your business, then move on."

Hearing the tone in Gideon's voice, Vernon became somewhat offended. "Damn, boy. You all growed up now and think you can just talk to your uncle any olé way." Still trying to laugh it off, Vernon once again turned to his men. "Would you look at that, boys? This Negro got a badge and now he thinks he's special. Like the white folks are really gonna treat him any different."

Turning back to Gideon, Vernon suddenly became serious. "Now, you listen here, boy. Me and my crew have been camped outside of your little town for some time now. We done seen quite a few familiar quick hands ride by.

Johnny Rocco, Sebastian Cole. And word travels fast. I heard the Bodine brothers already gott'em selves killed. No real loss there. Just more white folk I ain't gotta deal with. Saw some other faces I don't know with guns hung low, but no worries. I'm not here for them."

With his patience running thin, Gideon attempted to stay calm. "Uncle Vern, it was nice of you to visit, but there's nothing here for you, so why don't you just turn your horse back around and go back home?"

Turning back to his crew, Vernon once again laughed. "You here that, boys? He say they ain't noth'n here for us." Now Vernon was getting a bit angry as he turned back to face Gideon. "Oh, there's something here for us all right. Fifty-five thousand in reward money for that white boy's head. And with or without your help, I aim to get it. Now, the way I see it, you stand'n next to that white devil wearing a confederate hat, I could very easily misunderstand your allegiance. You either with your family or you not."

Looking up at Vernon, Gideon momentarily felt a sense of sadness. "Uncle Vern, it doesn't have to be this way. I'm not against you, but I have a job to do and that's to keep men like you from coming into my town and killing people."

Once again Vernon turned to his men and laughed. "Are you hearing this, boys? My nephew has a job to do. He say he gonna try and stop me from putt'n food on my table. How bout that? Little Gideon all growed up and now he thinks he's a man."

Swinging back around and peering down at Gideon, Vernon continued with the family connection. "Now, you listen here, boy. I took you and yo mama in like you's was my own and I treated you like a son. I taught you everything you know, including how to use that there gun. And besides, what do you care about these white folks for? They certainly don't care 'bout us black folk."

Listening to Vernon, Gideon knew he was trying to play off his family ties, but Gideon was older and wiser now and wasn't about to back down. "Uncle Vern, not everyone thinks like you. Most people around these parts are respectful of one another."

Bringing his temper down a few notches, Vernon attempted to reason his thought process. "Gideon, you're my nephew and I love you like family should, but either that badge has gone to your head or you been bake'n out here in this Texas sun for too long."

Trying to keep his momentum going, Vernon continued his banter. "Boy, this here is Texas. Nothing but Confederate lovers round these parts." Continuing with his abusive words, Vernon turned his anger toward Jubal. "And right about now, I'm just itch'n to shoot that white trash standing beside you."

Once again Gideon attempted to take Vernon's words in stride. "You're right, Uncle Vern. This here is Texas and things are changing. I didn't get this badge by stealing it. I got it by earning it and I proudly wear it. These people rely on me and I'm not gonna let you take that from me."

With a heavy sigh, Vernon could feel his cause was going nowhere. "So, you think'n bout stick'n up for that white boy over your own family even though he got a bounty?"

With some determination, Gideon stood his ground. "I don't see it like that, Uncle Vern. I'm standing for this badge and all that it represents, and if that means going against my own kin in order to protect this town, then so be it."

With the conversation coming to an end, Vernon said his peace. "Listen here, Nephew, as sure as the sun rises and chases the moon away, I'm gonna shoot me that white boy as soon as he shows his ugly face." With that said, Vernon and his men turned their horses and headed back out of town.

With Vernon and his men gone, Gideon took a few minutes to sit down and breathe. Still reeling from the tension, Jubal sat down beside him. "Boy howdy, Gideon. I thought my pa and brothers were bad, but seeing some of yer kin folk, my brood ain't got nutt'n on you. I'm really sorry I had to see that, but now what?"

Thinking through his thoughts, Gideon was almost at his end. "I don't know, Jubal. I just don't know. Every time I think things can't get any worse, they do. It's one thing to scheme and plot against bounty hunters and killers, but Vernon is family. He was like a second father to me after my pa was killed.

He was right. I can't deny him that. After my pa died, my ma and I made it up north to where my uncle Vern and aunt Sarah lived with their two sons. They didn't have much. Just a cabin way back in the woods. Vern wasn't a bad guy back then. Although his older brother was supposedly killed by some fur trappers by accident, he just seemed to absorb it and continue on. There wasn't much space for us, but they accommodated us as much as they could. The difference between my pa and Vernon was that my pa taught me how to be a good person, but Vern taught me how to kill. It wasn't long before the war found us. Don't really know what happened. I was out tracking down some food one day and when I returned, the cabin had been burned to the ground with my aunt Sarah inside. Vern and Nato looked like hell. He never told me exactly what happened, but it was bad. Vern buried his wife and two sons that day. Ever since then, Vern and Nato have had a hatred for white folks."

Listening to Gideon's story and feeling compassion for his friend, Jubal could sympathize. "So, what happened? Why didn't you go with them?"

Gideon thought for a moment as he reminisced back to an earlier time. "Well, Vern wanted me to join his little gang, but like I said, my pa taught me how to be a good person. When the war started, the Yanks needed good trackers, so I enlisted. Vern didn't really oppose the idea because he figured I would eventually be killing Johnny Rebs."

It was late so Jubal said goodnight while Gideon sat for a moment to collect his thoughts. After Jubal was gone, Gideon took in the night air as he tried to clear his mind. As he took a few deep breaths, Nato came riding up. Not knowing his intentions, Gideon quickly stood up in preparation. Looking tired and worn out, Nato sat atop his horse as he began to speak. "Listen, Gideon. Vernon told me to hang around tonight to see if that white boy shows up. Just so you know, I didn't wanna come here. Your uncle is getting older and even more hateful, but he's also getting more stubborn. He knows all these young guns are just hang'n around waiting for that white boy and he just don't care. Like I said, he's getting older and he doesn't have his useful speed anymore. Gideon, he's not gonna listen to anything you have to say, and if you try and stand in his way, he's gonna kill you. I just thought I would let you know."

Just then, several shots rang out as the two men looked around with concern. When Gideon ran toward the gunfire, he found a wounded Jubal standing over the Flying Dutchman. The Dutchman had been shot and was bleeding heavily from his stomach, but he was still alive. Seeing Jubal's wound was only a scratch, Gideon breathed easy, then made his inquiry. "Jubal, you okay? What the hell happened?"

Glancing down at the Dutchman, Jubal holstered his gun. "Well, I was headed over to Fynn's place because I thought I saw some shadows mov'n around, and this dang fool came sneaking up from behind. If'n it wasn't for his spurs flap'n, he would've put a hole in my back for sure."

Bending down to get a better look at the Dutchman's wound, Gideon saw it was a gut shot. Peering up at Gideon, the Dutchman started to quiver as the life started to slowly vacate his body. Glaring into his eyes, Gideon gave an unsympathetic smile. "Well now, Dutchman, leave it up to Satan to go back on a deal."

Before the Dutchman could respond, his eyes slowly closed and he was gone.

As Gideon stood up, he turned to see Nato staring with an unconcerned look. With his anger on high, he lashed out at his uncle. "Was this the plan, Nato? Keep me occupied long enough for this coward to back shoot my deputy?"

With a short pause, Nato gave a humble response. "Gideon, I swear, I didn't know anything about this. I just thought I would talk to you about Vern. We're getting old, but he just won't stop. I'm getting tired of being in this saddle fifteen hours a day galloping around from state to state tracking down bounties. Vern has become so crazy with hatred, but he won't listen to reason. I'm done, Gideon. I'm just done."

While Nato slowly rode out of town, Jon was just arriving at his wife's gravesite. During his travels, he decided to spend the night before moving onto Presidio. He figured it was the only place to welcome peace into his heart and, at the same time, get some sleep because his nightmares wouldn't dare haunt him. Since Mexico, Jon had gotten plenty of rest, but the spirits that haunted his nightmares gave him very little sleep. Knowing what his situation was, he already knew what was waiting for him in Presidio, so he needed to be at his best.

After a peaceful night's rest, Jon stood over the graves of his wife and children in the morning while thinking about the final steps of his last adventure. There was no sorrow or pain. There was no shame or regret. And there were no prayers. Just a few simple words said out loud. "I'll be seeing all of you soon."

While Jon was waking up to what he thought was his final visit to an earthly gravesite, Gideon and Jubal stood outside their office watching the sun rise and enjoying their morning coffee. Suddenly, a lone rider appeared at the end of town. His horse looked tired and was moving slow as he made his way down the center of the street. The man riding the horse was partially slumped over and had his head down to where you couldn't see his face. While Gideon and Jubal watched, the man got closer and closer. It was early and most businesses that were still operating weren't open yet, which meant there weren't many people on the street. Just one or two of the locals getting ready to start the day.

As the rider approached, he stopped in front of the sheriff's office. He still had his head down so the brim of his hat covered his face. Not knowing who or what the man wanted, Jubal placed his hand on his gun as a precaution. In a moment, Jubal glanced over at Gideon who was smiling. When he turned his attention back to the rider, the mysterious man had lifted his head and was now peering down at Jubal. "If you're not gonna use that gun, Deputy, I suggest you take your hand off it."

Looking at the man, Jubal nearly fell on the ground. "Oh, my dear Lord. You're Kenna James. My God, Gideon, you know who this is? It's Kenna James."

While Jubal was busy babbling, Kenna climbed down from his horse to face the two men. He listened as Jubal went on and on. "Mr. James, I'm so sorry. I didn't mean anything by it. Please, accept my apologies, sir, Mr. Kenna James, sir."

Jubal then turned to Gideon, who was waiting for Jubal's excitement to subside. "Please Gideon, help me out here, will'ya? It's Kenna James."

Now that Jubal was coming down off his high, Gideon was able to get a few words in. He shook Kenna's hand as the two old friends shared an embrace. "Good to see you, Kenna. It's been too long. This is my good friend and deputy, Jubal. Don't let the Confederate hat fool you. He's a really good man."

Taking a moment to look his old friend up and down, Gideon let out a small laugh. "You look like hell rode you hard and broke you. Why don't you come on in and have some fresh coffee?"

When the three men walked back into the office, Jubal poured a cup of coffee for Kenna, then refilled his and Gideon's cup. Shaking off the trail dust, Kenna sat down as he placed his coffee down on Gideon's desk. "Not meaning any offense there, Deputy, but why the hat?"

Taking a sip of his coffee, Jubal gave a short and honest answer. "Well Mr. James, It's a family thing, and besides, I can't afford a new one."

After a brief pause, Kenna laughed and then stood up to shake Jubal's hand. "Well, damn, can't get much more genuine then that. Any friend of Gideon is also a friend of mine."

With a tired look about him, Kenna turned to Gideon. "Gideon, we can get together later today and I'll buy you boys a drink, but for now, I've been riding all night and I'm tired. I need a drink of good whiskey, a nice hot bath, and a beautiful whore. Not necessarily in that order."

Happy that his friend was in town, Gideon laughed and shook his head. "Same old Kenna. Well, the Lucy Goosy saloon serves the best whiskey in town. As for the other two, you're in luck. Molly's place just reopened their doors and they will treat you like a king. Not that I'm speaking from personal experience, mind you. The hotel is right down the street and it's booking up fast with some of your favorite people. But don't worry, I've already reserved you a room. Top floor. Can see the whole town and it's easily defended, if you're wondering."

With a big smile on his face, Kenna glanced over at Jubal, then back at Gideon. "Well boys, you really know how to welcome a friend. So I'll see you boys later today."

While Kenna was busy getting his desires fulfilled, Gideon and Jubal walked the town. Still feeling his enthusiasm, Jubal's emotions took over again.

"Gideon, you knew Kenna was coming and didn't tell me? Dang nabit, I must have looked sillier than a bear being chased by a bunch of bees. Damn it, Gideon, why'd you do that to me?"

Smiling and laughing, Gideon felt a little guilty as he apologized. "I'm sorry, Jubal. If I would have known you were such a big fan, I would've definitely told you he was coming, but your reaction was priceless. And just to let you know, I have a few more tricks up my sleeve."

When the two men got to the end of town, they stopped in to visit the Bauernshubs. They lived in a small house that belonged to the original mayor but had been sold several times as the town of Presidio evolved. While Gideon and Jubal removed their hats, Mr. Bauernshub invited them in as Mrs. Bauernshub offered the men breakfast. As usual, Gideon was humbled and declined, but Jubal had no problem sitting down and digging into a plate of potatoes and eggs.

While Jubal fed his early morning hunger, Gideon had a talk with Andrew. "Andrew, I just wanted to take the opportunity to try and talk you into taking your family on a trip. Maybe visit some relatives or friends until all this bad business is done and Presidio can get back to being a nice town again."

Appreciating Gideon's concern, Andrew was a strong-minded man and didn't mind voicing his opinions. "Sheriff, there's a lot of bad everywhere. If I were to run every time something bad happened, then what kind of life would that be for my family?"

Admiring the philosophy, Gideon continued to try and press the seriousness of the current town situation. "Sir, some of the businesses have temporarily closed and most of the families who have small children have gone elsewhere. And if it's your store you're worried about, I ashore you, Jubal and I will watch over it for you."

Andrew appreciated Gideon and his kind gesture, but it was falling on deaf ears. "Sheriff, my wife and I give thanks every day for your dedicated service and we pray for the safety of you and Jubal, but the Bauernshubs have never run from anything. Being from Germany, our family has endured many trials." After a brief pause, Andrew took a deep breath and continued. "Believe me,

Sheriff, my wife and I aren't blind to what's been happening lately. Mr. Hayden's men have frequented our store and have bought many supplies from us and they've paid good money. Now, I've heard the rumors and I know Presidio is starting to fill up with some dangerous and questionable men, but with all due respect to you, Sheriff, we're not involved with any of it and we refuse to be intimidated by Mr. Hayden, these bounty hunters, or anyone else, mind you."

Gideon knew Andrew was a tough old bird, but now he gained an all new respect for the man. As he shook his hand, Gideon commented on his resolve. "Andrew, I applaud your honesty, sir, and I respect your decision."

Just then, Gino and Summer came out from the back room and approached Gideon. They were a little older now, but still infatuated over his badge and gun. Still in her bashful stage, Summer stood quietly while Gino smiled with excitement. "Sheriff, you gonna kill all the bad guys?" Before Gideon could answer, Andrew scolded the little boy. He then had Gino and Summer return to the back room to finish their chores.

Finishing up his breakfast, Jubal stood up and groaned like a bear. "Mrs. Dorothy, if'n you don't mind me say'n, ma'am, you sure know your way around a stove. I thank ya kindly, ma'am."

As Gideon and Jubal were leaving, Andrew apologized for Gino. "Sheriff, my son looks up to you and I hope you can pardon his enthusiasm."

With a smile on his face, Gideon placed his hat back on his head. "No, sir. No apologies necessary. You have two fantastic children and a very nice family. And we shall do everything in our power to keep you safe."

The sun was up and shining bright and the town of Presidios was now in full swing. Gideon and Jubal walked and talked as they greeted people, then headed for the Lucy Goosy for a visit with Ms. Lita. It was still early, so whiskey was out and coffee was in. Fresh out of the pot, Ms. Lita poured three cups. There was nobody in the bar yet, so the three sat and enjoyed each other's company.

Sipping on her coffee, Ms. Lita voiced her concerns. "Gideon, I gotta say, between all of Hayden's men, the bounty hunters, and the various stragglers coming in and out of town, I'm really doing quite well, even though I could do without the trouble. Not that I want Hayden's people in my place, but they're keeping my cash register full."

Before Gideon could comment, the saloon doors swung open and in walked a bold-looking female with fiery red hair, tight pants and top, and the gun she wore hung low on her thigh. She had the face of an angel, but her gun let people know all they needed to know about her. As her eyes adjusted to the dim room, she walked past Gideon and Jubal without saying a word and made her way to the other end of the bar. Fixed on her hips swinging from side to side, Jubal's eyes were mesmerized as she purposely flaunted her bottom. Even Ms. Lita was a bit taken by the woman, but before she could react, the women yelled for service. "Bar keep! Where the hell are you?"

Feeling a bit snubbed, Gideon nudged Jubal in order to snap him back to reality. Taking a sip of his coffee, Jubal smiled as his humiliation seeped out. "Dang, Gideon, that's a woman that could make love to a man then kill'em if'n she wasn't satisfied."

Being a little surprised at Jubal's comments, Gideon could do nothing but smile. "That just wasn't right, Jubal. Her coming in here like she owns the place. I think I'm gonna have to say something to her."

Feeling somewhat insulted, Ms. Lita had already rushed down to the woman to serve her an early morning whiskey and beer. With a full head of steam, Gideon readied himself for his encounter as he walked to the end of the bar. Stopping just short of the demanding female, Gideon paused for a moment, then spoke. "Don't you think it's a little too early to be drinking?"

After gulping down her whiskey, the woman turned to face Gideon in order to rebuke his comment. "Don't you think I'm a little too old to be told what to do?"

Feeling uptight, Gideon could see his efforts were going to be pointless. "Just a little friendly advice, sweetheart. We don't like your kind in here. I'm afraid I'm gonna have to ask you to leave, please."

Feeling even more contempt for Gideon, the woman smiled as she took a drink of her beer. "Well now, being a man of color, I could probably say the same for you. But looking at that badge, you have me curious. What's it like being a black sheriff in a state that fought for the Confederacy?"

Now Gideon felt things were getting a little too personal, so he moved his hand down and rested it on the butt of his gun. "Now, I'm only gonna ask you one more time, lady. You need to go."

With one last gulp, the woman finished her beer and stood up to face the man who chose to antagonize her. As she glanced down at Gideon's gun hand, then back up at him, she smiled as she peered into his eyes. "Good day to die, Sheriff. But too bad I love you too much to shoot you." Just then, the woman embraced Gideon as she gave him a big hug and kiss. "It's been a long time, handsome. Was wondering where the hell you been hiding."

By now, Jubal and Ms. Lita were breathing a sigh of relief as Ms. Lita came from behind the bar and Jubal walked over. Feeling happy, Gideon turned to introduce the mysterious woman. "Lita, Jubal, I'd like you to meet the one and only Ms. Rayna Jane."

Still feeling a bit giddy, Rayna shook Lita's hand, then turned to Jubal for a little play time. As she got up close and personal, Jubal began to blush. Caressing her hand across Jubal's cheek, Rayna whispered into his ear. "Now, Deputy, I saw you watching my ass shake when I walked by. Shame on you." Giving Jubal a light peck on his cheek, Rayna backed away laughing. "Don't worry, Deputy, I'm just fun'un ya."

With her hospitality back in swing, Ms. Lita grabbed a bottle of her best whiskey as the four sat down at one of the tables. Hoping to keep an open mind and not fall into the jealous trap, Ms. Lita poured the drinks. "So, how did you two meet?"

After playing his practical joke and noticing Lita was not amused, Gideon was ready to explain. "Well, after the war, the military put me in charge of hunting down war criminals. So, I was in this no-good godforsaken town just across the border and I was looking for a man called Blaze. He was a lieutenant during the war and went rogue. He and some of his men attacked homesteaders, robbing and killing them, then burned their houses down to cover up the crimes. Anyway, I tracked him to a little boom town down south and as usual,

Just then, a fight broke out inside the Lucy Goosy, with people yelling and screaming at each other. Gideon and Jubal could hear chairs being thrown and bottles of whiskey being broke. Just as they got to the door, Indigo came out the door head first and landed in the street. Afterward, Solomon came slowly walking out. Gideon tried to intercede so it could be a fair fight, but Solomon was having no part of it. When Indigo finally collected himself, he stood up and faced off against the behemoth. Before Solomon could prepare himself, Indigo withdrew his gun and fired. The bullet seemed to hit Solomon in his torso, then bounce off as it harmlessly ricocheted into the air. Stunned that Solomon didn't go down, Indigo payed the ultimate price. Within those few short seconds of disbelief, Solomon withdrew his gun and fired three shots into Indigo's chest.

Stunned at the events that unfolded in front of them, Gideon and Jubal could only look on as astonished spectators. They watched in horror as Solomon pulled out a very large knife and, with absolutely no emotions, cut off Indigo's head. Calmly walking over to Gideon, Solomon dropped the severed head at his feet. Looking on in awe, Gideon was doubting his own eyes, but before he could react, Solomon pulled out a Wanted poster with Indigo's name and picture and handed to him.

Gideon studied the poster, then glanced back up at Solomon. "I don't even have this yet, so how did you get it?"

With an intense stare, Solomon stood like a quiet mountain and said nothing. Once again, Gideon studied the poster, then gave it to Jubal. "All right then. Jubal will escort you over to the bank and get your money."

Gideon then turned to Jubal, who was trying hard not to panic as he felt no desire to be anywhere near Solomon. "Gideon, can't we just give him a note to take to the bank?"

While the big man turned to walk away, Gideon handed off the Wanted poster with a frustrated look. "No note, Jubal. Just follow him over to the bank so we can get this issue resolved, and on the way, have Orville clean this mess up."

While Solomon made his way to the bank, Jubal sank back into the urban legend. "Gideon, I trust you completely, but are you sure Belle knew what she was talk'n about?" Slowly walking away but looking back for a favorable reaction, Jubal waited, but Gideon had no encouraging words to give.

While Jubal was meeting with Satan's child at the bank, Gideon walked into the bar to see if Lita was okay. As he looked around at the damage, Lita was busy picking up tables and chairs. After Gideon helped her put the Lucy Goosy back together, Lita stepped back behind the bar and poured Gideon a drink. "Gideon, I know you have your hands full, but walking dead or not, you gotta do something about that man or whatever he is. He's libel to destroy this town and take us all down to hell."

Gideon welcomed the drink as he took a second to breathe and swallow it down. "We were just here. What in God's name happened?"

Just then, Rico came walking over and ordered a bottle. "Sorry, Sheriff. If I'd known my friend was wanted, I would've killed him myself."

After Lita placed the bottle on the bar in disgust, Rico slapped down some money, then took the bottle with him.

Still feeling some contempt, Lita explained what happen. "They all showed up shortly after you and Jubal left. Whatever he is, that dang fool Solomon came in here and handed Rico's friend a Wanted poster. When the guy stood up, Solomon grabbed him and started tossing him around like a damn rag doll. As you can see, he landed on his head outside."

With a heartfelt touch, Gideon reached across the bar and placed his hand on Lita's cheek. "I promise, one way or another, this will all come to an end soon."

After a few more brief words with Lita, Gideon left to go back to his office. With the antics of Solomon still fresh in his thoughts, he noticed an eerie unnatural silence after making his exit from the Lucy Goosy. As he looked around the town, he saw that everybody had stopped what they were doing and was staring toward the edge of town. As Gideon looked on, he saw Jon sitting quietly on his horse.

While all eyes were on him, Jon was staring back at the bounty hunters that were staggered along both sides of the streets. Some he recognized and some new faces he didn't. Jon was well aware that bounty hunters and gun fighters were usually one in the same. They all had their pride and they all aspire to be known as the best. So arriving at that conclusion, he figured nobody would try and back shoot him.

Just as Jon started to move his horse forward, a light rain started to fall. The townspeople looked on as dark clouds started to roll in from behind Jon as though he was bringing the storm with him. With the wind starting to blow hard, dirt and dust from the ground began to swirl as the townspeople attempted to shield their eyes. A quick flash of lightning, then a strong roar of thunder quickly placed the wary people on edge as they quickly sought refuge indoors. Just abruptly as the rain started, it suddenly became fierce and started to downpour. With the force of the storm becoming powerful, even the bounty hunters decided their showdown with Jon could wait. Most of them made their way to the Lucy Goosy, while others simply responded back to the hotel.

Gideon stood and watched as Jon casually stopped in front of the sheriff's office, then tied his horse off and walked in. Taking a deep breath and feeling a bit frustrated, Gideon took a look around and saw that the streets were now empty. Knowing his last encounter with Jon didn't go well, he prepared himself mentally, then walked into his office. When he walked in, he saw that Jon had poured himself a shot of whiskey and was relaxing as though he had no worries.

With his voice a little raised, Gideon frustrations came bellowing out. "Well, you really know how to make an entrance. By the way, help yourself to my bottle."

Before Jon could say anything, Gideon slammed the door behind him, then snatched the bottle of whiskey out of Jon's hand and placed it on his desk. "For the love of God, Jon. What the hell are you doing here? Did you see those killers out there? They're here to kill you. Why, you might ask? Because you're a wanted man, Jon. The state of Texas placed five thousand dollars over your head, and Hayden added another fifty thousand. So, I will pose to you the same question. What the hell are you doing here?"

Looking like he just didn't care, Jon sat down and poured two glasses of whiskey. He then handed one to Gideon and gave a short grunt. "You know why I'm here. I'm going to kill Hayden, and I'm wondering should I be worried about you standing in my way?"

With his anger at its peak, Gideon slung the glass of whiskey against the wall, shattering it to pieces. With his raised voice morphing into a shout, Gideon tried to be the voice of reason. "Damn it, Jon! It was your idea I take this job, or don't you remember back when you thought life was all fun and games? I have a job to do, Jon! How the hell is it going to look if I don't arrest you? Damn it, how the hell is it going to look if I try and stop one of those man killers out there from killing you? Tell me, Jon. Did you think any of this through, or maybe you just don't give a damn? Is that it? You just don't give a damn? Innocent people in this town could get hurt or killed, but all you want is your goddamn revenge. I hurt, Jon. I hurt every day I wake up, knowing Emily and the children aren't here anymore. But we have a system in place. You use to be a part of that system. It's called law and order, Jon."

Taking a short pause to catch his breath, Gideon lowered his voice a few notches and attempted to offer an observation. "There was a time you would carry the hammer of justice and destroy anybody who would take the path of destruction. Now look at you. There's no more justice. Just you with the hammer on your own path of destruction."

Jon sat and listened as Gideon's tirade came to an end, but he had no intentions of staying quiet. Then, in a low even voice, he responded. "I know you still have a job to do, Gideon, and I'm not asking for your help or protection. I'm asking as a friend to let me deal with Hayden, then you can do whatever you feel is right. I promise I will accept whatever consequences the state of Texas has to offer."

Gideon listened as Jon seemed to have no concern about the bounty hunters or the aftermath of killing Hayden, but there was something else wrong. It wasn't what Jon said that bothered him. It was what he didn't say. "You selfish bastard. You're not worried about any consequences because you're not planning on leaving here alive, are you? You plan to kill Hayden in hopes that one of those bounty hunters kills you. You dirty, rotten, selfish bastard."

Just then, the door swung open and a winded Jubal walked in. Before his eyes could adjust to the room, he informed Gideon of his conversation.

"Gideon, I can hear you scream'n all the way from down the street."

Before Jubal could continue, his eyes rested upon Jon. "Oh, my word. Jon? You came back. Gideon, what's going on?"

With his patience just about at its end, Gideon took a deep breath and sat down. With a bit more calm, he poured Jubal and Jon a drink along with himself. "Close the door, Jubal, and have a seat. As you can see, the day we've been dreading has now arrived."

While Jubal was pulling another chair over, Jon challenged him with a question. "Think a moment, Jubal. If a man kills all of your friends and tries to kill you, then kills your entire family, what would you do?"

Thinking for a moment, Jubal placed the chair next to Jon and sat down to ponder the question. "Well, during the war, members of my family along with many of my friends were killed. And when that Yank soldier murdered my brother, Ollie, well, it took everything decent inside me not to hunt him down after the war and kill'em. Jon, I know yer hurt'n and this probably ain't gonna be much comfort to ya, but the Bible says vengeance is mine saith the Lord. If'n ya don't mind me say'n, Jon. Kill'n Hayden out of vengeance isn't gonna bring your family back."

As a friend, Jon respected Jubal's opinion as he let his words sink in, but Gideon wasn't too quick to let him off the hook. "Go ahead, Jon. Tell him. Or should I?"

With his mouth running dry, Jon reached over and poured himself another drink. With his frustration showing again, Gideon waited as Jon found comfort in the bottle. Jubal waited for a response, but Jon had nothing to say, so Gideon informed Jubal of his theory. "Mr. Texas Ranger here has the idea of gunning down Hayden, then taking on every bounty hunter and gunfighter he can find until one of them puts him out of his misery, which means our friend here has no plans on leaving Presidio alive. Apparently he wants to go out in a blaze of glory."

Being surprised by what he heard, Jubal was appalled. As he looked at Jon with displeasure, thoughts of anger ran through his mind. "That's it? That's your master plan? Your endgame? Gun down Hayden, then commit suicide by gunfight? Jon, I never thought ya a coward, but that's a coward's way out."

Counting Jubal as a good friend, Jon wasn't offended by his words. "I appreciate your faith, Jubal, but whatever person you knew me as before is gone. There's nothing left of Jon Mason."

Sad to hear his friend say those types of words, Jubal felt the need to go for a walk. "Gideon, I'll leave you two to talk while I go check on the banks." Feeling bothered by the conversation, Jubal walked out with a sense of sadness in his heart.

After Jubal was gone, Gideon continued his verbal attack. "Jon, what the hell are you? Who the hell are you? In case you're unaware, stories travel fast in these parts. Word has it you killed a couple of locals up north, then beat up one of their whores. Also heard you shot a boy's finger off just north of the border. What the hell, Jon? Beating up on women and maiming children? Is that a part of your grand scheme of things?"

Tired and not wanting to hear anymore of Gideon's abuse, Jon stood up to once again ask his friend to stand down. "One more time, Gideon. Do I need to worry about you standing in my way?"

Feeling more frustrated and disappointed than ever, Gideon attempted one last plea of reason. "Ever since Hayden found out you were coming, he hasn't left that hotel. He still has a lot of men here, but the bulk of his men are already gone further north. I've already sent out warnings to all the territories. Most of his remaining men are camped outside of town. They roam in and out of Presidio periodically. You can't miss them. We also have the who's who of fast draws just waiting to take a crack at you. As for me, I have the added bonus of Colonel Pittman being back in town, but I don't think he's here for you. I have eyes on him at all times. He's over at the Chinese bath house as we speak."

Counting on Jon having some sort of sense of mental stability within him, Gideon decided to try and make a deal. In the most calm and serene voice he could conjure up, Gideon was hoping Jon could hear the sincerity in his words. "Listen, Jon. Hayden is waiting on one of these gunfighters to gun you down so he can swoop in and finish whatever business he has here."

Gideon took a moment to watch for any signs of Jon listening to reason, but it didn't seem he was interested, so Gideon continued his verbal barrage of subtle suggestion. Walking over to the window, Gideon looked out and saw the townspeople reverting back to their everyday lives. With more frustration starting to settle in, Gideon took a deep breath and spoke. "Jon, it's midday. Looks like the storm is starting to loosen its grip and the streets are full of people you use to care about and protect. If you go after Hayden now, you'll risk a lot of people being hurt or killed. I'm not gonna lie, Jon. I've nearly lost control of this town. Hayden has the men and the upper hand. Some of the businesses have closed and folks without ties to Presidio have packed up and left. It's all I can do to reassure the remaining businesses and residents that everything will be okay."

As Jon listened, Gideon could finally see something in him he hadn't seen in a long time: compassion. With the mood starting to swing his way, Gideon laid out his plan, hoping Jon would agree. "Jon, I underestimated Hayden and I'm sorry for that, because it cost your family their lives. I can't change that, but we can work together to deal with the person responsible. The last time we spoke, I let you ride off knowing you were going on a killing spree. I think maybe deep down inside, I wanted you to find those killers and enact your own justice."

Beginning to feel drained, Gideon poured two drinks and handed one to Jon. After gulping his drink down, Gideon glanced over at Jon, who hadn't drank his yet. Peering back at Gideon, Jon smiled. "Should I throw mine against the wall like you did?"

With a smile and a quick laugh, Gideon felt a bit of relief. "No. I expect you to drink it and listen to my plan."

While Jon enjoyed the smooth whiskey going down his throat, Gideon remained devoted to convincing him to listen to reason. "Jon, if you go out there now, it's going to be a blood bath. Tomorrow is God's day and come sunup, the streets will be empty. So, you let me have tonight and I will stand by your side tomorrow. Whatever happens, we'll leave it in God's hands to sort it out."

Feeling confident Jon would accept his terms, Gideon held out his hand. "Deal?"

Before indulging in a reunion of friendship, Jon had questions. "Gideon, by no means are you a stupid man, so I'm trying to figure out your angle. Besides the folks in this town not being around, nothing is going to change between now and tomorrow. You're still gonna have Hayden and a large contingent of his men, along with a bunch of bloodthirsty money-grubbing bounty hunters to deal with. Not to mention an ex-Confederate Colonel, who for some reason wants your head. And you're willing to toss your badge and duties aside to face down those impossible odds?"

With his hand still extended, Gideon smiled. "Well, why don't you shake my hand and let me take care of balancing the playing field?"

After thinking about the offer, Jon agreed and shook Gideon's hand. "Gideon, come tomorrow morning at first light, Hayden is going to die and whoever stands in my way will have to go down with him."

Jon was done talking, so he turned and grabbed what was left of Gideon's bottle and made himself comfortable in one of the overnight beds. With much relief, Gideon let out a deep breath and left to see Lita. Knowing Lita would want to see Jon, Gideon knew she would try and talk some more sense into him, so he figured he would have her bring some food over. And just for good measure, Gideon planned on Jubal staying with Jon all night.

After leaving Jon to his bottle, Gideon walked over to the Lucy Goosy to see Lita. To his surprise, he saw Jubal sitting at a table drowning in a bottle of whiskey. After momentarily staring at Jubal and being disturbed by what he was looking at, Gideon walked over to the bar to speak with Lita.

Before Gideon could talk, Lita spoke first. "My God, Gideon, what's going on? People are starting to talk and they're scared. Hell have no fury like a woman scorned, but what about a man whose family was murdered. People are saying Jon is back in town and he brought that viscous storm with him."

Before answering, Gideon glanced over his shoulder at Jubal, then turned his attentions back to Lita. "Lita, I can't go into it right now, but I need you to take some hot food over to the jail. Jon is there and you can sit and talk awhile. In the meantime, I gotta get Jubal sober and up to speed, so can you make me some coffee?"

Seeing Gideon was pressed for time, Lita didn't bother to ask questions. She quickly had Tommy make some fresh coffee while she rustled up her best steak dinner. While Lita and Tommy were busy with the request, Gideon walked over and sat down with Jubal. As Jubal drank down one of several glasses of whiskey, Gideon's anger started to surface. "Is this it? Getting drunk during work hours? We knew Jon was coming back to Presidio. And we knew it wasn't going to be easy."

Having no interest in lectures, Jubal took a moment and poured two drinks and slid one across the table to Gideon. He then raised his glass in the air for a toast. "Here's to not knowing what the hell is going on."

After watching Jubal gulp his drink down, Gideon became even angrier. "Jubal, Jon needs us and I need you."

By now, Jubal had finished half the bottle as Tommy came walking over with a full pot of hot coffee. After Tommy placed the coffee on the table, Gideon reached across the table and grabbed the bottle of whiskey and told Tommy to take it away. Reluctantly doing so, Tommy took the bottle from Gideon and quickly walked back behind the bar.

Watching his bottle being taken away, Jubal pushed back with some angry words. "Now, what the hell did ya go and do a dang thing like that fer? I paid for that there bottle and I'm gonna drink it."

With pushback of his own, Gideon responded with words of reason. "Jubal, I'm the sheriff and I'm in charge of this town, and as long as you wear that deputy badge, I'm in charge of you. Now, I need you sober so we can help Jon."

After the two men took a breather from the verbal sparring, Gideon poured a cup of coffee for Jubal and laid in in front of him. "Now, start drinking this coffee so we can get back to work."

With a few more seconds of staring down Gideon, Jubal had had enough. "Jon don't need our help. Hell, he's got this whole thing figured out. As for you, I don't think you need me around because you seem to keep me in the dark about everything."

While Gideon was busy taking in the second round of Jubal's verbal abuse,

Jubal removed his badge and tossed it on the table. "Here ya go, Mr. In-Charge Sheriff. I don't work fer ya no more."

Feeling like he had just lost a good friend, Gideon stared at the badge, realizing it was the second time a badge had been tossed back into his face. While Gideon was busy thinking of a new strategy, Jubal motioned to Tommy to bring his bottle back.

As Tommy once again nervously walked to the table, he slowly placed the half-empty bottle down in front of Jubal, then quickly returned to the bar. Time had run out for Gideon, so once again his anger took over. As Jubal reached for the bottle, Gideon quickly reached across the table and grabbed his hand. "No wonder you sons of bitches lost the war. Is this how you coward Johnny Rebs acted when things got tough? You just rolled over and played dead? Buried your sorrows in a bottle? You let your family down and now you let your friends down."

Realizing his grip was getting tighter, Gideon let go of Jubal's hand and sat back in his seat. With a smile on his face, Gideon continued his verbal beat down. "Just look at you. A total waste of a man. Now what are you going to do, Mr. I Don't Have A Job So I'm Just Gonna Sit Here and Cry About My Woes? The way I see it, Jubal, you have two choices. You have a half-bottle of whiskey sitting in front of you and a full pot of coffee. Which one you choose will determine who you are for the rest of your life."

After a few seconds of staring at a silent Jubal, Gideon stood up and walked outside. Just short of shedding a tear, he decided to catch his breath and sit down while he watched the townspeople move about. After a few minutes of breathing in some fresh air, the saloon doors slowly swung open. With his badge pinned to his chest and a cup of coffee in his hand, Jubal came walking out and sat down next Gideon. "If'n you were any other man, I'd hit you harder than a back-kicking mule, then put a bullet between your balls. And by the way, that boy Tommy can't make a good pot of coffee no how."

After listening to Jubal, Gideon glanced over and smiled. "You know I didn't mean any of it. I just needed that anger inside of you to sober you up so you could think straight."

ROBERT L. LeBrun

Looking down at the ground and kicking a few lose rocks into the street, Jubal took a sip of his coffee and made a sour face. "Dang fool. This coffee taste like pig slop." After a quick laugh, Jubal got down to business. "I know ya didn't mean anything by those words, but I tell ya what, you'd do well being one of them there psychiatrist. In any case, let me know the plan so I don't go shoot'n the wrong dang people."

After explaining the plan to Jubal, Gideon asked him to keep Jon occupied for the remainder of the day and overnight.

Feeling confident with Jubal back in the loop, Gideon left to meet Rayna for lunch. Unfortunately, the hotel had the only restaurant still open. So, at the risk of running into Zachariah Hayden, Gideon headed that way. The storm had subsided and the sun was out, so along the way he stopped to talk with Thomas about some recent suspicions. Afterward, he continued on to the hotel. As he approached, several men were coming out. Logan Slade, Johnny Rocco and Brice. No doubt headed for the Lucy Goosy. Gideon watched as the three men joked and laughed while they walked along.

Before meeting with Rayna, Gideon stopped to speak with Mr. Hinklemeyer, but quickly noticed some of the town's main gossip culprits were there whispering to each other. After a brief hiatus, some of the ladies who were suffering from gossip withdrawal found their way back to Mr. Hinklemeyer. Mrs. Becket, who always enjoyed her mental chess and flirtatious mind games with Gideon, was leading the way. "Well now, ladies, look who has graced our presence. Our very own fine-looking sheriff. Shame on you, Sheriff Gideon. You haven't been coming around lately to check on our little o' bank. And don't get me wrong, Sheriff, my husband and I simply adore Deputy Jubal, but he just doesn't have, well, shall we say, he doesn't possess your very fine qualities."

As Mrs. Becket was busy checking out Gideon's manhood, the other women giggled behind their handheld fans. Before Gideon could talk to Mr. Hinklemeyer, he had to defend himself against Mrs. Becket. "Mrs. Becket, I have nothing but respect for you and your husband, and I'm sorry if you think I'm somehow neglecting my duties as your sheriff, but I do believe Jubal is perfectly capable of checking in on your bank from time to time."

Once again, Mrs. Becket took a few naughty seconds to undress Gideon with her eyes. "Don't worry, Sheriff. I know you've been very busy lately. What, with all these bad men in our town, maybe you could swing by the house to make sure I'm okay. Our house is so big and Mr. Becket is such a heavy sleeper. You and I could, well, you know, we could check the other bedrooms for anything suspicious."

As the conversation reached its peak, Mrs. Becket took a step forward and stood on her toes in order to wrap her arms around Gideon and whisper softly into his ear. "I'm confident you know your way around a bedroom, and if I may add, I could surely make your most ferocious dreams come true."

Gideon could feel the breath of Mrs. Becket tingling in his ear and for a brief moment imagined what it would be like, but he quickly shook off the overwhelming feeling and got back to the business at hand. Unwrapping the arms of Mrs. Becket, Gideon stood his ground. "Mrs. Becket, please, I'm sure you have a very lovely house and I'm also sure your husband maintains its safety, so there's no real reason for me to visit you in the middle of the night. I appreciate the offer, though. But if you like, I can send Jubal to check on you. I know for a fact he takes a bath every Thursday night, so he could swing by afterward if you prefer."

With some aggravation starting to set in, Mrs. Becket took a step back as she heavily exhaled to show her contentment for Gideon's attitude. "Sheriff, I don't find you to be the bit least funny, and I don't appreciate you coming on to me. I won't tell my husband this time, but don't let it happen again. Come, ladies, we have other people to visit."

As the women turned their heads up and walked out, Gideon turned to Mr. Hinklemeyer and burst out laughing. "Hinklemeyer, do yourself a favor. Unless you're a glutton for punishment, don't ever marry a woman like that because she can never be satisfied."

With a blank look on his face left over from being privy to such a heated conversation, Mr. Hinklemeyer just stared at Gideon as though he envied his masculinity. "Um, sure, Sheriff. Whatever you say."

After discussing the hotel guests, Mr. Hinklemeyer once again repeatedly expressed his displeasure with the current situation. But Gideon assured him that the hotel guests would one by one start to vacate their rooms. Afterward, he inquired about his lunch date with Rayna. "Listen, Hinklemeyer, I'm supposed to be having lunch with Ms. Rayna Jane. Has she arrived yet?"

Mr. Hinklemeyer took a moment to look at his guest book, then turned his attention back to Gideon. "Yes sir, Sheriff. She arrived a little while ago and she's waiting for you in the dining area."

Feeling vindicated for fending off Mrs. Becket, Gideon made his way to the dining area. There were a few local people having lunch and Rayna was sitting at a table in the far corner of the room. Gearing up to have an enjoyable lunch with his friend, Gideon walked over and sat down. "I'm so glad you came, Rayna. Thank you for being here for me."

With a smile on her face, Rayna reached over and took Gideon by the hand. "Gideon, you know if you just say the word, I would come running. Besides, I didn't have anything else going on. I had just nabbed me a horse thief when I got your telegram. So, Lita told me a little of what's been going on, and by the way, you have great taste in women. Lita is a real hoot. I really like her."

After the waiter set the table and took their orders, Gideon filled in the missing blanks. "Well, I'm sure Lita told you about Hayden and his little treasure hunting quest. But I'm not sure how much she told you about Jon."

Taking a sip of coffee, Rayna thought for a moment. "Well, she told me he was once a Texas Ranger, and those boys ain't nothing to play with. She said this Hayden fella ambushed a bunch of them, then killed their families."

Slouching back in his chair, hearing those words brought back some sad memories for Gideon. "Well, somehow Jon survived the attack, but he had gone missing. When he finally came back, he found out Hayden had his entire family wiped out. His wife, who was pregnant, and three children. Hayden hired a man named Rico to do the job. Rico is here in town and now Jon is here to kill Rico and send Hayden back to hell where he came from. He's my friend and a good man, Rayna. His family was like my family and now they're gone and Jon's unjustly wanted."

Before Rayna could respond, Kenna James walked in. With a smile on his face, he approached and sat down next to Rayna. "Hello, beautiful. Been too long. To be exact, four years, three months, five days, six hours, and forty-three minutes. I could probably give you the seconds but they go by so fast. I remember it well because I was standing in that quaint little church listening to my best man here tell me why I should just give you a little more time, but you never showed."

Just then, the waiter came over and poured Kenna some coffee. Feeling a bit mischievous, Rayna gave a devious smile. "Well damn, Kenna, if I'd known your feelings were so delicate, I wouldn't have agreed to marry you in the first dang place, you big lush."

Wanting to get one up, Kenna slightly raised his voice. "If I'd known you were so rebellious, reckless, and irresponsible, I wouldn't have asked you."

Suddenly the two stood up and pointed their fingers in each other's face while getting loud with their words. Gideon sat for a moment and enjoyed his coffee, but eventually it was time to separate the two. "Okay, okay, okay, you two. Can we be civil for a few minutes and afterward, you can go someplace private and scream at each other all you want."

Kenna huffed and puffed while Rayna stuck her tongue out, but the two agreed with Gideon and sat back down. The waiter who was waiting for the spectacle to come to an end was finally able to place their food on the table. While enjoying their food, the three talked more about the plan Gideon had, and although Kenna had some doubts, he was willing to listen. "Gideon, I was over at Molly's place and they were telling me a little about your friend Jon. Texas Ranger with a very large bounty on his head and faster with a gun then anybody they've seen. You have some of the fastest guns in town looking to take your friend down and collect that reward. And then there's this fellow named Hayden. I heard he's got a bunch of hired guns camped just outside of town. I gotta say, Gideon, this ain't sounding good. I hope your friend doesn't mistake me for one of those killers out there."

Chewing on a piece of bread, Rayna decided to chime in. "Gideon, I hate to agree with Kenna, but he's right. You have a pretty volatile situation and if everything winds up going sideways, you're gonna have a shooting gallery in your streets. And if your boy turns on us, well, it could get ugly."

Finishing with her bread, Rayna turned her attention to Kenna. "And who the hell is Molly and why were you there?"

Conveniently, Kenna had a mouth full of food as he pointed his finger at his face, signaling to Rayna he couldn't speak.

By now, Gideon wanted to try and lay out the shaky plan he had. "Both of you listen. Jon isn't going to turn on anybody. And Kenna, those ladies were right. He's one of the fastest guns I've ever seen because he was taught by the best. He's only here for one reason and that's to kill Rico and Haydon. That's it. I can assure you, he doesn't care about those bounty hunters and he'll only draw on somebody in defense of himself."

Kenna listened, but there was a certain word that would get any gunfighters attention more than any other word in the dictionary. "Gideon, what did you mean when you said he was taught by the best?"

Taking a deep breath, Gideon took a drink of his coffee, then softly placed the cup down. "You remember the name Roy Wesley?"

Kenna thought for a moment, then smiled. "Oh yeah. Major Roy Wesley. That was the fool that faced off against a battalion of Johnny Rebs down at the Rio Grande. Dang fool took a cannonball to the head. Legendary soldier named Jacob took over and they fought their way back to Fort Riley, Kansas. By the time they arrived, he had only a handful of men left. I briefly met Jacob back during the war. Very few men impress me, but he is definitely one to remember."

After taking a sip of coffee, Gideon smiled as he continued his story. "Well, somehow Jon fell into their laps during the war and Jacob took a liking to him. He wound up saving Jacob's life a couple of times, so Jacob took him in like a son and taught him just about everything he knew, including how to use a gun. And now, here we are."

Jacob was a very well-respected man, especially with a gun, so there was nothing more to discuss, but Rayna had a good point. "Listen, fellas, forget all this talk about the war and who the best is. We're here now because Gideon asked us for help, so let us in on your plan."

By now, everyone was finished their lunch as the waiter poured more coffee and took away the dishes. Before Gideon continued explaining his plan, there was one more thing he had to add into the mix. "Listen. You both have a pretty good idea of the situation, but there's one more person you need to know about. Colonel Augusta Pittman is in town and he's working for Hayden. He's not here for Jon, although I wouldn't put it past him to try and collect the bounty, but he's also the one Hayden hired to kill the Rangers. I think he's back in town for me. I have some little friends watching him at all times, but he's a snake so just be careful."

Feeling a little uncertainty inside, Rayna had heard of the colonel. "Damn! Even I know that name. Heard all about his wartime exploits. Real butcher, that man is. Women, children—I don't think it really mattered to him. He just liked to kill."

Now that everyone was on the same page, it was time for Gideon to explain his proposition. "Kenna, when you think of bounty hunters and gun fighters, what's the first thing that comes across your mind?"

With a smile on his face, Kenna already knew the answer. "Egos and the desire to be the best."

Gideon then turned his attention to Rayna. "So, Rayna. Think about who's in town and what their goal is."

"Well, damn, Gideon. You got the best gun fighters alive and there all gunning for your friend."

Before Gideon could concur, Kenna interceded. "You're right, but only one person can collect the money, so with all these egos running around, there's bound to be a few fights. Question is, how long can you keep Jon from killing Hayden?"

Finishing off his cup of coffee, Gideon thought for a moment. "Well, he's over at my office for now and I'll have Jubal keep him busy for tonight, but tomorrow is another day. We have the rest of the day and tonight to sabotage as many plans as possible. Rayna, I'm going to need you to play the flirt, and Kenna and I are going to be opposite of each other playing the go between."

Standing up and reaching into his pocket, Gideon placed some money on the table. "So, can I count on a couple of old friends?"

With smiles, Kenna and Rayna stood up and agreed to the plan. On the way out, Rayna couldn't contain her excitement. "Damn, this might be more fun than I thought."

As the three exited the hotel, Jubal came running over with some not-so-good news. "Gideon, you better come quick. A bunch of kids threw some horse dung at Solomon and now he's terrorizing the townsfolk."

As Gideon ran toward the ruckus, Jubal, Kenna, and Rayna followed behind. As they rounded the corner, Gideon saw the massive man breaking windows and trying to fight some of the store owners. Aware of the reputation of the massive man, Kenna and Rayna had heard the stories and was eager to help, but Gideon expressed his desire to handle the situation himself.

With his back turned, Solomon continued to destroy whatever he could get his hands on, but unbeknownst to him, Gideon had quietly walked up from behind. With a raised voice, Gideon called him out. "Eugene Horowitz!"

When Solomon heard that name, he froze for a moment, then slowly turned to face Gideon. Feeling a bit nervous, Gideon smiled as he studied the colossal man. "That's right, Eugene. I know who you are. As a matter of fact, I know all about you. You've done a lot of damage here, Eugene. You seem to do a lot of damage everywhere you go. Terrorizing people. Killing people. You have everybody thinking you're already dead and that you can't be killed. They call you the devil's gun. They say you're faster than Satan himself, but I say they're wrong."

By now, Solomon was done thinking about how much of Presidio he could destroy and he was now solely focused on Gideon. Gideon watched as Solomon pulled back his jacket to expose his gun and readied himself to draw. But Gideon wasn't finished antagonizing the big man. "You sure you want to do this, Eugene? They say when you shake hands with the devil, you have to pay the consequences."

With a monstrous voice sounding like it came from the depths of hell, Solomon finally spoke. "The devil tried to shake hands with me, but I was too evil for him so he turned me away."

Just when Solomon finished his last word, he withdrew his gun with quickness and speed, but it wasn't enough. With all the banter Gideon threw out, it was just enough to throw Solomon off what was really important: being the fastest. As soon as Solomon's gun hand twitched, Gideon withdrew his gun with accuracy and hair-trigger speed, purposely shooting Solomon in his groin. The pain struck Solomon instantly, dropping the big man to the ground.

Jubal, who was worried Solomon was going to collect another soul, was stunned. As Gideon holstered his gun, he casually walked over to the massive man. Kicking Solomon's gun off to the side, Gideon stood over top the now not-so-intimidating Solomon. "So, Eugene. Is this it? Is this where your story comes to an end?"

Lying on his back, Solomon grumbled in pain. Feeling a bit angry, Gideon continued his onslaught. "You unfairly and unjustly killed many men during your time, Eugene. What do you have to say for yourself?"

Once again Solomon had pain but no words. Not knowing the full scope of what Gideon was doing, it was a surprise to everyone when he withdrew his gun and pointed at Solomon's head. "This is for all the people you cheated out of life." Feeling no remorse, Gideon put two bullets in Solomon's head, then watched him breathe his last breath.

When Jubal walked over, he watched as Gideon bent down and tore open Solomon's shirt, exposing a steal plate that protected his torso. "This was what he was looking for in the back of Hank Conner's store. But when he couldn't find what he needed, he paid a visit to the blacksmith shop. When Indigo shot him dead center and it bounced off, I got to thinking. So, on my way to the hotel earlier, I stopped to talk to Thomas. Thomas didn't think anything of it when Solomon paid him for the materials. So, this is our mythical bounty hunter. Nothing but a fraud."

Feeling even more astonished, Jubal breathed a sigh of relief. "Well, I'll be. That Solomon was a fake the whole time, and the story of him being dead was just a tall tale. Dang it, Gideon, I was duped again. I knew that couldn't be true, but I guess I let my imagination get the better of me."

But before any celebrating could start, Gideon heard some loud clapping coming from behind. When he turned, he saw Vernon standing off to the side, smiling as he slowly clapped his hands. "I knew you had it in you the whole time, boy. Damn proud of you. Always heard about that Solomon character. Heard he was a tough old bird, but you sniffed him out. Damn fine work, Nephew."

By now, most of the people who witnessed the spectacle had retreated indoors. But Vernon was there to collect his prize. As he walked over, he stopped about ten feet short of Gideon. "Now you know what I'm here for. With all these killers dropping dead like flies, I figure my work has gotten a little easier."

Gideon stared at Vernon for a moment, but was reluctant to make any sudden moves. "Uncle Vern, I asked you kindly to leave my town and you refused to heed my warning. There's nothing here for you, so please, just go."

But Vernon had no intentions of leaving and he had every intention of pressing his nephew into making a mistake. "I know that white boy is here. You probably gott'em hidden away in your jail. Now, you listen here, Nephew. I didn't come here to leave emptyhanded and if I have to, I'll go through you to get that money. Now, boy, I taught you how to use that gun, so are you really gonna draw down on your sweet old uncle?"

Once again, Gideon thought back to a better time with his uncle and came to the conclusion of only one ending. "Good-bye, Uncle Vern."

After hearing Gideon's disappointing words, Vernon's smile turned into a frown as he withdrew his gun. With an expeditious speed, Vern was agile, quick, and ferocious with his draw, but his years of tutorage became apparent. In a blink of an eye, Gideon's gun was out of his holster and firing several shots before Vernon could fire one. As Gideon's bullets passed through Vernon's body, his eyes widened as he momentarily stood fast, then dropped to the ground.

Holstering his gun, Gideon walked over and knelt down. Holding Vernon in his arms, Vernon stared up at him as a tear rolled down his face. Spitting up blood, he spoke his last words. "Gideon, be smart, boy. These white folk are never gonna accept a Negro with a badge." Gideon didn't say anything. All he could do was watch Vernon's eyes slowly closed as his life slipped away.

With an overwhelming sadness planted deep down inside, Gideon stood up and turned to Nato who was looking on. "I'm sorry, Uncle Nato, but please, no more. Just take Uncle Vern back home and see that he gets a decent burial."

Nato had no words, but more importantly, he had no desire to stay in Presidio. So, at Gideon's request, Nato and Wardell wrapped Vern's body in a blanket and laid him over his horse. Without looking back, Nato and Wardell along with the Cajun slowly left town.

Feeling satisfied with his actions and without missing a beat, Gideon informed Jubal about the evening plans. "Jubal, have Orville remove the head of Mr. Horowitz and bury it in a separate grave. And please say nothing to Hinklemeyer. He's liable to start running around spreading rumors about a headless horseman. And Jubal, I have the utmost confidence in you to keep Jon from coming out tonight when he hears gunfire. That'll be one least itchy trigger finger I have to worry about. You already know the plan, so Kenna, Rayna, and I are going to be a little busy." After making sure Jubal understood the severity in keeping Jon tucked away, Gideon walked over to Rayna. "You may want to change into something a little bit more alluring."

While Rayna was busy becoming ladylike, Gideon and Kenna walked over to the Lucy Goosy in order to figure out their next move. When they arrived, they took up a position at the end of the bar closest to the door. Lita was busy serving some of the local card players, but quickly finished when she saw Gideon walk in. As she poured some drinks, Kenna glanced around the room and saw Brice sitting at a table playing cards with several other locals, while Johnny Rocco and Logan Slade stood at the end of the bar enjoying their drinks and some of the women. Before he could turn back around, Brice glanced up and spotted him. Realizing a confrontation was inevitable, Kenna quickly let Gideon know about the problem. Trying not to further the situation, Kenna took a sip of his whiskey in hopes Brice wouldn't create a scene. But Brice had other ideas in mind.

As Gideon and Kenna stood quietly, Brice came walking up from behind. "Well, well, well. If it isn't the great Kenna James." After a pause, Brice realized Kenna wasn't paying him any mind. So Brice continued his banter in an attempt to provoke a response. "Hey, boy. You need to turn around and face me when I talk to you."

After another pause, Kenna reluctantly placed his whiskey down and turned to face Brice. "First off, I'm older than you, and second, I'm not your boy. So do yourself a favor and walk your stupid ass back over to your table and have a seat, boy."

Those words didn't sit well with Brice but then again, there was nothing Kenna could have said that would have sat well with Brice and both men knew it. Hearing his words being turned against him, Brice walked toward the door, then stopped and turned to face Kenna. "You've been avoiding me for way too long, Kenna. I think it's about time we find out who stays and who goes."

Unfortunately Kenna knew what that meant, but wasn't looking forward to facing off against his former protégé. As Brice turned to walk out the door, Kenna finished his whiskey and reluctantly followed. Thinking he may need the services of Orville again, Gideon also walked out. Once they were outside, Brice moved far enough away in order to start the show down. When Kenna stepped into the street, the people who were out quickly moved indoors.

While Brice was waiting, Kenna tried to talk some sense into him. "Where did I go wrong, Brice? I thought I was doing right by you in teaching you how to defend yourself. So, why? Why bother with me?"

Brice wasn't really prepared to talk, but he accommodated Kenna with a sincere and honest answer. "Because as long as you're around, I'll always be second to you. And I'm real tired of being second."

After a few more seconds of pause, Brice finalized his decision with what he thought would be his last words to Kenna. "Thanks for everything, Kenna, but it's time for you to die."

While staring each other down, Kenna and Brice stood still for a moment. Then Brice went for his gun. He was quick, but not quick enough. With unbelievable speed, Kenna withdrew his gun and strategically shot Brice twice in his arm and once in his gun hand. With his arm bleeding uncontrollably, Brice dropped to his knees while trying to control the pain. As Kenna holstered his gun, Gideon walked over and helped Brice up. Disgusted with the young man's decisions, he asked some of the local men to escort him over to Doc's office.

While some of Presidio's men grabbed ahold of Brice, Gideon questioned Kenna's actions. "So, why Mr. Nice Guy? Why not just kill him now, because you know he'll eventually find you again."

Kenna paused for a moment as he watched Brice be carried off. "Well, he was my creation, so he's also my responsibility. That arm of his is no good anymore, so the way I figure, by the time he learns to shoot using his other arm, I'll either be dead or just too old to care."

While Gideon and Kenna stepped back into the Lucy Goosy, Hinklemeyer was busy on his break paying a visit to one of his favorite taboo places: the Chinese bath house. Besides hot baths, sex, and opium, some of the girls along with the owner had become quite the entrepreneurs, trading customers' information and secrets in exchange for other valuables. Because most customers tend to become very relaxed, they drop their defenses, thinking the Chinese never repeat what they hear. But as the town's biggest gossip and trader of information, Mr. Hinklemeyer had the market cornered when it came to his network of gossipers and any intelligence they may have to trade.

During the visit from Hinklemeyer, it just so happened that Colonel Pittman was also indulging in some overdue needs of a personal nature. The colonel would utilize opium to battle the pain in which he suffered on occasions. And since the loss of his wife, he also embraced a hot bath along with the companionship offered by the young girls. As Hinklemeyer stood talking to the owner, Mr. Chung, some of the girls came running down the steps giggling and pointing to the upstairs because they knew Hinkemeyer was there and wanted to trade some goodies for information.

Whenever Mr. Hinklemeyer paid the Chinese bathhouse a visit, he always took along a satchel filled with bags of candies and the latest perfumes and colognes. As the girls approached, Mr. Hinklemeyer could tell they were very amused and excited. With permission from Mr. Chung, the girls guided Hinklemeyer up the steps and down a long narrow hallway. As they got closer to the door at the end, their excitement started to subside because they needed to be calm. Placing their fingers to their lips, the girls signaled Hinklemeyer to be very quiet.

As the girls slowly opened the door, they entered into a large room with several smaller rooms cordoned off with curtains. The colonel was in the largest of the rooms and had already taken his hot bath and was finishing up with having his way with one of the young ladies. Hinklemeyer could hear the colonel speaking to the young lady in a low voice as the girls urged him to slightly pull the curtain back. Feeling a bit intrigued, Hinklemeyer was giddy with emotion and pulled the curtain just enough for him to peek through. With his eyes wide, he was astonished by what he saw. The colonel was nude and had just gotten up from the small cot, which was supplied to every room for post-bath activities. With his nervous heart starting to beat faster, Hinklemeyer got a glimpse of the colonel's mysterious wartime injuries. Years before, Jacob and Zeke had used the colonel's own sword to prominently carve the word *coward* in large, bold letters into the colonel's chest and across his upper back. They also cut of his scrotum so as to leave him feeling less than a man and unable to reproduce. Hinklemeyer's heart continued to throb as he looked on with excitement, knowing the information would be disastrous for a man like Pittman and his reputation.

After a few seconds of watching the colonel get dressed, Mr. Hinklemeyer and the girls made their way back downstairs to see Mr. Chung. With such valuable information, Hinklemeyer was elated to give Mr. Chung a bottle of perfume along with some cologne and candy.

While Mr. Hinklemeyer was making his exit and spreading the word, Gideon and Kenna were at the Lucy Goosy waiting for the arrival of Rayna. Being late afternoon, Tommy was filling in for Ms. Lita and starting to get pretty busy, so a few of the saloon girls filled in and helped out. Just then, Rayna appeared at the top of the steps accompanied by Ms. Lita. Rayna was wearing a beautiful custom white dress with black and gold lace, which left just enough to the imagination. It had belonged to Ms. Lita from her younger days and it was perfect for Gideon's plan. It was cut low so it showed just enough of Rayna's cleavage to keep the men interested, and it wasn't elongated so the dress also showed off her legs. As she slowly walked down the steps, she caught every man's attention, including Kenna.

Seeing his friend's reaction, Gideon watched as Kenna's eyes were fixated on Rayna. "Boy howdy, Kenna. Rayna can really turn some heads when she isn't killing people." Gideon let out a small laugh as Kenna's eyes followed Rayna all the way down the steps.

When Rayna reached the bottom, the whistles and the dirty talk started to spring up. Thinking she may be a new saloon girl, most of the men couldn't wait to try her out. With all smiles, Ms. Lita quickly stepped behind the bar to lend a hand to Tommy while Rayna made her way through the gauntlet of wolves to the other side where Gideon and Kenna stood waiting. As she approached, Rayna could see the sparks going off in Kenna's eyes and decided to have a little fun. Brushing up against him, Rayna began to start her tease. "Well now, Mr. Kenna James, been a while since I've had the pleasure of seeing that look on your face. As a matter of fact, been a while since you've undressed me with those big eyes of yours."

Unable to find the words, Kenna was still in awe and was speechless, but Gideon was enjoying every moment. "Damn, Rayna, I gotta say, I'm sorry I've never seen this side of you, 'cause if I had, it might've been me standing alone at that altar."

Hearing those words, suddenly Kenna snapped out of his daydream and came alive. "Gideon, are you trying to flirt with my girl right in front of me? Because that's just not right."

Continuing with his fun, Gideon gave a quick smile as he glanced over at Kenna. "Hell yeah. Just look at her. But more importantly, look at everyone else. She has the attention of every man in this place, including Logan Slade and Johnny Rocco."

Before the trio could continue their conversation, the saloon doors swung open and in walked the Sicilian. Trying as smooth as possible, he walked over to a table in the back and motioned one of the saloon girls over with the thought of ordering a bottle of whiskey. His idea was to wait out Jon, knowing that any man who claimed to be any kind of a man would eventually come to the local watering hole to have a drink.

Just as the Sicilian got comfortable, the saloon doors once again opened again and in walked Sebastian Cole. Cole didn't have to try to be smooth because his demeanor spoke volumes. He waited a few seconds for his eyes to adjust, then walked to the end of the bar. Always a serious man, most people wouldn't even stare for more than a second or two.

Just like a game, Gideon took a mental note on where all the players were and what they were doing. After waiting a few more minutes, Gideon shifted his eyes to Rayna. Without saying a word, Rayna knew it was time to go to work. Stepping into her best ladylike walk, she went right for the Sicilian. Normally Italians were known to be ladies' men, but this particular Sicilian was all business. He enjoyed his whiskey and killing and there was no room for a woman, but Rayna was unaware of his beliefs and really didn't care.

As the little man sat quietly drinking, a promiscuous Rayna Jane came calling. Using her sexy legs, she approached the Sicilian and placed her foot up on one of the chairs, showing him some of her upper thigh along with a sexy garter belt. She then bent over toward him, placing her breasts inches from his face as she grabbed his bottle of whiskey and took a healthy swig. With a pucker of her lips, she placed the bottle back down in front of him. In the softest voice she could speak with, she started the game. "Hey, handsome. May I join you?"

Looking a bit confused, the short, balding man placed his hand in the air and got the attention of one of the saloon girls. After signaling for another glass, the Sicilian poured Rayna a drink and invited her to sit in the chair, which faced the bar.

While Rayna was acting as eye candy for her first target, Gideon walked over to Logan and Johnny in order to get them riled. Seeing that they were already drinking whiskey, Gideon ordered them two beers. Not expecting Gideon's random kindness, the two men accepted the gift and thanked the sheriff. With a smile on his face, Gideon raised his glass for a toast. "Here's to the not-so-handsome men in this world."

After taking a drink, Gideon glanced over at Rayna. "How about that, fellas? How the hell does somebody like a short, balding man attract a fine-looking woman like that? I bet he doesn't even have what it takes to bed down such a prize."

After a few more minutes of talk, Gideon locked eyes with Rayna. Utilizing the excuse that the whiskey bottle was a bit low, Rayna momentarily excused herself and walked over to the bar where Gideon was. While she was busy looking good for Logan and Johnny, it was time for Kenna to get involved. While Gideon was busy provoking Logan and Johnny and Rayna was busy getting their juices flowing, Kenna walked over and sat down next to the Sicilian. The Sicilian was familiar with Kenna and didn't take kindly to him inviting himself to sit, but before he could react, Kenna spoke up. "Hey, friend, I don't know how it is over in your country, but here we fight for our women. Especially one so beautiful like that little Philly you were just chatting with. Now, look over there. It's obvious those two boys aim to coerce that pretty little thing away from you so they can take her upstairs for some fun. Now, before you say anything, I heard you were the fastest man around. Be a damn shame if those two boys made you look like a fool. Just so you know, in a town like this, rumors get started off a wink of an eye."

Knowing the little Sicilian man was starting to look aggravated, Kenna smiled from ear to ear as he got up and walked back to the bar.

After a few more seconds of simmering, the Sicilian got up and walked over to Rayna. By now, Logan and Johnny was in full swing with their sweet talk and had started to flirt with her. As the Sicilian approached, he grabbed Rayna by her arm and spun her around. Before Rayna could say something, Logan grabbed the Sicilian and shoved him back. "Whoa now, mister. Where we're from, we don't go grabbing our women like that."

With a shocked look on his face, the Sicilian was stunned. Such a young man with very little respect for his elders, but it didn't matter. As far as he was concerned, Logan could die just as fast as anyone else. With a heavy accent, the Sicilian spoke with confidence. "You're not too young to die, boy. The lady is with me."

Just then, the Sicilian withdrew both of his guns and spun them around up and down and side to side to try and intimidate the youngster. After he was finish with his display of tricks, Logan turned to Johnny and burst into a laugh. Afterward, he turned back to the Sicilian. "Old man, this here is America and we care nothing about your stupid circus tricks. Now, if you would like to step outside, I'll show you what it's really like to face down death."

The Sicilian took the laughing as an insult and was not amused by Logan's words, so after a few seconds of staring Logan down, he turned to walk outside and motioned Logan to follow. With a smile on his face, Logan glanced over at Johnny, then walked out behind the Sicilian. Johnny gulped down what was left of his beer, then followed along with Gideon and Kenna.

When the men got outside, the Sicilian walked off some distance, then turned to face Logan. Looking on, most of the townspeople quickly got indoors. But the bounty hunters who were in town lined up to watch their competition because no matter who won the fight, they could easily gain information on how fast the winner was.

Staring at the Sicilian, Logan decided to have some fun. "It's not too late, old man. You can just turn and walk away and take your ass back to wherever you came from."

But the Sicilian wasn't laughing. Although he was deadly with both left and right draws, he took a deep breath and decided to go with his left hand, which he thought was a bit faster. In a blink of an eye, the Sicilian drew down on Logan as Logan withdrew his gun with deadly speed. As the bullets flew, Logan was struck in the neck and fell backward, while the Sicilian was hit dead center of his chest and was dead before he hit the ground.

Johnny ran over to Logan as he lay on the ground choking in his own blood. He tried to talk, but all he could do was smile as his eyes rolled back into their sockets. A few more seconds of choking and he was gone. Not really feeling any loss, Johnny figured two fewer bounty hunters was good for him, so he walked back into the bar and ordered another drink.

After all the commotion was over, the townspeople slowly came back out and went about their business. As one of the store owners passed by, Gideon asked him to fetch Orville. While Gideon glanced over at Kenna, Kenna had two fingers up, signaling to Gideon, *two down*.

Walking back into the bar, Gideon and Kenna ordered some more drinks, then signaled to Rayna to restart the game. Knowing she already had Johnny on the hook, she decided to approach Sebastian Cole. She knew Cole by reputation and had heard he was a very hard man, but she had a job to do and it was show time. By now, Cole was keeping to himself while sitting at a table enjoying a bottle of whiskey. Swaying her hips in a smooth back and forth motion, Rayna walked over and attempted to start a conversation, but Sebastian wanted no parts of her.

Just like she did for the Sicilian, she placed her foot up on one of the chairs in order to show some upper thigh and bent over just far enough to flaunt her breasts. "Hey there, fella. How about some company?"

Taking a drink of his whiskey, Sebastian slammed his glass down on the table, giving Rayna the idea of his displeasure. "And then what? You casually get up and walk over to the bar and try and persuade ol' Johnny Rocco to defend your honor?" Before Rayna could respond, Sebastian continued. "Listen, lady, I know who you are and you're no saloon girl. As a matter of fact, I was there when you gunned down the Mendoza brothers over in Louisiana territory."

With a smile beginning to form on his face, Sebastian poured himself another glass of whiskey then leaned back in his chair. "You just happened to beat me to them. That was a pretty good score for you. They were worth three thousand a piece. So, why don't you just walk your pretty little ass back over there and tell your sheriff friend and Mr. Kenna James that I'm not interested in playing their little game. And when that Texas Ranger friend of theirs shows his face, I'm going to finish up my business here and move on."

A little stunned but also flattered, Rayna smiled with pride. "Well now, Mr. Sebastian Cole, aren't you something? I thank you for recognizing my talent and I'll just be leaving you alone now."

Walking back over to the bar, Rayna locked eyes with Gideon and gave a subtle shake of her head. No. As she approached the bar, she poured herself a whiskey. "Damn! I knew Cole was a hard man, but I figured he wouldn't turn down companionship." After drinking her whiskey, Rayna explained. "He knows what we're doing and he wants no parts of it. He recognized me from a couple of previous bounties and I'll tell ya this, Gideon, that man is all business. He's here for one reason only, and that's to kill your friend, Jon."

Shaking his head in frustration, Gideon glanced over at Kenna. "Figures. Out of all the people here to kill Jon, he was the one I was most worried about."

Finishing off his beer, Kenna looked around. "Well, there's no other players here, and Johnny Rocco is probably not going to hang around much longer, so now what?"

Looking around, Gideon glanced over at Cole while Cole nodded his head and smiled back. "Well, I guess we wait."

While the trio was busy plotting their next move, Colonel Pittman was feeling refreshed as he made his exit from the bath house. Just as he stopped to take a breath and light his pipe, he noticed two men pointing in his direction and laughing. Momentarily placing his pipe back into his pocket, the colonel approached the two men. "Good evening, gentlemen. May I be of assistance to either of you tonight?"

As the two men continued to smile and laugh, one of them stepped forward. "We ain't got no beef with you, Pittman. Just like you, we here for that Texas Ranger."

Glancing around, Colonel Pittman took a deep breath as he inquired about the laughter. "I normally pride myself on keeping apprised of the more name-worthy gunfighters, but just by chance, I happen to know who the both of you are. You see, cowards like yourselves don't like to face down your acquisitions, but instead shoot them in the back. Reputations like that tend to get around quick. You are the Darby brothers, and may I ask what, pray tell, are you laughing about?"

The colonel was correct. The two men were Joe Darby and his brother Burt. Uneducated and failing at just about everything they've tried in life, they decided to try their hand at bounty hunting. While Burt was the quiet one, Joe always did all the talking. After smiling and looking back at his brother, Joe turned back around to face the colonel. "Well now, ain't you someth'n, talk'n 'bout cowards and reputations. Me and my brother done heard 'bout you and yer military dishonor carved into yer body. And we also heard you ain't got no balls."

Once again, both men burst out into laughter as the colonel was stunned at the revelation. As the two brothers continued to point and laugh, Colonel Pittman took a few steps back as he stared at the dirty and dingy duo. Not really giving any warning, the colonel withdrew his gun before the brothers even knew it was coming. After several shots, the two brothers fell to the ground dead. They didn't have to worry about being failures ever again.

While the colonel quietly slipped away into the night, Jubal was at the jail occupying Jon's time. Both men were quiet while they sat and listened to the town of Presidio and the sounds of everyday business. Jon had heard the gunfire coming from several directions and was up looking out the window. "What'ya think, Jubal? Wanna take a walk?"

Thinking about their last conversation, Jubal was busy making some coffee and wasn't really in the mood to talk, but since it was going to be a long night, he decided it would be best if he stayed friendly. "Jon, you gave your word to Gideon that you would sit tight for the night. Now, I'm pretty sure if'n you attempt to walk out that door, I'm not going to be able to stop you. But I would appreciate if'n you honor your promise 'cause the Jon I knew would do just that."

Still watching the people of Presidio conduct their business, Jon turned to face Jubal. "I'm sorry Jubal, but the man you knew no longer exists. I'm not here to cause you or Gideon any trouble, but if Gideon is in trouble, don't you think we should try and help?"

Before Jubal could answer, the door swung open and in walked Lita with two steak dinners. After laying the tray on the desk, she turned to face Jon. After taking a few seconds to look him up and down, the tears started to fall down her face as she took a step forward and gave him a big hug. She hung on longer than usual then afterward, kissed him on his cheek, and took a step back. "Dear God, just look at you. I can't figure it out, but you look different."

Before he could answer, Lita grabbed him by the hand and led him to the desk where Jubal was already eating. "Jon, please sit down and eat, and I'll be back to talk to you later. Right now, I have to get back and help Gideon."

Hearing that Gideon was okay, Jon relaxed as he sat down and began to eat. By the time Lita got back to the bar, Donovan MacCabe had just walked in and sat down to play some cards. After the earlier gunfight, some of the local cowhands wondered back in and was itching to lose their money. Before he could sit down, Donovan locked eyes with Rayna. Standing at the bar and seeing Donovan looking her way, Rayna motioned him to the back of the room. As she made her way over to a little dark nook, Donovan followed behind. Gideon and Kenna watched with interest as Rayna toiled and pulled on Donovan's clothing. While Rayna kept Donovan busy, Kenna walked over and started working on Johnny Rocco. Unfortunately, Johnny had been drinking all afternoon, so Kenna knew it wouldn't be hard to get him motivated.

As Johnny took a drink, Kenna went to work. "Can you believe that? I really thought you had that fine-looking thing earlier. I'm guessing you seeing your friend get gunned down, you're not feeling confident enough to be with such a beautiful woman like that."

Just when Kenna finished his words, Rayna came wondering over to order some drinks. While there, she gave Johnny a smile and started flirting with him again.

While Kenna and Rayna were working on Johnny, Gideon made his way over to Donovan and introduced himself. As Donovan sat in the far corner of the bar awaiting his prize to return, Gideon sat down across from him. "Mr. MacCabe, my name is Gideon and I'm the Sheriff of Presidio."

Already irritated that Gideon was blocking his view, Donovan spoke up. "Listen, Sheriff, I'm just here having some drinks with the local female help, so if you don't mind, I'd like for you to leave."

Gideon smiled because Donovan was already halfway to where he needed him to be. "Okay, but I have to say, I doubt if that pretty young lady is coming back here to sit with you. I think she took your money and is buying somebody else a drink with it."

As Gideon got up to walk away, Donovan glanced over to the bar and saw Rayna having fun with Johnny Rocco. Donovan was familiar with Johnny and didn't think much of him, but now he was interfering in his personal business. Frustrated and now angry, Donovan got up and walked over to the bar. When he approached, he stepped in front of Rayna and stood face to face with Johnny. "Hey, Johnny. Been a while. What the hell do you think you're doing?"

Just as familiar Donovan was with Johnny, Johnny had the same knowledge of Donovan. And being drunk, Johnny was in no mood. Not wasting any time, Johnny placed his hand on Donovan's chest and pushed him backward. "MacCabe, you need to take your silly ass out that door and don't look back."

Attempting to turn his attention back to Rayna, Johnny glanced over and noticed Rayna and Gideon had already created some space. Now, Johnny was really upset. But before he could react, Donovan came across with a right hook and knocked Johnny to the ground. "You're right, Rocco. I am gonna walk out that door, but I'll be waiting for you on the other side."

As Donovan turned to walk out, Johnny withdrew his gun and pulled the hammer back. Hearing the click of Johnny's gun, Donovan stopped and turned around. "I'll be outside, Rocco. Outside."

While Donovan turned and walked out, Johnny Rocco holstered his gun, then slowly picked himself up off the floor. As he wiped the blood from his bottom lip, he smiled and took a shot of whiskey.

Feeling as though she was doing something wrong, Lita watched with guilt, then turned to plead with Gideon. "Gideon, I know what we're trying to do, but you can't let this happen."

As Gideon stood quiet, Lita once again begged him to stop Johnny from walking out the door. "Gideon! He's in no shape. Please, for the love of God, he can't defend himself." But Lita's words fell on deaf ears, considering Gideon wasn't about to miss the opportunity to get rid of one more killer.

As Johnny started toward the door, Gideon and Kenna watched with no regret. As Johnny made his wobbly exit, Gideon and Kenna quickly followed behind. Patiently waiting for his target to exit, Donovan was already in the street when Johnny stumbled out of the saloon doors. As the two men stared at each other, Kenna suddenly stepped in front of Johnny and faced off against Donovan. "Well, aren't you a real big man, MacCabe? Gonna gun down a man whose been drinking all day."

Donovan wasn't thrilled about Kenna interfering and came right back with some words of his own. "Get out of my way, Kenna, or I'll make you my next target."

Kenna looked back at Johnny and realized the liquor and the punch in the face had started to take its toll as he watched Johnny sway back and forth. He then turned his attention back to Donovan. "I don't like you, MacCabe. Why don't you make me your first target?"

Not caring who he faced off against, Donovan stood staring at Kenna for a moment as he looked him up and down trying to assess any weakness. Then, in a blink of an eye, he withdrew his gun and fired, but it was too late. Kenna's draw was just a bit faster as he fired one shot, striking Donovan in the chest while the shot from Donovan harmlessly grazed Kenna in his left arm. Dropping to the ground, Donovan took one last look up at the sky before closing his eyes and breathing his last breath.

During the spectacle, Lita, Rayna, and Sebastian Cole had walked out to watch the show down. Afterward, Lita was somewhat pleased with the outcome, but Rayna was furious as she approached Gideon. "Gideon, what the hell? I gotta where this silly little girl getup while Kenna gets to have all the fun? That ain't right, Gideon. That just ain't right."

As Rayna turned to walk back into the Lucy Goosy, Lita followed behind, smiling and feeling better that it was Donovan lying dead on the ground instead of Johnny or Kenna. Worried about his friend Kenna, Gideon walked over to look at his arm and to make sure he was okay. Seeing that it wasn't serious, he gave Kenna a frustrated look. "That wasn't the plan, Kenna. You could've gotten yourself killed."

Glancing down at his arm, then back up to Gideon, Kenna smiled. "Then Rayna would've really been angry at you."

Although Donovan was lying on the ground dead, an ungrateful Johnny Rocco had some words for Kenna. With a slightly slurred speech, Johnny laid into him. "I didn't need your help, James. I could've taken him myself."

Listening to the half-drunk thankless Johnny Rocco, Kenna had no words for him. Instead, he swung his right arm around and hit Johnny in his jaw.

Temporarily stunned, Johnny looked at Kenna while Kenna scolded him. "Now, you look here, you stupid bastard. You owe me and I intend to collect right now. You're gonna walk your ass over to that hotel you're staying at and pack your belongings. And then you're gonna get the hell out of Presidio. If not, we can settle our differences right here right now."

Shaking off the punch to his face, Johnny took a few seconds to size Kenna up but wanted no parts of him. So, he tucked his tail between his legs and did exactly what Kenna demanded.

As Gideon and Kenna took a moment to smile and laugh, Sebastian Cole was looking on with thoughts of anger. When they turned to walk back into the Lucy Goosy, they saw Sebastian peering at then with disgust. After a few seconds of staring each other down, Sebastian turned and walked away. Knowing Sebastian was onto their plan, there was nothing they could do but continue in hopes Cole wouldn't get in their way. It was getting late and it seemed there wasn't going to be any more opportunities to induce gunfights, so Gideon decided to make some rounds around town while Kenna went to try and smooth things over with Rayna.

First stop for Gideon was to visit the Bauernshubs. By now, Hinklemeyer and his rumor mill network had spread the word about Colonel Pittman and his unfortunate battle wounds. In talking about the colonel, Mr. Bauernshub advised Gideon the nature of the embarrassing scars. After hearing of the colonel's misfortune, Gideon stepped aside to speak with Gino and Summer. After some head nods and some pointing down the street, Gideon smiled and thanked the two children with two lollipops.

As the sky gave off an array of faded colors, the sun started to set and various businesses were finishing up with their last customers of the day. After Gideon made his last rounds, he headed to the far side of the town to an old two-story barn, which used to double as a holding facility for grains and hay. The Quinn family owned it but had since closed shop and moved north away from the violent border. Now it acted as a playground for the children of Presidio who enjoyed playing hide and seek. Gino and Summer often spent their free time there when they weren't doing chores and running up and down the streets of Presidio.

Keeping a vigilant eye on the surrounding area, Gideon waited until the sun fell behind the distant landscape. As he stood in the shadows of an adjacent building, he watched as the vacant barn came to life with movement. While Gideon investigated the mysterious activities, four of Zachariah's men came from behind with guns out. Being enclosed by four men, Gideon had no choice but to conform to their demands. While one of the men shoved his gun into Gideon's gut, the other hit him from behind, knocking him to the ground. After disarming him, they pulled Gideon inside and tied him across an old slaughter table. With a bit of force, one of the men ripped Gideon's shirt off and threw it to the ground. Being stretched across a table with hands tied and back exposed, there was nothing Gideon could do but wait.

As the darkness settled in, a light fog started to roll into town and engulf the old barn. As Gideon lay stretched out and helpless, he could hear the clicking of spurs as they seemed to get closer. Suddenly Colonel Pittman came walking through the back door with his confidence riding high. Feeling as though everything was going his way, he stopped just within the door and smiled as he looked at Gideon with eagerness. "Well now. This is more like it, Negro. I bet it's been a long time since you've been in any type of position to get horse whipped."

Before Gideon could answer, the colonel reached around one of the stalls and pulled out an old horse whip and studied it. "But then again, it's been a long time since I've been in any position to horse whip me a Negro."

As the colonel conducted a small practice swing, the whip snapped like a loud crackling of a fire. "Well, damn, boy, we're gonna have us some fun."

After listening to the colonel, Gideon decided to try and reason with the madman. "Pittman, you don't have to do this. You can just walk away now before this goes too far."

Still feeling he had the upper hand, the colonel took a moment and glanced around at the other men. "If I'm not mistaken, boy, I do believe I'm the one giving the commands. Now Sheriff, we both know this isn't going to end well for you. But since we have time, allow me to appeal to your more patient nature so as to explain the severity of your situation."

While the colonel slowly circled Gideon, he began to explain about Zachariah Hayden. "You see, Sheriff, if it were up to me, I would just shoot you down like the dirty dog you are, but unfortunately my employer won't allow me to have such fun."

Wanting to exact maximum fear, the colonel kept circling around Gideon as to make him feel anxious and intimidated while he continued to explain. "Seems to be you laid your grubby hands on the wrong person. Mr. Hayden didn't appreciate being slapped around by you. Therefore, he instructed me to chop your hands off so he can hang them on his wall. But before I do, I want to introduce to you one of my associates."

Pointing the whip at one of his men, the colonel continued to speak with confidence. "This gentleman is a good friend of mine. His name is Harry, and he used to be a butcher before the war. His pappy was a butcher and his grand-pappy was a butcher. Now, I plan to take you back to the good old days and whip you until you scream and beg me for mercy. Then, after your back is swelled and bleeding and your hands are removed from your arms, I will un-ceremoniously place a bullet in your head. From there, these fine men are going to separate your head from your body and hang it outside of your office for everyone to see tomorrow morning. And for the rest of your body, well ol' Harry here is going to chop you into little bitty pieces and feed you to the hogs. Would be fitting, because I heard hogs like dark meat."

When the colonel had finished his little speech, he cracked his whip one more time in order to let Gideon know it was time. Just then, a woman's voice sounded out as though it was an angel descending down from the heavens. It was Lita, bursting through the front door with her double-barrel shotgun and targeting anyone who attempted to challenge her. "Okay, boys, the party is over, so let's see some of those hands in the air."

With a quick response to the demands, two of the men tried to draw their guns, but Lita wasn't the only party crasher. Rayna Jane and Andrew Bauernshub had snuck in through the second floor and had rifles pointed down at the men, and so began an all-out firefight. The two men who tried to draw their guns were shot dead by Rayna and Andrew. Harry attempted to run for cover, but Lita let her two barrels lose and nearly chopped the man in half. Seeing the situation was hopeless, the fourth man quickly placed his hands in the air and surrendered.

While Andrew kept his sights aimed at the last man, Rayna made her way down some old rotted steps and out the back door. After all the shooting, Lita quickly untied Gideon from the table with a very unhappy discord. "Gideon, are you okay? My God, I can't believe you actually went through with this outrageous plan."

Feeling the aches and pains of being tied down, Gideon stood up straight as he rubbed the rope marks from his wrists. After strapping his gun belt back on, he picked up what was left of his shirt and placed it over his shoulders. "Damn, I just had this shirt cleaned and pressed."

Looking around at the carnage, he didn't see the one man he was looking for. "Anybody get Pittman?"

Just then, Rayna came walking back in with a discouraging look on her face. Disappointed with the outcome, she gave the bad news. "Sorry, Gideon, that slimy snake slithered out the back door and disappeared into the fog."

By now, Andrew had made his way down to the first floor and, along with Rayna, had his rifle sights pointed at the last man. "What'ya think, Sheriff? Should we escort this fella to the jail?"

Breathing out some frustration, Gideon approached the man with anger in his eyes. Grabbing him by his collar, Gideon violently shoved the hired gun up against the wall. Still breathing heavy, he didn't say anything, but just stared into the man's eyes. After a few seconds of violent thoughts, Gideon let the man go. "No. No need for that. I don't need him stinking up my jail. Besides, I need him to crawl his way back to Pittman and Hayden to give them a message."

Just then, Gideon pulled his gun and shot the man in both legs. As the man fell to the ground in pain, Gideon had some last words. "You tell those two snakes I'll be waiting for them. You let them know, come morning light, the world according to Hayden is coming to an end."

While the man slowly crawled out of the barn and into the night, Andrew realized things were going to get worse. "Well, Sheriff, I'm glad you're alright, but I need to get back to my family now."

After thanking Andrew and shaking his hand, Gideon turned to Lita and Rayna. "Well now. You two seem to be making a habit of pulling me out of harm's way."

With a big smile, Gideon leaned over and gave Rayna a kiss on her cheek. "Thank you."

Afterward, Rayna gave a smile and a nod and walked toward the door. "I guess I'll go get some sleep. Come morning light, I think it's gonna get real interesting around here, to say the least. By the way, Gideon, you wouldn't happen to know Kenna's room number?" After happily receiving the requested information, Rayna hurried along to the hotel and a surprise rendezvous with Kenna James.

With Andrew headed home to his family and Rayna perusing her naughty thoughts, Gideon and Lita glanced around at an empty barn. As the two stood silent, Gideon peered into Lita's eyes. "Lita, it's hard for a man like me to count on somebody in times of need and I have to say, from day one I set foot in this town, you've made me feel special. I just wanted to say thank you."

With a smile on her face, Lita peered back into Gideon's eyes. "I just have to know one thing. Of all places, how the hell did you know Pittman would show up here tonight?"

Once again Gideon glanced around and spotted a pile of hay, so he took Lita by the hand as they made themselves comfortable. "Well, when Pittman arrived back in town, I figured I would have somebody keep an eye on him. But it couldn't be anyone he would notice. As you know, when they're not doing chores, Gino and Summer run from one end of the town to another. So, I spoke to the Bauernshubs and they were okay with them filtering information back to me on where Pittman would frequent. And before you go giving me a lecture, I also had Belle keep an eye on the children. She makes her rounds around town every day, and I knew Pittman wouldn't even think twice about her. Anyway, come to find out, Gino and Summer were in here hiding when Pittman came in to check the place out. They told me he looked the place over pretty good and even came back later in the day and hung a whip in one of the stalls."

While Lita absorbed the information, she couldn't help but feel concerned for Gideon's safety. "You took a huge chance, Gideon, and I'm not too comfortable with that."

Placing his hand on her cheek, once again Gideon peered into the eyes of Lita. "I know. But like I said, very few people I trust with my life."

Sharing a passionate kiss, Gideon gently rolled over on top of Lita and embraced the moment. Feeling Gideon's strong body, Lita placed her arms around him as she accepted his advance. "Well now, cowboy. Been a long time since I had a roll around in the hay. Guess my talk with Jon can wait."

After throwing his ripped shirt aside, Gideon smiled while he briefly thought about the up-and-coming day. "Come tomorrow, Orville's gonna have my head, so right about now, a roll in the hay sounds about nice."

While Gideon and Lita enjoyed their time in the barn, Jubal sat with Jon at the jail. Still working on a bottle of whiskey, Jon wasn't bothered, but Jubal still had fresh thoughts of their last conversation. In order to break the silence, Jubal set up a board of checkers.

While the two men engaged in a friendly game, Jon finally spoke. "If I remember correctly, you use to be pretty good at this game."

Listening to Jon, Jubal smiled with pride. "Well, I did take second place last year at the county fair. But I'm not trying to blow my own whistle."

While the two men strategically moved their game pieces around on the board, Jon also strategically maneuvered his words around while continuing the conversation. "If I'm not mistaken, that was rifle and shotgun fire we heard off in the distance. Could be trouble."

Once again, Jubal cracked a smile while capturing one of Jon's game pieces. "Now Jon, you know as well as I do, you gave your word not to leave here until morning. And although your brain has gone loco, I would like to think your word is still honorable."

After the ending of one game and the beginning of another, the two men poured drink after drink as Jon continued to press the issue. "Gideon could need some help. He's been gone a while."

Once again Jubal not only applied strategy to the board game but also to the mind game Jon was attempting play. "It's late, and I'm sure by now Gideon is probably in bed sleeping. He probably took care of any problems that occurred earlier and is in bed dreaming about better days."

After a few more games and drinks, the two men grew tired and put the board away. Now it was just one-on-one talk, and Jubal had concerns. While the two men continued to empty out the liquor bottle, talking seem to become easier and Jubal had no intentions of holding back. "Jon, I know you're hurting. It must really destroy you day after day thinking about your wife and children dying at the hands of a madman. But you decided to go the way of the law. You waited a long time for that Texas Ranger badge and you knew what it meant to wear it."

Keeping their friendship in mind, Jon listened and waited for Jubal to say his peace and then it was his turn. "I know you think it was war, Jubal, but your entire family was killed. Doesn't that at least bother you sometimes?"

Once again Jubal could feel the mind game coming back, so with a big sigh he responded, "Listen, Jon. Without getting into great detail, the only kin I ever cared about was my brother Ollie. And yes, he was killed during the war, but he didn't deserve to die the way he did. I remember the man who killed him like it was yesterday. After the war, it took a little digging, but I was able to find out who he was. He lives up north somewhere in Kansas. There was a time after the war when every day I thought about paying that son of a bitch a visit, and every time I mustered up the gumption to go, God would snap me back into my place. Revenge belongith to me sayith the Lord. Now, I've never known you to be a church-going man, but I've also never known you to be a violent criminal hell bent on death and destruction. So, come first light when you walk out that door, seems to me you're gonna have to make a choice."

After Jubal was finished, Jon didn't say anything because Jubal had finally put their conversation to rest. After losing the mind game, Jon drank down what was left of his drink and laid back onto his cot and closed his eyes. The rest of the early morning hours were quiet in Presidio, as only the crickets could be heard.

Thinking back on their conversation, Jon knew Jubal was right. Come morning light meant decision time, but in his mind, the decision had already been made: Find Rico and kill him, then send Zachariah Hayden back to hell. As Jon's body began to relax, he was finally able to fall asleep. Between the late night and early morning hours and the liquor, Jon was able to get a peaceful night's sleep with no bad dreams or wandering spirits to haunt his thoughts. The idea was to get a few hours' sleep, then get up just before the sun breached the darkness and finish his quest.

While the early morning hours passed, the streets were silent as the town of Presidio slept. After a few hours of much-needed rest, it was time for Jon's final battle. As Jon opened his eyes and sat up, he slumped over and rested his head in his hands. While sitting on the edge of the cot, he contemplated his actions on what he thought would be his final day alive. Between thoughts, he watched as Jubal sounded like he was sawing wood with his constant snoring. When Jon finally got up, he strapped on his gun belt and his shotgun, then quietly walked toward the door. Afterward, he stopped and turned to say good-bye to a friend. Looking back at Jubal who was still sleeping, he softly spoke some words. "You're a good man, Jubal. Maybe we'll meet again in another life."

After walking out, Jon quietly closed the door and headed for the hotel with hopes that he would find his targets and put an end to Presidio's deadly problems. It wasn't quite sunup yet, but there was just enough light to see as Jon made his way down the street. Along the way, he had to walk past Molly's place, which was a mecca for tired and horny souls. As he approached, he could see a man waiting for an unknown reason as he sat outside on a bench. Jon could see he was a good-looking man with a bit of moxie about him, but realizing he may be a bounty hunter, he slowed his pace and kept an eye on him.

As Jon slowly walked by, the man spoke out as his wait came to an end. "I heard you Texas Ranger boys are hard to kill."

By now, Jon's slow walk had come to a stop as he turned to face the man. Still sitting down, the man continued to speak. "When I was little, my ma and pa would drag me into church. That old preacher man with his Bible in his hand would just stand up at that podium and scream out the Lord's words, and

I remember my folks would just be so amazed. But not me. You know what that old preacher man told me one day? He said boy, you gonna go straight to hell when you grow up 'cause I can see the evil in your eyes. Yeah, do you believe the balls on that guy? That's what he said."

Jon watched as the man finished his story, then slowly got up and walked out into the street. With a suave look about him, he took up a position just far enough away to draw. Before Jon could say anything, the mysterious man decided to continue his banter. "I gotta say, all that time I spent in church, I did learn one thing. The Bible says to do onto others before they can kill you. You see, I knew you'd be coming for Hayden sometime soon."

Listening to the man and keeping an eye on his gun hand, Jon cautiously watched while the man continued to speak. "I just wanted to make sure I got to you before that idiot Sebastian Cole. That man is sneakier than a fox lurking around a hen house."

As Jon looked on, the outspoken man could see he was a little anxious and had an agenda in mind. But the mysterious man had his own plans, so he continued to talk. Letting out a small chuckle, the man finally revealed who he was. "I'm guessing you don't know me, but I know you. And I got to know that pretty little wife of yours too. Boy howdy, she tasted so good. Her lips were nice and soft, and boy, did she have spunk. I like lots of spunk."

While the man smiled and laughed, Jon began to realize he was face to face with the first of his targets. Like whiskey pouring into an old tin cup, Jon could feel the hatred pouring out of what was left of his soul. "Well now, I was beginning to wonder if you were around town, and here you are."

Still smiling, Rico decided to prolong their exchange of words by keeping Jon's family as the subject. "Of course. Mr. Hayden has deep pockets, and the money he's going to pay me for killing you will set me up for a very nice life. And after I kill you, I might kill that Sheriff and buy that little piece of property your family is buried on just so I can dig up their bones and feed'em to the wild dogs. That's the least I can do, considering you killed all of my men."

Rico was hoping his taunting would be enough to distract Jon, but his hopes were dashed when his fast draw was to no avail. As he drew his gun,

Jon's lightning speed was already in motion. Almost simultaneously, the last thing Rico felt was the bullet that shattered his teeth and the bullet that parted his eyes. With both bullets hitting their intended targets, Rico was dead before he fell to the ground.

As Jon approached Rico who was now lying on the ground dead, the shots had jolted Gideon and Lita awake as both jumped up out of their hay-made bed. Rushing to put their clothes on, Gideon and Lita ran out of the barn and toward the unmistakable sounds. The gunfire also awoke some of the hotel guests, including a much-curious Zachariah Hayden. Thinking Jon had finally met his demise, he quickly got dressed and made his exit from the hotel. By now, Jubal was awake and realized Jon was gone, so he, too, came running.

With the morning sun starting to shine its light on the old buildings and dusty street, Gideon and Lita came from one direction as Jubal arrived from another. After a few seconds of assessing the situation, it was clear Jon kept his promise and was now ready to end it all. Before anyone could react, Zachariah Hayden walked out of the hotel and approached the scene. Pointing his finger at Jon, Zachariah started making demands. "Sheriff, that man is wanted by the law and I want him arrested."

With Zachariah in his sights, Jon placed his hand on his gun as though he was about to draw, but Gideon intervened and stepped in front of Hayden in order to protect him. "Now, wait a minute, Jon. You can't do this. It would be cold-blooded murder."

Jon heard Gideon's words, but at this point it didn't matter. Taking his time, Jon withdrew his gun and pulled the hammer back. "I kept my word, Gideon, and now I need you to keep yours. Get out of my way."

Before Gideon could react, Zachariah stepped out from behind his temporary guardian. "Go ahead, boy. But only if you're ready to shoot an unarmed man."

To everyone's surprise, Jon hesitated as the hatred continued to consume his thoughts. "My family was unarmed, and so were the twenty-four Texas Rangers you killed."

As the tensions began to rise, Colonel Pittman exited the hotel and quickly approached. Tucking in his shirt and aligning his clothing as he walked, it wasn't long before he inserted himself into the already volatile situation. "Well now, I was unaware of your little soiree. My apologies for being late to the party."

With the arrival of the colonel dressed and ready for action, Zachariah felt a little more at ease as he breathed a sigh of relief. "Not a problem, Colonel. The sheriff here was just about to do his job and arrest this criminal."

Faced with having to decide between duty and friendship, Gideon had to make the quick decision to go on the offensive. Giving Jon a credible glance, he slightly raised his voice and gave Jon a command. "Jon, you need to trust me, so holster your gun."

Understanding the look Gideon gave, Jon reluctantly holstered his gun for the moment in order to determine what Gideon was going to do.

Maneuvering themselves around, Colonel Pittman and Zachariah were now facing off against Gideon, Jon, and Jubal, while Lita moved off to the side. With Colonel Pittman by his side, Zachariah wasn't going to let anyone control the conversation. So once again with confidence, he continued to make demands. "Now Sheriff, I'm an educated man and I have various degrees in law, so I suggest you place this man under arrest because if you don't, not even your friends in Washington are going to be able to help you."

Glancing over at Jon with a smile, then turning back toward Zachariah, Gideon decided to make a stand. "I'm a not-so-educated man, but I have degrees in killing people. Now, this man may be wanted in other territories, but he's not wanted in this town. And I don't give a damn about your empty threats anymore, Hayden."

Smiling back at Gideon as though he had just fallen into a trap, Zachariah gladly responded with the idea of one last crusade for the Confederacy. "Well Sheriff, seeing how I'm an opportunist, I was hoping you would refuse. Now you give me no choice but to kill you and your friends. So, what'ya say we have one last battle for the pride of ol' Dixie?"

Like a mental chess game, Gideon was anticipating every move. "Hayden, I think you're right. Just a good old-fashioned hoe-down. Last man standing gets the town of Presidio and bragging rights."

Feeling as though he baited Gideon into an impossible-to-win fight, those were just the words Zachariah wanted to here. In a bold voice, he described the bleak future of Presidio. "I don't like much about you, Sheriff, but I'm beginning to think you have style. You're outnumbered, outgunned, and outclassed, but you seem to think you have an honest chance to survive my onslaught. I like you're thinking and even remotely respect it, but your vanity will be short-lived. You have a set of nuts on you, but as you lowlife people always say, ain't gonna save you no how. In a few hours, my men are going to come storming in here and they're going to lay waste and chop this town to pieces. And when they're finished, there will be nothing left to brag about."

After everything was said and done, Zachariah, along with the colonel, returned to the hotel while Gideon responded back to his office, followed by Jon and Jubal. There were no patrons coming into town, nor were there any townspeople, so Lita had no reason to open the Lucy Goosy. The night before, Andrew Barenshrub made his rounds and evacuated the town by order of the sheriff.

With a worried look, Gideon sat at his desk thinking while Jon and Jubal sat staring at him. With the thought of letting Zachariah walk away still fresh in his thoughts, Jon spoke up. "Gideon, you said you wouldn't get in my way. You should've let me kill him."

Still in deep thought, Gideon didn't answer, but Jubal could see the worry. "Gideon, you said you had a plan. You still have a plan, right?"

Once again, Gideon stayed silent, but now it was Jon with the inquiries. "I'm not sure what kind of plan Jubal is talking about, but Hayden was right. He has us outmanned and outgunned. I saw his men camped outside of town yesterday on the way in. There's plenty of them left with pack mules filled with guns and ammo."

Before anything else could be said, the door opened as Kenna and Rayna walked in. While they took a seat, Jubal headed for the coffee pot. While Jubal readied some coffee, Kenna added his worries to the conversation. "Rayna told me what happened last night. Damn shame Pittman got away. Without him, I think Hayden would have packed up and left by now."

As the room fell quiet, Jubal poured the coffee for everyone. After a few sips, Gideon was ready to talk. "Jon, let me start by saying I can't apologize enough. I've been underestimating Hayden ever since he's set foot in Presidio and it cost people their lives."

Feeling disgusted about himself, Gideon got up and paced the floor. "You were right. I should have just let you end it by putting a bullet between his eyes, but in the back of my mind, I knew there had to be a better way. I know, deep down, he still yearns for the war because his family had a lot invested, but they lost and his pride can't handle that. So I decided to use his hatred for me to lead him right where he wanted to go. One final battle. This way, Jon doesn't hang for murder and we can show the people of Presidio that even in our darkest hours, good can prevail over evil."

Even with the inspirational words, everyone was still feeling a bit over-whelmed, and Rayna wasn't one to stay quiet. "Gideon, I love you like a brother, but I think you've done lost your mind. Hayden has an army of men about to descend on your town like a herd of angry buffalo, and I'm thinking our five guns are probably gonna be of no consequence."

Before Gideon could speak, Jon also had some disturbing words. "Gideon, I don't think there's anyone who could've predicted the events that have un-folded in this town, and I wouldn't begrudge anyone who just wanted to ride out. I would actually encourage all of you to do just that. Just let me do what I came here to do and come tomorrow, you can have your town back."

Like the heads of a round table, it seemed everyone had a comment to make, including Kenna. "Jon, we're here because Gideon asked us to be here, and although I would like nothing better than to take you up on your advice, Rayna and I aren't going to leave Gideon to fight this battle alone. So, with that said, has anyone given any thought to Sebastian Cole? He's still a player in this game, and I can't see him sticking his neck out for anybody sitting in this room."

Once again Rayna couldn't hold her thoughts or her sarcasm. "Gideon, Kenna's right. Hayden is the cash cow and Cole can't collect his bounty unless Hayden makes it out of this mess alive. So, Cole is definitely going to be an issue, and you already know about the small army of hired guns. There's no doubt they're gonna come at us from all sides."

Listening to everyone's concerns, Gideon grabbed another cup of coffee and sat down. As he looked around at the daunting looks he was getting, he tried to relay some positive thoughts. "Listen, you're right. All of you. We're here and our fight is now. Some of the fastest guns I know are sitting in this room, but I know that's not going to be good enough. Not only do we have the fastest guns, but I think our other advantage is our brains. We have the luxury of thinking for ourselves, where Hayden's men don't. He points and they go."

After taking a sip of his coffee, Gideon continued with his encouragement. "Now, listen. Hayden is over confident because he thinks he has us outnumbered, so he's not going to have any type of strategy to his plan. He wants to take it back to old school like two opposing forces. Us on one side and him on the other. He's going to come at us from just one direction."

After everyone shared their feeling s and worries, Jon decided to go along with whatever Gideon was planning. Besides, he had no plans on leaving Presidio alive. "All right, Gideon. I'm in. It's your show, so let's hear it."

Even with a plan in place and all his encouraging words, Gideon was still feeling a little worried, but he couldn't let the others see his doubt. So in his most serious voice, he gave everyone a duty. "I'm sure by now Hayden and Pittman have already ridden out to meet with his men, so we only have a couple of hours at best. Jubal, I need you to go to the edge of town and keep a look out. They'll be coming in from the east. I've already made arrangements with Flynn, so the rest of us will grab rifles and ammo and strategically place them in certain areas. The idea is to keep moving. Don't get pinned down and don't give them a sitting target. If necessary, we'll move in and out of the storefronts for cover."

After Gideon was done talking, everyone took a deep breath and got up to leave. Looking around, Gideon could still see the disheartening looks, so he had some last words. "I promise, we will not falter from this battle."

After everyone made their exit, Gideon pulled Jon aside to talk. Before walking out the door, Gideon placed his hand on Jon's shoulder and smiled.

"That damn Hayden seems to be a menace that looms over this town like a dark cloud. But his days are numbered. I promise."

As Gideon patted Jon on his back and walked out, his words stayed behind with Jon. In that moment, Jon realized everything in his life had come down to this one last battle. Reminiscing about the El Capitan, he briefly remembered the words spoken by the Old One: *You must defeat the dark cloud which follows you, and only then will you be able to fulfill your destiny.* Taking a minute to think about it, Jon realized Zachariah Hayden must be the dark cloud that consumed his family, and to kill Hayden would finally give him the opportunity to leave this world and rejoin his wife and children.

As Jon shook off his feelings from the past, he walked out to see everyone had come to an abrupt stop. While the air was swirling with a faint whistle, the wind blew the tumbleweeds from one end of town to the other. As Jon took a moment to glance around, he saw why everyone was silent. Sebastian Cole had come out of the hotel and was now standing in the street and facing off against the five protectors of Presidio.

As they stood staring at the deadly gunfighter, he made no bones about staring back. Not wanting any of his friends to get hurt, Jon wasted no time in stepping out into the street. "It's me you want, Cole. They don't have anything to do with it."

The tension was thick as the stare downs continued, but before anyone could respond, Sebastian Cole spoke some surprising words. "You're worth a lot of money to me and I have half a mind to just sit back and watch your friends get slaughtered and then just swoop in for the kill. But there's something about you, boy. And for the life of me, I just can't figure out why these four people are so hell bent on facing down an army of men just to save a ratchet soul like you."

As Jon listened, his fingers started to twitch, but he was unsure why Sebastian Cole was squandering time by talking. He knew there wasn't much time left, so he tried to push the action. "Cole, you're only going to get one chance and that chance is now. So stop your yap'n and make your move."

Listening to Jon started to become amusing to Sebastian, but the gunfighter had other plans. Glancing down at the ground and then back up at
Jon, Sebastian spoke some last words. "Boy, it's just not your time to die,
which is a damn shame because it would've been nice to add you to my col-
lection of kills."

Watching the gunfighter in disbelief, Jon looked on as he walked over and
climbed up onto his horse and guided it over to where Gideon was standing.
Peering down at Gideon, Sebastian Cole said his peace. "Sheriff, by no means
am I a coward, nor am I the brightest guy around, but I'm smart enough to
know when it's time for me to leave. That's how I stay alive in this dirty business. So for now, I bid you and your deputy safe travels." As he pointed his
horse west, he tipped his hat to Kenna and Rayna, then rode out.

While Jon was still busy trying to fathom Sebastian Cole's decision,
Gideon sent Jubal to stand watch at the end of town. He then sent Kenna and
Rayna over to the gun shop to collect the rifles and ammo. While the others
were gone, Gideon stayed to talk with Jon. He was glad that his friend was
okay, but he could also see the disappointment on his face. As the two men
stood in the middle of the street, Gideon took a deep breath before speaking.
"That was it for you, wasn't it? You thought you were gonna cash out and leave
this world, didn't you?"

Shaking his head, Jon was just coming down from his testosterone high.
"I gotta say, Gideon. Out of all the bounty hunters I heard was in town, Cole
was the one I was most looking forward to. His name seems to pop up the
most when it comes to speed. But to answer your question, I still have one
more person to kill before I go anywhere."

With his frustration starting to seep out, Gideon scolded Jon for his
words. "Damn it, Jon, I need you. Not just to face off against Hayden and his
men, but because you're more like a brother to me than a friend. It seems like
the more I try and keep you alive, the more you try to orchestrate your own
demise. And it's not just me. Most of the folks in Presidio look up to you,
damn it. Now, please, for the love of God, help me help you so we can get
through this."

With his heart being worn on his sleeve, Gideon walked toward the gunsmith shop, leaving Jon to grasp the powerful words. Taking a moment to glance around town, Jon saw nothing but emptiness, which was how he felt inside. Empty. No feeling or emotion, not even anger. Even the pain he felt for his family was gone. As he continued to look around, he spotted the neglected, worn-down church he had once married his beautiful bride in. He was quick to remember his wedding, which was the last time he had stepped foot in the aged, decrepit building. Looking toward the east end of town, he could see Jubal was still on post, so he decided to take a few minutes to visit the ailing chapel.

As Jon approached, he stood tall as he took in the overall view of the building. The small bell tower had been destroyed from a previous storm and the unsympathetic seasons had brutalized the facade. The few windows it had were boarded up, but the door with its missing lock was open as though the run-down church was inviting him in as an old friend. Pushing the door slowly, Jon listened to the rusted hinges creak with every movement. Standing in the dark doorway, he looked around at the neglected sanctuary. It was clear Father Time was just as unkind to the inside as it was to the exterior. But it didn't matter. He could picture Emily smiling as she recited her wedding vows. He also remembered Doc Micah sitting in the front row, trying to hold back his tears.

As Jon took a few steps in, he remembered Doc Micah consoling him about fear as he told the story of Jesus. He also remembered the joy he had felt when Doc endorsed his desire to become a Texas Ranger. Taking a seat in one of the dusty worn-out pews, Jon glanced up at the old faded statue of Jesus, which was still perched behind the water damaged pulpit. Through the years, water had leaked through the roof missing the statue of Christ but completely saturating the once-beautiful wood-carved podium. A few more seconds of staring and then Jon heard a voice from behind. As he turned, he could see a dark-skinned man wearing a faded robe smiling back at him. Jon recognized the garment from his younger days of living with Father Andres and Santos. They wore the same type of robe as friars.

When Jon stood up, the priest greeted him with kind words. "My friend, welcome. I am humbled you have come to visit."

After standing up to greet the man, Jon held out his hand for a handshake. "My apologies, sir. My name is Jon Mason, and I didn't mean to intrude. I was just taking a walk down memory lane."

While Jon stood waiting for the priest to shake hands, the priest chose not to extend the courtesy. Instead, he glanced down at Jon's hand, then guided his attention back up to Jon. "No apology needed, my friend, but you must accept mine. For I am not worthy to shake the hand of such a great man."

Jon wasn't sure what the priest meant, but he accepted his decision and withdrew the gesture. With dark brown skin and an unfamiliar accent, Jon wasn't familiar with his nationality and inquired about the priest's origins. In response, the priest gave Jon a smile and purposely kept his reply short. "My name is Jeremiah, and I come from a place where dreams and nightmares collide. So, Jon Mason, how may this humble servant of God be of help to you?"

Glancing back at the statue of Jesus, Jon gave a straight-forward comment. "Well Pastor, I wasn't really looking for help. I guess I came in to get some quiet time so I could think. You see, my wife and I were married in this church years ago and now she's gone. She was murdered along with my children, and the man responsible is here in this town and I'm going to kill him."

Hearing Jon spiel out his grief, Jeremiah listened but did not judge. Instead, he attempted to offer some words of wisdom. "So, Jon Mason, you are looking for Jesus to approve of your revenge?"

Turning back around to face Jeremiah, Jon gave a quaint smile. "No, sir. I'm not looking for permission from anyone. I already know what I'm going to do and I'm not really interested in being saved or forgiven."

Taking a moment to sit and rest, Jeremiah attempted to guide a lost soul in the right direction as he responded to Jon's heartless words. "I must say, Jon Mason, your words are troublesome. You have an eternal battle within you, so let me just say, only God has the right to enact revenge. As for your family, nobody is ever completely gone. They live on in your heart and in your memories. Just close your eyes, Jon Mason, and you can feel your family deep within yourself."

Before Jeremiah could continue, Jon became a bit bothered and decided to interrupt. "Pastor, I appreciate what you're trying to do, but I think I'm beyond help and I don't think God cares enough to grant me peace."

While the conversation was starting to take its toll on Jon, Jeremiah continued with his advice and guidance. "Please, Jon Mason. History teaches us that many people before you came to the same conclusion that God had abandoned them, but in the end they found out they were wrong. God has not abandoned you, my friend. He will never turn his back on you. He has been with you all of your life. Even in your darkest of hours, he will shine a light of hope for you."

Listening to Jeremiah, Jon smiled, then let out a small laugh. "You sound like two old priests I use to know. They were good men and they, too, lived by the word of God."

Realizing the mind of a fool could not be reasoned with, Jeremiah stood up to face Jon. In a stern voice, he spoke out with some urgency and warning. "Listen to me, Jon Mason. Do not follow the dark angel down a path of no return. He will lead you into darkness and you will be forever lost."

Once again Jon listened to the words Jeremiah was speaking, but they were in vain. With a respectful nod, Jon turned and walked toward the door. Before leaving, he turned and had some final words for Jeremiah. "Pastor, you may want to leave town. There's going to be some very bad men arriving soon and I wouldn't want to see you get hurt."

Now it was Jeremiah listening to words that were in vain. With confidence in his heart, Jeremiah gave a bold and decisive response. "I am a servant of God and I run from no man."

After so much time dealing with cowards posing as men, Jon admired the courage of Jeremiah. Realizing Jeremiah was a man who relied on the strength of his faith, he decided to give some words of encouragement. "Sir, most of the folks of Presidio are warmhearted, so after this is all over, there's a good chance they'll help you fix this place up."

With a smile on his face, Jeremiah once again shined with confidence. "Do not let your eyes deceive you, Jon Mason. This is a house of God and it is always perfect."

With the conversation at its end, Jon had nothing left to say, so he turned and walked out. Walking through what looked like a ghost town, he began to once again reminisce. He thought about when he first arrived in Presidio and how the streets were full of life while the store owners swept their fronts and sold their goods. As he took a moment to glance back at the old church, he noticed the front door was now shut and boarded up. Not thinking anything of it, he looked around and saw Jubal still manning his post at the edge of town.

Arriving back at Gideon's office, Jon saw Gideon and Kenna setting up barriers that stretched across the street. The idea was to use the barriers as cover during the first wave of attacks in order to kill as many of Hayden's men as possible. Afterward, they would retreat to the storefronts while the remainder of Hayden's men took cover. With Hayden's men busy regrouping, Gideon and company would navigate forward, utilizing staged rifles they had strategically placed earlier.

Even against insurmountable odds, Gideon felt they had the advantage by not underestimating the opposing force and being better prepared. While Kenna and Rayna sat off to the side waiting for the inevitable, Gideon and Jon sat and shared a conversation. Attempting to relieve some of the tension, Gideon decided to speak first. "Jon, I know your life consists of many bad happenings and there's a number of things about you I just don't understand. I know Jacob seems to think there's something mysterious about you, and when a man such as Jacob speaks, people like me often listen. With that said, I don't believe in all the lost spirit and ghost stories, but when we make it out of here, I would appreciate if you and I could just sit and have a heart-to-heart talk over some drinks."

Before Jon could respond, Jubal quickly came running down the street. Breathing heavy, he took up a position behind a barrel. "Gideon, I can see the dust kick'n up. They're on the way."

Still breathing heavy and with his nerves on edge, Jubal stated his opinion. "If'n we ride out now, I don't think anyone would think bad of us. If'n we don't, I think we're gonna get real bloody on this one."

Trying hard to force a smile, Gideon glanced over at Jubal. "Well, old friend, I don't think this is anything we haven't faced down before. I'm just glad we're fighting on the same side."

Just then, Kenna and Rayna trotted over and took their positions.

Trying to lighten the mood, Kenna glanced over at Jubal, who was still proudly displaying his Confederate hat. "Jubal, when this is all over, I'm gonna get you a new hat. Preferably something with a bit more, well, you know, a little more style."

In response, Jubal gave a gracious smile. "Well, I appreciate that, Mr. James, but let's not count our turkeys before they start to gobble. I'd like to try and make it out'a here in one piece, if"n ya don't mind me say'n."

As the five brave souls sat quietly for a few more minutes, they knelt down behind their barriers staring toward the east end of town and waiting. After a few minutes of watching the tumbleweeds blow back and forth across the street, they could see the dust start to stir at the edge of town. Then out of the dust came the first wave of Zachariah Hayden's men. The first squad of men had arrived in town riding in formation with Colonel Pittman behind them, ready to call out commands. Pulling their horses to a stop, the intimidating group of men sat tall in their saddles, waiting on the command from their leader to attack. As the men waited, a second squad of men came riding in and, just as prominent, waited confidently and proudly for their orders.

Being in the war, Gideon, Kenna, and Jubal knew what the formations meant. It was partly a scare tactic to intimidate the enemy and to show force before coordinating an attack. While the five sat waiting, Jubal made a very important observation. "Gideon, seems to be a few people missing from the party. What'ya think?"

Taking a few seconds to look, Gideon came to the same conclusion. "You're right. According to Jon, there should be more men, and I don't see Hayden."

While the men pondered the revelation, Rayna spoke up with an idea. "Listen, fellas. I don't mean to leave ya'll short, but I'm more of a close-range shooter, so why don't I just fall back and cover ya'll backsides?"

Knowing they would be short one rifle, everyone agreed it would be better than the alternative of being caught off guard in a crossfire. So Rayna collected an extra rifle along with some ammunition and fell back, taking up a position toward the west end of town.

Like the calm before the storm, it suddenly became quiet with only a light breeze blowing around the tumbleweeds—and then it happened. Colonel Pittman raised his arm in the air, then loudly shouted the command. "Ready your firearms, men. Charge!"

As the first line of attack came galloping down the middle of town, Gideon raised his rifle and gave his counter command. "Fire."

While the bullets from Hayden's men began to shred some of the barriers, the return fire from the four heroes struck their targets. Some of the men fell to the ground dead while other were badly wounded. As the dust from the ground kicked up, it started to become more difficult to see past the first line of attack. The other men along with Colonel Pittman had temporarily disappeared behind the commotion. Then, out of all the confusion, came the second line of men. Barreling down on the four defenders and firing at will, Gideon and company attempted to return fire, but with no good results. Some of the men broke through the barriers, while others used their horses to jump over. Quickly turning their horses, Hayden's men came charging back through while firing their guns. Taking a bullet to his leg, Kenna fell back against the barrel he was hiding behind but continued to fight. Jubal and Gideon were able to get off one shot each, which killed one of the men and wounded another. With his lightning speed and deadly accuracy, Jon withdrew his six-shooter and killed two more of Hayden's men. While the last of the men retreated, Gideon tended to Kenna, with Jon and Jubal standing watch.

Hearing all the gunfire, Rayna came running back over and found Kenna lying on the ground with Gideon tying a piece of cloth around the wound. Taking a personal interest in tormenting Kenna, Rayna scolded the wounded gunfighter. "Just look at you, you lazy ol' hound dog. Wouldn't it figure I'd find you lay'n about."

Feeling the pain of his wound, Kenna's face cringed as he tried to push out a smile. "Well now. Just when I thought you didn't care. Thanks for the vote of confidence, sweetheart."

Before anybody could continue, Colonel Pittman gave the order for the second squad to attack. Dismounting their horses, the men from the previous attack took refuge behind anything they could find. With plenty of ammunition, they laid down suppressive fire as the men from the second squad galloped toward what was left of the barriers and fired everything they had. While Jon and Jubal fired back, Gideon and Rayna propped Kenna up in order for him to try and help.

Once again Jon and Jubal were able to pick off a few of Hayden's men, but the barrage of bullets coming their way was just too much to handle. With their horses in a full gallop, Hayden's men closed quickly as rifle fire shredded the remaining barriers. Once again Hayden's men easily broke through the line, causing mayhem. Unloading his rifle, Gideon continued to fire, killing more of Hayden's men while Jubal attempted to reload. Before he could fire a new round of shots, Jubal was shot several times.

As Hayden's men quickly turned to make another pass, Gideon knew it was time to seek shelter elsewhere. So, as planned, they moved to take shelter along the storefronts. While Rayna helped Kenna get to the north side of town, Gideon and Jon helped Jubal get to the south side. While Jubal leaned on Jon for support, Gideon attempted to shield the two friends but took a bullet to the side of his body.

While Hayden's men made their second pass, they bypassed the rubble in the street and made their way back up through town. With the defenders of Presidio separated and wounded, the rest of Hayden's men dismounted their horses in order to ready their ground attack. Taking cover behind barrels, water troughs, and structural beams, Hayden's men regrouped and reloaded.

Well-armed and well prepared, Hayden's men zeroed in on anything that moved. With a fire fight in full force, Jon attempted to advance toward Hayden's men in order to utilize the rifles that were strategically placed, but was quickly targeted, so he took up a defensive position inside one of the vacant shops. With Kenna and Rayna pinned down across the street and Gideon and Jubal wounded, Jon was beginning to think Gideon's plan wasn't the best course of action.

As the bullets continued to batter the already-damaged storefronts, Gideon was able to help Jubal by wrapping his wounds in order to stop the bleeding. Trying to keep Jubal calm, Gideon attempted a bit of humor. "Not bad for a Johnny Reb. How are you doing?"

Feeling the pain as he laughed, Jubal smiled while trying to be upbeat. "Thanks, Yank. I'll take that as a compliment."

While Gideon listened to the bullets tearing apart the buildings, a small glass sitting on the counter caught his eye. As he stared at it, it began to vibrate. After a few seconds, the glass vibrated its way to the edge of the counter and fell off. Afterward, Jubal noticed some of the hanging signs and photos starting to vibrate off the nails they were hanging on. While looking bewildered, Jubal became intrigued as both men could hear a faint rumbling sound. "Gideon, what the hell is that noise?"

Feeling a bit confused, Gideon thought for a second as the sound became louder. "I've only heard that sound one time in my life and it wasn't a pleasant one."

By now, the sound had become prominent enough for Hayden's men to hear, so they temporarily suspended their shooting, knowing something inconceivable was coming their way. With no gunfire aimed at him, Gideon pulled himself up and peeked out the window. He looked toward the west end of town where the sound was coming from and saw a large amount of dust advancing toward Presidio. Scooting himself backward, Gideon grabbed Jubal and dragged him behind the counter. "Lot of dust coming this way."

With the sound growing louder and the room starting to shake, Jubal took a wild guess. "What is it, Gideon? Dust storm?"

Before Gideon could answer, a thousand head of cattle stormed into town, trampling and destroying everything in their path as they powered their way through Presidio. While the buildings and ground trembled and shook, Gideon glanced over at Jubal and smiled. "Stampede."

Over on the north side of town, Rayna stood staring out the window of the dress shop at the massive amounts of beef easily disposing of anything and anybody in their path.

While Rayna was giving Kenna a verbal description of the destructive scene, Kenna hobbled his way over to the dresses using a makeshift crutch he made from a piece of wood. When Rayna turned around, Kenna was holding up a beautiful pink gown. "Would really like to see you in this."

Smiling from ear to ear, Rayna walked over and gently took the garment from Kenna. Glancing into a nearby mirror, she placed it against her body and spun around. "Well now, you have some good taste, Mr. Kenna James. I can see myself wearing this for you."

As the two shared a passionate kiss, Jon was still nestled in the vacant building, wondering where the herd of cattle came from. He watched as the steers rampaged through town, laying waste to anything in their path. Hayden's men, who thought they had the upper hand, were quickly dismissed when the mighty beasts descended onto the town. Some were able to quickly retreat within the safe walls of some of the storefronts, while others attempted to take cover behind some frivolous objects that were no match for the tons of beef. Yet others aspired to try and outrun the stampede, but their feeble attempts were met with a horrible death.

As the herd started to thin out, many of Hayden's men lay dead in the street. When the stampede was over, the remainder of Hayden's men retreated back to the east end of town to regroup. While they were busy getting new orders from the colonel, Gideon peeked through a fairly big hole in the wall in order to talk with Jon, who was next door. "Jon, are you okay?"

With his sarcasm still intact, Jon immediately replied. "Was this a part of your plan, Gideon? Where the hell did the cattle come from?"

Feeling some temporary relief, Gideon thought for a moment and then smiled. "Well, I don't remember placing an order for that much steak, but they got Hayden's men off our asses for now."

In the past Jon would have welcomed Gideon's sense of humor, but all he could see was his chance of killing Zachariah Hayden slipping away. "Gideon, we tried it your way, but I don't think things are working out in our favor. Kenna took a bullet to the leg and you have some pretty hefty bleeding coming from your side. And I don't think Jubal is in any shape to continue the fight. It looks like Hayden's men are lining up to come at us again, so when they do, I'm going out the back. If I can find Hayden and kill'em, I think this will all end."

With his frustration starting to replace his temporary relief, Gideon came back with some words of his own. "Listen to me, Jon. We need you. When Hayden's men come rushing down that street, we're gonna need every gun we have to stop them."

Pausing for a breath, Gideon continued his argument. "Jon, please tell me you're not thinking about deserting your friends in our darkest moments. I promise, we will get Hayden."

As desperate as Jon was to get Hayden, he knew with Jubal badly hurt and Kenna down to one leg, they wouldn't stand a chance against the rest of Hayden's men. "All right, Gideon. We'll face them head-on, but if I die, I'm coming back to haunt you."

Even though it had been a while since he heard humor coming from his friend, Gideon smiled as he and Jon shared a small fragment of laughter.

Before Hayden's men could refocus their efforts, Rayna retrieved some of the staged rifles and ammo that were hidden earlier in the day. Gideon also had the same idea and knew that he had placed two rifles on the counter where Jon was. "Jon, look over on the countertop and grab the two rifles. Keep one for you and pass the other to me."

Listening to Gideon, Jon crawled over to the old dusty counter and grabbed both rifles, along with the ammunition. Keeping himself low, he made his way back to the hole in the wall. "Take both of them, Gideon. Give one to Jubal and you keep one."

With some curiosity, Gideon took the rifles and ammo. "What about you? Aren't you gonna need one?"

Having no concern for himself, Jon didn't reply right away. Instead, he took up a position at the window and glanced up the street. "No, I'm okay. I'll be okay."

With the remainder of his men regrouping, the next sound everybody heard was Colonel Pittman shouting out an order. "Ready yourselves, men. Charge!"

With Kenna and Rayna already in position on the north side, Gideon and Jon prepared to meet force with force on the south side. Waiting for the inevitable, Gideon, Jon, Kenna, and Rayna watched as Hayden's men came galloping down the street, blasting away at the storefronts. But before they could get close, their force was met by another force. Like the four horsemen of the apocalypse, Jacob, Zeke, Harvey, and Shelby came charging in from the west and unloaded everything they had onto the unsuspecting enemy. With nowhere to run or hide, it was a fight to the death as the battle raged in the streets of Presidio. With Jacob and company battling on horseback and Gideon and company firing from the ground, many of Hayden's men were easily eliminated.

Looking around at Hayden's small army lying on the ground, Jacob had Harvey and Shelby join Milky Way, who was rounding up the cattle while Zeke checked around town for any stragglers. After the dust had cleared, Jon came out to greet his mentor and friend. "Not that I'm trying to be ungrateful, Jacob, but what the hell are you doing here?"

With a smile on his face, Jacob gave his usual sarcastic answer. "I was invited to this party."

By now, Rayna had also come out, with Kenna hobbling behind with his homemade crutch. Before any introductions could be spoken, Gideon emerged from the battered building, with Jubal leaning on him for support. As the two made their way to the middle of the street, they were greeted with smiles.

After surveying the surrounding area and seeing all the dead bodies, Gideon turned to Jacob with a smile. "About damn time. Where the hell have you been?"

With a well-deserved handshake, Jacob responded with more humor. "Well, I had to drop some cattle off to a friend of mine, and this town just happened to be in my way. Good to see you too, Gideon, but you don't seem to be looking too good." Pointing at Gideon's side, Jacob gave his concerning thoughts. "You should probably have that looked at."

Glancing over at Jubal, Jacob shook his head. "You look like hell, Jubal, but I'm glad you're still with us."

As the friends were discussing the outcome of their battles, Zeke was busy snooping around town. While checking the old storage barn, he heard the door slowly creak open behind him. When he turned, he saw Colonel Pittman in the doorway staring him down. "Well now, look who we have here. I seem to remember something you said to me years ago. Maybe we'll meet on the battlefield another time. You remember saying that, boy?"

As the colonel stepped inside the door, he closed it behind him for a little one-on-one privacy. Looking at the sword hanging off Zeke's side, the colonel let out a small smirk. "I see you still have my ancestor's sword. Very considerate of you to return my property."

With a smile on his face, Zeke started to laugh. "Well, Colonel, you're only half correct. I did say we would meet again, but I can promise you, it wasn't to return this cheap piece of Spanish steel." Pulling the relic from its holder, Zeke admired the sword for a few seconds. "Although, it does give me pleasure know'n I took it from a Confederate swine like you."

Placing the sword back into its holder, Zeke and his arrogance faced off against the colonel and his smugness. "I keep hear'n you the fastest gun around, which can't be true 'cause I'm the fastest, period. Been look'n forward to this, Colonel."

Smiling as though he was about to feast on a Thanksgiving dinner, the colonel spoke in very clear terms. "Well, my young Negro friend. You were right. This is our battlefield as we meet for the last time."

A few moments of staring each other down, and the two men drew their guns and fired. Colonel Pittman was grazed across his neck and stumbled backward, but quickly recovered as he gave Zeke a look of evil. Staring back at the colonel, Zeke smiled and then let out a small laugh. "Well, well, Colonel. What'ya think 'bout that? Lot faster than you thought I was."

Glaring at Zeke as though he was looking at a dead man, the colonel didn't say anything as Zeke suddenly felt a warm sensation running down his body. As he looked down, he saw his own blood starting to saturate his clothes. The colonel's bullet had ripped through Zeke's gut and made its exit out of his back. Feeling his body becoming week, Zeke's started to sway as he staggered back a step. Not wanting to show weakness or fear, he took one last look at the colonel and smiled before falling to his knees.

With the spoils of war at his fingertips, it was now Colonel Pittman with the arrogant attitude. After holstering his gun, he walked over to Zeke, who was now struggling to stop the blood flow from his stomach. "Now, what were you saying? Oh, yeah. Well, well, boy, what do you think about that?"

Zeke didn't want to give the colonel any more pleasure than what he was already bolstering, so he tried not to look up at him. But Colonel Pittman, in all his glory, wanted to make sure Zeke was thoroughly humiliated, so he placed his boot on Zeke's shoulder and pushed him backward to the ground. Lying on his back, Zeke had no choice but to look up at his nemesis. As Zeke's body started to turn cold, he began to tremor as the blood continued to flow from his stomach. Standing over top of him with a cold-hearted smile, the colonel looked down and gave Zeke some last words. "Don't worry, boy. I shot you exactly where I wanted so you would live just long enough for you to tell your friends who killed your sorry ass."

With no more words, the colonel bent over and unsnapped the sword from Zeke's waist and proudly walked out with it.

Thinking the battle was over and Presidio was safe, Jacob was about to say his good-byes when suddenly Hayden and the last of his men came riding into town with a covered wagon. With astonished looks on their faces, the defenders of Presidio were stunned to see more men. With his anger still fresh on his mind, Jon wanted nothing more than to get closer so he could end Zachariah Hayden's life. But just when he thought about moving forward, some of Hayden's men maneuvered into an attack formation. Before anyone could react, another man pulled the cover from the wagon to reveal one of the Civil War's most ferocious weapons.

Horrified at the sight, Jacob's eyes widened as the glare of the sun bounced off its multiple barrels. "Dear God. It's a Gatling gun." Able to fire four hundred rounds per minute, one man could easily take out an entire company of men.

With no alternative, Gideon and Jon grabbed Jubal while Jacob and Rayna latched onto Kenna, but before they could run, the men on horseback charged while the man on the wagon opened fired. While the Gatling gun began its mass destruction, the defenders fell victim to its carnage.

In the course of trying to help Jubal, Gideon took another bullet to his leg and fell to the ground. Watching his friend go down, Jon had no recourse but to turn and face the oncoming horsemen. Trying to stay one step ahead of the incoming bullets, Jon withdrew his gun with lightning speed and killed two of the men before a third one was able to return fire, striking Jon in the shoulder. With the Gatling gun still raining down bullets, the remaining horsemen retreated back to safety. Before she could get Kenna to safety, two of the Gatling bullets struck Rayna in the back with massive force, knocking her unconscious to the ground. Thinking Rayna may be dead, Jacob continued to help Kenna to the temporary safety of the dress shop.

Once again Gideon, Jon, and Jubal retreated to the shops on the south side of town while Jacob and Kenna were occupying the dress shop on the north side of town. With the Gatling gun silent, it gave everybody time to catch their breath and assess their wounds. As Presidio lay quiet, Jon stood watch at one of the busted-out windows while Jacob took a position in the doorway of the dress shop. Looking across the street at each other, the two men shook their heads in disbelief. The menacing results of just one weapon were too inconceivable to absorb.

While looking around, Jacob noticed Rayna was still breathing, but he knew once he stepped out into the open, Hayden's man on the wagon would gun him down in seconds. Getting Jon's attention, Jacob yelled to him to try and draw their fire. Understanding the plan, Jon glanced up the street and saw some of Hayden's men still on horseback, so he grabbed a rifle. Thinking he could quickly get off one shot, he scurried out the door and took aim. One shot, one kill. As one of the horsemen fell to the ground dead, another pivoted the Gatling gun and threw down a barrage of bullets in Jon's direction. With bullets nearly missing, Jon ducked back into the vacant storefront where he was at earlier.

In the midst of chaos caused by one man, Jacob was able to run out and drag Rayna back to safety. She was breathing, which was good, but Jacob couldn't tell how bad her wounds were. While Kenna held her tight, she slowly opened her eyes. After a few seconds, Rayna was able to barely speak with a faded voice. "Kenna, what the hell are you doing? If I remember correctly, we have a fight to finish."

After hearing her voice, Jacob and Kenna figured her wounds weren't life-threatening, but they were still serious enough to need a doctor.

Knowing they were unable to confront a Gatling gun head on, Jacob had to think quickly. With Hayden's men in his line of sight, Jacob thought it best to sneak out the back and try and come from behind. Knowing Rayna wasn't going to last much longer, Jacob made the decision to enact his plan.

While Jacob was busy moving quietly through the rear alleys, Jon was coming to his own conclusions. With Jubal badly hurt and now Gideon shot for a second time, Jon felt he had no other choice but to make a sacrifice in order to save his friends. It was time to end the makeshift war, but before making any rash decisions, he peeked through the hole in the wall and got Gideon's attention. "Gideon, how are you and Jubal holding up?"

Unable to stop the bleeding, Gideon glanced down at his wounds. "Well, my leg is okay for now, but my side is starting to become a problem. And I think Jubal's arm may be broken." With a heavy heart, Gideon attempted to apologize. "I'm sorry, Jon. I definitely wasn't expecting anything like this."

As Jon listened to Gideon's words, he wasn't upset or angry, but instead felt sorrow. He was sorry his friends had to be a part of something he felt was between him and a madman. "Please, Gideon. No apologies. I was talking to your new pastor earlier at the church and he was right. God always shines his light and that light for me is my family. They still live in my heart and my thoughts, and no matter how hard he tries, Hayden can never take that away from me."

Gideon didn't say anything, but listening to Jon, it almost sounded as though he was contemplating something unthinkable. "Jon, are you all right? There is no new pastor. That church has been closed for years. The town council passed a resolution to take that old church down before it falls down and kills somebody."

Hearing those words, Jon thought back to what the pastor said. He came from a place where dreams and nightmares collide. The unique sounding pastor seemed to be a dream, but Jon was beginning to live the end of his nightmare.

Thinking about the conversation with Jeremiah, Jon smiled as the thought of his family filled his thoughts. "Yes, Gideon. For the first time in a long time, I'm okay."

Not wanting to talk anymore, Jon slid himself away from the hole and over to the door. Peeking out into the street, Jon took inventory of his ammo and guns as he took a quick count of Hayden's remaining men. As he sat quietly, he reached into his pocket and pulled out the letter given to him by Doc Micah and read it over again. As he thought about the man he called Pa, tears started to form as he spoke to himself. "I'm sorry, Pa. I could never be like you. You were right all along. Violence just brings more violence and it never ends."

After a few moments of thought, Jon reached into another pocket and pulled out the necklace that belonged to Father Andres. In studying the necklace, he thought about the lessons taught by the padre then apologized to God. "I spoke to you many times, Lord. If you spoke back, you did it in a way I just couldn't understand, and for that, I am truly sorry."

While Jon was busy coming to terms with his decisions, Jacob had successfully made it to the east end of town. Seeing the old storage barn and its location, his thoughts was to enter in through the rear door, then come out the front behind what was left of Hayden's men. Pulling his gun from his holster, he slowly opened the door and walked in. Looking around, there were several dark corners, but all seemed well. As he crept through the over-sized building, he turned to see Zeke lying on barn floor. Quickly holstering his gun, he ran over and knelt down beside the boy he raised into a man. It was a relief to see Zeke still breathing, but he had lost a lot of blood and Jacob could see the bullet wound was life-threatening.

Trying not to be too loud, Jacob sat Zeke up against the wall and whispered his name. "Zeke." After no response, Jacob lightly slapped his cheek to try and revive him. "Zeke."

Finally there was a flicker as Zeke slowly opened his eyes. With a faded voice, he tried to speak. "Hey, Pops. I knew you'd come."

With a smile on his face, Jacob tried to reassure him. "Listen, Zeke, save your strength. You're gonna be all right, but I have to get you out of here. Okay?"

Shaking his head no, Zeke glanced down at his wound. "No, Pops. I'm not go'n nowhere. We both know that, but its okay."

With Zeke starting to fade, Jacob knew he was running out of time, but he still had one question. "Zeke, who did this?"

With blood starting to spew from his mouth, Zeke smiled as he spoke his last words. "You tell Jon I be way faster than those Texas Ranga boys."

As Jacob held Zeke, he watched what was left of his life fade away as he closed his eyes for the last time. Feeling heartbroken, Jacob looked around and realized Zeke wasn't wearing his sword. It was then Jacob realized he wasn't alone in the barn.

Slowly standing up, he turned to find Colonel Pittman proudly wearing his prized sword and smiling. "Well, well. If it isn't my old friend, Jacob Jabari. I've been waiting a long time for this day and here we are."

Trying to keep his rage from taking over, Jacob stayed calm in the wake of the coming storm. "I see you know my name. It's always a good thing to know the name of the man who kills you."

With a sparkle in his eyes and arrogance on his breath, the colonel smiled. "Jacob, I'm certainly glad you feel that way because I didn't wait all these years just to be deprived of my prize. You see, after the war, I started hearing about a so-called Yankee hero who raided a Confederate camp and generated maximum destruction with the utilization of just a few men. And then an old cattle baron friend of mine gave me your name."

After watching Zeke die, Jacob was in no mood for talk, but felt a need to respond to the colonel's remarks. "Colonel, I never meant for my exploits to be glorified, but it was my intention to make sure everyone knew exactly what kind of man you were. Just a no-good hateful coward who deserved everything you received."

Listening to Jacob's words and thinking back to that dreadful night enraged the colonel as his voice became raised. "You attacked my camp and my men without mercy, held me down, and used my own sword to carve that abomination into my body. But that wasn't good enough. No, you had to take my balls and deprive me of my future offspring. My wife and I had plans for a son. A son who would have done his father proud. A son who would have grown to possibly fight another war with my proud name leading the way. But I became a monster in the eyes of my own wife. She refused to lay with me. She couldn't even look me in my eyes or feel any love for me. And when she took sick, she just gave up and died because she didn't have the guts to leave me. You did this to me. You and that pathetic lump of a rotting corpse who stole my sword. Every time you stuck that sword into my body, I swore to the all mighty God above that I would hunt you down and kill you. And now here we are."

Having absolutely no sympathy for his enemy, Jacob listened to the pathetic words of the colonel, but kept his anger in check. Speaking in a slow, calm voice, he offered his last words. "Colonel, your arrogance is only second to your ignorance."

Feeling their conversation had reached its end, Jacob stared at the colonel as Colonel Pittman stared back with a burning hatred in his heart. With each man staring the other down, neither knew just how fast the other was. But there was no more waiting. With speed the likes which no man has ever seen, Colonel Pittman withdrew his gun and fired. But it was of no consequence. Jacob's draw was so fast, the colonel's naked eye never saw it coming. By the time Colonel Pittman fired his gun, Jacob's bullet was already entering dead center of the colonel's stomach.

As Colonel Pittman slowly dropped to his knees, he fired another harmless shot at the ground, then fell backward. With blood gushing out, the colonel was now at the mercy of his greatest foe. As Colonel Pittman glanced up, Jacob was now peering down at him. "Just like you did to Zeke, I shot you exactly where I wanted, except I'm not going to give you the time to say your peace." Pointing his gun at Colonel Pittman's head, Jacob slowly pulled the hammer back.

Staring death in the eyes, Colonel Pittman could do nothing but smile. "Well done, Jacob. You've proven to be my greatest challenge."

As Colonel Pittman closed his eyes, Jacob pulled the trigger and ended his life.

With the killing of Colonel Pittman, one of Hayden's horsemen was aroused. As he climbed down from his horse to investigate the gunshots, he made his way to the barn and slowly opened the door where Jacob was already waiting. Utilizing Colonel Pittman's sword, Jacob quietly pulled the man inside and stabbed him through and through. With a heavy heart, Jacob took a few minutes to retreat back to Zeke's body and hold him in remembrance of all they had been through.

While Jacob was busy grieving the loss of his adopted son, Jon was preparing for his final resolution with Zachariah Hayden and his men. Before making his final stand, he closed his eyes and pictured Emily and the children. While reminiscing about happier times, he let out a deep sigh and smiled. After his brief heart felt moment, he stood up and asked Gideon a final question. Raising his voice so Gideon could hear, Jon blurted out his words. "Gideon, answer me this. Does anyone know where the love of God goes when there's nothing left to do but die?"

Thinking about what Jon was asking, Gideon realized what he was about to do. But before he could react, Jon kicked open the door and walked out into the middle of the street. With his six-shooter in one hand and his sawed-off shotgun in the other, he made his intentions quite clear. Firing everything he had, Jon started his trek toward the last of Hayden's men and the deadly Gatling gun. With Jubal's wounds taking their toll and Kenna trying desperately to keep Rayna alive, Gideon attempted to stand in order to get to the door and help Jon. Hobbling to the door with his loaded rifle, Gideon made his exit and unloaded everything he had as Jon made his way up the middle of the street. As the Gatling gun peppered the street with bullets, the remainder of Hayden's men joined in. With Jon working his way up the middle of the street, Gideon chose a path along the storefronts working his way up the south side. With each man firing with precision and accuracy, the battle continued with bullets coming from every direction.

Hearing the battle rage on, Jacob made his exit and saw the devastation taking place. Only armed with his six-shooter, he faced off against several of Hayden's men who realized he had somehow got behind them. Realizing their vulnerability, they turned and attempted to keep Jacob from getting to the Gatling gun. Like two dominating forces opposing each other, Jon and Gideon pushed forward against insurmountable odds as Jacob battled his way from the opposite direction. Emptying his six-shooter and then his shot gun, Jon struck several of Hayden's men, but with the devastating array of bullets being fired back, he was shot several times. With the Gatling gun ripping holes in his body, Jon moved forward, twisting and turning and moving side to side, picking up any weapon he could find.

Trying to give Jon a fighting chance, Gideon moved from cover to cover as he killed more of Hayden's men, but not before taking another bullet to his leg. Falling to the ground, he quickly dragged himself to cover as he continued to fire in the direction of the Gatling gun. With Gideon pinned down, Jon was left to his fate. With only a few men left along with the Gatling gun, Jon was riddled with bullets and couldn't go anymore. While Jon fought to stay standing, Jacob eliminated the rest of Hayden's horsemen, then took aim at the final man. Realizing everyone else was dead, the man who controlled the Gatling gun turned just in time to take a bullet to the face.

With Hayden's men dead along with Colonel Pittman, the streets of Presidio were quiet as Jacob ran over to Jon, who was now kneeling on the ground. With Jon's body perforated with bullets, Jacob tried to think of a way to help, but it was too late. Jon had no purpose left. Thinking about his journey's end, he welcomed the familiar voice of his old friend Jacob. "It's over, Jon. It's all over."

But before Jon could respond, Zachariah Hayden came walking up from behind with a gun pointed directly at Jon's head. With his arrogance at its peak, Zachariah smiled as he sang a demented tune. "One, two, I see you. Three, four, you're such a bore. Five, six, I'm full of tricks. Seven, eight, you'll never escape. Nine, ten, you're dead again."

Still holding on to Jon, Jacob could do nothing but watch Hayden play out his sick, sadistic game.

Flipping his gun from one hand to another, Zachariah smiled as he pulled the hammer back. "It didn't have to be like this, Ranger Mason. All I wanted was the necklace, which you deemed worthless."

Even with his wounds, Jon was still able to utilize his brain to buy some time. With his voice starting to quiver and fade, he could barely lift his head as he smiled. "You were right, Hayden. The necklace was the key. It led me to the final piece of the puzzle. In your wildest dreams, you could never imagine. Such a beautiful story and it was right in front of me the whole time, but you'll never find it."

Intrigued by Jon's words, Zachariah's curiosity got the best of him. "I'm going kill you, Ranger, and afterward, I'm going to snatch that necklace from your dead body. Then, I'm going to happily claim what is rightfully mine."

Feeling more confident than ever, Zachariah decided to push a little further. "So, what is it about that equation keeps me from claiming one of the most legendary treasures ever to have existed?"

Pointing at Zachariah, Jon slowly raised his arm. "Come closer."

Convinced nothing could happen, Zachariah bent down in order to hear what Jon had to say. With a smile on his face and his last bit of energy, Jon flicked his wrist as a small derringer snapped out from beneath his sleeve and shot Zachariah Hayden between his eyes. The point-blank shot blew his brains out of the back of his head as Hayden dropped to the ground dead.

Seeing Zachariah's brains splattered all over the ground, Jacob was more than impressed. "I see my advice of more than one gun didn't go to waste."

Not hearing a sarcastic response, Jacob turned his attention back to Jon. But with his eyes closed, Jon's thoughts faded away.

Over the next few days, Belle was busy patching everyone up as Presidio slowly got back to being the township it used to be. The banks were open for business and shop owners welcomed their customers with open arms. The money was flowing as customers scurried to buy much-needed supplies. With the worst of days behind them, the parents let their children dominate the streets again as they ran up and down playing and laughing.

With Rayna in bed resting, Kenna made his way to the bar where Gideon and Jubal were waiting with drinks. Placing a fancy Stetson hat down on the bar, Kenna picked his drink up and gulped it down. "Jubal, I do believe I promised you a nice hat when this was all over, and I always make good on my word."

With a worried look on his face, Jubal glanced down at the hat, then back up at Kenna. "Well dang, Mr. James, sir. That's mighty kind of you, but that looks like the hat that devil Hayden wore."

Smiling from ear to ear, Kenna ordered another round of drinks. "Well, Jubal, you're right. It wasn't easy, but I was able to make a deal with Mr. Orville. He's a pretty tough negotiator, but I was able to wear him down."

With his concerns starting to disappear, Jubal removed his old, dusty, dingy Confederate hat and slowly placed it down on the bar. Thinking respectful thoughts of his family, he picked up the Stetson and placed it on his head. "Well, I reck'n it's time to leave the past in the past."

Smiling and laughing, Gideon raised his glass for a toast. "Jubal, you look damn good. Here's to better times."

With the whiskey flowing, the Lucy Goosy was doing quite well as Lita was running from one end of the bar to the other. Just then, the saloon doors opened and in walked Jacob. Taking one look at Jubal, he walked over and poured himself a drink and smiled. "Jubal, you're looking mighty important. Glad to see that hat is being put to good use."

Looking around the room, Jacob shook his head with pride. "Gideon, congratulations. Looks like your town is recovering just fine."

Looking around the room, Gideon smiled, but inside his heart was mourning. "Yeah, Presidio took on much damage and a lot of people died for it, but in the end I guess you're right. Time doesn't stand still for no man and we have to move on."

By now, Lita had gotten some of her saloon girls to take over so she could join her friends. As she poured one last round of drinks, she poured two extra, then raised her glass. "To the loved ones we've lost. May their souls never be forgotten."

After drinking down their liquor, Gideon quietly placed his glass down on the bar next to the two extra glasses. "I guess it's about that time. Is everybody ready?" Turning to face the door, one by one, the friends walked out.

The bar stayed open, but many of the patrons had filtered out in order to follow the heroes to their destination. Most of the businesses had temporarily closed while many of the townspeople made their way down to the end of town where Orville was waiting at the entrance of Presidio's cemetery. Since Orville was the town's undertaker, he was also the closest thing they had to a priest. With caskets lying in two side-by-side graves, the townspeople looked on as the funeral services started. While Orville gave a makeshift sermon, Presidio's heroes listened while praying for answers to why such good men had to die at the hands of a maniac.

After all the words were spoken, Jacob leaned forward and placed the sword on top of Zeke's casket. Turning to Gideon, he shook Gideon's hand. "Well, Harvey and the boys are waiting for me. We still have a thousand head of cattle to get to market."

Smiling at Jacob, Gideon was happy on the outside but sad on the inside. "Jacob, thank you. I fear things would have turned out somewhat different if you hadn't helped us. God, forgive me, I'm so sorry about Zeke."

Feeling a bit relieved, Jacob looked back at Zeke's grave. "It saddens me to say, but some people are just better off dead. Zeke had a lot of anger inside and he could never quite deal with it. At least now there's some comfort in knowing he's at peace. As for Jon, he died doing what he did best: killing people. There's only one outcome for a man like that."

Glancing over to the grave next to Zeke, Jacob read the tombstone. It had just one word: Justice. "I see you picked something befitting for our friend."

Turning his attention to the grave, Gideon smiled. "Yes. I thought so to. That's how he lived his life and that's how I wanted the people of Presidio to remember him."

Placing flowers at the foot of both the graves, Lita began to cry. After a few moments of trying to console her, Gideon asked Jubal and Kenna to escort her back to the Lucy Goosy. After praying a silent prayer over the graves, Gideon turned to walk Jacob to his horse. "So, besides running cattle and horses, what's next for you?"

With a gleam in his eye and a smile from ear to ear, Jacob had thoughts of younger days. "Oh, some years ago I met a young señorita down Mexico. Long story short, she saved my life and I've always had that itch to go back. After this last drive, I think I'll wonder across the border and maybe see how she's doing."

As they arrived at Jacob's horse, Gideon gave a smile and once again the two men shook hands. "Thanks again, Jacob. For everything. And tell Harvey and the boys to stop by and visit once in a while."

Climbing up on his horse, Jacob took a deep breath and took a suspicious glance around town. "I'll give them the invite, but I'm guessing you won't be needing our help anytime soon. Seems to me you have a guardian angel watching over Presidio."

After watching Jacob ride away, Gideon walked over to the Lucy Goosy. When he arrived, Lita had a hug and a drink waiting for him. While Gideon was receiving his affection, Jubal and Kenna stood at the bar admiring Jubal's new hat. Suddenly, the saloon doors swung open and in walked Harley Daniels. As he looked around the room, his eyes found their way to Gideon. With his usual mean look hanging off his face, he pulled his drooping gun belt up and walked toward the bar. Not wanting any trouble, Gideon attempted to give a pleasant smile and greeted the angry-looking farmer. "Hey, Harley. How are you?"

Looking meaner than a hungry wolf, Harley looked Gideon up and down, then turned his attentions to Lita. But before he could speak, Lita posted her warning. "Now, you listen here, Harley. It's been a difficult day, so I don't need any trouble out of you."

Not really caring what Lita had to say, Harley slapped some money down on the counter and placed his order. "Gimme a bottle. And not that horse piss you sell dem good for nutt'n drifters and cow hands that slitha through here."

Not expecting the strange demand, Lita thought for a moment, then reached down beneath the bar and pulled out a fresh bottle of high-grade whiskey. After placing it on the bar, Harley snatched the bottle then turned to face Gideon. "Sheriff, you probably think I have issues, but I knowed a good man when I see'em. You and dem there friends of yers put ya'll lives on the line for this here town, so I'm here to tell ya thank'ya."

After handing the bottle of liquor to Gideon, Harley held out his hand in friendship. After cautiously shaking the hand of the man who had no quarrels of expressing his hatred, Gideon thanked Harley for the gift. "Well, damn, Harley. That's mighty kind of you. Why don't you stay and have a drink with us?"

With a few of his teeth missing, Harley gave a half-smile. I thank ya kindly fer the hospitality, but I have work to get to. Sheriff, you stop by anytime an me and my misses will fix you up some cow an grits."

After Harley walked out, everyone just looked around at each other and laughed. Afterward, Lita was the first to get her words out. "Well, I'll be. Doesn't that just beat all? Harley Daniels buying the first black sheriff of Texas one of my finest bottles of whiskey and then inviting him to sit down and have a meal together."

After gulping down what was left in his glass, Jubal set his sights on Gideon's gifted bottle. "Well, I guess you just can't rule anything out nowadays. Come on, Gideon, don't be stingy. Open her up so we can all get a taste."

After a few more laughs, it was time for Kenna to say his good-byes. "Gideon, I'd like to say it's been fun, but I can't. So I'll just say it's been damn interesting. I'm headed up Nebraska way to take Brice back to his folks. He should be okay since he isn't a threat anymore. Maybe along the way we can work out some of that hatred he seems to have for me." After one last drink, Kenna gave Lita a hug and a kiss, then turned to Jubal and shook his hand. "Jubal, you're a damn fine man and one hell of a friend."

With the bar getting more crowded by the hour, Lita went back to helping with the customers while Jubal left to make rounds around town. Walking out the door, Gideon glanced over at Brice, who was sitting in a wagon that was hitched and ready to go. As he turned to face Kenna, he shook his hand, then handed him the half-bottle of liquor. "Here, take this. It may help to calm the beast."

Accepting the bottle, Kenna smiled, then gave Gideon a hug. "We seem to make it through some of the toughest situations, but I have a feeling our luck may run out one day. But until that time, you can always count on me to come running if you need me. By the way, when Rayna is well enough to ride, she's going to meet me in California. Who knows, there may be another wedding in the works."

Feeling the gratitude, Gideon nodded his head and said his good-byes. "You're a good friend, Kenna, and I love you like a brother. And I'll make sure Rayna gets the best care. Take good care of yourself and don't be a stranger."

Gideon took a few minutes and watched his friend as he guided the loaded wagon out of town. Looking around town at the people conducting their everyday business, Gideon glanced down at his badge and shook his head with a smile, knowing there would be many more adventures for the town of Presidio.

After taking in the day's events, Gideon walked over to Belle's office to wrap up some unpleasant business. When he arrived, she was at her desk doing some unfortunate paperwork. Filled with emotions, Belle stood up and walked around her desk to give Gideon a hug. "Gideon, I'm so sorry. I hope you're not disappointed that I wasn't at the funeral. I just couldn't bear to stand there and watch the caskets being lowered into the ground. And besides, there wasn't anyone available to tend to Rayna."

With his usual charm, Gideon understood as he held on to the saddened doctor. "Belle, don't worry about that. We all know you've had your hands full for the past few days. You have to be exhausted."

Looking down at the paper Belle had in her hand, Gideon's heart sank. "Is that it?"

Feeling a bit upset, Belle handed the paper to Gideon. "Yes, that's it. One certified certificate of death for Jon Mason."

Taking the certificate from Belle, Gideon took a minute to look it over. "Since there's no next of kin, I just have to forward the information to the governor's office. So, how is your guest doing?"

Turning to sit back down, Belle pushed out a smile. "Oh, she's a real hoot. She's been asking for you. Go take a peek."

Anxious to see Rayna, Gideon walked into the back room and found her wide awake. "Hey, how are you feeling?"

Feeling a bit frustrated and embarrassed, Rayna gave her answer. "Never thought I would be shot with a Gatling gun. I feel like I've been run over by one of those locomotives. My God, I don't know how you boys made it through that damn war. I could really use a whiskey, but Doc seems to be a Ms. Goody Two Shoes and won't give me any."

Letting out a small laugh, Gideon took a seat beside the bed. "Well, I wouldn't be too hard on Doc Belle. She did take the time to save your life. Besides, I just happen to have a little snip in my pocket."

Reaching into the pocket of his jacket, Gideon pulled out a small flask and handed it to Rayna. "You just never know when an emergency like this might pop up."

With some much-needed relief, Rayna was happy to take a swig of the magic elixir. "Damn, that's good stuff. I'm guessing Kenna is gone by now?"

After taking a drink for himself, Gideon tucked the flask back into his pocket. "He just left a little while ago. He's dropping Brice off with his folks, then moving onto California. He says you're supposed to meet him there."

Having all smiles on her face, Rayna's voice became giddy. "As fast as I can get out of this bed, I'm gonna hop a train and be on my way. You know I love that man, Gideon, but he can really pluck my last nerve someth'n awful."

Taking Rayna by her hand, Gideon leaned over and gave her a kiss on the cheek. "Listen to what Belle tells you and get well soon. I'll be back to visit and if she tells me you've been good, I'll make sure I bring my little flask filled with that magical goodness."

As Gideon got up to leave, Rayna had some consoling words for her friend. "Gideon, I'm really sorry about your friend Jon."

With his grief starting to fade, Gideon gave a small thank-you smile. "Don't you worry about me. You just concentrate on healing and getting better."

With Jon's death certificate in his hand, Gideon left out and made his way to the post office to make his notifications. After taking care of his brief business, he walked back to his office where Jubal was waiting. Jubal had just made a fresh pot of coffee and could see by the look on his face Gideon could use a stiff cup. With an inquiring look, Jubal had an idea of what was bothering Gideon, but decided to ask the question anyway. "Is it done?"

Gladly accepting the coffee from Jubal, Gideon took a seat at his desk. "Yes. Just came from the post office. Didn't really feel good about it. I guess I'm still in a bit of a shock that we actually have to do something like this."

Still feeling mournful but needing to change the subject, Gideon scolded Jubal for being up and walking around. "Jubal, Belle said you need to stay off that leg for a few days, and besides, didn't she give you some crutches to use?"

Realizing Gideon was just being a concerned friend, Jubal responded in his usual way of looking at life. "Well, them there crutches are for the lame, and besides, you know I can't sit still for more than a few minutes. You just never know what sidewinder will come wondering into town and cause us grief."

Shaking his head as he took a sip of his coffee, Gideon gave a small grin. "Well, let's hope that all the sidewinders got the message to stay out of our little town." Raising his cup of coffee, Gideon gave a hopeful toast. "Here's to some peace and quiet. We definitely earned it."

As days turned into weeks, which turned into months, Gideon got his wish as Presidio remained quiet and peaceful. Except for the locals who drank too much, cow hands, and card cheats, the town of Presidio remained free of any serious outlaws.

It had been two months since the dramatic showdown and Rayna's wounds had finally healed enough for her to travel. Anxious to catch her train, she came busting through the saloon doors looking for Gideon. Seeing Gideon at the bar talking to Lita, she pranced over and slammed her hand down on the counter. "Well, howdy, ya'll. I gotta say, I love Belle, but damn, she can be a hard woman. Lita, I need me a whiskey and I need it fast. Set us up, darl'n."

Happy to see Rayna in good spirits, Lita pulled out a fresh bottle and poured everyone a drink. As the three shared some laughs, Jubal came hobbling in. All of his wounds were healed, but he was still walking with a bit of a limp. "Looks like I'm just in time for the party."

The Lucy Goosy was filled with customers and the town of Presidio flourished as the money flowed. Rayna was ecstatic to finally be up and walking around, but it was time to say good-bye. Giving Lita and Jubal big hugs, she then turned her attention to Gideon. "Well, cowboy, I guess this is it. Kenna has a ticket waiting for me up in San Antonio, so I gotta get my cute little derriere mov'n along."

Placing his half-empty glass of whiskey down on the bar, Gideon took a deep breath. "Rayna, you're the best. Thank you for all your help. I didn't expect things to turn out the way they did, but I'm glad you and Kenna are okay."

Happy about his friends full recovery but sorry to see her go, Gideon escorting Rayna from the bar where Thomas had her horse saddled and waiting for her. After all the hugs and kisses, she hopped up on her horse and made her exit out of town as she hooted and hollered all the way. Watching Rayna ride out gave Gideon a sense of emptiness, but in his heart he was happy knowing she was headed for Kenna.

Just when Gideon was about to turn and walk back into the bar, two of Molly's girls came walking by. Laughing and giggling, they greeted Gideon with their flirtatious talk. "Hey, Sheriff, nice day to pay us a visit. Why don't you stop by later so we can treat you right?"

Tipping his hat and smiling, Gideon didn't mind the flirting as the two women continued to eyeball their prey. "Well, ladies, that's a mighty tempting offer, but I'm sure somehow, someway, Hinklemeyer would catch wind of it and that would put me in a bit of hot water with the mayor, not to mention Lita."

As the two women twisted and turned their bodies like little school girls, they admired Gideon for his humbleness. While turning to walk away, one of the women turned back around to express their concerns. "Well, Sheriff, if you don't feel the need to visit us for personal reasons, you may want to walk over and help Ms. Molly out. She has her hands full with an unruly customer, if you know what I mean."

Watching the two women walk away, Gideon took a long, deep breath, then walked over to his office. As he walked in, Jubal could tell something was wrong. "You okay, Gideon?"

Like a strong wind, Gideon blew past Jubal and walked into the back room. When he came back out, he was carrying a small black leather bag by his side. "Trouble at Molly's. Hold the fort, Jubal. I'm probably going to be a while."

As Gideon hastily made his way over to Molly's place, he tipped his hat and greeted people, but avoided having any conversations. When he arrived, he could tell Molly was trying to exercise her last bit of patience. "Gideon, you better get up there and get'em before he plucks my last nerve. I swear that man is just like his pa. Straight as an arrow and stubborn as a damn mule stuck in mud. And he stinks. He won't let any of us giv'em a bath. He smells like death dumped him into a pile of cow dung, then dried him out inside a dang outhouse. He won't eat. He's wasting away to noth'n. And on top of everything else, he keeps drinking all my damn good whiskey."

With a smile on his face, Gideon temporarily placed his bag down. "Don't mind if I do."

After Gideon helped himself to a glass of liquid courage, Molly continued her loud reasoning. "It's been two months and I can't be have'en no man in my room for that long without hav'n some sex. Could bring a bad name to my whore house. Besides that, women like me aren't known for keeping our mouths shut. We like to wrap our lips around certain things. Catch what I'm say'n, big boy?"

Shaking his head while trying not to blush, Gideon was finally able to respond to Molly's comments. "Molly, you're the only person who could help me pull this off and I really appreciate you and your girls for doing me this one favor."

Knowing she had Gideon by his pride, Molly decided to take advantage and get her fun on. Swaying her hips from side to side, she stepped up and wrapped her arms around Gideon's shoulders. With her delicate caress and soft voice, Molly stood on her toes and whispered into Gideon's ear. "Lita is a fine woman, but sometimes a man like you needs to scratch that itch with someone a little more wild and fun, so just know that you owe me big time and I may come'a collect'n one day."

Feeling the strain of the intense moment, Gideon quickly gave Molly a kiss on the cheek. "You keep trying, Molly, 'cause one day I may call your bluff. Now, excuse me while I go take care of your problem."

Picking up his bag, Gideon walked up the steps and headed for Molly's bedroom. Before he opened the door, he could hear some of the other customers enjoying their bedroom time as he took a deep breath. When he opened the door and walked in, his nose got a whiff of what Molly was talking about. "You may not be dead, but you sure do smell like you are."

Lying in Molly's bed with a half-empty bottle in his hand wearing urine-stained clothing was what was left of a broken Jon Mason. Lifting his head up to briefly look at Gideon, Jon flopped back down because he had nothing to say. But Gideon wasn't there to sympathize. Pulling up a chair, he began his reproach. "What the hell, Jon? You got what you wanted. Hayden's dead and the people of Presidio can sleep knowing you gave your life for them."

Still not wanting to talk, Jon sat up and took a swig from his bottle as Gideon watched with disgust. "I gotta say it, Jon. You are one lucky bastard. Only guy I know who is blessed by God but works for the devil. You single-handedly faced down a Gatling gun and took nine bullets, none of which hit any organs or major arteries. By every sense of the word, you should be dead, but you're not."

Hearing Gideon talk about death, Jon finally responded with a raised voice. "You should've just let me die. Why didn't you just let me die? Why, Gideon?"

Taking a moment to look around, Gideon tried to stay calm. "Jon, you're drunk, so I understand you're not thinking straight. You can't stay here forever, which means sooner or later, you're gonna have to walk out that door. And if you're not aware of the fact, dead man or not, you will still have a price on your head."

Swinging his free hand around in the air while speaking in a slurred voice, Jon lashed out with words of defiance. "Well, maybe you're not aware of the fact, but I just don't give a damn. Now, get the hell out."

Taking a few moments to think about Jon and his present condition, Gideon reached into his black bag and pulled out the Bowie knife that belonged to Gunny. "Here, take this. I think Gunny would have wanted you to have it. You remember Gunny, don't you? Texas Ranger? Best of the best? Never back down from a fight? One town, one Ranger? Is any of this sounding familiar to you?"

Once again, Jon had no words as he watched the ceiling spin around. The only interest he had was getting to the bottom of the bottle in his hand and not throwing it back up.

Being unable to reason with a drunken man, Gideon placed the knife on the table beside the bed. Exhaling his frustration as he got up, he took one last look at Jon, then walked out.

Feeling even worse than he did before Gideon's visit, Jon took a long guzzle, then slouched back down in bed. Going over the conversation in his mind, Jon thought about Gideon's words as they swirled around in his thoughts. With his emotions way out of balance, Jon mustered up enough strength to roll over and grab the knife from the bedside table. Reminiscing about his friend Gunny and his unforgettable way of looking at life, the tears started to fall. Starting to feel very sick from the whiskey, Jon sat up on the edge of the bed and attempted to dry his eyes, but the tears kept coming. Glancing down at the knife, Jon's blurry vision was finally able to focus in on the inscription. *Best of the best, Texas Rangers*. Feeling angrier as the seconds ticked away, Jon through the nearly empty bottle of whiskey against the wall.

Hearing the glass shatter from downstairs, Molly came running up to check on Jon. When she walked in, she saw the mess on the floor and became livid. With her anger reaching its max, she began her tirade. "Now, you listen hear, you no-good backwards ass. I work very hard at my trade and I run one of the classiest whore houses in this territory, and you have no right to destroy my belongings. Especially with my best whiskey."

With her hand on her hips and shaking her head, Molly became even more insulting. "Just look at you. I lost count how many times you done pissed yourself. You've been hiding in here like a coward for two months and beating yourself up with your self-pity and for what?"

Jon's focus was in and out and he could hear the words, but just didn't care to listen. As he swayed back and forth, his thought process was shaky at best. Desperately trying to get through to him, Molly sat down and continued in a more calming voice. "Listen, Jon. I understand you've been through a lot. Probably more than anybody I know, but you gotta find strength. Not a whole lot of people know this about me, but I was married once. Yeah, we lived back east. I loved that man with all my heart. He was a business man and worked hard like every other business man did. We had it all. Big house, money, prestige, high society friends. We lived a great life. Parties and get-togethers, and every now and then he would take me on a romantic picnic."

Momentarily glancing up into the air, Molly continued to reminisce. "Yeah, life was good to us. We even talked about having children someday. And then came the bad business dealings. Investments went belly up and the bank took it all. After several long talks and promising each other we would be okay, that stupid son of a bitch took our last bit of change and went to the saloon and got stone drunk. After his silly ass drank down a bottle of cheap poison, he stole a shotgun from behind the bar and stumbled out into the woods. That fool blew his dang brains out. They found him the next day half-eaten from the buzzards."

After listening to Molly's downfall, Jon became a little more attentive to what Molly was saying, but he remained silent as she spoke her mind. "There I was. Alone with no idea how I was gonna survive. And those so-called friends I mentioned earlier, well, they turned out to be a bunch of phonies. They turned their backs faster than a cheating card shark taking you broke. Boy, you talk about some cold-hearted weasels. I wound up selling the only possessions I had, which was my jewelry. I sold my entire wardrobe and just kept the clothes on my back. I bought a one-way ticket west and arrived in a little hole called Shackelford, Texas. I had dreams, but I couldn't do anything until I got a job. Well, wouldn't you know it? The only skill set I had was lying on my back. So what the hell, it was time to forget about where I came from and concentrate on where I was going, so I landed a job in the local saloon. Now, listen. Come to find out, I had another skill set I didn't realize I had. Listening to my husband all those years conduct his business ventures gave me all I needed. The saloon I worked in was run piss-poor by a local swine named Willie Walker. Just another dirty old man, but he took one look at me and fell in love. Problem was, he was so stupid, he'd be lucky to dress himself in the morning. Anyway, after a while of defending myself against his advances, I took inventory of what he had and explained to him how much he was losing by not becoming more organized. And that was it. I got off my back and became management. All that I learned from my husband started to kick in and within a year we were the biggest saloon in town with the best whores available. I handled the books and I did all the hiring. Old man Walker ran the bar side and I ran the whores. Couple years later, Mr. Walker died and I just didn't have the taste to hang around anymore. By then, I had made my own investments, so once again, I found myself moving in order to make a better life for myself. After the war, I wound up here in Presidio."

After listening to Molly's story, Jon was still silent, but he felt something he hadn't felt in a long time: compassion and sympathy. Being done with her story, Molly got up with the hopes her words penetrated Jon's thoughts. Looking down at Jon, who was now squirming in his own sorrow, Molly had some last words. "Jon, I didn't know Emily personally, but just hearing people talk about her, she seemed to be a mighty fine woman. Strong willed. If she walked through this door right now and saw you like this, what'ya think her thoughts would be?"

After Molly left, Jon fell back down into his bed and closed his eyes as he tried to forget about all the sadness.

The next morning before sunrise, Molly came frantically knocking at Gideon's door. Half-asleep and wearing just a pair of pants, Gideon opened his door to find an anxious Molly staring back. Running her eyes up and down Gideon's body, Molly had to remind herself why she was there. "Jon's asking for you and he won't tell me why."

Rubbing the sleep from his eyes, Gideon threw on the rest of his clothes and accompanied Molly back to her place. It was still dark and all the businesses were closed with nobody around except the crickets. When Gideon arrived, Molly tended to business while Gideon walked upstairs to talk with Jon. When Gideon walked in, he could see Jon was a mess.

With no clothes on and crying, Jon was at the window peering out into the darkness. "I need you, Gideon. I need you to help me over to Mr. Chungs."

Not knowing why but eagerly willing to help, Gideon helped Jon put his filthy clothes back on. Jon could barely walk, so working as a team, Gideon and Molly carried him over to Chungs bath house. Once there, Gideon had to knock several times in order for Mr. Chung to finally get to the door and open it. Still being half-asleep and upset, Mr. Chung hastily opened the door and started venting his anger in his native language. With Mr. Chung upset and cussing, Gideon and Molly pushed their way through the doorway with Jon and sat him down in the nearest chair.

Standing up straight, it was time for Gideon to explain. "Mr. Chung, please forgive our early morning intrusion. I'm not quite sure why we're here, but if you can just be patient, I'm sure my friend here can explain."

Feeling very weak, Jon reached into his pocket and pulled out the jade coin he had saved from his previous visit and handed to Mr. Chung.

Feeling a bit calmer, Mr. Chung momentarily studied the coin, then turned his attention to Gideon. "Tomorrow morning, you come back."

With a little uncertainty but still not knowing what else to do, Gideon reluctantly agreed.

After the departure of Gideon and Molly, Mr. Chung went to work. Each girl had their own coin, so he knew the coin had come from Jinjing. Wasting no time, Mr. Chung gathered some of his workers and carried Jon into one of the back rooms. He then gathered some wild herb and spices and combined them into a pot and added some water. After letting the mix simmer, he looked around to make sure nobody was looking, then proceeded to pull a small burlap bag out of a hidden hole in the floorboard. Inside was a long-forgotten root only grown in a certain province of China. After cutting a small piece, he placed it into the pot and watched as a greenish blue smoke began to form. Just a few more minutes and it was ready.

Wasting no time, Mr. Chung force fed the liquid substance to Jon. Using all of the strength he had left, Jon struggled to sit up as he drank down the mysterious potion. Cringing his face, he attempted to push Mr. Chung's hand away, but Mr. Chung was persistent. He continued to force Jon to drink it all. Afterward, Jon laid back as the awful taste dominated his taste buds.

"My God, if I'm not dead, please, kill me now." Coughing and gagging, Jon tried to spit the bad taste out, but it was too late. The liquid had coated the inside of his mouth and there was no getting away from the aftertaste. Still cringing and coughing, Jon glanced up at Mr. Chung. "Can I at least get a swig of whiskey, please?"

While Jon was busy trying to cope with the bad flavor, Mr. Chung pulled the coin out and held it up for Jon to see. "Where you get coin? You tell me now."

Attempting once again to hold himself up, Jon focused his blurry vision on the coin. "Last time I was here, girl named Jinjing. Why do you ask?"

Looking down at the coin, then back up at Jon, Mr. Chung clarified his questioning. "Coin very special. Only for special person. Not everybody get one."

Calling on some of his workers to assist, they helped Jon to his feet and carried him upstairs. Once they escorted him to a room, they laid him on a bed and drew a hot bath. As Jon lay still on the bed, Jinjing, with her silent steps, came walking in to tend to the bath. After adding some perfumes and scents, she moved gracefully around the room and lit candles. From there, it was time to care for Jon and his needs. First thing was first. Helping Jon to his feet, she stripped him of his smelly clothing, then helped him into the hot bath. Then it was her turn. She undid the see through silky garment she was wearing, then joined Jon for his bath.

Feeling Jinjing and her soft hands, Jon inquired about the coin. "I gave the coin to Mr. Chung, but what does it mean?"

Jinjing continued to pour the hot water down Jon's back as she rubbed his aching body with her delicate hands. "They special coin. It mean trouble. It mean you need help. Only for special people."

As Jon began to relax, he slumped down into the bosoms of Jinjing. "So, what's on the coin and why me?"

Still rubbing his body, Jinjing leaned forward to rest her head on Jon's warm back. "Coin say who you are. Dog trustworthy and protective. Horse independent. Must have freedom no matter what cost. You special, Jon Mason. When I look in eyes, I don't see man. I see something I no understand."

The rest of the night was all about healing Jon's body and spiritual being. Jinjing tended to Jon's every need—love, passion, lust, and any other desires that presented themselves. Jinjing used her body, mind, and soul in order to strike a balance within Jon's spirit. Connecting to his emotions, she took away his sadness, hatred, and pain, and replaced them with love, compassion, and humanity.

The next morning just before sun up, Gideon was up and out the door. Not knowing what to expect, he knew the Chinese people were an ancient people and specialized in healing the body and mind. With hopes of success, Gideon carried his black bag with a hat box and boots and hurried over to the Chinese bath house with the anticipation of seeing his old friend. When he arrived, Mr. Chung let him in and guided him upstairs to a back room. Wanting to allow some privacy, Mr. Chung didn't stay and left Gideon to conduct his business.

After knocking on the door several times, Gideon noticed the door wasn't locked and it could be easily pushed open. As Gideon slowly pushed the door open, he could see Jon once again standing by the window and staring out into the eerie darkness. Entering the room, Gideon noticed Jon was wearing a faded white bath gown, which stretched down to the floor. "Jon? You okay?"

Turning around to face Gideon, Jon was clean shaved with his hair combed back and was looking healthier than ever before. "For the first time, Gideon, I'm feeling really good. I won't go into specifics, but something happened last night. I can't really explain it, but I feel strong again. My mind seems to be in line with my body."

Gideon was certainly impressed with the man standing in front of him, but feeling a bit awkward, Gideon smiled as he looked Jon up and down. "Well, I gotta say, you look and sound fantastic, but your wardrobe needs a little work."

Checking himself out, Jon glanced down at the garment that was provided to him. "Yeah, I guess you're right, but it's definitely better than what I was wearing. Guess I'll have to head over to the general store later."

Walking further into the room, Gideon placed his bag and box down and sat on a chair and crossed his arms. "Aren't you forgetting something? You're a dead man. You can't go anywhere."

Looking around the room, Jon walked over to the bed and sat down. "So, you expect me to just stay here forever? I mean, don't get me wrong. Last night was incredible, but I can't stay here."

After a few moments of thought, Gideon reached down and opened his bag of goodies, then pulled out some black clothing and tossed it to Jon. Black pants, beige shirt, and black vest, along with some long underwear and socks. "Here, try these on and tell me what you think."

After getting dressed, Jon walked over to a full-length mirror to see how he looked. "Not bad. I like the black. Very ominous looking. So, now what?"

With a brand-new pair of black leather boots in his hand, Gideon got up and walked over to the mirror. Looking at Jon in the mirror, Gideon began to walk around him while looking him up and down. "You're right. You look ominous. Black suits you well. I like it."

After handing Jon the boots, Gideon walked back over and picked up his box, which had a surprise in it for Jon. As he opened the box, Gideon pulled out a newly purchased black Stetson hat. Smiling with pride, he handed it to Jon. "Wouldn't you know it, Hayden had a wad of money on his person when you parted his eyebrows, so I told Orville I needed it for the town's expenses. He wasn't too happy, but with all the other dead bodies, he wound up making out pretty damn good."

Looking down at the hat, Jon felt grateful. Placing it on his head, he turned to look in the mirror. "Gideon, this is too much. You should've used the money for Presidio."

Taking a few steps back and shaking his head, Gideon once again looked Jon up and down. "Black is beautiful, baby. You look damn good, if I may say so myself."

Jon was feeling good and looking good, but the question still remained. What was he going to do? Alive, he was an outlaw with a price on his head. Dead, he had to live in seclusion, not ever telling people who he was. As Jon pondered the situation, he turned to Gideon. "I'm kind of at a loss of words. Any suggestions on where I go from here?"

With a plan already in the works, Gideon thought for a few moments, then smiled. "Well, while you've been drowning in Molly's booze for the past couple of months, I've been doing a lot of thinking. Normal everyday people feel helpless when the odds are against them or when they're outnumbered and the law isn't around to help. Towns are still being overrun by outlaws. The military has their hands full. Most local sheriffs are either paid to look the other way or just too weak to stop the ruthlessness."

With Jon still glancing into the mirror, Gideon reached down into his bag and pulled out a black mask. "Try this on."

Turning his attentions back to Gideon, Jon looked down at the mask. "Really? Of all things, you want me to wear a mask?"

With a big sigh, Gideon handed the mask to Jon. "Stop your bitch'n and humor me. Just try it on."

Not believing what he was hearing, Jon slowly took the mask and wrapped it around his face. It covered nearly everything from his head down to his eyes. After positioning the mask on his face, Jon placed his hat back on his head, then turned to face the mirror. "I'm not an outlaw, Gideon, but you want me to run around looking like a bank robber?"

With Jon's outfit coming together, so was Gideon's plan. "No, Jon. That mask is going to represent justice. You can be the perfect lawman. Make your own rules and answer to nobody. You can be the voice of the oppressed. You can be their hero. I'm not telling you to be an avenging angel, but be the guy you've always dreamed about. The guy that shields people from harm. Be the guy that evil fears. Be the people's champion."

Once again Gideon reached down into his bag of gifts and pulled out a certificate and handed it to Jon. "This is your official death certificate. I sent a copy off to the governor's office yesterday. You are officially dead and there are only a few people who know the truth, and I aim to keep it that way. That mask will hide who you are, but I have something that will let people know you're one of the good guys." Reaching into his pocket, Gideon pulled out Jon's Texas Ranger badge and held it up. "Remember this? I knew the last guy that wore this badge. He wore it with pride and honor."

With some disbelief, Jon reached out and took the badge into his hand as he examined it. "I thought this was gone forever. I remember tossing it to you. I just can't believe you kept it all this time."

Taking a moment to pin the badge to his chest, Jon could feel his pride returning. "A masked man with a badge? What makes you so sure people will believe their eyes?"

Once again Gideon had no shortage of answers. "People will believe what they see. Their hearts will race when they see the mask, but then they'll see the Texas Ranger badge and they'll know you're a friend."

Looking at the entire outfit, Jon was beginning to like the idea, but still had his reservations. "I don't know, Gideon. Half of me is saying yes, while the other half has doubts."

Still looking at himself in the mirror, Jon's sarcasm returned. "So, am I supposed to be a masked crusader without a gun or a horse?"

With a smile on his face, Gideon reached into his bag and pulled out one last thing. "Of course not. I have your gun belt here."

Jon took one look at the gun belt given to him by Jacob and smiled. With his heart starting to beat faster, he wasted no time in strapping it on. Now his outfit was almost complete. The gun that was given to him by Jacob was long gone, but Gideon had one last gift, compliments of Zachariah Hayden's money, which he no longer had use for: a Remington outlaw .45 nickel-plated with a walnut grip. Gideon had Flynn special order it.

Seeing Jon suddenly come alive again with excitement, Gideon had one more trick hiding up his sleeve. Walking over to the window and looking out,

Gideon felt a bit concerned with the arrival of daylight. "Jon, I have one more thing to show you. It's starting to get light out, so we'll have to stick to the back alleyways."

While Gideon and Jon weaved their way in and out of the alleyways, the town of Presidio was starting to wake up. The merchants were opening their doors and getting their goods ready to sell while the townspeople moved about in a frenzy. Eventually Gideon guided Jon to the stables where Thomas was waiting. Seeing the masked man, Thomas was nervous, but took comfort with the presence of Gideon. As Thomas stood staring with his nerves on edge, Gideon gave him some relief. "Thomas, this is my friend, and don't let the mask fool you. He will soon be everybody's friend."

For a moment, Thomas couldn't take his eyes of Jon. There was something familiar about him, but the intimate feeling passed. Glancing at Gideon, Thomas was no longer afraid.

Thomas knew why Gideon had come, so he guided the two men to the back of the stables to a portion of the building rarely used and unknown to the people of Presidio. There were a few old stalls with supplies being stored and an area where Thomas would often sleep. Lighting a lantern, Thomas guided the men over to one of the stalls. Looking on, Jon couldn't believe what he was looking at. Standing tall with her stunning beauty, the elusive white thoroughbred was not only enchanting but captivating. While the beauty was busy casting her provocative spell on Jon, Gideon waited with respect, knowing the two were somehow engaged in an instant connection of their souls.

After a few emotional moments, Jon was finally able to speak. "What happened? How did she get here?"

Taking a deep breath, Gideon glanced at Thomas, then turned back to Jon. "Well, she wandered into town a few days ago. It was early enough so there wasn't anybody around. When she showed up at the stables, Thomas said he nearly fainted. He did a great job getting her inside before anybody saw her, and he's been doing a wonderful job taking care of her. Call me crazy, but I think she's here for you."

Once again Jon gazed at the brilliant white beauty as she moved about and neighed. "Why me? So many men have been chasing her from one end of Texas to the other and nobody has even gotten close to her. Most people think she's a myth. Some people say she's just an old wise tale handed down by the Indians. But here she is. Why me? What makes me so special? She's royalty. She commands dignity and respect. She moves as though she doesn't put forth any effort, and yet she's the fastest horse anybody has ever seen." Reaching out his hand, Jon gently rubbed the Mare's nose.

Feeling the conversation was getting a little more personal, Gideon turned to Thomas. "Please, Thomas, can we have a few minutes?"

Understanding the moment, Thomas smiled as he watched Jon align his thoughts with the legendary mare. "Mister, I don't know who you are, but you surely a lucky man."

As Thomas turned and walked out, Gideon continued the conversation. "Jon, I've stopped trying to question what my eyes can't understand. I'm starting to learn to just go with not being too inquisitive. I once said when everything was said and done, you and I would sit down and have a conversation. But I'm not interested in having that conversation anymore. There's happenings going on which I just can't comprehend and I'm okay with that, but I need you to be the man you were born to be. I need you to do what you were born to do so I can sleep soundly at night knowing I did the right thing by not overstepping my boundaries and discovering things I have no right to know about."

Listening to Gideon, Jon knew he could never explain half the events that happened in the past, so with a smile on his face, he shook Gideon's hand. "So, you think she'll let me ride her?"

Feeling relieved, Gideon took a breath and walked around to the other stall. With curiosity, Jon watched as Gideon pulled out a black leather saddle with saddlebags. "Wouldn't you know it? Our friend Hayden was also kind enough to buy you a nice new saddle equipped with new saddlebags. So, why don't we put your question to the test?"

Not knowing what to expect, the two men cautiously opened the stall and coerced the mare out into the open. Gideon stood by calming the magnificent beast while Jon gently placed the saddle on. Realizing she had accepted the terms, Jon and Gideon took a step back. Jon looked on in awe as Gideon was finally able to ask the question. "So, what are you going to name her?"

With no ideas going through his mind, Jon took a step back and made some observations. "Well, she seems to have a glow about her. Very divine. Like a natural brilliance. But elegant in every way. Just being allowed to be in her presence, I feel humbled."

After a few more seconds of thought, Jon glanced down at the necklace Zachariah Hayden risked everything for. "I think I'll call her Silver."

With such a befitting name, Gideon's thoughts became aroused. "Yes, you are correct. She has an illustrious shine like silver. Jon, I don't think you could be more perfect in your thinking."

Before Jon could test out his theory of riding, Gideon had one more surprise. Walking over to the back door, he opened it up and in walked Jubal. Wearing his Stetson hat, he was very well dressed and looking good. Being happy to see his old friend, Jubal smiled as he approached and shook Jon's hand. "Jon, it's damn good to see you. It's nice to have you back with us because I've missed you someth'n awful. Welcome back from the dead."

Feeling good about Jubal's words, Jon immediately noticed Jubal was wearing Gideon's sheriff badge. "Thanks, Jubal. I see you changed your style a bit. You're wearing some mighty fine-looking clothing. And I see you're also wearing Gideon's badge."

Feeling a bit confused, Jon turned to Gideon. "Did I miss something? Are you not the sheriff anymore?"

Feeling excited, Gideon directed his attention to Jubal and gave Jon the news. "Jon, I present to you Presidio's finest new sheriff."

Once again, Jon shook Jubal's hand and wished him well. Afterward, he turned back to Gideon. "What happened? What about you?"

With a smile and good thoughts, Gideon explained. "Well, I had to submit a full report to the governor's office, and when I say they were happy, I mean they were impressed. They offered me a new position." Pulling back his jacket,

Gideon was sporting a brand new shiny badge. One that was engraved with the words *United States Marshal*.

Jon glanced down at the badge as the shine radiated from it. "I don't know what to say, Gideon."

Instead of words, Jon leaned in and gave Gideon a hug. "Congratulations. You're gonna make the best damn marshal this territory has ever known."

After all the smiles, handshakes, and praise, it was now time to put Silver to the test. Gideon and Jubal swung open the rear stable doors as Jon led her out into a fenced in corral. Once outside, Jon leaned into Silver while taking a few deep breaths. With a gentle voice, he spoke some soft words. "Easy, girl. You're okay. I won't let anyone hurt you. I know you're full of pride, but it's time for you to help me move on. You've been trying to tell me something for a very long time, so let's see where our adventures take us."

With his heart racing, Jon took his time as he slowly mounted his royal steed. Sitting atop, he leaned over and stroked her mane as she proceeded to prance around the corral. With a kick here and there, Silver grunted and puffed but in the end, she knew she belonged to Jon and their spirits were going to be forever intertwined. Watching Jon gallop around the yard, Gideon and Jubal whistled and cheered him on, and after a few minutes of riding, Jon came to a stop and dismounted. Gideon and Jubal could see the exuberance on his face as Jon tried to catch his breath. Leading Silver back into the stable, Jon filled a bucket with some water and let her drink. Turning to his friends, it seemed Jon was filled with exciting energy. Watching Jon come back to life, Gideon momentarily thought about the words of Chief Machakm. He would know Hok'ee when he saw Hok'ee.

There wasn't much more to say, so Jubal said his good-byes and left so the two old friends could have their last words. Half-joking, Jon got back to being Jon. "Well, I guess I'll have to stay one step ahead of the jailer."

With a smile on his face, Gideon let out a small laugh. "I think the jailer will be the least of your worries. By the way, ever since our private war, your Indian friend has been camped outside of town for the past couple of weeks. He's really scaring the hell out of people."

Once again Jon smiled as his sarcasm seeped out. "I wouldn't worry too much about him. He's harmless. He only likes to kill bad people."

With a deep brotherly love for one another, Jon shook Gideon's hand and gave him a hug. "Thanks, Gideon. I'll be around if you need me."

With a sense of pride, Gideon peered into the mask of his friend. "I know you will."

Finally able to come to the realization of his existence, Jon mounted Silver and readied himself to be seen by all. With Jon riding high, Gideon led Silver through the stable and to the front where Thomas was waiting. As Thomas swung open the doors, Jon emerged from the dark stable into the streets of Presidio. Seeing the masked man with Gideon, the townspeople stopped to look on as their hearts sank with worry.

Looking around, Gideon began to reassure the nervous onlookers. "It's all right, folks. He's a friend. He'll always be a friend."

After a few shaky moments, the people of Presidio realized the masked man was wearing a Texas Ranger badge. As they drew near to get a closer look at the newest defender of Texas, Silver gave out a screeching yell as she danced around in a circle, giving the people of Presidio a chance to see her glory. While the people of Presidio were busy being impressed, Gideon watched with admiration as his brother at heart disappeared out of town like the wind. "Giv'em hell, Jon. Giv'em hell."

While watching Jon ride off into history, Gideon was approached by Gino and Summer. Feeling a tug on his arm, Gideon glanced down at the two little spies who helped him save the town. With a lot of curiosity, Gino didn't hesitate to speak up. "Who was that masked man, Sheriff? Is he alone?"

With pride in his heart, Gideon knelt down to face the two Presidio heroes. "Well, he doesn't have a name anymore, son. He's definitely not a lone Ranger, because he'll never be alone. And when you need him, he'll always be around, so what'ya say we call him the Forever Ranger."

As Jon reached the outskirts of town, the warrior Indian was there waiting. Sitting atop his beautiful Pinto, he waited for Jon to approach. Knowing he was wearing a mask, Jon slowed his ride and approached with caution. Thinking his Indian friend would have more answers, Jon came to a stop and held up his hand in peace, showing the Indian the bracelet he was given as a young boy. Jon waited for a response, but the warrior Indian just stared. Finally, the mysterious Indian held up his hand in peace. "Cheveyo, you still seek guidance, but I am not the one to teach you."

Listening to the warrior, Jon was a bit disappointed. "Then why are you here? What is your purpose for following me and protecting me?"

The warrior Indian paused for a moment as he looked deep inside of Jon's soul. "You are Cheveyo. It is not my place to rule over you but to direct you to the Old One. You must go to understand your place."

Trying to avoid the thought of trekking back to the El Capitan, Jon knew his Indian friend was right. Jon remembered the Old One and his words about coming back to seek answers, and so it was time. But before the long trip, Jon decided to take a trip north to see an old friend and to settle some business. After a few days' ride, he arrived at the Red River and purposely stayed in the open as to be seen from all direction. After a few minutes of waiting, Jon could see Two Feathers with his war party riding hard in his direction. As they trampled across the water in Comanche fashion, they came to an abrupt stop in front of Jon.

Not knowing what to think about the mask, Two Feathers exercised caution. "Masked man, why do you trespass on our land?"

Without saying a word, Jon held up the palm of his hand for Two Feathers to see. Recognizing the large scar to be the scar of the man who made him a promise, Two Feathers ordered his men to retreat back across the river. Once his men were gone, Two Feathers spoke. "I hear of great battle. Battle where many men die. The one they call evil is no more."

Knowing there was a good chance Two Feathers already had the information, Jon still needed to convey his friendship. "I've given you my blood and I've delivered on my promise. For now on, your battles will become my battles and we will fight together to protect your lands."

Accepting Jon's word as bond, Two Feathers glanced at Jon's magnificent thoroughbred. "You ride great white spirit. My father was right. You are

Hok'ee. You keep promise to avenge the death of Seven Bulls. Let there be peace between my people and you."

With that said Two Feathers turned his horse north and rode back across the Red River.

Feeling a little more at ease with himself, Jon turned southwest and headed for the El Capitan. He stuck to the woods whenever possible and tried to avoid the main trails. After a few days, he found himself in familiar territory. He was at the base of the El Capitan. As he looked around, the sun was going down, but he had no intentions of waiting until morning. With the wind starting to howl, Jon dismounted as Silver became spooked. Gently stroking her neck, Jon once again spoke some soft words. "It's okay, girl. We're gonna be just fine. You'll see. I promise. I'll be back soon."

Starting his ascent up the mountain, Jon finally reached the familiar plateau, but with the darkness came blindness. There was no light coming from the moon, so Jon could no longer see where he was going. Thinking of Father Andres, Jon remembered his words. *No matter which direction you come from, the Old One will find you.* After a few minutes of listening to the wind blow through the trees and the fainted screams of long lost souls, Jon saw the familiar light up ahead. As he approached the cave, he entered with caution. With his eyes focused on the Old One sitting by the fire, Jon walked in and sat down. With the old scrolls in his hand, he watched as the Old One rocked back and forth with his eyes closed as he chanted and sang words, which Jon didn't understand. Then suddenly, he stopped. As he slowly opened his eyes, the Old One peered at Jon through the fire. Taking the scrolls from Jon, he began to speak. "I see you have returned, Cheveyo. You have conquered the black cloud, which has taken away all you hold close to your heart. You have also tamed the white spirit, which you ride, and now your souls are forever intertwined."

Jon had many questions, but he had accepted and learned to have respect and patience for the Old One. "Old friend, as you can see, I now wear a mask to hide my identity, but I need to know who I am and what is destined for me. I've read the scrolls, but I need to hear your words."

Once again the Old One started to sway, but there was no chant. Instead, he began to speak words of wisdom to Jon. "Cheveyo, you have worn many disguises in the past and so the mask you wear now is just a continuation of the life you have chosen."

The words spoken by the old Indian were bothersome, but Jon kept his attitude in check as he continued to press for information. "I didn't create nor did I choose this life. But I defended what I thought was right and I lost everyone I loved. How is that a continuation of my life?"

Understanding Jon's frustration, the Old One momentarily came to a stop and pulled some silver dust from a pouch. Throwing it into the fire, the fire momentarily turned blue as the flames rose up high. Once the fire receded, the Old One spoke. "Cheveyo, you must first see your past before you can understand your future."

Before Jon could respond, the Old One waved his hand over the fire as he began to chant. Beginning to feel the effects of heavy eyes, Jon's eyes closed as he slowly fell backward. Once again Jon was awakened but couldn't move as the Old One began to tell his story. "Cheveyo, you have been born many times, but with each life you have chosen violence and revenge. But in your darkest of hours, your heart desired counsel with the Creator and you sought his knowledge, and so he casts his pity upon you. The Master is always watching, and so he has endured your relentless disobedience by calling upon you to fight against the evil in this world. The necklace you wear is of great importance. It was presented to you many moons ago, but you chose to ignore its great significance. But as time went on, you were given many tests, which you have failed. Many times you have been to the mountain and many times you have chosen to abuse the power given to you. You sought revenge rather than to protect."

Just then, a young man appeared to Jon. He wielded great wealth, but was rambunctious in nature. He disguised himself as a soldier, but was unsatisfied with the violence. He then resorted to wearing rags as he attempted to disguise himself as a pauper. But he could gain no satisfaction. The young man than turned old and withered away as a man of God. Suddenly, another scene started to develop. It was a young boy. Very frail in nature. He wielded great power and used it for revenge. Jon could see the boy as he disguised himself by wearing the skin of a jaguar. The boy then returned to his native village and killed those who bathed themselves in evil."

One by one as the scenes continued to play themselves out, Jon could hear the Old One speak. "Cheveyo, upon your return to the mountain, the mountain did not welcome you back. The Master was furious and so once again, you were cast out as a ghost and cursed to roam the land. My heart was broken as I begged the Creator to have mercy. But once again, you sought revenge. In your anger, you appeared to the holy men as a tribesman and led them to the mountain of wealth. It was then they realized the mountain was a sacred place of great power and importance. So, they devised a plan to rid the Earth of all who knew of such a place. They promised the evil soldiers great wealth to kill many tribes and other priests, but the soldiers were blinded by greed and could not see the deceit and treachery. The holy men gave bountiful food and wine with poison, and the soldiers were no more.

"Knowing others would come, the holy men became the protectors of the mountain, but their mortal bodies were no match for the passage of time. For they did their best to conceal the knowledge of this hallowed ground."

As the Old One finished with his story, Jon's consciousness was restored as he sat up straight. Shaking off the temporary drowsiness, he now understood who he was but still had questions about his future. "So, now what? Am I finished? Do I stay here?"

In his attempt to control the flow of information, the Old One didn't answer right away. With an intense stare, he peered into the fire as though he was waiting for a resolution. As the fire crackled and spit out sparks, the Old One turned to Jon. "Cheveyo, you are not finished with this life. Your story has been handed down through the generations and has been changed from tongue to tongue. And will continue to be told as future generations learn of your existence. You must take the path which has opened and serve the Creator, who has given you much wisdom and strength."

As the winds outside the cave started to wield their powers, the fire suddenly sprang up and lit up the entire cave, which had expanded. Jon could hear all the lost souls start to cry out for help, but there was no relief for them. The ground started to rumble and shake as the cave became angry as though it had been waiting a lifetime for this moment. As quickly as it started, the rumblings came to an end with many dark passageways being exposed. With his emotions in a frenzy, Jon stood up and looked around. His thoughts were rapid with each passage having a different treasure exposed to the light. While Jon walked to each opening, he gazed upon the tender each passage had to offer.

When he turned to the Old One, Jon gave a quaint smile. "Old friend, I'm not here for prosperity. I came to you seeking answers."

Looking upon Jon with pride, the Old One gave a surprise response. "Cheveyo, you have witnessed your past and now you must decide your future. Within life itself, you must choose the correct path. Only then will you find meaning. Now, before you are many passageways. Some filled with much wealth and others filled with death. You must decide on which path to take. Only then will you learn the fate of your future."

Looking around the massive cave, there were many passageways to choose from, but Jon needed to determine the right one because the wrong choice could mean death. As Jon walked around, he carefully examined the contents of each opening. Some had jewels piled high to the ceiling, yet others had gold that cluttered the passageway. Some had silver and yet others had nothing but darkness. As Jon peered down one of the dark passages, he could smell the aroma of death. While looking intently down another dark passage, he could hear horrifying screams coming from deep within the bowels of the mountain. As he moved from one passage to another, he would briefly admire the riches each opening had to offer, but he wasn't sure what would happen if he chose such meaningless wealth.

Thinking he could ask for advice, Jon paused as he turned to the Old One. But the Old One was well prepared for Jon's quest. "Cheveyo, before your venturous spirit inquires of me, allow me to guide your thoughts. I cannot answer your questions. I cannot encourage you or make suggestion of which path to take. As in life, you must make the decision to follow a righteous path and become the person the Master has envisioned you to be."

Listening to the words of the Old One, Jon continued to walk along the cave walls and glance down each passageway. After a few more minutes of contemplating, he stopped and turned to face the Old One. "I've made my decision. My choice does not lie within this cave or on this mountain. My choice is within my own heart. Although I have lost much, I have accepted my decisions that I have made in life, so I choose the path I have already been living."

Hearing those words, the cave once again grumbled and moaned as the many passage ways started to disappear. After a few moments, the cave dwindled back down to its original small size with only one passageway left. It was dark and dusty, and Jon could see it hadn't been entered for many centuries.

As the Old One approached, he placed his hand on Jon's shoulder. "Come, Cheveyo. You have made a wise decision."

As the Old One guided Jon into the dark passage, Jon lit a nearby torch so he could see better. Afterward, he realized it was an old mine shaft. Through the many spiders and their webs, he saw the worn-out rusty rails equipped with long-forgotten carts. As they carefully weaved their way down into the belly of the mountain, the dust spiraled down from the ceiling and the walls. Suddenly, the narrow passage opened up as Jon entered into the main chamber of the mythical mountain. His heart began to pound as his eyes widened with the sight of such wonders. In front of him flowed the fabled river of silver that once flowed freely down the sides of the El Capitan. Chunks of silver were bountiful as they lay strung across the floor of the cavern. Looking around, he could see the walls were laden with silver dust, with some flaking off over the years and compiling piles of silver against the walls of the cavern. With a smile on his face, Jon glanced back at the Old One. "I just can't believe this. I gotta hand it to him. Hayden was right all along. He knew it was here and he knew he was close when he saw my necklace."

Jon continued to look around as he shook his head with disgust. "So, this is it. This is what so-called dreams are made of. This is what so many people came here looking for and gave their life for. No wonder the Spanish were so pissed off at those Franciscan monks."

After a few minutes of allowing Jon to take in the spectacle, the Old One led him over to a smaller room within the main chamber. There, Jon found what looked like human remains. The room was dark, but as he lit what he thought was a small bowl of incendiary powder, the fire quickly spread around the entire room lighting up what was obviously a treasure room but, more importantly, revealing twelve bodies. But not just any twelve bodies. Sitting upright at a Camelot-style round table were the original twelve Franciscan monks. With plates and goblets made of pure silver sitting on the table, it appeared they enjoyed one last meal together before taking the same poison given to the Spanish soldiers. While glancing around the room, Jon saw silver crosses hanging off the walls along with crates of silver stacked against each side of the cavern. Even the exquisite table and chairs seemed to be partially made up of silver with silver ornate gargoyles built into the legs and arms.

While Jon was wondering why, the Old One spoke out. "Do you remember, Cheveyo? Out of revenge against the Creator, It was you who led them to this place. But you were not responsible for their fate. Like so many others, the black cloud consumed them because of their many sins. Their fate was sealed when they were overwhelmed with greed. After realizing no man could handle such power and wealth, they took it upon themselves to seal the mines forever and to become the protectors of the mountain. But the mountain refused them. They were of flesh and blood and had betrayed their faith, so the Creator turned from them."

With a bit of guilt starting to set in, Jon looked at each monk as though he could remember their faces. "You said I made a wise choice, so why show me this? Am I to suffer the same fate? Is this why you brought me down here? To condemn me?"

Jon watched as the Old One exited the room and walked over to a small campfire, which was already lit and going strong. As the Old One sat down, Jon sat down across from him. With the Old One tossing silver dust into the fire, the fire turned every color of the rainbow. After chanting a few words, the Old One turned to Jon. "For those who seek righteousness, they will find it, but only one will fulfill the destiny of protecting this sacred ground. Cheveyo, you have earned this right. You are now the keeper of the mountain. You will now carry out your destiny and embrace your future."

With every word the Old One spoke came new questions for Jon. But with Jon becoming more comfortable with his new self, some of his old self started to seep out. "So, I'm supposed to somehow protect the secret of this mountain, take on all the bad guys, help those who are in need, defend the innocent, and somehow keep from getting myself killed in the process?"

Recognizing the sarcasm of Jon, the Old One still had an answer for him. "You are not alone, Cheveyo. The mighty warrior who has watched over you is waiting."

Working their way back up the mineshaft, the two found themselves back at the small cave. The night had passed and now it was early morning. There was no fire, so the cave was damp and cold as the outside winds assaulted the cavern. As Jon made his way to the entrance, he turned to ask one more question, but the Old One was gone. Standing at the mouth of the cave, Jon shouted out. "Wait. What about you? Will you be here?"

Jon waited for a few seconds, then he could hear the faded voice of the Old One. "My time is done, Cheveyo. You are the new guardian of the mountain. The Creator has called me home."

Thinking about the challenge, Jon had never backed down from any responsibility and he wasn't about to start. The Old One was gone, but with his exit came a gift for Jon. Looking down at his feet, he noticed a small crate leaning up against the mouth of the cave. With much curiosity, Jon opened the crate and found it filled with ammunition. Feeling a bit confused, he realized the bullets weren't ordinary bullets; they were made from the finest silver. With a delightful smile, Jon accepted the gift and his fate and was looking forward to his future. After loading up his gun belt, he gathered the rest of the ammo and started his trek back down the mountain.

When he got to the bottom, the warrior Indian was there waiting with Silver. Taking a minute to mount his powerful steed, Jon began to get more acquainted with his new friend. "So, it's just you and I against the world?"

With his usual stern face, the warrior Indian spoke. "You shall face the perils of this world and I shall watch over you as I always have."

Looking around in every direction, Jon gathered his thoughts. "Well, I happen to know a little border town that could use our help, so what'ya say we head that way?"

Before galloping away, the warrior Indian displayed a rare smile. "I like what you say. You, me against world. Would be good battle."

Staring at the warrior Indian, Jon let out a small laugh. "We're definitely gonna have to work on your sense of humor. By the way, if we're gonna be fighting side by side, is there a name for you I should be using?"

The warrior Indian paused for a moment while thinking about the question, then gave his answer. "When I was boy, my father call me Bruto."

Taking a few seconds to let the name sink in, Jon let out a small grunt. "Bruto? Sounds barbaric. What does it mean?"

Taking a moment to reflect, the warrior Indian spoke. "It mean many. I come from many tribe."

With a grin on his face, Jon chuckled. "Well now, you're just as messed up as I am. So in Indian terms, what's another word for Bruto?"

Taking another moment, the warrior Indian thought about it then came up with his best answer. "Tonto."

With the word comfortably rolling off his tongue, Jon spoke the name several times. "I like it. Tonto it is."

With the idea of a masked crusader and an Indian roaming around Texas and fighting for justice, it didn't take long for the people of Presidio to spread the word from town to town. As with every rumor, there's usually a little bit of truth. And for the Forever Ranger, it was no different. As the word spread, some people believed, while others just scarfed at the idea. But as with any story, seeing was believing.

Days later on the U.S./Mexican border, a small township was being terrorized by several bandits who had been robbing and killing weary travelers. With their spoils, they would enter the small town of San Luisito and terrorize the tiny community and would often claim the town as their own. The residents had no taste for violence and would often give into whatever demands were placed on them.

During one of their violent exploits, three bandits destroyed several storefronts and raided the bar for whiskey. They also killed several of the town's men and had their way with their wives. While they were busy doing as much damage as possible, a light fog started to roll in. While the townspeople did their best to hide, the bandits continued to scavenge the town. Having no safety concerns for anyone, including themselves, they continued to shoot at the air and anything else that moved. But they finally noticed and eerie silence after realizing the townspeople were more afraid of something other than them. While looking around, they noticed all the townspeople had disappeared in doors and they were now alone in the street. Looking down the center of town, one of the men noticed a masked man and his Indian friend sitting atop their horses. With the fog, they had quietly slipped into town unannounced and without vanity. After alerting his two amigos, all three men stopped what they were doing and faced off against the intruders.

With elegance and grace, Jon and Tonto simultaneously dismounted and walked toward the three bandits. With confidence in their body movements, they stopped a short distance from the three adversaries. With an intense staring contest, one of the bandits finally spoke. "Gringo, I see you wear a mask and a badge. Why? Who are you? What do you want here?"

Feeling no need to respond, Jon's silence made the marauder angry. While one bandit attempted to engage in conversation, another was looking beyond the masked man. "Señor, you have some fine-looking horses. Why don't you give them to us and your guns, and we will let you leave here with your life."

Once again, Jon remained silent, which intensified the situation.

With a smirk on his face, the third bandit was also annoyed and spoke up. "Señor, my friend is being kind, but me, not so much. I'm gonna cut off your balls and feed them to you. Then I think I will make you watch while I scalp your Indian."

Growing tired of the three bandits, Tonto didn't take kindly to their words. With a hatchet in one hand and a very large knife in the other, he swung them both with lightning speed as he threw both weapons and chopped down two of the bandits while the third watched in horror. With just one bandit left, Tonto casually walked over to a nearby bench and sat down. From a pouch hanging off his side, he pulled out a pipe and lit it, then placed it in his mouth.

Glancing down at his two sidekicks who were now dead, the last bandit became even angrier as he tried to use intimidation. Facing off against Jon, the bandit attempted to be bold. "Gringo, you may have heard of me. My name is Emiliano and I am the greatest trick shooter in all of Mexico."

Taking a page out of Gunny's playbook, Jon laughed at the man. "Well now, friend, that's one of your problems right there. We're not in Mexico, and there's no trick to dying."

Knowing Jon was mocking him, Emiliano wasn't laughing, nor was he impressed. Infuriated, he attempted to withdraw his gun, but Jon was second to none when it came to speed. With Emiliano's gun still in its holster, Jon's bullets were already fired, striking Emiliano in both hands. With agonizing pain, Emiliano dropped to his knees.

After holstering his gun, Jon walked over to the struggling bandit, who was now hopelessly kneeling down. Still on his knees, Emiliano glanced up at Jon and begged him for mercy. "Masked man, please. We are the same. Can we deal?"

Feeling no pity for a person who would so easily destroy and kill, Jon looked down at Emiliano. "Wrong again. I'm nothing like you and I'm in no mood to deal."

Feeling as though he was running out of options, Emiliano attempted to appeal to Jon's good nature. "Please, señor. You seem to be a man with heart. I am just a poor farmer. Please, take pity."

With a smug look on his face, Jon continued to peer down at Emiliano. "What is it about Mexican banditos? They all claim to be poor farmers right before they die."

Hearing those words, Emiliano was unaware Tonto had quietly walked up from behind. With one swift swing, he struck Emiliano with a hatchet, chopping his head off. He then turned his attention to Jon. "If you're gonna shoot, then shoot. No talk. Hok'ee have too many words."

With a grin on his face, Jon let out a small laugh. "Not bad. Your humorous attempt reminds me of an old friend of mine. And next time, leave a bad guy for me."

Feeling dry from the ride, Jon motioned Tonto over to the nearby saloon. Along the way, he picked up several bottles of whiskey, which the three bandits had stolen earlier in the day. Entering the bar, the customers were on edge but calm. Having a masked man and an Indian walk into the bar wasn't exactly a normal everyday thing for them.

While Jon and Tonto stood in the doorway, the bartender finally spoke up. "Well, come on in, friends. Damnest thing I ever saw. Those three bandits have been terroriz'n this town for a long dang time. Kill'n and steal'n and rape'n like it were nutt'n."

As Jon and Tonto approached the bar, the old bartender kept talking. "Mister, I ain't ever seened nobody draw as fast as you. Especially against that there feller, Emiliano. You knowed what they call that there feller? They called him DOA 'cause he kills every dang body that crosses him."

Placing the bottles of liquor on the bar, Jon asked for two glasses. But before the old man broke out the celebration glasses, he glanced over at a sign that was hanging on the wall. Looking back at the sign, Jon read it out loud. "We allow whores, beggars, and dogs, but no Indians."

Turning back around to face the old man, the old bartender could see the two heroes were disappointed, so he quickly amended the situation. Taking a minute to walk around the bar, the old man ripped the sign from the wall and tossed it aside. "That takes care of that. You boys are welcome here anytime."

Smiling from ear to ear, the old man walked back behind the bar and gladly poured two drinks. After watching the two heroes down their drinks, the old man quickly filled their glasses again. Once again the two heroes quickly downed their two drinks as they prepared to say their good-byes. Grabbing one of the bottles of whiskey, Jon asked the old bartender the price.

Glancing down at the bottle, the old man became hesitant. Scratching his head and nervously rubbing the back of his neck, the old man finally gave his answer. "Well, mister, you boys really did us a favor, but that bottle happens to be one of the more expensive whiskeys. I'm really sorry, mister, but this town isn't exactly rich, so I just can't give it away."

Before the old man could do anymore wiggling around, Jon pulled out three bullets and placed them on the bar. "I understand, old man, so this ought to cover it."

Glancing down at the bullets, the old man picked one up and bit it. "Dang, that there be real silver. Hey. Where'd you get someth'n like that, mister?"

Before Jon could respond, he heard a familiar thunderous noise outside. It sounded like a large number of horses arriving into town, which meant more bandits.

Glancing over at Tonto, Jon pulled out his revolver and checked to make sure he was loaded, then placed it back into its holster. Thinking they would be in for a horrific gun fight, Jon and Tonto turned to walk out the door. The bartender, along with the few customers, knew all too well the sound of many horses arriving into town meant violence and destruction. As Jon pushed open the saloon doors, he walked out and was met by a United States platoon of cavalry soldiers. Commanded by Colonel Isadore Shaw, they rode into town and took up a position lining both sides of the street creating a gauntlet of horses and men. As Jon and Tonto stood fast, the soldiers looked upon them with curiosity. After a few uncomfortable moments of staring, a lieutenant guided the heroes' horses over to them and handed them the reins. "Gentlemen, word travels fast in these parts, so my colonel wanted to meet you in person."

Taking a few more seconds to fathom the request, Jon and Tonto mounted their horses and guided them over to Colonel Shaw. Hoping the colonel wouldn't recognize him, Jon stared but didn't say a word. With Izzy staring back, he peered into the masked man's eyes and saw nothing but justice. Seeing the mask didn't bother the colonel because the man in front of him wore a Texas Ranger badge and that's all he needed to know. With a feeling of familiarity, Izzy greeted the hero with a salute. After a cautious salute back from Jon, Izzy smiled. "I see, you and your Indian friend are doing a damn fine job. And it's an honor to know the mask you were stands for justice."

Looking around at the gauntlet of men, Jon and Tonto guided their horses down the center as each man gave a respectful salute to the duo. When they arrived at the end of the line, both men turned their horses to face the platoon of men. Letting out a thunderous scream, Silver reared back onto her hind legs as Jon yelled out. "Hi, Ho, Silver."

Along with his Indian friend, Jon went on to be a champion for the people. Riding tall on his gleaming white horse named Silver, he became the who's who in fast draws. His heroic gunfights became legendary and the people spoke about his exploits until they became legendary folklore.

After his last cattle drive, Jacob finally took his trip down to Mexico and found his señorita. After buying some land and starting his own ranch, he invited Harvey, Shelby, and Milky Way to help him grow it into one of the largest beef ranches in South America.

Gideon and Lita were married with Jubal conducting the ceremony as the justice of the peace. Afterward, they combined their money and took full ownership of Jon's old property. They built their house next to the graves so they could easily watch over them. From the porch, Lita hung the wind chimes Gideon had saved so when the wind blew, they could almost hear the children playing. Unfortunately, time wasn't on their side. Tragedy struck a few years later when Lita took sick and quietly passed away in her sleep.

Jubal lived up to the expectations of the people and remained the sheriff of Presidio until it was time for him to retire. He decided to let the younger generation take over, but he continued to reside in Presidio with his hero status and live out a quiet life.

Keeping his heroes close to his heart, Gino grew up to be the next sheriff of Presidio. With Jubal's blessing and guidance, he became the people's sheriff. He was well liked and respected by all, and when it came to defending the town, he was brave in his actions while facing down some of the most ruthless of outlaws.

Summer decided to take a more educational approach in life. She went onto college and received her degree in politics. She then set her sights on the governor's race for Texas and won. She fought hard for Texas, never letting the dirty politics get in the way of protecting the citizens of her fine state.

As for the old cow pass, it had become a major thoroughfare, with the great oaks standing tall and strong for everyone to admire but never knowing their true meaning.

With the years going by, the days of the rough and tough outlaws came to an end as Jon and Tonto disappeared into the landscape of the old west. With the industrial age rapidly growing and evolving, a new kind of transportation was invented. For those who could afford them, the horseless carriage, which was later named the automobile, started to litter the American landscape.

As the turn of the century came, a more modern Presidio with new gun laws overtook old traditions. But that didn't stop Gideon from wearing his gun belt and carrying his rifle by his side whenever he left his house. With his age and a defiant attitude being of no factor but hearing the old stories of the battle for Presidio, local law enforcement gave Gideon his due respect and allowed him to keep his firearms handy. Gideon didn't believe in modernization and never adapted to modern times, so whenever he had to go someplace, he would always hitch up his horse and wagon.

One day while riding into town, Gideon noticed a young boy sitting on the side of the road. As he got closer, he could see the boy was alone and frightened, so he pulled his wagon to the side and stopped. Peering down at the boy, he could tell the boy was distressed. With his raggedy clothing and some apprehension, the boy quietly stared back at Gideon. After a few seconds, Gideon signaled the boy to climb up. After the boy got into the wagon, Gideon noticed he was wearing some Indian beads around his wrist. He then took notice of a familiar worn-out leather necklace he was wearing. "So, boy, where are your parents?"

The boy didn't answer at first and thought for a few seconds before responding. "I don't know, sir. I don't think I have any."

As Gideon smiled, an automobile sped by and honked the horn, signaling for Gideon to get off the road. Shaking his head with frustration, a rebellious Gideon raised his fist in defiance at the speeding pile of steel. He then turned his attention back to his passenger. "They call that progress. I call it horse shit. You have a name, boy?"

Once again the boy paused for a moment before giving an answer. "My name is Jon."

As his horse trotted along pulling the wagon, Gideon took a deep breath and smiled. Before continuing the conversation, he reached into his pocket and pulled out a cigar. Placing it in his mouth and lighting it with a match, he took a few puffs, then turned his attention back to Jon. "Well, Jon, let me tell you a little story about a young man and a magical mountain."

With Texas leaving behind its more turbulent days, the outlaws of the past live on in romanticized stories while the true heroes tend to get lost in the confusion. But where ever a dark cloud looms, the Forever Ranger will be there to answer the call for help.

By now, you, being the reader of this novel, should know the rest of the story.

CPSIA information can be obtained
at www.ICGtesting.com
Printed in the USA
BVHW071528191219
567146BV00005B/16/P